THE

IMMORTAL

KNIGHT

CHRONICLES

Vampire Knight
Vampire Heretic
Vampire Impaler

DAN DAVIS

VAMPIRE

KNIGHT

The Immortal Knight Chronicles
Book 4

Richard of Ashbury
and the Hundred Years War
1346 - 1377

1

A King's Command

THE MESSENGER WOKE ME before dawn. It was Saturday 26th August 1346 and there would be a grand battle that day between the kings of France and England. And, although I did not know it that morning, by nightfall I would discover a new and terrible immortal enemy in the midst of the French army.

"What was that?" I asked the figure standing over me in the dark. He had spoken before I was fully awake.

"His Grace summons you, sir," one of the King's men said, speaking softly but with some urgency.

It was dark inside the church in the small village of Wadicourt.

"Where is the King now?" I asked, rubbing my eyes.

"His Grace is yet in the other village, sir," the messenger said. "In Crecy."

I climbed to my feet and stretched the aches from my muscles. Over the decades, I had become accustomed to sleeping in my armour, when necessary. The mail hauberks from my youth had slowly been replaced by various other forms of armour. Many of my men wore coats riveted or sewn with small plates to provide protection. Those of us who could afford it though wore larger, close-fitted iron pieces. Sleeping in a breastplate and back plate along with armour on the front of my legs and the outsides of my arms, and armoured feet and gauntlets, took some getting used to. After decades of campaigning experience, along with my immortal strength and endurance, I was capable of getting a fair night's sleep in it.

I left my helm with a page and stepped around the sleeping bodies on the floor of the church. It was damp outside and colder than an August morning deserved to be but it would soon warm up once the day got going.

We traipsed across the ridge following the rutted track between the two villages, walking past thousands of English men-at-arms and archers beginning to bestir themselves. Scores of campfires were being lit along the slope. Few of us expected the battle to start any time soon. Still, many men were eager to arm themselves immediately upon waking and the sounds of steel plate and mail clanging filled the air, along with gruff complaints, coughing and the clearing of throats and the odd bark of laughter. Every man in the army wore a steel helm of some kind and although most were darkened with grime or painted, still they glinted in the gloom.

I approached the village of Crecy, walking past a windmill at the top of the ridge, its furled sails stationary in the dawn light as if it was some giant sentinel watching over us. In between the thatched houses and kitchen gardens, soldiers and servants busied themselves by fetching water from the stream running at the back of the village. Beyond the village to the south was a woodland, deep in shadow. Young pages led groups of horses to and from the stream, or brushed them down, or walked them to warm them up. Many were led back behind the ridge to the wagon park where they would be both safe and out of the way, assuming the French came at us from the way we were expecting.

The messenger led me past the King's pavilion tent into the small church. It was stifling inside and dark despite the candles and packed with men in armour. A priest was concluding a mass and I waited by the door for it to finish.

"Is that you, Richard?" the King asked as I approached. His helm, with its ring of gold around it, stood higher than almost all of the priests and lords surrounding him.

King Edward III of England had grown into a very fine man. Already wearing his harness, clad in the finest plate armour and helm, he was ready for the battle and yet appeared relaxed and comfortable. The King's surcoat was quartered with the red field and three golden lions of England and the blue field and gold lilies of France. His visor was even affixed, though he had it hinged up so that his face was exposed.

"Your Grace," I said, bowing.

"Come closer, sir," the King said.

The lords clustered all around him were unwelcoming, begrudging the attention I was receiving. For many of them, it would be a day for them to shine before their enemies and peers, to win renown and solidify their already-glowing reputations as fighting lords of England.

The King brought me a step further away from the crowd and waved away one of his priests who made to follow.

"We will fight in three battles, as planned, with most of the bowmen on the flanks and some in front of the men-at-arms. The first two battles will form a line across the ridge, two thirds of the way up," he said, speaking clearly but softly, so that his words would not carry. When he said battle, he was referring to our formations. A *battaile* was a semi-independent division and our armies were almost always divided into the van, middle and rear guards, or battles. "My battle will hold behind the main line, on the ridge in the centre, forming the reserve. You will keep your own bowmen with you and the rest of your company at the edge of my battle on the centre of the ridge. I would ask that you stay within earshot."

I nodded, and attempted to keep my disappointment from my face at being held in the rear. My men would be frustrated at being so far from the action. Not least because that meant thousands of Englishmen would plunder dead Frenchmen before they could. Assuming, of course, that we won the field.

"You have a specific task for me in mind, Your Grace?" I asked. I had known Edward for many years and even though I kept my true strength and speed hidden from mortals, the King knew me as a consummate knight who could be trusted with any task. It would not be the first time he had given me special instructions for swinging a battle in our favour.

The King lowered his voice further and turned his back on the great lords waiting on him. "The Prince fights in the van on the right, by this village. You will have noted how the slope on that flank is gentler, easier. Our enemies will press him hard. Perhaps, if events necessitate it, you might consider providing him with just a little support?"

"I understand, Your Grace."

He pursed his lips, cleared his throat and punched his fist into my breastplate. "I know, Richard."

When he turned back to the great lords of his kingdom, our conference was over and I had been dismissed. Pushing through the priests and lords who ignored me or scowled at me, I went back to prepare my men.

I was posing as a mortal, as always, and as a somewhat impoverished knight at that. Edward had favoured me ever since I helped him to take control of his crown from the traitor Mortimer sixteen years earlier.

Yet, I was a man with an invented lineage, pretending that I was the latest in a line of minor knights who had fought for Henry III and Edward I. The lords considered my pedigree to be non-existent. And the great men of the realm disliked my closeness with Edward, from the days of his youth through to that morning in France when he was in his prime at the age of thirty-four.

More than their needless petty jealousies, though, I was beginning to run into the problem that I always encountered.

The fact that I had apparently not aged in the sixteen years since I came to prominence was now often commented on, and the young men who had laughed and joked with me over wine when we were twenty years old were now beginning to go grey and bald and fat.

Eva, who had once been my wife, had told me that I unnerved many men just with my presence. She suspected that they sensed there was something different about me, something wrong. Something dangerous. For young men, that is all very well. Exciting, even. But old men grow suspicious and bitter and so it would soon be time for me to move on. To remove myself from England and the English for twenty or thirty years so that most of the men who knew me would die. Then I would return and perhaps once more claim to be the son of the man I had pretended to be.

The other members of the Order of the White Dagger, especially the former monk Stephen Gossett and my friend the former Templar knight Thomas de Vimory, had urged me to leave before it drew any further attention to me that might endanger the Order itself.

"You already arouse great suspicion, sir!" Stephen had said at our last meeting in London. "We agreed to this. You agreed, Richard. You agreed!"

Though he claimed his concern was for the continued secrecy of the Order, I suspected he was more worried that his growing mercantile empire in London would be threatened. He was right that I had sworn to flee when the whispers against me started.

But I could not leave King Edward. Not when he was poised to smash the French and reclaim some or all of the lands that the English crown had held in my youth, over a hundred and fifty years earlier.

Not yet.

It was early morning when my company assembled from the places around the villages where they had slept. There were eighteen men-at-arms and twenty-nine archers in my company and before I spoke to them all I relayed the essence of our orders to the leading men in my company.

Many in my company were drawn from the few capable men on my estate, along with a few retainers I had picked up over the years. A couple were pardoned criminals and more were already professional soldiers looking for hire when I found them. However they had come into it, they stayed for the money, as well as for the love of it. They were men who made war for their private profit, neither knights nor squires but men of little worth who would not do a thing without their six pence a day and thirty marks a year.

Together, we had fought for years in Brittany, on the far north-western tip of France. A rugged land in places but a fertile one and a good place for small companies of men to commit mischief. We helped to take towns and win small battles, and we raided and lived off the land.

"The King wants us in the rearguard?" Black Walter cried. "Don't he know we can win this battle for him, sir?"

Walter was one of my best men but he was a mortal who had no inkling that I was anything other than a capable knight. He was a commoner and had such a simplistic and shallow view of the world that for many years I had thought him a halfwit. Even then, I had recognised his unusual ability, strength and courage when it came to feats of arms and so I had equipped him with good armour and commanded him to fight as my squire. He even rode superbly, despite never mounting a decent horse until he was a man grown.

His father had been from the Welsh Marches in the far west of England, and his hair and beard were shiny as obsidian and his skin somewhat swarthy. Walter denied that he was a Welshman by blood but most of my men liked to doubt him. I trusted him to watch my back in battle and tried to avoid speaking to him otherwise.

"Hold your tongue, Walt," Thomas said. "The King will ultimately send the rear guard into the fray to turn the tide of the battle and so win the day."

Sir Thomas had been fighting at my side for close to a hundred years and we knew each other like brothers. He so often spoke my own mind that I rarely needed to disagree with him.

"Come on, Walt, you know this," said John, grinning. "It is precisely because we are so well regarded by the King that he wishes to use us in the most critical moment."

"That is right and true, John," Hugh said, eagerly. "Surely, our company shall carry the day."

John and Hugh were the newest and youngest members of the Order of the White Dagger. Formerly a member of the Knights Templar, Thomas and I had freed Sir John and the squire Hugh from gaol in France when the French King had arrested and prosecuted their order. I had been reluctant to offer them the Gift but allowed myself to be persuaded.

John was a tall, fair, handsome and chivalrous man who had always fought and acted honourably, despite being a Frenchman on his mother's side. Thankfully, his father had been one of the Anglo-Normans of Ireland, which meant he was almost a proper Englishman.

Hugh, a Frenchman by birth, was a squire when we found him thirty years earlier and he remained a dutiful though unimaginative fellow. I found it impossible to think of him as anything other than a young man, even though he was over fifty, because of the wide-eyed earnestness he had somehow retained.

"Aye, sirs, I suppose you be right enough about that," Walt said, cheering at the thought of being able to fight by the end of the day.

"What about my lads, sir?" Rob Hawthorn asked.

Another mortal, like Walter, he commanded my archers. Once, Rob was a wild youth, much taken with brawling and chasing women. By the time my company left Brittany, he had become as steady and trustworthy as a commoner could be. He was not tall but he had an archer's build. John had once cried that Rob was built like the Minotaur. Once the myth was explained to the archers, they found it highly amusing. "Can I take my men to join the flanks of the van? Or the middle?"

"You are all to stay with me throughout the battle and you will hold on to your arrows until we need them," I said. Rob nodded, pressing his lips together. I continued. "Right then, you all know what you are about. Get the men some food, make sure they are well watered. Get the weapons sharpened and armour repaired. Make sure the servants keep our horses ready at the rear."

"Horses, Sir Richard?" Walt said, scratching his face under the edge of his mail aventail. "Ain't we all fighting on foot today?"

"Indeed we are, Walt. And yet one never knows how a battle may turn." I raised my voice so that the rest of the men could hear me. "Make yourselves ready. John, set my banner on the right of the vanguard, at the front, so that we may advance without hindrance when the time comes. I shall see you all there, men. God be with you all today."

"Stick by Sir Richard," John cried, "and we'll get to murder a dozen Frenchmen apiece."

The entire company cheered, bringing bemused glances from the other men gathering on the ridge.

While they busied themselves, I glanced at Thomas and we walked a few paces away down the slope, looking down the hill and out across the valley.

"What is our true task?" Thomas asked when we could not be overheard.

"The king wants us to protect the Prince," I replied.

Thomas narrowed his eyes. "And yet Prince Edward commands the vanguard while we shall be in the rear."

"By honouring the Prince with such responsibility," I said, attempting to gather the strands of my thoughts into what I believed was the truth behind the King's words, "a victory this day will establish the Prince of Wales as a great warrior. He will be famed across Christendom as a mighty king in waiting. His reputation will be made. All will know that England has a bright future."

"Only if we win," Thomas pointed out.

"Well, yes," I said. "And only if the Prince lives through the day, more to the point."

Thomas took a deep breath and then sighed. "He will be hard pressed indeed down there. Gentle slope that side. If I was charging our lines, mounted, with my lance couched and looking for an Englishman to impale, that is where I would do it."

We stood looking along the slope, imagining thousands of knights charging our men.

"Imagine if they took him," I said. "What would England's future be then?"

"So why are we to be held back from him at all?" Thomas asked. "We can protect him from the start."

"His victory must not be tainted with my name. Although Suffolk is my lord, all men know that I am the King's man. The victory must belong to the Prince. If he is in danger, we shall save him for as long as we need to. But we shall not say that is what we have done. We shall deny it. And so shall our men."

"A shame."

"We will know," I said. "God will know."

He bowed his head and turned to look out once more. "Dear Lord, here they come."

2

The King's Campaign

THE BATTLE WE WERE SOON to fight had been a long time coming. King Edward had needed to obtain an enormous amount of money, to raise thousands of men along with purveying the victuals to supply them, and then ship that army across the channel.

We had been through it before, in 1338 and 1344, when we had relied on our Flemish, Breton and German allies but their endless dithering, fickle nature, and endless petty demands had scuppered our attempts. Now we would invade France properly.

With Englishmen.

To find the funds, Edward had forced loans from the Church and from towns all across the country. Foreign clergymen, some of whom were astonishingly wealthy, were fleeced three ways from Sunday, which all true born English folk rejoiced to see.

But all this was still nowhere near enough and so Edward had borrowed money from a syndicate of London merchants led by none other than my immortal friend Stephen Gosset.

It was of course not right for the wealth of the Order of the White Dagger to be employed in funding a mortal's war but finding immortals had proved incredibly difficult and we increasingly expressed doubt that there were any left to be found. Besides, it was the King of England who needed the money, and Edward III had turned out to be rather a good one.

Stephen wanted to provide the funding because he claimed we would, eventually, recoup our investment many times over and also that it would buy favour from the Crown that would enable us to leverage even more influence. That is to say, it appealed to his ambition.

And I wanted to fight. If that meant loaning a king some of our massive wealth, so be it.

The King wanted a vast army of twenty thousand men and so he implemented the innovation that was compulsory military service. Every man in the kingdom was expected to serve based on his level of income. If you made five pounds a year then you would be expected to fight as an archer, with all the necessary equipment and ability that entailed. Men who earned ten pounds a year would fight as a hobelar, those fellows who formed a versatile light cavalry of sorts which we used for scouting and foraging and anything requiring rapid mobility. Those who were assessed as having an income of twenty-five pounds were required to serve as a man-at-arms, with proper weapons and armour and a horse, along with the necessary servants to support him on campaign.

The king required every man to serve not merely in defence of the realm against invasion but also if we were to fight on the Continent. Also, any man who claimed to be too old or ill to fight would have to provide a substitute or pay a fine instead of their service. It was a shrewd move on Edward's part but in other years, before and since, he would have faced opposition to his money-raising schemes. It was only the fact that so many of his lords were looking forward to the fight that he got away with little more than grumbling.

In spite of my considerable secret wealth and immortality, I was playing the part of a minor gentleman who was lucky enough to have been knighted during fighting overseas before returning to England as a young man.

As I had done a number of times already, I left England for twenty years and then posed as the son of the man I had formally been. This time, a few older fellows here and there had given me hard stares before swearing that I was the spitting image of my father. It was a simple enough thing to pull off successfully because who would truly suspect I was the very same man? It was hardly credible.

Very soon after my most recent return, I had moved immediately into supporting the young King Edward just as it appeared he was being usurped by the traitor Roger Mortimer, the new husband of the King's mother.

When he was aged just seventeen, I had urged the powerless king to act before it was too late and together with a group of young lords we seized Mortimer in Nottingham and hanged the traitor a few weeks later. Edward subsequently favoured me considerably and I had fought for him in various ways ever since.

But, as we stood to prepare for battle outside the village of Crecy, that night in Nottingham had been sixteen years before and the time was drawing near for me to flee once more. My apparent youthfulness was remarked upon by men who were beginning to feel the ravages of time in their aching limbs and the tightness of their clothes across the belly. It is merely a matter of eating beef every day and drinking good wine, I would say, but increasingly my words fell on deaf ears. Even the King was beginning to look at me askance, though for now he protected me against the detrimental effects of rumour by his continued favouring of me with tasks of a military nature.

For Edward, I had fought against the old enemy the Scots, in the Low Countries and in Brittany against the French and their allies. During the Battle of Sluys off the coast of Flanders, I had led my men across the bloody decks to take ship after ship, winning considerable glory and fame for myself and my men. In that great victory we slaughtered tens of thousands of Frenchmen but due to the weakness and untrustworthiness of our allies the Flemish, we could not take advantage of it and so the war foundered.

In Brittany, for many years, I took and defended towns and raided for supplies to provide for garrisons. The mortal men who survived that crucible with me became as hard as iron and it was those men who were with me at Crecy. Men-at-arms and archers who had learned to fight as a unit whether we were on our own or fighting with other companies in a more significant battle.

My men believed me to be blessed.

Or cursed.

Some said I was protected by an angel or by God Himself, while others whispered that I had done a deal with the Devil. But all had seen me recover from wounds that they swore would have killed King Arthur or Alexander and, whatever the cause, ultimately, they thought that I was blessed with that most precious of all soldierly traits. Luck. And they all loved to serve me because as every soldier knows, luck is contagious. And the regular plunder also helped.

And so I came back from Brittany to join the King's army in Normandy for the invasion of France, bringing my small force of hardened veterans with me.

Edward had not, in fact, managed to bring an army of the size he had intended. The treacherous Scots were massing in the North and thousands of Englishmen had to be left behind to face them. Similarly, there was thought to be great risk of French attacks by sea on the southern English coast and so the King ensured that the men of the coastal towns stay where they were to resist. What is more, a diversionary force was sent to Flanders to distract the French and to drag them to their north-eastern border.

Our main force landed from 12th July 1346 and spread out into the countryside, only to discover that the villages, towns, manors and monasteries were abandoned; the people fleeing into the woods and marshes at our approach. Immediately after stepping ashore, King Edward, God bless him, proclaimed that, out of compassion for the fate of his people of France, none of us should molest any old man, woman or child, or rob any church or burn any building on pain of immediate death or horrific mutilation.

It was a fine sentiment and he even offered forty shillings to anyone who discovered men breaking the King's orders, which proved that the King perceived the essentially mercenary nature of the common man.

Of course, every village, town, manor and monastery with twenty miles was burned to the ground on the first or second day but at least he tried. The fires were so widespread that on the first night in Normandy we lit up the sky so brightly that the reddish glow filling the horizon all around was enough to play dice by.

And so we continued. We rampaged across Normandy, heading always east with the coast on our left, sometimes so close we could smell it but other times ranging miles inland.

Those poor people. They would have been King Edward's subjects, had their lords but sworn fealty to him as their rightful lord but I suppose they knew he could not protect them from King Philip. England was considered a poor and weak kingdom and France was the mightiest in Christendom. What is more, Normandy bordered the core of the Kingdom of France, whereas Brittany and Gascony were further removed. All the King of France had to do was lean from his palace window and reach out his arm to take Normandy. They were loyal to him and so we burned the duchy from one end to the other.

Before then, though, we had taken the city of Caen. It had to be taken because the garrison inside was big enough to cut our supply line and threaten our rear if we left them in there. What is more, it was immensely rich and somewhat vulnerably located.

Even before we landed, we knew where we were headed and it was within striking distance from the coast. Still, few of us expected the siege to be over quickly.

Caen was a vast city and even the men who had never seen it knew that it was one of the biggest in the whole country, not counting Paris of course.

"It is bigger even than London," I had said to my men.

"It never is, sir," said Black Walter, a man of astonishing ignorance and impudence who I liked to keep at my side because he was so good at killing my enemies, despite him being a mortal man.

"Wait until you see it," I said.

The castle on the north side was formidable and they had high, thick walls around the city itself. Those walls, we saw when we approached, had been draped with colourful banners to display to us that it was defended by powerful and wealthy men. Atop the walls, standing shoulder to shoulder, were those who would defend their homes with crossbows and rocks and, if it came to it, swords and spears and daggers. Inside, Caen was packed with magnificent homes and enormous churches with grand spires jutting up in every quarter and on either side of the city were two abbeys, both huge and fancy and with high walls that joined with the ones ringing the city.

"I stand corrected, sir," Black Walter had said.

"This was William the Conqueror's city, Walt. The bastard robbed Saxon England from top to bottom and spent all our gold enriching this city here."

"Pardon me for asking, sir," Walt said, "but ain't you come from Normans yourself?"

In fact, I was descended by blood from Earl Robert de Ferrers and through him to a lord who had fought for the Normans at Hastings but I never revealed such things to mortals.

"My mother was as English as they come," I said, which was true. "And my father's line, well, that was all a long time ago. I am as English as you are, Walt."

"If you say so, sir," he said.

"But Walt's a Welshman, sir," Rob said, in a false whisper. It made the men laugh and Walt cursed the lot of them.

To the south of the city was a large island in the centre of two broad rivers that flowed around Caen. The island was filled with splendid houses and ornately carved churches and even had plenty of green, open spaces. All of our eyes were drawn towards it because it alone out of everything in sight was unprotected by walls. Of course, the rivers served as a moat of sorts but we knew from our approach how tidal the rivers were and also that such watercourses tended to be slow and shallow at low tide. Still, even if we took and looted that island, the rest of Caen would remain untouched.

I knew how it would play out. As I explained to my men, we would dig in, offer terms which they would refuse and we would fling rocks at the walls for months until it became clear no French army was coming to relieve them and then they would surrender.

I was proved wrong almost immediately.

On the very first day, before our vanguard even established themselves around the walls, groups of archers drifted closer and closer to the city. Some of them noticed that the inhabitants of the town were fleeing across the stone bridge that linked it to the wealthy island. The cannier ones saw that there was a steady stream of soldiers, too, pushing their way out of the city and into that island. It made no sense at all for the French to contest that island. All it was good for was plunder.

More and more of our archers stopped preparing camp and drifted closer to stare, confused, as the French soldiers barged through the denizens. After a while, our men began jeering and mocking them. And then, without any orders being given by anyone, groups of archers started an assault on the bridges, on the island and on the city that the Normans seemed to be abandoning. Archers waded through the river, and used barges and boats, to approach the island and bridges, and other Englishmen hacked their way into the city and assaulted the bridge to the island from the rear.

"Have you ever seen anything like this before?" I asked Thomas, looking down on the madness from afar.

"An impregnable city being abandoned for no reason?" he replied. "One could argue Baghdad ninety years ago but..."

"Come now, that is hardly the same thing," I said.

"Indeed, it is not," he allowed. "And I can only think that God has driven the Normans mad."

It was hard to argue with that. My immortal knight John and his immortal squire Hugh, both former Templars, charged in amongst the heaviest of the fighting, leading Rob Hawthorn and my archers deeper into the fray. Black Walter begged me to give him leave to join in.

"Old Tommy here can watch your back all right, sir," Walt said, in a pleading tone. "Almost good as I can, sir."

I laughed, because Old Tommy was the affectionate name my company had awarded to

Sir Thomas the former high-ranking Templar who was about a hundred and fifty years old and who had fought in more battles and killed more men than anyone alive, other than me.

"Go on then, Walt. But if you get killed, do not come to me complaining of it."

Despite not being a straightforward assault, for the enemy fought hard, it was one of the unlikeliest victories I have ever witnessed, or even heard about. For days after Caen was plundered from basements to belfries, I saw many a man laughing and shaking his head in wonder.

After that, it was all marching and plunder, marching on a broad front and going always east and north and east again. Following the coast.

"We are heading to Paris," some fools would say. "We shall make Paris into England."

"We are heading to a port on the coast," the wiser would answer.

"But where?"

No one knew.

We were practically unchallenged the entire way until we reached the River Seine. We wanted to cross at the city of Rouen but the bridge had been destroyed by the canny French. There was talk of taking the town but Paris and King Philip were so close that it would have been foolhardy to dig in for a siege. What we feared as much as anything was being cut off from the coast. If we could reach the coast, we could reach our ships and then we were as good as back in England, or so we felt.

We headed upstream for another place to cross but after doing nothing for weeks the French finally made some tactical decisions. Every bridge or ford was destroyed or defended. Some we contested but, as Edward feared committing to any one place and being trapped, we were always driven back.

And then we were so close to Paris that those who stood in the right place or climbed trees or spires could see it on the horizon and everyone else could smell it when the wind blew the stench in our direction. So close to Paris that when we burned the hunting lodges and mansions of great nobles everywhere about, the smoke billowed into the sky and announced that we were so close that we could be at the gates if we so wished. No doubt the Parisians panicked, as they are a people prone to hysteria. And yet still King Philip did not attack us.

We knew from reports that he had been raising an army for weeks but where was it?

In the meantime, we brought more havoc to the country as our army, spread out for miles in a number of groups, probed the river until we reached the town of Poissy. The garrison had fled after wrecking their bridge but our men repaired the span and we were across.

Only to find ourselves now trapped by the River Somme.

Again, all bridges were destroyed or guarded and suddenly we felt the noose tightening. The word was that Philip's army had taken so long to assemble because it was so vast. An army created for a single purpose; to crush the English and grind us into dust once and for all.

My men began to feel the ravages of the march. They grew hungry and tired. Bone-tired from never getting enough rest. Their feet were in a bad way. The horses were suffering. We ran out of meat and the men grumbled that the dried peas sat heavy in their guts.

"Be grateful that you have boiled peas," I upbraided them. "You lucky bastards ate onions yesterday. You should be on your knees thanking God for those onions."

My weak jests were always tolerated and perhaps even appreciated but it grew increasingly difficult to keep their spirits raised.

"We will thank God, sir," cried John so that all in our company could hear. "We will thank Him when we scythe through the French knights like they are sheaths of wheat and take their stinking spiced sausages for ourselves."

They cheered that, at least, even though John was almost a Frenchman himself. My men were common as muck but they knew John first as a man who had risked his own life for all of them in battles past. I thumped John on his armoured shoulder as I made off, grateful as ever for his God-given charm.

Still, our army as a whole seemed to contract and shrink and the rambunctiousness of the march became pensiveness and men's eyes drooped and shadowed. Soon, we were cornered by the Somme and I had to lead my men in the crossing of a ford at low tide. Our archers drove the waiting enemy away from the water's edge and when I waded ashore with Thomas and John at my side, we carved our way into the French and held them as more English men-at-arms and archers crossed.

It was hard fought for a while but then the French fled and our entire army, including all our scores of wagons and thousands of horses, made it across in a single tide which may just have been the most remarkable moment of the whole campaign.

For a day or so we stayed on the river because the French army had come up and thousands upon thousands of them stared across at us from the other side. They could have forded the river, for they had the numbers on us, and we waited for them to attack.

In the end, they quietly went away again. My men shouted their thanks for the day of rest across the river at the retreating French, to much laughter. In truth, our army was still exhausted and low on supplies.

We marched on, hoping to drive on through and join with the Flemish.

But it was not to be.

King Philip had finally acted decisively to pin us in place with his numbers and so Edward found an excellent position to defend.

The ridge between the villages of Crecy and Wadicourt, with a slope at our front and to the flanks and woods behind.

"This will do very nicely," I had said to Thomas from atop the hill after the King had made his decision.

He shook his head. "It is unseemly to be so cheerful when so many Christians will likely die in this valley."

"I have known you too long, sir," I replied, "and watched you too often rejoice in the blood you have spilled to believe that your disapproval runs deep."

Thomas spluttered in protest. It was his French blood that made him so melancholic but that was understandable considering we were going to be fighting his countrymen. Having said that, John and Hugh did not appear overly concerned that morning as John went amongst my men to jokingly berate them for their lax standards. I watched from afar how the squire Hugh followed closely at John's side, all the while gazing at him in adoration.

They had both been very young men when Thomas and I had rescued them from a French gaol, saving them from execution. It had been about thirty-five years since that night and yet in many ways they had both retained their youthful manner. Thomas had been old when he had become one of us so perhaps that better explained his grim mood.

The mortals in my company seemed happy enough, although, being commoners, they lacked the depth of character necessary for considering such things and so it was to be expected. They wanted to win, to fight well in the eyes of their friends, the King, and God, in that order, and then to plunder the dead or take a man for ransom. They were not troubled by the whys and wherefores.

And so, after a night of preparation and my brief morning meeting with the King, we stood ready to face the onslaught of the massed ranks of French nobility.

The common archer and man-at-arms knew one thing as well as any knight amongst them.

That if we broke, we would be slaughtered to a man.

3

Crecy

EVERY ENGLISHMAN WAS ORDERED to fight on foot. King Edward himself walked amongst us, speaking to the men-at-arms, the archers and even the occasional Welshman.

What is more, he took the time to personally adjust our dispositions even within the individual battles. Many of the knights and lords who trailed after him also engaged the men in similar fashion and so the bonds of friendship and loyalty and duty were strengthened before the horror of the battle was to begin.

The army's priests went from man to man, blessing them. Our soldiers would be hard pressed by the massing ranks of the French knights and if any of us broke, we would all certainly be lost because it was only when an army fled that a right slaughter could occur. We needed to hold against whatever onslaught we suffered, no matter how long and how terrible it was.

For all of our recent victories against towns and small detachments, none of us was under any illusion about the enemy that day. The Frankish knight, armoured and mounted and delivering a thunderous combined charge with their enormous war horses, was the most devastating force on Earth. They were famed as Christendom's finest troops right across Europe and far beyond. Nothing could stand against the French knight when used properly. Not massed ranks of savage pagan Lithuanians in the north, nor the horse armies of the Turks of the East.

King Edward took his position near the top of the ridge, with the huge windmill behind. His bodyguards, lords, messengers, marshals, secretaries, heralds, and servants surrounded him. Each of the lords had their own men on hand, so that there were scores of men about the King in the centre of the rear battle. My company was many yards down the hill and I would certainly not be within earshot of the King unless I moved back.

"The men will stay here," I said to Thomas and the other key men of the company, "and you shall accompany me further up the hill."

The first of the French standard bearers arranged themselves in the valley a couple of miles away to the south, their colourful fabrics rippling in the wind. Behind them, thousands upon thousands of soldiers emerged from the roads and deployed in formation. Even after midday, they were still deploying.

"By God, sir," Rob Hawthorn, the leader of my archers said to me. "How many of them are there?"

"A good few, Rob, a good few. But we should have an arrow or two for each of them, what say you?"

He frowned. "Aye, that may be, sir."

We had fought smaller battles before, my company and I, while in Brittany, and one or two of them had begun with similar respective positions, writ small. A few hundred English against a thousand or two French. And we had always come away from them rather well.

But however keenly they are fought, a small scrap is a world away from a mass battle. It is often a slower affair on account of the masses of men and horses that must be arranged but the momentousness of the occasion stirs men's hearts, for good and for ill.

On that ridge by Crecy we held an advantageous position and yet it was by no means unassailable. What passes for hills in that part of France would not count as a molehill in Derbyshire.

The men knew it was to be the sort of battle they had heard of all their lives but had never really fought. These men had battled for their lives in Scotland, Wales, or Brittany, climbed town walls as the denizens fought to resist, forded freezing rivers while under attack, faced down charges from mounted men-at-arms. And all of those events were filled with moments that they would boast of when drunk, or weep for when very drunk, or recall in silence before the next action.

And yet that morning outside Crecy, there was a feeling in the air. Every man knew that his king's fate hung in the balance. And so, England's fate hung in the balance.

I wondered if the French felt that also. Indeed, they would have felt the desecration we had committed against the sanctity of their God-given lands and the people who served them. A knight's duty was to protect his lord, his king, and his people and the French had been held back from us for so long. They must have been desperate to do their duty and run us down.

"Will they come?" Thomas asked, looking at the sky.

John laughed. "Of course they will, brother. How can they not?"

Walt scratched his armpit through the mail there. "Why do you say it so certain, sir?"

John shrugged. "They must, that is all. They simply must."

I knew what he meant. It was what knights had lived for, since the days of Charlemagne. To charge the enemies that despoiled the earth with their presence.

The bannerets of France were rich and prominent knights who had made a career of war and commanded sections of cavalry in battle and flew their banner, which was a rectangular flag bearing their arms as opposed to the triangular pennon of an ordinary knight.

These men too often recruited their own companies and some did so among their dependents and neighbours like we did in England. But that was unusual. Most of the French army was made up of hundreds or thousands of individual noblemen and gentlemen, each one with his own personal retinue of a squire and a page and often no more than that.

When they mustered in France, they would line up wearing their armour ready for inspection by the officers of the Crown. The archers had to show they could use their bows. Horses were valued and branded so they could not be swapped for poor ones later, with the useless horses sent away and the man rebuked or fined. These men were then assigned to one great nobleman or another for the duration of the campaign. This meant that they would be fighting alongside men they did not know.

But despite all these weaknesses in organisation when compared to our superbly professional armies, the ordinary French peasant and the knights and lords, all threw themselves into the army with great heart for they loved the Crown and wished to do their duty.

Although King Philip himself was not loved, the idea of kingship had to be served. Our hearts compelled us to do so. Of course, the hope for financial reward and personal glory was just as important for some men.

Knighthood was yet a glorious thing, especially for the French. The ballads of the day yet celebrated knighthood as an idea, an ideal, more than it did the act of war. Not just knights but the common folk were able to recognise the banners and blazons of the most famous knights of the realm. Membership of the chivalric orders was much coveted by French and English alike.

Before every great battle, young men-at-arms queued up in their scores or even in their hundreds to be knighted on an occasion that would do them great honour if they survived and they sought to cement their newly-won status by challenging enemies to jousts between the lines.

Men wanted to be knights even if they did not want to be a soldier because they knew it would win them respect from their peers. The ideals of knighthood were perhaps rarely reflected in the practice of war itself but it was a knight's greatest duty to fight in a war for his king and fulfilling that duty felt truly glorious. Riding amongst your brother knights with the cacophony of horses' hoofs and armour and the trumpets and kettle drums, the brilliant colours of the pennants and banners snapping in the wind above your head. There was nothing like it for feeling right and true and powerful.

But changes were already on the horizon. Indeed, many were already present and being felt.

Men who were not knights still became great soldiers. Of course, our great armies were always commanded by the King, or a duke, a count, or an earl. But an experienced English squire could find himself leading a company and commanding knights even when he himself had not been dubbed. And, indeed, a mere knight could find himself in command of counts and barons if the King so ordered it. Something unthinkable in my youth. And men like Black Walter, who never wanted nor expected nor deserved to be knighted, could fight alongside them and be as skilled as any of them and just as well equipped.

Again, in my youth, we had a far greater expectation that battles would be decided by knights fighting knights from horseback under agreed and understood codes of behaviour. But the lessons learned over the years, especially from combat against the horse archers of the Steppe and the slippery Saracen cavalry, meant that we came to favour mobility and victory over honour. And so all of the men and even the archers used horses for mobility but all would dismount for combat itself. Most of my men had coursers, light and swift and trained for war. We needed at least two and ideally three horses each. The archers tended to ride rounceys or hobbies which could vary in quality from the sublime to the God awful.

When I was young, swords were worn and used by what would later be known as gentlemen whereas commoners were more likely to be armed with no more than spears and bows. But even archers had swords by the time we were fighting in France, though plenty preferred axes, maces or hammers and could afford to buy or loot whatever they liked.

Armour, too, had changed almost beyond recognition. Once, we had worn mail from head to toe, with a surcoat over the top in our colours. But by Crecy, we knights and lords mostly wore steel breastplates and back-pieces, along with close fitting plate covering our limbs and only the insides and exposed parts protected by pieces of mail. The steel would discolour and rust something terrible and pages and servants had to scrub them every night that they could to keep them in good order.

Our helms had changed from the old style to a lighter, rounded one called a basinet which protected the top and back of the head and was fitted with a gorget to protect the throat. A movable, conical visor hinged at the top or side meant one could open the helm to breathe, speak and see clearly. A basic style of basinet was worn by almost everyone, even the spearmen and garrison troops. Though for the rest of their armour they often wore a habergeon, which was a mail jacket that a man could shrug on by himself. Some men could only afford, or simply preferred, to fight in a layered linen coat which was easily good enough to stop all but the most terrible of cuts.

Their trumpets sounded in the distance, the blasts brought to us on the wind and calling in ever more of them from miles around.

The foremost of them was an enormous mass of crossbowmen, growing ever larger.

"There be the Genoese, sir," Rob said, unnecessarily pointing at them with his unstrung

18

bow.

Black Walt pointed down the hill at the numerous cannons being prepared on the flanks of the archers at the extreme ends of the battlefield. "What do you reckon our smoking monsters will make of them?"

The dozens of small cannons were protected by a line of parked wagons on either flank, the bizarre, squat things pointing out between them. Most were *ribalds*, cannons constructed from clusters of narrow iron barrels attached to a wooden frame that fired out iron rods. Some had four, or eight, or a dozen barrels. There were a handful of *bombards* amongst them, which were single, more substantial, iron barrels that shot out larger iron arrows or clusters of balls.

"The cannon will do nothing," I said, confidently. "A cacophony of thunder, belching foul smoke and nothing to show for it other than to frighten the birds. Same as we saw in Scotland."

Thomas coughed and spoke under his breath. "That was over twenty years ago, Richard."

Most of my men had been babes in arms or barely much older at the time.

"These devices are ever improved by the cunningest Italian minds, Richard," John said, his smile wide. "One day soon we shall see these ribalds or the bombards wreaking havoc upon an enemy army, mark my words, sir."

"Nonsense, John," I replied. "I have heard those very same words for how many years past? And, let me tell you, the Tartars used trebuchets to launch barrels filled with oil, *naphtha*, black powder, and the like which would explode upon impact with the ground and throw terrible fire directly onto the men nearby. I have urged the King to seek out these proven weapons but, sadly, he has fallen for the deceits of these Italians who have promised devastation for decades and yet who deliver only smoke and belch out ever more vague promises."

My men chuckled at me, for they had heard it all before. What I could never tell the mortals amongst them was that I had witnessed the effects of these Eastern weapons with my own eyes.

Some part of me still enjoyed being well-regarded and respected by other men. It was a terrible weakness of character and one I would soon seek to eradicate altogether, but I even drew satisfaction from the approval of commoners like Rob Hawthorn and Black Walter, men who served me and would be far beneath me in every sense even had I been a mortal knight

Our own trumpeters sounded the call to arms once more, as if there was an Englishman in all France who was not prepared and ready to meet the enemy.

"God Almighty," Rob said, "they don't half love their bleating."

"It is a wonderful sound," I said, loudly. "It rather stirs the blood, does it not?"

"What's the point of stirred blood if we be all the way back here?" I heard Black Walter mumble. I chose not to respond to his grumbling.

"There's too many of them to assemble properly before nightfall," Thomas said, with what was possibly more hope than judgement. "Do you not see, Sir Richard?"

I looked at the height of the Sun and held out my fingers to measure the distance between what was probably the horizon and the Sun itself. "There is a good few hours yet. All depends on how keen they are."

A little while later, it clouded over and a light but steady rain began to fall.

"Surely," Thomas said, "surely, they will not attack this evening."

Men cried out up and down the line as the French trumpets sounded, the kettledrums resounded and the Genoese crossbowmen began marching forward, closing the distance toward our forward battles.

Our archers, on the flanks of the battles, began stringing their bows from their horned nocks and readying their arrows. Their linen arrow bags were coated with wax to keep the arrows dry. Those bags were bulky things, stiffened by a wicker frame so that the fletchings did not crush each other.

They wore their lords livery over their brown, russet, or undyed tunics. The surcoats displayed the yellows, reds, blues, or greens of their lord's colours, scores of different styles from every county and hundred in England. But all were faded and most filthy with mud and food and wine stains.

As the Genoese came within the farthest range of their weapons, in groups they began to shoot their bows. Once they had shot, they would reload and advance further. In this way, they made their way closer and closer while unleashing a steady stream of bolts at us.

Sadly for them, their bolts mostly fell short of our lines.

The English bowmen, however, were in their element. Those men could shoot a dozen arrows a minute, if they had to and if they had enough arrows. They rarely did shoot at such a rate. Doing so would use tens of thousands of arrows in a couple of minutes and although that would cause an orgy of destruction it would also use up wagonloads of ammunition and leave the archers with little to do. What they tended to do instead was loose a mass volley of one or two shots and then they would pick their targets, being mindful of how many arrows they had left and how many enemies were on the field.

Still, they swiftly shot down hundreds of the Genoese. The mercenary crossbowmen stood in formations that were as loose as their vast numbers would allow so that our arrows would be more likely to fall on empty ground rather than on a man. Yet they dropped, killed and wounded, faster then I had expected to see.

"Quite a harvest this year," Hal Brampton, one of my men-at-arms, quipped. "Sizeable crop of crossbowmen we be scything down, is it not?"

"Do my eyes deceive me," Rob Hawthorn said, "or have the Italians gone and forgotten their bloody shields?"

I squinted into the crowd for a moment. "By God, how right you are. Is there a shield amongst the lot of them?"

Rob laughed in disbelief, as did the others. And well they might, for part of the strength of the Genoese was that each man carried an enormous and quite sturdy personal shield which would protect him from return shots while reloading or marching. But these thousands of men had no shields at all.

"Why ain't their bows reaching our lads?" Walt asked Rob. "They be in the range of them now, ain't it so?"

"Their cords are wet," Rob said, nodding once. "That rain fair soaked them through. Ain't so easy to restring a crossbow as is a real bow." He patted his own weapon like it was a faithful old hound. The hemp bow string was coated with wax but that only went so far in keeping the things dry, so archers kept them rolled away in a leather pouch on their belts, along with a spare or two. Some even kept a coil of cord under their steel helms.

"Hate this bit," Walt complained. "When the archers just stand there and shoot at each other for bloody ages while we hang about with nothing to do."

"Patience is a conquering virtue, Walt," I said.

Walt sighed. "Want to get on with the real fighting, is all, sir."

Rob and my other archers were offended on behalf of their profession. One of them, Deryk, cried out at Walt.

"Should you not be down amongst your brother Welshmen, Walter?"

"Shut your damned mouth, Deryk Crookley, or you shall find it filled with my knuckles and your own black teeth."

Our trumpets sounded and orders were shouted and relayed by heralds and sergeants that our bowmen were to increase the pace.

Before any man could respond, a great cacophony split the air along with billowing smoke and fire, as our cannons began firing, one after another and often many at once.

The ribalds and bombards spat their fire and their iron arrows and pellets down at the Genoese. How many of them were killed by the cannon, I could not say, as the arrows began to take them apart at the same time. Italians fell all across the field, and the foremost among them began backing away into their fellows behind.

I shot a hand out to grab Thomas by the armour of his upper arm. "They are going to break."

"Begging your pardon, sir, but not them lads," Rob said. "Genoese don't break, don't they say? Retreat in good order, the Genoese."

For a while, it seemed that he was right, for the Italians steadied themselves despite the astonishing number of them that fell to English arrows. Still, they were on edge and shuffling in that way that men do before they lose heart.

"Quick charge would do for the lot of them," I said to no one in particular. "It would be well if we had a hundred men mounted and ready for just such a moment. See them off once and for—"

The cannons sounded again. Not as many as before, perhaps merely a dozen of the squat little beasts coughed out their fire. It was impossible to tell if any of the projectiles even reached their targets but the fear of the machines was enough to do the job that a hundred charging men and horse would have done.

The Genoese broke.

Some of them at the fronts and edges of their formations backed further and further into the men behind, forcing those men to edge back themselves until some men turned and walked toward the rear, pushing past men still loading and shooting. More and more followed until the walking turned into running as fast as they were able with their large bows. Some men tripped and fell and—if they had any—their friends helped them up. All the while, the arrows fell upon them, driving them away.

A cheer went up from all the English battles as our men jeered the fleeing Italians, for it is a sight to stir the heart when your enemy breaks.

"You ain't looking happy, sir," Black Walt said from beside me. "You neither, Tom."

"It was good work," I replied. "Yet now we face the true test. See, there, how they are already making ready. Look at them, the magnificent bastards."

The French mounted men-at-arms moved forward on their great destriers and in their bright colours and shining steel. They were so many, massing together in a curved, broken front that stretched halfway across the vale and many more ranks pushed in from the rear.

"Once the Italians get free, the true battle shall begin," Thomas confirmed.

Instead, the French pushed into the fleeing Genoese and the mounted men's weapons were drawn and they began laying about them. Cutting down the Genoese, who could put up no defence against the onslaught.

"What are they doing?" Rob shouted, outraged at the sight of archers falling to knights, which was a deep-rooted fear for all bowmen. "They slay their own men."

Walt scoffed. "Shouldn't have run, should they. Bloody cowards." We ignored him.

"They are not their own men," I said to Rob. "We are watching Frenchmen murdering Italians."

It was a horror of a sight but we did not have long to ponder it, for the French had their blood up and in no time they barged through the Genoese and came charging in a chaotic mass straight across the field toward our first battle on the right.

"Here they come," Rob said to his archers. "Now let's see our lads do their work."

I had loved English bowmen for over one hundred years but only in the wars against the belligerent Scots and the factions in Brittany had they begun to come into their own. Successive English armies had included more and more bowmen in their ranks to the point where we had twice as many of them as we had men-at-arms. With masses of spearmen supporting them, our archers could shoot their powerful bows into enemy horse and men at will. We had done so before in Brittany but never on such a scale.

And we had likewise never faced an enemy of the scale and quality of the French nobility, the knights and squires of the greatest nation in Christendom and perhaps of anywhere on Earth. It was impossible not to be moved to fear by the sight, even though their initial charge was as ragged as any I had seen.

As they came within range of our foremost bowmen, the orders were given to shoot.

Arrows darted up in their hundreds and fell in amongst those riders.

The arrows the bows shot were murderous bloody things. A yard long and thick so that they did not snap when the massive force of the bow thrust them skyward. At their head was the small, dense bodkin point which could penetrate mail armour and force its way through visors or between sheets of plate.

Horses fell, stumbling and throwing their riders as they tumbled or sank to their knees and keeled over. Men were hit and rode on, or else veered away. Others were spilled from their saddles like the hand of God had swatted them. The fallen impeded the charge of those behind.

Our cannon fired. I jumped in fear at the sudden noise, as did many of those around me.

It terrified the charging horses and disrupted them further as they turned to flee from the appalling crashing thunder and evil stench.

And yet through it all, the courageous and the lucky reached our first battle in their dozens and then in the hundreds. All along the front line of the English battle, horses swerved and their riders hacked down on our men in a whirling storm of steel. A terrific clangour filled the air, growing louder even than the roaring cries of the men.

The first battle, on the right, was packed with great lords, their banners held high above where they stood.

In the very centre was the tallest banner.

That of Prince Edward.

Already at sixteen, the young man himself stood a head taller than most of the other men around him and he made for an unmistakeable and irresistible target.

"Going for the Prince, ain't they, sir?" Walt said. "Great bloody pack of the lordly bastards. Perhaps we might have a wander down there and lend a hand now, sir?"

"All is well," I said, though it certainly seemed as though the fighting was heaviest where the Prince was. I chanced a look behind me at the King, who stood watching all impassively.

More French came from the rear, streaming in as if there was no end to them. Our arrows fell in their thousands, coming in an endless stream. Those shooting from further away on the farthest flanks aimed up so their arrows dropped from a height into the massed French and the bowmen but those closest to the men-at-arms shot at the mounted knights before them.

Small groups of riders in the dozens attempted repeated charges against the archers on the wings but the tightly packed spearmen formed a wall of points that horses would die on, while the archers picked off the charging men at will.

The French edged away from the wings and clustered further in the centre where they could engage with our men-at-arms but this only served to give our archers even more of an oblique angle to shoot from, so that even men fifty yards back from the fighting were dropping from the arrow storm while they waited their turn at the English.

Still, they were skilled and brave and they were so many, and they forced their way into the Prince's battle right at its heart.

Right where the Prince stood, fighting for his life, for his people and for the love of glory.

The sky grew darker. Surely, many a man ventured, surely the French would have to break off soon. And yet still, they fought with a mad fury, sensing that all they needed to do was to break through the lines or to kill the Prince and they would have victory.

The Prince's banner fell.

A great intake of breath went up all around us and a rumbling growl began from our men as the horror of it dawned on them.

"He's fallen, by God," Black Walter said. "There, told you so."

"Hold your damned tongue," I snapped. "A banner is not the man."

Sure enough, in a few moments the banner was heaved aloft again and ten thousand Englishmen roared.

I sidled away from my men so that I was within hailing distance from the King as a knight came panting up the hill, covered in the grime of battle.

The messenger dropped to a knee in front of King Edward.

"Get up, sir, and relay your message," said one of the King's men.

When he stood, I saw wild fear in his eyes. "Your Grace, the Earl of Northampton begs you send the reserve to assist the Prince, who is sorely pressed. All about him, men are falling and the Prince can do only so much. Please, Your Grace. We must have more men, or the Prince is in the gravest of danger."

King Edward barely blinked. "Is my son dead or injured? Does he lay upon the earth, felled?"

"No, Your Grace, but he is hard pressed. Hard pressed, indeed."

The King radiated disapproval. "Hard pressed? You return to Northampton and those that sent you and you tell him to beg me for nought while my son yet lives. Tell them also that they are fighting so that my son may win his spurs and so that this victory may be his alone. Do you hear me well, sir? Then go now."

The poor man withered and bowed as deeply as he was able, mumbling his confirmation as he backed away.

Watching carefully, I noted how the King looked out from his helm, searching for someone and I pushed my way forward to appear at his side while more celebrated knights and lords than I protested in outrage.

"Your Grace?"

"Richard," he said, using his private voice, "I wonder if you might take your company forward a little way?"

"At once, Your Grace."

He turned away, dismissing me, but I noted how his eyes locked onto his son's wavering banner down below.

I pushed through the courtiers and called to my men. "We shall push forward now." I grabbed my senior archer. "Rob, keep your men to our rear but ensure they stay with me. You will be close to the enemy but hold your shots for now. I know it will much pain them but they will not shoot near the Prince and yet keep them in place in case the bastards break through our line."

The archers carried a variety of secondary weapons. Most of the younger lads wore cheap swords that were liable to bend or break if they struck a piece of armour at an odd angle. Older men could afford better weapons or had learned to favour a hammer or mace. Every one of them, though, wore a long dagger which was the sweetest thing there was for slipping through a man's armour and right into his offal, or to open his veins. Even the ones who barely knew one end of a sword from the other had grown up with a dagger in his palm and by God did they like to use them.

Rob nodded. "They'll not wander off, sir."

"Walt," I said, "you stay by my side and do not get carried away like last time."

"Don't know to what you be referring to, sir, but you can trust me, sir."

I raised a hand to Thomas, who lifted his hilt in salute. John grinned from ear to ear as he drew his sword and kissed the base of the blade. He and Hugh clapped each other on the shoulders before closing their visors.

Leading them, I pushed down the hill toward the battle while Walt shouted out for men to make way. He had a loud voice when he needed it, uncouth as it was. In no time, we were in amongst the wounded and the exhausted who sat or lay upon the ground while their servants tended to them. Some men guzzled water or wine. Others cried out in pain. We passed a knight who was having a great dent hammered out of his breastplate while he directed his servants and swigged from a cup of wine.

"Good evening, Sir Richard," he grinned, raising his cup to me. "Rare old fight, this one. Have at it, sir. Have at it!"

I nodded and continued on, pushing into the massed ranks of men. The sound grew until hearing a single voice in amongst the shouting and clash of arms grew impossible. Keeping my eyes fixed on the Prince's banner, I shoved and yanked men aside, calling out that I was on the King's business, for all the good it did.

The masses around me surged like a wave and, all of a sudden, there he was.

Prince Edward.

The sixteen-year-old prince fought like a lion fending off dogs. From afar and in his armour and similar red and blue quartered surcoat, the Prince looked exactly like his father. His magnificent harness was covered in muck and his armour much bashed about but the Prince stood tall and thrust at a horseman with a broken lance in one hand and swung a mace in his left at a French knight who rushed him on foot.

At his side, Sir Humphrey Ingham, a strong knight but a sour bastard, held the Prince's great banner aloft with an arm wrapped around the pole while he slashed at the French with a drastically bent sword. Even as I watched, more French horsemen pushed their way into the clear space before him. But the Prince smashed his mace into the helm of the man charging on foot and a moment later stepped forward and thrust the tip of the broken lance into the groin of the mounted man with such force that it threw the man down even as it rent his loins apart. The horse reared in panic but the Prince swatted its thrashing hooves away with his mace and stepped aside to knock a lance away from his chest.

In the space he created for himself, he half turned to those men being pushed back beside him.

"Come, my lords!" The Prince shouted, breathing raggedly. "For England!"

In response, the great cry of our people went up. "Saint George!"

"Prince Edward!" I shouted as my battle cry, for my heart was greatly stirred by the young lord's heroism and his skill. "For the Prince! Prince Edward!"

I hurled myself into the fray beside the heir to the throne and Thomas and John were with me, as was Walter, who put himself in harm's way for me many a time, though he was but a mortal man. Bless his black heart.

Humphrey Ingham, the Prince's friend, fought like a lion even with the hindrance of the great banner, throwing his body before Edward's time and again so that he became much battered.

For a time, I all but lost myself in the battle. The enemy faltered and returned, time and again. And we threw them back, time and again.

Night was almost upon us when the heat went out of the enemy. Prince Edward stepped closer and, exhausted beyond speaking, briefly placed a hand upon my shoulder. I clapped him on his arm, with a little too much enthusiasm, and he staggered away.

John grabbed me, leaned his helm against mine and shouted through the metal into my ear. "Now is the time, is it not? Now we should rush out and finish them?"

I looked to Thomas close behind us, who chopped his hand down in a signal that meant we should not act.

"Still too many," Thomas cried to John. "How many more do they have out there? Ten thousand mounted?"

"Numbers count for nought!" I shouted. "Remember the Mongols, Thomas."

I could tell by the set of his shoulders that he scoffed at me because he thought I was half mad with the urge to kill more men.

"King Philip holds the other side of the field," he said. "We had the best of it today. Perhaps we shall decide this tomorrow, no?"

"They will flee, the damned—" I said, in half a growl and caught myself before I spoke an insult aimed at all Frenchmen. "Come, the Prince is safe for now. Come, all of you, come."

I led them out of the fray, back up of the hill.

Black Walter flipped up his visor, panting next to me. "French still coming, ain't they, sir? Should we not stay with the Prince until he be safe and well?"

"Be quiet, Walt."

Almost to the King, I turned and looked out at the heaving to and fro of the battlefield.

It was clear to me that we had triumphed over the French. No matter how often the mounted French charged, fell back, rallied and charged again, their attacks could not break us.

We stood and watched, all of us wondering when would be the right moment to throw a good portion of our reserves into the fight on the front lines.

I coughed and pushed through the powerful knights until I drew close to the King. "I wonder if we might advance and engage now, Your Grace?"

Edward pondered it for a moment, as if the thought had not occurred to him, and as if every Englishman in France had not been urging him to do so for hours.

He nodded once.

"Let us be about our business," the King said, his voice raised, and the cry went up to advance down the slope and join the slaughter.

For slaughter it seemed to be. We were giving no quarter, no ransoms were taken, and no corpses were stripped of riches. Even the archers restrained themselves, somehow overcoming the natural acquisitiveness of the common man in order to continue killing French knights and nobles.

It was when we were fully engaged and the field was strewn with corpses, that one of the most remarkable things happened.

A charge of knights came full pelt for our centre, right where the King's banner was held aloft. They were in the very finest armour, riding the most magnificent beasts, and in their centre was a great lord in all his finery.

As they drew close, I realised in shock that they were shouting the war cry "Prague!" and those men around me called out in surprise that this was the John, the blind King of Bohemia. Once a formidable warrior, he was about fifty years old and had been blind for years after losing his sight on crusade against the pagan Lithuanians, and so no one had expected to see him fighting.

Yet there he was, charging headlong toward his death. John of Bohemia's bodyguards were slaughtered and the blind old soldier was surrounded by our men, dragged from his horse, and killed. By God, it must have made those poor men sick to their stomachs to kill a king rather than take him for ransom.

Darkness was falling. At the rear and edges of the masses of French cavalry, I watched small groups failing to reform and peel away from the main body.

"We have to finish them," Thomas said to me. "Now, before they escape."

I was surprised to hear him, a Frenchman originally from a place not far to the south, near Paris, urging us to kill his countrymen. But then Thomas had been amongst the English for almost a hundred years and a century was enough time to turn even a Frenchman sensible.

"Yes, yes," John said, "now is the time."

His good-hearted squire Hugh raised his axe above his head. "Let us kill the damned bastards."

That surprised me even more but then the reasons for their passion became clearer. I recalled how they and their brother Templars had been persecuted by a French king. It had been almost forty years since we had rescued John and Hugh from execution at the hands of the fourth King Philip, and it was that king's nephew, Philip VI who we faced across the battlefield that day.

Thomas especially wished we had saved more Templars but John and Hugh were all we could manage. To save their lives, I had granted them the Gift of my blood and we had welcomed both into the Order of the White Dagger.

John had been a very fine addition to the Order. He was a well-made young man, well-spoken and chivalrous. He retained his vows of poverty and chastity, so he claimed at least, and I had never met a man who did not like him. As a man often disliked by my peers, it was a wonder to me.

Hugh was a born follower but there was nothing wrong with that. Almost every man on Earth is the same and he was skilled in war and dutiful in nature.

I pushed my way back toward the King's massive dragon banner once more and forced my way through the press of men who wished to defend him with their person. A few fellows attempted to stop me but I did not allow them to.

"Your Grace," I called out when nearing him. "Might we not now mount and drive them off?"

William de Bohun, the Earl of Northampton, answered me. "The command to retrieve the horses has been given, Richard. Do you think we are fools or children who need you to hold our hands? Take yourself back to the fighting where you may be useful."

A few men about us chuckled. I ignored them all.

"Your Grace? Is that not the standard of King Philip out there at the rear?"

"Of course it is," Northampton said, irritated. "Are you as blind as the dead King of Bohemia, man?"

More laughter.

"We can kill Philip," I said, using my battlefield voice. "Or take him, if you prefer. Your Grace."

The laughter died and the King turned to me. "You will wait until our main charge begins. If you and your men can find a way through, then you may take my cousin the King of France."

"I will, Your Grace."

He reached out and grasped my arm as I turned. He leaned in close and I heard him over the terrible din. "God be with you."

"And with you, sire."

Northampton spoke up again, aiming his remarks at Edward but speaking loud enough for all about us to hear. "Philip will never surrender himself to a mere knight."

"Then that will be his choice," King Edward said, allowing his irritation to show. "Go, now, Richard."

28

With a bow of my head and a final glance at the Earl of Northampton, I began to push my way out of the King's circle and back to my men.

Sir John Chandos clapped an armoured arm around my shoulders. "Richard," he shouted in my ear. "The King said to take him, yes? He is worth everything alive. Dead, he brings us nothing."

I liked Chandos. He reminded me of myself. A Derbyshire knight barely above a commoner, he had risen as high as the likes of us could rise. He was about twenty-six or so and yet his tactical ability was evident to those of us who were able to recognise it. I had taken him under my wing when he was younger but now he was reaching the prime of his life and he was growing to consider himself as a greater man than I.

"I will treat Philip as gently as a babe in arms," I said, pushing Chandos away to arm's length. "But babies sometimes get dropped on their heads."

He looked concerned as I turned away but I wanted Chandos to know that his patronising advice was unwelcome.

When I returned to my company, I dragged our wide-eyed pages to me and shouted for them to bring our horses up immediately.

"We join the counter charge?" Thomas asked.

"The King has issued a command to me. This company will follow close behind the counter charge in the centre. When the lines clash, we shall punch our way through and we shall take King Philip in the name of Edward."

"My God," John said, a grin forming across his face.

"Rob?" I called to the leader of my archers. "You will stay close behind us, save your arrows if you can. When we reach the banner of the King of France, you may kill the horses of the King and his bodyguard. But please, Mister Hawthorn, do not murder a king this evening."

Rob nodded. "We'll give you dead horses, Sir Richard."

I have always appreciated the simplicity of the lower classes.

Darkness was falling and we were running out of time to complete our victory. The haste with which hundreds of horses were brought forward was impressive and was a testament to the fact that the professionalism of our army extended from top to bottom. My company mounted just as the first line of English cavalry formed and charged at the French. They were themselves readying for yet another desperate and foolhardy charge at us, no doubt because they witnessed the relative disorder in our lines as the horses were brought up.

"Stay together. Stay under our banner. And take no man but Philip." I urged my men before closing my visor.

We were going to capture a king.

4

The Black Knight

IT WAS WONDERFUL TO BE mounted again. To rise up above the heads of men on foot and so see that much further. Feeling the power of the animal beneath me and the mass of those beside me as we advanced behind the English men-at-arms. They smashed into the French and the sound of metal clashing echoed through the dusk. Banners waved everywhere and rallying cries filled the air as groups of men were broken apart before desperate attempts to reform.

All the while, I kept my sight fixed upon the banner of Philip; a vivid blue covered in countless emblems of the bright yellow fleur-de-lis.

Beside it was the Oriflamme itself, the ancient and holy battle standard of the French crown. Bright red and unadorned but long and narrow, with two enormous streamers doubling its length and flown from a gilded lance. Flying it over the battlefield meant that no quarter was to be given, echoing the orders of Edward for the English.

I aimed directly at those banners and, after ensuring that Thomas, John, Hugh, Walt, Ralf, and Simon were with me, I forced our way through the press of men and horse until we reached Philip's companions and bodyguard.

Touchingly, there remained some levies of townsfolk on foot about the French king and they were being cut to pieces even as the lords and knights of France turned and fled from everywhere else on the field.

Our advance was halted by a line of beautifully armoured men on enormous horses. They looked like they had been untouched by the fighting and I meant to change that forthwith. As we clashed with them, a few arrows slipped by me to hammer into the flesh of the French horses. The man before me struggled to control his maddened destrier and I shoved him sideways from his saddle, sending him down into the deep shadows between the horses.

I pushed through deeper and found myself surrounded on all sides, though it was increasingly difficult to tell. Men were losing the breath necessary to shout through their visors and the growing darkness was dulling heraldic colours and designs.

But I could see King Philip clearly now.

He looked magnificent and I was thrilled to be so close to him. To be the one to capture him would be a great honour.

We were close, and his men were falling all around him. When a gap opened up, my archers hit his horse with a volley of arrows, some slipping through its protective coverings and it went down, taking the King with him. A cry went up from both sides and we heaved forward against the mass of men protecting him but they pushed back at us with equal ferocity. In mere moments, Philip was up on a fresh horse and his men took up their battle cry with renewed vigour.

"*Montjoie Saint Denis!*"

While the English, including Thomas and John behind me, roared for Saint George.

I hacked and shoved further in, closer and closer to Philip. My armour received terrible punishment and my entire body would be a mass of deep bruises in the morning unless I could sup on a goodly amount of blood after the battle.

And that was when I saw him.

A French knight hacking his way toward me. He wore black over his old-fashioned armour and he was followed by a handful of men-at-arms also in black.

One of the pair of squires bore a banner of plain black with no emblem or image upon it. He threw down the English who stood against him with such ease that I was astonished to see it.

Philip used the opportunity to begin to withdraw and, seeing this, I shouted at my men to bring him down. My command was passed back to my archers who loosed a volley at the group of bodyguards. A roar went up. Philip had an arrow shaft jutting from a gap in his visor and his new horse was also wounded and both man and rider fell.

Good God, I thought, *we have killed the King of France.*

But they pulled him up and cheered as they helped him to mount a third horse. The mass of loyal men dragged the mounted King away toward safety.

As the French pulled back, space was created and the fighting intensified at once. The knight with the black banner swung his polearm at Thomas and knocked my friend senseless on the back of his horse.

John shouted and jabbed at the attacker with a broken lance. The man-at-arms bearing the black banner whirled his hammer down on Walt's horse's head with such force that the animal was killed. It dropped like a stone, throwing Walt down with it. John's lance was ripped from his grasp and tossed spinning over the heads of the riders swirling behind.

Hugh rushed in with his axe and smashed the breastplate of the black knight, who reeled from the blow before returning one of his own with such speed and power that it crashed against Hugh's helm. He fell to his knees, dazed or dead.

Such strength was inhuman. I could barely believe what I was seeing but there it was.

These men were surely immortals.

Charging my horse at them, I raised my weapon and thrust it at the squire with the black banner. I noted his red shield with three white escutcheons hanging from his shoulder. It seemed familiar but I had no time to think on it as, somehow, he swiped my attack away with the head of his hammer and struck me on the shoulder so quickly I did not see the blow coming.

Instinct caused me to lean away and so the rising backhanded blow merely clipped the top of my conical helm rather than hit me clean on the side of the head. Even so, it knocked me momentarily senseless.

I was falling.

The bastards had struck my horse and he was dropping.

When I looked up, the three men-at-arms beneath the black banner were riding away after the King.

John helped Hugh to his feet but he was unsteady indeed, despite the immortal blood in his veins.

"Get after them!" I shouted at my company.

"King Philip?" Thomas asked, lifting his visor and peering about, clearly still dazed from the blow to his head.

"The knight with the black banner!" I shouted, pointing with my weapon. "And his squires."

My archers were mounted on all kinds of horses but mostly hobbies that would not fare well when fighting through the mad swirling cavalry before us, of both sides. I watched John force his horse forward and raise his sword above his head.

"Saint George!" John cried with primal harshness. He was outraged that they had so wounded Hugh, who was very dear to John. He was an honourable man.

John was the finest horsemen of us all and mounted on the biggest, strongest destrier. He could force his way ahead through the crowd while I brought up the company.

I lifted my visor and raised my voice. "John, hear me. Get after him, John. Slow him down, if you can. Yet be wary."

"Wary?" John cried, with outrage in his voice.

I reached across and grasped John's arm. "You can see that he is one of us, John, do you not see it? In receipt of the Gift. One of William's creations. His squires also."

"Of course they are," John snapped, still angry, before calming himself somewhat. "I will stop him, Richard."

"We are taking the knight of the black banner and his men," I called to my company.

"Twenty marks to the man who takes one alive. Ten for each one dead."

They all roared their approval and we chased them through the battlefield. A handful of my archers, the best riders, pulled ahead of us. They wanted the money and they wanted the glory, too.

The sun had set and it was almost full night but there was just enough light to see by, though my vision was severely limited by my visor. I could just make out John and a couple of archers racing ahead of me, taking their own paths through the chaos in pursuit of our quarry.

The black banner was still held aloft by the small group fleeing amongst the rest and yet almost all the banners began to look similarly dark. I forced myself to clamp my eyes upon the one I wanted and trusted my horse and my instinct to avoid whatever came in front of us.

Likewise, I had to trust that enough of my company remained with me. As far as I was concerned, my archers were worth their weight in silver, for they could bring down a knight in armour with a well-placed arrow to the man's horse. I prayed to God that we would catch them before they escaped.

Years, I had searched for William's hidden immortals and now I had three of them almost within my grasp. I could barely contain the passion rising in my throat and I roared a wordless cry. It was echoed by my men behind me, crying for Saint George and some calling my name as their war-cry. It stirred my heart greatly to hear it.

We were charged in the flank by a group of knights from Hainault. Their shouts and the drumming of their horse's hooves filled the air at the same moment they hit my company. I avoided the lance aimed for me but a charging horse's shoulder collided with my destrier's head and neck and we were knocked quite desperately aside. It is a wonder my magnificent animal did not fall and instead we recovered, wheeled about and charged into the affray. I assume they believed we were in pursuit of King Philip for, after only a short engagement to delay us, they fell back and rode away.

It was growing difficult to see anything at all but I hurried on, with ever fewer of my men behind me.

"John!" I called, lifting my visor. "John!" The noise of the battle was growing ever quieter but still I barely made out his answering cry from up ahead.

An isolated farmhouse appeared before us. The structure and the building around it had formed some sort of nexus for the fleeing Frenchmen, perhaps seeking to hide overnight or to use the structures to mount some kind of defence against their pursuers. And the English had swarmed here, the foolish ones perhaps expecting to find food and the more experienced-aware that the place would likely have been commandeered by some lord before or during the battle—looking for wealth they could carry away.

I lifted my visor again and left it up so I could see better in the darkness.

Men shouted and fought all around. A pair of men even struggled high up on the thatched roof, grappling and sliding down the sides. They could have been men of either side, perhaps fighting to the death over a ring or a chicken. There was madness in the air already when I saw a flash of yellow and turned to see a man attempting to fire the barn.

In the light of the growing fire, I saw the black knight.

I saw so much in a single instant.

Far across the yard, the figures like ravens against the flame. On the ground, bodies writhed and died.

The black knight's helm was gone but he was silhouetted against the fire and I could make out no features.

But I knew it was him, for he held a grown man aloft in his hands as if his victim weighed no more than a rag doll.

And it was John that he held in his grasp. John was also without his helm and indeed his armour seemed to hang off him in tatters, with buckles and straps hanging down.

My friend and companion struggled to free himself but he was dripping with blood from injuries elsewhere on his body.

The black knight brought John's neck to his mouth with a savage jerk and began drinking from what must have been a gaping wound. He pulled back, tearing a long strand of skin and flesh and blood with it. As he did so, John let out a terrible, mournful cry.

I rode blindly toward the knight, determined to destroy this monster, to smite him with a single mighty blow. The rage filled me.

Something hit me in the face.

Then I was falling, the flames and silhouetted figures twisting as I tumbled to the ground.

Even as I crashed into the compacted earth and the pain hit me, I had a dreadful realisation of what must have happened.

As if I was some impetuous young fool in his first campaign, I had left my visor up as I attacked.

And a crossbow bolt had hit me in the face.

The shaft jutted from my cheek and hot blood gushed into my throat and I was wracked by coughing. Crawling on all fours, I had to hang my head down to let the blood pour out of my face rather than fill my throat and drown me. My eyes streamed so that it was hard to see and I groaned, unable to speak. Still, I got to my feet and stepped forward into the blurred streaks of shadow and flame.

"Sir Richard!"

Friendly voices surrounded me and hands were on me.

I recognised the voice of Black Walter, the commoner who was not an immortal and who did not know anything about the existence of the Gift, or the Order. But he was strong and did not know hesitation.

"Walt? Pull this bolt from my face!" At least, so I tried to speak but instead it came out as a series of grunts and ended in wet coughing.

Frustrated, I grabbed the slippery bolt in my fist and began to draw it out.

"No, no, no!" Walt and my other men shouted at me and they seized my arms so that I could not pull it from my face.

I was strong but was held by half a dozen English archers who were as strong as mortals could be and they heaved my arm away from my face. I almost screamed in frustration because I knew that once I got the bolt out and I could consume a mortal's blood, I would heal my wound and I could return to the fight.

"Leave him be!" Thomas shouted. "Move back, you fools. Spread out and stand guard. Catch your horses."

He forced me to kneel, bade me hold still and muttered a prayer as he pulled the wooden shaft from my head. It was excruciating and I felt the shattered bones of my cheek crunching and grinding as the iron point of the bolt made its way back out. More blood and chunks fell into the back of my mouth and I shook as I held my breath and braced myself against Thomas, fighting the urge to jerk away from the source of the agony.

With a wet, sucking sound, he pulled it clear and held it up to the firelight. The barn and the farmhouse were both burning with enormously tall, bright flames and their heat washed over me in waves.

Holding a palm over the ruin of my face, I attempted to speak but Thomas hushed me. "Blood. Yes, Richard, I know. Come."

He guided me into the shadow of a chest-high stone wall, sat me down and dragged a dying French spearman into my lap. He was probably a locally raised levy, called to defend his homeland and his town from the invading English brutes. He had a deep laceration in his skull and his movements were weak and he was clearly dying from his wounds. Thomas said another prayer but mercifully for me did not wait until he was finished before slitting the spearman's throat and holding the wound up to my face.

I drank down his blood, swallowing as much of my own as I did his.

And yet I felt it working in my belly before I had finished drinking. The strength of it filled me, lessened my pain. I felt or perhaps merely imagined the bones of my face knitting back together.

"John?" I asked, the moment I was able.

Thomas helped me to my feet and escorted me to him. Our company had already cleaned him up somewhat and bound his wounds even though he was dead.

And dead he was, with no hope of recovery. His head had been severed almost all the way through and his eyes stared lifelessly, reflecting the light from the fires that were already burning themselves out.

Hugh cradled the body of his brother, friend, and closest companion, weeping freely over him. They had been together, knight and squire, friend and brother, for over thirty years. And now Hugh was alone.

"Two of Rob's archers also fell," Thomas said, his voice flat. "Deryk Crookley and Paul Gipping."

It was my fault that John was dead. And two of the best archers. I had sent them on ahead, alone, without considering that even an immortal knight like John might be vastly outmatched by the men he was pursuing.

Even at the last moment, when John was still alive, I could have stopped it if only I had pulled my visor into place.

Decades, I had been searching and waiting for the chance to find and face down one of William's immortals and when it finally happened I was somehow unprepared and useless.

It was an irreparable personal failure.

"I could not stop them," Thomas said, his voice flat with his own sense of failure. "And then when they fled, I lost them in the darkness."

"As God is my witness," I said, "I shall find the knight of the black banner and his men."

"I swear it also," Thomas said.

"And I," Hugh said, wiping his eyes.

"I shall find them," I continued, "and tear their God damned hearts out."

5

Duty

"BY GOD, SIR!" Black Walt said in the pre-dawn murk the next morning. "Your face, sir. It is a miracle, sir."

"Avert your eyes from my face, Walt," I growled at him, for I was still in pain and had hardly slept as we lay by the smouldering ruins of that farmhouse. "Else it shall be a miracle if you live to see the sunrise this day."

He ducked away in false obsequiousness but I could hear him muttering under his breath as he went.

It was dank but not cold and the sun would burn away the damp when it rose. Smoke drifted through the morning. Normally, blackbirds, warblers and song thrushes would be chorusing at that hour but all I could hear was the cawing of a hundred malicious crows off in the shadows, already feasting on the carcases of the fallen.

I hid my healed face behind my visor, hoping that my soldiers would assume my wound was shamefully hideous, and gathered my company. We had lost men due to my foolishness but those that remained seemed not to blame me. Indeed, they all wanted to take their own revenge for John and Deryk and Paul. Their bodies we wrapped up as best we could and brought them with us for proper burial later.

I knew we had little chance of finding our prey by that point but I also knew that our chances would dwindle to nought if we delayed much longer. We assumed that the French would withdraw but we did not know whether they would contest the field again that very day. Some battles ran over more than one day and I thought that perhaps the French, who undoubtedly outnumbered us, might have another crack of the whip.

"It may be that the black banner knight laid low in the darkness nearby and may yet be within our grasp," I told my men. "We must get after them now, before they can get further away."

My company was ready almost immediately for they had no camp to break and little equipment. We had not gone far and were picking our way through the pre-dawn gloom when a cry went up from Black Walter and Rob the archer.

"What is it?" I asked, approaching to where they had stopped, looking south. There was a slight rise in the land there, and a line of trees across the horizon forming a darker band of black beneath the lightening sky.

"Listen, sir," Rob muttered. "Men marching. Hundreds."

"Marching? Not riding?" I strained to hear anything through my helm as Black Walter removed his own.

"Sounds like thousands to me."

"Where?" I asked.

They both pondered it, heads tilted to one side, listening. Rob pointed and Walt nodded in agreement.

"Coming up from the south," Rob said, "up the Abbeville road, I reckon."

It seemed as though the French would contest the field once again and they were making an early start of it, hoping to catch us unprepared.

"God damned bastards," I said, as Thomas came up beside me.

"The French have returned?" he asked, his visor open but his features lost in shadow. I detected a hint of pride in his voice, along with the frustration. "We must warn the King."

"If we do, we will lose the black banner," I replied. "Lose our chance to take revenge for John."

"I wish to kill that black knight. I wish it with all my heart," Thomas said. "Yet it is our duty to warn the King."

"Other men will send word," Walter said. "Perhaps word is sent already."

"Or one of us can return," I said, "bringing word of this fresh attack."

Thomas turned to me and though I could not make out his features, I knew him so well that I could imagine precisely how they were set. "None of us would be heeded by the lords. None but you."

"They would listen to you, Thomas. You are a knight."

"I am French. And they know me as a squire in your service."

"Very well," I said, growing frustrated, "I will return to the King and you will continue the pursuit."

"We ain't going to leave you alone, Sir Richard," Walt said, with his infuriating, base sense of honour. I ignored him.

"You know that I am not afraid of an honourable death," Thomas said, "but I do not hope that we can best the men we pursue without you there."

I almost growled at him. "What then would you have me do, sir?"

"It is our duty to return to our lines, raise the alarm, and join the battle."

I grumbled but I knew he was right. My men were frustrated also and they had no wish to fight another battle after the exertion of the day before but they did as I commanded and returned with us.

"Where have you been?" the Earl of Northampton said to me when I reached the village of Crecy as the sun was almost up.

"In pursuit of our enemies."

He scoffed as his men finished dressing him in the final pieces of his armour, most of which he had apparently slept in. "Did you even make an attempt on seizing Philip?"

I recalled how my men had killed Philip's horses, twice, and had even put an arrow in him, driving him and his men from the field and confirming our victory for King Edward. Perhaps de Bohun saw something of the violence I felt bubbling up within me and he addressed me again in a more agreeable tone.

"We are grateful for your bringing us news of the French attack," he said.

More and more men were coming in from the south, bringing word of the massing French troops.

"My lord!" one lightly-armoured squire on a fast horse cried, riding close and calling out. "They are two thousand strong. And, my lord, they are all levies and all are on foot."

Northampton's face lit up in joy and he turned to the other lords within hailing distance. "Suffolk! Warwick! Did you hear? Two thousand local levies!"

"It is a ruse," Warwick said, confidently. "They are drawing us in for a counter attack."

"Never, my lords," I said. "The French are not sufficient in cunning to bait such a trap."

Sir John Chandos mounted his horse. "Sir Richard is correct, my lords. Shall we slaughter them to a man and then return to break our fast?"

Our cavalry could not have been more thrilled at the opportunity to run down the enemy formations. It was the perfect situation for mounted men-at-arms to bring to bear the heavy cavalry charge and hundreds of us formed up in lines with remarkable ease and as the sun came up we thundered across the battlefield, already churned by yesterday's struggle, and crashed into the front ranks of local levy troops.

They were astonished by our attack and they crumbled almost immediately.

When they turned to run, we forced ourselves in amongst them and cut them to pieces. I broke off quickly and returned to my company but the English pursued the fleeing commoners for miles as they scattered in all directions.

By the time I reached my men, the sun was fully up. The field was strewn with bodies and with men and horses wandering, dazed and wounded, singly and in groups.

It seemed that the dead were all French, or at least practically all of the men-at-arms were. Heralds from both sides picked their way through the field, checking bodies for identifying heraldry as clerks marked down lists of the deceased. There were hundreds of dead English archers and Welsh spearmen being prepared for burial.

"We may continue the pursuit of the knight of the black banner now," I said to Thomas and the rest of my men. "But in which direction should we go?"

"South, sir," Black Walt said. "Let us get back to the edge of Paris."

"And what is your reasoning, Walt?"

"Good plunder, ain't there."

I ignored him. "Thomas? Rob?"

"I heard from some of the other lads that the French knights and lords ran on past Abbeville to Amiens, sir," Rob said. "So they reckon."

"If that is so," Thomas replied, "it would be madness for us to ride that way. There must be ten thousand men-at-arms in that direction."

"And yet if our quarry is there, we will go nonetheless," I insisted. "Assuming the men will follow?" I looked at Rob and Walt.

Walt grinned. "Try and stop them, sir."

Rob was more circumspect. He scratched his nose. "Might do it with a bit of encouragement, sir."

I resolved to promise generous sums of prize money but a royal sergeant rode hard toward me and my heart sank. And it was as I feared.

"King Edward requests that you attend him at his quarters in the village of Crecy, Sir Richard," the sergeant said. "Immediately, if you please."

It seemed that God did not wish me to pursue the knight of the black banner. I cursed Him even though I knew it must have been punishment for some sin or other that I had committed. It was hard to know which it might be, as I committed so many.

Prince Edward was leaving the King's tent on the edge of the village of Crecy as I approached. He was surrounded by a gaggle of young lords and he towered over almost all of them. Clad in his magnificent armour, he looked every bit the picture of the chosen prince, the hope of a new generation. The Prince had fought like a Greek hero. I knew looking at him that morning, serious and alert and paying his sycophantic knights like Sir Humphrey Ingham polite yet distant attention, that he would make a superb King of England, just like his father.

"Sir Richard!" he called, surprising me and startling his lords. "They caused you no trouble this morning, I take it?"

"It was like hunting sheep, Your Grace."

He laughed. "And yet they say you do not enjoy hunting of any sort, sir."

"I enjoy hunting well enough, Your Grace. It is simply that I prefer hunting the King's enemies."

Prince Edward nodded at his followers. "A very fine thing to say, sir. And you are in luck, for the King has need of your preferred kind of hunting. God be with you, Richard."

I bowed. "God be with you, Your Grace."

He moved off as if he had a specific task of his own to complete, and I am sure that he did for he was no paper prince but a useful lord and contributor to the campaign. Already at sixteen years of age he was a better man than most. His competence and rightness made us all feel hopeful and secure about the future of England.

His knights hurried after him like goslings after a goose. One of them, Sir Humphrey, turned to glare at me before he went. He had fought well on the field by the Prince's side, bearing his banner, and yet it had been my company that had come to the rescue. No doubt he felt the glory that should have been all his had been stolen by me.

Ah well, I thought. *Another enemy to add to the list.*

"Richard, good. Tomorrow, we shall move northeast along the coast," King Edward said without preamble as I ducked inside the open-sided tent.

All the lords surrounding the King turned to me also. A few of them scowled. I grinned back because I knew it would annoy them.

"We are heading for Wissant, Your Grace?" I asked, stepping forward. A couple of the lords begrudgingly moved aside. Wissant was a common landing place for those crossing from England. It made sense to me that we would want to take it when we disembarked for home.

"You want to leave France, Richard?" Edward asked, seeming to be cross with me. I suspected that he was feigning displeasure but it is hard to know where kings are concerned. Some of the sanest ones are still quite mad by ordinary standards.

"In fact, Your Grace, I would like to ride further into the country."

"Oh? Do you have some heroic deeds in mind? Or are you simply looking for pillage?"

I considered requesting his leave for the pursuit of the knight of the black banner but I could not think of a reason good enough. Clearly, I could not say that he was a blood-drinking immortal so powerful that he and his men had easily slaughtered John, who was himself a blood-drinking immortal knight.

If I suggested that I wanted revenge for John's death, he would dismiss my needs without a thought, for as far as anyone else would be concerned, I had lost a man on the battlefield. No crime had been committed. He may even explicitly forbid me from pursuing the French knight.

If on the other hand I said nothing, perhaps I could find time for my own purposes.

"As you say, Your Grace," I replied.

He glanced at me but I kept my face expressionless and he continued.

"That is well, as I would have your men advance ahead of the vanguard. You shall start today and we shall start behind you tomorrow. Go no further than Calais. The French have withdrawn into their towns, stiffened the garrisons and are no doubt improving their defences but there may be some attempts to delay us or divert us. If you encounter any force who will not withdraw from you, fix them in position and send a man to Northampton who will come up to you in strength enough to drive them away. And ensure you go no further than twenty miles from the coast. Is that all clear, Richard?"

How in the name of God will I know how many miles I am from the coast, I wondered.

"Perfectly clear, Your Grace," I said, bowing.

In the end, it was a disappointingly routine duty and though we ran off a few local squires, we rode through a quiet and empty country. Anyone with any sense had long since fled far from our advancing army and even the fools hid in the woods and dells and ditches at our approach.

Behind my company, the English army advanced in a broad front stretching from the coast deep inland, and they burned every house, barn, outhouse and field so that the sky was filled with smoke. We ignored every walled town, other than to burn their crops and suburbs to the ground, other than a small place called Etaples which was quickly taken, sacked, and then burned. Every market town and tiny village in our line of advance was turned to charcoal and smoke. When the army reached the settlement of Wissant, where I had expected we would embark for England, we instead destroyed it utterly.

Ten miles further up the coast was the small port town of Calais. It was well-known for two things. The first being that the place was a damned nest of pirates and the second that its people reeked of herring.

And yet it would be hard to imagine a small town that was better defended than Calais. As it was so close to the border of Flanders, it had become the stoutest fortress in the area. The first element in its favour was the fact it was surrounded by water. On the north side was the harbour and between that and the town was a wall, a moat and a fortified dyke. The other three sides had walls and a wide double moat. Beyond the moat was a marsh that teemed with fowl and wading birds but was sodden, boggy and crossed by rivers and tidal inundations. A dangerous place to cross even for locals and the marshland was vast. The approach to the town was by causeways that were anything but trustworthy.

The town itself was a perfect rectangle of high walls and the massive castle in the north-west corner was separated from the town by even more walls, moats and ditches. What is more, the place was well garrisoned and stocked with vast stores, because it existed in constant readiness for a siege by the Flemings, who wanted more than anything to take the place for themselves but never had the resources or the courage to make the attempt.

And it was Calais, of all bloody places, that King Edward decided to take.

6

The Lady Cecilia

"IT'S THE FLEMISH, ain't it," Black Walt said, picking gristle out of his teeth. "Everyone knows."

The leading men of my company sat at the table in my newly built home in the English camp outside Calais which had been named Villeneuve-la-Hardie in early summer 1347.

We had been besieging Calais for nine months and, in fact, to call Villeneuve a camp was rather absurd. It had become a town and a fortification as grand as any in England, outside of London. Villeneuve had a population of over ten thousand men, and hundreds or perhaps even thousands of women. In the cold autumn, we had dug our defences all around Calais to defend ourselves from assault by any French forces coming up from Paris to relieve the siege. Within our own lines, we built the temporary town.

We knew we would be there for a long time and so considerable effort was made to ensure we could pass the ravages of winter in some sort of comfort. The King had a quite considerable mansion of two storeys built from massive timbers and the great lords each attempted to outdo the other with their own homes around the royal residence.

Not simply grand homes but we also had market halls, public buildings, bathhouses, stables and thousands of hovels thrown up the soldiers made from whatever brushwood and reeds they could bring in from the land all around. We cut down every tree and bush for miles in every direction.

We had in effect created a new and vast English town that happened to be located in France. But ten thousand men could not survive for long on the countryside thereabouts, bountiful though it was. Supplies came from England by a steady stream of ships bringing fuel, food, ale, and everything else needed by a town and an army. Much of it was landed up the coast at Gravelines and then brought overland from Flanders. My company had been active over the months by patrolling that route and escorting the supplies because the French attempted time and again to cut us off. Whenever we were given leave to do so, we raided deep into the French lands.

Even so, I could find little trace of the knight with the black banner.

Our new town sucked supplies from all across England via the ports of the south in hundreds of ships. It was a town that housed some of the richest and hungriest men of England and the meat markets and the cloth markets of Villeneuve were as well stocked as any in the region. We were maintained in our position only by an enormous effort of support by our people. The English were proud of us and willed us toward the victory that would come from taking Calais for England.

Before the full depths of winter struck, we made an attempt to storm the town. I had urged those lords who would listen to me that we should simply take the place so we could spend the winter within the walls rather than without. And I believed that a victory would free me to take up active search for the blood drinking knight.

"How would you suggest we do it?" Northampton had asked me, scoffing. "The land is waterlogged so we cannot undermine the walls. Breaking them would take months anyway, even with the largest trebuchets."

It amused me to be so condescended by young men who had a fraction of my experience. "We storm them," I had said, shrugging at their concerns. "Our men are well rested now. We make hundreds of long ladders and make a rush on the place from all directions. Our archers would be up them in no time."

"The archers?" Northampton had cried, appalled.

In the end, the King listened to me but he also heeded the warnings of his faithful lords, who convinced him that a complicated plan to take the town from the seaward side would be most likely to succeed. They arranged dozens of small vessels to be packed with me and with huge ladders. The assault failed.

Then they built the trebuchets that Northampton and the others demanded and they even brought over a dozen cannon. For weeks and then months they chipped away at the walls but there was hardly any effect. We received an influx of fresh men before Christmas, when it was getting icy, but the half-hearted attempts to storm the walls all failed. By the time of the deep freeze at the end of February, we had entirely given up and all settled in and waited for the townsfolk to starve.

There were some of us who wondered what all this great effort was for. Was Calais really worth it? We accepted that taking Paris was out of the question but many of the veterans could not understand why we did not withdraw before winter and return in spring to engage in more raiding.

"It's the Flemish," Black Walt repeated. "Got to be."

My house was a sturdy one, with two chambers and a loft above for storage. The small bedchamber at the rear was a private space for me and where I would bleed myself to provide blood for Thomas every few days, away from the prying eyes of our company. The main chamber was a larger space with a fire which I used for company business which meant in essence it was where we drank ale and talked and played dice every night.

"The King would not do all this just for the Flemings," Rob countered. "It must be for England's benefit."

"Aye," said Hal, "but what's good for Flanders be good for England."

Fair Simon lifted his head, confusion on his face. "We ain't going to hand the keys of Calais over to the Flemings, are we, Sir Richard?"

"Of course not," I said. Though I thought that Edward was the kind of king who would do anything if it served his ultimate purposes. Whatever those were.

"You see, Walt!" Simon snapped. "You don't know what you're talking about."

"And you cannot hold your drink, lad. Why don't you have a lie down before you hurt yourself, eh?" Walt cuffed his mouth. "I never said he would hand it over, did I? What I do say is that we were supposed to be taking possession of Normandy, were we not? I know we cannot secure so much land but if we want a city or a port, why not one in Normandy? Well, we know why. The King needs the Flemings. And so we take Calais, no matter the cost, because the Flemings want it. When you bargain with a man, best you hold what he wants so you may get what you want. Right?"

Black Walt was fundamentally ignorant about matters above the interests of his class but he was wily enough to see that the patterns of human relationships were in essence the same even when writ large on a geopolitical scale. Still, I was bored of the endless talk.

"Hold your flapping tongue, Walt," I said. "Do not concern yourself with the intentions of your betters. If you must speak, tell us of the time the Mayor of Spalding caught you in his bed with all three of his daughters."

Merely mentioning the tale brought smiles and laughter from most of the men but Walt shook his head. "How many times have you blasted fools heard me tell it? I grow weary of it and thus you have gone and spoilt what was once nought but a cherished memory. No, no, do not crow at me, you oafish band. I have a greater tale I would have us hear, if Sir Richard would deign to tell it. What say you, Sir Richard? If I was a sinful man, which praise God I am not, I would place a wager that Fair Simon, Ralf, and perhaps even Adam, ain't never had the pleasure of hearing the tale of the storming of Nottingham and the taking of the traitor at the right hand of our great king when he was but a young man in danger of losing his crown to the usurper."

"Dear God Almighty," I groaned. "I am nowhere near drunk enough for your goading to work, Walt, you ignorant sot and to even make the attempt demonstrates no more than your own inebriation."

"But this is a special occasion, sir!" he cried, staring at each of us in turn with an idiot grin on his face. "It's a Tuesday."

"You are embarrassing yourself, Walt. We are riding to Gravelines on the morrow and I will need you sober and well rested, do you hear me?"

My men, impudent commoners that they were, cried as one that they must have my tale or else their hearts should break and other such nonsense. The more I cursed them, the more resolute they became.

I waved them into what passed for silence. "Someone bring me some wine, then," I said and they cheered their victory.

Yet before I could begin, a messenger arrived stating that the King requested my presence, immediately. It was late in the day and so I was confident we must be facing a military crisis of some kind.

Calling Thomas, and Rob to me, I told them to get the men sober and ready them for action. I did not envy their task for it would be all but impossible.

"Walter, brush yourself off and come with me," I said and followed the messenger to the King's grand residence.

In all the time we had been besieging Calais, I had been seeking the knight of the black banner. I did not have leave from the King to venture far from our lines but I did what we always did in the Order and that was to pay for information. Using tactics employed by the Assassins of Alamut and the Mongols, we cultivated relationships with merchants, jounglers, tinkers and other travellers who could come across enemy lines without rousing very much suspicion.

Initially, I had been hopeful. But all our possible roads to the immortal killer of John led, in the end, to a dead end.

Stephen stayed in London for most of the time and used his existing agents and contacts to ask questions and to recruit further men. We spent a fortune in bribes and in hush money.

All for nought, so far.

After winter had passed, I was expecting the trail to magically grow fresh once more and yet every day into summer I knew that I had failed again. My failure in the battle had led to the failure in the search for the knight. My lack of success was no doubt due to my sinfulness. I had sinned by my complacency, my vanity. For decades, I had fought in battles where no man could harm me. Only when outnumbered and cut off had I felt my life at risk and even then, I was rarely concerned.

And so I had grown lazy and vain.

I had become arrogant.

Lost my way.

And I knew that I could redeem myself, in the eyes of God and in the eyes of the men and the woman of my Order, by slaying the knight of the black banner and his men.

But I had to find him first.

When we reached King Edward's mansion, I was called into the hall without a moment's delay.

Edward and his men were at the far end, seated about the long table, outnumbered by attentive servants. The day's ordinary business had been dealt with and I was relieved to see the men of the court were in good cheer, for once. Wine and morsels of food were consumed as the lords conversed loudly amongst themselves. They ignored me as I took the offered seat at the King's side.

"I have a request to make of you, Richard," the King said, gripping a letter in his hand.

"Name it, Your Grace."

"One of the Queen's friends, the Lady Cecilia Comines has been widowed and requires an escort back to England. There is a ship waiting at Gravelines but the lady is at her husband's estate in Hainault."

"I am sorry to hear of her husband's death. Was he at Crecy?"

"No," the King smiled, "he was with the Flemish forces and never made it to us. His death was due to a sudden bloody flux. And the Lady Cecilia cannot stay in Hainault in the current circumstances and she requires an escort to the coast."

"Forgive me, sir, but is her brother not Sir Humphrey Ingham?"

"Humphrey is back in England. You are the steadiest man I know and you shall not allow any harm to come to her, nor shall you allow her to be dishonoured or insulted in any way. You shall travel with the protection of a letter which states you will undertake no action which would alter the war or any treaty or truce. Do you accept?"

I bowed, for how could I deny my king? "I am honoured to accept, Your Grace."

As I left the royal presence, Walter fell in beside me with his eyes popping out of his head and a broad, idiot grin on his face.

"The Lady Cecilia is said to be the most beautiful woman this side of the Rhine, Sir Richard!"

I chose not to ask what great beauty was on the other side of the Rhine and instead sighed at his ignorance. "Every bloody lord with a spare shilling will pay troubadours to spread word of his daughter's beauty far and wide. In this way, he increases her market value. Do you see?"

"Clever bastards," Walt said, nodding. "But that ain't true of Lady Cecilia, Sir Richard, not in the least bit true. You know Garrulous Gilbert what's with Dagworth's company? He seen her with his own eye, so he did. He swore upon God's teeth that she was more beautiful than a dewdrop on a red rose lit by a midsummer dawn."

I knew the man Walt referred to and his epithet was an ironic one. "Gilbert has not had a tongue in his head for over six years, Walt. Not since that Breton knight had it cut out."

"He speaks with his *hands*, sir. Gestures in a most eloquent fashion. And Gilbert says she's got a bosom like the Lady Helen."

"Lady Helen who?"

"The Lady Helen of Troy, sir."

"And Helen had a fine bosom, did she, Walt?"

He shook his head in despair at my ignorance. "Stands to reason, sir. It is wisdom itself. Why else would them Greeks have run after her like that if she ain't got no apples in her barrel?"

"You have not an ounce of wisdom in your soul, you fool."

"Yes, sir. But what is better than wisdom? A woman. And what is better than a good woman? Nothing."

I cursed his idiocy even as I chuckled but damn me if the fool was not entirely right about the Lady Cecilia.

***

"Might this not be a fine opportunity for ranging inland a little?" Thomas suggested as we rode. "By which I mean we can make enquiries regarding the knight of the black banner?"

"I know your meaning, Thomas," I said. "We must do as the King commands."

He said nothing. A silence full of meaning, which I supplied for myself. We had seen kings come and go and while they ruled, they were everything to the kingdom and to each of us that served him. But then the king would be dead, and his courtiers would be dead, and new men would take their places. Why did the likes of us, who outlived them all one after the other, need to follow the wishes of even the greatest of mortals, when we had our own quest that spanned lifetimes?

I had no answer for Thomas back then, nor even one for myself, other than I felt it was my duty. It was the duty of all men to follow the word of their king, even if that king was young and the man was old. Why should it be any different for us when it came down to it? Fulfilling one's duty is all one can hope for in life.

Of course, it is when duty battles with duty that a man's heart is filled with anguish. But I had been asked a favour by a king, and a good one at that, and so I would see it through.

I escorted the Lady and her servants from a small manor house in Hainault back to Calais. It was not a long way but of course tensions were high and there was an air of lawlessness and fear everywhere we went, although that may have been as much to do with my men—veteran brutes that they were—as it did with the state of France. The entire task would have been a simple one and indeed a rather pleasant break from the fetid air of the army had it not been for one thing.

The Lady Cecilia herself.

For it was true that she was a great beauty. Her skin was pale as milk and her hair fair as sunlight, with lips like ripe cherries and eyes as big and bright and blue as a clear sky over Dove Dale. The moment I saw her, I knew I was in trouble. She was a lady and a widow still in mourning for her husband but I had bedded ladies before, married, widowed and maid alike, when they were lusty enough to make pursuit easy. There would be no privacy to be had on the road, however, and so I resolved to restrain myself lest it cause me further problems with the courtiers. Any more scandals and rumours around me and Edward would be forced to cast me aside. It would therefore be best if I attempted no seduction at all, not even a subtle one.

And then I discovered that I need not have concerned myself with such thoughts.

"The King sent you?" she said, somehow managing to look down her pretty little nose at me while avoiding eye contact of any kind. "The King sent you and you alone?"

"I have a number of armed men who serve me who will also provide your protection on the road, my lady."

"Those appalling villeins?" she said, her sweet lips turning sour at the corners. "But where is the Earl of Northampton?"

"He is with the King, my lady."

"Surely, Warwick has come for me?"

"The Earl of Warwick is with the King in Calais, my lady, and with your permission I shall escort you there forthwith."

"You most certainly do not have my permission. Summon Lancaster. He may escort me."

"I am afraid he is otherwise engaged, my lady."

"How dare you take that tone with me. I shall not stand for it. You must send for Kent, immediately. Even Stafford would do. Come, come, the sooner you set off with my instructions, the sooner a man of the proper rank shall return. I cannot stand to stay in this ghastly place an hour longer than necessary."

I stepped closer to her and she fell silent, looking warily up at me. Her servants drew nearer, ready to pull her away.

"We are leaving now, my lady," I said with a pleasant smile on my face. "Please mount your horse and instruct your servants and ladies to do the same, or else I shall instruct my appalling villeins to truss them up and carry you all to Calais like bolts of Flemish cloth."

She hesitated for a good long moment and I knew I had her.

"The King shall hear about this," she said, in a far softer voice. "And the Queen, also."

"I am certain that your woes will be the very essence of their attention once we reach Calais. Shall we begin, Lady Cecilia?"

She tossed her head up and rolled her eyes, not deigning to reply.

By the time we made off, it was already late in the day but we had to get moving if we were to reach the first stopping point. My men were ranging all around the Lady's company on their coursers or hobbies, other than Walt who lurked as always within striking distance of my back. I urged my horse forward and called out that we were leaving immediately and that anything or anyone not packed up and mounted would be left behind.

"Do not hurry the lady so," a hulking great servant said to me in a dismissive tone as he tightened a strap across a horse's flank. He did not even look up from where he stood. His voice was as gruff as his manner and I resisted the urge to lean down and strike him with the back of my hand.

"I do not hurry the lady," I replied, my tone level. "I hurried her servants. I hurried you, did you hear, little man?"

Prideful men who consider themselves to be large fellows hate nothing more than to be called small. And so it was with this servant, who glared at me with open hostility.

Instead of pushing him further, I laughed and rode away, turning to Walt as he came up with me.

"Watch that man, Walt."

"I clocked the cove before you ever conversed with him," Walt replied. "His name's Eustace. They call him the Steward and so he is but he's built like a fighter and no mistake. Right bruiser, that one, sir."

"Yes, thank you for your assessment."

Now that Walt mentioned it, I noted how this Eustace fellow stayed close to the Lady and watched her always from the corner of one eye. I should have seen it before but he was undoubtedly an experienced soldier, or a bailiff used to bashing skulls in, or perhaps a former ruffian, but it was perfectly ordinary for a noble to have guards and armed servants and arguably it was vital considering the state of the country.

"Well, Sir Richard?" Walt asked, raising an eyebrow and jerking his head back with a sly look on his face.

I knew what the sordid ruffian was getting at but I pretended ignorance. "What is it that you are asking, Walter?"

He grinned. "You doubted what old Gilbert said about the lady, sir, but now you know that he ain't one to tell a lie and, so help me God, neither be I. That dear lady is a ripe one and no mistake. Wheresoever she goes, the men all about her, common folk and lords alike, must be bending God's ear with all the praying for forgiveness they be doing once she passes by."

"Do not speak of your betters in such a manner," I said, repulsed by his vulgarity. "In fact, do not speak of the Lady Cecilia at all from now on, excepting practical matters."

"Right you are, sir," Walt replied, cheerfully. "So, speaking practically, my lord, how about we inveigle the Lady's wagon into a ditch at a likely spot on the way, so as you can take her into the woods and give her the green gown?"

I do not know what disturbed me more. The fact that Walt's depraved mind so closely mimicked my own, or that I was desperately tempted to take him up on the offer of assistance.

But my reservations remained. Even if I could somehow seduce the woman into civility, I could not imagine her softening so far as to allow me to lift her skirts and attempting to do so and failing could have dire social consequences for me. As it was, it appeared that she was resolved to be insulted by my every action and indeed by my presence and even the maintenance of the utmost public courtesy would only go so far to lessen the blow.

Besides, she would never be left alone. Not by her ladies, nor by her servants. And certainly not by her bodyguard.

"He's watching you like a hawk, sir," Walter said when we stopped at a local manor for the night. "Black beady eyes on him, ain't they, sir. Like a rabid badger."

The little manor hall was a dark and smoky place in need of repair but the lord was a loyal Fleming and so was an ally of ours, though he was away with the army. His servants provided dried herring in abundance and plenty of bread, though the wine was two years old and on the turn. The ale was good, though, and that was enough for my men.

"See that the bowmen are on watch all around and come back for some ale, Walter," I said.

When he was gone I smoothed myself down as well as I could and made my way to the table where Lady Cecilia was eating. She did not look pleased to see me.

"My Lady, I hope that everything is to your satisfaction." I continued before she could voice her displeasure. "We shall rise before first light and look to make the rest of the journey before nightfall tomorrow. I pray you sleep well." I bowed and turned to leave.

"Sir," she said, her voice softer than before. I turned back. "I know that your only concern is for my personal safety and I wish to say that I am grateful for your efforts."

Surprised, I was about to make a gracious reply but she continued speaking.

"And that is why I know you shall grant my request that you and your men shall sleep outside the manor house tonight."

"Come again?"

"I think you heard me perfectly well. I could not possibly sleep for a moment all night long, knowing that such men sleep under the same roof."

I rubbed the corner of my eye. "My men will behave themselves, my lady. Some shall be outside through the night to watch all approaches at all hours. Those not on watch shall sleep within the hall. You shall have the master bedchamber on the floor above. Have no fear, for I shall stand guard myself at your door all night long."

Her face flushed and she gaped at me. Behind her, the steward Eustace stomped forward.

"I shall be the man standing guard over the lady," he said, his voice a growl.

Making a show of it, I raised my eyebrows dramatically. "Oh, it is like that, is it? Well, in that case, do not allow me to stop you."

Her ladies gasped and the Lady Cecilia jumped to her feet, slamming her hands upon the table in a most unladylike fashion, causing the cups to wobble mightily. "It is most certainly not like anything, you unchivalrous oaf. Oh, I cannot eat another morsel, you have upset me so. I must retire to my chamber lest I strike you for your impudence."

I bowed. "I would greatly savour any blow to my person that you could strike, my lady."

She screwed up her mouth and I was certain she was about to toss her wine in my face but her ladies bustled her away from the table toward the stairs at the rear.

I bowed again, grinning as I stood up. The stocky steward glared at me with red murder in his black eyes.

"Eustace, is it?" I said, brightly. "I thought you were to stand guard at the lady's door? Well, hop to it, man. Hop to it, I say. We would not wish harm to come to such a delightful creature, would we? Come, come, good steward, be about your business."

Gritting his teeth, he backed away while fixing me with that dark look.

"You will let me know if you need me to stand watch in your stead, will you not? I hear many a man of advanced years struggles to remain wakeful in the darkest hours."

He hesitated, his face growing a vivid purple, but then he turned and strode off up the stairs.

When I turned to head back outside, I caught Thomas' eye. He shook his head in disapproval. After so long, I could read his mind in just that one look.

Making enemies at every turn, Richard, he would have said.

I shrugged, indicating that I cared nothing if some slab-brained steward thought himself an enemy.

Thomas was unimpressed.

Through the night, as I lay on my back on two old mattresses at the top of the hall, I considered climbing the stairs to check on Lady Cecilia. I would have had to bully old Eustace away but I knew he could be overpowered with ease and perhaps even without much fuss. Once he was removed, I would politely ask if there was anything she needed.

I imagined that she might ask one of her ladies to open the door to me, where I might be admitted into the dimly lit room. I pictured a single candle burning beside the bed and the Lady, sitting up with her hair uncovered, to ask if I might not sit upon the bed to converse with her. It seemed to me that if I could get so far then it would be a simple enough matter to be invited to disrobe entirely and to join her in the bed and beneath the sheets. I thought it likely that her servants would vacate the bed but that was not always the case and if the red-haired girl were there with us then I would certainly allow her to remain. The older ladies were welcome to feign sleep upon the truckle bed. The lady herself had no children, so perhaps her marriage had been a loveless one. It might be that I could awaken a desire in her that was hitherto unknown to herself and so I would proceed slowly and lovingly, caressing her. Stroking her blonde hair and the perfect pale skin of her cheeks as they flushed with desire. Her chest, too, would be flushed when she removed her underclothes and bared herself to me.

Black Walter kicked my feet again.

"Begging your pardon, sir, but it's almost sunrise."

"Damn your tongue, Walter," I cursed. "Damn your eyes, too."

"Yes, sir," he said. "Glad you slept well, sir."

It was an overcast day and we set off under a low sky with very few words spoken. Lady Cecilia appeared just in time, wrapped tightly in a heavy cloak with her hood up. Eustace heaved her into the saddle and we were away. I set a smart pace so that we would make it safely back to our territory before dark.

"A rather bad track for rain," Thomas said, looking at the gathering black clouds.

It was much travelled and the surface was deeply pitted and the soil loose. It would certainly turn into a morass if heavy rain were to fall.

"It may hold off yet," I said.

The rainstorm hit us before midday, driving us all to the shelter of a nearby copse. Mud pooled and spattered everywhere in mere moments and there was no chance of making headway through it. Beyond the copse I could make out the reed-thatched roof of a low cottage and I raised a finger to point at it, about to suggest to the Lady Cecilia that she seek shelter within, when a fox burst from a bush beneath the lady's horse. As much as the surprising streak of red at its hooves, the sudden shouts of warning from the men all around caused the horse to bolt away. Lady Cecilia held on while the animal thundered across a field, flinging mud and crops behind it as it went. I was after her right away, my courser gaining on the palfrey and all would have been well but for the idiot bloody fox veering back across the path of the already frightened horse.

It reared and then bucked, throwing the poor girl over its neck, causing her to fall very heavily.

Flinging myself from the saddle, I stooped to the mud and lifted the woman into my arms. She was dazed and caked in dark mud but she was awake and mumbling something. I wiped the muck from her eyes and started back to the cottage I had seen, crying out orders for water to be heated and for clean cloth to be readied.

"I shall take her," Eustace said, scowling as he lumbered up to us.

"You shall not," I replied. "I will place her within, where her ladies can care for her."

The cottage was cold and dark and clearly had been abandoned. But only recently, for it was clean and had no smell of mould. There were plenty enough such emptied homes in those parts where armies tramped back and forth looking to take everything a man had and those who could live with distant family readily did so.

"Make a bed of your cloaks by the hearth," I commanded. "Build the fire hot, for she is soaked through."

I laid her down and saw with relief that her eyes were open.

"I am well," she said, faintly. Her eyes closed.

"Glad as it makes me to hear that, my lady, you took a bad fall and must rest. Your ladies will see to you now and you and they shall send to me if you need anything it is in my power to provide."

She reached up and placed a hand on my cheek, leaving a wet smear of mud.

Eustace lurked in the background like an old storm-struck tree trunk. "My lady shivers. You must leave."

"As must you," I said and dragged him from the cottage and pushed him away while I closed the door. "Thomas, Walt, Rob. I believe we will be forced to shelter hereabouts for the night. Even if the rain lets up, I doubt the lady will be ready to travel before day's end."

"Begging your pardon, sir," Rob said, snatching off his hat. "Is the lady much harmed?"

I pondered it, for I had seen how she had landed on her head and neck and such falls had ended the strength of many a man in my sight. "No, no. She will be well by morning, I am sure of it."

All my men sighed with relief and many grinned. "God be praised," Rob said and many of them took up the prayer.

It is my experience, earned through many centuries of observation, that most men would do almost anything for any woman. A beautiful young woman of the nobility may have men of all ages and all classes gladly laying down their lives for her, should she wish it. This is the proper way of things, for women carry our civilisation within their wombs, and each and every one of us knows this to be true.

Eustace glared at me and I turned on him.

"Where were you, Steward Eustace?" I said softly, advancing slowly. "Why was your hand not wrapped about her bridle? You will damned well do your duty the next time or I'll see you punished myself."

He did not retreat but stood his ground and simply glowered in response.

A group of sodden archers hurried over, their arms full of twigs, branches, and broken dead wood. "Firewood, Sir Richard!"

"Well done, lads," I said. "Leave it by the door for the ladies, will you and fetch more. We shall need to strip that little wood clean, as the Lady must be warm through the night."

"Right you are, sir!" the men cried, happy beyond measure.

It was a sodden afternoon, with nothing to do but huddle against a tree or a wall. Some of the men took turns within the empty pigsty, empty wood store and the outbuildings but I resigned myself to being wet through to the bone and staying that way. Just as night fell, the rain began easing off but a steady wind came up with it and chilled us mightily. I kept moving around between the groups of my men to check at least one of them was alert to danger but mostly it was to keep myself warm and my thoughts away from the memory of holding Lady Cecilia in my arms as she stared up at me with those big blue eyes.

"Begging your pardon, Sir Richard." It was Reginald, one of Rob's bowmen, approaching with one of the Lady's servants huddled under a thick cloak. "The lady here has a message for you directly, sir, from her Ladyship herself, sir."

"My Lady would speak with you, Sir Richard," the woman said. "As soon as your duties allow."

"I shall return with you immediately, good woman."

I ducked in through the doorway and stood for a moment as the warmth from the fire and the silence from the cessation of the wind enveloped me. It was like stepping into an altogether different world from the one outside.

Lady Cecilia reclined where I had last seen her, bundled up by the roaring fire. One servant attended her, while the others were nowhere to be seen.

"Where is Eustace, good woman?" I said to the young red-head who was tucking the blankets up higher over the injured woman.

"I sent him away to see to the other servants," Cecilia said, her voice clear. "I could not stand his ceaseless lurking. And besides, I now know that I am perfectly safe in your care." She glanced at her servant who finished fussing and moved away. "Come closer, Sir Richard.

Down here, where I can see you."

I did as I was bid and knelt close beside her on one knee. The firelight shone upon her face like gold on marble and her eyes glittered.

Swallowing, I spoke softly. "How may I be of service, my lady?"

She reached out from her bundled coverings and placed a lovely hand upon the back of mine. Those eyes of hers snared mine in their gaze and I could not look away. "I simply wished to thank you for what you did for me and also to beg your pardon for my rude manner."

"No pardon is necessary, my lady, but of course you would have it."

She smiled and gently patted my hand. It stayed there. "An explanation, then? You see, your reputation preceded you and I had been led to believe that you were a most uncouth and unchivalrous knight. It is known that King Edward favours you for your martial abilities but it is said that you entirely lacked even the most rudimentary courtly standards."

Whatever my facial expression was, she laughed lightly at it before continuing.

"But I see that these were slanderous words spread by your enemies and that you are as true a knight as any in Christendom."

I bowed my head, tearing my eyes from hers for but a moment before fixing on them again. "Your generous words have moved me, my lady."

"Then kiss me," she said.

I was startled but a woman does not need to tell me such a thing twice.

Bending to kiss her upon the cheek, she grasped my head between her hands and pulled my mouth down onto hers. Her lips were soft and warm and delightful beyond measure. I had my hands planted either side of her, lest I fall down upon her with the weight of my body. She kissed me deeply, opening her mouth and putting her tongue into mine and her fingers dug into my hair like she intended to never let go. She moaned with passion into my mouth, bringing forth a groan of my own, the sounds resonating between us, while her hands moved from my hair to my face and my neck, touching and stroking me while her lips worked on mine.

She pushed me away, gasping and eyes shining.

"You must go now," she said, breathlessly, grasping one of my hands to her chest with both of her. "Lest our servants start talking."

I did not know what to say, so I said nothing as I stood, gazing down at her.

The young red-haired woman took my arm and led me away to the door. The girl was looking at me with passion in her eyes while biting her lower lip and I almost asked her to come outside with me before cooling my ardour. At the door, I turned and remembered my manners.

"I shall pray you rest well, Lady Cecilia, and wake fully recovered for the journey tomorrow."

"Good night, Richard," she said softly.

In the morning, she carefully ignored me and we continued on, our horses splashing through the remnants of the rain and sinking into the mud. The wind helped to rid the street of the water and then the sun came out and the surface firmed up so that by late afternoon we came to Gravelines. Thomas would take over leadership of the company while I returned to England.

"It is my duty to cross with you to England. My men shall remain but I also have business in London."

"You continue to honour me with your protection, sir, and I have so little to offer in return."

"Your company is more than enough, my lady. The crossing should be swift if the wind remains as it is but the journey can be tedious unless one has diversions."

She blushed and looked down, covering her face with a lovely hand. "I should greatly wish to share a ship with you for the crossing, dear Richard," she said, speaking softly. "Yet my good name is the only thing of any value that remains to me."

"I understand, my lady," I said. "I shall ensure that you and your household reach your estates but I shall do so from afar."

"A true knight, indeed," she said, starting to reach for my cheek before pulling her hand back to place it over her heart.

After we embarked, I barely saw her, even from a distance. But I kept my word and made certain that there were no delays in ports. Our ships both travelled around Kent into the Thames and the port of London. The crossing was as easy as any I have undertaken and I have crossed that channel more times than I care to count.

London was teeming with ships, as ever, with large and small cogs with single masts, the fatter hulks and even a handful of huge Genoese carracks with sleek sides, two masts and more than one sail. They brought all manner of goods from Italy and beyond and in return brought English wool across to Flanders or back home, for our wool was rightly prized for its quality. Between the great ships, hundreds of wherries taxied passengers to and from ships, and across and up or down the Thames.

While I waited on the dockside for her to disembark, her brother, Sir Humphrey, rode up with a dozen men on expensive horses, crowding the space. Walt cursed them for their rudeness but I forestalled him.

"Sir Humphrey," I said, walking directly to his horse. The men around him put their hands on their swords but Sir Humphrey waved them back and called out to me in return.

"Richard?" He frowned, looking between me and the ship. "You travelled with the Lady Cecilia?"

"But of course!" I said, purposefully misunderstanding the specifics of his insinuation. "Did not the King himself order me to protect the lady and see her home safe, sir? I am not a man to shirk his duty."

Sir Humphrey curled his lip and furrowed his brow. "Where is she? Where is my sister, man?"

"I assume she is yet to disembark. I just arrived from my own ship." I jerked my thumb down river and he visibly relaxed and even began to smile a little. Then he looked up and the smile spread across his face.

"Cecilia!" he cried, and fairly leapt from his saddle to run to her.

She was a vision as she stepped onto the dock helped by her servants and a swarm of bowing sailors. She and her brother embraced and he directed a dozen questions at her before she could answer the first one. Eventually, she laughed and pushed him away.

"I am well, I am well. All is well." She looked at me, then, for the first time but so directly that it was certain she knew precisely where I was. "Thanks entirely to Sir Richard's chivalrous attentions."

"I am sure," Sir Humphrey said, all but growling. "I shall have to thank you in some way, sir. Are you going to that manor of yours directly?"

It was clear he was prompting me to make my departure and now that I would be robbed of my planned, passionate farewell with his sister, I was liable to get going forthwith. "I have a house in London and shall stay there until my business here is complete. Then I must return to my company in Villeneuve. Lady Cecilia, I am glad to see you well and back in the arms of your family. If there is anything I can do for you, you need but ask it. Good day, my lady. My lord."

He all but growled at my presumption yet she beamed at me in open affection. It stirred my heart but it was tinged with sadness. She seemed to be perfect. A woman grown, strong and forthright but kind and filled with physical passion tempered with the wisdom to control it. If only she could be my wife, I thought, as I rode away on my rented horse. But I knew just as she would that her destiny was to marry some great lord, perhaps even an earl, and bear him many children.

"To Master Stephen's house, sir?" Walter asked as we plodded by the carts teeming with barrels of salt cod and herring.

"It is my house, Walt," I said. "And no, I am beyond filthy and in need of a bath. I shall cross to Southwark and go home later. Go home and tell Stephen to have my chambers prepared and to ready a fine feast. And good wine."

Walt nodded. "My old man used to say, God rest his soul, if you cannot have a woman, son, then you might as well have a drink."

I shook my head. "I see that you come from a long line of wise fools."

Yet it was I who was the fool for sending Walt away from my side.

7

The Assassin

SOAKING IN STEAMING HOT water, I leaned back against the side of the tub and sighed. I could not recall the last time I had taken a bath. Certainly not during the campaign and not for some time before then. It was somewhat indulgent of me but then I did so hate coming to London at all and anything I could do to balance the unpleasantness was perfectly acceptable, as far as I was concerned.

The Southwark stews, on the south side of the Thames across from the City of London, served as the bathhouses for anyone who could pay for them. While they were all private establishments, some were more affordable than others. The one I utilised was the most expensive of them all and thus I enjoyed the privacy of my own small room and a woman to serve me as I bathed. It was a well-made room, lit by small windows high up on the exterior wall and a decorative, iron-framed lantern on an ornate dressing table. The floor was tiled quite finely in a white and green pattern evoking the sensuality of nature, an effect enhanced by the fresh lavender and other herbs filling the room with delightful scents.

A most welcoming woman scrubbed my shoulders with a sponge and good Spanish soap, kneading my flesh as she washed. Try as I might, I could not cease thinking of Cecilia. She had bewitched me utterly and no matter if I directed my thoughts to the conduct of the war or the possibilities for our search for the immortal Frenchman, I found myself recalling moments that I passed with the lady, and even fantasising about conversations that we might one day enjoy. Absurdly, I even pictured myself married to her and sharing the truly intimate relationship that comes from daily sharing a bed, a home, and a partnership with another.

And, as was as natural and inevitable as the changing of the seasons, I sinfully indulged in base, lustful daydreams where I stripped Cecilia of her clothing while she smiled up adoringly at me.

"That feels remarkably restorative, Pernille," I muttered.

"I do apologise, good sir, but as I have previously expressed to you, I don't be doing that sort of thing no more."

Surprised, I noticed that I was idly stroking one of her hands as she worked on my neck. "My apologies, Pernille. Upon my oath, it was not my intention to initiate~" I broke off from my explanation as I saw that my intention was in fact jutting up above the surface of the grey water.

"And besides," Pernille continued, as if I had not spoken, "I am far too ancient to excite a young man such as yourself."

I stopped, because I knew then that she wanted me to talk her into it. Quite suddenly the wantonness of her subtle proposition turned my incidental lust into a fervour and I grasped her hand firmly in mine, pulling her gently but firmly closer to me by an inch or two.

"My dear, I am a hundred and eighty years of age and you are nought but a spring chicken to my eyes. I would be honoured if you would share the pleasures of this bath with me."

She assumed I was joking about my age, of course, and she laughed even though there was no jest to be found in my remark. "I shall call one of the younger girls, my lord. One more suited to your needs. Surely, you cannot wish to waste your coin and your ardour on the likes of me."

"By all means, call one of your girls in to serve us both while we recline in the waters. Come, come. You are perfection itself."

"Oh, you are spouting flattery, sire, as surely you must know that beneath my clothes my body is quite unbecoming."

"I would never pursue a woman who does not desire me in turn, Pernille, so do nothing that would not please you. But you can see in my eyes that I speak truth when I say I want no woman here more than I want you."

At that, she disrobed and we made love very slowly in the waters. If I had to guess, I would have said she was aged between thirty and thirty-five and she was quite lovely in body and in spirit.

"I truly have not lain with a man here for some years," she said later, reclining in my arms as one of the servants let cold water out from the tub and opened the brass tap to allow the hot water to fill up to the brim once more.

"Then I am honoured by your generosity." It was her job to make men feel wanted, and special, and I suspected that she recited the same words a few times a week. Even so, I was ever contented to be deceived by a comely woman.

"There is something unusual about you, my lord," she said, trailing a finger over the back of my hand where it rested on the rim of the tub. "And I do not speak of your talents in the ways of love, which are quite remarkable."

I sighed, as she was rapidly spoiling my relaxed mood with her professional patter. No doubt she wanted me to ask for her the next time I returned but I wanted a few more moments of peace before I went back to doing my duty to the King, and to my Order and my oath. And I wanted her to be quiet so I could think of Cecilia and imagine that one day it might be her reclining in my arms.

There was a cry from somewhere else in the building, rising over the usual hubbub and occasional barks of laughter.

Something about it called for my attention.

It was the sound of a woman protesting in outrage. After laughter and cries of passion, that was the most common noise to hear in that place and yet there was a tone of terror in it.

Pernille was attuned to the sounds of her bordello also and her body tensed at the cry.

"Go see what that's about, Maggie, dear," she said, her demeanour suddenly serious and commanding, to the young woman attending us. Maggie nodded and went to the door.

A shout of warning went up from beyond the room, far closer than before, and it was accompanied by the sound of a man's feet approaching along the floorboards.

My instincts kicked in and I pushed Pernille away from me and stood in the tub, looking for my clothing. The rules of the establishment were that no weapons were allowed within and so my sword was in the guardroom along with the two burly porters who dealt with trouble using stout clubs when necessary. No doubt, I thought, they would soon put an end to whatever the trouble was but still I felt somewhat vulnerable as I stood there with the water streaming from my naked flesh, knowing that I was entirely unarmed.

My instincts were always good and they had been honed further by the many decades of danger I had lived. And they had not failed me.

The door to the soak room burst open, striking young Maggie and knocking her aside as a huge fellow barged through with an angry expression on his face and a drawn sword in his hand. Pernille, moving with admirable speed, hopped from the tub, her heavy breasts swinging beneath her, and retreated to the corner, dragging Maggie with her.

The attacker was not interested in the women.

Indeed, he did not even take a moment to look at the naked one and instead had eyes only for me as he paused in the doorway.

My first impression was that he was taller than me, and considerably stouter. He wore the clothing of a middling townsman yet was bareheaded and his hair was unkempt and he sported a rather wild beard, which was really quite unusual at the time.

His eyes were filled with the fury of violence and as he looked rather like a wild bear wearing a tunic I did not waste time attempting to forestall him with words.

Instead, I jumped from the water across the room, away from him, trying to reach my clothing and the knife that was on my belt so that I would at least have something sharp and steel that I could stick the bastard with.

My lead foot, wet as it was, slipped from under me as I landed on the tiled floor and I fell hard, banging my elbow and hip and jarring me to the bone. What often saved me in a fight was my instinct to always be moving and even as I fell, I twisted and rolled and sprang back to my feet. And a lucky thing it was, too, as the bear-like fellow was already slashing his blade down at my naked back.

He caught me with a glancing blow, cutting me obliquely across the skin over my shoulder blade. I cried out in surprise more than pain, as I had not for a moment imagined such a beast of a man would move so swiftly and I knew then that he was an immortal. He had to be.

I glanced behind me as I changed direction, bounced off the wall and dived for the neat piles of my clothing upon the dressing table. The man was growling as he thrust his blade into the air, judging very well just where I was heading.

The point punctured my flank, low on my ribcage, penetrating quite deeply before my momentum pulled me from the blade and I crashed into the table, grabbing hold of it and crying out from the terrible pain shooting through me.

There was no hesitation from him and he followed me with a stride that brought him to striking distance. Before he could finish me off, I grabbed the heavy lantern on the table top and swung it with all my strength at his head. He ducked but still it struck him good and proper right on his crown and the blow shook him down to his toes. Such a blow would have smitten a mortal man and likely would have felled a warhorse but it did little more than slow my would-be murderer. As his sword point waved, I steeled myself, batted it aside with my forearm and charged into him. I lifted him with my shoulder and carried him across the width of the room until his back crashed into the opposite wall. It was such a terrible impact, even through the heft of the sturdy man's flesh, that the force of it knocked the wind from me and I fell back and down to the floor, as did the other man. The women were screaming.

Before I could recover, he was somehow throwing himself on top of me. My wound was deep and blood was pouring down my side and I felt my strength leaking out of me along with it. The great big bastard forced me down beneath him as I tried to squirm away on my back. He brought the edge of his sword to bear and pushed it down toward my throat. I reached up and stopped the blade by grasping it with both hands, taking the weight upon my palms. He heaved down and the edge sliced through my flesh. His face was contorted in rage and his lips pulled back in a sneer, baring his yellow teeth. A stream of blood gushed from the top of his head where I had split his skull with the lamp. I was strong enough to resist his downward force but he began to saw his sword back and forth and the blade sliced down to the bones of my hands and I knew then that he would cut through my hands and drive the blade through my neck.

His head burst apart. Cloven in two from above by a blade. Pink brains and blood showered down on my face and I twisted his body from me.

Above me stood my man, Walter, looking quite concerned.

"Good Christ, sir," he shouted, "you be in a right bad way."

"God love you, man," I said.

He was grinning at the terrified women, feasting his ignoble eyes upon Pernille's flesh even as she cowered in fear and disgust. The dead man twitched and blood gushed from the large gap between both sides of his head.

"Help me into my clothes," I commanded, "quickly, man."

Walt jumped to help me to my feet. "Sir, I must say your wounds are grievous. Sit here and I shall fetch a surgeon to bind you up."

"No surgeon. Help me to the house. I will recover there."

"As you command, Sir Richard. But should we not wait for the bailiffs? This bastard done killed the stew's porters down at the door. I cannot flee from the body or else they shall say I am guilty of murder myself."

He was quite right. But I knew that I needed blood or else I would not be long for the world and I had no wish to be caught up in an inquest. It would be possible to bribe the right men to keep my name from public mention but only if I was not seen with the body by too many people, and already I could hear folk gathering from elsewhere in the stew.

"We shall do what is right and no harm shall come to you, Walt," I said, hurting quite badly, "as long as you help me to dress and get me out of here."

"Right you are, sir," Walt said, then immediately shaking out my shirt.

"Leave my purse for the ladies."

"Ladies?" He looked around, confused. "The whores? How much?"

"Leave the purse," I hissed. They would know what I wanted in return. "And for the love of God, remove your blade from the man's head."

***

"You must have some idea who he was," Stephen said, pacing back and forth across the width of his solar on the second floor of his house.

It was our house, in fact, belonging to the Order of the White Dagger. We had taken turns to reside there over the decades, though I had used it the least because the decadence and stench of London made my skin crawl. But Stephen lived there publicly and had spent most of the previous century living there, on and off, and as such it was imbued with his personal taste. Having said that, Stephen would rather have by his bedside twenty books, bound in black or red, of Aristotle and his philosophy than rich robes or costly fiddles or gay harps. What décor I could see was far too modern for me to feel comfortable at the best of times and I was already feeling unnerved by my recent close brush with death.

I lay back on a day-bed with a cup of tepid blood in my hand, generously donated by three of Stephen's servants. We always employed servants, in the London house, and also in our smaller residence in Bristol where Eva preferred to live, who agreed to be bled every few days so that someone provided blood once every other day. That volume and at that frequency was enough to keep Stephen or Eva in fine fettle. We explained to the servants when we employed them that bloodletting was necessary for maintaining the good health and proper behaviour and always they had accepted it, for it was a common practice.

"I have no idea who he was, Stephen. How many more times would you like me to say so?"

"And you are certain he was one of us?" He strode away across the chamber as he spoke.

"He was one of William's creations, yes."

Stephen turned on his heel. "Could it be that one of William's men created another? One of the revenants, as the Assassins made in Alamut?"

"I suppose it is possible. The revenants were quite raving mad but they were also burned quite rapidly by sunlight, far more even than you and Eva are. Our fellow today wore no hat or hood and his face was quite unburned."

"Not much daylight in the stews, though, I take it?" he said it lightly, not looking at me.

"Do not pretend you are ignorant on the matter, Stephen. But he must have arrived in the stews through the streets in sunlight."

"We do not truly know where he came from, do we. Perhaps he was lying in wait for you."

"I thought you were the master of reason and I was the dullard soldier? If you recall, the porters were slain when he forced his way into the building. He came from outside. Hence, he came through the streets and was not burned by the sun. Therefore, he was not a second-generation revenant but a direct spawn of William."

Stephen inclined his head for a moment. "And where did he come from before he walked the streets of London, I wonder? Was he English?"

"I told you. He did not speak a word."

"Did he *look* like an Englishman?"

"An English hermit, perhaps. The brute was in dire need of a barber's services."

"And yet he had the build and the skill of a man-at-arms."

"I would not necessarily say so. We did not engage in much swordplay. His build would have made him suitable as the bailiff of a hundred in the northern Marches. A brute, as I say, not necessarily a warrior."

Stephen nodded and continued his pacing. "I shall ask the city watchmen which gate he entered through. Perhaps that will give us a clue about where he came from. Assuming one of the oafs recalls our Assassin."

"Unless he came by ship," I muttered.

Stephen stopped and turned to me. "How did he smell?"

"How did he *smell*?" I sighed. "Stephen, I do wonder about you."

"Think, Richard," he said, approaching and speaking earnestly. "Did he smell of the road? When he grasped you, did he smell like horses? Or did he smell like the sea?"

I laughed. "You have not been on a long voyage for so long. You have forgotten that you would step ashore reeking of stale sweat, vomit, and piss."

"And is that how he smelled?"

I scoffed. "I really do not recall, Stephen, but why do you not pay a visit to the coroner and ask if you can smell the corpse."

He grinned. "What a wonderful idea." Tapping his fingers on his chin, he turned and wandered away.

"Oh, Stephen. Our money can only turn so many heads and close so many mouths. If you go around sniffing corpses then you shall arouse more suspicion than we can cope with."

"Is finding the origin of our assassin not of the utmost importance? Surely, he was sent by the very man we are pursuing? If we can track the path of the assassin back to its source, will it not lead us to the knight we seek in France?" He came close again, dropping to a knee next to me. "What if we cannot find our quarry in France or further afield because he somehow got by us and came to England? The black knight could be in London, Richard."

I nodded, galled that I had not come to the same conclusions myself. "Very well. Do whatever you have to. But, for God's sake, go nowhere without protection, Stephen."

He airily wafted my concerns away. "Oh, I shall be fine."

I shot my hand out and grasped his wrist. "I am returning to the siege, Stephen and shall not be here to keep you safe. That brute would have killed me if Walt had not hewed his skull in half at the very last moment. What if the assassin had come for you first? You have been living comfortably for so long that you have forgotten what it is to be afraid. It is time you remembered."

Stephen was nothing if he was not a survivor at heart and so he listened to me and swore he would arm his porters and servants, hire soldiers to guard the house and to guard his person when he went about on business.

I hoped that the black knight was not in England, as Stephen feared. My duty to the King, and to the men of my company, required me to return to the siege of Calais.

My oath to find the immortal spawn of my brother William would have to continue in France.

8

The Siege of Calais

A WARM SUMMER CAME and inside Calais the townsfolk starved. Like all who suffer in a besieged town, they ate all the horses, then the dogs, the cats and finally the rats and mice. After that, in their desperation they began to boil up and chew on anything leather. I have been that hungry myself many times down the centuries and it is a kind of madness that grips you and convinces you that you may draw sustenance from gnawing on your own shoes.

Then their wells inside the city began to dry up. Disease broke out within the walls.

We knew how bad it was inside because we intercepted a letter from the commander of Calais to King Philip. A brave Genoese rowed out of the harbour one morning in late June but he was caught and his letter brought to King Edward who read it aloud to us right away.

"We can now find no more food in the town unless we eat men's flesh," Edward read from the letter. "None of the officers have forgotten your entreaties to hold out until we may fight no more and that day is almost upon us. Yet we shall not surrender. Every man here has sworn to rush from the gates to fight our way through the English lines until each one of us lies dead."

As he read this, I turned to Thomas behind me. "Take some men and keep watch on the gates until you are relieved." When I straightened again, I caught Northampton's eye and he nodded once at me.

"Unless you can find some other solution, this is the last letter that you will receive from me, for your loyal town shall be lost and all of us that are within it," Edward said. He finished reading it but spoke no more of the content. Then he called his servants. "I shall seal this with my personal seal and then we shall forward it to my cousin Philip."

A few of the lords laughed at the thought of the King of France receiving such a dire letter with Edward's seal on it but most of us, I am sure, felt sickened by the plight of our enemies within the town.

In response, Philip organised and launched a great relief convoy of eight armed barges that he hoped could sneak into the harbour without us noticing. I have no idea what the French were thinking because we easily captured the supplies ourselves, which was a boon to us and served to utterly break the will of the leaders within the walls.

The leaders of Calais rounded up all their wives, daughters and mothers. They gathered their young sons and their aged fathers. They collected their injured and sick brothers.

And they threw them out of the gates.

It was not an unknown tactic, of course, but it was no less sickening to see for all that. For the sort of men who become the leaders of a town, their primary duty is their duty to their lord. To their king. That duty was greater than the one they felt to their own families.

When I saw the huddled, shuffling, gaunt women with their children clinging to their knees creeping out of the gates, I wondered if Englishmen would have acted in the same way. Our people have always been more independently minded than those from other nations. Not as independent as the Welsh, Scots or Irish, thank God, but certainly more so than the French. The English have always had the best possible balance between civic duty, royal loyalty, and individual freedom. The French, on the other hand, were always more collectivist or, as one might say, subservient.

But we were not going to take on responsibility for the families of the men who had defied us for months. King Edward was under no legal or moral duty to accept those useless mouths expelled by the fathers of Calais. What was worse, though, was that he refused to allow them through our lines and inland to where Philip could care for them.

And so those poor women, those weeping children and weak old men, huddled in the ditches between our lines and the town's defences, starved.

"Let them burden King Philip, Your Grace," I pleaded to Edward one night after I could take their wailing no longer.

"My lords have always whispered in my ear that you are too cruel and unchivalrous to keep at my side," the King said in response. "But they do not know you like I do. You have always had this absurd weakness. A hidden softness. And because of your weakness, you would have me show weakness when Christendom is watching. No, Richard. They had their chance to surrender months ago. Now they must suffer the consequences."

I wanted to argue. Protest that compassion was not weakness but a virtue and it would be a most Christian and decent thing to let the women and children through our lines.

But just as he knew me, I knew him. I had known him since before he was twenty years old. And I knew that when he had that dark look in his eye, nothing could divert him from his royal cruelty.

I rode away with my men to raid the country for as many days as it took for the last of the refugees to perish.

It did not take long.

By this point, we had been outside Calais for ten months and our army had been growing since spring. The town that we had created to contain them all also grew beyond our defensive lines and so we had to extend them further. By July, we had over five thousand men-at-arms with their horses and servants, along with seven thousand infantry made up from levied townsfolk and Welsh spearmen, plus what I was told was twenty thousand archers. In all my years fighting, I had never known an English army the size of it. Indeed, we would not raise such a force and send it to France for another two hundred years or so.

And what were we going to do with all those men?

The French were coming for us again. King Philip had raised a massive force and he meant to drive us into the sea and so wipe away all we had accomplished since that morning near Crecy almost a year before. He marched it right up to our camp at the end of July and we all knew we would have another fine battle to decide the fate of France. Philip was said to have eleven thousand men-at-arms, more than twice as many as we had. We all wondered if our archers would be able to cut them down as they had at Crecy.

"What is he waiting for?" Walt asked me as we looked up at the distant escarpment miles to the south where thousands of Frenchmen stood, silhouetted against the bright blue skies beyond. Their banners and pennants fluttered and whipped in the steady wind.

"Would you attack us?" Thomas asked. "If you were Philip?"

"I wouldn't attack us," Rob said, "if I was Charlemagne himself, sir."

"Philip is no Charlemagne," I said. "But we must do our duty and provoke them into attack."

My company and many others skirmished with groups of Frenchmen who strayed from their lines. We shot a great many arrows but they were fearful of us. And rightly so.

Our defences were simply too strong and the French took less than a day to decide they would not attack us after all. In fact, they sent word to Edward that it was not a battle they wanted, but peace. And so a truce was declared and my company fell back from the French. My archers were disappointed, for their favourite sport was shooting the horses of French cavalry.

The two sides negotiated for days. Thomas and I got close enough to watch the French delegation closely but we saw no one who might be the knight of the black banner.

"Look," Thomas said, nudging me with his elbow. "It is Sir Geoffrey."

"Who?" I asked.

"Geoffrey de Charny," he said, pointing at a well-built lord in a very fine red coat. He was fine-featured, with a square jaw and piercing eyes. "Do you see? Standing between the Duke of Bourbon and the Duke of Athens."

"Hmm," I said. "The man does not seem to be particularly impressive."

Out of the corner of my eye I saw Thomas turn and stare at me.

"Perhaps you should introduce yourself," Thomas said. "If we are considering one day inviting him to join the Order of the White Dagger."

"Look at him, Thomas," I said. "Why would he ever give away his fortunate life in order to take up a future with us? When Dukes wish to consult an expert on chivalry, they send for that man there. He has founded more than one monastery. He keeps company with the great lords of his kingdom."

"So do you, Richard."

I snorted. *Yes,* I thought yet did not speak aloud, *yes but Charny's lords respect him.*

"I think we must aim a little lower than the living embodiment of chivalry, Thomas."

He laughed a little and nodded. "Very well. Let us look elsewhere."

The negotiations dragged on. The French proposed that we march from our camp and fight an open battle. Of course, Edward could never have given up our impregnable position but the ploy was a clever one because it made the King of England appear to contradict his chivalrous reputation as a man of honour. We wondered how our king would handle the matter but in the end he was saved from having to make a decision.

For the commanders of Calais, the men who had thrown their wives and children out to starve to miserable deaths within sight and earshot of their precious town, declared at sundown on the first day of August, that they were surrendering.

In the dark of the night, the French army under Philip set fire to their tents, spoiled their food and water, and marched away before sunrise. The King of France abandoned his most loyal subjects to their fate.

The lords of Calais requested a negotiation of terms but Edward's message to them was quite clear. There will be no terms. Their surrender would be complete, and England would take everything they had and would kill every man they wished to.

"You cannot mean to put all these knights and squires to the sword, Your Grace?" Northampton said to the King that day.

"I would prefer their heads," Edward said. "But I will be content with hanging."

"They simply did their duty to their king," the capable knight Walter Mauny said. "Just as any of your loyal captains would have done in their place."

"Ransom them, Your Grace," Suffolk said. My lord the Earl of Suffolk had once been a prisoner of King Philip a few years before and had ultimately been ransomed.

I said nothing. It was not as though Edward did not know that the chivalrous thing to do would be to ransom them but he was resolute and I knew from the set of his arms and the look in his eyes that nothing his lifelong companions could say would move him.

William Bohun the Earl of Northampton came around the backs of the men surrounding the King and approached me. He reached out and grasped my upper arm, attempting to drag me away from the rest. When he found that he could not budge me so much as an inch, he lowered his head and muttered. "I would speak with you, sir." I followed him a few paces away. "You must add your voice to ours, Richard. Make him see reason."

I shrugged. "Why should I care what happens to those men? They defied us. They must now die."

He peered up at me, squinting. When he spoke, he did so slowly, as one might explain the operation of a watermill to a simpleton. "It is not the men but the convention we must protect, Richard. It is clear that this war will drag on further, perhaps for years. What if you yourself are captured one day? You scoff but you are often deep within enemy territory with no support and it is highly likely you will be taken. Do you wish to be ransomed or murdered outright in revenge for this atrocity which we are about to commit?"

Northampton clearly had a poor consideration for my intellect and my morality.

"Try someone else, Bohun," I said, shaking his gloved fingers from my arm.

"I can help you," he said. He said it in a way that was loaded with meaning of some sort so I turned back. "Yes indeed, I can help you to find the man you are looking for."

"Where is he?" I asked.

"If you help me," he said, "I will help you."

"Fine. I will persuade him. Now, tell me."

The Earl of Northampton smiled and spread his arms. "If you tell me who it is that you seek, I will find out for you."

I laughed. "You promise a thing that you do not possess. You know nothing, my lord."

"I know that you are always asking questions. Seeking the knights who killed your squire. Wherever they have gone I will find them for you."

In the end, I did as Northampton proposed and had a few choice words with King Edward. I did not know if the Earl would truly be able to help me to find the black banner but having a favour owed to you by a great lord of the realm could be worth more than money, if one knew how to use it.

Edward allowed the lords of Calais to live, although he took everything they owned other than their Earthly lives.

When the French were dragged out, the English entered and raised Edward's standard from the walls to the sound of horns and trumpets as our great king rode within. The booty was dragged out and gathered in one place to be properly accounted for. Calais was filled to the brim with the profits from decades of enthusiastic piracy and there was a remarkable amount of money, silver, and other goods and valuables. I received coats, furs, quilts, tablecloths, necklaces, silver goblets and linen. I had it all sent to Eva's house in Bristol.

Edward held on to a few of the richest leaders but all the other survivors were given a hunk of bread, a cup of wine and a kick up the arse as we sent them south into France without a penny to their names. Those emaciated, humiliated men were an announcement to the people of France that their king could not protect them and that they would do well to consider welcoming a king who could.

Calais was thus emptied completely of Frenchmen and immediately repopulated with Englishmen and the city became a true part of England from that day on for over two hundred years.

The war was not over. Indeed, it grew heated again, for I was ordered to begin making deeper raids into France in preparation for our army's next advance. Not just my company, of course. Henry of Lancaster led a huge force to capture a town thirty miles away. Even the Prince of Wales, God love him, rode at the head of a raiding party into Artois. He made a lot of noise and burned plenty but no one wanted him to range too far from safety. He was our golden prince, after all.

And I was free to take up my hunt for the immortal knight once more.

***

The search for the knight of the black banner continued and yet it foundered as we entered the autumn of 1347. People still travelled in bad weather, of course they did, but with nothing like the frequency of the summer. And the banditry and general lawlessness that gripped France following the loss of the battle continued.

But then at the end of September, a truce was agreed by both sides which was to last until July 1348. Of course, Philip wanted a truce because he had no hope of beating us militarily. But my men could not understand it. They felt as though they had been cheated of their ultimate victory and I could understand why that was their view but I explained that we had reached somewhat of a strategic impasse and the nine-month break would allow a reduction of the appalling cost and logistical effort it took to keep our vast army in the field.

They were just annoyed that they were going to miss out on all that booty.

It meant that my operations in France were suddenly curtailed. We were going home, and a few men were pulling back into Calais but maintaining my company in the field was out of the question. It would threaten the treaty and to defy it would be treasonous.

When we returned to England, I gave the men of my company their final payments and dismissed them. They returned to their homes and their families, if they had them. Some claimed they were now rich enough to find a wife and start a family. Others went into the degenerate filth of London to spend their relatively huge wealth on drink and women and to waste the rest.

For a time, I returned home and set things in order there. It was a terribly wet summer and the rain fell and fell and there was never enough time between downpours for anything to dry out so that everyone and everything was damp all the time, even indoors. My fields turned to mud and the wheat and barley was much battered by the deluge. The common people grew tense because they could sense that a famine may have been coming.

King Edward and the lords of England, on the other hand, spent that wet summer in a series of sumptuous tourneys across the country. In many ways, Edward was on top of the world. And why would he not be? He was thirty-five years old, and a fifteen-month campaign had brought him the glory that he had been seeking for so long. The leaders of England were rather joyful after such a series of victories. Our small nation had bested the mighty France again and again, in battle and in tactical manoeuvres, overall strategy and even in politics. As soon as winter was over, the tournaments began at Reading, Bury St. Edmunds,

Lincoln, Eltham and Lichfield. It was an endless cycle of feasting, competition, dancing, drinking and travelling. Round and round the country they went in an orgy of consumption and splendour.

"As much as I respect the King and the young lords he has cultivated," Thomas said to me during a feast at Windsor in July, "I despise witnessing how they squander their wealth and deck out their bodies with the trappings of frippery, buffoonery and lust."

"Keep your voice down," I warned him, aware that he had unusually consumed rather a lot of wine.

"They celebrate themselves, Richard," he continued, heeding me not at all. "Not one of them seem to realise that their victories were a gift from God, who is the true benefactor of the chivalry of England."

I took his cup from him and pressed food into his hand. "Eat some bread, brother."

Although I was sympathetic with his opinion, I could not hold those elaborate displays against Edward, for he was behaving precisely as a king should. He was demonstrating his power and his majesty to the people of his kingdom, from the great to the common folk. A king's magnificence reflects onto those he rules and so every man no matter how lowly rejoiced to see the astonishing pageantry and splendour.

Thomas saw empty glamour and vanity but then he still carried within him the heart of a monk and his personal distaste for rampant consumption blinded him to the necessity of it. A king who acts with frugality is not loved by the common man. The pageantry *was* kingship, perhaps just as much as victory in battle was. Both ends of the scale enabled and enhanced the other.

But my pride was mostly in how my people were growing in stature on the world stage. The lords of Christendom had witnessed the King repeatedly overcome the first ranked military power west of Constantinople. The English had become the foremost warriors of Europe and suddenly every prince in Christendom cried out for Edward's attention, whether it was to arbitrate disputes between kingdoms or to offer him marriages for his children or beg for military aid.

The King of Castile betrothed his heir to the Princess Joan who was fourteen years old and as pretty as a picture and as charming as any of her lauded ancestors.

While dreading to hear of it as if I was a young girl myself, I kept an ear out for news of any betrothal that Lady Cecilia might have made to some lord or other but there was nothing. She was almost never travelling with the court and never when I was in attendance, although I was sure that was merely bad luck.

Oftentimes a widow could postpone her next marriage by claiming to still be consumed by grief for her last husband but when a lady was as great a prize as Cecilia, that could only get her so far. I had little doubt that her brother Sir Humphrey was doing everything in his power to arrange a match.

Their family was not a great one and their family was small, surviving the generations with just an heir or two but their wealth was considerable and her beauty was famed so it was likely she could find an older man looking to replace a dead wife or a young lordling who would not object to an older widow, considering all her other attributes.

More than once I sat down to pen a letter to her but I always stared at the confused words in my appalling hand and ended up tossing the letter across the chamber in irritation. What was it that I wanted from her? Her love, of course, but I knew that would never be possible for even if in some mad passion she wanted me, I could never condemn her to a marriage with an ageless knight who could never give her children. It could never lead to happiness.

And so, with the war on hold and the search for the black knight finding only shadows, I commanded that the members of the Order of the White Dagger meet at our house in London to discuss what was to be done next.

***

Myself, Thomas, Hugh, Stephen and Eva were in attendance. Without the good humour and energy of John, it seemed to me to be rather quiet and dour in the hall as we ate up our bread and drank off the wine.

I dismissed the servants for a while so that we could speak freely and I commanded Stephen to provide a full account of his search. And Stephen swore blind that he was doing everything he could to locate the knight but there was the fundamental problem that we had so little to go on.

"I did discover the truth about the squire of the black banner knight who held the red shield," Stephen said. "As you stated, the shield was red with three white sub-ordinary escutcheons and this being the blazon of Sir Geoffrey de Charny, one of the most famed knights in Christendom, we believed it may have been painted in order to distract or deceive us or others on the battlefield. However, the shield truly *was* one of de Charny's. This does not incriminate the great knight himself, of course, because the shield had in fact been stolen."

"*Stolen* from de Charny?" I was suspicious. "Who would steal a shield?"

It was true that Sir Geoffrey de Charny was one of the most famous knights in Christendom. A lord who was honoured for his chivalrous acts in peace and in war. But the story of a stolen shield seemed like something a guilty man would make up to defend himself in court.

"A man in need of one?" Eva said.

"Sir Geoffrey was not at Crecy," I said to Stephen. "So how could his shield have been?"

"I am cognisant," Stephen said, holding his palms up to me. "I had the story from one of de Charny's squires but, even though de Charny's reputation is impeccable, of course I would not take such a thing on face value. On the day before the battle, Sir Geoffrey's second-best shield was found to be lost and the squire gave the servants a sound thrashing for the loss. And de Charny was diverted from the battlefield itself by King Philip and so he was not present. Other witnesses confirm that de Charny had his squires and servants whipped around that time, presumably for the lost shield."

"How far away was he?" I asked.

Stephen nodded. "The heralds state that de Charny was not present and my contacts say he was on his way to Flanders on the day of the battle. A servant in the King's household said Sir Geoffrey was tasked with ensuring the Flemings could not come to our aid. Sir Geoffrey's squire, on the other hand, suggested King Philip was jealous of the fame and glory that his lowly knight would no doubt win against the English and so he sent him away."

"Both can be true," I muttered. "But why would anyone steal it at all? Who would have the opportunity to do so?"

"As for opportunity," Stephen replied, "there were tens of thousands of Frenchmen roaming north of Paris during those few days before the battle. As to why take it all, I do not know. Perhaps it was misdirection, as we thought. Or perhaps it was meant to inspire those who saw it. Whether they thought de Charny was present or not, laying eyes upon a famed standard could stir the hearts of lesser men, could it not?"

I smiled at Stephen's woeful attempts to appear wise in the ways of war.

"Indeed," Thomas said earnestly, for he somehow remained free from cynicism despite decades of experience, "and ever since, the French have said that if Sir Geoffrey de Charny *had* been present, the battle would have been won."

I scoffed. "Even a perfect knight like de Charny could not have changed the course of that battle."

"Is he?" Stephen asked, jerking his head up to look at me.

"Is who what?"

"Is Sir Geoffrey the perfect knight, as they say? Or were you speaking in jest? It is often rather difficult to tell, Richard."

"In jest, yes, but it is not entirely untrue. He fights as well as anyone, in tourney and in battle and acts with honour, so far as I know."

"He is a man filled with the experience of years, as much as a mortal man can be," Thomas added. "His family blazon of a red field represents Iron, and the god Mars who was the pagan god of war. He is gifted with profound wisdom and the spirit of adventure and by common repute, a knight more skilled in the art of war than any man in France."

"An exaggeration," I muttered. "Most probably."

"Well then," Stephen said, speaking carefully and watching us closely, "would he not be an ideal member of the Order?"

Thomas snapped his head up at that.

"Have you two been speaking about this?" I asked Stephen and Thomas.

"Indeed, we have not, Richard," Stephen said, his face the picture of sincerity. Thomas would not meet my eye.

"As you well know, Stephen, I would not make a man one of us," I said, "without him being on point of death, as Thomas was, or if he begged me for it knowing everything that it would entail, as you did. And I cannot see Geoffrey de Charny giving up all he has to join us, no matter how honourable we know our cause to be."

"But if, in the wars to come, he is cut down when you are near," Stephen said, "perhaps then you might—"

I spoke over him. "It would be an extremely unlikely confluence of chance that I be on hand for the man to draw his last breath, and also be alone with him long enough to administer half a gallon of my own blood to his lips, do you not think, Stephen? A man of his standing would be attended by a dozen servants, and many peers."

Stephen sighed. "I understand. You have it right, of course. But as Thomas and I have been reiterating for many years now, we need more men, Richard. As our difficulties in finding the black banner knight demonstrate rather well. With more men, men who were absolutely trusted with the knowledge of what we truly seek, we could have eyes and ears all across France. And you also have agreed to find us some men, have you not? Men of high quality, as you have said. If such a situation as his death was to occur while you…"

"Yes, yes," I said, irritated with his presumptuousness and also knowing that what he wanted would never come to pass. "But enough of Sir Geoffrey de Charny. What about the trail of the bloody immortal, Stephen?"

He looked down at his wax tablet, as if hoping that answers would appear there. "We expected that the black banner or his men would commit more murders in order to obtain their blood. But every occurrence I have been able to investigate has led nowhere."

"Perhaps he has his own blood slaves," Eva suggested. "We have managed to go entirely undetected for all this time. It is not a difficult thing to procure blood, if you have means and a few private moments."

I slumped, growing disheartened by the extended failure. I had been so close and yet my momentary lapse in forgetting to close my visor had cost me so dearly. "More likely he has fled France for some other land. He could have crossed into Aragon and beyond, gone over the Alps to Italy and from there, to anywhere."

"Would he flee so far?" Hugh said, ever hopeful. "Why was he here, fighting in that battle at all? Where did he come from?"

We had no answers.

"What of the assassin?" I said. "Stephen, what came of the dead man in the Southwark stews? Where did his trail lead?"

Stephen hung his head. "It seems he came to the stews from London, as he was seen crossing the bridge. Also, he had no known lodging in the city. So we can conclude that he came either from ship to London or by land from elsewhere in the country beyond the city."

"And?" I said. "Which was it?"

"None admitted to his coming by ship. But, as you know, it is possible to smuggle ashore many a hidden cargo, including a man, should a shipmaster wish it. But my agents have always been trustworthy before. And so I believe the brute who attacked you was an

Englishman from somewhere beyond London."

"From where beyond London?"

"Ah," Stephen said. "Of that, I do not know. There was no sighting of him coming in through any of the gates. And none from any road to here, either."

"Dear God, Stephen."

"Come, Richard," Thomas said. "It is hardly Stephen's fault that the assassin kept to the shadows."

My frustration grew into anger and although I felt the urge to rant and threaten them all, I resisted it.

They had superior strength and speed and health than mortal men, but their minds had not been enhanced along with their bodies and so I could not expect them to have done any more. Although railing at him further would be futile, I knew it was Stephen's fault, if it was any man's. It was he who ran our core network of spies.

But, there was one other resource we had not yet tapped.

"If you are not competent to complete this task, I shall ask Eva to do so."

Stephen's eyes bulged and he babbled out a series of notions as to why it should not be done. "But, Richard, Eva's agents are far fewer than mine. No offence meant, good woman, but it is true. It would take weeks for relevant messages to reach your people and then weeks more before they could act. Besides, the information that your agents provide is of a more general sort, mostly for trading purposes. And also, the fact that you are a woman means you would find it vastly more difficult to operate away from home if you needed to travel to meet them in foreign parts as I have done when necessary."

"I have managed well enough in years gone by," Eva said, fixing him with a steady look. "And have counselled you in many a matter when you have needed it."

Stephen scoffed and threw up his arms. "A woman's counsel? It was a woman's counsel that brought mankind to woe, did it not? A woman's counsel was it that threw Adam out of Paradise, where he had been so merry and at ease. And also—"

"That's quite enough of that, Stephen," I said, cutting him off as he searched in vain for some other objection. "You have failed. What is more, you have told us, in essence, that you do not expect to ever be successful. And so Eva shall find the man and then we shall go to him, take him, and force him to tell all about the others that he knows. Now, we will start again afresh, under Eva's direction."

Eva simply nodded. "I will begin immediately."

I had embarrassed Stephen in front of the others and he grew sullen. It is good to consider the effects your words may have on your followers but you should always ensure they are men of character who can accept your criticisms and continue to do their duty. Stephen was quite brilliant but he was never emotionally robust. Perhaps it was due to his common birth that he lacked the depth of character that a man of good breeding will tend to have. Or perhaps it was his lack of dutifulness that was his main weakness of character. He never comprehended, not truly, that doing one's duty lifts up one's soul to greater heights than self-interest ever could. Stephen was always keenly aware of his lowborn blood and I believe he resented being beholden to anyone, even~astonishing as it may seem~to a king. It was a flaw that would eventually have disastrous consequences, as he pushed and needled England further away from the proper, natural hierarchies designed by God and toward ungodly, destructive notions of egalitarianism. But that would unravel in the centuries to come and I had only a glint of it at the time.

"I wanted to ask you Stephen," Thomas said, "and you also, Eva. Have you heard about this pestilence growing in the south?"

Stephen nodded. "The merchants are all in a blaze about it. Word has stopped coming out of Italy but many ports were closed, last we heard."

Eva sighed. "It appears this will disrupt our search."

"Nonsense," I said. "When is there not some pestilences striking down armies and ports and cities and towns? This summer is already the wettest I can recall and no doubt has caused foul air to rise in the heat of the south. This new bloody flux or murderous fever or whatever it is will burn itself out without affecting any of us much at all."

But I could not have been more wrong.

The Great Mortality had come.

9

The Black Death

I WAS HAPPY, because I had received a letter from Lady Cecilia.

Dearest Richard, I pray my words find you well. I had hoped so to see you at court this past winter and spring yet found you always absent which caused my heart to be full heavy. I shall be staying at the Tower in London in early June as a guest of the Queen. If you could spare the time and effort away from your important duties on your estates to join me there, it would make me the happiest woman on earth.

As ancient as I was, upon reading the words I leapt in the air and whooped with joy, scaring the messenger and bringing Walt running with his dagger drawn.

It was all I could do to contain my excitement in the following days and every time I recalled that there could be no happy marriage for us, I simply pushed the thought away.

And when I saw her, I forgot it entirely.

After arriving absurdly early and sending word of it to the lady, I stood in the entrance to the gardens in the southwestern corner of the walls, beneath the White Tower. It had stopped raining after days and days and though everything was damp, the sun came out and the world sparkled. The ornamental fruit trees shone with vivid green, though the blossom on them had all been blasted off by the rains and there would be no fruit for the royal cooks to use in the fall.

She was more beautiful than ever and her smile at seeing me took my breath away. She was a vision and I for a few moments I was simply, idiotically happy.

"Sir Richard," she said as I bowed. "It gladdens my heart that you came."

I smiled. "My heart is glad also, my lady."

We were not alone, of course, and her servants followed closely and mine drifted along as far away from me as they would go. And the Tower was busy with other lords and ladies within and without and so our meeting was not some secret liaison but an opportunity to converse and become acquainted, as those who might be disposed to a marriage will often do.

We talked of small things, such as the appalling weather, and ignored unsavoury topics such as the necessary leanness of the coming winter for many in the land. It had been a long while since I had spoken of my favourite ballads and favoured foods and I was rusty with it, doing so was a pleasant change from discussing war and siegecraft. In truth, any topic would have been joyful with her clear voice in my ears and gorgeous face delighting my vision.

"I am afraid I was blessed with an ear for music," I said when she asked me to sing a verse, "but cursed with a voice that causes children to weep and milk to curdle."

She laughed. "In that case, I will beg your pardon and recall my request. Shall we head into the rose garden, Richard? The air beneath these trees is very close, do you not think?"

On our way across to the new rose garden, Cecilia took my arm and leaned on me a little. It was a pleasant feeling. I wondered if I plucked one of the roses and presented it to the lady whether King Edward would have my head plucked from my shoulders.

"Why are you unmarried, Richard?" she asked.

"An interesting question, my lady," I said, temporising so I could gather my thoughts. "I have concentrated on waging war rather than on love."

"Love?" she said, as if she was shocked. "But what has love to do with marriage, sir?"

I glanced down and saw that she had a twinkle in her eye.

"You did not marry for love, my lady?" I asked.

She sighed. "Dear me, Richard. I had no choice in my husband. I thought that I would be blessed with children and that I could love them, at least. But God decided otherwise."

I swallowed. "I pray that you are so blessed in your next marriage, my lady."

She grasped my arm and looked me in the eye. "If I ever marry again it shall be for love. Children are a blessing but my heart wants only the companionship of an honourable man."

"An honourable man," I repeated, my mouth dry. Was that what I was? Was it something I could ever be? "Well, my lady, I sincerely hope that—"

Before I could continue, a great crowd came bustling from the royal apartments. For half a moment, I thought we were under attack but then I realised it was a member of the royal family, surrounded by an enormous number of ladies, servants and guards. The party was rushing across the courtyard and through the gardens.

Cecilia and I at once moved aside to allow the swishing wave of garish frocks and nattering nobles past us.

"Sir Richard!" Princess Joan called to me from the centre of the pack, shouting over the enormous noise.

The chattering died down as the chaotic procession slowed to a stop right before us.

78

Princess Joan was fourteen years old and about to embark on the journey that would take her away from England, possibly forever, to a foreign kingdom. It was the duty of such ladies to undertake such things but surely there was never a one of them who did not find it a hard task. Still, one day soon she could expect to become the wife of the heir to that foreign throne and bear him sons. Her husband would one day be king and she would be the queen and her sons would be kings after them.

And she would be travelling in style. All the talk for weeks had been the size of Joan's trousseau which was said to entirely fill one of the four ships that would take her and her retinue south to Iberia. The princess would be travelling in as much comfort as was possible in those days and she would be well protected. I had even spoken to a few of the two hundred veteran archers escorting her, for I knew them from Brittany and from Calais. They were hard men, as hard as they come, forged in the fire of battle where they had seen the weaker of them, their brothers and cousins and friends, struck down by blade or sickness, so that only the strongest survived. Being chosen to protect King Edward's precious daughter brought them more pride than their hearts could bear and more than one of them had tears in his eyes when he spoke of his new duty.

I bowed low. "I am honoured that you remember me, my lady."

"How could I forget you, sir," she said, smiling and pushing her way through the ranks of formidable matrons. Joan turned to the Lady Cecilia. "When I was but a girl, Sir Richard instructed me in methods by which to improve my riding. He was so effective that I beat Isabella in a race across country." She laughed. "The King was most displeased with me for that and he banned both of us from riding for a year. Of course, he never enforced it. I was so very sorry to hear that you bore the brunt of his displeasure when it was entirely at my insistence that you addressed me on the matter at all."

"Not at all, my lady," I said, unable to keep a straight face. "Your father merely sent me to Brittany for years with an army consisting of two dozen men. But I do not mind that now I hear how you finally bested your sister." I winked at her and she giggled until her matronly companion growled a warning.

"I am leaving for Castile," Joan blurted out to Cecilia.

"So I hear, my lady," Cecilia said. "You must be very happy."

Her smile grew tighter but Joan was clearly excited as much as she was worried about leaving her family, forever, to set up in a foreign court. Such a thing requires courage from a woman and she faced her future with fortitude. "I am happy. I cannot wait to embark upon the journey. They say that Castile is a beautiful land."

"It is, my lady," I said.

"Oh, you have not been there? Truly?"

"Not for some time. Yet I remember it well and my memories are fond ones. They are a fine people."

Cecilia lowered her voice and looked up at me through her eyelashes. "I am sure it is the fine ladies that you recall so well, Richard."

Joan gasped, thrilled at Cecilia's teasing. "Is it true, Richard?" Then her face fell. "Are the ladies as beautiful as they say?"

I bowed. "They are indeed lovely, my lady, but there is not one amongst them who could hold a candle to you." Joan's face lit up as her outraged companions huffed and dragged her away from us. "God bless you in your marriage, my lady."

"And you in yours," she said as she went, grinning at Cecilia and attempting a wink. "Remember to keep your lower legs in contact with the horse at all times, Lady Cecilia."

"Good God," Cecilia said, shocked, as Joan disappeared into the hall. "She is as uncouth as you are. No wonder she is so taken with you. If only you were a Spanish prince, Richard, I think you would have had an infatuated English princess for a wife."

I tried not to laugh, for Cecilia seemed to be rather jealous but I had nothing but fatherly affection for the dear child.

Poor Joan, the little angel. I heard what happened much later from one of those archers. On her way to Castile, they put in at Bordeaux and her grand party was warned by the mayor there was a terrible sickness in the town and he advised that they leave.

Instead, they stayed. They had no idea what was in store.

But the archers, who were supposed to be housed in the town, noticed what was happening around them. Doors swung free in the wind and the homes were deserted. There were hundreds of bodies being buried in unmarked pits and the stench of death and decay began to waft over them. A wary bunch, they begged the leaders of the party to put out to sea immediately but they were rebuffed and then ignored. The archers explained how the sick people of the town were covered with swollen sores that emitted the fetid smell of putrefaction. In response, the noble leaders said that they would be safe in the castle, away from the town and the archers were instructed to keep to the town and to stop bothering the nobles. It did no good, and archers and lords alike fell ill and began dropping dead.

The leader of the party tried to save the precious and terrified Joan by fleeing to an estate in the country which would be free, they hoped, from the miasmas covering the town. That leader never made it, dying on the way from the terrible and unknown disease. I cannot imagine dear little Joan's terror. I imagine how she prayed in those days. I picture her in her bedchamber in the country, praying and praying to be spared as those around her died one by one.

A few days later, and in unimaginable agony, sweet little Joan died all by herself.

There were a handful of survivors from her party and these men made their way back to England as quickly as they could, hoping to bring warning of the terrible pestilence travelling the land.

By the time the first of them reached us, the pestilence was already ravaging England.

***

There had for some time been ever-growing certainty about that terrible illness affecting the cities down in Italy and even rumours that it was spreading northward. I had dismissed it all so easily when I first heard and I know for certain that I was not alone. Few of us paid it much heed.

Few of us, that is, until the rumours became certain reports that the pestilence had reached England, finally. Even then, I do not know of anyone who thought it would be anything like the way it turned out. Still, people had enough sense to take proper precautions in case it reached their town or village or manor. The most sensible ones focused on praying that they and their loved ones would be spared and the wealthier sort took pains to make donations or undertake charitable works in order to head off the Lord's wrath, as it were.

As soon as it became clear that it would be a true pestilence, a plague, I returned to my manors in Suffolk to make my people ready. Lady Cecilia did the same and we parted in quite a hurried fashion. As I turned, from my horse, to look down on her before I rode away, a profound sense of dread descended upon me and I felt certain that she would succumb to this unknown sickness that crept toward us. For a moment, I considered insisting that she come with me to my lands so that I could better protect her but good sense returned to counter my romantic notions. As a widow, she had full responsibility for her own lands and she would certainly have rejected my offer. Besides, how could I have protected her against something that I could not see and did not understand?

Still, I regularly recalled the sight of her standing in her elaborate robe and headdress in the courtyard at the Tower for a long time afterwards.

I was the lord of two estates in the county of Suffolk, which stood and still stands on the eastern coast of England, northeast of London between the counties of Essex and Norfolk. The county was a fine place, as far as lowland, southern England goes, with bounteous green fields and leafy woodlands and gently rolling hills. It was no Derbyshire, of course, but then what is? The people were good and honest and toiled as hard as any ever did. The two manors of Hawkedon and Hartest did not make me rich but the land was so productive that I could provide a core of fighting men and afford most of whatever I needed. Whenever more was required, I obtained it from the Order's coffers.

The most important man a lord of the manor could employ was his steward, for all else flowed from him. My steward ran both estates, though a sub-steward was present at Hartest, the smaller of the two and in effect made all daily decisions. Both places were old but neither was a castle and they were rather comfortable. Other lords would invest in stone walls and towers but I could see very little chance of a new French invasion or armed uprisings against the King and his lords and so I sought always to make improvements to the domestic quarters, the kitchens and storerooms, or the workshops. I even had two chapels built. In particular, I added a new wing to Hawkedon, my primary manor, with two floors, and stayed there almost exclusively in as much privacy as I could maintain. The smaller manor of Hartest was better for hunting and when I was there I spent as much time as I could riding in the woods. Hunting was a social activity as much as a practical one but I preferred to provide meat for my table following excursions with as few others as possible. Mortals engage in ceaseless prattling about the most inconsequential topics and I can only feign interest for so long.

There was little I could do to shut myself away for as long as I wished, for my tenants came to me with a great many manorial issues. One man had not properly delved his drainage ditches and caused other men's crops to get flooded from the terrible rains and he had to be punished and make amends. There were so many cases of cattle and pigs straying and damaging crops or property that I quickly lost count. I had a few instances of poaching to deal with. It was never something I cared about but I had to pretend outrage and issue relatively steep fines. It was expected and if a lord was too lenient then the villeins and freemen did not like it, not one bit, even as they grumbled about the fines. There were greater crimes, and those committed by my own people against those from neighbouring manors, that I had to hear about but which were outside of my jurisdiction and would need to be deferred to the sheriff's court later in the year.

Of course, the talk from everyone was focused on the dreaded pestilence.

Many wanted to hear how the plague had affected London and were almost disappointed when I assured them that it had not occurred there before I had left it.

"What can we do to prepare, my lord?" the stewards and senior servants asked me in Hawkedon Hall.

I had no idea but I pretended that I did. "The pestilence is caused by bad air and so we must clean, brush, and wash all rooms and paths."

This they did with enthusiasm and returned to me, asking if they were now safe.

"The pestilence is caused also by rising miasmas from bogs and although our wetlands grow every day with these rains, we must now all avoid these places."

They nodded, keen to do so, for everyone knew that such places caused sickness at the best of times.

"But, my lord," my steward said, "the pestilence is also spread by the bad airs emanating from unwashed persons and from the foul breath of careless folk."

"Yes indeed," I said, "and so we must each make the greatest of efforts to wash our linen and our bodies as much as we are able. We shall send to the market at Lavenham and Framlingham for as much soap as possible."

My steward sucked air in through his teeth. "Hard to get soap in Lavenham, my lord, in these times."

"We shall go to Norwich if we have to."

"Very good, my lord," he said, though he seemed unhappy. "What about foreigners, my lord? Bringing their pestilential airs with them?"

"Quite right. We shall forbid anyone from Norfolk or Essex from coming into the manors without exception."

"Especially Essex, my lord."

"As you say, good steward. Anyone from the south or from the coast shall be strictly turned away from the borders."

"And also, my lord," the steward continued, "we must post sentries on the wells, at all hours. And the stream, also, I should think. Sentries night and day, sir."

"Sentries? But why, man?"

"But ain't you heard, my lord, that the pestilence is begun most of all by the Jews, what come creeping out from their low places to poison the wells of good Christian folk in the night so that we all fall dead by dinner?"

I sighed, for the Jews had been expelled from England decades before. It was common knowledge that plenty of them had changed their names and hidden themselves amongst the population, pretending to be Christians but continuing their dark rites in secret. No one ever met one of these secret Jews but everyone knew they were there amongst the townsfolk.

"If that is the case," I said, "surely they would be intent on destroying London, or Bristol, or Oxford, or York. Not Hawkedon and Hartest."

He sniffed, looking over his shoulder before turning back to me. "Colchester's got them new foreigners, sir. Might be they creep up here in the night."

"The Flemish weavers? They are good Christians, not Jews."

"Still foreign, sir."

"Post your sentries, then. But for God's sake ensure they are not armed or they will like as not spear Mistress Heyward when she comes to collect water one morning."

It was a Monday when the first people fell ill in Hawkedon and we all knew what it was, though at first there was still a tragic hope that it was an ordinary affliction that would pass.

A mere three days after the illness came, the first of my people died in blistering agony.

The villeins and freemen stayed in their homes and I stayed in my manor. What could I do? I was powerless. It was tempting to administer my blood to some of the pestilent but I saw how that path might save a life, or not, but would likely lead to my own downfall. Men and women grew suspicious of everything as they watched in helplessness as their parents and their children died first. But the strong and healthy, in the prime of their lives, died also.

I begged for our priests to come and to pray and to visit each of my people, especially the afflicted, and this some of them did. One kindly old priest rode from home to home, dealing out blessing and rites for four days without rest before dying in the night of the fifth.

In desperation, I sent for the finest physicians in the county and to the neighbouring ones, promising that I would pay whatever cost was asked. Just one of my men returned successfully and the doddery old fellow with a fat, red face that he brought back with him claimed to be a physician of the highest learning, although I had never heard of him. I met him in the confines of my solar in my private wing at Hawkedon, and had him sit with me while I asked what experience he had.

"I come from Ely," he said, proudly. "Where I have successfully kept the pestilence at bay throughout this plague."

"Indeed?" I replied, impressed. "Ely is an island in the pestilential fens and yet it is free from the spreading mortality?"

"Well," he said, spreading his stubby-fingered hands, "I have treated a great number of the afflicted. Some have even survived."

"What is the method of treatment? It seems to me that the servants die in more ways than I can understand. Some die where they stand and some few lay abed for a week and then rise, weakened but alive. What can be done, sir?"

He nodded, sagely. "It is a confusing story indeed. It seems as though it may afflict the victim in one of three ways. Most commonly, they fall ill with a fever that hits them very hard indeed. A day or two later, they break out in the boils, clustered in the armpits and groin. Many of these I have seen and they may grow to the size of an apple in a single night. If the sufferer is able to speak he will complain of blinding headaches and violent chills while his body sweats freely and uncontrollably. Within five or six days from the first signs of sickness, they will be dead."

"God preserve us," I said. "This is how my people have been dying, yes."

He held up a finger. "That is merely the first of the three forms, as I stated. Another form is rather better and if God decrees that I become afflicted, this is the form I wish to receive."

"Ah!" I said. "So, this is the gentler form?"

He laughed so hard that his face turned purple. "Dear me, no. I speak of those who die with almost no warning. Surely you have heard of these, sir? A man will kiss his wife goodnight in fine health and be discovered dead in the morning. You may soon find yourself witnessing a man or woman or child suddenly fall to the ground and begin a terrible shaking, with limbs and features rigid and quivering most violently. When you go to their aid, you will discover that they are quite dead, perhaps with putrefied blood oozing from their various orifices. It strikes with such rapidity that the suffering is certainly over quickly. Thanks to God's mercy."

I gripped my hands together in front of me. "There was a third form of death, you said?"

"Yes indeed. One where you might say it falls between the other kinds. It is preceded by terrible coughing which brings up enormous amounts of blood before their end. These poor souls take just two or three days from their first bloody cough to their burial but those days will be filled with agony as they struggle for every breath. They will vomit up their stomach contents, and then whatever water, ale, or wine you can get into them and then quickly it is blood that they vomit, almost ceaselessly. Their fingers turn black and die, as do the toes. No doubt the rest of them would follow in like fashion, if their body was not emptied of blood. This is perhaps the worst form of the pestilence."

There was nothing I could say in response. My instinct was to pray to God but there was a profound sense that He was not listening to our prayers. Worse, it was hard to avoid the feeling that we were all being punished by Him. But what monstrous sins had those living in that time committed that the people I had known earlier had not?

A letter arrived at my home from Stephen in the hands of a young messenger who shook as he stood before me.

"Are you suffering from the pestilence, son?"

The messenger looked horrified. "Oh, no, sir. Thanks be to God. Simply cold and weary from the hard riding and…" He hung his head. "My father and my sister died not three days past, sir. Yet I am hale and in fine health, praise God, sir."

I took a full step backwards. And then another.

"You are one of Stephen Gossett's servants, yes?"

"Indeed, sir. And a fine master he is, sir. None better in all Christendom, so we all say, sir, especially in these days. Fair as the day is—"

"Yes, yes, I'm sure," I muttered as I broke Stephen's seal. Then I froze as I read the words, before calling one of my own servants over. "Escort this young man to the kitchens, see him fed well, give him good ale and provisions for his journey back to London. Give him a good, fresh horse. The black rouncey." I stepped forward and placed a hand on the young fellow's shoulder. "Tell your master I am coming immediately. That is all."

As they left, I read the letter again.

Richard. Regretfully, Sir Thomas and Lady Eva are struck down by the pestilence. They yet live. Please come at once. Your faithful servant, Stephen Gossett.

10

Pestilence

I RODE TO LONDON with all haste, taking Walter and a handful of healthy servants. The roads had degenerated since I last travelled them, with the surfaces washed out and pitted so deeply with eroded pits they were like elongated ponds. Worse, the ways had not been cleared of all the wild growth from weeds and bushes and felled trees blocked the way. Most were natural deadfalls but one seemed felled with a purpose.

"Robbers done it, sir," Walt said, riding to me with his sword drawn after investigating the trunk.

"I doubt they will attack us, Walt," I replied, though I drew my own sword and watched the undergrowth closely for the next mile or two.

We saw few other travellers and those that we passed we kept a distance from and they kept away from us, almost all covering their mouths and noses as they did so.

Rushing, we made the distance in three days which was as swiftly as anyone could hope for. Even so, I was fighting to control my distress over every mile. I had already lost John and now I was at risk of losing my dearest companion and the woman I had loved for longer than any other. Eva was no longer my wife and what passion we had once experienced was by then a century past but the thought of losing her was almost more than I could bear.

When I arrived at the townhouse, I did not pause to change or even to wash but strode into the house, scattering servants while I cried out for Stephen. He came clattering down the main stairs, banging to a stop on the steps before reaching the bottom.

"Richard, thank God. They are this way."

I followed, taking the steps two at a time, up to the rooms on the uppermost floor. Though it was a bright day outside, it was dark in the bedchamber and it took a moment for my eyes to adjust to the lamplight. I had slept in those rooms before and recalled how the windows allowed a pleasant view over the Thames and the ships that filled it. Now, they were shuttered and covered with heavy, dark cloth.

Stephen ushered me fully inside the larger of the two rooms and closed the door behind me. "The doctors said not to allow the bad air into the chambers," he explained, speaking softly.

Servants moved away from the bed as I approached, pulling back the linen curtain. A single candle, fixed to one of the bedposts, gave enough light to see that Eva lay within, her hair loose, wet with sweat and plastered to the sheets. Her face was waxy and pale and translucent as marble. The stench was quite foul. The only sign that she lived was her breathing, which was shallow and rapid.

"Eva?" I said, quietly.

She stirred and groaned and then fell silent.

"Is it truly the pestilence?" I asked Stephen, reaching down to touch her brow. It was fiercely hot and slick with sweat.

"She has the signs," Stephen said, then rushed to explain. "So the doctors tell me."

I pulled back the sheets. "Avert your eyes, Stephen," I said.

An old woman appeared as if from nowhere at my side, grabbing at my arm with her sharp little fingers. "How dare you, sir. You must not. It is unseemly, sir."

"She is my wife," I said to the servant, which gave her pause. I did not add that she had left me eighty years before but nevertheless she *had* been my wife for forty years before that and I knew her body almost as well as I knew my own.

"It is true," Stephen said, over his shoulder. His definition of truth was always a loose one.

"Even so," the old servant said, firmly.

"You are quite right, good woman," I said. "Would you be good enough to help me bare her shoulder?"

She peeled back the sheets and I lifted Eva's arm.

"Here, sir," the servant said, and handed me a lamp.

Holding it close, I saw the enormous black pustule half-filling her armpit.

"Dear God," I muttered. "There are more?" I asked. "Her nether regions?"

The old woman coughed to indicate that she did not think it seemly to discuss it but she then whispered. "Yes, sir."

"How long?" I asked Stephen as I covered Eva again. "How long has she been like this?"

"Come with me," he said and led me across into the second chamber. Hugh, the squire, knelt at the side of Thomas' bed in prayer.

He got to his feet in that stiff-legged way that a man does when he has been at prayer for many hours.

"Sir Richard. Thank you for coming, sir. I know that Sir Thomas would be greatly pleased that you have come."

"How is he?"

Hugh took a deep breath. "The physicians say it is the strangest case they have seen. Thomas and the Lady Eva both, sir. How they are afflicted by the pestilence and yet cling to life, neither dying nor recovering, as some are said to do." Hugh glanced at Stephen then back to me. "Of course, we cannot tell the physicians about the Gift. Surely it is the blood that preserves them so, my lord?"

I nodded, patting him on the shoulder as I crossed to the bed.

Thomas looked like a dead man. His aged face had sunken further, and he was thin as a skeleton.

"Others I have seen suffering from this affliction," I said, "were crying out and raving from their pain."

"They have done so, many times," Hugh said. "After the blood."

"You have given them blood," I said, seeking confirmation, "and it does not cure them."

"For a time," Stephen said, softly. "It rouses them enough to accept a little broth, perhaps some morsels of bread soaked in milk or ale. The black blisters recede and they are often able to converse. And then their anguish begins anew. Eventually, they fall into this state of deathlessness until we rouse them again."

"Perhaps more blood would help? Increase the number and size of the draughts."

Stephen shook his head, sadly. "At first, I filled them both with so much that they vomited it back up. I also gave them blood once they woke, and again twice every hour, but still they fall back into this. I attempted giving them blood the instant they collapse, thus bringing them back to health over and over in quick succession. But there was no increase in effectiveness. Always, they return to this. And now, half my servants have fallen to the pestilence and more have fled this house and the city. I tell the survivors that bleeding them daily is what is keeping them free of the plague but every soul in the city grows suspicious."

"Suspicious of you?"

He waved away my concern. "Suspicious of everyone, of everything. Fear reigns, now. Ancient superstitions half-forgotten are being spoken once more. But my servants trust me and those that remain will continue to be loyal. I ensure I take very good care of them, with the best food I can find, hot fires to keep them warm and dry, even physicians for their families, if the bastard piss prophets can be enticed to attend anyone any more. No, my servants will be here to supply us with blood until this plague passes and our friends recover from their affliction."

"When the plague passes, they will also recover?"

"So the physicians said."

Hugh dared to speak up. "Some say it will never pass. We are dying one after the other until all will have perished and so this is surely the end of the world."

Increasingly, I feared that very thing. It certainly seemed far worse than I could have imagined, had I not ridden across some of the country and seen the horrors of London. Still, it is a leader's duty to provide strength and hope and so I searched for something comforting to say.

"It is a hard time, yes. As hard as any I have seen. Yet order remains in the streets, does it not? The dead do not lay in their beds but are buried by their loved ones and their neighbours. This is a pestilence, no more."

"What have we done to deserve it, sir?" Hugh asked.

"A great deal of evil," I said.

"And yet children have done no evil and they die also. Even more so."

"Some are saying," Stephen replied, "that God slays the children to punish the parents. And that the inexplicably random nature of the death is itself punishment for the wickedness of humanity as a whole."

"But if God is just, why would He do that?" Hugh asked, close to despair.

I wished to snap at him to ask a bloody priest but I held my tongue.

Stephen had an answer, as always. "One of the physicians told me the pestilential miasmas are due to a particular alignment of the heavens, and that God has no hand in this at all. That it is as natural as a storm."

"Of course it is God," I said. "He did it before, did he not? When he sent the Great Flood of Noah to cleanse the Earth."

Stephen bowed. "Of course."

Hugh was not satisfied. "But why—"

"Enough," I said. "Let us rouse them so I can cure them with my own blood. They have suffered enough, whether God wills it or not."

I decided that Thomas would be first. If anything went badly wrong, it would be he that bore the brunt rather than Eva. And I knew that he would not want it any other way.

Using the instrument, I bled myself into a cup.

"Should I..?" Stephen began, reaching out to take it.

I ignored him and sat on the edge of the bed. "Thomas?" I called. "Thomas, it is Richard."

He groaned and muttered.

"Come on, now, old man," I said brusquely as I lifted his head up. The hair at the back of his head was sodden with sweat and a strong, foul stench gusted up to my nose. My stomach churned.

I poured some into his mouth and he stirred himself, slurping at it in a most disgusting fashion. The effects began almost at once and he reached up to grasp my hand and tip the rest of the cup into his mouth while he gulped it down.

Thomas opened his eyes and gasped, then clutched at his stomach while he thrashed his head side to side. After a few moments, he sighed and sank back.

He looked at me.

"Richard."

"Thomas, thank God. You have returned to us."

"Yes, yes," he said. "What took you so long?"

"How do you feel?" I asked.

He considered it for a moment and sat up. I moved back as he pulled back the covers and got to his feet, standing in his sweat-soaked shirt. "I feel well," he said, speaking slowly and wiping his lips. "This was your blood, Richard?"

"You can tell the difference?"

"I have been drinking mortal's blood every day, or near enough. It is difficult to recall clearly. But yes, I believe this does feel different." Hope dawned on his aged features. "By God, I feel hearty indeed."

"Praise God," I said, turning to Stephen. "Now, let us see to Eva."

I was gratified when it went much the same as with Thomas. When Eva awoke and confirmed that she felt fully well, I gave her time to wash and be dressed and waited downstairs in the hall, drinking wine. Stephen's servants managed to find enough fresh produce in London to make for us a rather impressive impromptu feast to celebrate and first Thomas and then Eva joined us while the dishes were served.

Our first course was an array of boiled meats in sauces, of which my favourite was an excellent beef pottage in wine with herbs and spices. After that, we had meats in jelly with roast kid, and a dish of roast heron and one of woodcock which I devoured almost entirely by myself. The third course brought us dozens of small, delicate sparrows and swallows with bowls of fruit compotes, cooked with huge amounts of sugar. After that, when I declared I could eat no more, they brought out a half dozen cheeses which I tucked into with heroic vigour and good cheer.

"Bring us *hypocras*," I called to the servants, which was a spiced red wine that the produced with such alacrity that they must certainly have anticipated my order.

Stephen laughed. "Of course it was ready, Richard. Do you not think that I know you well enough, after all this time together?"

"Let us drink to your good health, my dear friends," I said to Thomas and Eva, raising my cup, and we did so drink.

"And to friends departed," Hugh said, raising his cup. We drank to John, who all of us missed.

"I must say, I am quite relieved to be rid of that terrible affliction," Thomas said. "I never felt anything like it in all my days."

Eva nodded. "And I never wish to again," she said. "It feels like..." she trailed off, staring into nothing.

"Well," I said, "it is all over now and all I can say is that I apologise for not being here sooner."

"You came as soon as you were summoned," Stephen said. "What more can a man do, Richard?"

Summoned. It irked me that he would use such a term when I was his superior in every way but I was in such a high mood that I let it pass. I often wonder what might have come to pass had I destroyed Stephen in his early days, instead of letting such moments pass and pass.

In no time, we were well on the way to pleasant intoxication.

"This was a fine meal, Stephen," Thomas said, "considering the circumstances."

"What do you mean?" Stephen replied, growing rambunctious with the wine in his belly. "This would be a fine meal in any circumstances."

Thomas shrugged. "For an English merchant, perhaps that is so. Speaking as a Frenchman of noble breeding, however, all I will say is that I look forward to when this pestilence passes and we can get some decent food in this hall."

As gibes go, it was rather close to the bone but Stephen laughed it off and so we all felt able to join in with the laughter.

Thomas was still chuckling when he popped some bread into his mouth and began coughing. I jumped up, thinking he was choking on his food, and thumped him on his back.

He coughed up a handful of bright, frothy blood.

We all stared at his hand, shining in the lamplight.

Thomas whispered the short prayer.

"God, no."

I turned to Eva. I will never forget the look of dread in her eyes.

His face contorted in pain, Thomas clutched at his guts and vomited onto the table before collapsing in a shaking fit.

Stephen called for his people and the servants came running.

"Eva," I said, kneeling by her. "It may not return for you."

"No," she said, "it has come again. I can feel it. Your blood, Richard. It did not work."

***

We tried everything that any of us could think of. I gave them more blood, of course. We gave them mortal blood soon after mine, or before, or both before and after. Stephen had the idea of concentrating my blood by heating it gently for some time. That seemed, if anything, to lessen its potency.

Nothing worked.

"We shall find a cure," I said, looking down on Eva, in her bed as the sickness descended upon her once again. "I shall not rest until I do."

"I know, Richard," she replied, patting my arm before turning away from me. I got up and trudged down to the hall.

Sitting with Stephen later with my head in my hands, I felt truly defeated. More than I ever had before. The pestilence was an enemy that I could not fight.

"There must be something," I said, for the thousandth time. "Must be some way to strengthen my blood."

Stephen shrugged. "What flows through your veins is already the most powerful substance on Earth. Yours and your brother's. And as much as I should like to empty him of his, he is not even in Christendom."

"It would take years to follow him to Cathay, Stephen, if that is what you are suggesting."

"I suggest nothing of the sort, sir," he replied, as if he was affronted. "Even if William was here, there is nothing to indicate that his power is any greater than yours. Is there?"

As tired as I was, I knew that Stephen was pushing me for information. He always was. It was his nature.

In fact, I had long suspected that my brother William was stronger than me. Whether it was a factor of the blood in our veins or something else, I did not know but I felt it nonetheless. Perhaps Stephen sensed it too, in some way, and was seeking confirmation.

"We are equals, my brother and I, but if he were here I would string him from the beam there and drain every drop on the chance alone that it could help Eva. And Thomas." I thought for a moment, and idly spoke the next thought that popped into my head. "It is a shame that he killed our father so long ago, or else I could fetch him from Derbyshire and see if he is any stronger than his sons. Alas, William poisoned him when—"

I stopped speaking when I recalled something I had not thought of in quite some time.

If you do return to Christendom, you should seek our grandfather. The Ancient One. The old Lord de Ferrers was not our father's true father. Our true grandfather lives, and he is thousands of years old, Richard. Thousands! The things he has seen. The power that he has. You would learn a lot from him, brother, if you would but go to him. Our grandfather is in Swabia. In a forest, living in a cave. The locals live in terror of him.

"If power is what we need, there is one who may be stronger than I."

"Your brother?"

I scowled. "No, Stephen. Back in Baghdad, in that charnel house of a gateway, I made a deal with William. He told me of the immortals he had made in France and I agreed to not pursue him until he returned to Christendom."

Stephen nodded. He knew all this.

"William also told me something else. He told me that he had discovered our true ancestry. That my natural father was not descended from the de Ferrers family line but had been fathered by an immortal himself. A man who is thousands of years old."

Stephen sat bolt upright. "But you cannot make children, Richard. Neither you nor William."

"Our grandfather did. As did our father. That is why I think he may have more power in his blood than I do. The strength to create life. Perhaps it has strength enough to cure this cursed pestilence."

"Just a moment, please," Stephen said, shaking his head and closing his eyes. "Are you saying that your grandfather yet lives?"

I sat back and spread my hands. "I am relating William's words. As far as I know, he does not lie. To me, at least. But he may be mistaken or confused. He claimed to have visited him."

"Where?"

"Swabia."

"A fair distance from here, Richard. Where in Swabia?"

"In a forest. He lives in a cave."

Stephen stared. "That is it? How can we find him?"

"I would go to Swabia and search, I suppose. Ask around."

"How big is Swabia?"

I shrugged. "Big enough."

"It must surely be the size of Wales and just as mountainous."

"Even more so. And thickly wooded."

Stephen rubbed his eyes. "We must certainly seek this man out but I do not see how it will help us with Thomas and Eva. How long will it take us to travel to Swabia?"

"I can move quickly when I need to."

"Even so, how will we find one cave in a forest the size of Wales?"

"My brother found him. I will find him."

Stephen stood up. "You speak as though you have already decided."

"Do I?" I asked. "I suppose I have. Do you have a better idea?"

He waved his hands in the air as if he hoped to scoop one up out of the ether. "There must be one."

"Perhaps there is but until it occurs to us, I shall do this. Alone."

"Alone?" Stephen was appalled. "Take Hugh with you, at the very least."

Hugh was a good squire and a fair fighter but my instinct was that he was not up to such a challenge. "I shall take almost nothing but food and travel quickly."

"Take Black Walter with you, at least."

"Walt?" I said. "He is mortal. And ignorant. Close to useless."

"He saved your life once, did he not? You underestimate him, Richard."

"I doubt that is possible but you are correct, I shall need someone to take turns on watch and I suppose he is marginally more useful than a goose." I stood. "I will make preparations immediately. I will take Black Walter with me but no other servants. We will move swiftly that way. You and Hugh will stay here and keep our companions alive."

He looked stunned so I strode over and grasped him by the shoulders.

"Keep them alive, Stephen."

His eyes were wide. "I will."

I was going to cross a Europe deep in the grip of the worst plague it had ever known, in the faint hope of finding a hermit who apparently claimed to be thousands of years old as well as my grandfather. And I was going based on the word of my brother, who I had sworn to kill.

I must have been mad.

1 1

Land of the Dead

THE PORTS WERE CLOSED. No ships in or out across all southern England. I knew that it would be foolhardy to travel to the south coast and try to force passage across the English Channel from there, even though that would have been the quickest crossing. Instead, I headed north and east, up into that flat, marshy land called East Anglia. Although it was a fertile land, good for wheat, sheep and cattle, it was wet at the best of times and it had been raining steadily for weeks. When we travelled through it was as though the North Sea had risen up from the east to claim the land for itself. Roads were washed out. Rivers burst their banks and spread out to turn fields into lakes, ruining all crops not on the higher land. And that was few and far between. The landscape was often as flat as a table top.

"How will they eat?" Walt asked as we passed yet another field turned to bog. A man stood on a spit of land running to a cluster of houses, staring at the disaster. "How will they survive winter?"

"They will not."

There were fowl in the reedy ponds and wading birds on the mud flats. Deer in the woodlands. But unless there were enough survivors of the pestilence to hunt for them through the winter, the people would not fare well.

When we reached the coast, it took days of following it from town to town to find someone willing and able to cross to the continent. Even in that remote place, Walt proved useful. Well did he know the taverns in every town, and every hosteller and bar-maid, and these directed us to those who might have helped.

A few fishermen claimed to be able to make the journey but their boats were in appalling condition. Most simply refused to approach us, let alone converse. I considered stealing a boat and leaving a bag of coin but I could never have sailed it and Walt barely had wits enough to navigate his way up a gangplank.

It was a merchant who volunteered his ship, sailing master and small crew in exchange for an appalling amount of money. Due to the closure of so many ports, trade was so diminished as to be non-existent but still he was canny enough to know a desperate man when he saw one. We sold him our horses, as there was no possibility of taking them aboard the tub. Anticipating such a thing, we had not brought our best horses. Still, the awful price I got for them made me more irritated at the merchant than I had any right to be.

"Good idea, this, my lord," the merchant said as we agreed our terms, blustering in the loud voice merchants use when attempting to make a sale. "Get away from the pestilence to where it is safe."

"Do you take me for a fool? It is far worse everywhere south of England, as you well know."

His face turned white and he lowered his voice. "Then why do you wish to go there, sir?"

"I hear Ghent has an excellent brothel house just off the market square."

He went away, mumbling something about petty lordlings and Walter sidled up to me.

"That place ain't all it's cracked up to be, sir. Especially nowadays, I'd wager."

"Be quiet, Walt."

The crossing was remarkably unpleasant. It rained either all day or all night and sometimes both and the boat was seaworthy enough but it had a strange and at times quite alarming propensity to roll like a barrel.

Black Walt was completely unaffected by the motion, which was irritating in the extreme. We crept down the coast, taking advantage of the wind when it blew where we wanted and waiting it out when it did not. We sat in one cove for three days somewhere off the coast of Essex with the sky low and grey and the land lower and greyer. Local men on the land cried out that we were not to land under any circumstances. They made sure that we saw the huge longbows in their hands.

Blustering wind whistled and rushed through the mass of rigging like the wailing of a thousand widows. The boats rolled and pitched in the waves with relentless regularity, up and down, rolling one way and back the other. On every horizon, nothing but a haze like powdered bone. No man who was not a sailor knew whether we were being blown out to sea, on to the shore, or were making no headway at all. Such is the sea. Some moments out of a thousand, when all is well and the sun shines and the wind is stiff and steady and the ship ploughs through the waves toward home, it is of the purest joy. At all other times, it is deep misery that must be endured.

Eventually, we crossed the waters and were out of sight of land for a disturbingly long time and I was sure we would end up in Denmark, despite the sailing master's assurances.

And yet he put us down on the coast of Flanders, just as he had said he would.

"Got to row you off onto the beach from here," he said as his ship bobbed at anchor off the coast. "We'll do it as the tide turns."

"If this is anywhere *other* than Flanders," I promised him, "when I return to England I shall castrate you and throw you into the sea so the fish can feast on your ruined nether parts."

He swallowed, hard. "This is bloody Flanders, my lord. I know these waters. Southwest is a fishing village called Eastend, and beyond that is France. Up the coast, northeast, the mud flats and shoals go on for miles. There is a harbour just up the way at a village they call Bruges-on-sea. You might find horses to purchase there, elsewise it's a walk into Bruges proper for you."

Walt shrugged. "Seems to know his business, sir."

"We shall see," I said, giving the master the full force of my death-stare.

The cold winter sea churned beneath the prow like the frothing mouth of a blown horse. Icy wind sliced through my clothes and chilled me to the bone.

We splashed ashore in the half-light of a grey dawn, wearing our padded armour coats and struggling to keep our over-sized packs from getting completely soaked.

"Going to be right hard buying decent horses for anything other than a king's ransom," Walt said as we trudged along the track to the nearest village. "But I reckon we can like as not help ourselves to a brace of them from some little lord's stables hereabouts."

"We are not thieves, Walt," I chided. "And the Flemings are our allies."

Walt scratched at his chin. "Seems like they're allies with King Edward in fighting the French but me and you are just a pair of foreigners traipsing through their lands uninvited."

"Nevertheless."

He shrugged and hitched his packs higher on his shoulders.

We were turned away from the village of Eastend by men with spears and crossbows who did not believe, or did not care, that we were English.

"Let us try Bruges," I said to Walt. He raised his eyebrows but said nothing.

The path to Bruges was almost empty and we met few travellers. The town was one of the biggest and busiest markets on the Continent, teeming with wealthy merchants and stuffed with skilled craftsmen, drawing locals from the lands all around and traders from everywhere in the world, when times were good. And yet it seemed as though we were almost alone as we approached the outskirts and suburbs. Even Walt was disturbed.

"Seems like things ain't going to go well for us in there, sir," he said, nodding at the walls and roofs in the distance.

"Nothing ventured, nothing gained," I replied.

A short while later, we passed by a father and his son sitting on their cart by the side of the road.

"Way's closed," the man said, turning to spit. Where one of his eyes used to be was a weeping sore that he dabbed at with a filthy rag.

"Do you mean to say that the town is not admitting travellers?" I asked him.

It seemed, as he squinted at me, that his French was not very good. "Way's closed," he repeated.

Walt plucked at my elbow. "Best make our way to a manor off in the country, what say you, sir?"

I shook Walt off. "They likely did not admit him on account of the appalling pustules in his eye, fearing him to be a plague carrier."

Walt wrinkled his nose. "What if the townsfolk detain us?"

"We shall not allow that to happen," I replied, tapping my sword. "Come on, you coward."

The men on the gate were suspicious but once they saw we were healthy and had coin to spend, they welcomed us like we were old friends, directing us to the places where we might purchase what we needed.

"Is the brothel house still open?" Walt asked but I shoved him in through the gate and apologised to the porters.

"Of course it will not be open, Walter. Besides, we have no time for that sort of thing, man. And you will certainly catch the plague in such a place. And catch it in your nether regions, like as not, causing your pestilential member to drop off by the middle of next week."

He nevertheless disappeared from our inn during the night, returning bleary-eyed but happy before sunrise and dozed in the saddle the next day.

Our four horses were good enough for the task and I felt hopeful as we set off because finding good mounts for the journey had been playing on my mind since leaving London. The rain threatened throughout the morning, fell lightly in the afternoon and ceased before sunset.

It was quiet on the road.

South of Bruges, in peaceful years gone by, that same road in late-summer was thronged with merchants and messengers, villeins and freemen, churchmen and beggars and endless servants. The road would be filled from edge to edge with carts piled with produce, riders with lords, children with chickens.

But not that day.

We came across a small group of poor folk wrapped in cloaks and hoods who retreated far into a field as we passed them and watched us for a good long while with dark looks until we were away around the next bend.

Walt turned in his saddle before settling down again. "I reckon we'll be finding trouble before long, sir."

The houses on the side of the road were silent and cold. Whether they had been abandoned or were filled with the dead, entombed unburied in their bedchambers, I could not say for we had no intention of entering any of them.

"What tongue do the folks around these parts speak?" Walt asked as we made camp for the night in a scrubby copse of coppiced ash and hazel a few miles from a village.

I covered my eyes and stifled a groan and cursed myself for not bringing Hugh along instead of Walt.

"You have been to this country before, Walt," I said. "Their tongue is Flemish. Most folk in the towns have French and the learned know Latin, just as it is everywhere. How did you converse with the pestilential harlot during your sordid excursion last night?"

"Oh, you don't have to speak to them, sir. You give them the coins and point at what you want."

"I am sure you do. It surprises me that the establishment is allowed to function at all, considering the keenness with which the men guard the doors to the town."

He shrugged. "Only a couple of old dears in there now, seeing to the locals. Fellow before me was keen as mustard on account of his wife died a few days ago and now he can get his end away again. Ain't take him too long, I tell you that much, he was in and out and looking happy as a pig in shit before I had time to sit down and take a sip of beer."

"Is that so?" I said, getting up to move further away from him. "I believe I shall prepare my own meal this evening, Walter."

Many a man of the knightly classes would despair at the notion of a meal consisting of a hunk of bread, a mouthful of cheese and a few slices of sausage, even if they were on campaign, and yet to me it has always been the simplest fare which brings the most nourishment to body and soul.

I had thought him asleep but Walt's weary voice drifted out of the darkness on the other side of the embers. "Sir?" he began, "is it true that you don't know the way? Only, our lad Hugh reckoned you don't know the way to this land called Swabia but I said Sir Richard wouldn't set out on such a quest without knowing where he was headed and no mistake."

"I do know the way," I replied. "It is to the south. We shall find our way the same way we do everywhere we go, Walt. By asking the way from one place to the next until we arrive."

The extended silence led me to hope he had fallen asleep but then he spoke. "How far south is Swabia, then?" I was about to hazard a guess but he continued speaking. "Long way, ain't it, sir. Long way to go to find a man who you say has a cure for the pestilence when it might be a lot of threshing for no nuts, if you catch my meaning, sir."

I caught his meaning well enough. Black Walter was unnerved by our venture. He was frightened by the creeping death all around, even if he was too simple-minded to know it in himself. And I was leading him further into unknown lands that were peopled with folk he did not know when all man's natural inclination when threatened with disease is to withdraw into a safe place. Into the arms of family and one's own home.

"All will be well, Walter," I assured him. "Rest easy, now, for all will be well."

In fact, it would not be well. Not at all. Especially for Black Walter.

***

From Bruges, we made for Ghent, which was an even larger town. In fact, it was one of the largest and richest towns I had ever seen, rivalling Paris and was even larger, perhaps, than London. Unlike London, however, it was an almost pleasant place, as far as cities go. While London was just as mercenary and grasping at its heart, it was a magnet primarily for the poor, useless, desperate, degenerate, and the sinful, where Ghent was committed wholly to commerce and the people within were hard working and respectable.

Though there is no getting away from the fact that commerce is a soulless and empty pursuit, it is impossible to deny the benefits that it brought the people of Ghent. Merchants and their wives wore the finest clothes in colourful, embroidered cloth and the homes they built were tall and elegantly apportioned, some rising as if straight from the waters of the river. Their churches were impressive and the cathedral truly glorious. An enormous bell tower, still unfinished with empty scaffolding up two sides, soared above every other structure other than the cathedral's tower and the tower of the Church of Saint Nicholas. Within the city, a man could find the answer to all his needs, if he had enough silver. My needs were to obtain as great a quantity of salted and dried meats as could be carried.

"You may not enter," the porter said from the other side of the bridge.

"We carry no pestilence," I replied in French. "Our coin is good. I wish to spend a great deal of it."

The conversation was shouted across the short span of the bridge because the porter's guards had ordered us to stop on the far side. Not that I would have forced the issue but two of the men held crossbows which they loaded and held ready and that demonstrated quite well that they meant what they said.

"None may enter," he replied.

"Do you have the pestilence?" I called out.

"No!" the porter snapped. "And we shall keep it this way. Be off with you, you French dogs."

Walt snorted. "Charming folk, the Flemish, ain't they."

I sighed. "They are merely protecting themselves." Raising my voice, I held a purse, heavy with coins, aloft. "This is for the men who allow us entry."

Three of the guards turned to the porter with hopeful expressions on their faces but the man cursed me and assured us that no man would enter, not for all the silver in England.

"What did he say about England?" Walt asked, putting his hand to his sword.

"Never mind that, Walter. We shall try the town of Brussels, further to the east. It has high walls but the men are not so full of their own importance as these bastards. We shall be there tomorrow before nightfall if we make good time."

The land all around Ghent was marshy but usually firm enough for them to raise so many sheep that the landscape seemed to be made from wool. Yet the rains had turned those grassy fields to ponds and the sheep were long gone. After another night sleeping like outlaws in the trees, we continued on the road to Brussels. It rose above the marshy land and so the going was far easier and we made it soon after midday.

Brussels was open and they welcomed us, for visitors had been fewer than they had ever known it.

"Pah!" a red-faced old innkeeper said. "That pestilence will never come to Brussels. We are good folk here, good folk, I say." He lowered his voice and glanced over his shoulder. "Other than my wife. She will certainly be afflicted. But, such is life." He shrugged.

His wife showed us to our bedchamber and she was a strongly built, rather handsome young woman who seemed perfectly decent to me.

"What on earth do you suppose that fellow meant about his wife?" I asked Walt over our beer and food later that evening.

"She be a harlot, sir," Walt said, hunched low over his pie and speaking with his mouth full, spraying flecks of pastry and gravy over the table.

I looked at the woman as she carried mugs of beer to a group of inebriated guildsmen on the other side of the ale room. "She seems to be a perfectly ordinary ale-wife."

Walt shook his head, still without looking up at me. "Pinched my arse, sir."

"She did what?"

"Earlier, sir, when you were looking at the bed. She pinched my arse and give me a saucy wink, she did."

"Why on earth would she pinch your arse and not mine?"

He considered it for a while before pointing at me with his knife. "You're too good for her, sir. A knight such as yourself is. You're pretending you're just an ordinary squire of middling means but it's clear as day from your bearing and manner that you're a man with noble blood and a practised harlot don't want to be getting involved with the upper crust or it'll be more than fines she'll be paying in court."

After regarding me warily for a moment, he continued to attack the meat within his pie.

"Are you mocking me, Walter?"

He looked up, aghast, radiating innocence. "Me, sir? Never, sir. Wouldn't even occur to me, sir."

I nodded slowly and he let out a breath before guzzling his beer and studiously picking the chunks of liver from every corner of the pastry crust.

It occurred to me that Stephen may have been right about Walter. I had perhaps been underestimating the depth of the cunning in my companion for many years. Never having spent so much time alone in his company before, I had always assumed his occasionally perceptive observations on the world were mere chance but I felt like I had just had a glimpse of his true self. His mask had slipped and the man beneath was illuminated.

Walt burped, cuffed his mouth and picked at something deep within his nose. I could not decide if he was truly so uncouth or if he was playing it up in the hope of throwing me off.

"What do you think of me, Walt?" I asked him.

He froze, one finger up his nostril. "Sir?" he replied, pulling it out.

"Do you wish me to repeat myself?"

"Just don't understand what you want from me, sir."

"You do not hold out much hope for our success in this venture, do you?"

He shrugged. "Seems like you always win when it comes to a fight, sir."

"Ah. But it seems like I always lose when it comes to everything else?"

"Don't rightly know about that, sir. But we been looking for the knight of the black banner for a long old time. Two years, is it? And we can't find him nowhere. Now, with this new fellow, you reckon you'll go to some distant land you ain't ever even been to before and find a man you ain't never met and who you don't even know the name of. Don't seem possible, is all."

I nodded. "I would agree with you but for the fact that the knight of the black banner knows we are looking for him and he is hiding. He is most probably travelling around from place to place. Or he was one of the knights of France who has put away his black banner and his black armour and is posing as an ordinary lord, in plain sight. Whereas the man we are searching for lives in a cave, and so can be found in one place. Hiding, perhaps, yet known to the folk of the surrounding area as a wolf man. As something ancient and terrible. All we need do is find stories of this wolf man in the towns and villages and search the local woods for traces of such a creature until we find him. It should be rather simple. Not easy, perhaps, but simple."

Walt scratched his face. "I suppose I don't really need to understand it, do I, sir."

A wise fool, indeed. "No, Walter."

He nodded, downed the rest of his beer, glanced around at the innkeeper for a moment and lowered his voice. "Right then, sir. That cuckold seems busy. I got to meet the alewife in the cellar about now so I will most likely see you on the morrow."

After Brussels, we headed south and passed through a landscape that I would come to know over four centuries later through battles at Quatre Bras and Waterloo. All I knew then was that it was Wallonia and that the villages and hamlets were terrified of outsiders. They hid from us or threatened us from a distance to keep away and we were glad to do so.

Our way south was hindered by the Ardennes, a land of dense forest and awkward hills, much fought over by Charlemagne. Assuming it might be hard going, I still decided to cut through the region rather than going around it by heading directly east but we found the road into a valley blocked by felled trunks. It was manned by a group of villeins who were wet and mud-stained but were armed with spears and bows and a few put on their helms as I approached on my horse. Walt was behind me to my left with the two pack horses.

"Good day, good fellows," I said. "We wish to pass through this land on our journey to the south."

"French, are you?" the lead man asked from behind their barricade. He gripped his spear so hard that his fingers were white.

Whether they considered themselves to be friends or enemies of the French, I could not guess, as in that area it could have been either.

"How much is it to pass?" I asked.

"Answer the question, Frenchman!" another fellow called from the rear.

I grinned. "Why, we are Englishmen and friends to all the folk of these parts."

"English!" they cried, and levelled their weapons at us and all began talking at once. Some to each other, most shouting insults and curses at us. I had no idea what the English had done to them but it mattered not.

"Please," I said, holding up my empty hands. "By God, will you listen? We mean no harm."

Walt rode forward from behind me. "Come on, sir," he shouted. "Let's be off from—"

I watched a crossbowman aim at Walt and I drew my sword. The bow clanked and the bolt shot straight and flew true. Without thinking, I swung my sword and knocked the bolt aside with a terrible clang that jarred my arm to my shoulder. Our horses, untrained in the ways of war, decided that they would much rather be elsewhere and we retreated, dragging our other horses after us until we were well clear of the men and their barricade.

"By God, sir," Walt said, "you knocked the bolt right out of the air."

"By God, so I did," I replied, laughing.

"We should go back there and slaughter the lot of them," Walt said, his face clouding over. "They would have murdered me, sir. Murdered me!"

"They were simply protecting their families from the pestilence. Even that fellow who sent a shot at you may not have meant to do so. You know what the levies are like. No nerves at all."

"Even so. It is the principle of the thing. The insult of it can't go unpunished, sir."

I must admit, I was tempted, and Walt could see it on my face. With a start, I realised that he was attempting to manipulate me by putting it in terms he thought I would respond to. *Do my men truly see me as prickly as all that,* I wondered.

"It is not worth the lost time," I said, finally. "We shall go back to the crossroads."

He said nothing but I sensed he had lost a little of the regard he held me in. For some reason, that bothered me.

***

"Paris is filled with the dead," the priest said. "Fifty thousand, at least. Some say one hundred thousand. Rouen, too, is destroyed. Amiens has filled its graveyards, dug new ones, and filled those, too. The dead lie now in their beds, corrupted. Everywhere in France, it is the same."

We met him on the road and, unlike most other travellers we had seen, he was keen for our company. His name was Simon and he was heading home to Strasbourg from his parish in Normandy, where he swore that every one of his parishioners had died. The man had lost his horse at some point and was walking in shoes that were almost entirely worn away and his feet were in a terrible, disgusting state.

"Flanders yet fares well," I said. "They closed their towns."

Simon shook his head. "Sensible folk, the Flemish. Bunch of bastards. They do not have the pestilence at all? That is good."

Walt spoke up. "It's there alright. Cattle wandering without herdsmen in the fields. Barns and wine-cellars standing wide open. House after house empty and few people to be found anywhere. Fields lying uncultivated. It's there, sir."

"Ah. As it is all across France." He shook his head. "What did Man do to deserve such punishment? Are we not punished enough with our daily travails?"

"Some are saying this is the end of all things, brother," I said. "What do you say to that?"

"It may well be so," he replied, sighing and looking up at the darkness. "For how can those that live now go on in a world such as this? Perhaps when we are all dead, we shall all then rise and see Heaven made upon the Earth." He put his head in his hands and sobbed.

Walt leaned forward and held out a skin. "Some wine to ease your suffering, sir?"

Simon jerked up and snatched it from him. "Praise God," he said.

We each of us drank and in the morning we found that Simon had stolen one of our horses and some of our food and wine.

"I shall murder him," Walt said, shaking where he stood. "I'll bloody tear his throat out."

"Not before I do," I said.

But he had sold us a duck. He was most certainly not on the road to Strasbourg and we never found him before we doubled back and went on our original way again.

"All is well," I said. "We have one spare mount and coin enough to yet to buy another."

In truth, I cursed myself for trusting any soul and resolved not to let any man near us again. Walt was furious with himself and with me and he was mercifully silent for days on end.

We came to a small town named Saarbrucken where we found the people dying in great numbers of the sickness and so we did not enter for long. Bodies were being born in great numbers to the churches. Few spoke to us at all, save to warn us off but they did so without any malice. The dead were everywhere and the living were broken. Curates and parish clerks could barely keep up and they looked as though they were dead on their feet.

Passing on as quickly as we were able, we came to a well-fortified city called Stuttgart, where the buildings were grand and clean but the people were miserable and fearful.

A hooded monk, old and drawn, hobbled over to us with his hands folded into his belly.

"This is our punishment. All must repent. Confess. And repent."

"Yes, yes," I said, trying to ignore him.

"Do you know of the tale of a wild man of Swabia? A man like a wolf. Some call him the Ancient One."

The monk lurched away from me, muttering a prayer before seeming to lose his thoughts. "A ball of fire was seen above Vienna! Pestilential flame. The bishop exorcised it from the skies, praise God, and it fell to the ground. Praise God. A pillar of flame rises above

Paris, from the depths of the city into the Heavens. Fire!" He stood as upright as he seemed able and raised his hands as he spoke.

"Stand back from him, sir," Walter said, drawing me away. "He has the plague."

I noticed then that the man's hands were black and rotten. Someone nearby shouted for the guards. As he was dragged away, his hood fell down and a woman screamed at the ruin of his face.

"He was a leper," I said to Walt. "Not a plague carrier."

Walt shrugged. "Same thing, ain't it?"

Heading further into the town, I kept an eye out for any man who might be likely to help me. A well-travelled man would be best, respectable in ordinary times but in dire need of silver and gold.

"Have you seen her?" a little girl with a pink face asked me in the marketplace. She was well dressed and the servant who was supposed to be taking care of the girl was instead arguing with a wine merchant about his prices. The child was perhaps ten years old and had spoken in good French, no doubt having heard me conversing with Walter.

"Have I seen who?" I asked the little girl.

She lowered her voice. "The *Pest Jungfrau*."

"The Plague Maiden?" I said. "I never heard of her before. Who is she?"

The pale little girl was as delicate as a winter flower. Her big grey eyes filled her face. "A ghost. She flies across the land as a blue flame, spreading the plague. She flies from the mouths of the dying to look for her next hale body to fill with death. My mother died. My father will die, also. I think that I shall die soon."

"Take heart, dear girl. You may yet—"

The servant woman whipped about, seized the child's arm and dragged her away while giving me an evil glare.

"Poor child," I said to Walt. "How potent is their fantasy. People are so impressionable, they can die of imagination itself."

"*Have* you seen it, sir? The Plague Maiden?"

"For God's sake, Walt."

Stuttgart had taken the view that the pestilence was a punishment from God and that their only salvation could come from being free from sin. The town fathers had acted to shore up moral standards by forcing unmarried cohabiting couples to either marry or separate. Swearing, playing dice and working on the Sabbath became crimes punishable by the harshest fines and penalties. No bells were to be rung at funerals, no mourning clothes were to be worn and there were to be no more gatherings at the houses of the dead to honour the departed souls. New graveyards were dug and all the plague dead were taken there rather than to their family plots.

Men came to close the market even while we were negotiating our purchases and they turfed us out.

"It has been noted that deaths are more numerous about the marketplaces," one of the kindlier officials explained in English. "And so we close the marketplaces. God be with you."

"Please!" I said. "We are travelling south, seeking tales of a wolf man. Some call him the Ancient One."

"By God," the man said. "You are madmen."

"Perhaps but have you heard of such a man?"

He shook his head, looking around to check that his fellows were not listening, and lowered his voice before speaking. "There is a wolf man in the *Schwarzwald*. Or many of them, perhaps. The tales are told to children to stop them going into the forest. It does not work."

"In the *Schwarzwald*? The Black Forest? We have heard much talk of this place. Can you direct us to it?"

He scoffed. "It begins here," he replied, pointing to the southwestern gate.

"Begins?" I said. "Where does it end?" I had a feeling I would not like the answer.

"I do not know. A hundred miles? Two weeks on horseback? The hills are large and many. The forest is dense and ancient. I must go now."

"Thank you for your—"

He grabbed my shoulder. "Do *not* go into the *Schwarzwald*." Before I could answer, he turned and strode away.

"What now, sir?" Walt asked.

"We go into the Black Forest."

1 2

The Black Forest

AN ANCIENT FALLEN fir tree allowed us the space to look out across the wooded mountain ranges to the south. The track we had taken up the hill wound its way down the other side and disappeared amongst the deep green needles of the pines below us. On the other side of the narrow valley rose hill after hill, growing fainter until they were lost in a white mist and merged with the sky. Smoke drifted above the dense canopy here and there. Somewhere, perhaps miles distant, a single axe blade smacked steadily into a trunk, the sound echoing between the hills. I could make out a handful of shapes that might be houses.

"God help us," Walt said. "We have no hope. None."

"Nonsense, man. We must keep on to the next village. And then the next. Someone will know of the Ancient One."

He mumbled under his breath as I led my horse on down the track but I heard him clearly enough. "I'll be the bloody ancient one at this rate."

After Stuttgart, we had asked in the marketplace of a very fine little town named Calw about the man that we sought and had been led by a leather worker to an old woodsman who sat drinking in a beer hall. Only after buying him a half-dozen mugs of ale did his tongue loosen. The leather worker, whose name was Conrad, explained to me in French what the old man was saying.

"He says this Ancient One, the man who is sometimes a wolf, lives deep in the forest. That all woodsmen know to leave his lands alone and to fell no trees there."

"Ask him where, man. Where?"

"He says it would be very bad for you to go to this place."

"Surely, that is my business. Tell him I wish to know. I will pay him for the knowledge. I shall pay you, also, if you get the truth out of him."

"He says he swore to his father never to reveal this secret. He cannot do it for any money. He wishes us to leave now."

Walt cleared his throat and leaned into my ear. "Could always beat it out of him, sir?"

I shook my head. We would need a translator willing to participate in a crime and if we were caught we would be strung up by the local lord and his bailiffs.

"If he knows of the Ancient One, others will also know. We will continue."

Conrad agreed to act as our translator and guide, for a sizable sum, and so we went south and a little to the west, into the dark beneath the trees. Three days, we had picked our way into the northern Black Forest, before reaching that high ridge and looking out at the seemingly impenetrable mass of deep green.

Our guide, Conrad, had lost his parents and sister to the pestilence and his father's business was almost entirely without custom. He claimed he was unafraid of the forest and that the people were perfectly reasonable folk. When it came to the stories of the Wolf Man, he said he had heard them from other children growing up but his parents had forbidden him to speak of such nonsense. It was all a little close to heathenry for good Christian people. But no one knew any details. Only the hunters, the charcoal makers, the woodsmen and swineherds knew the details and most of them would never speak of such things openly and never to outsiders.

"All I need is one man who knows," I replied. "One man who knows on which mountain to search. Which valley to scour."

On the fourth day, we came to Hausach, a small village nestled on the flat bottom of a steep-sided valley.

It seemed as though everyone was dead.

The graveyard was lined with freshly-filled graves and a long trench had been dug as if ready to accept a host of bodies. Yet it was empty, and the sides had begun to crumble into the waterlogged hole.

"We should not enter this place," Conrad said, in between muttered prayers.

"He ain't wrong, sir," Walt said, speaking softly. "Horses are nervy."

"Nonsense," I said. "We have walked through pestilential lands before and remain free from the sickness. Come, now."

But nothing could convince our guide to continue on and Conrad took his payment and fled back to Calw as fast as his pony would carry him.

Walt climbed back into his saddle. "Well, I suppose we don't need one who speaks the local tongue if everyone is dead."

The next village was far smaller and seemed as though it had been abandoned for over a year.

"We need to find local people, Walter. They must be out there in the hills and under the trees but how can we find them?"

"Never many people in the woods in the best of days, is there, sir. If you want people, you find a town. To find a town, you follow the widest tracks."

"That will take us away from the deep woods," I argued. "And I know my grandfather is here. Somewhere. I can feel him."

Walt frowned and looked at me strangely before shrugging. "Going forward sometimes means going backward. You said that to me years ago."

"I very much doubt it. But we must find local people so let us go on."

On the empty road to Freiburg, a rainstorm began late in the afternoon that was heavy enough to make travelling further almost impossible and we walked our horses into the trees to look for a dense copse or ideally a rocky cliff to shelter against until it passed. A track led to a very fine stopping place consisting of a short defile that was narrow enough for a few tree trunks to have been thrown across them to create a crude roof.

We slowed as we approached because someone was already there.

Loosening my cloak, I checked that my weapons were free to be drawn quickly and let my horse trail far behind me to make space. Walter began to draw his sword but I waved him back. Walking into a travellers' camp with a drawn sword is as sure a way as any to start a fight.

"Good evening," I called out in French, raising my voice over the cacophony of the ongoing deluge. "We are simple travellers, seeking shelter."

Between the ten- or twelve-foot high rock outcrops on either side and beneath the roof was no more than a small family and a smoky little fire sputtering in the rain. A man stood with his son and behind them was the wife and a young girl. They were all soaked through and fearful.

"God be with you, good fellow. May we share your fire?" I asked as I approached, smiling. "We shall build it higher. We have food that we will share with you. We do not have the pestilence, as I am sure you can see. Lower your hood, Walt, show them your face."

The wife hissed something but the man looked us over and nodded. Presumably my wealth was obvious enough to allay his initial fears. The son glared with open hostility but was dutiful enough to follow the lead of his father as they took their seats on the logs around the fire.

"My name is Richard and my servant is Walter. Where do you come from, sir?" I asked as we settled ourselves.

The wife glared at the husband and he hesitated but he knew that to not answer at all would be extremely rude.

"Basel."

"Ah," I said. "You are heading north?"

Again, he hesitated before answering. "East." His French was heavily accented.

Walt busied himself splitting logs to one side and I left him to it.

"Is it bad in Basel?" I asked. He said nothing. "Of course, it is bad everywhere. Is the pestilence lesser in the East? We are heading southward but I do not know what our final destination will be as I am searching for a man, for a story of a man. Perhaps you have heard of a wildman who lives in the woods hereabouts? Some call him the Ancient One, or the Wolf Man. Have any other travellers mentioned such a man?"

The husband was confused and his wife scowled at his side. The son's eyes were wide with anger which was clearly aimed at me. He saw me as a threat to the safety of his family, which I most certainly was.

"We have heard nothing like that," the woman said, in rather good French, though there was something about it that made me look closer at her, and all of them.

The light was poor, her clothes were heavy and her hair was entirely covered. And she was drenched but she had a particular look to her. Pretty, in fact, and younger than her demeanour had suggested but her complexion was dark. It was a look that the husband had also, and of course the children were the same.

"What was your profession in Basel, sir?" I asked.

Both the wife and the son looked frightened and glanced at the husband, who clenched his jaw for a moment before looking down at his hands. His wife tutted and turned away. The son glared at his father with contempt, which he then turned on me.

"Are you Jews?" I asked but I already knew the answer. Walt stopped chopping wood and stared at them.

"We are travellers, heading east," the husband said, not meeting my eye.

"You are travelling alone? Just the four of you? How do you mean to protect yourself against those who would do you harm?"

The boy jumped to his feet, eyes filled with emotion. The father pulled him down while his mother scolded him. The little girl continued to bury her face in her mother's flank.

It was perhaps an unfair question to ask because clearly they had no protection and little hope of getting wherever it was they were going. Even in the best of times it would have been unlikely that a man such as he would have been able to long protect his woman on the wilder stretches of road. And at that time, when it appeared to be the end of the world and the civilising effects of the law was falling to pieces about us, they had no hope at all.

"Why do you not hire guards?" I asked him.

He scoffed and rolled his eyes, which was a strange response.

"Not all Jews are wealthy," the woman said, glancing at her husband. I took this to be a barbed comment aimed at her husband's failings but he nodded vigorously.

"We be very poor people, sir, and have nothing to offer anyone."

Now he had raised my suspicions, for no Jew took pride in his poverty, as a good Christian might.

"Not all wealth comes in the form of coin and gold, sir," I said, looking at his pretty young wife.

He looked horrified but she sat up straighter and held my gaze. The boy again stirred himself as if he was about to leap to his mother's defence but she muttered some foreign words to him and he sullenly stayed where he was.

"Perhaps we could pay you, then," the wife said, straightening the sides of her headdress and smoothing her clothing over her body. Even through the thick woollen layers, her womanly shape was quite apparent.

Despite myself, my ardour was raised. Without conscious thought, I entertained the idea of taking the woman to some sheltered spot close by to lay with her. It would have to be done against a tree or over some fallen trunk. She was offering herself in return for ongoing protection on the road, or even out of the hope that I would not murder her family that very night and take her anyway, before killing her, too. Rather rapidly, my ardour cooled.

The husband was looking down, while the woman looked at me steadily. She shook, ever so slightly. The strength of a woman, in what she is willing to suffer to protect her family, is the most powerfully-felt force in the world. Yet it is worthless without the physical and moral strength of a man to protect her. And her man was a weakling.

"I cannot travel with you eastwards," I said, "as my task takes me elsewhere. If we had been headed in the same direction, I would have protected you without any form of payment." The woman sagged, then, looking down. She took a deep breath. "But I would urge you to spend whatever coin you have to hire proper guards to escort you."

"We did," the wife said, glaring at me again. "They robbed us on the third day. They took all of our money, our jewellery. They even took my husband's and my son's weapons. Could you not escort us, good sir? Some of the way at least?"

"I can do no more than wish that God goes with you."

They nodded, sadly.

Walt approached and began to build up the fire.

"Was it you?" he asked them. "Was it you what poisoned the wells?"

"Walter," I chided him. "We are guests at their fire, are we not?"

He was surprised. "But they be Jews, sir. I mean no harm by asking but ain't it a fair question? I just want to know, is all."

"We poison nothing," the man said. "Never. Nothing."

I nodded. "It would not be the likes of these good folk, Walt. It would have been the elders and the priests of their tribe who did the poisoning. Besides, the learned physicians are certain that the pestilence is due to miasmas released from within the Earth, due to an alignment of the planets."

"Our elders poisoned nothing," the man said, sullenly. "We are innocent."

Walt scoffed. "The Jews might be many things but they ain't innocent, sir. We let you live in our towns, let you grow rich off our backs. You people are like fleas infesting our clothes, feasting on our blood. And this is how you repay us?"

Him and his boy stirred again but I knew they would do nothing. They were weaklings and soon they would be taken on the road and they would be murdered, for one reason or another.

"Leave them be, Walt," I said. "You are right that their people are never to be trusted by good Christian folk but here before us is nothing but a poor family who need our charity."

"Charity is for Christians, sir," Walt said, with such certainty that I hesitated to correct him. Possibly he was right, for I was never much of a theologian. "What was your profession, sir? Were you a money lender?"

"I am a goldsmith," he said, with pride.

"There you are, then, Sir Richard," Walt said, immensely pleased with himself. "A bloody goldsmith. What more do you want, eh? I never understood none of it my whole life. What do you want to live in our towns for anyway, goldsmith? Living protected by our walls, protected by our soldiers, eating our bread what we grew with our own hands. And what do we get for it?" He held up a hand and counted off on his fingers. "You steal our babies for your blood magic, you poison our fountains and wells and kill us off for no reason, you creep about at night changing into animals, you pretend to be one of us when it suits you while at the same time you demand special treatment because you ain't Christians, and... and..." he flailed around, desperate to find a fifth outrage so he could close his thumb also. "And usury. I cannot fathom why we allow them in our kingdoms at all, Sir Richard, can you? Of all the people of the world, the least trustworthy of all are—"

"All right, Walt," I said, "that's quite enough of your philosophising for one night, I think." I turned to the woman. "I do apologise for my servant. You will please excuse his shamelessness and general uncouthness. His intellectual deficiencies come not only from the lowness of his birth but I fear he is also halfway to being a Welshman."

The rain eased off and then stopped halfway through the night. Walt and I took turns to sleep because even though the man was weak, his son or the wife had enough heart to run us through and steal our horses if we let our guard down. Jews were devious, it was common knowledge, and I still wondered if the man could be trusted. They, too, watched us warily through to morning.

As we packed our belongings and prepared the horses in the halflight beneath the saturated, heavy forest, I watched askance as they loaded their sawbacked old pony.

"You said your guards stole everything from you," I said. It was quite clear that they had secreted something of value on their persons that the guards did not find, which they then used to purchase the packhorse and other supplies. If they had remaining valuables then I meant to impress on them that they needed to invest in protection, in spite of their previous failure in that regard. "How much do you have left?"

"Nothing," the man said, bitterly. "Be on your way, now."

"You cheeky bastard," Walt said, placing his hand on his sword hilt. "You be speaking to a great lord and you will show him the proper respect or I'll knock you into next week. You and your shit-brained boy. Hear that, lad? You want a thrashing and all, I take it?"

Stepping between them, I spoke to my soldier servant. "Peace, Walter."

He muttered under his breath but calmed himself and carried on doing his duty.

"Go on, then," I said to the family, indicating the track back to the road. The man pushed his wife and the girl ahead of him and I was pleased to see his fear that I would do him harm. The boy led the horse by me and I stepped in his way. He was about thirteen and had his mother's good looks though he had the weak build and narrow chest of his people. His bitterness and anger and fear were understandable, considering what was happening in the world.

"Your father cannot protect your mother and sister," I said to him and I handed over one of my swords.

The lad was shocked but he snatched it quickly enough and hurried by me. He did not thank me.

"Why in the name of God did you do that, Sir Richard?" Walt asked, incredulous.

"It was a useless old sword," I said.

"I liked that sword," Walt said.

Blamed as they were for the plague, Jews were soon being massacred from Toulon to Barcelona and from Flanders to Basel and Strasbourg. Many were burned in their homes by the terrified townsfolk who believed that they were protecting themselves and their families while also taking revenge for the Christian deaths already caused. Others were executed by their towns or hacked down by angry mobs.

The Church pronounced that Jews were innocent of spreading the plague and the nobility of Europe issued edicts condemning the violence and sought to protect the victims.

In some places, such as Mainz, the Jews took the initiative and murdered the townsfolk first, resulting in massive reprisals from the populace. In more generous places, the Jews were given the chance to renounce their faith and become Christians, which many did. Those that did not were then righteously slaughtered. Tensions were so high that in other towns the Jews barricaded themselves in their own homes before killing themselves and their families rather than to allow the townsfolk the satisfaction of committing the acts themselves. Some even burned their homes down around themselves to deny the Christians the plunder of their worldly goods.

In time, the massacres lost momentum and ceased. Perhaps the townsfolk finally noticed that the Jewish people also died from the pestilence in great numbers. And it is the nature of mass hysteria that its manic energies cannot be maintained for long.

All of this began the eastward movement of Europe's Jewry to Poland and Russia. I do not know why the Poles gave refuge to the Jews. Walt had questioned why they wanted to live in Christian towns at all but it was clear to me. The Saracens had conquered the Holy Land and being subjugated by the Mohammedans was far worse than living amongst us, good and tolerant Christian folk. Still, they did not truly belong anywhere in Europe and they never would do, because it was not their land. They would always be regarded as strangers amongst us.

As I rode away that morning, I reflected that their plight as a people in some small way reflected my own. I was a man who did not belong but who had nowhere else to go. I existed within my society while forever being outside of it. In order to avoid persecution, I was forced to sometimes pretend to be something that I was not. Perhaps that was why I felt such sympathy for them, despite their dourness and possible hand in causing or spreading the pestilence.

It is likely that the family we met were murdered by robbers before they had gotten very much further along the road to the East. In the dark depths of that plague, strangers of any kind meant danger for desperate locals and had little value beyond what could be taken from them.

Shortly after our encounter with those poor people, Walter and I fell to calamity and sudden violence.

***

It was an ordinary enough village, from a distance. A small number of painted timber houses, some rather large, clustered about a fine stone church. The river was clear and fresh and swift flowing before widening and slowing as it passed by the village.

"Graves, sir," Walt said, nodding to them as if I had not seen it. As if I had not already smelt the death.

"Let us pray that some yet live," I said.

It seemed at first that the place had fallen entirely but there was woodsmoke in the air and a large goat stood tethered to a post in a garden, chewing and watching us pass with its evil eyes. In the village square before the church, I felt other eyes on me. Human eyes, I was certain of it.

"Good day," I called out, in as friendly a shout as possible, hoping one of the survivors spoke French. "We are simple travellers looking to purchase supplies. Can you help us, please?"

A scraping sound brought me around to face the church as a priest emerged in his robe, wiping his mouth on a cloth. When I raised my hand in greeting, he smiled and came out from the church door, holding his cloth to his mouth.

"You are welcome," he said from behind his cloth. "Welcome indeed, sirs, to Wolfach. You come from France? In the name of God, I pray that you have news of how the plague fares there?"

"France, yes," I replied. "My name is Richard and this is my servant."

The priest was looking at me very strangely and I thought that he had detected the form of Norman French I spoke and perhaps even suspected that I was an Englishmen. His own version of French was quite different from mine, rather idiosyncratic in truth, with strange turns of phrase and I had to listen carefully to catch his meanings.

"Ah, pray forgive my manners. It has been the most trying time I have ever known and my mind is not what it was. My name is Peter. You must be hungry and tired from the road. Come, come. We shall find you something."

I dismounted and made for the church.

"No," Peter said. "Not there. We shall go to the inn. My brother is the innkeeper and he will have what we need."

The priest was a well-made fellow and no mistake. Almost of a height with me and broad in the shoulder. Still, not all men who are built for war are suited to it and he seemed to have the manner of a village priest, though he did look fair harrowed by the deaths. The doors to most of the houses were closed and marked with a cross.

"Have many survived, sir?" I asked. Our horses hooves echoed from the plastered walls of the houses.

"Some yet live and breathe, praise God," Peter said. "Enough to keep us alive, as long as no more perish. The dead are with the gods and the village will go on. And that is what matters." He raised his voice as we approached the inn. "Christman! We have visitors."

Before we reached the door, a huge man emerged. He had the look of his brother but taller, broader, with a skull like a granite boulder and arms like tree trunks. He wore a leather apron spattered with blood. When he spoke to his brother in their guttural tongue, his voice was as deep as the lowing of a bullock. After giving us a hostile glare, he ducked back inside.

"So many have died," Peter said. "We who are left must take on the work of the dead. The slaughterman and his sons died months ago. Here, let us sit on the benches out front so we do not have to smell the stench within. I have had my fill of death."

Walt tied the horses and began brushing them down rather than join me and the priest at the bench outside the inn. I knew then that Walt felt it too.

Something was wrong.

"Your brother is a giant, I see," I said to Peter as we sat. I made sure to face the doorway so the innkeeper could not come up behind me. "Are all men in these parts so well made, sir?"

He tilted his head. "Not all. Our father is a large man and all men grow from their father's seed. You yourself come from good stock."

I nodded. "Your father lives?"

Peter looked up at the sky. "Our father lives in another place and we do not know if he lives or if he has died. But I think that he lives." He looked at me suddenly. "To where do you go?"

"We are looking for the town named Freiburg. It is south of here, is that correct?"

"Southwest, beyond this valley toward the Rhine. Three days on good horses, if you are not running. What business do you have there? Are you expected by anyone?"

I sat back and allowed my right hand to fall into my lap so that it was close to my dagger. "Our business is that we are looking for a man." From the corner of my eye, I saw Walt turn to me and shake his head ever so slightly. I knew he trusted this man not a bit and neither did I but he was the first local we had found for days and even if he meant trouble, I thought we could fight our way out. Even the largest mortal, like his brother, was little when

115

compared to my immortal strength.

"A man, you say?" Peter replied, speaking with forced lightness. "What man is that?"

"In truth, I do not know if he is a man at all. For they call him the Ancient One and also the Wolf Man."

The priest froze and stayed perfectly still. It seemed as though the very air around us stopped moving and a silence descended over the village. "Where did you hear those names? Why do you seek him?"

"I would be delighted to tell you. If you know where I might find him. What did you say the name of this village is, sir?"

He chewed on his bottom lip before replying. "Wolfach."

"Wolfach, I see. And is that name related to the tales of the—"

I was cut short by a cry of warning from Walt.

"Watch out, sir!"

The giant brother, Christman, came charging around the corner of the inn behind me, moving with such speed that I barely had time to register the sight of him. His face, contorted with rage into a savage grin, filled my vision as I jumped up, knocking the bench down behind me and swinging the heavy pine table into the great charging mass.

It crashed into him but he knocked it aside without slowing and threw his weight onto me, wrapping his monstrous great arms about me and dragging me to the floor.

His grip was inhuman.

He held me from behind, so that his back was upon the ground and my heels drummed against the floor. Both of my arms trapped against my body, I struggled and heaved against him. The air was crushed from my chest and I fought for a breath. He may as well have been made from stone. Never, in all my life, had I felt such strength. Not even William's immortals had been so possessed with might. I used the back of my head to hammer at him but met only the flesh of his chest and shoulder.

From the corner of my eye I saw Peter rush to Walt and knock him down with a single blow.

Christman the giant squeezed hard, panting his bloody breath into my ear. I fought to strike him, any part of him, with my feet. Tried to roll him over so I might stand and throw him. I could find no purchase.

I was dying. Suffocating. My vision growing dark at the edges.

Walt leapt up, ran quickly to the nearest saddle and grabbed for a weapon. It was not there. I had gifted it to the boy on the road.

Peter stepped up behind him and stabbed a dagger into his back, over and over. Stabbing him in the chest and belly as he fell beneath the hooves of the terrified horses. Stabbed him a dozen times.

The giant grunted and squeezed harder, popping ribs and dislocating one of my shoulders.

I could not take a breath.

The world turned black.

1 3

The Ancient One

THE PAIN told me that I was not dead.

Not yet.

I came back to myself slowly. Somehow, I sensed that I had been out cold for some time. Men on either side of me, holding me up between them, dragged me forward deeper into the blackness of a tunnel. The bare rock on either side and the rough floor beneath suggested I was in a cave.

My hands were bound. I was naked and shivering. The pain in my crushed chest and disjointed shoulder burned as they jostled me, handling me roughly as if I was a bag of meat.

My captors were Peter the false priest and Christman the giant who had crushed my body. I wondered if one of them was the Ancient One I was searching for.

Or if they taking me to him.

Either way, I felt a deep horror of how I had been bested and overpowered by those men. I was at their mercy.

There was no question of overpowering them. And yet I would not allow them to do whatever they were intending to do to me. I imagined that they were going to slaughter me. It seemed as though they were bringing me into some foul pagan grotto where I would be sacrificed.

It was the only explanation. The oppressive chill of the place seeped into my bones and the mass of the hard stone above bore down on me from all around. My bare feet dragged on the cold, damp gravel floor. Close echoes of their footsteps sounded in my ears.

I resolved to break free the moment they reached whatever destination they had in mind.

Perhaps they intended to chant their way through some depraved pagan ritual before slitting my throat but in case they proceeded without ceremony I would have to take the first hint of an opportunity.

Even if fighting were hopeless, even if it ultimately led to my death, I would not allow myself to die on my knees.

Light.

Up ahead, the walls reflected the yellow of candlelight and the hurried steps of my captors slowed. The smell of woodsmoke filled the cave and I imagined that they had some pagan fire up ahead that they would use to burn me alive.

I forced myself to relax, lest they sense I was about to break free and tear their heathen hearts from their chests.

We rounded a final corner whereupon they halted, threw me forward with considerable force so that I landed on my front with my bound arms outstretched before me. The impact jarred me to the bone.

Before I could even catch my breath, I heard Peter and Christman retreating rapidly back the way we had come. None had spoken a word.

When I rolled over, I was struck by an image of domesticity.

A young woman leaning over a blackened pot that was suspended over a small hearth fire. She paid me no mind at all as she stirred the contents and the smell of food wafted from the pot. She wore a simple dress and her hair was covered.

Ordinary domestic furniture completed the space, with a table and two stools, a long bench for the preparation of food and the storage of earthenware. It was merely the fact that the walls of this home were rough-hewn, natural stone that demonstrated I was still within the cave.

I was thoroughly confused.

"What is this?" I asked in French, my voice loud.

The woman glanced at me with no expression on her face. I was startled to see that she was quite lovely. After resting her eyes on me, she glanced over her shoulder and then moved to the bench, turning her back to me.

A figure stirred in the long shadow of a bed set back into a dark alcove on the far side of the cave. I began shifting back, ready to spring to my feet and fight my way free.

"No."

The voice of the shadow was a rumble.

It was him.

The Ancient One.

His form was mere shadow and did not move. He spoke no more and yet I was overwhelmed by a terrible oppressive menace emanating from him.

"I have been looking for you," I said. "I doubted you were real."

He said nothing.

"Do you understand French?" I asked the figure. "I sought you out. I came here to find you. I have questions that I would ask of you."

The shadow stirred and rose. And rose. The man was massive. Tall, broad of shoulder, with a mass of brown hair on his head and a dense beard over a massive jaw. His eyes were deeply wrinkled beneath a jutting brow line and cheekbones. The way he moved was unnerving. He had the fluidity and stillness of a cat stalking a rodent.

"My name is Richard," I said. "My brother William spoke to me of you."

He grunted something and the young woman stepped away behind him without a word, her head lowered. When he moved around the fire toward me, I saw his full stature. He wore no more than a shirt, belted at his waist, and his legs and feet were bare.

His body radiated immense physical power. There was not an ounce of fat on him. The muscles of his legs were ridged and striated. His forearms were likewise crossed with bulging veins and deep ridges, as well as dark patterns on the skin in the form of dots and short lines arranged in clusters.

The Ancient One crouched, his feet crunching the surface of sand on the compacted dirt floor. The face before mine appeared at first to be that of a robust man aged about forty years old and although his vigour was that of a younger man while his skin also had weathered lines about the eyes, like those of an aged shipmaster.

Those eyes were wide and his terrible gaze was difficult to withstand but I stared back.

My doubts that he was something other than an immortal, like me and my brother, evaporated.

But was he truly our grandfather, as William had claimed? Perhaps he did look like us, in some ways. Sheared and dressed properly, he could have passed for a noble in any court in Christendom.

He snorted and stood, rising above me and looking down.

"You are weak."

His voice was deep and effortlessly powerful. It took me a moment to decipher the words, as they were so heavily accented but he did speak French, of a sort. Every time he spoke, he would use some words in a form of Latin that I could barely comprehend, some words of Greek and other words in languages I did not know and often the order of the words in the sentences were unconventional. It took me time to restructure his sentences into something meaningful but the more he spoke the more I understood him.

"No. I am not weak," I said. "Your men surprised me. I could have freed myself. I hoped that they would bring me to you. I was looking for you."

"Weakness fills you. Pours from you."

He turned his back on me and returned to the bed.

The woman crossed to him and sat on his thigh while he snaked an arm around her waist. He stared at me while she stared through the fire blankly, in the manner of men who have seen too much of war.

I got to one knee, watching him closely for a reaction. When there was none, I stood fully upright before them in my nakedness.

As far as I was concerned, I was the strongest man in the world, other than that monster innkeeper called Christman, the Ancient One before me and, perhaps, William.

My body was powerful and yet my chest and shoulder ached from being crushed and dislocated. Still, I would not allow him to dismiss me so easily.

"Try my strength, then," I said, thrusting up my jaw and looking down my nose. My hands were bound but I was determined to show that I did not fear him. That I could best him.

In truth, he unnerved me.

My whole reason for seeking him out was in the hope that his blood at least would be stronger than mine but I did not expect him to be so imposing and disturbing in demeanour. Few men had ever frightened me. I did not mean to challenge him so in his home but his condemnation had wounded my pride.

He chose not to take me up on my offer. Instead, he looked me up and down, his lip curled and eyebrows raised. His eyes lingered on the mass of bruising on my chest and shoulder.

"Drink."

He spoke and shoved the woman away from him.

With a blank face she pulled up one of her sleeves, revealing a mass of crisscrossing white and pink scar tissue from her wrist to the inside of her elbow.

There was no hesitation before she sliced into her flesh and drained her blood into a wooden cup. This, she handed to me without a word or expression. With my wrists bound together, I lifted it to my lips and drank. It was warm and delicious.

Perhaps there was a hint of disgust in her eyes when she took the cup back from me, or perhaps I imagined it.

She turned away and then busied herself with serving the food at a table in the corner opposite to that of the bed.

Her blood worked on me quickly. My ribs cracked back into place with a sound like the snapping of a bundle of sticks. I rolled my shoulder around and it popped back into place. In mere moments my breathing was returned to normal, the pain was gone and I was at full strength once more.

The Ancient One approached, moving fluidly like a wolf on the hunt, and pulled a short knife from his belt.

I tensed, dreading that he was about to plunge it into my heart or across my throat. Perhaps it would be my only chance to overpower him, I thought, and if I had him at my mercy I could force him to answer my questions.

He came forward and I raised my hands, ready to grapple with him.

Instead, he gently took my hands and cut through the bonds at my wrist with a few expert strokes.

All the while he looked at me. He was taller than I was and his hands were bigger than mine. I was conscious of my nakedness but I was determined to show no shame and no fear, neither.

When the woman had served the food, she brought me a linen shirt that I pulled on gratefully. She provided no belt and so it hung loose over me but it was better than nothing and I took the stool at the table across from the man who may have been my grandfather.

She brought a bowl of water for me to wash my hands, provided linen to dry them and then served the meal. The mutton and cabbage stew was surprisingly savoury, full of salt and sugar and other spices and I spooned it in just as soon as he began to eat. The hard oatcake served alongside was swiftly softened in the broth and helped to fill my belly.

When all was served, the woman busied herself cleaning the bench, took a pail and walked away into the darkness of the tunnel.

"I came from England," I said, not knowing where else to start. "There is a pestilence. A plague. A great mortality. Across the whole land. The worst the world has ever known."

He scoffed at that and I thought I saw the hint of a smile beneath his beard. "No."

"I assure you, it is quite terrible. Every other man, woman, child. Dead."

He nodded. "Many times, this has happened. When I first conquered this land, the men die before my sword cuts them down."

"When you conquered this land? Do you mean the village? When was that?"

He sat back and picked at his teeth while he looked at me. "Why come to me?"

"My people are dying. My companions. You see, William my brother and I made them immortal with our own blood, many years ago. Two of my companions have fallen ill with this pestilence but drinking human blood does not cure them, as it does for anything else that has ever ailed them. Rather, it cures them for only a few hours but it is not long before they fall ill again."

His face unreadable, he watched me as I spoke and I did not know if he understood anything that I was saying.

"Before my brother William went away to the East, he told me about you. That is to say, he told me that you were powerful. More powerful than I could imagine, he said. Whether he spoke the truth, I do not know, and yet I came to ask if *your* blood can heal my people."

It was far from the fine speech of introduction that I had rehearsed during the journey to find him but he was so strange that I did not know how to speak to him.

The Ancient One held my gaze. "William told me he made many such men by emptying them of some blood and giving them his to drink. I know what manner of servants you make with this act. Your blood will heal these men."

"And yet it does not. I gave them as much as I could spare and it was not enough."

For a long moment it seemed that he doubted me and then he looked disgusted. "You are weak."

I gripped the edges of the thick table. "I am strong."

"Strength would heal. Heal all ills. If your blood does not heal? This means there is no strength."

"No strength in me?"

He nodded, and gestured with the fingertips of one hand at my heart. "In your blood."

"How can that be? Surely there is some remedy that you know of? Some method of extracting the necessary potency from your blood that I could employ to heal my people?"

He frowned, not following me at all. I tried again.

"Would you give me your blood?" I asked.

"You ask your host for a gift?" he said, mocking me.

It was not merely difficult to understand his words but his meaning was confusing.

"I could give you something in return," I ventured. "I would pay any price."

"Any?"

"Well," I said, thinking of his knife, "almost any."

He snorted and shook his head. Though I struggled to comprehend him, it was clear that I was a profound disappointment to him. Or, at least, that he thought very little of me. Although preening courtiers often looked down on me, it had been such a long time since any man that I respected had displayed such open contempt for my character.

"I apologise, sir." I said, sensing finally that I had rushed headlong into a social transgression by asking for something immediately. Where I had merely hoped to explain why I was searching for him so that he would understand I meant him no harm, in truth I had acted with enormous impropriety. "I would like to speak of myself to you and also to seek your wisdom. I have many questions. Do you know about me? Do you know who I am? My name is Richard."

He inclined his head and touched his fingertips to his chest. "Priskos."

It was a strange name, to my ears at least, and sounded Greek. Whether it was his original given name, or one he had taken for himself, or a title of some sort, I did not know.

"Thank you for welcoming me into your home, Priskos, and for sharing your table with me. Forgive me if I am mistaken but my brother William told me that you were our grandfather. I do not know how such a thing could be possible. My natural father was Robert de Ferrers, an earl of England. A man of Norman birth who traced his ancestors back to before the conquest of England. How could you be his father?"

The woman came back with her pail, heaved it up onto the bench and busied herself cleaning up the meal.

Priskos barely glanced at her, preferring to regard me closely. "Sleep, now," he said after a while, and pointed to the blankets that the woman had laid against one bare stone wall. I would have to sleep on the floor, like a dog or a child.

What could I say? There was so much more to be said. I still did not even know if he could truly help me and time was wasting. Every night I spent away was another night that Eva spent in torment. Assuming she yet lived.

And the men who had ambushed me had murdered Walter.

It was entirely my fault. I should never have trusted that damned priest but he had outwitted me. I should have suspected that he was an immortal. One of William's, at least. And I should never have underestimated the huge innkeeper. My complacency had led to Walter's death and so, even with everything else, I had to find justice for Walter.

How could I get it? Other than taking revenge on the men who had captured me and dragged me hither to the Ancient One.

I was loathe to capitulate so easily to his demands and yet I was a guest and I wanted something from him. Either I had to comply with his commands or defeat him by force.

Even if I could overpower him without his men coming to his aid, I suspected after speaking to him that torturing the knowledge out of him would prove ineffective.

And there was something deeply unnerving about the man. He radiated violence like a wild animal. Like he truly was a wolf wearing the skin of a man.

"Very well," I said. "We can continue our discussion in the morning."

Priskos barely responded, as if it was of no interest to him at all. He grunted something at the woman and retired to his bed while she finished tidying away, extinguished all the candles and went to join him in his bed.

The bare rock floor beneath the blankets was more comfortable than I had expected due to the layer of sand and I quickly fell asleep. I awoke at some point in the night to the sound of vigorous yet brief rutting from across the cave. It was cold.

I wrapped myself tighter, rolled over and thought of Cecilia until I drifted off again. I recalled the way her eyes narrowed and her lips twitched in response to some jest I had made, and how her bosom swelled beneath her dress. *If I ever marry again it shall be for love. Children are a blessing but my heart wants only the companionship of an honourable man.* I resolved once again that I would ask her brother for her hand as soon as I returned. Assuming that she survived the pestilence, of course.

For all I knew, lying in that dark cave so far from home, the whole world could be on its way to annihilation.

As I drifted back to sleep, I wondered if I would even survive my meeting with Priskos, whether I challenged him or not.

***

The cave was empty when I woke in the morning. A lamp was burning on the table but a slither of daylight lanced across the rear wall of the cave from some unseen crevice amongst the folds of the rock roof high above.

Tentatively, I felt my way to the exit and emerged, blinking, into green and orange sunlight. The woodland came right up to the opening and the understorey layer had presumably been allowed to remain dense as a form of concealment.

In no more than my linen shirt and with bare feet, I pushed through off the side of the track to void my bowels. As I was kicking the leaf litter over it, the young woman came crashing through the undergrowth with a bundle of firewood slung over her shoulder, her

124

fair hair unbound, flowing as she bounded past. She wrinkled her nose but otherwise paid me no heed. It dawned on me that I had taken a shit on what amounted to her doorstep and I hurried after her.

"Good morning, good woman," I said. "May I carry that for you?"

She glanced over her shoulder but kept going until she reached a chopping block in small clearing and then dumped it all on the carpet of brown and yellow leaves littering the floor.

Dappled sunlight fell across her hair as she bent to the bundle.

"Allow me, madame," I insisted, dropping to one knee as I untied the bundle and eyed the axe stuck into the block. "Is your husband abroad this morning?"

She pursed her lips in a most fetching manner, then tucked a stray strand of hair behind her ear. It seemed that she understood no French and I did not even bother attempting English. I doubted a commoner such as her would understand much Latin.

Commoner though she must certainly have been to live such a life, she was as pretty as a princess. Although, I had seen plenty of princesses in my time and few enough could hold a candle to that girl waving a bee away from her face that morning in the Black Forest. Perhaps I was love-sick for Cecilia but that girl was strong, womanly, and made a dutiful wife even in a ridiculous dark cave in the woods and I was struck by the outrageousness of it all.

Where was her family, I thought. What on Earth was this Priskos doing with her?

I took up the axe and she stepped back as I swung, splitting the log in one blow.

"We were not properly introduced, madame. My name is Richard."

She bit her lip and looked down, clasping her hands.

"Would you tell me your name, my dear? Where are you from? May I ask how you came to live here?"

The woman looked around. A cold wind gusted through the canopy with a sound like the breaking of waves. After a moment, she opened her mouth to speak to me but then clamped it closed, threw her head down and hunched her shoulders.

Priskos strode toward us from out of the undergrowth. He did not hurry and his face was emotionless so his intentions were unclear but the woman's demeanour caused me concern. I gripped the axe, ready to defend myself.

Instead, he drew to a stop in front of her, placed a finger on her chin and tipped her head up. Her jaw was set and her eyes had returned to that blank stare I had seen on her before, as if she was looking through him. Without a word from either of them, she turned and walked by me, going off into the woods.

Without looking at me, Priskos held out one hand and I knew what he wanted. I handed over the axe, which he took and held by his side.

"You must leave," he said.

I could not allow that. There was no possibility of me leaving empty handed after all I had been through to reach him.

"I will leave when you have told me what I need to know."

Priskos stepped closer to me. His features were even clearer in the daylight and I peered with fascination at his eyes and his nose. Did he look like me? I thought I could see William in his features. The nose was the same. Those eyes were impossibly cold and clear. Perhaps it was my imagination but his eyes seemed to look into me. I felt like a child before him.

"Go home," he said.

"I need your help, sir," I replied. "Priskos, please. You know why I came. Can you help me to find a cure for the pestilence for my people?" I glanced at the bushes that the young woman had walked beyond. "One of them is a woman. My wife."

It was not quite true, of course. We had been married once and though my feelings for her were quite profound, we had not lived together nor laid together as man and wife for a hundred years.

He lifted the axe. I tensed, ready to leap forward to grapple with him. Instead, he rested the haft on his shoulder and tilted his head.

"Your blood cures all."

I stifled a frustrated sigh. We were going in circles. "I have no wish to quarrel with you but I assure you that it does not, sir."

He frowned. "Then, you are weak."

Again, he had said it. He spoke with such certainty that it was like a judgement from a king, or from God Himself.

Even as a child, few had ever called me weak. If anyone but Priskos had accused me of such a thing, I would have laughed in his face, and then crushed him.

But the conviction of his repeated accusation wounded me deeply.

"I am strong," I said, sounding like an impudent child even to myself. In response, he sneered. That made my blood boil. "Try my strength, then," I snapped, and stepped up to him. "Try it, sir. Try me."

For a moment, he appeared shocked and I was certain that he was going to explode with violence.

He laughed in my face and clamped a massive hand on my shoulder. "You should not *be*. I did not wish to make you. Your father did not know what you are. Your brother did not know. You are ignorant. But this not of your making." He thumped me on the arm with a friendly blow as powerful as a kick from a horse. "Come."

With a casual flick of his wrist, he buried the axe in the chopping block so quickly that I barely saw it. The head of the axe was buried almost to the hafting.

I followed Priskos back into his cave, where he indicated I should sit at his table once again. He served me with strong beer and sat in front of me.

"Your father? He is my son. I did not intend to make him." He turned to look at the entrance to his curiously domestic cave. "A man needs woman. Many years, I have been here, in this place. I take woman, she serves me until she grows old and weak. Then I take new woman."

He drank a gulp from his beer and wiped his lips and beard.

Many questions sprang to mind and I chose one. "What happens to the old woman?"

"I honour her."

"How do you honour her?"

"I drink her. I bury her."

My stomach churned, even though I had suspected it would be something like that.

"But why not let them go, sir? When they have fulfilled their usefulness to you? Surely they can do you no harm? Would it not be more honourable to let them live?"

He pressed his lips together as he regarded me. I was beginning to perceive that when he looked at me in such a manner, he was thinking one thing about me.

Weak.

"Blood gives strength. An old woman's blood is weak but this *honours* them. This is their final duty to their lord. Their offering. Their sacrifice."

I wanted to ask about the woman he had in his power now but I was already, in my heart, intending to rescue her from him and I did not wish to alert him to my concern for her.

"You said my father was your son," I said instead. "But who was my grandmother?"

He took a deep breath and a slight smile appeared beneath his beard. "Cunning woman. She bested me." He laughed, like a growl. "First in thousand years."

I wondered how old he was. "How did she best you?"

"I choose to not spill seed into woman. I choose not to make sons." He shrugged. "In this, some of times, I fail. I fill a woman. When her belly grows, I drink her. Take new woman."

"If your woman gets with child, you kill her?" It was monstrous. He was a beast. A demon. "Why? Why not allow them to bear children?"

He shook his head. "I make bad sons."

"Bad how?"

He licked his lips and pressed them together before answering. "Some are weak in mind, like Christman. Some are quick and wise but fall to ambition, as did Caesar. Some try to kill me, their father, as Peter one day will. I see it in him. Some sons conquer world, like Alexander."

I was beginning to suspect that this man was himself quite mad. Perhaps he was my ancestor but how could I trust anything he said?

"Your sons conquered the world?" I asked.

Clearly, he detected the disbelief in my voice as he responded with a rueful smile. "So much is forgotten. You know it not."

"Indeed, please tell me. Help me to understand." When he yet hesitated, I continued. "You told it to William, sir. Why will you not tell it to me?"

"Your brother is like me. Your brother is man like his ancestors. Like my great sons."

I was insulted. "And what am I?"

He looked closely at me. "A Christian." He grimaced and turned to spit on his own floor.

"I am, sir. And proudly so. What else could I be? And William is a Christian also. For a time, he believed himself to be Christ reborn. Or an angel, perhaps. And then he claimed to be some incarnation of Adam, the first man, and he sought to recreate Eden upon the Earth. Did he claim to be something else when he came to you? I fear, sir, that he has no shame. He will speak whatever the listener wishes to hear, if it means he gets what he wants in return."

Priskos held himself very still. "No man deceives me. In here," Priskos thumped his chest, "William is conqueror. A man to remake world."

"I thought you said you killed sons like that."

He sighed. "They all fall to ruin if I do not. Once, I took kingdom to make it strong. I made mighty son. Philip was his name. His son was stronger, in some ways, but also he was mad. He conquered much and did much war but he could not conquer his own heart. His name was Alexander. William is like this. He burns with fire that destroys everything it touches and then it will destroy him, also. I had to put an end to his life to save his people."

I almost laughed in his face. Surely, I thought, this was proof of his madness. He believed that Alexander of Macedon was his grandson and although it sent a thrill through me to imagine that I was of the same blood as the most famed conqueror in all the world, I was sure of its impossibility. At least, it was highly implausible. How could this man who lived in a cold cave with a single woman to serve him have once been a mighty king?

"If you believed that William is like Alexander of Macedon, why did you let him leave here instead of killing him? What do you want from your sons and their sons?"

"It is every man's duty to conquer all before him. To make his name and his deeds live on in minds of his people and in blood of his sons. But sons of my sons make none of their own. Line shrivels to nothing and this drives great men mad. Alexander could make no sons, and so he brought his wife to his companion. But this is no good. Without sons, no man is complete. They destroy themselves. They grow angered at me. William will do this. It is his nature to do so. If he becomes an Alexander, I will put an end to him, also."

"And what about me?" I asked. "Do you mean to put an end to me?"

He regarded me. "You are not Alexander. You are not Caesar, nor are you Hattusili, Atreus, or Cleomenes. No."

Although I did not know some of the names he mentioned, I knew of course that I was being gravely insulted. I struggled to contain my anger. "What am I, then?"

"A man like Peter. One born to serve."

Whether he was attempting to anger me or it was merely incidental I did not know but it was having that effect on me.

Born to serve.

Was it true, I wondered? Was that all I was? A dutiful knight, when I could have been so much more?

"I am a knight," I said. "I serve a lord. I serve a king. But this is the order of things. Not servitude but duty, sir."

"I know what is a knight. One who serves. A servant is a slave. Slaves have traded honour for life."

I scoffed. "What about Peter, then? He serves you and so you do not kill him? Why did you allow him to be born at all?"

Priskos held my gaze. "A lord needs men to serve him. Who better than sons?"

"Is that why you allowed my father to live when he was born?"

The Ancient One shrugged. "A mistake."

So easy for him to rip my heart open. He had called me weak, called me a natural servant, and said my father's existence—and therefore my own—was a mistake.

Already, I was beginning to hate the Ancient One.

With great effort, I remained seated by gripping the edges of the table. "How then did I come to be born? Who was the cunning woman who bested you?"

He furrowed his brow and looked through me into his past.

"I took woman I should not have taken. The daughter of lord. Yet I saw her, travelling through woodland far to north. I do not take daughters of great men. Trouble follows, always. I take strongest common women, as their fathers are afraid and if they come with their spears and torches, I slaughter them. Yet, lords have many swords and their men cause endless mischief."

His eyes wrinkled as he continued.

"But this girl. I saw her. I had to have her." He made a gesture to show how helpless he had been and then snatched at the air. "I take her. She fights me, for years she fights but I *break* her. Then, she loves me." His grin turned into a laugh. "She tricks me. Years, she tricks me, loves me in her words and deeds but holds hate in her heart." He nodded to himself. "Strong, strong woman. She seduced me with food, with water. All poisoned. That night, I spill my seed in her, for she has taken my heart and I have lost my mind in her. A woman's power. Belladonna, hemlock, you know these? I wake, fighting to breathe. She slits my throat." He used a finger to trace a line from ear to ear, and then he jabbed his thumb into his chest. "She pierces my heart. She flees."

He shook his head, sighing but he had a smile on his face.

"How could you survive such injuries?"

"She do good work on me. But I am strong. I come back. She flee north and west, returned to her people. They put her with lord for husband. Her belly must have already been big. Some weak men stand such things, if it brings him wealth and name of another greater than him. She flees across water, to the land of Britain."

"You let her go?"

"Perhaps I should have killed her. Killed child. But she fought. She won her life. My people would have sung songs of her."

"And that child was my father, Robert? So he was not the son of the old Lord de

Ferrers?" I laughed in disbelief. I knew of course that a great many are deceived about the identity of their true fathers. After all, it had happened to me. And yet my father had also been a bastard, unknown to him. I wished that the old sod had known it before William had killed him. "Robert de Ferrers was not an Alexander either."

Priskos nodded. "No. So be it."

"But why? Why are *you* the way you are? Why is it like this? Why can I live on as I am, ageless and powerful, yet I cannot become a father? Why does our blood have such power that when a mortal drinks it, they gain our strength? Why?"

Priskos pointed up. The darkness of the jagged rock ceiling was like an infinite void. "Gods make it so."

I hung my head in my hands. "That is it? You do not know why you have this power?"

He frowned and jabbed a thumb into his chest. "I *know*. It is Sky Father who was my father. I am half god." He pointed a finger at me. "You have Sky Father in your veins."

I shook my head and scoffed. "The Sky Father? Is that it? I had hoped you would have true knowledge about our origins rather than some pagan nonsense about—"

I did not even see him move.

It was no more than a blur and a noise and then pain. He threw the table aside with such force that it smashed upon the wall with an almighty crash. His hands were around my throat and he hoisted me aloft as they squeezed into my neck under my jaw.

The strength in his fingers was inhuman and I could do nothing to resist them. I kicked out and struck at his arms but it was like fighting with an oak. Blood rushed in my ears and my vision darkened.

He tossed me to the floor like a rag and I clutched at the dry dirt as if to hang on to the Earth itself. Soon, my breath came back to me and I looked up at him.

"You worship the god of the wrong people," Priskos said. He pointed at me. "Your gods are the gods of sky, of thunder and lightning. Your gods are Sun and Moon and gods of lake and river. Your dead god is desert god, for desert people. God of death and of weakness. God of word, not deed. You must cast him off."

I sat up, rubbing my neck. I should have been angry but the fact that I had insulted him first gave me pause.

Also, I was quite terrified of his power. His strength was so far beyond my own that I was stunned.

Climbing to my feet, I looked him in the eye.

"You have it wrong," I said, warily. It was a risk to challenge him but I could not allow his insults against God to go uncontested. "Jesus is for all of us. For all of mankind. His message is for each of us as individual men and women, so that we may be saved and reborn."

We stood glaring at each other. Priskos kept his eyes on mine but turned to spit on the floor.

"You are fool amongst fools. But you do not know. Their victory is almost complete.

Their madness conquered the strength of Rome when their strength of arms was too weak. They made great empire rot from the inside. They drove apart families with their lies. Jesus Christ was not one of *us*." He slapped his chest. "His words were never meant for you, for any of us. And yet you have them in your heart all same, corrupting you, making you weak. You must throw off dead god."

It was like the Devil was speaking to me, tempting me away from the light of Jesus Christ.

"I am a faithful servant of God and His son Jesus Christ," I said. "And I shall not waver in my devotion."

I thought he would be angry and braced myself for another assault. Instead, he seemed saddened. I felt I had disappointed him once more.

The woman came in, then and began to clear out the hearth. She took no notice of us or the smashed table.

"Did *you* ever make immortals by feeding them your blood? Did any of your sons or their sons? If mortals are drained of blood and then they drink from us, they become like us."

"This I have done."

"And what happened to them? You must have many sons and grandsons. And they must have made many immortals. Where are they all?"

"They fall."

"They are all dead?" I asked. "What about the men who brought me here? They are your sons, are they not?"

He scratched at his beard. "You must go home."

"I wish to," I replied. "Once you tell me how to save my people."

"Your ears are bad. Your blood saves them."

"But it does not!"

"Then your blood is weak."

I took a deep breath before replying. "Can my blood be made strong?"

He hesitated. "You drink blood of your enemies, yes?"

I nodded. "To heal wounds. To restore myself after battle."

"Seek more enemies. Strong men. Destroy them. Drink them."

"And that will make me stronger?" I asked, imagining finding and killing men, not because I was wounded and they were my enemies but because I wanted strength for myself. "But I cannot slaughter innocent men."

He scowled at that. "Then do not."

"Drinking the blood of strong men makes me stronger? More than the blood of weak men?"

He frowned. "But of course."

"What makes a man strong?"

"You do not know?"

"The strength of his arm or the strength of his will? Or do you mean a powerful, wealthy man?"

Priskos tilted his head. "These are all the same thing."

"Once, perhaps," I replied. "Not always today."

He nodded. "This world is mad. The weakness of your dead god infests the hearts of men. Weakness is worshipped. Failure is worshipped. Meekness celebrated. A world of weak men." His levelled his finger at my face. "This is your world."

"My world is a great one. We have built things that your barbarian people, whoever they were, could not comprehend. Have you seen the Cathedral of Notre-Dame in Paris? Or the one in Chartres? Once, I won a battle in the shadow of the Cathedral of Lincoln, an edifice more magnificent than any other. The spire reaches halfway to Heaven. It is a monument to the glory of God."

Priskos scoffed. "A monument to madness."

"How can you say such things? These achievements are greater than any other. What did your world create that was half so glorious and everlasting?"

"We created you. All of you. You come from us. We worshipped the gods and we gloried in the feats of men. Our monuments were the songs that were sung of them."

"Songs? Your songs are forgotten. Our castles and cathedrals will stand for ever."

His mouth twitched at the corners. "They will crumble to dust. Our songs are sung still. Names changed, tales twisted. And sung still."

I wished I had not come. It was all so abstruse and what little I did comprehend was hard to take.

"Yes, yes, very well," I said. "So I must kill and drink strong men to strengthen my blood. Their blood is best."

Priskos spread his hands and sat back a little. "Best? Well, the best blood is not of men."

I sighed, rubbing my eyes. "What?"

He smiled. "Best blood of all is blood of child."

I kept my eyes on him but it was clear he did not speak in jest. "A child's blood is stronger than a man's? How can that be so?"

"Child's blood hold's all force of life. What child may become is in blood. Drink this blood, take whole life. A babe's blood is best. From mother's belly, from breast. Or blood of girl who soon becomes woman."

"By God," I said. "By God, I shall never do such evil."

He snorted. "No. I know this."

I knew what he meant when he said it. *Weak.*

"William drank the blood of my brother's children," I said, suddenly recalling it. "My half-brother who was the son of my mother. William killed him, and his wife, and he tore apart—" I broke off, unable to speak of the horror.

Priskos regarded me coldly. "William understand this. William will take what needs to be taken. He will travel path to greatness. To everlasting fame. To glory."

"If doing evil is the price for your idea of greatness, I shall never pay it."

"Then you fail."

I nodded slowly, growing angry. "Because I am weak."

His smile grew into a grin, showing big yellow teeth. "It is law. Weak die. Strong live."

I shook my head. "As a knight, it is my duty to defend the weak from the strong."

"Yes, yes," he said, nodding. "This good, yes. This how we make our people safe. Our own people. Outsiders we destroy. This why to protect your people, you must become strong. Stay strong. Always."

"Very well," I said. "I understand."

Priskos seemed doubtful about my understanding but he did not pursue it any further.

"Enough, now. You will learn this, or you will die."

As I watched the woman, whose name I still did not know, bustling about the cave that was her prison, I resolved two things.

First, I decided that I would escape.

And I swore that I would rescue that woman and save her from her confinement at the hands of the monster who was my grandfather.

A true knight would save a maiden from the dragon. Arthur's knights, Sir Gawain and Sir Percival, would have risked all to rescue a lady from imprisonment. Lancelot's son, virtuous Galahad, would never have hesitated to do what was required.

One hundred and eighty years old, I was, and still a bloody fool.

14

Rescuing the Maiden

IN THE DARK of the night, I lay awake listening to the steady breathing of the man who could kill me at will and trying to get up the nerve to make my escape.

After eating a fair meal with me in something close to silence at midday, Priskos had disappeared outside for hours.

I wondered then what he did to occupy his days. What purpose he had taken for himself. Did he spend his hours praying to his strange gods? Was he practising his skill at arms? Contemplating the great mysteries? Whatever it was, it seemed to be an empty life and a lonely one.

In his absence, I considered fleeing but did not know if I would run right into him in the woods outside. The woman would not speak to me and made an effort to be wherever I was not. Priskos returned before dark without a word and gestured that I should sleep on the floor again before he and the woman turned in.

I thought it likely that he would allow me to leave, should I ask it of him. But he had admitted to murdering his own sons and grandsons before and even more he had suggested that he felt it was some sort of duty to do so. He claimed that he had allowed William to leave but was that true or had William outwitted Priskos, as our grandmother had once done? And even if he had allowed William to leave, clearly he thought much less of me than he did my brother.

I was keenly aware that I was at his mercy, so fleeing in the night was a risk as it would certainly violate basic rules of hospitality to do so. Yet staying in the hope of being released may have been no safer and as taking action is almost always better than not doing so, I was certain that I would flee into the woodland. I believed that I could get miles away before sunrise, steal a horse and be away for good.

But the thought of leaving that woman there alone with him weighed heavily upon me. How could I in good conscience leave her in such a condition when I knew she was there against her will, facing certain death when he grew bored with her or when her belly swelled with a child?

And yet taking her with me would be an appalling risk. She would slow my progress so much that I doubted we could get away.

I knew what a chivalrous knight would do. But my noble act for that woman may well end up condemning my dear Eva and my closest friend Thomas to an agonising death. Back and forth, my mind went, playing through all the possibilities. Perhaps I could restrain Priskos in his bed? But if I failed then that would certainly seal my fate. I had considered poisoning his meal, as my grandmother had done but even if I could have found the correct plants, I had no idea how to prepare them so that their presence would go undetected in his beer. I knew that my best chance would be to dash his brains out with a rock while he slept, and then to perhaps burn his body so that he could not recover. But even though the man was clearly evil, I was not prepared to murder him in his bed.

Just as I was erring on the side of cowardice, she stirred in her bed and then climbed from it. I could see from the light of the single candle that she pulled a shawl around her shoulders and stepped by me on her way out of the cave.

I took it as a sign from God to do the honourable thing. It seemed as though He wanted me to save her, that He was testing my faith and my honour, and I resolved to do as the Lord commanded.

Priskos continued to snore, his breathing regular and steady. I carefully slipped from my blanket and crept after her. As I saw the light grey outline of the world beyond, I heard her passing water near the mouth of the cave. She was startled when I appeared and I held my hands out to show I meant no harm.

Still, she held herself very still.

"I am leaving, now," I said, pointing at myself and then out into the dark woodland. "Will you come with me?"

Without hesitation, she grasped one of my hands and dragged me out into the world.

Dear God, I thought, give our feet wings and guide our way through the darkness.

We rushed headlong into the abyssal black shadow, our bare feet pounding the forest floor hard and fast and not caring that we cut our feet on the stones and twigs and thorns on the path. She seemed to somehow know where to go and so I allowed her to lead me for the time being, hoping as I did merely to get as far from the cave as possible before he began his pursuit, assuming he did do so. Would he wake once he sensed the warmth beside him turn cold? Or would he snore away in oblivion until the dawn?

Branches whipped my face and I stumbled on a rock, rolling my ankle and hobbling for a few steps until I recovered. She fell, later, and I helped her up to find her drenched in sweat and shaking from the cold and the exertion. How much further could she flee at such a pace? Her breathing was heavy and she fought for air. The unchivalrous thought that I should leave her was motivated by fear and I shook it off.

"Come," I said, softly, "we must continue on. As long as we can."

How much she understood, I still did not know, but she caught my meaning well enough. Soon, I was the one dragging her along as her pace slowed further and further. At last, it was unavoidable that I scoop her up into my arms so that I could keep moving with rapid, short steps. She buried her head in my neck but also I felt that she looked over my shoulder, behind me, watching for the pursuit that would surely come.

It was not long before my own breathing grew laboured and loud. While it felt as though I had run for uncounted hours, the sun was beginning to brighten the sky above the trees to the west. The shadows grew deeper even as the greys and purples of the pre-dawn edged the trunks and boulders all around.

"Is there a village?" I asked. "Near here? Horses? Where?"

For the first time in a while, she lifted her head and looked around with alarm. "*Die klamm!*" she said, pointing ahead. "The gorge!"

I had brought us to the edge of a shallow ravine. I could not see the bottom as it was too dark, though I could not hear a river below. Even if it was dry, I doubted climbing down into it would be the best decision.

"Which way?" I asked.

She pointed north and I hurried that way, being sure to keep the gorge on my right and to watch my forward step as best I could so that I did not stumble headlong into a side channel or some other fissure.

The sky grew lighter and my heart thumped in my chest like a drum. Although I did not wish to stop for long, I had to catch my breath for a moment and stretch my back while I put her down.

"Is there a village?" I asked, panting, "This way?"

"This way," she said, echoing me. The daylight was growing with every moment and I saw the fear and the determination on her face.

"Very well. Are you ready, my dear?"

"Osanna," she said, touching her fingers to her chest.

"A lovely name. Where is your own village? Is it far? Do they have horses for riding there?"

Before she could answer, something rushed from the darkness and struck me from behind.

I fell, hard. As I rolled and jumped to my feet I was smacked in the side of the head and my vision exploded. I drifted in and out of wakefulness as I was savaged and beaten bloody. It was so sudden that I felt little pain, just the sense of being thrashed. I had been trampled by horses more than once in my life and it was far worse even than that. Ribs snapped. It hurt to breathe. I lashed out and caught my attacker on his head and in response my forearm was grasped in a grip of iron and then my bones were snapped like twigs just above my wrist. I was screaming in anger and fear. My head hit a rock, or perhaps my skull was cracked with the back of an axe but I felt and heard the bones of my head breaking.

When I returned to consciousness, Priskos stood over me. I could barely move from the agony of my ruined body. It was light enough to see by but my vision was badly blurred. When I attempted to curse him, all I could manage was a strange moan. My jaw was broken.

He reached down and picked me up by the neck and held me in front of him. My arms did not appear to work and I was as helpless as a baby.

Without a word, he did something to my face, pushing his fingers against my cheeks. Only later, as I recalled the events, was it that I realised that he had pushed my left eyeball back inside my shattered eye socket.

Hoisting me up further, he twisted and threw me into the ravine.

***

A noise woke me. Some steady sound at the edge of my consciousness pulling me back into wakefulness. Perhaps it was the smell of blood that roused me.

Though the ravine was in deep shadow, it was full daylight high above.

I was face down in soft leaf litter. I knew I was dying. Pain held me rigid but I forced myself to lift my head and look around.

The sound was the wheezing breath coming from the woman lying near me.

Her throat had been cut or punctured and her chest was covered with blood. Her eyes were open and her mouth moved.

I groaned and her eyes flicked toward me.

Behind her eyes, I saw terrible agony and hatred for me, who had failed her so completely.

With great effort, I dragged myself through the leaf litter toward her an inch at a time. The smell of cold, damp fungus in the leaf litter filled my smashed nose.

Osanna might have died at any moment and yet she clung to life, even though she surely knew she had no hope.

She lay motionless on her back. Not even her fingers twitched. It was such a fall from the edge of the ravine above that it was likely she had broken her back in the fall, if Priskos had not snapped it himself before throwing her down. Her legs were twisted and perhaps her pelvis was broken.

Pulling myself up to her, I believed I knew why he had done this to her. He had even cut her throat for me.

He meant for me to drink from her.

If I did nothing, she would certainly die and then I would die also.

That did little to make me feel better but my choice was really quite simple. Did I want to live or did I want to die?

I shifted myself, inch by inch, up to her throat and clamped my mouth over her wound. She was already cold to the touch and her blood sticky and thick about the wound but when I sucked, the hot blood flowed into my mouth.

It was not very long before her breathing stopped and her heart ceased beating. My belly was full enough and I turned over. Already, I felt the blood working in me and still I lost consciousness.

"Sir Richard," a voice said. It had been saying it repeatedly but I had been unable to respond. A hand slapped my face lightly.

I was cold and I shivered. It was late in the day and I had lain in shadow for hours in no more than a bloody undershirt.

"Walter?" I said, my voice a harsh croak.

Walt was alive? How could it be?

"Thank the Lord," Walt said. "Thought you was a goner, sir."

"Help me up," I muttered.

He had already carried me away from Osanna's body and he had mercifully laid a cloak over her face and chest.

"I saw you die," I said to Walt.

"And die I did, sir. Then those fellows, Peter and his giant brother Christman, poured a great cup of hot blood down my throat and then I was dead no longer. Peter told me some fanciful tales, so he did, and then later he told me my master needed me. Told me to take you home. Brought me nearby, gave me back our horses and even packs with supplies and pointed me to you. The horses are up there, sir, if you can try to stand?"

Priskos was up there somewhere, likely already back in his cave. After all he had done, I wished nothing more than to find him and kill him. Then again, he was stronger than I could have imagined. Attempting to take revenge on him would have certainly led to my death. And he had allowed me to live when he could so easily have killed me. Through that act, I sensed that he had gifted me life. I would be foolish to throw it away.

I got to my feet.

"Let us be gone from this damned black place."

It was a long way back.

To strengthen my blood, I had to find men, kill them, and drink their blood.

According to Priskos, if I killed enough of them, I would be able to save the lives of Eva and Thomas with the power of the blood in my veins.

15

Becoming the Dragon

I WANTED TO BE GONE from that evil land, with its close hills and black shadows beneath unnaturally upright trees.

On and on it went.

It seemed to me that we were followed and watched, from the darkness of twisted roots and moss-covered rocks beside the winding tracks. I pushed us onward, allowing little rest.

Every other step, I saw the dying face of Osanna, staring at me in condemnation of my failure.

Walter had died for me but he had been reborn as an immortal. I owed him a frank and full explanation of what that meant.

"What fanciful tales did Peter tell you?" I asked. "Why did they bring you back from the point of death? They must have done so immediately."

Walt shrugged. "Peter said you might need a strong servant, if his father ever decided to let you go."

"What if he did not let me go?"

"Funny, sir. That's what I asked the fellow. Peter said if that happened, they would just have to kill me along with you."

"He explained that you needed to drink human blood from now on?"

Walt scratched his chin. "He said a lot of stuff what sounded like drivel. Lot of talk about living forever and whatnot. Wasn't following the fellow all that close, truth be told, sir. I never put much stock in the tripe that priests babble on about. I kept asking that giant what it was all about, on account that innkeepers tend to be the salt of the earth, but I reckon that big lad was simple. Proper simple. Never said nothing."

"What about when they let you go? When they gave you these horses?"

"He said you had gone and betrayed his father and you deserved death but you had to be saved. He was right angered about it. Bitter fellow, that Peter. Still, told me to do my duty and get you out."

It took a few days to explain it all to Walt, going over some of my life story a number of times before we left the *Schwarzwald* proper.

He took it rather well.

I did not, however, trust Walt with the knowledge that the blood of infants and young women was the most potent of all. He was not an evil man, far from it, but commoners have always lacked the restraint that comes more naturally to the better-born.

"So, he said you had been too *good*, sir?" Walt said, furrowing his brow. "You been too chivalrous and honourable and the like and so the blood what is in your veins lacks the strength to heal them? That what he said, then, is it, sir?"

We had ridden far to the north and the Rhine valley was down to the west. I was searching for a route down from the hills so we could head back to the lands of civilised Frenchmen who I could murder.

"Not in so many words. But yes."

"Bit of a surprise, that, though. Seeing how you killed about three score men before my own eyes since I first met you, sir."

"Perhaps I should have drunk their blood before I killed them."

"Can't see that sort of thing going down well with old King Edward, sir."

"No."

"But what if he was wrong, sir? The ancient gentleman. Perhaps it is not that your blood is weaker than his but this plague is worse than anything he has seen before in all his long years?"

"It oft surprises me how your profound ignorance does not hinder your ability to reason."

He picked something from his nose. "Yes, sir."

"I cannot know whether it will work. Yet there is nothing else but to try."

"You mean we have to kill some strong fellows and drink their blood, sir?" He curled his lip into a disgusted snarl as he spoke. He was not one to shy away from a little murder when necessary but the thought of drinking a man's blood was anathema even to a man like Walt.

"Do you recall that I fought in Spain and the Holy Land with Eva as my squire?"

"How could I forget that part, sir?" He shook his head.

"For a time, because she needed blood every two or three days, as you now do, we would find wrongdoers in the camps or amongst our enemies and slay them so that she might drink from them."

"Dead men are revenged by their friends. You just got to do so. Dangerous work for you and the lady, sir."

"Perhaps. They were wild days, and men died everywhere from one thing or another."

"Wilder than these?"

"You know war as well as any mortal. You know how it is with companies moving from place to place, with disease in the camps, men deserting or fighting to death over some woman. If one is careful to take the worst, it can be done."

"Sounds like Brittany."

I grunted. "It does, that."

The germ of an idea began to grow. I had fought and killed from one side of the world to the other, leading men, following lords. Priskos had thought me weak for doing my duty but I had led warbands and caused havoc for almost two centuries. It was what I was best at. It was what I should have been doing all along, no matter what else my duty required of me.

"So, you and the Lady Eva was married, sir?" Walt shook his head. "You know how to pick them and that be the truth. The Lady Eva has a right majestic pair on her."

"Do try to hold your tongue until we pass through this forest. I should hate to have to cut it out."

"Won't it just grow back, sir?"

"Good God, I hope not."

North of Strasbourg, in a wild, wooded place, we were set upon by robbers.

It looked like a dangerous place and I was already on edge. The sky was close and the shadows pressed in from beneath the trees and rocks.

"Any chance you relate that story now, sir?" Walt asked. "The one where you captured Mortimer in Nottingham, when King Edward was young? I should like to hear it, sir."

"Hush, Walter. Watch the flanks."

He sighed, because I often chided him with such warnings in dangerous places and usually nothing happened.

A shout pierced the air. Harsh and guttural, echoing along the trackway. We drew our weapons just as a score of desperate men descended on us from both sides of the road, all suddenly screaming their battle cries.

We cut them down to a man. Walt fought like the Devil himself, racing from the dead to the living to run the next one through with a mad joy on his face. I followed the last of them through the trees, spearing one in the spine and jumping from my horse to follow the last two on foot where I killed them with my sword.

Both pitiful creatures wept and begged. They were so thin and filthy. I killed them without a word and drank from them both.

Their blood filled me with strength. I was used to drinking it when wounded or exhausted and much of the power of the blood went into restoring me. But, drinking those men when I was uninjured and fresh, I felt how the full potency of the blood seeped into my bones.

I had a purpose. I would kill and drink, kill and drink, the strength from my next victim building upon that of my last so that I would grow to match the strength of the immortals Peter and Christman, who were apparently my uncles.

I would grow to be a match for my brother William whenever he returned.

If I drank enough powerful men, perhaps I could one day return to Priskos and beat the filthy bastard to death and throw his shrivelled carcass into a ravine.

Those scrawny, desperate robbers on the road had been a start but I would have to find warriors and lords, if I was to become what I needed to become.

Returning to the site of the villeins' ambush, I found a wild-eyed Black Walter standing over the whimpering forms of the wounded survivors.

They would not survive for much longer.

"You must drink their blood, Walt."

"God forgive me," he said, but in the end, he did not require much coaxing. Walt was a born survivor. Willing to pay the price for life, whatever it was.

I showed him how it was best and easiest to drink from the neck or wrist of a body where the heart still fluttered with vestiges of life and he sank his teeth into the wounds and gulped it down. Even when he heaved and vomited it back up, he drank once more.

All the men died and we left them to rot on the side of the road. Whether they had any families left alive nearby to bury them, I neither knew nor cared.

"Cold blood does not work?" he asked me later, when the bodies were miles behind us.

I recalled submerging myself into a vat of congealing blood beneath the hills of Palestine, so many years before.

"It works to heal you and will maintain your health. But it is not so potent as blood from a living man. And it congeals in your mouth and belly and it is quite foul."

"Living blood it is, then." He was quiet for some time. "What if those men had not come along? I would make ill?"

"You would grow weaker, the sunlight would burn and blister your skin even more than when you are satiated. And your pallor would take an ever greener tint."

"Green?"

"There was an immortal monk that I kept prisoner once. He would turn the colour of mould and rotting pears. As I recall, Eva would take on the hue of a mint leaf."

"Never been a man admired for my features. And I can keep my skin shrouded so as to not blister in sunlight."

"You would also lose your mind. Although, in your case it would prove difficult to tell."

"We always knew something was queer with you, sir."

"Who is we?"

"All of us. The lads. The men and the archers both. You and Old Tom and John and Hugh. Something off. Something to do with blood magic."

I scoffed. "How could you possibly know that?"

"The company servants would get bled regular, right? The young lads. Yet their blood would get taken off. We thought it was blood magic. What else could it have been? You was burning the blood, praying to Satan for your strength and your youth. All the lads thought so. Well, not so much that anyone would have done a thing about it. But that was what was said."

And I had thought us so clever. So subtle and cunning. But I should have known how a company of men can talk and talk so that a bunch of fools can together arrive at wisdom.

"Damn your eyes, the lot of you."

"Yes, sir. But what do we do for blood if we find no more desperate men?"

"If there are no men to kill and your time for blood is come, you may drink of mine. And my blood will keep you hale and steady. But we are now heading into pestilential France, where all men are desperate and two lone Englishmen will be welcomed not."

And I was more right about that than I expected.

***

As we rode across the county, the weather grew wetter and wilder almost every day. I hunched in my saddle and plodded onward with nought but the thoughts in my head and the rain drumming against my hood or my hat. Always on my mind, of course, was the dead girl, whose life I had cut short through my witless romantic notions.

And often I pondered the condemnation that Priskos expressed over my worshipping of Jesus. He had called cathedrals monuments to folly. As if worshipping God was folly.

Your dead god is desert god, for desert people. God of death and of weakness. God of word, not deed. You must cast him off.

How could such blasphemy be truth? Of course, he was older than Jesus and from a pagan land somewhere to the east. And Alexander had been a pagan, as had Caesar, and yet they were sung of in ballads as heroes that upheld a kind of chivalric ideal. If they could be chivalrous without worshipping God, was it possible for me, also? I did not know what to make of it, only that I found it horrifying and intriguing in equal measure.

South of the fortified city of Luxembourg, we came to the outskirts of town where a large and bizarre group filled the road in a long procession ahead of us. They wore robes and sombre clothes with red crosses on their fronts and backs and almost all were men but there were some women at the rear. All wore hoods or caps, also with a red cross on, and they marched in silence with their eyes on the ground.

"Monks?" Walt ventured.

They moved in a long procession, like a chain, walking two by two. Two or even three hundred of them. At the front, down by the town, the leaders of the procession held aloft banners of purple velvet. As the first of them reached the town, the church bell began to sound and it kept on with its ringing, over and over, as if it would never cease.

We followed the strange procession right into the market square, where they filed into a large circle and the townsfolk came out and surrounded them.

In the centre, many men stripped themselves to the waist so that they wore nothing more than a linen skirt down to the ankles. Their outer garments were laid reverentially in a big pile to one side of the open space within their circle, and I watched in confusion as pestilential townsfolk were dragged and carried to the mound of clothing where they took turns laying upon it while others prayed over them.

The robed worshippers began to march around and around the circle in a procession. In the centre, a powerful old man with a big beard held his hands aloft and chanted something.

All of a sudden, he cried out a command and all the marching people threw themselves to the ground, most violently, face down with their arms outstretched as if crucified to the floor.

The leader stalked among them and thrashed them on their bare backs with a switch, one at a time. Not all received such a punishment but a good number of them did. When he was done, he ordered them to their feet and each of them produced a heavy scourge from a bag on their belts. It was a short wooden rod with two or three leather thongs dangling from it and each thong was tipped with metal studs. With another command from the big bearded fellow, they each began to beat their backs and breasts in time.

The leader and three of his attendants walked amongst the madmen, urging them to have strength and to pray harder.

On the far side of the square, the folk parted and a sobbing mother stepped forward into the magic circle carrying a bundle which she placed in the centre and wailed. A flap of cloth fell back and I saw that it was a dead child, not more than a year old, already turned black with putrefaction. Prayers were said over the poor thing and its mother but no matter how she wailed and how they prayed, the baby did not return to life and the mother was dragged away.

All the while, the mad worshippers continued to whip themselves bloody. And then they began to chant a prayer in time to their thrashing of themselves.

"What in the name of God is happening here?" I asked a tall man who stood far to the rear.

His eyes were shining, rimmed with tears, as he turned to me. "They mortify their flesh. Praise God!"

"Who are these men? Where do they come from?"

"The Brotherhood of the Flagellants," one man said.

"They come to us from the East," said another.

"From Bavaria."

"Hungary," said a woman. "So I heard."

"They said with their own mouths they was come from Nuremberg, Martha. Why don't you ever listen?"

I interrupted their argument. "What do they hope to accomplish through such acts?"

No one wished to speak the words until one young fellow turned and answered with a sob. "To end the plague!"

Their pace accelerated and the Flagellants threw themselves to the floor again and got to their feet to continue to the thrashing.

"What nonsense," I said, far too loudly, for a dozen or more townsfolk turned and gave me the evil eye. Some even cursed me.

"We should go, sir," Walt said, for he had a nose for trouble. Perhaps I should have listened but the orgy of self-mutilation fascinated me to such an extent that I could not draw my eyes from them. The fronts and backs of both the men and the women were beginning to spit more and more and the smell of blood was in the air as it was sprayed and spattered toward the crowd on all sides. Women were as enthusiastic as any of the men, their bared breasts bouncing and bloody as they whipped their flails around their flanks onto their fronts.

The big man in the centre, along with his three burly attendants, called out orders and lead the chanting prayer.

"Why do the leaders not mortify their own flesh?" I asked the folk about me.

Sensing criticism, they scoffed and scorned to answer.

"He is the Master," a lad who spoken before told me.

The Master shouted a command and the Flagellants threw themselves to the ground once more and fell silent but for their panting and wincing while the leaders strode amongst them, whipping a few of them.

"Should this Master not suffer his own punishments?" I said, speaking far louder than I intended. My voice filled the quiet square and the Master whipped his head around to me.

His eyes locked on mine.

Walt whispered. "We should go, sir."

"You!" the Master shouted, raising a finger to point at me.

A great rustling sounded as every face in the town square turned to mine.

"What great sinner is this?" he roared. "What great sinner is this that dares to interrupt our sacred rites?"

Walt began to turn his horse. "Time to retreat, sir?"

"I think so," I said and attempted to turn my horse about through the crowd.

"Yes!" the Master cried. "Yes, see how the sinner flees before our righteousness. Flee, you murderers and robbers. None you shall find but endless woe. The wrath of God on you shall fall."

I turned back to him.

"Richard. Sir," Walt muttered, looking at the outraged faces all around us. "My lord. We must—"

I sat upright and called across the square. "And who are you? Who are you to make such pronouncements? You who command these mad fools to beat themselves bloody while you yourself stand unharmed?"

A collective intake of breath echoed around the square and the faces turned back to him.

The Master's face above his beard turned the colour of boiled beetroot. Without a word, and keeping his gaze fixed upon mine, he untied the rope about his robes and shrugged off the clothes from his torso. The flesh of his muscular upper body and fat belly were white as chalk.

White, that is, other than the mass of red welts, pink scar tissue and weeping, pussy wounds that covered his back, chest and shoulders.

The crowd turned back to me as the Master, triumphant, raised a hand to me once more.

"You shall know what it is to suffer for your sins. Bring him here!"

All at once, the townsfolk all around me surged forward, their faces grim and wild with righteousness. Hands grabbed my horse's bridle and tail and, already nervous, he began to panic. I fought him as the hands reached for my ankles.

"Unhand me!" I roared.

Walt was swearing at the men and women that grabbed at him. The crowd began to shout their encouragement and their rage built into a roar that filled the square.

I leaned over and punched the face of the man who had my right leg but three more grabbed hold of my forearm and began to heave me down from my saddle. I held on with my knees and yanked a dagger from my belt with my off hand and stabbed it down, striking flesh. They released me, shouting in anger that I had drawn blood.

More surged forward.

I realised that I was about to be ripped to pieces by a mob of mad, French peasants.

A rage filled me. A rage unlike any I had known. A rage that caused me to shake and growl like a bear.

My mind filled with visions of Priskos. His words. His assault on me. That violation.

I pictured my friend John being slaughtered by the black knight. I recalled the assassin that came so close to killing me in the Southwark stews.

Felt the agony of the bolt that had struck me in the face.

Saw Osanna's dying eyes fixing on mine.

Back in England, Eva and Thomas died in agony, over and over again, and only I could save them.

There was no decision. It was all instinct and blind rage.

I drew my sword and, screaming a wordless battle cry, I slashed down at the mob. My blade cut into the flesh of the faces of the nearest men. Blood sprayed up to splash across the crowd. My horse tried to flee but there was no way out. A young man leapt up behind me and I thrust my dagger around my flank and into his, sending him to his death. My blades stabbed down, left and right, killing and maiming men and women who still came at me.

Walt fought them also, with sword and dagger, so that the screams of the dying merged with the shouts of the madmen all around.

When one fell, two more took his place. It was as though there was no end to them. No satiating their lust for blood.

And there was likewise no bounds for mine.

It was a slaughter. They died and they died and I killed them with joy.

Without warning, it seemed, their hatred turned to panic.

Dozens were dead, scores were blinded or maimed, and instead of pushing forward the ones closest to us began to fight to get away. Pushing against the crowds behind to escape the terror that was my sword. My horse wheeled and rushed into whatever spaces formed, causing more panic. And their panic spread. Like soldiers breaking on the field, or a herd of animals sensing a predator in their midst, the townsfolk finally understood, on some primal level, that they were facing something that could not be faced. They were fighting something that could not be beaten. Like a living plague, I charged from the dead to the living, bringing agonies and swift death.

The crowds parted before me and streamed away through the side streets, pushing the aged and the children before them and trampling those that fell.

My horse was wheeling and breathing in terror, so I climbed down and pushed him away. Walt stayed mounted, controlling his horse, while he chased away the rest of the madmen nearest to him.

The Flagellants alone had not fled, and I stalked toward them, wiping blood from my eyes and licking it from my hands.

A dozen of them rushed me with their flails and walking sticks. I smashed their skulls with my sword and threw them aside as I approached the Master, who stood his ground and prayed. His three attendants chanted some mad prayer and came at me with willow switches in one hand and wooden crucifixes in the other. I stabbed the first in his guts, cut the right hand off the next and the third dropped to his knees, weeping and praying to God with his head bowed like an invitation. With one swing, I cut off his head and kicked over his body.

The Master shook and tears streamed down his face into his beard.

I dropped my sword and seized him by the shoulders.

"Who am I?" I said, my voice low like a growl. It did not sound like my own. "Who am I? I am a sinner. I am a murderer. I am the wrath of God."

I sank my teeth into his neck and ripped out a chunk of flesh that I spat onto the ground. He screamed as I sucked the blood from his neck.

Walt grabbed me by the shoulder.

"People will see, lord."

"Let them see."

"These folk will talk."

"Let them talk!" I snarled. "Let them all talk. Let all France talk and let them tremble at the word of our coming. Soon, I will kill my way across France and they will fear me."

I drank more from the dying man until his heart stopped and I threw him down and raised my voice.

"Englishmen will drink the blood of the French." I shouted it so my voice echoed hard from the houses walling off the square. "Spread the word. The English will drink the blood of the French until we find the knight of the black banner. Spread the word. You fear the pestilence? *I* am the pestilence. I am Richard of Hawkedon and I will murder every soul in France until I find the knight of the black banner. We are the English and we will bring death to France!"

Walt recovered our horses and together we rode slowly out of town with eyes peeping from shuttered windows and half-open doors all around us.

We left scores dead and a market square drenched in blood.

It was a start. But I needed more.

1 6

Strength

"DO YOU FEEL stronger, sir?" Walt asked.

We had made it to the border of Normandy, coming at it from the south, and would soon be within striking distance to the coast. Then it would be a matter of finding a ship that would sail us home. I wondered whether Eva and Thomas yet lived.

Our camp was once more made amongst the trees away from the road. The weather had turned with the seasons and everything was wet. It reeked of mushrooms and brown leaves stuck to everything. My shoes were rotted almost away and the fires never dried us completely.

"Stronger?" I considered it. "Somewhat, perhaps."

Northern France had been ravaged by the plague such that it seemed at times that everyone was dead. Entire villages were empty. Others had no children or old folk. Everywhere was misery.

Walt sighed. "We need to kill more people, then."

I shook my head. "Killing these poor, starving villeins will not make me stronger. Not by much, at least."

Priskos had told me that the best blood came from unborn babies, and children, and from pregnant mothers, and from young maidens just into womanhood.

And also from great warriors.

Try as I might, I could not imagine killing babies, women and girls. Not even to save the lives of my companions.

I had tried.

In one hamlet, a starving girl of fourteen or so was alone in taking care of her very young brother and another little girl. Looking down at them after they came to beg for food, I considered cutting their throats.

"I will lay with you for some bread, lord," she said without looking at me, her skinny arms wrapped about her.

We rode on after I gave her all the food in my pack. Walt shook his head at my idiocy but I saw him quietly hand the boy an entire cheese. I was pleased to note that I yet retained some sense of morality. Did that mean I would never be strong enough to beat William?

"Could we not take some people and drink from them at will? As you do with your servants, sir."

"That is one way, indeed. It seems that is the way of many immortals that I have killed. It helps them to maintain the illusion of normality for the mortal world, just as it does for our order."

"So, am I now a part of the Order of the White Dagger, sir?"

"Good God, I suppose I shall have to swear you into it." In truth, I did not wish to sully the quality of our order with the likes of Black Walter, so that was all I said.

"You reckon we should take some slaves from the locals, then?"

"Priskos claims that one's power grows by drinking the blood of one who dies as you drink. They release their essence into you at the point of death."

Walt frowned. "That true, sir? It's better when they die?"

"I believe I have noticed a difference."

"Do you think that's what your brother William has been doing these centuries past, and that when he returns from the East he will be stronger than you?"

"Shut up, Walt."

There was nothing for it but to seek out strong men. And to kill them.

We found an ancient tower a few miles from Normandy outside a place called Senonches. The village was dead. It was surrounded for miles by dense oak woodland, all turned to gold and brown and decay.

The tower, though, was guarded by men.

It had been built probably centuries before and was no doubt even older than I was. The mortar between the stones needed repairing and grass and weeds grew from the cracks. A wooden palisade surrounded it, far newer but still rotting.

We reached it at dusk.

Smoke rose from within the walls and the sound of men's laughter drifted across the cleared ground to the trees where Walt and I crouched. Our horses tethered in a clearing half a mile behind us, we were dressed for war.

"How many, you reckon?" Walt asked.

"It does not matter."

I stood and walked across the soggy ground, pulling a cheap helm down over my head.

Walt followed quickly. I considered going to the gates of the palisade but I knew I could not convince the men within to open the door so I aimed directly for the nearest corner of the stone tower. The ground was soft underfoot and I sank down into an ancient ditch up to my knees and fought my way out, emerging in a fouler mood.

Climbing the ancient walls was simple enough but not easy. Not in a wonky helm, and a gambeson with a sword dangling at my hip. I scraped the steel against the stones as I climbed, and I could hear Walt doing the same. If I could have taken both hands from the wall I would have ripped the useless helm off and thrown it down but I was committed.

As I rolled over the battlements, I knocked a stone from the wall onto the wooden boards of the roof, making a great bang. I helped Walt over and heard a noise behind me.

The hatchway onto the roof was opened by a man who stared, open-mouthed, as I ran at him across the roof. He pulled the hatch shut but I yanked it open before he could bar it and I jumped through into the chamber below.

The fall was greater than I expected it to be and I landed heavily, falling onto my face. I rolled and jumped up as the first man and another came at me. They were proper men-at-arms but they were not armoured and I wasted no time in stabbing the first in his chest. Walt slipped down the ladder and sank his dagger into the neck of the second.

Removing our helms, we each drank from the man we had killed until he was dead.

Walt stared at me with joy in his eyes as his man fell at his feet.

I nodded to him and we ran down to the chamber below.

To my surprise, it was a bedchamber, dominated by a great four-post piece with a sagging canopy. An old man lay abed with his sheets drawn up to his chin.

The door burst open and Walt killed the man as he came through. Three or four men behind, coming up the stairwell, turned and fled at the sight of it. Walt followed and I knew that he would have no trouble, for he had been a savage fighter even before being gifted with the strength of the immortals.

"Invaders," the ancient lord in his bed muttered. "Murderers."

"Who are you, old man?" I asked, crossing to him.

He raised his chin, exposing a wrinkled neck and unshaved white whiskers sprouting from his chin. "I am the lord of this place. Sir Pierre of Senoches. This is my tower. You shall leave, or die."

"Killed many men, have you? In your younger days, I mean."

He quivered. "Every death I brought was in honourable war. Your vengeance means nothing."

"Vengeance?" I replied. "You misunderstand, sir. I am not here for justice. You have not wronged me in any way. I am pleased that you were a strong knight. I honour you."

I slit his throat and drank his blood. It tasted old and wrong, for he was riddled with the diseases of the aged, but I hoped that some of the power he had in his youth had gone into me.

In the bailey below, I found Walt drinking from a dying man while two others huddled against the base of a section of the damp palisade, staring at us in horror and fury.

"Fight for your lives, you cowards," I said to them. "Where are your weapons? Fight and die with honour or die in the mud like worms."

They were mere men-at-arms, retainers in the employ of an impoverished lord whose tenants were all dead or gone. And yet they fought like heroes, thrusting with their spears and wrestling us with daggers in hand as they fell to our strength. We drank heartily from them and I felt my power grow.

At the coast, four days later, a company of eight men stopped us as we went from village to village to find a boat capable of crossing the channel so late in the year. I knew at once that the men who surrounded us were veterans of the recent wars. They were grim and wild-eyed. Most were scarred, missing fingers or an eye. Thin, desperate and iron-hard men.

It felt good to kill them, to cut them open and taste their strength. I could almost taste the evil acts that they had committed to survive the years of war and plague.

On the wide banks of the Seine where it becomes the sea, we found our way home. A trader and his family dragged their boat back into the water in exchange for a heavy bag of silver and for our horses. The crossing was unpleasant in the extreme and I thought for certain we would be dashed against the cliffs of Dieppe or sunk in the churning dark waters. But the winds, strong as they were, turned mostly in our favour so that we made the crossing in five wild days.

We went overland to London with all the haste we could manage and arrived in the middle of November, having been away for little more than three months. With my heart in my mouth I rode into the courtyard, threw myself from my horse and hammered on the door of the house, shouting for Stephen.

Eva and Thomas were alive.

Opening my veins for them, they drank.

Each drank so much of me that I fell to my knees and then myself collapsed and was only revived through hot spiced wine and three cups of servant's blood.

Praise God, they were cured.

After two days with no relapse into sickness, dearest Eva wept with relief and embraced me closely.

When I was certain they were truly well, I told them what had happened. What I had done.

And Thomas was furious.

1 7

Recruitment

"YOU DID *what?*" Thomas asked me, his eyes shining.

"It was the only way."

Two days after my return, sure as we could be that they would not fall back into sickness, we ate in the hall.

After dismissing the servants, I had relayed the events of our journey to the south. Walt sat in silence and kept shovelling food into his face. We had both grown thinner but I had appetite solely for wine.

Elbows on the table, Thomas lowered his face into his hands.

"You murdered good men to save our lives?" he asked, without looking up. "I would rather have died."

Hugh, sitting beside him, patted Thomas on the back.

Stephen drummed his fingers on the table. "Hardly *murders*, were they, Thomas? It sounds to me as though Richard and Walter defended themselves when attacked, as any man would have done."

"And the knight in the tower?" Thomas asked, lifting his face. He seemed tired. Drawn. Months of illness had taken their toll, perhaps not to his immortal body but certainly to his soul and to his heart. "That knight and his men were no threat to you."

"Enemies," I said, waving my cup and spilling wine over the side. "Enemies of England who would have fought us one way or another, one day."

"There is a truce," Thomas said. "You know they did not deserve their deaths."

His ingratitude was beginning to grate on me and I stared at him, feeling the anger burn in my chest.

"Well," Eva said, placing a hand on my forearm. "It is done now. The strength Richard gained through these actions has cured us and now we can go on, Thomas."

"Yes, yes," he said, bowing his head. "I am not ungrateful. It is simply that... for so long you have ensured we act entirely within the terms of the truces arranged between the kings. We do nothing that might risk them. And now..."

"I understand. As you benefit from my actions, you feel as though you had a hand in them. Do not trouble yourself with guilt. If there is sin here, it is mine."

He was unhappy and wished to say more but he was tired in his heart and he merely nodded.

I was irritated by his weakness.

Yes, I had sinned by killing when I had not needed to and I would have to atone. My sins had brought Thomas back from a terrible living death, and Eva too. They had wakened from an endless nightmare only thanks to my acting more like my brother and Priskos instead of by the code of chivalry.

A part of me had expected Thomas to fall to his knees and express everlasting gratitude for his deliverance. Part of me wanted him to do so.

"What I struggle to comprehend," Stephen began, "is that there are clearly many more immortals in the world than we knew of."

I nodded. "Yes, there are three more. Priskos, Peter the false priest, and the giant Christman."

Stephen opened his arms. "Are you certain? It is astonishing to think of this blood. The blood from you, Richard, that you have given to us." He rolled up his sleeves and examined the veins of his wrists, touching the skin reverently. "This blood that is in us, comes from so great a pedigree. It is the blood that flowed in the veins of Alexander. In the veins of Caesar. Think of what this blood has accomplished." He looked at us, eyes shining joy and not a little hint of madness. "This turns so much of history on its head, does it not? How many men like us have been turning the wheels of history down the centuries? How many famed ancients have been of this blood? It could be hundreds. Thousands."

"Only if this old man was speaking the truth," Eva pointed out. "He may be as mad as William."

I nodded. "Priskos may have been lying but I do not believe so. Mad, perhaps. But not a liar. And his strength." I closed my eyes and suppressed a shudder. "I cannot convey to you the power in him."

Hugh had his fingers across his mouth. "Surely, Richard, he cannot be that much stronger than you."

I scoffed at his ignorance. "Consider the chasm that exists between each of you and a mortal man." I looked around at each of them to see them nod as they recalled it. "That was what I felt when I struggled against the giant Christman. Perhaps that would also be the distance in strength between myself and Peter, the other son of Priskos. But the father himself." I grasped the edge of the table as I pictured him holding me aloft. "His fingers were iron. His arms unbending as an ancient oak. One might as well attempt to fight a mountain."

"Like a god," Stephen muttered.

"What was that?" Thomas said.

Stephen sat upright. "The pagans believed in gods that walked amongst mortals. They had stories of Hercules and Mars and Jupiter. Gods who acted like men, who could defeat monsters and cut down men like wheat."

Thomas snorted. "Pagan nonsense."

"Of course," Stephen said, waving his hand.

"He criticised God," I said, almost blurting it out. "He said that Jesus Christ was a god of death. The god of a desert people who was never meant for us."

"Disgraceful," Thomas said. "Surely, Richard, you put no stock in such blasphemy."

"Of course not," I lied. "And yet, Alexander displayed knightly virtue in his conquest of the East, and in his conduct with his enemies, and with women. And Alexander was a pagan."

Thomas scowled. "He had no choice but to be a pagan. We have no such excuse. The truth and the light has since been revealed to us. To all mankind. For the sake of our souls, we must worship God and His son Jesus Christ. You see what becomes of a man who has not welcomed Jesus into his heart. This Priskos is a brute. A savage. And it is because he rejects God. Only through God can man rise up to take his place above the creatures of the earth, else we are condemned to forever act like beasts. All pagans were like this before Christ and all pagans are like this in the world today."

"You are right, of course," I said. Though I still had my doubts.

"Are we going to kill them?" Eva asked, looking at me. "Priskos and his sons."

I finished my cup and filled it again. Placing the jug carefully back on the table top, I picked up my wine and took a great gulp.

"The Order of the White Dagger exists to find and to destroy the immortals that William has made and to kill my brother for the evil that he has wrought in the world." I took another drink. "Priskos has done evil. Perhaps even greater evil than William. But he and his sons are sitting in a quiet corner of the world, doing harm only to the villages and people in the vicinity. One day, it may be necessary to cleanse them from the Earth also. Until that day, we may ignore them."

Stephen held up a finger, tilting his head. "Could Priskos or the sons be the progenitors of the black banner knight and his men?"

"He knew nothing about all that. He knew that William was granting the Gift to others and he even suggested he might have to kill William, if he caused too much trouble."

They all sat up at that.

"So," Stephen said, a small smile on his face, "why not let Priskos kill William?"

"He might not act for five hundred years, Stephen. Only once William unmakes the world, which we must not allow. And it is *our* duty. Would you allow another to fulfil your duties merely because they offered?"

He did not answer, which spoke loudly on what he thought of duty.

"What of the pestilence?" Eva asked. "How does it go across the sea?"

I shook my head, unable to describe it.

"Bad," Walt said, his mouth full of boiled pork. "Exceeding bad, Lady Eva."

"Here, also," she said.

Stephen sighed. "So many have died and yet the numbers of new deaths diminish. It seems that this is not the end of days after all."

"Plagues lessen in winter," I pointed out, "only to return in spring."

Thomas and Hugh nodded. We had seen it in many campaigns.

"The people are stunned," Hugh said. "It seems that the living are thankful beyond measure for their own lives, even while there is not a soul alive who is not terribly bereaved. It is beyond comprehension. There is nothing to be made from it. It is beyond reason, is it not? And so, as I say, the people everywhere seem dazed." He shook his head in wonder and placed a hand over his eyes, for he was a gentle soul, in truth.

"That may be so," Stephen said to me. "Order has not broken down in England. We still receive reports from the few yet travelling. Those that survive go on. In some places, half of the folk perished, so we are told. In others, merely a third, or fewer. And yet some villages seem to have been entirely lost. Our king and queen and the princes live. Most of the great men of the realm have so far survived. The soldiers, too, have fared better than others. It seems, from what we can tell, that the poorest, the oldest and youngest have died where the rich and the strong have lived."

"Good," I said, nodding and banging the table with my fingers. "Very good. As it should be. England goes on. When they are ready, King Edward and the Prince can go on with their war."

Hugh frowned. "Their war, sir? Is it not our war, also?"

"Not any more, Hugh."

"What about us?" Thomas said. "What shall we do if we are not fighting for Edward?"

I drank off my wine. "We shall winter here. Grow strong and healthy and wait for the weather to change."

"And then?" Eva said.

"We shall revive my old company of archers and men-at-arms and lead them into France. Not for Edward. Not to fight Philip. We will find the knight of the black banner and this time nothing shall stop us. If we must, we will burn all France to the ground."

***

Eva came to me a few days later as I rested in my chamber. Rain pattered on the tiles above and on the walls outside but the chamber was warmed by the fire in my hearth and from the fire in the chamber below. One of the greatest creations ever developed in my long life is most certainly the chimney stack.

"Am I intruding?" Eva asked at the door.

"You could never intrude on me, Eva."

She smiled and shook her head. "What if you were privately entertaining the comely Lady Cecilia?"

I hesitated, surprised to hear her mention the name, before I recovered. "Well then I would most certainly endeavour to privately entertain you both, simultaneously, to the best of my abilities."

She scoffed, presumably at my abilities, and took the seat I held for her. "Do you mean to marry her?"

I sighed as I sat opposite. The green glass in the windows let in light and kept out the damp weather. Best of all, I could not see out across the cesspool that was London.

"Why would you ask me that?"

"I know you escorted her back from Flanders. You visited her at the Tower. She has written you four letters in these past three months."

A laugh escaped my lips. "You have been keeping note of my romantic liaisons?"

"I keep note of everything." She peered at me. "Of everyone."

"I had no idea you already maintained so many agents."

"When will you give me an answer?"

"Is it your business to receive one?"

She frowned. "My business? I care for you, Richard. I would see you happy."

I sighed. "I see." The rain gusted against the window. "Would you like a drink?" I poured us some wine but my hand shook, spilling the blood-dark liquid onto the table. "How can I marry the woman, Eva? She would get no sons from me. No daughters neither. She would age and wither while I went on. How can any of us condemn a mortal into such a life?"

"Have you told her that you cannot marry her?"

I wiped my finger in the dark wine spilled on the table. "I have discouraged her. Reminded her that I am good only for war and not for marriage. She knows I am beneath her, surely."

Eva shook her head at my stupidity. "You may as well attempt to fend off a bear with a honeyed chicken."

"What do you mean?"

She scoffed. "Tell her you will not marry her and then cease all contact. That is the kindest thing. Or..."

"Or what?"

"Would it be the worst life for her? You would not be such a bad husband. She is old. She bore no children in her first marriage. Her brother is wealthy but her name is not that great. Sir Humphrey Ingham is known to be a prickly bore and many a lord has already been put off by him, whereas you would never be intimidated by him. Cecilia is no doubt aware of that."

"She is not old," I said. "Anyway, I leave for France in the spring and I will not return until the task is complete. One way or the other."

"What if she is unmarried when you return?"

"She will not be."

"You do not have to allow your oath to drive you from happiness, Richard. You might have twenty or thirty years of contentment with Cecilia. Do not throw it away because you believe that you know what she wants better than she herself does."

"But I am a monster. I cannot allow her to enter into such a life without knowledge of all the facts."

"In what way are you a monster?"

"Come, now. You have seen the things I have done."

"I have done the things you have done. I do not consider myself a monster. And I do not consider you one, either."

"You might have done the odd monstrous act, Eva. But I come from a monster. Directly. It is in my blood."

She pursed her lips, frowning. "Perhaps the sins of the fathers will be visited on the sons for those who hate God, as Priskos claimed to do. But you are a good Christian."

I scoffed. "Never that."

"You *were* not. Not when I met you. But you have changed over the years. You have gown devout in your faith."

"Nonsense."

"It is Thomas," Eva said. "Did you know that? His love of God, his loyalty and respect for the Church. After decades together, his piety has rubbed off on you."

"God forbid."

She shook her head. "Admit it, Richard. You strive to be a good Christian, do you not?"

I sighed. "If I do, that may be that is why I have failed to find the black knight. I have been overly dutiful. Overly courteous to the kings and lords I have served. Perhaps I should be the one who is served by kings and lords. Let me be the monster and I will find the black knight and be feared also."

"Do you think Cecilia would like that?" Eva asked. "For you to be monstrous? Or would she rather marry to the man you are in your heart. A good and decent knight."

"She shall have neither." I drank my wine and poured another. "Perhaps I will write to let her know I will be gone for a long time. She will be free to forget me and perhaps it will not break her heart."

She laughed a little. "I doubt her heart is so fragile. I suspect she has a half-dozen other suitors dangling by threads."

"But you said—"

"Visit her, you coward. Do not write. But also do not tell her that you are taking your company to Brittany. Word would very likely get back to the King that you are jeopardising his treaties."

"I may be a fool when it comes to the ways of women," I said, "but I am not a drooling simpleton."

Eva nodded slowly as she considered my words, then shrugged. "Why are you willing to risk starting the war again? To risk falling out of favour with the King, likely forever?"

"For the rest of his mortal life, do you mean? Perhaps I have of late been overly concerned with the King's purposes, rather than those of the Order."

"And yet having the King's ear has helped us, has it not?" Eva asked. "You have said so repeatedly for fifty years. Social position unlocks doors that even wealth cannot."

"That is what I have told myself," I replied, "and whenever any of you had doubts, that was my response. Now, I wonder if I was not avoiding my true duty by waging war against the Scots and the Welsh and all the rest. It was simpler to do so rather than to carry out my true duty."

"For so long it seemed reasonable to believe that there were no more immortals left. Other than William. And our Order had to strive to maintain and develop our resources in the meantime."

"You mean to say that it was difficult to find them and so we gave up. No, no. That is not it. I should say that *I* gave up. Ceased trying. If I wished it, I could recruit hundreds of men and cut a swathe through France and we could torture our way to the truth. *Someone* would know. This is what I should have done decades ago, in the time of the first Edward, instead of amusing myself by killing barbarian Scots."

"You would bring the King's fury down on us."

I nodded. "So be it. One day, his son will be the King, and his son after him. While we will endure. What is the King, any king, compared to us?"

"A man powerful enough to wield the might of an entire kingdom."

That was true. "We have power, also. One of us is equal to hundred mortal men."

"Two or three, perhaps."

"A dozen. A score."

"Even if that were the case, it would mean we could defeat how many soldiers sent against us? Perhaps five hundred at the most? How many soldiers can a king raise?"

"I shall create more members of our Order."

"I see. How many? Who will they be?"

Her precise questions irritated me, as they always had done. I recalled how much I hated her damned practicality. "I do not know. Whatever is needed."

"How many, Richard?"

"A hundred, if need be."

She scoffed. "A hundred?"

"Damn you, woman, I shall make a thousand immortals and burn France to the ground."

"Very well," she said, "and who will these men be? Men you can trust, you have always said. Men who you could be certain will never turn on you, never betray us."

"Yes, yes," I said, waving my hand at her. "Why must your arguments always be so bloody well-reasoned?"

She smiled, and for a moment it was like we were man and wife again. But then we both recalled our separation and our smiles dropped.

"How fare you, Eva?" I asked.

Eva took a long, slow breath. She closed her eyes for a long moment and opened them again.

"I wanted to die. It was as though I descended into Hell, and climbed back out again, day after day."

"It cannot imagine the torment. Yet you endured."

"I did."

I reached across the table and held her hand. "In time, the memory shall fade."

She pulled her hand away. "You are changed," she said.

"I am?"

"You descended into Hell, also. You did it for us. You faced the demon of the abyss but it has hardened your heart. You fell. You died. You came back with these notions that you are monstrous, that you will burn and destroy. Death changed you."

I shrugged. "I have died before."

"You pass it off lightly but whatever you went through in that cave, with that man, has taken its toll on you. Can I even call him a man? The way you spoke of him. His power is terrible, is it not?"

"It is."

"You fear it."

I hesitated. "Yes."

"You have always had anger, Richard. You cloak it in jest, or courtliness, or chivalrousness. Even then, many can sense the danger in you. It makes men, even knights and lords, fear you. Fear what you might do. And yet when I look at you now I see that the anger has grown. It swells in your breast, it moves your limbs. It is closer to the surface and even I fear what might be should it burst forth."

I drank my wine. "I would never harm you."

"What did the Ancient One infest you with, Richard? Our Order exists to destroy men like him and yet you dismiss any notion of doing so."

"I created the Order to kill William and the ones he created. Priskos is something else."

"Something worse. At the least he is a killer of women and there is nothing honourable about that."

I gripped my cup so tightly that my wine spilled. Osanna would have lived a few more years if not for my idiot meddling. "Leave it, woman."

She licked her lips and swallowed. "Is it not worth discussing again? Unlike the black knight, unlike William, we know where these ones reside. Perhaps we should recruit an army, travel to Swabia and destroy him and his spawn."

"He deserves death." Even as I said it, I was not certain it was true. Was there much difference between his monstrous actions and my own? Perhaps he did deserve death and I did, too. "Even with an army, I am not sure we would be enough to stop him."

"Surely, that cannot be."

"Stephen said Priskos seemed like a pagan god walking the earth. He spoke truer than I cared to admit. Could a thousand knights stop him? I swear that I do not know."

"I have never known you not to seek revenge on every enemy. If you wanted to do it, you would find a way."

"I may need centuries to grow strong enough. And first, I must find and destroy the black knight. Then William. When that is done, I shall visit Priskos once more."

Eva peered at me closely. "What about the others? His sons, Peter and Christman? Perhaps you feel a certain kinship with them?"

She was right but I denied it, even to myself. "The only kinship that I feel is with you. And Thomas, and Hugh. And Stephen."

She smiled. "That is well."

"So, all else will have to wait. The black knight must fall. I shall recruit my old company," I said, "and take them to France. Some of them, I am sure, would make reliable members of the Order."

"More commoners like Walt?" she asked. "You have always resisted it. You have not yet made Walt swear the Order's oath, have you?"

"These are desperate times. I will bring Walt into the Order and I shall make more of us. A select few, I think. Some of them fight better than knights I have known."

"How will you turn some of your company and not others? Surely, you will have to grant them all the Gift at the same time or none at all? You know what commoners are like. They have no restraint. How will you manage it?"

I laughed. "Will you stop thrusting your damned questions at me, my lady? Sometimes, a man must act and concern himself with the detail later."

She tilted her head and regarded me with a look. With her eyes alone, she expressed a thought as clear as if she had spoken it. "What do you mean, sometimes?"

I laughed again, because despite everything, I knew I was going to war again. A war on my terms.

And, whether I was a knight or a monster, there was nothing I loved more than that.

***

Rob Hawthorn had been one of the wilder ones in his youth, when he fought for me in Brittany. Fighting and drinking like a madman, and he had been even worse with women. But he was a natural leader in spite of his carousing in the towns, for when we were fighting there was no steadier soul in the company.

Once when I led my men into an ambush near Rostrenen in Brittany I saw him standing alone, isolated from the rest of us, with two mounted men charging at him. I called out that he should run, or at least throw himself down. While I bellowed for the other archers to shoot, Rob put an arrow into one man's neck, and then calmly pulled another arrow from his bag, nocked it and shot the second man's horse in the nose, throwing the rider. Rob strolled up and cut the Frenchman's throat. When he turned around to us, he was grinning from ear to ear. It's fair to say that the rest of the men loved him for his steadiness and bravado and his legend amongst them grew until he commanded all of my archers.

It had been hardly a blink of my eye and there I was approaching his rather fine house where small children played in the yard, terrorising the chickens.

"Praise God, Sir Richard," Rob said, "I got your message, sir. I am greatly honoured by your presence." Touchingly, he was wearing what I sure was his very best clothing, as did his wife Agnes and his children.

Rob looked incredibly uncomfortable and stiff. His wife was a pretty young girl who watched all of her children like a hawk, without seeming to pay them any mind at all. She appeared nervous, as it was unusual for a lord to attend a commoner.

It would have made sense for me to invite Rob to the manor, or else simply instruct him by messenger. Agnes must have wondered what business I could possibly have in store for her husband.

"You honour me," I said, warmly, "by inviting me into your home. Please forgive me for bringing Walter, here, Rob. I am afraid, madame, that Walt's table manners are quite appalling. I will understand perfectly if you decided to relegate him to the servants table and in fact that may be for the best."

Walt hung his head in shame. "My lord Richard speaks the truth, madame. I ain't fit for proper company."

Rob laughed as he approached Walt and clapped him on the shoulder. "Black Walter, it is a wonder that you are still alive."

Walt glanced at me. "You don't know the half of it, Rob."

Rob had done well for himself. He had saved enough of the money he had earned during his years fighting to set himself up well in a three-bay house with a good-sized hall. The outside was covered in smooth plaster, freshly painted. Inside the dark hall, the central fire burned well with little smoke, and the mouth-watering smells of food filled the air. Rob gave me the best seat at the head of his table and he sat on my right while Agnes sat on my left and Walt sat opposite. The children sat at their own table nearby and Rob's servants busied themselves with the food, directed by Agnes. It was a well-ordered home. The plastered walls inside were even painted a bright white, and the rushes on the floor were mixed with copious amounts of lavender and other fresh herbs. The table was well laid with bowls, ceramic jugs and even silver serving spoons.

The food was good, hearty stuff and well-prepared. They must have spent a considerable sum on the fish and the meat and spices, perhaps in honour of my dining with them. We spoke of men we had known who had died, during the wars and during the Pestilence. The deaths of so many local landowners had been a benefit to men like Rob who had been able to buy up parcels for very little and his future was looking rather bright.

"God spared many of our family," Rob said, indicating his wife. "My wife's brother and his children excepted, of course." Agnes lowered her head in grief.

"There has never been anything like it in all the world," I said, though I thought of Priskos as I said it and recalled how he claimed to have seen even greater mortalities during his long life. "Though it is passed, now, and we may at last continue with our lives."

Rob seemed to catch a deeper meaning in my words and looked at me keenly.

Rob's eldest son approached toward the end of the meal. "Excuse me, sir," he said as he sidled up to me.

"Dick, leave the lord alone," Rob said.

"It is well," I said, smiling. "You are a well-made lad. How may I be of service, Master Dick?"

"Father says often that he saved your life in the wars against the French and swears he speaks true but my mate Will down Scatborough way reckons that ain't nought but a bunch of gooseberries."

"Richard Hawthorn!" Agnes snapped. "You mind your tongue, young man and beg the pardon of Sir Richard this very instant. Pray, forgive us, my lord, and know that he shall be thoroughly whipped for his impudence."

I tried and failed to keep a straight face. "Forgive me, madame. You must do as you see fit but do not thrash the lad on my account. Rob, may your boy join us at table?"

Rob had his own hand across his mouth as he nodded his assent and shifted aside on the bench, catching a look of some sort from his wife as the young master sat next to me.

"Dick, you should know that it is indeed the truth that your good father did save my life in the war and not merely once but many a time." I spoke a lie but it was not dishonest in spirit, for had I been mortal then Rob's loyal actions would have indeed saved me. "Once, a French knight's lance caught me just so, on my flank, and forced apart my armour where the buckles had loosened during battle. The lance sliced deep into the flesh of my belly and I do not mind admitting to you, young master, that the wound laid me low. Blood soaked me, belly and loins, and I would surely have perished that day, had your father not carried me, armour and all, upon his shoulder, away from the danger. He found me wine, clean water, and later he even persuaded a surgeon to come to heal me."

Young Dick's face was a mask of enraptured attention.

"You will have seen your father shoot, so you will well know what a fine archer he is. But you may not know that he has the strength of five men, and the courage of a lion. Do you know that I fought with the greatest Earls of England and even with Prince Edward of Woodstock and yet, I swear, lad, that there is no man I would rather have fighting at my side than Robert Hawthorn."

The boy slowly turned away from me, eyes bulging, to look up at his father.

After the meal, Rob offered to show me the new orchard he had planted and at once I agreed. The moment we were out of earshot of his house, he turned to me.

"Where?" he asked. "When?"

"Dartmouth," I replied. "Four weeks, if you can make it."

"I will be there. Who joins us?"

"So many of our company fell to the pestilence. Yet I hope we will have Hal, Ralf Thorns, Reg, Osmund, and Fair Simon, at the least. Also, Diggory and Fred Blackthorpe, if they are still at their farm. Gerald Crowfield is said to have returned, finally. Adam Lamarsh, if he is not in gaol. I would hope also to get Roger, Osbert, Watkyn, Jake, and Stan. I have sent a messenger to each but would you consider speaking to them?"

"I'll get them there, sir."

"Hear me, Robert," I said. "This raid is not sanctioned by the King. In truth, if the King were to know, he would likely forbid it."

"This is a personal quest, sir?"

"I never stopped hunting the man with the black banner, who killed our men that day near Crecy. Yet, I grew complacent. I did not try enough. No longer. I will tear France to pieces to look for him and then I will take revenge."

Rob's face grew tight. Unclenching his jaw, he nodded. "Deryk Crookley was my cousin, sir. And I fought with Paul since we were lads. The whole company loved them like brothers, Sir John, too, and were heartsore indeed when they got killed. All of us who remain will join you. Do not doubt that, sir."

His easy commitment worried me. I wished to make him understand what he was agreeing to.

"We will be alone, Rob. We will be cut off from supplies and if we wish to retreat, we shall have to fight our way through. But we shall be a small enough band to evade pursuit while we live off the land and we will move rapidly. I do not know how long we will be there. How long it will be before we return home."

Rob looked back at his house. It was a good home. A home that all men wanted. A dutiful wife, a strong son, pretty daughters. I felt a keen stab of jealousy for the kind of life that I wanted more than any other. Though I knew it could never be, I thought for a moment that I would even live as a common man if I could have such a family. Without a home, without sons, I would never feel truly whole, no matter how many centuries I lived or how much glory I won in battle.

Rob sighed and chewed his lip. "Agnes will not understand."

I nodded. She would be right to be confused and hurt by him leaving. She would feel betrayed and rejected. Agnes would feel abandoned. By God, she would *be* abandoned. Rob was a man who had everything he needed to be happy and fulfilled. He had an heir to carry his name and continue the family, he had daughters to bring him joy, and his young wife could no doubt bear him more. He had over forty contiguous acres and more elsewhere in the hundred he had bought up. Already a man of good standing, and chief tithingman, he could easily become the bailiff of the hundred in time and his son would grow up to take full advantage of his father's wealth and status. Who knew how far young Dick would rise with such a start and with his father to guide him? His daughters might make excellent marriages, to merchants or lawyers or even the poorer sort of esquires.

It was certainly everything a man needed to be happy and fulfilled.

Except, of course, it was not.

A man also needed war. If you had fought in battle, and if you enjoyed it, then it was something you could never throw off. Even though war would bring you discomfort, pain, terror, and misery, it would also take you to a state of being that was far beyond anything that could be found in peace. Men like Rob knew, even if he may never have been able to put it into words, that war brought a man closer to God. It also brought you further into the world so that colours were more vivid and edges were sharper, before, during and after a battle. It brought you closer to the men you fought beside, the men you marched and rode with through burning sun and freezing rain, the men you shared your last piece of stale bread with, the men who picked you up when you were broken and roared your name when you won glory. It brought you closer to your brothers in arms than you were even to your wife and your children, or your father and the brothers you were raised with. Once you tasted that life, you could never be complete without it.

Even though it might leave his family without a husband and father, Rob Hawthorn could not resist going to war. He *had* to.

And he was right. His wife would never understand.

***

Although I knew that the best thing to do would be to cut off Lady Cecilia from all contact, I could not help but call on her before I left. Being cruel to be kind, I should have sent a terse letter but I could not bear the idea of her thinking badly of me and so I kept her dangling by a thread.

It was astonishing that she had rejected so many suitors as she was not growing any younger and she had to marry soon else her value would decline so far that she might spend the rest of her days as a widow before entering a convent. And that, I thought, would truly be a terrible waste.

Though I had only ever treated her rather badly, Cecilia seemed overjoyed to see me and rushed across the hall to me when I entered. She looked wonderful and if anything was even lovelier than I remembered. Truly, I marvelled as she approached, she was of elegant deportment and very pleasing and amiable in bearing. She displayed well the manners of the court and was so dignified in behaviour that she was more than worthy of reverence.

She held my hands and looked up at me expectantly, as if she hoped I would ask for her hand in marriage there and then.

"I must go away," I admitted. "For a long time."

"I see," she said, dropping my hands.

Of course, the poor woman was expecting I had come to ask her, simply to be disappointed once more. At least, I thought, it would be the last disappointment she would get from me, for surely she would accept one of her other proposals while I was gone. Especially if the King publicly denounced me once he heard where I had gone and what I was doing.

She escorted me to a fine chair in her hall and I sat while the servants brought food and wine before withdrawing to a respectful distance. I reflected that the lovely place I was in could have been mine. The servants could have served me and Cecilia every day and I could have shared her chamber every night. It would become my place and hers and our marriage would be a place for our hearts.

But it would forever be empty, of children and of hope for the future.

"Because I do not know for how long I will be away," I said, "I thought it best that I come. To speak to you."

"How kind," she said, pressing her lips together. "And where is it that you go, sir?"

"I am afraid I cannot say."

"Oh?" She was angry. "So it appears that you have said all that you came to say, sir, and you may now take your leave."

"My lady, you must understand that I do not tell you in order to protect you."

She laughed, bitterly. "You protect yourself, Richard. Do not pretend otherwise with me. I am not some two-penny prostitute who will nod and smile at your lies."

I paused, astonished at her vulgarity. Clearly, I had wounded her grievously.

"It is to France that I must go," I admitted, "but I cannot say more than that. Truly."

"France?" She gasped. "Has the war taken some new course I am not aware of?"

"No, no. Nothing of that sort."

"Then why do you go, sir? Is it merely to be free of me?"

"Cecilia, please. How can you say such a thing? It would not be fair to you for us to be married, we have spoken of this."

"You have spoken of it but it did not make sense then and it makes less sense now. You are running off to some woman in Normandy, I know it. Do not deny it."

"Where did you get this notion? I have no woman, my lady. None but you."

She scoffed at my words. "But you do not *have* me, do you, Richard."

"I wish that I could. But we cannot be married."

She came to me and knelt before me. "Not in law perhaps. But who shall give a lover any law? Love is a greater law than any written by mortal man. We could pretend to be married," she said, speaking softly. "Just for one night."

She looked up at me with those huge, dark eyes and long black lashes. Her pink lips were slightly parted and her breathing fast and shallow.

I wish I could say that I did the honourable thing.

But I am not as chivalrous as all that.

Her wanton passion and her remarkable ability in the bedchamber was startling to partake in. Tearing off her clothes with the help of her red-headed servant, she stood before me in joy and pride in her own nakedness. It was all I could do to keep up with her. She used her mouth over every inch of my skin and demanded the same from me. I was only too pleased to oblige. In fact, I obliged her all of the night and half of the next day. Thus in this heaven I took my delight and smothered her with kisses upon kisses until gradually I came to know the purest bliss.

While she rested in between bouts of passion, she had her maidservants bring us wine and fruit and she never once troubled to cover herself. We spoke of small things and laughed, though she also attempted to tease more from me regarding how long I would be absent, though she protested she was but making idle conversation.

"You were so very terse with me when first we met, My Lady," I said as she reclined in my arms. "I would never have known how sweet your lips could be."

She raised herself on one elbow and turned to peer at me, right close. "Men may shield their bodies with brigandines and mail but women must use cunning."

"Ah, so you were merely acting the hard-hearted creature when in truth you wanted me from the moment you laid eyes on me?"

She slapped her hand on my chest over my heart and poked me there with her sharp nail. "I had heard how you were a raging barbarian, sir. A vicious monster who delighted in murder and the ravaging of women. I had to show you with the cold steel of my words that I was not a lady to be trifled with or to be taken advantage of."

"And yet your cold steel warmed when you felt my mighty arms about you."

"Ha!" she scoffed and pinched my skin. "It was not your mighty arms but your kindness, sir, your gentleness that showed me what sort of man you truly were. A chivalrous man. A knight in your heart."

She kissed me on the spot where she had twisted and poked at me.

"Come here, then," I said, pulling her to me. But she pushed me off and reached away from me to find refreshment from the bedside. After wine and fruit, she aroused my passions from me once more with her breasts, her hair, mouth and hands.

Although I was in Heaven itself, by midday I had to take my leave or I risked missing my own boat. When I raised the issue, she commanded me to leave without saying farewell and pushed me from her chamber before I could say more than a few words. The lady was wiping her eyes as she heaved her door shut with a slam.

A porter at her front door gave me an eyeful of judgement as I left the house but I heroically resisted knocking his teeth out and slamming his head into the wooden frame.

"Good day, sir," he muttered, bowing his head.

Outside, the sky pressed down like a sheet of melted lead. I dragged myself into my saddle, as weary and heartsick as a king that just lost his kingdom.

"You alright, sir?" Walt asked me on the road to the coast. "You look a little worse for wear."

"Shut up, Walt."

My company awaited us.

I had the immortal warriors Thomas, Hugh and Walt. I had twenty-one veteran archers commanded by Rob Hawthorn. With nine men-at-arms, their squires and the servants, I had fifty-two men.

Fifty-two men with which to invade France and find the knight of the black banner.

This time, I thought, *I will not fail. No matter the cost.*

But I had more to lose than I knew.

1 8

Brittany

MY COMPANY CROSSED from Dover to Calais. My men brought their armour and weapons, we brought food and wine and equipment. I even brought across our best horses, which cost a fortune and quite ruined them for days afterward. It took five ships to get us all across and to avoid suspicion each left on a different day so that we appeared to be no more than the ordinary traffic to our little piece of England on the French coast.

It was still ours.

Earlier, in July 1348, the first truce ended and King Philip sent his greatest knight, Sir Geoffrey de Charny, against us. The Burgundian knight who had borne the Oriflamme in the army that fell back from Calais in 1347 was one of the commanders of an army sent to cut off Calais from our allies in Flanders. They were hampered by the terrible summer rains that had so threatened to spoil Edward's endless tourneys in England.

De Charny built a fort outside Calais and cut that road through the marshes to Gravelines that I had spent months keeping open the year before. But the appearance of the pestilence had cut short his campaign before he could follow up on his initial moves. Instead, the French moved to attack the cities of Flanders and so cut off our vital allies not just from Calais but from the entire war and that was where they had focused ever since.

My men claimed it was not for strategic reasons but because they were afraid of us and demoralised with their endless failures whenever the French went up against us.

Either way, Calais remained in English hands and so we crossed to there.

The town was a hive of activity and regular shipments brought a steady supply of timber, building stone and lime so that construction and repair could continue apace. What is more, bows and arrows were stocked in great abundance, as were spears and lances. Carts and wagons were unloaded in pieces, and oxen were driven down narrow gangplanks with much bellowing and cursing. A significant fraction of it all was organised by Stephen and the merchants who operated on his behalf. He was making a great deal of profit from the venture, while also fulfilling the King's strategic objectives.

And smuggling an entire company over in amongst it all.

I claimed to all who questioned me that we were on royal business and presented papers forged by Stephen and Eva as proof. The letters and their forged seals worked and we were soon through the gates heading south into France.

As the French forces were concentrated in the great estates around Paris and the armies were in Flanders to the east, we instead went west into Normandy.

My goal initially was to head for Brittany where I and many of my men knew the land, the towns and the people. Also, English allies held almost the entire coastal area and so there were many places we could be welcomed. And it was a place that we could always fall back to, should we need to do so.

Indeed, one of the King's Lieutenants in Brittany was Sir Thomas Dagworth, a man who we had fought with and who I hoped could be relied upon to provide me shelter and support. Of course, should he decide otherwise then I would most likely be driven from the duchy altogether. I hoped that would not be the case. In my favour was the fact that Dagworth had only about five hundred men in total and so my force of veterans would surely be most welcome, even if I insisted that I would remain independent of his command.

And I would most certainly insist so.

We made excellent time travelling across country and almost all local forces who came out to us simply stood and watched us go by. We set no fires and raided no homes. Well, few enough. I assured my men that there would be plenty of time for that. We made it in under three weeks and were in a very presentable condition when we came to Dagworth's castle.

Dagworth was originally from a village called Bradwell in the northern part of the county of Essex in England, which was not far from my manors in Suffolk and where many of the men in my company were from. I hoped the fact that they hailed from the same region of England would encourage him to welcome us as comrades.

Thankfully, he was surprised but pleased that we had joined him. He had fewer than three hundred men at arms and two hundred archers which was hardly enough to control the surrounding area, let alone impose his will on the entire Duchy of Brittany, which was larger than the entire country of Wales and had a population of hundreds of thousands.

Dagworth welcomed me to his table, along with Walt, and fed us very well indeed. The rest of my men crowded amongst the garrison down in the hall and grew increasingly raucous as the beer flowed.

"You are doing well, I see," I said after the fourth course of meats and sitting back to drink my wine.

Some of his men grinned and said that was very true but Dagworth grimaced.

"I do as well as I can. The damned *routiers* take and take from the country so that many of the common folk suffer even more from the soldiers than they did from the pestilence."

"Surely not. How bad has it become?"

Dagworth pressed his lips together, glancing at his men. Some shrugged, others grinned, and Dagworth nodded.

"Most of the inland castles were taken by the various captains that we have out of necessity employed. Many of them, unfortunately, are led by and made up of German, Dutch and Flemish mercenaries. I do not mind admitting to you, Richard, that I have very little control over them. Even more so than when you were here last, they increasingly act like little kings, lording it over the common folk of the towns they occupy and the lands about them. They are all ransoming the districts that they control. In return for payments to the mercenary captains, the inhabitants are not too badly assaulted by the companies occupying their area and, if they are lucky, they are defended from the other captains in neighbouring districts and from the wandering bands that go from place to place."

"It at least sounds to be more formalised than when I was last here. Before Crecy."

Dagworth sighed. "Indeed. They are dug in like ticks. Each garrison captain has marked out his own ransomed district and informs those in surrounding districts. Where they fall into disagreement about the borders, it is the inhabitants that suffer but it has settled somewhat into stability."

Walt grunted. "Sounds like a good deal to me, sir. Our king ain't paying for the garrisons but we have loyal men keeping the castles for us all the same."

Dagworth nodded. "Except they are no longer kept for us so much as kept out of the hands of the French. And should King Philip or one of the Dukes decide to roust them out one by one, what could they do to resist? And as I do not pay them, I have no control over them. And the common folk suffer. Dear God, how they suffer. I wonder if there will be any remaining to rule over once the war is won."

Once the war is won.

The words, so often spoken, hung heavy over us all like a curse. When the captains and lords spoke them, it was with hope and expectation that Edward would someday be the King of France and her dominions and his loyal men would all be great lords, living in peace and abundance. When the common soldiers spoke the same words, it was said flippantly as if they knew that the good times of plunder and murder would never end.

Once the war is won, when Hell freezes over.

"With your permission, Sir Thomas, I should like to take a tour of these towns. Inspect their defences. Speak to the commanders of the companies."

Dagworth sat back, chewing on the roast leg of a heron. "If it were anyone else, Richard, I would laugh in his face. As it is you, I believe you might just be able to do it. But tell me, sir, why would you do this for me? Anyone of these rogues could turn on you."

"I seek a man. A particular knight who I saw at Crecy. A knight with a plain black banner, fighting for the French. No one knows who he is, where he is from or where he has gone, but I mean to find him and put an end to him."

"All this?" Dagworth said, gesturing out of the window at my company. "All this effort. This expense. For one man?"

"A knight, his squires and any who associate with him, yes indeed, sir. It is a matter of honour."

He nodded, slowly. "I will write you a letter, though I doubt it will open as many doors as you might hope."

I shrugged. "Any door I need open I shall break into pieces."

***

"He complains about the *routiers*," Walt said as we rode west, further into Brittany, "and yet he's robbing his own lands three ways from Sunday and all, ain't he?"

I had to agree with Walt that the people of Dagworth's lands seemed broken and destitute. Bridges were not being maintained and roads were washed out all over. The thatch on houses was rotten and sagging, as if they lacked the will or the wealth to repair their own homes. Fields were fallow and meadows grew wild with no livestock to eat it.

"The English," Thomas pronounced grandly, "are excellent at making themselves rich from others' misfortune."

Rob laughed at him. "It's us that's making the misfortune, too, Tom."

That brought a cheer from the others and Thomas and Hugh scowled at them. Neither was a Breton and yet they must have sympathised with the people of the duchy even more than I did.

Our destination was the fortress of Becherel in the northwest of the duchy, a castle under the command of Hugh Calveley and his band of *routiers*.

His men refused me entry.

"I come under the authority of Sir Thomas Dagworth," I called up to the wall. At my side was Walt, Thomas, Hugh and Rob. The rest of the company held far back but within sight so that the men in the castle would know I was not attempting a ruse but also that I was not to be trifled with.

A few moments later came the shouted reply, along with a round of mocking laughter. "You can shove Dagworth's authority up your arse."

"When I get inside your walls," I said, "I am going to strike that man so hard he shall wake up in the infirmary pissing blood. Tell your master that Richard of Hawkedon is here."

The laughter faded into nothing and half an hour later the great doors were opened and Sir Hugh Calveley waved me in himself.

"Richard!" he cried. "What a delightful surprise."

"Sir Hugh," I replied. "Bring me that man."

His face coloured. "What man would that be?"

"You know what man."

"It was a jest, Richard. They did not know who you were. Thought you were one of Knolles' men come to bother us again."

"Bring me the man."

"Richard, I cannot—"

"A commoner cannot treat a knight with such disrespect and avoid punishment, can he, Hugh?"

"Why go to such trouble over a bloody archer?"

"Trouble? There will only be trouble if you deny me."

He nodded to one of his men who went away into the base of the tower and a few moments later a big man with a ratty face came stumbling out. He had the massive shoulders of an archer and was a veteran of perhaps forty-five.

"What do you say to Sir Richard, Esmond?"

Esmond looked down. "Beg your pardon, my lord."

I walked slowly toward him and he began edging away until the man-at-arms behind shoved him on the back. "Are you ready to receive a blow that will rupture your bowels?" I placed my hand on his shoulder and lowered my head. "Are you, man?"

He shook and nodded.

With a stomp of my foot, I thrust my fist toward his belly, shouting in his face. I stopped the blow before it connected but he fell back, crying out and tripping over his feet. He fell into a heap.

The courtyard erupted into laughter and Esmond was helped up, dusted off and led away while the others mocked him.

"Come on," Sir Hugh said, "let's get you fed and find out what the bloody Hell you are doing in my lands."

His table was not so well stocked as Dagworth's but he had an astonishing amount of fish, from the river and from the sea, as well as wading birds and fowl.

"All the fisherman in Dinard died," Sir Hugh said. "But more fisherman came." He pointed his dagger at me and waved the point around. "The lords all around complain that their peasants have died from the pestilence or say that we murdered them or starved them. But, mark me, Richard, mark me. There are always more peasants." He opened his arms. "And they come. They come from wherever the bloody Hell they come from. Like flies on a cow turd."

"Are you calling your lands a cow turd, Hugh?" I asked.

He scowled. "Why have you come, Richard? What do you mean to do with those men you have out there? You will never take this castle, you know that, surely? We outnumber you ten to one."

"More like three to one, Hugh, and those odds would not be enough to save you if that was my intention."

He scoffed but did not argue. "Why, then?"

"I seek a man. A knight who fought by Philip at Crecy. A knight with an all black banner."

Hugh shook his head. "And this knight is here?"

"He may be. What do you know of him?"

"Nothing. No knight I know of has a black banner. Who would have a black blazon, sir?"

"The heralds did not know him. None knows him. And yet he exists. He was there. Someone in France must know him."

"Then why not seek him in France?"

"Someone is helping him. Keeping him hidden. Or else he is a known knight who fought incognito to protect his identity. Who would do such a thing? What if it was a man who should have been fighting for England. Perhaps he was a Fleming? Or a Breton? Perhaps, God forbid, an Englishman."

Sir Hugh scowled. "I was not at Crecy."

I leaned forward. "Precisely, Hugh. Precisely."

His jaw dropped. Then he laughed, wiping a hand across his brow. "Come now, sir. Come. You cannot suspect I would fight against the King? Why would I do such a thing?"

I pursed my lips. "Who knows how the mind of a traitor works? But no, of course it could not be you, Calveley. You are as loyal as a..." I trailed off, leaving the unspoken word *dog* to fill the gap. "As loyal as any dutiful knight in the kingdom. All I ask is that you keep an eye out for word of the black banner. I will pay handsomely for any true word that leads me to him."

"Handsomely?" he said, looking me up and down. "Is that so?"

I sighed and took out a purse which I emptied into one hand. A cascade of sapphires, rubies and emeralds filled my palm. Hugh's eyes grew.

"While you and the other captains have been gathering men and castles these last few years, I have been gathering gems, gold and silver."

It was somewhat true but most of the gems I had taken from the grave of a Mongol lord a hundred years earlier on the other side of the world.

"I shall send word," Hugh said, licking his lips and nodding. "All my men will ask wherever we go."

I poured the gems carefully back into the purse. "I want only true word, now. There shall be no payment for false words and threads that lead to nothing."

"If he is here, we shall have him for you."

With one English captain in my pocket, I went looking for more.

***

We crossed back and forth across Brittany, sometimes raiding the lands of those *routiers* who denied us entry or tried to chase us off.

My men were good and I led them well.

Still, some men fell to wounds or sickness. Fair Simon took a scratch on the forearm in a scrap with some of Robert Knolles' men at a place called Gravelle down near the Loire. When he fell, he tumbled head first into a patch of boggy ground which was never good but the lads cleaned him up, cleaned and dressed the wound and we went on our way. He tried to hide it for a day but his sweating gave him away and when they pulled his arm from beneath his coat the stench was overwhelming.

"Am I going to die, lord?" he asked me.

"Yes. Say your prayers, lad. We will all be here with you when you go."

"Oh," he said, looking down. "That's good, then."

We lost Ralf Thorns in an ambush near Vannes when I stupidly split my forces in an attempt to surround an enemy who was not there. We all make mistakes but it was old Ralf who paid the price.

Adam Lamarsh came down with the flux and he emptied himself inside out between dawn and dusk one day on the banks of the Vilaine.

One by one, we lost archers and men-at-arms. One of the servants fled, looking to make for the coast. I ordered them to bring him back so I could talk some sense into the man but they brought him back dead. They protested that it was an accident and I accepted them at their word but I knew they had punished his disloyalty with death.

As the leaves turned to gold and yellow and brown in that first year, we tallied up nine dead.

Thomas was worried. "We are not yet beyond Brittany and yet we have lost so many. We must take on more men."

"Plenty of *routiers* about, sir," Walt said. "God knows, they would follow you."

"Men I do not know. Do not trust. I will take none on. We yet have enough to see off any trouble that comes our way."

"What about, you know, sir," Walt said, lowering his voice. "Giving some of the lads the old Gift, then?"

I scoffed. "Whenever the thought crosses my mind, I take one look at you and it puts the matter to rest."

He pursed his lips and nodded slowly. "Fair enough, sir. Fair enough."

In the second year, we lost thirteen more. Never a good number and it meant we were down from over fifty men to just thirty. With so few, there was less we could attempt and so less we could achieve.

"Would you not consider it now, sir?" Hugh asked me after we buried another archer beneath an old oak in northern Poitou. He lowered his voice as the other men trudged away from the grave. "Giving the common men the Gift?"

It was raining lightly. Our men were weary and wounded and needed somewhere to rest through the winter. We had to take a fortress and use that to wait out the bad weather but my men were hardly capable of defending themselves, let alone launching a ferocious attack on a walled town or tower.

"I thought you agreed with Thomas?"

Hugh nodded. "We should bring some men from the other companies into ours, yes. You say you would not trust them but we would watch each new man like a hawk. But also, sir, I think it would be a great boon to us if you would consider turning a few more men-at-arms, at least. There are so few left."

"Most of our archers fight as well with a sword or mace as any man-at-arms," I said. But my company suddenly appeared small and the men round-shouldered and tired. They could not keep up with the immortals. Still, they were savages at heart and once they were given the gift, I suspected I would have to fight to control them and some I would have to kill anyway.

"Find me a knight who has no family or future and I will consider him. Not these ruffians, Hugh."

My resolve lasted as long as it took for most of my remaining men to be slaughtered.

19

Immortal Company

WE ASSAULTED A SMALL fortified town under the command of a tough old French knight named Charles of Coussey who had three times as many men as I did and all of them veterans.

But I wanted Charles. I needed to take him. Rumours had circulated for months that he was murdering local girls but that was far from an uncommon occurrence for *routiers*. Only when word came from Sir Hugh Calveley that this Charles of Coussey was stealing young women from villages, marrying them and then murdering them before taking another, was I struck by the similarities to the vile Priskos.

"It could be him," I said to Thomas. "The black banner knight himself."

"Or one of his men," Thomas replied.

"We must take him."

It was late October in 1351 and I intended to take the town and fortress at Tiffauges, discover whether Sir Charles was the man we sought and then, either way, use the town for the winter.

I had but thirty men remaining and just twenty-four of them were fighters. Tiffauges was a small town but the fortress was far beyond our strength if we attempted any sort of frontal assault. The archers favoured drawing the enemy out and ambushing them but they had seventy men and would not send all out at once, leaving us with the rest within the walls being on high alert.

Walt wanted us to launch an attack on the walls during the dark of the night. He thought we could kill enough men in their beds before they could form against us. But they would be spread in houses throughout the little town, along with the poor townsfolk who suffered under the *routier* occupation.

"It would be chaos," I said to Walt.

He nodded, blank-faced, not seeing a problem.

After many days exploring the land all about, I came to a decision.

"The town is too well defended for us to take it. It is too large for us, anyway. We shall find somewhere else to overwinter. All we need is to take Sir Charles. If he is the knight we seek, we shall take revenge for John and our brothers. If not, we shall ransom him back to his men, if they will pay for him."

Thomas coughed. "What about justice for the women he has killed?"

"We are not here for them," I snapped.

He was a wily old knight, that was certain, and he was happy enough where he was, all tucked up safe in the town's keep, on the little hill looking down on the few houses and the church below. But his men had to come out to look for food and take tribute from the starving villages all around.

These men we took.

We took their horses, their food and their wine. We took their lives and their blood.

From Charles of Coussey's perspective, he had sent out a handful of men who did not return. Such things were common enough. Men desert for better lords all the time. So Coussey sent more riders in their stead but this time he sent fully half his force. Almost forty riders.

"This is madness," Thomas said as we watched their approach from the ridge in the woods two miles from town. "We cannot defeat so many."

"You and I could take that many all by ourselves," I said, turning from him.

But they were expecting an ambush in the woods. Of course they were. And they broke into three groups, the first riding along the road while the others came behind, separated by over a hundred yards.

"Should we call it off, sir?" Rob asked me. His men were concealed on both sides of the road, ready with their arrows.

"No," I said, though my heart raced at the thought of what was about to happen. "Bring down as many of the first group as you can then withdraw up the hill. We shall make a stand and take them as they come for us. They will give up before long and ride home to tell Sir Charles about us."

My complacency was going to cost my men dearly.

Our arrows flitted into the first group of riders. All eleven of them were hit with an arrow to either horse or man. But the survivors raced straight for us with cries of red murder in their throats and the other two groups came galloping to their companions' aid.

I did what I could to forestall them, as did Thomas, Hugh and Walt. But our enemies were so spread out between the trees that we could not reach and slay enough of them before the riders overtook us and ran down my fleeing archers. Stout and brave fellows that they were, they fought the mounted men with their bows, their swords, and even their bare hands. But many fell and no matter how many enemies I killed, they refused to flee from us. I killed man after man but I also saw my own men lying dead or crying out in agony and I wondered if I would have any men left to salvage from the utter disaster.

And then I saw him.

Up the hill, on a white horse, with his sword blade raised and visor up, roaring in fury and in victory.

It was Sir Charles de Coussey himself urging his men on from horseback in very fine armour and the most magnificent clothing. He was a big, burly fellow, gesturing theatrically. His fitted surcoat was a vivid yellow with a black cross emblazoned on it.

That was why the enemy were fighting with such uncommon ferocity. That was why my men were being slaughtered.

Their lord was amongst them.

He had been leading the third group of riders and had charged through the trees up the hill to the ridge to cut off my men and kill them all. Charles de Coussey was filled also with a ferocious energy and vigour and made an inspiring sight.

I was moving before I considered the bodyguard around him. I ran as though my armour was nothing, closing the distance in mere seconds and pushing through his men without attacking them.

A growl of rage grew in my throat and I speared my blade through the neck of de Coussey's horse and sawed it out, spilling the hot blood from the terrified beast. I yanked de Coussey from the saddle and stamped my foot on his face through the open visor. His nose crunched and I pushed my weight on him so that he could not rise.

His men came at me all at once and I fought them off for a few moments before Thomas, Hugh and Walt caught up with me and killed the bodyguards. The remaining enemies fled back through the wood toward the town and I let them go. Charles de Coussey was suffocating on his own blood but we got him upright and he coughed it out well enough while he was trussed up tight.

"Send to the servants beyond the ridge and have them bring up the horses," I said to Walt. "Thomas, Hugh. Let us find any man of us who yet lives."

"It is Rob, sir!" Hugh called a few moments later from just along the hill.

I went crashing through the undergrowth and found him on his back, coughing up blood all over Hugh. A broken lance point had taken him in the gut, front to back.

"We shall remove it," I said. "Hold him steady, Hugh."

Rob grimaced as he spoke. "No point. I'm done for."

"Yes," I replied, hurrying to remove the armour from my left arm. "You will die. But if you wish it, you can be reborn stronger than before."

He was confused and dying and did not understand, especially when we slid the lance from his guts, being careful to hold the wound tight so we did not rip him apart. In his confusion and agony, he followed our directions and drank down the blood that I gave him.

I poured it in and he drank and was turned.

So many more were close to death. I had a choice to make. Grant the gift of immortality to the dying remnants of my company or resign myself to failure. Recruiting new men who would be willing to follow me as the others had would be close to impossible and, even if I could, it would set me back months or years.

There was no time to hesitate.

I offered life to my strong men-at-arms Hal, Reginald, Osmund, and Watkyn, and the archer Randulf. They all took the chance, though they knew it to be blood magic and they barely comprehended what they were agreeing to. Ultimately, though, it was as stark and simple a choice as the one I faced in whether to offer it. Few men, when offered life over death, ask to first see the terms.

We were safe enough in the darkness of those woods but it was a tense night, crouched in the undergrowth and tending to my poor soldiers as they lay in the leaf litter. It took a long time to turn so many but they all lived to see the dawn, other than poor Reg, who died writhing in agony after drinking my blood. For some men, the Gift simply does not take.

When the surviving archers understood what had happened to their brothers, they each wanted to join them in immortality. With those men, healthy as they were, I took the time to explain that they would be slaves to blood and that their chance for ordinary life would be over.

They wanted it anyway though I could see they were not considering the consequences. And because I needed them, I cursed them also by granting them the Gift of immortality. So the archers Osbert, Jake, Lambert, and Stan were soon welcomed into the brotherhood of the blood.

The six remaining servants I would not change because my men needed their blood to drink and, in fact, I required more of them just so I would have enough for the bloodletting needed to keep my men thriving.

I had lost fourteen men in the failed ambush, including some of my best. Men who had followed me for years. Men like Nicholas Gedding, who would sing ditties to his bow to make his mates laugh. And Roger Russet the sturdy man-at-arms who never said much but always did what he said he would do. Gerald Crowfield, another one who had been a stocky labourer when I found him but who had turned into a damned savage soldier after a few months in the crucible that was Brittany. And Fred and Digger Blackthorpe, brothers who had died protecting each other.

It was a disaster that would have been the end of most *routier* leaders. What soldiers would follow a lord so incompetent? But my company was not dead. I had lost so much but I had gained eight more immortals. Three men-at-arms and five archers.

These along with Walt, Thomas, and Hugh, made for a force equal in effective strength to a mortal one of perhaps three or four times its size. There were few companies in France capable of withstanding a dozen veteran immortals.

After the disastrous ambush, we had dragged Sir Charles de Coussey with us and although much of the time I had his head covered by a sack, I had not bothered to hide all of the bloodletting from him as I turned my men.

When, three days later and many miles away, I leaned him against an ash tree by a swollen river and removed his hood, he stared at me in horror. His eyes wide and wary and jittery.

"Yes," I said, smiling. "I am Satan himself. But I hear you are quite the murderer yourself, Charles." I wagged my finger at him.

He ground his teeth and glared but said nothing. Sweat ran down his face and his eyes seemed unfocused.

"Hungry are you, Charles?" I asked. "Thirsty? What a terrible host I am, not giving you water for so long. Dear me, and your nose is such a bloody mess it is a wonder you did not suffocate, sir. Here, watch me drink this wine." I slurped at it and smacked my lips. "Would you care for some?"

He nodded.

"What was that, Charles?"

"Yes." His voice was thick with his broken nose. "If you please."

"What a polite fellow you are." I had another sip. "Tell me, Charles. Are you the man I am looking for?"

He seemed to be somewhere between horrified and confused, which was understandable.

"What do you want?" he managed, blinking as the sweat ran into his eyes.

He did not look well at all and I nodded to Walt who crossed and gave Sir Charles a drink of water. He gulped it down, gasping. Thirst is a terrible thing and he was suffering mightily from it.

"All I want, Sir Charles, is to ask you some questions and then I shall ransom you back to your men. What do you think about that?"

He pursed his lips. "I know who you seek."

I raised my eyebrows. "Oh?"

"Everyone knows. You are Richard of Hawkedon and you seek a black armoured knight. You are offering a reward for him. I will tell you all I know in exchange for the wealth."

I laughed. "Your reward shall be that you will live. If your answers are true. If I think you are lying, I will gut you from hip to hip and leave you tied to that tree so you can watch the wild dogs eat your entrails. Now, what do you know?"

"The knight with the black banner. I saw him."

I shook my head. "I doubt that."

"It is the truth, sir. I saw him three years past, in Orleans, meeting with Jean de Clermont. He wore blackened armour, with a surcoat of a black field. His man held aloft a black banner also."

"Who was he? The black knight?"

"I know not. I swear it."

"Oh, you swear it? It must be true, then. Why were they meeting? Jean de Clermont is the lord of Chantilly and of Beaumont."

"De Clermont has been made a Marshal of France and he governs Poitou, the Saintonge, Angoumois, Périgord and Limousin for the new King John."

I whistled. "And the black knight was there? In armour? For the ceremony? What did he look like?"

"It was from afar, across the field. I did not see his face but they seemed to be on good terms, sir. On good terms. Jean de Clermont laughed at something the knight said. Other lords around me noted the knight and asked each other who he was but none there recognised him."

"What else can you tell me?"

De Coussey shifted in discomfort and looked like he was going to be sick. "Nothing. I beg your pardon but there is no more."

I watched him for a while. Thomas raised his eyebrows. Walt shrugged.

"I think I will kill you anyway," I said.

"Sir!" Thomas said. I went away with him a few paces. "Richard, you cannot kill him. You took him as your prisoner. He has given his word he would not flee. We have treated him very poorly already and we must not slay him."

"He is a murderer, Thomas. Even worse than I am. He kills women."

"It is nothing to do with him, Richard, nor his actions. To kill him would demean us. It would demean you. A chivalrous knight saves his own soul."

Walt was at my elbow. "Begging pardon, sirs. But the lads was all heart set on ransoming the bastard. Running low on coins, a bit."

"Very well, let us offer him back to his men. If they will have him."

His men did have him, though it was for a pittance as they swore they had not a penny more in the entire town. But Charles de Coussey seemed sick and dying when we handed him over outside his town and I did not expect him to live much longer so I did not feel too bad about it.

"What now?" Thomas asked.

"Now we must capture a Marshal of France, the governor of Poitou, the Saintonge, Angoumois, Périgord and Limousin. Jean de Clermont. For he has met the black knight, face to face."

Hugh looked to Thomas rather than me. "But does such a man not have a sizeable force?"

"Hundreds, perhaps," I said, lightly.

"Thousands," Thomas said. "Thousands of mounted men from the Loire to the Dordogne."

Walt looked around. "There's only a dozen of us, sir."

"A dozen immortals," I said.

"Even so, Richard, I do not think that we can make war with a Marshal of France."

"We shall not make war on him. We will burn his lands from the coast to the marshes. We will burn his forests and his vineyards. Destroy his villages and his mills."

"He will never come out himself."

"We will make him come. And then we will take him."

It was easier said than done.

***

I had my men make new banners and paint the design on what few shields we possessed.

"A field of red, with yellow flames beneath rising up to touch the white dagger in the centre of it all. We shall be the White Dagger Company. And we come from Hell. Let us let the people know."

Some were disquieted but most grinned like madmen at the thought of the fear it would instil in our enemies.

There was so much land to cover. We went from place to place, flying my banner, and causing what destruction we could. We took from the people and made ourselves rich, though we had to spend everything we took just to stay alive.

Local lords sent their men after us and some we killed and drank from, others we ran from. Because there was always the next village or valley to attack.

When things grew too difficult we travelled across to the next county or to the farthest reaches we could. Other times we went to ground or fell back into the chaos of Brittany.

The immortals were thrilled with their new strength and stamina. They wanted to slaughter every soul in France and make themselves kings. I needed the help of the steadier men to keep them in check and had to dominate a few with my own hand. I could depend utterly on Thomas, of course, and on Hugh who was ever the dutiful young squire even as he entered his sixties.

Getting the attention of such a great lord as Jean de Clermont was close to impossible. Especially as he was almost always in Paris. One year he spent in England and another year he spent near Calais, leading negotiations with the English. I was undecided on whether to chase him there or to continue on the path of destruction.

"The men do not wish to leave," I said to Thomas one winter. "They are revelling in their power, here in the Périgord."

I had taken an old fortress for my men and although it was cold and damp in places we sat by the crackling hearth fire and filled our bellies with warm, spiced wine.

Thomas watched the fire as he spoke. "You know you could order them to follow you. And they would. It is you who does not wish to leave."

"What are you saying?"

He looked at me. "You love this burning and looting."

"And you know its purpose."

Thomas rubbed his eyes. "You love it for its own sake."

"All I want is to find the black knight."

He sighed and looked to Heaven for a moment. "You are lost in it. You must find your way back to virtue."

I laughed. "You are mad, sir. You hang on to notions of chivalry. Do you not think that we are past that now?"

He stared at me, the fire flickering on the side of his face. He looked old. "I know you think you have gone beyond proper standards but we must hold on to our honour. It is not a line that one crosses but an ideal that one must always seek. We do this by following the code of honour that dictates our actions no matter how often we fall short."

"When I say that we are past chivalry, it is not only us that I speak of. You and I. Not us alone. How can you not see that the world has changed around us, Thomas? Where are the true knights, now? Who decides the battles? Brutes like Walt and archers like Rob. Mercenaries from Italy and massed levies from towns. The great lords seek earthly power. None care about crusades in the Holy Land. I tell you, there are no true knights left, Thomas. If there ever were any. It seemed as though, in my youth, that knights strove to achieve greatness for the glory of God and for their king. Now, they seek only to further their family name and consolidate power and wealth. It is all so base. Why should we alone hold ourselves to such ideals when no other does? By so doing we merely hobble ourselves while the monsters of the world have free reign."

"Perhaps all you say is true. But what other men do does not have to dictate your own actions. You can yet be virtuous. You can be chivalrous in war."

I shook my head as he spoke. "No, no. It is too late for all that, brother. There can be no chivalry in this war. It would not lead to victory and our oath to the Order of the White Dagger comes before all else."

"Then go to Calais! Find Clermont in the negotiations, charge in amongst the diplomats and cardinals and cut off his head. If you wanted to do it and cared nought for the consequences, none could stop you."

I looked away into the fire and Thomas scoffed.

"Precisely, sir," he said. "You are not so far gone as all that. You are a knight still in your heart and would not carry out such an act and call it victory."

I laughed, without humour. "Which is it, Thomas? You criticise me from both ends. Do I love pillage too much to be a knight or am I too virtuous to achieve victory? Make up your mind, sir."

"It is *you* that must make up your mind, sir. Will you have victory through honour? Or victory no matter the cost?" He bowed his head. "I will, of course, do as you command."

He left me alone to ponder it. Once, when I was a boy, I wanted only to be a knight. And then I wanted to fulfil the chivalric virtues through my actions. But over time, perhaps even before I had ever met Thomas, I had forgotten how to be courteous. I had grown arrogant and vain. And even then, I had not gone far enough to achieve the victories that I could have had if I had thrown off virtue entirely.

Virtue was all very well but perhaps it was more than I could afford when what I needed above all was victory.

King Edward had wanted victory and so he had thrown off knightly ideals on the battlefield. Using masses of archers instead of knights had led him to victory over the virtuous, chivalrous French.

Priskos my grandfather had conquered lands in ancient times before there were such notions as chivalry and Christian decency. He said that William would achieve greatness because he had thrown off the shackles of those very things.

Thomas was a knight from the days when it had still meant something. And so was I but I was also more than Thomas could ever be. I had the blood of heroes and conquerors in my veins. The blood of monsters and tyrants. Kings who had known victories that lived in legend.

"I will have victory, then," I said, speaking to the fire.

***

Four years, we burned those lands. Four, long, bloody years. We killed hundreds of men sent against us and still Jean de Clermont never came to deal with us directly. He was always with King John in Paris, or so we thought.

My men were a concern. They enjoyed the blood drinking and the slaughter of the men who tried to stop us, whether they were levies or mounted professionals. Rob and Walt managed to keep them in check but I fretted at times about what I had unleashed. Oft times in the night I would consider getting up and slaughtering them all rather than have them go on.

But I did not.

I needed them.

And I could not see much difference between them and me. If anything, I was worse because I had made them, I led them and I knew that it was not the honourable path in a way that they, as ignorant commoners, could not comprehend.

We wrought so much death and chaos that even the English in Gascony sent word that we were to be stopped. It was an order from Prince Edward himself, ruling over the many lords and factions of Gascony like he was already a king. There would be no safe haven in the south for us and I doubted whether I would have any lands in Suffolk to return to, if I ever succeeded in my quest.

By itself, it was not so much of a loss. But it meant that I would certainly never marry dear Cecilia, or any other lovely English woman for that matter. Not for a long time. I avoided seeking word of her but I got messages from Stephen and Eva every now and then, many months out of date but always Eva mentioned pointedly that Cecilia remained unmarried. I felt sorry for her. It happened with some women, who were more useful as a potential wife than an actual one and so were dangled until they grew too old and joined a convent.

It was such a terrible waste. Still, knowing as I did the lustful wantonness of the woman I expected she was enjoying the delights of the bedchamber while she yet could.

In 1355, we became trapped in the vast marshland in northern Poitou by a massive group of knights and spearmen. We had been surrounded and expertly pushed back into the boggy landscape close to the coast.

Jean de Clermont had not come himself but he had finally sent someone close to him named Rudolph de Rohan, a powerful lord who commanded de Clermont's troops and ruled over vast lands for his master the Marshal of France.

After so many years of practice, my men were as good as any could be at setting and springing ambushes. Those that had not the discipline for such work had long since been killed due to their own folly and so all that remained under me were cunning, strong-willed fellows. Despite being so heavily outnumbered, we remained confident that we would prevail. Indeed, we delighted at causing the enemy companies to dance to our tune.

The marshland was deceptive to men who had no direct experience of its fickle ways. There were dead men and dead horses down in the shallow waters, and hundreds of sheep and cows, too. Green grass would stretch for hundreds of yards in all directions but there might be just a single track through it capable of carrying a man and his mount.

We drew them in deeper and deeper until we ambushed our hunter Rudolph de Rohan. Two score of them charged my exposed archers only to ride headfirst into a sucking bog. As they abandoned their horses and struggled away on foot, our arrows killed them all.

Another dozen followed us into the darkness of a wood at sundown where my men charged their flank and speared them to death. When their friends came to retrieve the bodies, we killed them, too. From these men we took the best horses, the best weapons and armour, and we were soon the most well-equipped bandits in Christendom.

Rohan's men grew so dispirited that many began deserting their lord. Along with the casualties we inflicted, he had just forty-five soldiers when we finally surrounded and trapped his company.

Sheets of rain fell and soaked us thoroughly, washing the blood into the rivers and bog all around.

Though they fought to free themselves, we killed his men and made him watch while we drank the blood from his loyal captains and followers.

Lord de Rohan fought like the devil but we brought him down last of all and my men held him and revelled in his anguish. The lord was angry and he almost wept in despair as he witnessed us murdering and drinking his best men. He knew that his campaign against us had led to total and complete failure.

"So it is true," Rohan cried, disgusted and furious. "You are monsters. You are evil."

"Yes," I said. "And we mean to have your master, Clermont. You will lead us to him."

Rohan regained his composure. "No, no."

"I do not wish to *kill* him, Rohan," I said. "Merely to ask him questions about the black knight."

He blinked. "Who?"

I smiled and held my arms out. "You know who. The knight who wears black and bears a black banner. Your master Clermont has met with him, so I am told. I would so dearly love to meet him, also."

Rohan looked between me and Thomas and the others. "You are *friends* of the black knight?"

I was confused. "If he were my friend, I would know where he is."

Rohan frowned, looking around before staring at the ground at my feet. "I know of the black knight. He is evil. Like you. He drinks the blood of men. Like you."

"What did you say?"

Rohan took a deep breath before answering. "The black knight. He drinks the blood of his enemies. But you know that, do you not? You are all the same. All of you? Even you, sir?"

He had not seen me drink blood but I ignored his probing question.

"You know of him. So what is his name?" I said.

Rohan shook his head. "No one knows."

"De Clermont knows."

Rohan shrugged as best he could with my men holding him. "Perhaps. He is in Paris."

"Why is he in Paris?" I said. "Is he helping King John to assemble the army of France?"

Rohan hesitated and I knew it was true. "You will never reach him."

"I will kill the black banner knight and all of his men, no matter how far they are from me today, nor how well protected."

Rohan laughed bitterly but I did not understand why until later.

"Have you seen the black knight with your own eyes?" I asked.

"From afar."

I looked at Thomas. "Why is it always from afar?"

"He was meeting with the Dauphin." Rohan sneered. "I was not allowed near, of course."

Thomas and I exchange a puzzled look. "He was meeting with the prince? When was this? What year did you see him? Do you mean the new King John of France?"

He shook his head. "The prince who is the son of John. The young Charles, the Dauphin of Viennois, who will be John's successor."

"But he is just a boy."

"He is seventeen or eighteen years old," Rohan said. "And already a bright man. That is, so they say."

"I hear," Thomas said, "that the boy prince is a weakling. Pale, sickly, and strangely proportioned."

De Rohan paused but then nodded. "He is that, also."

"Who is the black knight, Rohan?" I asked. "What is his name?"

"I swear on all that is holy, I know not."

I stared at Rohan, unsure whether to torture him or not.

"We should let him go," Thomas said. "It would be the chivalrous thing to do."

"What is that to me?" I replied. "I think I shall cut him to pieces and scatter him in the bogs."

"Please," Rohan said. "Please, no. I have great wealth. Ransom me and you will be rich. All of you will be made rich, if you ransom me."

"We do not need your money," I said and saw how many of my men shot me hostile looks. "But I shall let you go. Find your master Clermont in Paris and tell him that I am coming for him. Tell him that nothing will stop me."

He scoffed but said that he would relay my message.

"And Rohan?" I said before we sent him off. "If I ever see you again, I shall kill you."

He laughed as he rode away.

We broke out of our encirclement and headed east for a time to get away from the mass of men sent to catch us. But we ran into more troops, and more. It seemed as though all of France was up in arms.

"Something significant is happening," I said to my men. "Something we have not seen for years. It is true. It can no longer be denied. France is going to war."

"Where?" Hugh asked. "Calais again?"

"They are gathering south of Paris. Garrisons are being strengthened in the south and west. There can be only one place. They mean to invade Gascony and to drive out the English once and for all."

"What do we do?" Thomas asked. "If Clermont and the black banner knight are with King John and with the Dauphin, they will be surrounded by an army. How do we get through that?"

"I must get myself captured by the English," I said. "Immediately."

2 0

The Prince's Campaign

IN EARLY DECEMBER 1355 the Prince of Wales called the leaders of his army to the fortress of la Reole overlooking the Garonne. It was Englishmen almost to a man but a handful of the best of the Gascons were also invited. Men who had fought with us for years and had neglected their own lands and lives to fight almost constantly for English interests. Proper soldiers, like the Captal de Buch, Auger de Montaut the Lord of Mussidan and Elie de Pommiers.

Although, most of the other Gascons were tucked up nice and warm in their homes and cuddled up to their wives or a soft servant girl, the bastards.

It was exceedingly cold when I walked up to the gates of the town of la Reole in my best clothes and spoke to the sergeants on the gate.

"My name is Richard of Hawkedon and the Prince has ordered me captured. And that is well because I would very much like to speak with him about an important matter." They gaped at me, their faces pale and lips blue from the cold. "It is a matter of considerable urgency, my good fellows."

The men looked at each other. "You what, sir?"

"I am the captain of the White Dagger Company. You may have heard of us?"

They held me in a small, cold room in the fortress of la Reole for three days without contact with any of my men or servants. Although I was fed and given wine, they did not provide me with a servant of any sort and it was quite clear that I was being treated as a prisoner, whatever my legal status might have been. Not that anyone would have cared to consider the law as far as I was concerned. In Gascony, the Prince of Wales' will was all the law any man would know.

I was brought into his presence eventually and they did me the courtesy of removing my chains and allowing me to wash. Still, my best tunic was filthy and threadbare and I am sure I looked quite the ruffian to the Prince when he looked up at me from the table at the top of the hall.

Their recent meal had been cleared away, though the smell of it yet filled the air and the tablecloth remained in place while the wine still flowed freely.

At the Prince's side were the Earls of Salisbury, Oxford and my own lord Robert Ufford the Earl of Suffolk, all scowling and casting disapproving looks. The Gascon lord Jean de Grailly, known as the Captal de Buch, stood with the other prominent Gascons still loyal to the English. Sir John Chandos stood to one side trying to keep the smile off his face.

With horror, I saw that Sir Humphrey Ingham, my dear Cecilia's brother was also in attendance. His glare radiated something between disgust and rage.

I smiled at him before turning back to the Prince.

"Your Grace," I said brightly as I was acknowledged, "my lords! What a pleasure it is to see you all here and all so hale and hearty at that. It has been far too long since I have seen you all."

A couple of them shook their heads while others turned to the Prince.

He scratched at his cheek while he regarded me. The young Edward truly did look well and I was pleased to see how he had continued to grow into a well-made man with all the stature and presence of any of his illustrious ancestors. If anything, he was taller even than his father. It was not hard to see the Lionheart in him, and of course he was every inch the Longshanks.

"What am I going to do with you, Richard?" he asked, sighing.

And, I noted, he was every bit as arrogant and condescending as those very same forefathers.

"Do with me, Your Grace?" I asked, pretending to be as innocent and guileless as a newborn lamb. "Why, I would expect that you might use me and my men in your imminent attacks into Languedoc."

They began to splutter in outrage until the Prince waved them into silence.

"What makes you think I mean to move now?" he asked, speaking mildly.

Because I have been doing this since before your great-grandfather was squeezed from the royal nethers, boy. I thought the words but did not speak them, though the temptation was great.

"Forgive me, Your Grace. I have been everywhere in France over the last few years and I have heard and seen a great deal. For instance, I have heard how the leading men of France are urging King John to strike back at their enemies in Normandy and Picardy and also down here in Gascony. It is no secret that the nobles feel dishonoured that the French Crown has been pushed back on all fronts and the lords wanted their king to throw back King Edward from Picardy and also smash you here in Gascony. And although King John continues to hesitate to commit himself, they insist that he take decisive action. As we speak, they are now raising an enormous sum through taxes which they will use to raise the King's army."

"What does all that have to with anything?" Salisbury asked, scowling.

A handsome man with a big nose, he was just a year or two older than the Prince but through his military competence had risen to become one of the most trusted English commanders. I had fought with his father, the old earl, when this Salisbury was just a boy but the man before me was one of the new generation that was far from impressed by my earlier exploits. I had stood near to the King as he knighted the eighteen-year-old Salisbury along with the Prince and a few others after we landed in France before Crecy. But I was swiftly realising that meant nothing to the new men.

"It is in the air, sir," I replied.

Their faces turned to a sea of frowns.

"What in God's name are you blathering about?" Sir Humphrey Ingham spluttered.

I lifted my arms. "War, my lord." I looked at each of them in turn. "I can smell it. I can taste it. It is all around us. It fills the air from Paris to the Périgord and every man, woman and child there knows that the war proper will be rising up just as soon as the French can muster their huge numbers of men from all the regions of the country. Even now, they are coming in, mounted and on foot. In dozens and hundreds." I smiled at them. "And of course, here you all are, my lords. The finest fighting men in all England, all gathered here in this one place. Why? Are you here to celebrate Christmas together?"

I got a few smiles from that but the Prince fixed me with a dark look.

"Richard, speak plainly, will you." My lord the Earl of Suffolk spoke up. "Are the French prepared to defend an assault from Gascony?"

"No, my lord," I said. "They are preparing to invade Gascony."

"Nonsense," Salisbury said, turning to the Prince. "We would have heard about this."

"My men have taken many messengers in the last few weeks, most heading south from Paris, and we questioned them quite vigorously. The French know, sirs, that Lancaster has summoned men to muster at Southampton after winter, with horse and equipment, ready to attack Brittany in the spring, as soon as the weather turns. They know also, that a second fleet is intending to sail from Plymouth to here, bringing supplies and more men to reinforce you."

"Good God," Suffolk said, raising his voice above the growing muttering. "Their agents have improved."

"If it is true," Ingham growled.

"And yet," I said, quickly before their attention wandered. "And yet, they do not suspect you plan to strike against *them* before spring."

"Who says we plan such a thing?" Salisbury asked.

I shrugged. "If you are not, then you damned well should be. The towns are well stocked and under-garrisoned. It will be spring or even summer before France's grand army can be brought to bear on you. If you divide your forces into three or four, each army will be large enough to raid at will. Even to take possession of many places, if you are willing to garrison them. If your armies remain close enough that, if threatened by a royal army of the French, you can withdraw and form together at one of a number of prearranged places."

They looked at me without speaking and I knew that I had either spoken their own plan to them or else I had outlined a better one. Either way, they seemed quietly impressed.

"He is yours, by law, Robert," the Prince said to the Earl of Suffolk. "What would you have us do with him?"

Suffolk bowed. "He may be my man by law," he said, glancing at me, "but we all know that he was only ever your father's man, Your Grace. Whatever crimes he may or may not have committed these last few years, I believe that the King has looked the other way in greater crimes, over the decades since he gained the Crown."

"Decades, yes," the Prince said, turning to look at me with narrowed eyes. "How is it that you continue to avoid the ravages of time, sir? Since I was a child, there has been talk where you are concerned of dark things indeed, though I shall not speak them."

"I shall," said Salisbury, looking down his fat nose at me. "I shall damned well speak them, if you will pardon me, Your Grace. It is witchcraft that is spoken of, when men speak Sir Richard's name. Witchcraft, blood magic, sorcery and demon-worship."

For a moment I considered remarking that it was cuckoldry that was spoken of when men spoke Salisbury's name, on account that his first wife had secretly married another before she married him. But I reflected that it was probably best not to mention it.

"I made no pact with the Devil," I said.

"You will wait to be asked a question before speaking again," the Prince said, growing angry.

The meeting was getting away from me once again. What could I do but bow and stay silent?

"My father always told me that I could rely on you, Sir Richard," the Prince said. "No matter how strange you are. No matter how violent your tendencies and how absurdly old-fashioned your manner of speech and style of clothing are, I could always rely on you to get the necessary work done when it comes to matters of war."

"He is a wise man, Your Grace."

"Perhaps he is," the Prince said, "or perhaps he *was*. Unfortunately for you, he is not here to protect you this time." He turned to his sergeants and gestured at me. "Take this man and lock him up until we are well gone from this place."

I forced myself into stillness as three armed soldiers moved to surround me. To resist might mean my death but even if it did not, it would be the end of me in the eyes of the lords of England.

Suffolk cleared his throat and I was pleased to see that he had remembered he was my lord. "What about his men, Your Grace?" he said.

"His men?"

"A score or so of them," Sir Humphrey Ingham said. "Brutes, the lot of them. The murderers and thieves who have slaughtered their way back and forth across this land for years. They must be taken, too, Your Grace."

"Must they, indeed?" the Prince said.

"They have slaughtered their way through the King's enemies, sir," Suffolk countered.

"And so have blackened the King's name," Sir Humphrey replied, sharply. "Their deeds reflect badly upon the English amongst our allies here in Gascony and in France and they should suffer the consequences."

The Prince raised his chin. "What would they be, Sir Humphrey?"

"That is not for me to say, Your Grace. But if it were, I would hang the lot of them, strike off their heads and stick them on pikes above the walls of Bordeaux."

"A waste, Your Grace," Suffolk said, "of their considerable talents and experience. We could use men such as they. Even a score of them."

"I am sure you are right, Suffolk, but I am yet inclined to hang them."

I held my tongue but glared at my lord.

Suffolk bowed. "Many of them are from my lands, Your Grace. Let me take them on. If they put a foot wrong, they shall hang."

"Fine, fine. If you can find Hawkedon's men, you may use them." The Prince gestured at me. "But I will have none of your mischief making, Sir Richard. You have caused enough havoc on your own. Take him away."

I could have fought my way free, perhaps. But to do so would have involved killing Englishmen and perhaps even a great lord or two. And then I would have truly been an outlaw. Any Englishman who saw me could have killed me and indeed they would have sent a large number of soldiers to hunt me down. It was trouble I wished to avoid.

So instead I bowed to the Prince and wished the lords well before I was escorted away from the hall by the sergeants. Suffolk caught my eye and winked, which was encouraging but I also saw Sir Humphrey's dark looks. He knew, I am sure, that his sister loved me and so Humphrey rejoiced at seeing me disgraced.

Far from the hall, the sergeants courteously asked me to step inside a small room above the armoury on the outside of the eastern wall and then slammed the door behind me.

I have been in worse prisons than the chamber they locked me inside. There was a straw mattress and I even had a slit window with which to look out at the men leaving over the next few days. While I waited, I fretted about my men. Thomas would lead them well, of that I had no doubt, but he was not like them. He did not understand how they thought and if they were pressed hard then I wondered if they would follow his commands.

Would they continue to respect the bloodletting schedule I had established? Or would they demand ever more from the servants? If they followed my orders then Walt and Rob would support Thomas and together they would control the others and all would be well.

Surely, they would be quick enough and wily enough to evade any men sent after them. Even though I had faith in them and their abilities, still I watched from the window and listened at all hours, fearing to witness them being dragged into the fortress to face justice.

On the third day, the Prince left. It was with rather more fanfare and general fuss than most nobles might but it was concluded efficiently and when the last of his long train of servants and soldiers had peeled away, I knew it was time for me to leave.

When the old man opened my door later that day with a big cup of wine and a loaf of bread, I stood to receive him. He was as wrinkled as a decrepit shoe and lame, dragging one foot from an old injury but he had a way about him that suggested he had once been a fighting man.

"Step back, sir," he said, as he had said before. "Stand to the window, sir, if you please." He pulled the door all the way open and stepped inside. "Go on, sir, if you want your wine, sir."

This time, however, I did not follow his instructions.

"I am afraid, sir," I said "that I shall be leaving now."

He looked alarmed and a darkness descended across his face. I had caught a glimpse of the man he used to be.

"We got guards. *Guards*. Soldiers on the walls, porters on the gates. You ain't getting out, sir. Now, what say you just move to the window and I'll not tell the steward nothing?"

"Do you enjoy your work, man?" I asked him.

"Can't fight no more," he said, shrugging. "Ain't got no family. Better here than dead in a ditch, sir."

"I am curious," I said, sliding slowly forward while keeping a reasonable tone, "about whether you can still ride well?"

"Ride?" he asked, confused.

I slid forward while smiling and holding my arms out.

"I could use a man like you. A trustworthy older man who has seen his share of action. You could help steady my wilder ones."

He frowned. "But I'm the assistant to the head steward of—"

All of a sudden, he noticed how close I was and he sucked down a huge gulp of air, ready to cry out for help.

My fist connected just under his ear as he turned. I intended to silence him but he collapsed like a sack of mud and his skull bounced hard on the stone floor. I considered tearing his neck open and drinking him dry. But that would have been most unchivalrous. And I thought I could probably do without his aged blood.

Taking the keys on his belt, I locked him in the room and crept carefully to the stairwell. I could have fought my way out, charging from guard to guard, knocking each on his arse. But sometimes, a man simply has to brass it out. I straightened up, brushed myself off and strode down the stairs like I was about official business.

It was clear that the Prince had not been committed to keeping me locked up for long. Perhaps Suffolk, before he left, had advised the garrison to stay away from me. Whatever the reason, I was not accosted. I nodded to servants and called out good day to the soldiers

I saw. A few frowned, possibly unsure of who I was, but I simply waved and smiled and nodded my way to the stables. I ordered a boy to prepare a horse and he jumped to it quite smartly. Mounted, I rode out through both gates and crossed the bridge out into the country with the farewells of the bemused porters in my ears.

I rode to find my company. I hoped that they had not turned into wild beasts without me.

We had a grand English raid to join.

***

When I found my company at our agreed meeting place two days later, they were in a state of high agitation.

We stood in a wooded hollow at the edge of a boggy field in the flood plain of the Garonne. It was very cold and they were irritable and hungry from waiting so long for me.

"Suffolk's men have been searching the valley for us," Walt said, glancing at Thomas. "Some of our lads want to kill the soldiers, sir. Have a bit of a drink of them, like."

Hugh edged closer and lowered his voice. "The brutes would not listen to reason, Sir Richard."

Thomas held his chin up. "I explained that you would prefer them not to."

I clapped him on the arm. "I am sure that you had to explain it at length. Well done, sir."

He nodded.

"My lord the Earl of Suffolk," I told them all, raising my voice, "has been given leave by the Prince to take us under his command."

They grumbled and cursed but I held my hand up before continuing.

"The Prince's armies are to undertake a series of raids, all along the border. There will be plunder like you would not believe. We will follow Suffolk's contingent and keep our heads down. I will take no orders, not from the Earl of Suffolk, and not even from the Prince himself. Not unless they are orders that suit me and suit our search."

This they cheered and I could see how their faces flushed with the prospect of blood and riches.

"But mark me well, you men." I waited until their faces dropped and they fell silent. "Mark me that my orders to you shall be obeyed. Every one, without delay or question. The English and the Gascons are off limits. We shall have plunder and, in time, we shall have a battle. But what we need above all is to bring the black knight to us. Wherever we meet him, be it in siege or in skirmish or in open battle, we shall find him and take revenge. That is why we are here. That is the only reason we are here. If any of you forget that, I shall have no more use for you. Do you understand me?"

They swore that they did and I took them at their word.

We joined the great raid.

There were over two thousand English soldiers, all told, and a few hundred Gascons. These men were divided between the various leaders and the leaders assigned planned routes for the march. Salisbury made for Sainte-Foy on the Dordogne River. Prince Edward made his headquarters at Libourne along with Chandos and Ingham. The Earl of Suffolk was directed to Saint-Emilion and my company followed.

From places of strength, each commander sent raiding companies outward as they advanced, to widen the frontiers of the destruction and to pull more lands into what was effectively English dominion. The poor French on the Gascon border had never known an assault like it.

Our columns pushed eastward into the Agenais. Warwick invaded the Lot Valley and took fortified monasteries and important bridges. A force led by Chandos and Ingham marched right up the Garonne and captured forts and castles all along the valley. The largest contingent was led by Suffolk, Oxford and Salisbury. Charging along the fertile and wealthy Dordogne we stormed fortresses in the barony of Turenne, taking Souillac and Beaulieu and many more.

It was ideal land for those who could fight like *routiers* and after the main forces moved on, that land became infested with bandits for almost two years.

Through it all, my company kept apart from the mortal men, making camp away from the others and keeping to ourselves. And when it was time to fight, we did as we wished, taking a village or a fortress whether another group had claimed it first or not.

The soldiers under Suffolk learned to keep away from us.

For a time, our detachment made as if we were going to assault the great town of Poitiers but then we swung south away from it, rode like the devil and assaulted the walls of Perigueux during the dark of the night. While we held the town, the French reinforced the castle and held it, so that both sides warred unceasingly and the townsfolk, caught in between, suffered greatly from the arrows, fire, and fury.

All of the great French lords of the border regions, whose duty it was to protect their people from the aggression of the English and Gascons, did nothing. The cowards cried that they could not act against us until King John's mighty army, yet assembling at Paris, arrived in the southwest.

What weakness they displayed. What a betrayal of their obligations. It would have been far better for their people and the lords' immortal souls if they had fought and died.

"What is the point of a lord saving his own life," Thomas asked me, "if he does not do his duty?"

Our assaults had taken eleven towns and seventeen castles in just a few weeks. It was nothing, perhaps, compared to the vastness of all France but still the local lords saw who was strong and who was weak. The Prince sent a stream of messages and bribes to the lords of the bordering regions until by spring a number of them transferred their allegiance from John King of France to Edward Lord of Gascony and future King of England. These lords brought almost fifty more towns and castles under English authority.

Prince Edward's successes in turn encouraged King Edward back in London to prepare his own invasion force so that he could assault from the north while the Prince of Wales attacked from the south. The Duke of Lancaster prepared for an invasion of Brittany.

The freezing weather finally passed and, in April, a detachment including my company raided deep in Quercy and laid siege to the fortified village of Fons and its royal garrison, and to the massive fortress of Cardaillac.

I recalled the name and realised it had once belonged to a knight named Bertrand I had travelled with from Constantinople to Karakorum. Sir Bertrand had been turned by William into an immortal and I had killed him in the entrance hall to a house in Baghdad. A sordid, low death for a mean bastard of a knight. And then the descendants of his cousins ruled Cardaillac, high on its cliff, until we came and assaulted it without warning. The locals put up a spirited defence but their spirit was not enough and we killed them almost to a man, ransoming the few survivors off to their families.

Local order collapsed following the raids and the country all about fell to banditry. The land there was so rich with crops and vineyards, it was as close to an Eden as one can get outside of England. Robbing the country blind and burning what could not be taken was as disgusting as it was delightful. Captain after captain peeled off from our main army and began taking places of their own while our companies raided deeper and deeper.

The locals despaired. Our soldiers were become depraved through decades of war and they, surrounded by abundance and safety until then, were like innocent lambs to the slaughter.

The southern parts of Poitou fell entirely into English and Gascon hands and the cities that remained free, like Poitiers itself and the ancient castle of Lusignan, turned inward to shore up their own defence and abandoned the other cities to their fate. And so, with France in great disunity, we picked them off one by one.

My own company even rode through the dilapidated walls of Poitiers and seized goods and men, including the Mayor of Poitiers himself who we stole away and then ransomed. It was so daring that we deserved everlasting fame for the act but the land was in such chaos, such an orgy of theft and destruction, that it was lost amongst a thousand other stories.

Still, we knew through it all that the French would come eventually. That there would be a reckoning for all the destruction. That fact led it all an even greater sense of urgency and madness.

All the while, in the north, the French army grew.

King John had summoned all those lords holding noble fiefs to join the army with a retinue and equipment appropriate to their status. The same was commanded from the towns who had to supply equipped infantry and crossbowmen.

Lancaster gathered an army of two-and-a-half thousand in Normandy from the garrisons of Brittany. It was a terribly small army but they were all veterans, all were mounted and two-thirds of them were our savage, brilliant archers. Moving swiftly, they plundered great riches in Normandy, took thousands of fine horses, and caused havoc before withdrawing for safety. King John offered battle and Lancaster declined, for his job had been to draw the French to him and in this, he had succeeded.

While in the southwest, our main army moved north toward the Loire. The Prince unfurled his great banner, quartered in red and blue with the arms of England of France.

And we began to burn.

We assaulted and looted abbeys. We crept across the county of La Marche like a plague, sacking town after town in the lands owned by the great Bourbon family. Soon, we crossed the River Creuse at Argenton and again the crossing was uncontested by the French.

"Where are they?" men asked each other.

"Do not ask," others said. "Make yourself rich while you can."

All the men knew that the French could easily outnumber our small army by two or three or more times and not even our veteran soldiers thought we could stand against that so deep into French territory. We were in the heart of France and could not run for the sea like we had always had before in Normandy and Brittany.

The army destroyed the town of Issoudun so thoroughly that much of it remained uninhabited for years after we were done with it. The small garrison sat in the keep and watched us from the walls. We did not bother them and they left us to it.

"They are *cowards*," Hugh said, with uncharacteristic venom. "They should come out and fight."

"They would die," Rob said, gesturing at the men on the walls. "And for what? For this little town?"

"Even so," Hugh said. "It would be the honourable thing to do."

"They are not knights, Hugh," Thomas said, softly.

"Even if they were," Walt said. "It'd be a stupid bloody knight who charges into this lot. That be a glorious death, Hugh? To be hacked apart by the sons of tanners and labourers?"

What could Hugh say? His sense of honour was offended every day by the sight of so many Englishmen destroying his beloved country. It was hard on both Hugh and Thomas but the older man had the strength of character to find some level of personal accommodation with the world as it was.

The French had received a fleet of galleys from Aragon and so King Edward found himself suddenly unable to cross to France and join up with the Prince. Instead, Lancaster was ordered to take his two thousand veterans south from Normandy to meet us in September.

Joining the two armies together was critical and yet it seemed to many of us to be impossible.

"Do you truly believe," Thomas asked me, "that Lancaster can lead so many men across two hundred miles of hostile country and make a rendezvous without being trapped and destroyed?"

"Only time will tell," I said, though I doubted it also.

We were watched and followed, day and night, by French scouts. The mounted men

198

were always watching from every horizon, relaying our movements and actions back to the French.

"Want us to kill them, sir?" Walt asked.

"Good God, no.

"They'll tell old King John where we be at."

I pinched my eyes and cursed the stupidity of the common man.

"We *want* them to see us, Walt. We want them to see how few we are, how spread out we are, how much loot we are weighted down with. We want the French to come. We need the King to bring the Dauphin and the other great lords so that the black knight comes with them."

"Right you are, sir." Walt lifted a hand and gave them a friendly wave.

They turned and galloped away in panic.

The local lords assembled their forces but still they kept away from us, preferring to hide on the other side of the Loire and wait for King John to bring enough proper soldiers from the rest of his lands to crush us.

And, finally, praise God, he was coming.

Our men reached the River Cher and put every building to the torch for a distance of twenty miles in all directions. The country burned.

Chandos and Ingham took a force to Aubigny where they clashed with a group of eighty French men-at-arms. The fighting was hard but the French were defeated, many captured and the rest driven off. Irritatingly, Humphrey Ingham won great plaudits from his skill and bravery in the sordid little scrap.

The Loire thereabouts was flat and boggy and the trees were of willow and alder on the higher patches of land among the endless reedbeds. After all the rain that summer the river was enormous. It was wide, deep and fast flowing and could not be forded.

We found that there was no way across.

The main body of our army came up behind the advance companies and occupied the burning towns and country.

"Where are the bloody French?" I asked Thomas, for the hundredth time. "Can they not see what we are doing to the heart of France? How can any king allow this to happen to his country? To his people?"

"Perhaps we should ride north," Thomas said, "and ask them?"

I nodded. "A fine notion. But we need not ride north. There are Frenchmen hereabouts, are there not?" I sat up in my saddle and turned to find the man who was my shadow. "Walt? Take Rob and bring us back a few French scouts, will you?"

Walt looked exasperated. "I thought you said we was to ignore them, sir?"

"Just bring me a damned Frenchman."

Before sundown, my company dragged three men back to us. They had ropes about their necks and all three had been beaten roughly about the face.

"Where is your king?" I asked them.

"We will tell you nothing," one of them said, his face rigid with fury and contempt. "Nothing."

"Very well," I said.

I sliced my dagger across his throat, lifted him and drank the blood from his neck while the other two men cowered and sobbed in horror. Before his heart stopped, I tossed him to my soldiers, who grabbed him and supped from the wound, passing him around like a wine skin.

"Now, sirs? What can you tell me about the location and the intentions of King John?"

They died the same way as their fellow scout but before their blood fed my company they admitted that the French would confront our army on the road to Tours.

"How far does that be, sir?" Rob asked.

"Tours? It is merely sixty or seventy miles west."

"That mean there's going to be a battle this week, sir?"

"It depends on the courage of the French."

Thomas and Hugh took no part in such brutality and though they rarely gave voice to it, their behaviour spoke loudly enough. I did not like disappointing Thomas but I needed victory, not honourable failure.

Sixty French men-at-arms and a few hundred infantry guarded the crossing of the Sauldre at Romorantin. The Prince decided that he had to drive them away and so ordered the taking of the walled town and its ancient keep.

"Why get bogged down with this bloody lot?" Walt asked while we watched the army assembling for the assault. "We always leave big towns or garrisons what burrow in to keeps like tics. Waste time here and the French army will cut us off."

"With any luck," I said, brightly.

Thomas answered Walt's questions properly. "We cannot allow a force made up of hundreds of men at our rear as we advance on Tours. If the French do stop us on the road we will have those men in that town attacking us from behind."

Rob nodded. "Still a risk to stay in place for so long. What if they hold out in there? Look at the size of the bloody walls, Tom."

"It certainly appears to be a tough place but it is old and will fall, in time. Perhaps this will be where the French catch us. This is what we want, is it not? Then we shall find the men we seek."

"He is right," I said. "We must have the heart of the black knight and then we shall rejoice, even if the cost is the destruction of our entire army and the death of every Englishman in France."

My men were appalled but I cared nothing for that. My enemy was so close now, I could almost taste him.

"While we're here," some of my men said, "perhaps we might get involved, Sir Richard? Lots of gold in that town. Women, too."

"And we would be of great help to our soldiers," Hugh said, eagerly.

"No," I snapped. "I need you all alive and well for the coming battle. I will not lose any of you in some pointless siege. Let the mortals spend their lives."

Thomas glanced at me and I was ready to tell him to take his chivalry and shove it up his arse but he simply turned away in silence.

In the end, it was a brutal assault on the little town. Our men stormed the walls and the garrison retreated into the citadel. Three long days of struggle, the Prince's army tried to winkle out those men inside. Our miners undermined the walls while our siege engineers threw up three moveable assault towers and the soldiers launched repeated attacks on the keep from every direction at once.

The men were exhausted but the Prince urged them all on. He swore that it had to be done swiftly or it would be the end of the army.

All the while I prayed to see the blue and yellow banner of the King of France appear on the distant horizon. But no one came to save the town and the assaults continued until the keep was set on fire. It burned all through the night and in the morning the garrison surrendered.

We headed for Tours.

The delay had cost us. The French were coming, out of sight somewhere to the north, every man knew it now. But where would they catch us? I considered sending a message north to let King John know where we were but that would have been treasonous and besides, it was hardly necessary.

Every mile on the road to Tours, with the River Cher on our left, I expected scouts to report that the way was blocked.

And yet we reached Tours unopposed.

"Perhaps I *should* send word," I muttered to Thomas. "Clearly, King John is a coward or utterly incompetent. Perhaps if he knew how tired we are, he would take heart and come to meet us in the open field?"

"Anything you did or said would be mistrusted by the French," Thomas replied. "They would certainly think you had been sent by the Prince and suspect a trap. It may even drive them away from us."

"God damn his cowardice."

Lancaster was on the other side of the Loire with his two thousand men but he could not cross to us and we could not cross to him, for the French had broken every damned bridge across the great river from Tours to Blois. It was a serious setback. Our armies were suddenly more likely than ever to be destroyed one by one, despite being so close as the crow flies.

The Prince, bold as a lion, decided to take the city.

Tours was big. It was well defended by the river and by walls and towers enclosing the city and the castle. The citizens had dug ditches and raised ramparts and palisades. We wanted to burn them out but the endless rain did not allow it. Men experienced with assaulting towns were thrown at the walls but they fell back every time.

And then the French came.

Finally, the combined French army crossed the Loire just thirty miles upstream at Blois and came charging down at us. We were suddenly at great risk of being caught tween Tours and the enormous army of the King and so the Prince did the only sensible thing he could.

He ordered us to flee.

The army abandoned everything that we did not need and charged south, crossing two small tributaries and making ten miles before dark caught us.

In the morning, we found that the French had sent envoys.

They wanted peace.

"Bloody cowards," I said. "We cannot have that."

"But we do not *need* a battle," Thomas pointed out. "We wished for the French army to come within close proximity so we could seek the black knight."

"Yes, yes," I said, irritated. "But how do we now find him if there are twenty thousand enemies spread across miles of country? I need to see his black banner held aloft, Thomas."

"There's truly more of them than us?" Walt asked.

"Twice as many, at least," Rob replied. "So the scouts are saying."

"That is what they always say," Hugh pointed out.

"I think this time it is true," I said.

"And every one of them a man-at-arms on fresh horses?" Walt frowned. "While we're saddle sore, injured, and wet to the bone? What are they afraid of?"

Rob and his archers laughed. "This," Rob said, stroking his bow stave.

Walt shook his head. "When will they bloody learn?"

"Learn what?" Rob said, offended. "How would *you* fight us?"

Walt shrugged. "Either do it or don't do it. But farting around it don't do nothing."

The envoys spoke at length to the Prince about truces and treaties. But the Prince replied that there would be no peace. The King of France was here with an army and if he wanted peace, he would have to fight for it.

It was a very fine sentiment, somewhat undermined by the fact that we immediately turned and ran south once more. King John had the local forces in addition to his own army of mounted men and also the young Dauphin had arrived with another thousand men-at-arms. The black knight *had* to be amongst them.

Our lords were desperate to join up with Lancaster's army in the west while King John attempted to get around us to the east and cut off our retreat. He was so close on our heels that his men reached our nightly stopping point just hours after we left it. And our brave Prince made a difficult decision.

He waited.

The Prince held his army at Chatellerault, in the hope that Lancaster could reach us there and cross while we held the bridge.

French scouts watched us and ours watched them. The great French army was somewhere to the northeast and heralds gathered between our armies as the inevitability of battle grew.

"Surely," I said to Thomas. "Surely, this is it. I cannot stand it any longer."

"You know how it goes," Thomas said. "There has to be the will to fight from both armies. We are getting tired, now. If Lancaster does not come? We will try to run. And King John? Will he have the courage of his ancestors? His kingdom is not a happy one."

"There will be no avoiding it now," I muttered. "Surely."

Yet his words concerned me. What if the French pulled away again and my enemy disappeared once more? "But let us find him now, Thomas. Let us go to the French. Find the black banner amongst them. And slay him there."

"You have been patient for years," Thomas said. "You can wait a few days longer."

"What if he flees, Thomas?" I said, almost pleadingly. "We could charge into the enemy now. Right now, Thomas. We could do it."

Thomas, God love him, nodded slowly. "Perhaps. He will likely be with the Dauphin. Deep within the army. Imagine it. The press of men and horse. Even our strength could not throw down thousands of horses and men. Our company will certainly be stopped before we can reach him. No, no. It cannot be done. You must wait, Richard. Take heart. Have patience, sir. Take the time to pray."

I scoffed in his face. "I will go alone, then. One man on a horse is nothing to them. I will call myself a Frenchman. There will be so many of them, they will not know the truth of it until I am in striking distance."

"You would assassinate him, and kill his men also? Even if you could achieve such a thing, you would give yourself away in doing the deed and the French would tear you apart."

"Possibly."

"Certainly."

"Then so be it! If he never leaves the side of the Dauphin, how can I hope to kill him?"

Thomas stroked his chin. He needed to shave. "You shall have to wait for the battle."

I hung my head. "You said there may be no battle."

"Eventually, there will always be a battle."

Thinking of Priskos, I imagined what Alexander would do. What would Caesar do? Would they act? They had commanded armies and I had one company. Patience and steadiness were virtues but I could wait no longer.

"I must make an attempt," I said. "If they are too strong, I shall return. But I must see the banner, Thomas. I need to see it. If I can reach it, I will."

"Take Walt with you."

"He will give me away with his presence. Even a fool can see that Walt is an Englishman. Look at his features, Thomas. Despite his colouring, he is the most English thing you ever saw, is he not? Or Welsh, perhaps, I will allow. But I am stronger now than I have ever been and need no man's help. I shall do it alone."

"You need a good man to watch your back."

"Perhaps you should come with me?"

He thought about it. "Without me, the company will turn feral. Even Rob cannot control them now."

I left them in the dark of the first night. I took Walt with me.

Leaving my men was a mistake.

In my wrath and my haste, I was throwing away the steady work I had done over the previous years to uncover as much as I had. Because I was so close, I could not temper my frustration but still I believed that I could not fail. Thinking of my immortal ancestors made me feel as invincible as Priskos, as vigorous as Caesar, and as mighty as Alexander.

Patience is a conquering virtue. And vanity is the deadliest sin.

21

Deception

BY MORNING, I WAS CLOSE enough to smell them. The French were moving around us along the roads to the east. Moving in their thousands, spread out over many miles. I rode into them and simply asked.

"Where is the knight of the black banner? Have you seen the Dauphin's mystery knight? You, sir? Do you know of the knight of the black banner? Where is he, sir?"

I asked a dozen, a score, a hundred, as I rode back along their lines. Some men were angry, calling me a dog, a swine, or an Englishman. From most of these, I simply rode on, calling out cheerfully and with encouraging words, before asking my questions again.

"Who has seen the Dauphin's black knight? Where is he?"

"With the damned Dauphin, you fool!" one man shouted, to much laughter.

"Where is the Dauphin?"

A series of shouts came back to me from knights, squires and pages.

"With the King."

"At home with your wife!"

"Up your arse!"

Their laughter filled the air as I rode on, trying to get deeper into the masses of riders coming the other way. We were cursed and damned for going in the wrong direction but I kept claiming that I had a message. Everywhere I looked it was more knights, lances and pennants, banners, and shining steel. The whole day passed in that way and by evening I was cursing myself for wasting my time.

"We'll go back home to the lads now, will we, sir?" Walt asked, speaking softly.

We watched as the enemy broke up into hundreds of tiny camps on whatever dry area of field, copse, or hedgerow they could find. Some lit fires but most did not bother. It was not cold.

"The King, the Dauphin, and our black knight will pass this way eventually. We will wait another day until–" I grabbed Walt. "Look, there. Is that not the blazon of Jean de Clermont?"

A rider cantered south beside the road in a coat emblazoned with the red and gold coat of arms that we knew so well. Behind him rode a squire and a young page.

"Is it?" Walt asked, with his nose in his pack. "Do you want some of this cheese before it goes bad?"

"Let us take him, Walt. Come on." I rode to intercept him and called out a greeting while waving my hand. "Thanks be to God, sir. I have been looking for you all day."

His face expressed deep irritation. "For me? Who are you, sir?"

"For your lord, sir. I have a message that I must give to him."

He sighed dramatically and rolled his eyes. "Very well. Hand it over. Who is it from?"

I had no letter, of course, and made no move. "It is a message I must relay in person. Where is your lord tonight?"

He eyed me closely, looking me up and down. I was quite filthy and everything from my clothes to my horse's caparison was plain and mismatching. "Who did you say you served, sir?"

"Pierre of Senoches," I replied, plucking a random name from my memory. "My lord owes yours a considerable debt and he finally is able to pay it."

The knight frowned, as well he might, for the debt was a fiction.

"Here, see for yourself." I pulled out the purse I kept close to my body at all times. "Come closer, sir and see."

He was very wary indeed but his curiosity got the best of him and he watched as I tipped the garnets, emeralds and sapphires into my palm.

"My God," he muttered. "Where did your lord come into such a fortune?"

"He took it from the English. The fools are so laden with treasure stolen from our brothers across France that they cannot move for it. We routed a company of them and took this and much more from them. Much more. Perhaps you would assist us in bringing the sum of the debt back to your lord?"

"More?" he asked, astonished.

I pointed into the trees. "Just a small chest, sir, but we cannot carry it between us," I jerked a thumb at Walt. "And our wagon cannot travel this road as it is. If you and your two men there would consider sharing the coin between you, we could bring it to Lord de Clermont all together?"

His face lit up at the prospect for enriching himself and bringing his lord a great prize. "Certainly, sir. Certainly."

I narrowed my eyes and tipped the gems carefully back into their purse. "Only if you swear that your men are trustworthy. I shall have none of it pilfered and so come up short in the final accounting."

"They are trustworthy," he said, with greed in his eyes. "I swear it, by God and upon my honour."

I nodded slowly. "Very well. If you say it, sir, I shall believe it. Come, we are camped not far into the woodland there."

He followed us, still wary, but his fears suppressed in the hope of easy booty. Perhaps the knight and his squire were intending to kill us when we gave them the gold to carry. Perhaps they were even going to do their duty. Whatever their intentions, I never gave them the chance to act upon them. When we were alone and two dozen yards from the edge of the wood, I threw myself at the knight and dragged him down while Walt bundled the squire to the ground. The little page almost got away but Walt charged him and plucked him from his horse. We had to beat them around rather a lot to get them to be silent. The page pissed himself, poor lad, and I told him to be silent or he would be killed. He nodded, eyes as wide as saucers. The squire remained insensible for some time.

"I have questions for you, sir," I said to the knight, who sat leaning back against a tree trunk.

He spat blood out and it dangled from his chin and dripped onto his chest. In the distance, men laughed in the darkness. His eyes darted left and right before coming to rest on me again.

"No one will come for you. But answer my questions and you shall go free."

"You are English," he said, bitterly. "I knew it."

"I am looking for the knight with the black banner."

He glanced at me, suddenly fearful. "I know nothing."

"And I know that your master is friends with him. Tell me where they are."

He scoffed and I held up a dagger to his face.

"I have skinned men alive," I said, which was not true. "I have become very good at it."

He licked his fat lips. "You are the man who has been searching for him all day."

"You heard about that? Who told you?"

"My lord was told. Earlier today. In my presence."

"What did they say?"

"They said that the Englishman Richard of Ashbury was looking for..." he trailed off.

Ashbury, I thought. I had not gone by the name for decades. No man alive knew me by that name, other than my immortals.

And William's.

"Was the black knight there with him?" He looked away and I grabbed his jaw with my hand and squeezed, staring into him. "Was he there?"

He nodded as best he could. I did not release him.

"Who is he? You saw him? You saw his face? Who is the man you saw? Who is the black knight?"

I pressed my dagger gently to the underside of his eyeball and held it there. His breathing became panting and tears welled in his eyes. He blinked and they flowed down over the point of my blade.

"Charny," he whispered, so softly it was like the hushing of a mother to a child.

"I did not hear you."

He gasped and blurted it out. "Geoffrey de Charny."

I sat back on my arse, staring. "I do not believe it."

"I swear it." He rubbed his face and touched his eye to check it was intact. "Sir Geoffrey de Charny. The black knight is Sir Geoffrey de Charny. It is a secret known only to some. To my lord and to the other great men. He uses the black banner to fight where he has been ordered not to by the King, and by the previous king. And so de Charny protects his honour."

I scoffed, almost disbelieving it still. "He protects his name, not his honour, you fool. Do you know what he is, son? What he *truly* is?"

The knight frowned. "He wishes to do what is right for the kingdom. For the Crown."

Oh?

"Not for the King?" I said. "But for the Crown? And what is right for the Crown but not for the King? Come on, out with it. No use holding back now. I truly will take your eye if you hesitate and take them both if you lie."

"To fight for the Dauphin," he blurted. "My lord Jean de Clermont and Geoffrey de Charny will help the Dauphin to do what the King cannot. We will push the English from France forever."

I shook my head. "He wants to put a puppet on the throne and so make a kingdom that my brother can take when he returns."

The knight frowned. "Your brother?"

Walt coughed. "Kill them now, sir? Have a little drink, like, before heading home to the lads?"

All three of the prisoners looked so weak and pathetic that I was disgusted by them. "We'll bind them. Gag them. Tie up their horses. Perhaps someone will find the fellows before they die of thirst."

Walt grumbled that it would be easier to do them in rather than muck about with ropes and whatnot. But after the revelation that Geoffrey de Charny was the black knight, I suddenly did not have the heart for murder. I had a vague sense that Thomas would have disapproved of it and I wanted to act chivalrously. And I thought that, so close to victory, I could afford to be magnanimous.

If I had known what was coming, what I had set in motion with my bull-headed blundering, I would have killed them all. Even the boy. It would have made no difference to the outcome but vengeance is a matter for the heart and the balls, not the head.

"Time to go home now, sir?" Walt asked when the men were trussed up tight. "Catch up with our lads?"

I looked around at the crow-black woodland. The sky above the trees was cloudy and there were no stars. Walt's immortal night vision was better than mine but I did not wish to go staggering about all the hours of darkness looking for our tiny company amongst ten thousand soldiers.

"In the morning. We know that Geoffrey de Charny is our enemy. And now he can hide no longer."

But hiding was not what that monster had in mind.

***

The French were everywhere even before dawn, creeping through the trees collecting firewood, looking for somewhere to shit, or to take a woman. There were plenty being dragged along with the armies, willingly or otherwise.

We walked our horses through the darkness in the general direction of the English army. As the morning grew brighter I noticed that some of the trees were already beginning to change into their autumn colours, mottling like rust on an old blade. Spiderwebs hung with glistening dew across every path, some with black spiders waiting in the centre for the flies to wake and come blundering to their doom.

The French voices all around us thinned and soon we heard Englishmen shouting insults, in the way that friends do.

I discovered that the Prince was still at Chatellerault and so our army had not moved. Three days, he had waited, hoping to strengthen his army with the men who could give him the edge in the coming battle.

It was not to be.

Lancaster could not make the meeting place. His two thousand veteran soldiers were stopped at every turn by guarded crossings and fortresses filled with large garrisons. And King John in the meantime, sent his army well in front of us to the south.

It took us all morning to pick our way beneath the trees, across fields and through two villages. My company was still encamped in the little wood where I had left them. Acorns crunched beneath my horse's hooves as we rode up toward the group of my men, all standing and watching me approach.

"Thank God, sir," Rob said

"Where is Thomas?" I asked, aghast that he had abandoned our brutes to themselves. Although, they seemed to be behaving themselves. If anything, they were a bit pensive. "What is it, Rob?"

"Letter came, sir. First thing this morning." He held it out to me. "From a bloody Frenchman, sir."

I yanked it from his hand and read it aloud to Walt, my heart racing ever more as I did so.

"To my brother knight Sir Richard of Hawkedon. After many years of searching, by the grace of God, I have finally discovered the identity of the knight of the black banner. This man fought in disguise at the battle at Crecy and his men also stole a shield from me bearing my coat of arms. Although I am certain of the truth of it, I cannot divulge this to you in writing. If you still wish to find this man, I shall be at the chapel in Liniers at midday today." I looked at Walt. "It is from Sir Geoffrey de Charny."

Walt looked at the sun above us as I screwed up the letter in my fist.

"Thomas said he had to go meet him," Rob said, backing up from me a step. "Took Hugh with him. Told us to give you that if you came back. Only been gone a little while, sir."

"It is from Geoffrey de Charny," I repeated to Rob, who nodded, fearful of my boiling rage. The rest of the men drifted toward me. "Listen, all of you. This is a ruse. A bloody trap. This bastard de Charny is the black knight. Do you hear, men? Thomas and Hugh have gone to meet the black knight but they do not know it. Mount your horses. Weapons and helms. We will kill de Charny and all who ride with him, do you hear me?"

My heart was in my mouth as we rode south through the woodland. My horse was sweating and exhausted but I pushed him harder.

Thoughts revolved in my head as I cursed myself to the rhythm of my horse's movement.

I was a fool. A damned fool. I had been so close and I had ruined everything. I had shown myself to my enemy by barking the words *black banner knight* up and down the French army.

Of course it had gotten back to him. Someone saw me, perhaps one of his own immortal squires. Someone who knew my true name. And then Geoffrey de Charny had set a trap for me.

A trap I would have walked into if not for finding Lord de Clermont's man. Perhaps I would have suspected the truth but Thomas thought he recognised in de Charny a truly chivalrous knight. An honourable man who brought forth the righteousness and decency in those he fought with.

Please, Thomas. Please, do not trust him.

We charged into the tiny village of Limiers. It was hardly more than a hamlet, with a smattering of cottages and gardens about a small wooden chapel.

The ground was much chewed up by hooves but there were no horses outside the building.

The chapel door stood flung open. A black chasm leading into emptiness within.

"Maybe Tom and Hugh chased after them?" Walt ventured, pointing along the road through the village which disappeared beyond hedgerows and hills. "Can you hear them horses galloping?"

Rob ordered some of the men to pursue the riders and others to stay with me.

I ignored them all and rushed through the open door.

The taste of blood filled the air. It was a small, dark place, with a square window high up over the shrine to some unknown local saint.

Thomas' body lay on the floor in a pool of blood. It flowed still from the tattered flesh across his neck.

My friend's head lay against the far wall next to the altar, with sunlight falling full on his anguished face. I stepped closer and saw how his expression in death was fixed in surprise and outrage.

"Sir!" Walt called from behind me, drawing my attention to our other dear companion. "I'll see if I can find a priest."

Hugh lay against the side wall, eyes wide and flicking about while his mouth worked in silence. His throat trickling blood from a great gash across the front of his neck.

Both of his arms had been cut off between the hand and elbow.

Hugh's eyes swam with tears and agony.

"Sir," he was trying to say. "Sir."

Blood issued from his lips and he coughed, spraying

I knelt in his blood and took his head in one hand. "Drink from me."

Shaking his head, he mouthed in despair. "No, no."

He held up the ruin of his arms before his eyes, staring at the space where his hands had been.

He preferred to die than live so disfigured.

I shook my head. "Forgive me, Hugh."

"De Charny," he said in a wet whisper, blood filling his mouth.

"I know," I said. "I know de Charny is the black knight. I swear to you I shall kill him. That's enough now, son."

"And... and..." He coughed, causing blood to spray up and the gash in his neck flapped open. I placed my hand over it, feeling the hot blood pump out beneath my palm to soak my hands in it.

"Rest easy now, good Hugh. Go to God, son. You have always done your duty. You fought well all your life. You lived with honour. Go to God. Go to God."

He closed his eyes. In a few moments, he was gone.

I looked up at the men of my company. Their faces reflected the misery and the anguish and the anger that boiled in my breast.

We buried them in the village

And I went to make a battle.

22

Poitiers

PRINCE EDWARD LED HIS ARMY south through the woodland with the intention of getting in front of the French army on the road to Poitiers as they crossed the Vienne. The forest was dense and dark and filled the land between two valleys.

It was a hard march. Forcing horses and wagons through dense woodland is difficult enough and doing it quickly was taxing in the extreme. Even so, the men managed to cover over twenty miles that day using the woodland tracks.

And the route kept our army hidden from the French scouts. They knew we were somewhere close by but they had no idea how close we were to them. In truth, neither did we, for our foremost groups stumbled upon the French rearguard quite suddenly and fought a sharp action. They were more surprised than our men, though, and seven-hundred French men-at-arms routed as the sun went down. Our army pulled back into the black shadows of the woodland.

It was safe within but we were between two rivers and there were no springs to be found in the wood from which to water the men and horses.

Before daybreak, we were already moving west, toward Poitiers, hoping to get away from the French army that we knew were nearby.

But the French were already drawn up in battle order on the plain before the city.

"By God, sir," Rob said as we observed them from the shelter of the woods. "Look at the bastards."

There were eighty-seven banners held aloft over the French army. Eighty-seven bannerets with their companies and God alone knew how many ordinary knights. Thousands of men-at-arms, plus infantry and crossbowmen.

"There will be no escape now," I said to Rob.

"Bloody hope so," said Walt.

"Won't the Prince try to flee anyway? We are outnumbered and outmatched."

"Our route to Gascony is blocked. We have nowhere else to go. And this is good battlefield territory."

It was good land to live on, too. Low hills covered with woods and green pasture. Miles and miles of abundant vineyards in every direction. A place made beautiful by the generations that had lived there since the days of the Romans. It would soon become a place for death.

The Prince conferred with his lords and led the army to a hilltop just north of a village named Nouaille. The French were about a mile away, just beyond the brow of another hill. And our army established itself in battle order.

Warwick and Oxford commanded the vanguard on the left, his far wing where the ground fell away into marshland toward the river. Salisbury commanded the right and Edward took the centre. We had about two thousand archers, three thousand men-at-arms and a few Gascons.

This would be our battleground.

Behind us, the wood of Nouaille gave us somewhere to retreat into, if we were overrun. In front was a thick hawthorn hedge which ran right across the hillside. Here and there were copses and scrub and everywhere across the hills were rows and rows of vines. On our right flank, where there were no natural defences, the archers dug deep trenches and pits to protect themselves from a mounted charge.

It was a good place to fight.

But the English were afraid. Fear was in the air. At Crecy, we had been as confident as an army could be.

On that hillside outside Poitiers, there was a sense of impending doom.

Every man was hungry but even worse was the thirst. After the twenty mile march the day before and the hundreds of hard miles before that, legs and arses were like jelly and thighs raw.

All the men knew we were outnumbered, with at least two of them for every one of us. Many were shaken by the fact we had missed meeting up with Lancaster. Those two thousand men were on everyone's minds and some were even convinced they would come to our rescue in time, no matter how much it was explained that was impossible.

Also missed, desperately, were the thousands we had left behind to guard Gascony. All of them sitting warm and dry for months, eating all the food, drinking the wine and bedding the women, while we stood shivering and thirsty waiting to die on a French hillside.

The French sent their priests and envoys out into the fields between the two armies.

Prince Edward and the leading nobles rode a little way forward toward them and they came closer to meet him.

I jumped on my horse.

"Sir?" Walt said.

"Stay here."

I rode out after the Prince and the great lords, feeling the eyes of the army on me. I was disgraced, an outcast, practically a criminal.

Ever since I had escaped my half-hearted imprisonment in Gascony, I had kept well away from the lords of the army. My presence was barely tolerated within the mass of the general soldiery but still, I rode out alone behind the great lords and their retinues and lurked where they could not see me without turning. No one else came to stop me. I knew none would dare.

A French cardinal came forward toward the Prince on foot with his arms stretched out, tears in his eyes.

"Your Grace," he said, voice quivering. "I beg of you that you listen."

Edward sighed. "Say it quickly. This is no time for a sermon."

The cardinal stuttered into his speech. "Your Grace, I beg that you consider the appalling deaths of the good Christians that shall happen in this place if battle is joined. Your men, there, so many good and decent men, will surely be slaughtered. Your royal person, your loyal nobles beside you, and the common folk that follow you, are in the gravest peril where you stand. Please, my lord, let you not tempt God with pride and vainglory. I beg you, in the name of God and by the honour of Christ and the Blessed Virgin to grant a short truce so that negotiations may be held. I swear to you that my brothers and I shall do all in our power to assist you to come to some accommodation in this matter. If you will allow it, we should have a conference between the kings of England and France and so avoid the terrible slaughter that you must suffer."

I laughed and a few men turned around to look at me.

"What are you doing here?" Salisbury growled, pointing his ample nose in my direction.

"You cannot mean to treat with the French, Your Grace?" I called out.

Edward turned and gave me a death stare. I gave him one back and mine was far more practised.

"Get him away from here," Edward said to Oxford, who nodded. However, he wisely made no move toward me.

The cardinal and his men glared at me. "Your Grace, a truce would be—"

"Yes, yes," Edward said, waving his hand. "I suppose a short negotiation would be in order. We owe it to God, do we not?"

The cardinal beamed. "Praise God! We shall at once return to the King of France. There is a hill just there, between the hedge and the vines, where two groups may sit in peace."

Bowing and praising God and the Prince, they left and rode away over the hill.

I shook my head as they went. "We hold a fine position," I said loudly as the lords turned in to each other.

214

"You do not hold anything," Salisbury called. "You are not welcome here."

Oxford nodded. "You may take yourself away from the Prince's presence. Immediately."

"We can kill them all," I shouted. "We can murder the lot of them, Your Grace. Why delay?"

Warwick sneered. "Our men need rest, you fool. This way, our men can recover from the march."

Humphrey Ingham took up the haranguing. "Hold your tongue, Hawkedon, you blustering bastard. You claim to know so much about—"

"There is no water here, sire," I said to Edward, projecting my voice over theirs. "Our men will have to ride to and from the rivers for as long as we stay in this place. All the enemy has to do is guard the banks and wait for us to die of thirst or attack. We must invite an attack now, today."

The Prince pursed his lips and looked back at our army. The men stood, spattered in filth and all cloth darkened and heavy with rain not yet dried. They looked anxiously down at their lord and future king.

"It is done, now," he said, his tone surprisingly reasonable. He looked at his lords. "Let us see what they have to offer. In the meantime, send companies to collect as much water as we can and have them drink while they are there."

They glared at me but again made no move to drive me away. Each of them had experience and they were good soldiers. But they knew my reputation. Most had seen me fight. They had heard my advices over the years to the King and to his nobles and they knew that whether my words were listened to or not, I was usually right.

But despite all that, the negotiations out between the armies lasted all day and continued after sundown. For all his confident talk, it was clear that Edward wanted to avoid a battle.

He, too, was infested with the sense that we could not win.

I had to force the battle or else I could not kill Geoffrey de Charny. I needed them to come for us and whether de Charny fought in the open or under the black banner, I would cut my way toward him and tear his heart out.

But only if there was battle.

The proposal from the French was galling. They said Edward had to surrender all his conquests in France over the last three years and he had to pay tens of thousands of pounds for the damage caused by the great raids. In return, the Prince asked to be betrothed to a daughter of King John, and she would bring the entire county of Angouleme as dowry.

"Absurd," I said when I heard the details but Edward seemed to be open to it.

When it went back to the French, they changed their minds and after sundown their message came back to us.

"You have destroyed too much of France to be paid for by any sum. You are trapped in your position, your men are exhausted from their ceaseless destruction and you are out of supplies. You have no source of water and so you cannot stay where you are. But you cannot escape. Any agreement you make with us would have to be confirmed by your father the King and in the meantime you would throw away our terms and continue your onslaught upon our soil. You will have no agreement from us."

"Why did they go through all this?" Oxford said. "Merely to throw it all back in our faces?"

"They are delaying because it suits them, you bloody preening fools," I said, unable to contain my anger at their stupidity. "We can only lose by such delay while they only gain. We eat the last of our supplies while their numbers continue to grow beyond that damned hill."

Although they knew it was true, they despised me for my disrespect towards them and they pretended I was not there.

The men of our army sat all through the day and in the night each man lay down on the ground and slept.

Thousands of men laying across the hillside beneath the stars. Small fires flickered everywhere. A few fellows gathered around a candle or two, talking in low voices. Pages and other servants traipsed back and forth through the mass of men, some holding lamps aloft as they went.

"How can there not be a battle?" the men in my company asked me. "How can we be here and them over there and not come to blows?"

"Ain't you daft sods never seen two blustering drunks?" Walt answered them. "The two biggest mouths in the alehouse, shouting each other hoarse and cursing each other's mother and puffing up their chests, only to allow themselves to be pulled away by their mates? Seems like that's what this is here, if you ask me. Two biggest bastards in the room, each afraid of getting his block knocked off."

"How do you make such men come to blows?" I asked Walt.

He shrugged. "No one wants to see that, do they, sir. Just want to finish your ale and go home to a woman, that time of night."

Rob leaned forward. "Some craven old bastards wait for a man to turn away before thumping him on the crown."

I nodded, the germ of an idea taking root.

"Nah," said Walt. "You want to drive your knuckles into a man's kidneys, if you be hitting from the back. Liable to break your hand, cracking him on the dome in such a manner."

"Unlike you, Walt, I ain't got experience hitting a fellow in the back."

The men laughed.

"Come now, Robert," Walt countered, "from what I hear it told, you like most of all to pound a man solely from behind."

I walked away while they roared and argued with each other. Most of the soldiers on the dark hill were quiet and pensive but men prepare for battle in a thousand ways and it has always been the same.

Some laugh and joke, others tremble and others weep. Many, I know, think of home and family and what they might go back to if they live through the next day. And they dread to never see it again.

Myself, I had no home. Not really. And yet I thought of Cecilia and the home that I might have had with her, for a time, if things had been different. If I had chosen differently. If there was any home at all, it was the house in London and if I had any family it was Eva and Stephen alone. Poor Thomas, and Hugh with him, were gone forever.

Both men, I had given a longer, ageless life than they would have had otherwise. But still they were dead because I had not done my duty protecting them from the danger I exposed them to.

I walked by an armourer who sat hammering dents from pieces of armour plate while another sharpened weapons nearby. Pages queued up for either one man or the other, their arms full of blades or helms.

I had lost John, and Thomas, and Hugh, to Geoffrey de Charny.

He had taken so much. His reputation as the greatest knight in Christendom irked me almost as much as anything else. The fame that he had cultivated had come from his prowess in battle and in tourneys and jousts. Prowess enhanced due to his immortal strength and speed. It was deceitful, dishonest and I wished I had done it.

The soldiers around me on that hillside joked and complained and said their private prayers.

My prayers would wait. Instead, I swore by God and Jesus and all His saints that I would have vengeance.

In the morning, a rider came to ask for a truce of one year. Prince Edward replied that he would agree to a truce extending from that day to next spring but no longer.

"They will give us no truce," I said, exasperated. "This is nought but to delay us further. We must force battle today or we will wither and die like vines in a drought."

"How can we force them to attack," Warwick said, "when they are seeking to delay."

I had been thinking about it. "The hotheads amongst the French lords will have been urging King John to attack us since yesterday, or even earlier. Especially the ones who were not at Crecy. They will see us as weak, needing only to be assaulted for us to crumble. They are surely being held back by cooler heads and the reticence of the King. All we need do is tip the balance."

"Yes, yes," Warwick said, scowling. "But *how*, man?"

"We turn our backs."

They stared at me.

"We withdraw." I smiled back at them. "At least, we should *appear* to be withdrawing. What can they see of us, from over the hill?"

They looked out across the rolling hills and hedges.

"Nothing," Oxford said.

"Their men see us," Salisbury said, nodding at the scores of riders atop the far hill a mile away. "And they will ride back, frantic, telling their masters all at once what they see. And they will surely act to catch us while we are in disorder."

Salisbury may have been a miserable bastard who disliked me intensely, but he was a damned fine soldier. He smiled and the others began nodding with him. Even Sir Humphrey Ingham, who seemed delighted by the proposition. Salisbury and Ingham turned expectantly to the Prince.

"Raise your men's banners aloft at the rear," Edward said to Warwick, "and have them advance them into the wood. Go with him, Humphrey."

They turned to make it happen, enjoying the prospect of tricking the French.

"Best tell the men, my lords," I said to them, loudly. "We would not want any of them thinking we were running away." I raised my voice. "Not when we are about to slaughter the French." A few of the common men near us raised their voices to cheer me and I grinned at them. "Pass the word, lads. The Prince is going to *trick* the French. But we are all staying right here. This hill is England, today, boys. Pass the word."

Salisbury nodded once at me and turned to make his way to the right flank.

I made my way to my company.

"Going to be a fight then, is it?" Walt said. He lowered his voice. "The lads are getting a bit thirsty, sir."

"I know. There will be a battle today if I have to ride out and charge the French alone. We shall be away from here tomorrow. They can drink then."

"If any of us live to see tomorrow," Walt said. "Sounds like there's a lot of French knights." He spat at his feet.

"We are in a very fine position. Do you see? Their numbers do not matter so much as they cannot get around our left due to the marshes and the hill. How will they get through those hedges, there?"

Walt frowned. Rob answered. "They'll have to come through the gaps where there's no hedge. They just have to. Proper hedges, them."

"And so they will have to come on in a narrow front there, and over there, and right here, before spreading out again to attack our front line."

Rob was grinning as he strung his bow. "They'll be all herded together. All nice and tight and packed in there. It'll be lovely work, lovely."

"It'll be a bloody slaughter, all right," Walt said, nodding. "And then they'll be through and they'll slaughter us in turn."

The priests came out and started to say Mass.

Many men-at-arms filed away up the hill with their lords.

Walt jerked his head at them. "Knights up there, sir. Knights dubbing their men, making them knights also. Great honour, that, if we win. Great honour for a loyal man to be so dubbed by his knightly lord." He looked at me expectantly.

"The day you are knighted, Walt, will be the day the notion has lost all its meaning."

He hung his head and walked away by himself.

Edward came forward on his magnificent horse and turned to his men. A hush fell on the army as we strained to hear his shouted words. He had a fine, loud voice and it carried well but the wind blew most of it away.

The Prince's men came around, shouting out the written orders as they went. "You shall keep strictest discipline in the lines! No man shall waste time securing prisoners! Do you hear? No prisoners to be taken."

Rob looked over his shoulder at Warwick's banners on our left as they waved rearward into the wood. "Supposing it *ain't* a trick, sir?"

"What's that, Rob?"

"Oh, nothing, sir."

"Spit it out, man."

"It proper looks like Warwick is retreating, don't it? Look at Ingham's banner, there. It's halfway to bloody Bordeaux. But still the enemy waits up there. And if the French don't attack now, then we might as well make it an actual retreat, right, sir? The rest of us can follow him?"

I had a sudden thought. Perhaps it was I who had been tricked by the Prince. Perhaps he had in fact ordered Warwick and Ingham to retreat and that was what he intended.

Aghast at the thought, I rode out through the rows of vines toward the French. "Fight me!" I shouted at the men on the far hill. "Come and fight, cowards. Any of you, come fight me. All of you, come to me and fight."

A mass of horsemen crept over the brow of the hill and began to cross the fields toward us. More and more appeared and streamed after the ones in front. I counted scores, then a hundred and when I saw it was perhaps five hundred men mounted on destriers with their lance points glinting and their pennants snapping in the wind, I turned and rode back toward the Prince.

"Here they come, Your Grace."

"Yes," Oxford said as I rode up, "thank you for you pointing it out."

"They are aiming for Warwick," I said, watching the Prince closely. He screwed up his face and turned to a man on a swift courser at his side. "Ride to Warwick! Tell him to hold his position against the assault."

"Look!" Chandos said, pointing with his sword. "Their men separate. Two columns."

I nodded, seeing the riders pick their way through the trees and bushes. "They mean to charge the archers on both flanks. Drive them away or kill them before the main assault."

"Oxford," the Prince snapped. "Lead the archers into the marsh around the left flank."

The Earl of Oxford blinked once and then charged his horse along the front lines toward the men. In the distance, the two columns of French cavalry formed as they drew closer to us, ready to smash into our formations.

They charged into the disarray on our left flank and penetrated the lines where Warwick's men had pulled back. They were fighting to hold the French from breaking through and sweeping in behind us. Out beyond them, on the farthest left flank, Oxford ordered the archers to slog out further into the marsh. The horses could not charge them there but they were able to shoot into the rear and flanks of the French horses. The horses died. Falling, throwing their riders, and panicking, the enemy horses took terrible damage from the storm of arrows and the attackers were driven off.

On our right, the enemy column came galloping up the hill toward our archers. The dense hawthorn hedge on that flank was broken only by a gap so narrow that no more than five riders abreast could make it through at once.

Our archers began shooting.

As the French squeezed through the gap, the arrows smashed into them causing terrible damage. Still, their armour protected many of them and they came on through the hedge and opened out into a wider front and, horses blowing, they readied to charge.

Salisbury ordered his men forward to meet them and our men-at-arms, hundreds of them, stepped rapidly forward with their visors down and their polearms raised. The French charged into them and our men hacked at the riders and horses with their long-handled hammers and axes and the enemy thrust with their lances.

My lord the Earl of Suffolk had his blood up and he rode down to the archers shouting at them to advance on the right and shoot into the flanks while he and his men guarded them.

The French assault was overwhelmed. So many fell, and yet they fought on.

Until they fled.

The assault on our right collapsed and they rode away while our men cheered and hurled insults after them. A few archers kept up shooting at the backs of the men riding away, taking down a handful more horses, until they were ordered to stop. So many dead and wounded French lay on the hillside in front of us. Some of the archers walked out to them until the Marshals of the army roared at them to get back into their formations.

"Why can't they grab a bit of loot, sir?" Rob asked.

"The battle has barely begun."

"Killed hundreds of them," Walt said.

"And here come thousands more," I said.

For the first proper assault was coming toward us across the rolling hills. They came on in good order, on foot, in all their glory. The banner at the centre of them all was that of the Dauphin. He was just eighteen years old and leading the vanguard, as our own prince had done at Crecy aged just sixteen. But their prince, the Dauphin, was a weak little streak of piss and ours was a damned hero.

When their well-ordered lines came to the hedge, they had to break up and come through the gaps to get to us. Once again, our archers unleashed a storm of iron and steel on them. Many fell, some dead, more wounded, as they emerged from those gaps.

But still they came on.

Thousands of French men-at-arms assaulted our lines. They fought us for hours. And a hard fight it was.

When they could make no headway against us, they retreated back down the hill.

Our men wanted to chase them away but we knew we had resisted but a portion of their army and our keenest men were held back.

Only later did we discover that the Dauphin was then spirited away from the battle. Some said it was on the orders of the King of France but in truth it was the actions of Jean de Clermont and the other conspirators who wished to place the young and weak Dauphin on the throne. The Duke of Orleans followed the Dauphin from the field, as did the Count of Anjou and the Count of Poitiers. And they took the entirety of the second line of battle with them. Thousands of French soldiers under the command of those men marched right off the field and away into France, abandoning their king to his fate.

A shocking, treasonous betrayal.

It cost the French a third of their army but still they had their third battle, the rearguard, commanded by King John himself and it was large enough by itself to match our entire army.

They came forward to the roar of trumpets and drums, his men shouting and cheering as they came.

"This lot seem keen," Walt said.

They held the King's banner aloft and beside it was the unfurled Oriflamme. The sacred, inspiring, red banner of the King of France since the days of Charlemagne which declared that no quarter was to be given.

Beside that was the banner of Geoffrey de Charny.

"Our enemy is with the French King," I called to my men.

John Chandos heard me shouting but misunderstood my words. "By God, Richard. We do not wish to kill King John."

"Shut your idiot mouth, Chandos. There will be a cold day in Hell before I need your battlefield advice."

The trumpets sounded over and over and the men beneath them roared like the sea in a storm. Their armour shone in an array of blue, gold, red, and silver. A riot of colour across the front.

They were keen. And they had every right to be. That third battle was filled with the finest knights in France.

And they were fresh.

We had been fighting for hours and our men leaned on their weapons or sat on the churned ground. Men breathed heavily and drank whatever last dregs could be found and ate any morsels their men had hidden away. Fighting saps the energy from your limbs. A minute feels like an hour. Two hours can finish a man for days. And yet our toughest test was coming.

Before the French knights came their crossbowmen. Hundreds and hundreds, perhaps thousands. Unlike at Crecy, these men held their enormous shields aloft as they came forward and so protected themselves from the arrows of our men. Our archers unleashed their arrows but they hit only wood and steel. Our men's volleys slowed until they all but stopped.

"Out of arrows, sir," Rob said.

I ignored him, keeping my eyes fixed on de Charny's banner. Like the Oriflamme and the King's banner, it was at the rear of the advancing French lines. I would have to smash through hundreds of knights without being swarmed by their number. *Unless*, I thought, *unless I can come at them from the rear.*

"Send for our horses," I said to Walt. "Take our men to the rear." I left them and pushed further to the centre. "Your Grace!" I shouted, shoving my way through the masses of men toward him. "Sire. They are held here. Fixed here. Horsemen can get around to their rear."

The Prince ordered the Captal de Buch to take fifty men from the reserve and whatever mounted archers had arrows around the right flank into the rear.

I turned to go with him and the Prince shouted at me. "You will remain, Richard."

"Fifty men will do nothing," I said, scowling. "I am taking my company, mounted, to charge the Oriflamme."

"You will not!" he shouted.

"I am going to kill de Charny. If you have any sense in your fat head you will send every man you can with me."

I turned and pushed my way through the men as the lords of England shouted their disapproval.

"To me, men," I called to my company. "Mount your horses. De Charny is there, do you see his banner? He holds the Oriflamme. We will kill any man who stands in our way, whether he be French, Gascon, or English. Whether he be knight, lord, or king. For Thomas! For Hugh! For the White Dagger!"

My men roared and I led them along the rear of our lines, throwing clods of earth as we galloped, sending archers scurrying and cursing us. At our farthest flank I turned to the north and rode on beyond the French. My men, not the finest riders and not on the finest horses, caught up with me. "There!" I said, pointing to the distant banners. "We stop for no man. Unfurl the banner! Get it aloft."

My great war banner was raised. The white dagger on the red field with golden flame reaching up.

"Death!" I shouted. "Death!"

My men shouted with me and we rode along the rear of the French lines to the centre, where the King's bodyguard turned to meet us. They were on foot and as our charge faltered, they surged around us. My horse was struck and he stumbled.

"De Charny! The Lord of Hell is here," I shouted. "Hell has come for you!"

My horse was killed and I threw myself off, stumbling into the arms of my archers Watkyn and Osbert, who pushed me upright again.

We cut our way through the masses, my men fighting like lions. Like demons.

My sword was yanked from my grasp and I took a mace from another man before smiting him with it. It was hot beyond belief in my armour. The sounds of clashing arms and men's cries filled my head. I was struck with weapons and gauntleted hands grasped at my shoulders, my helm. Pole weapons were shoved, unseen, between my legs, as enemies tried to trip me. Falling even once could very well mean death.

They were so many and my men were swarmed by French bodies. It was chaos. I saw Hal Brampton, my sturdy man-at-arms, go down under a dozen men and their daggers worked their way through his armpits and groin. His visor was pulled open and they stabbed him in his eyes and face until his screams stopped.

Osmund was overrun by my side and before I could reach him, he was borne away by masses of enemies. I cried out for Walt but I had no idea where he was. One of my archers, Lambert, stumbled in front of me. He had lost his helm and had a torrent of blood gushing from his skull.

"Get to the rear," I shouted at him. "I will restore you later."

He nodded and took one step away before a heavy bladed glaive swung down from nowhere and hewed his head in two down to the neck.

I was shoved forward, blows ringing on my back and shoulders. Enemies were all around me and I did not know if any friends remained. Had my entire company been killed or lost? It seemed as though I would never reach the French King. Never reach de Charny and the Oriflamme. Never kill the black knight.

And the English mounted knights came. Finally, the Prince had sent them after all and they smashed into the rear of King John's men, knocking down knights and squires and spearing them with their lances. The press of men was suffocating.

I surged forward, throwing enemy knights down before me. I hammered my mace into the King's standard bearer and he fell, along with the King's great banner.

"De Charny!"

He was there, with the pole of the Oriflamme in hand, striking down English knights like wheat. Finally, my enemy was before me.

His two men beside him were immortals also, their inhuman strength undeniable and irresistible.

I killed the first one, crashing my mace down on his shoulder until my weapon broke. I wrapped my arm around him while he hammered at my helm with his sword and I worked my dagger through the tattered mail beneath his armpit and through his ribs into his lung. I swirled it around, opening the wound and working my way toward his heart. His knees sagged and he fell against me. Reaching down, I tore off his helm, ready to stab him in the eyes.

It was Rudolph de Rohan. A lord who I had once held in my grasp before sending him back to his lord Clermont.

"You," I said, breathing heavily.

He had deceived me and I had let him go. I had never considered that he would have fought as a squire to a mere knight. But what did such things mean to immortals? I had been a fool again. I had wrought so much destruction and killed so many but I had still not killed enough.

Seeing me distracted, Rohan thrust up with his sword and it slid inside the armour of my right arm, cutting me deeply. Enraged, I stabbed him in the head and bore him to the ground.

Blood poured from my arm, soaking my sword-hand.

A cry of warning alerted me to the incoming blow but I managed no more than to see it coming and lean away.

A poleaxe hit me flush on the breastplate. The inhuman force knocked me onto my back and I could not breathe, nor see.

It was not a blow from a mortal man.

De Charny was on me. I got my arms up as he swung his poleaxe again down onto my head. The haft on it had broken and he gripped it close to the head of it, striking hard against my helm, my gauntlets, and my breastplate. Such force and fury that I could not block the blows, nor grasp the weapon or the man. I rolled to the side to get up but his weight and strength bore me down and he struck me so that my world turned dark.

It was suddenly bright.

My visor was gone and de Charny kneeled over me with his arms raised, the massive steel polearm over his head. I reached my hands up. Pieces of steel from my gauntlets were hanging down from the ragged leather gloves.

He was dragged away.

I climbed to my knees in time to see Rob twist de Charny's helm off his head before holding him down with his archer's strength, magnified by his immortal power.

And Walt sawed Geoffrey de Charny's head from his shoulders with a broken sword, crying out in an animal roar at the barbaric brutality of it.

I staggered forward as Walt lifted de Charny's severed head. The eyes were open for a moment and it seemed as though they focused on me in rage and in horror, just for a moment, before the eyes rolled back and the lids closed.

"My dear fellows," I said, hearing the emotion and exhaustion in my voice as I spoke. "Walt. Rob." I could say no more, overcome with the knowledge that they had saved me. Both men seemed to be in as bad a condition as I was and yet they stood and grasped my arms and grinned with me.

The King of France fought on with his youngest son, a lad named Philip. Almost all of his bodyguards had fallen. The English could have killed the King easily but they shouted at him to surrender and yanked his weapons away from him. A great press of English and Gascon men-at-arms pushed in on him but King John would not submit. The crowd about him were furious.

My wounds were painful and I wanted to drink blood. But I could see that he was going to get ripped apart and that was no way to treat a king.

"Everybody back!" I shouted in English. "Get back from him you bloody filthy dogs!"

A few parted and I pushed into the front of the crowd.

"Why do you not surrender, my lord?" I shouted in French, my voice carrying above all others.

"I shall surrender only to a knight," he shouted back. "As will my son."

"I am a knight," I said. "I swear it to God."

The crowd around us quietened as they watched.

He hesitated and then pulled off one of his gauntlets and held it out to me. I stepped forward and bowed as I took it in my left hand. I must have looked quite a sight. My armour dented and hanging off me. Blood streaming from beneath what remained.

"You are my prisoner. You shall be safe. Have no fear."

"My son also," King John said, and pulled the young Prince to his side.

"He's mine!" someone shouted behind me and surged forward to grab the King from me.

Another voice from the other side shouted. "He's mine!"

Then they all began shoving forward and I pushed back their grasping hands. Walt appeared by my side, and Rob also, slapping at the greedy bastards as they tried to take my prize from me.

King John raised his voice, though it shook as he spoke. "I am a great enough lord to make you all rich!"

We pushed against them. "Get off him, you faithless dogs!"

And then the Earl of Warwick and his men, all mounted, pushed through the crowd.

"Stand back on pain of death!" Warwick's men shouted. "On pain of death, I say!" Their swords were drawn.

The crowd backed away.

"You, too, Hawkedon," Warwick said.

"The King has surrendered to me," I said. "He is my prisoner and in my care."

Warwick sneered. "I will be damned before I allow you into the presence of the Prince ever again. Step back."

I recalled how I had spoken to Prince Edward and the great lords of the realm. It was a breach that I could never repair. And I realised I did not want to do so. It was irrelevant. My enemy was dead.

"I pledged to protect you and I have. The Earl of Warwick is an honourable man who will keep you safe. You and your son."

I bowed and stepped back while Warwick and his men dismounted, bowed low before King John and took him away. The men-at-arms, deprived of the riches and the spectacle, turned back to find other prisoners and to loot the bodies of the fall all around us.

"Walt," I said, "Rob. Where are the others?"

Rob hung his head. "Dead, sir."

"Hal? Osmund? I saw Watkyn fighting at the end, surely he is not dead?"

"All of them," Walt said.

Rob looked me in the eye. "To a man."

"Good God Almighty," I said, looking at the sky. "We must bury them."

My men had been spent in breaking through the French centre. Without their immortal strength and veteran skill, the battle could yet have swung in the favour of the French. Each of my men had fought and killed a dozen, a score, of enemy knights. They had helped me to cut a swathe deep into the royal retinue, bringing me to our immortal enemy. They had paid for my revenge, and the Prince's great victory, with their lives.

We buried Hal, Osmund, Lambert, Watkyn, Osbert, Randulf, Jake, and Stan. I said my prayers over them and gave them my thanks. Also, I gave thanks to God and humbly requested that He take care of my men. So many, I had sent to Him, both friends and foes, over the long years.

All told, the Prince's army lost no more than fifty men-at-arms and a few hundred archers and spearmen. There were hundreds of wounded, though, and every man who stood was exhausted beyond measure.

Well after the battle, I heard about the French losses from the heralds. Two-and-a-half thousand men-at-arms were struck dead on the field. Their armour and wealth was well stripped by the end of the day and, without coats of arms to go by, the heralds had difficulty identifying the bodies.

As well as Geoffrey de Charny, his ally the lord Jean de Clermont was killed and scores of other great lords and nobles. We took three thousand prisoners, including fourteen counts, twenty-one barons, and fourteen hundred knights. Marshals of France, Archbishops, the leaders of the kingdom, all were in our hands. Each one would be ransomed for a fortune.

But that was not for us.

Just before sundown, I led Walt and Rob to the top of the hill by the wood. Our brothers had been killed. We were exhausted and hurt. They wanted blood so I gave them each some of mine. Enough for them to recover. My arm was hurt but I would live so I could wait.

"How many times is it that you have saved my life now, Walter?"

He smiled. "A few, sir."

"Why?" I asked him.

He was confused and opened his mouth to answer. I wondered if he would say it was because I had lifted him up from his poverty and given him wealth. Or if it was because he thought he needed me, now that he was an immortal.

In the end, he shrugged. "It is my duty, sir."

Rob nodded slowly as Walt spoke.

"You are an honourable man, Rob," I said to him. "Trustworthy, loyal, and honourable."

He bowed his head. "Thank you, sir."

I had taken two rather fine swords from the field, having lost my own. These swords, I placed before me.

"Kneel. Both of you."

They did so, glancing sidelong at each other.

"This is your oath. You will safeguard to your uttermost the weak, the widow, and the helpless. You will be without fear in the face of your enemies. You will be loyal by word and deed and serve your lord. Be humble and courteous everywhere, especially to women. Serve Jesus Christ and protect those who worship in His name. Be the terror and dead of all evil-doers and be just and brave in battle."

They so swore and I struck each of them across the face with the flat of my hand to dub them. Then I presented each man with a sword.

I dragged them to their feet and embraced them in turn.

Walt had tears streaming down his cheeks. Rob looked astonished.

"Let us go home, brothers."

2 3

The Great Storm

"SO OUR ENEMIES are all dead," Stephen said. "It is over."

I thought of my brother, out there somewhere in the East. Destined to return. I thought of Priskos and his sons and wondered what it would mean for the future.

"For now, at least."

We made it home from Gascony to London by the summer of 1357. I was allowed to keep my land and my title but as I dare not show my face at court or call on any great lord, especially my own, the Earl of Suffolk, I was unsure what to do with it. It was beyond time for me to leave England but I delayed leaving.

We sat in the townhouse in London and ate well. Stephen, Eva, Walt, and Rob. The remaining members of the Order of the White Dagger.

Stephen nodded. "All this time it was Geoffrey de Charny and I did not have the wit to see it."

"You did see it. We all did. Yet he managed to turn our suspicion away from him with that business with the stolen shield. It was a mistake."

"A costly mistake," Stephen said. "Our dear friends. Dead, because of my failing."

"Yours, yes. And Eva's. And mine."

"He is dead," Eva said. "Him and his men. Whatever business they were up to, to put the Dauphin on the throne, is finished."

"And yet the Dauphin is regent while his father is the prisoner of King Edward," Thomas said. "Is that not precisely what they wanted?"

Walt spoke up. "But there ain't none of them alive to whisper in his ear none, is there."

"No immortals," I said. "Plenty of lords."

Walt shrugged. "Sounds about right, to me."

"What I still do not understand," Stephen said. "Is why they sent that ruffian to kill you in Southwark."

I shrugged. "He is dead. They are all dead. What does it matter?"

None had an answer for that.

"When do you mean to go away again?" Stephen asked. "Where will you go this time? To crusade against the northern pagans?"

I waved a hand. "Perhaps. For now, we shall return to Suffolk," I said to Walter and Rob. "You can be with be with your family for years yet, Rob."

He nodded, keen as mustard to get back to his wife and children.

"I will give you the manor at Hartest, Walt. You can be the lord there, now."

"Me, sir? I wouldn't know what to do with it."

"You will be all right. And you might even take a wife, now. Settle down for a few years."

"Don't want a wife, sir. The man who has no wife is no cuckold, and that's the truth."

"Not all women are deceitful, Walter. But, wife or no wife, you are a knight, now. No man may have position without duty. And so you will run it well and you will take care of your servants and tenants."

He held up his chin. "I will, sir. I surely will."

In the courtyard a few days later, Eva embraced me before I mounted my horse. She placed a hand against my cheek.

"I am so sorry about Thomas."

"Thank you."

She took her palm away from my face and took my hands in hers.

"You know that Lady Cecilia has married."

I took a deep breath. "I heard it on the way home. Some fat fool. Not a proper knight at all. Never been on campaign. Wealthy, though."

"I am certain she will be deeply unhappy."

I smiled. "I do not want that."

"She sounds like a lusty one. And lust is addicted to novelty. Perhaps you might have her anyway, when the fat fool is not looking."

"I do not want that, either," I said.

"Of course," Eva said, patting my hands. "Do you want me to kill him for you?"

I laughed and embraced her again before mounting my horse. "I think I have had enough killing for a while."

"Does that mean you do not consider yourself a monster after all?"

Before I rode away into the vile filth of London, I considered it.

"We shall see."

It seemed certain that I would not have to fight again for a long time. Perhaps decades.

But I was wrong.

*****

In late 1359, the King summoned me to Windsor Castle.

The war had gone remarkably well. After the Battle of Poitiers, Prince Edward had sent word of the victory back ahead of us.

"We take no pleasure in the slaughter of men," King Edward had said, which was a lie. "But we rejoice in God's bounty and we look forward to a just and early peace."

He seemed right to be so confident that, after yet another catastrophic defeat, the French would sue for peace on almost any terms. With all the leading men of the kingdom either dead or prisoners, their lands had fallen into chaos, anarchy, and rebellion.

After the battle, there was essentially no French army in the country and yet there were thousands of well-organised, highly experienced English armies in Brittany, Normandy, Calais, and Gascony. The French were surrounded and on their knees. In panic, they recruited townsmen to protect against the assault they were certain was coming for Paris.

But the English did not want Paris. Instead, our armies overran what little resistance remained near our strongholds.

The French commoners turned against the knights and nobles who had robbed them for years through endless taxation only to lose battle after battle or to run away in ignominy. And then they were informed, all across the land, that new taxes would be raised to pay for the enormous ransoms required to free their lords. What was more, the assaults of the English and Gascon free companies had increased now there was little threat of resistance.

The people had bent as far as they were able, and then they snapped.

Paris revolted. An eruption of violence took hold of the city as the merchants and common folk rose up against their lords and the Dauphin. They tried to force political changes through violence. The Dauphin attempted to negotiate and delay and said he would consider their demands.

He then ran away from Paris.

The capital city exploded in chaos again. Coinage collapsed. The mob sought to enforce their terms. They attacked royal buildings and set fire to noble's houses with burning arrows while they pillaged official's homes and rampaged through the streets.

Some lords cowered and prayed and pissed their underclothes. Others abandoned law and honour and took up banditry and murder, like the routiers of Brittany.

All through this, King John, still a prisoner of the English, attempted to negotiate his release, negotiate with his lords, with the Dauphin. He was still the King but he was not present in his kingdom and so little could be concluded.

King Edward wanted John to give huge concessions in return for being set free and meant to hold him for as long as it took to extract this from the French.

The political mess was so chaotic that it hampered diplomacy and the talking dragged on for months and years.

Truces were allowed, conferences were held, peace terms were negotiated almost endlessly. Edward wanted the world and he felt he could demand it. He was willing and able to launch more massive attacks on France.

And that was when he summoned me back to him. It was done quietly, and I was shown into his private chambers with no announcement.

"Dear God," King Edward said. "How do you do it, sir?"

I knew he was referring to my everlasting youth. "It is my innocent heart, Your Grace."

He scoffed and almost laughed but then his face fell. "How old are you, Richard?"

The King of England was in his late forties and looking rather as if his best years were far behind him.

"To be honest, Edward, I have lost count. But I must be fifty, I suppose."

"I am surrounded by young men. Or men who appear youthful." He shook his head. "You have the devil in you."

"Perhaps."

"My son says so."

"I would never disagree with the Prince, Your Grace."

He smiled. "I think you embarrassed him at Poitiers. I hear you shouted at him. Called him a fool in front of the army."

"Unforgivable actions."

"Spare me your false contrition. I do not need it."

"You called me here for something."

"I am going to war again." He did not sound pleased about the matter. "I will only get the victory God wishes if I take Paris."

"So it is true."

"I would have you with us."

Even though it was gratifying to hear it, I was surprised. "It is a great honour to offer my sword in service to you again, Your Grace. And yet, the lords of—"

"Are they the King of England, sir? Or am I?"

Inclining my head a little, I smiled. He had rarely been one for outbursts but the war had been hard on him, even if he had not been the one fighting it in person.

He cleared his throat. "You have always been able to achieve that which other knights would find difficult."

I knew that he meant I would do dishonourable things, if he asked me to. And I would achieve them and hold my tongue about it.

"Certainly, Your Grace. Whatever you require."

"If you do this and can manage to control yourself, you will be welcomed back in full honour."

That was not something I needed, or wanted. And I felt no desire to go to France again and do whatever it was that the King had in mind for me. Possibly, he wanted someone killed. Perhaps the Dauphin. Or perhaps even King John himself.

I sighed.

Edward scowled. "Are you ungrateful, sir? I offer you this chance at redemption and you can think only to huff and blow like an old maid? Damn you, then, Richard. And Damn Humphrey too. Leave me."

"Humphrey?" I said. "Sir Humphrey Ingham? What does he have to do with it?"

"He is the man who asked me to bring you back in."

"Why in God's name would he do that? He despises me."

"I always believed that Sir Humphrey Ingham regarded you highly. After all, he requested that you be the lucky one, of all the knights of the realm, to escort his lovely sister home after she was widowed the first time."

"Sir Humphrey asked for me personally? But why would he do that?"

"Practically begged me. I told him you were a rogue who could not be trusted with his sister but he insisted and as he had done well for me I granted his request. As I recall, now that I think of it, he put a word in with Suffolk and my son to ensure that you would be released from confinement when you were thrown into gaol before the Poitiers campaign."

"That is quite peculiar. The few occasions we have crossed paths in person, he gave every indication of despising me."

"Perhaps he does. Many do, Richard. But all men know that when you set your will to a task you see it completed. He was thinking of his sister's safety and who better to protect her from robbers and pirates than the biggest robber and pirate of them all."

"Thank you, Your Grace."

"And now, I expect, he wants you for his sister again."

"Cecilia is in trouble?"

"Trouble?" The King waved a hand. "Her second husband has suffered a tragic accident while riding. The fall killed him dead. Oh, do not worry, the Lady is well. But, of course, she bore him no children, she is now really rather old, and she is considered to be somewhat unlucky. It is the convent for her, that is for certain. Unless..."

"Unless some great, desperate fool is willing to take her as his wife."

The King smiled. "So, I shall see you again once you join the army in France, sir?"

***

I rode hard for Cecilia's home. When I arrived, it was as though she was waiting for me. Everything was ready. Food, wine. Her bedchamber.

Even though she was in the middle of her thirties, she was still quite lovely and had the energy and enthusiasm of a girl half her age.

We spoke little until we lay naked and tired on her sheets, looking up at the underside of the canopy. One of her maids brought wine and then left, leaving us to catch our breath in the candlelight.

"I missed you," I said.

"Clearly, sir," she replied. We laughed.

"I am very sorry about the untimely death of your late husband."

"Yes. I am in mourning."

Growing serious, I turned my head to look at her. She was not smiling.

"I wish I had not left you all those years ago. I hope your marriage was not too difficult for you."

She sighed. "He tried to get a child on me. I could not stand it. He soon gave up. Much preferred hunting and drinking."

"An often fatal combination."

"And boys."

I turned to look at her again. "He was a sodomite?"

She laughed, bitterly. "I do not think he went so far as that. He just enjoyed touching them a little."

"Dear God. I do not know what to say."

She reached over to her wine beside the bed and drank a sip. I ran my fingers idly down her flank as she turned and stretched herself out.

"He was a child himself, in truth. He was terrified of me, and rightly so. Still, I withstood him as long as I needed to," she said. "And when I knew you had returned, and Humphrey gave me leave, I broke my dear husband's neck."

Astonished, I began to lean over onto my elbow to ask if she was speaking truthfully.

She whipped around as fast as a striking snake.

I saw a glint of bright steel raised high.

Before I understood what was happening, she stabbed me through the chest, between collarbone and nipple, with a sword.

It ran right through me to the hilt, through the mattresses below and into the oak bed beneath. My blood welled up and flowed across my chest beneath the crosspiece.

The pain was incredible but it was nothing compared to the horror of what had happened.

I grabbed the sword and tried to pull it out. It was stuck fast.

She had missed my heart but only just and I could barely breathe. I coughed and sprayed blood over myself.

Cecilia was staring at me with wild victory in her blue eyes.

She laughed.

"I did it," she said to herself. "My God."

The betrayal was more than I could bear. Her laughter echoed in my empty soul. I grasped the sword hilt with both hands and, cutting my hands, heaved.

It slid slowly up through my body, slicing through flesh and bone and lacerating my organs as it followed the path. My body seemed to suck the blade into itself as if it did not want to come free.

As the sword came loose from the bed beneath me, Cecilia's laughter turned to a scream of horror.

"Eustace!" she shouted. "Eustace!"

Almost at once, the door to the chamber burst open and the damned steward marched in with sword in hand.

Cecilia, shamelessly naked, jabbed her finger me. "He frees himself!"

Eustace snapped at her to get back and stalked forward to finish me.

I gripped the blade and pulled it up and up, out of my sucking chest wound, hand under hand. The stocky steward rushed me and thrust with his sword where I lay. I rolled away across the bed just as I pulled the last of the steel from my body. Blood gushed out of me and filled my throat.

The steward rushed around the end of the bed, hooking a hand around the final post and aiming a cut at my face. I lurched back away from it and, holding the blade in both hands, blocked his next cut before falling back over a low table beside the bed and crashing into the wall. He stood back, watching me warily. It seemed as though he was afraid of me, even naked and bleeding. But I realised he was merely waiting for me die.

Angry, I stumbled forward with my sword in my hand.

Cecilia jumped on me and held on to my sword arm with her immortal strength.

"Now, you fool!" she yelled at Eustace.

He came forward, sword ready to strike.

Lifting her up, I threw Cecilia, naked, at Eustace. He lowered his blade and ducked and she hit his considerable mass with a thud and fell to the floor. I grabbed her by the hair and yanked her up and tossed her away against the wall.

Eustace rushed me like a bullock charging a half-open gate. I thrust my sword into his neck, sliding the blade down into his body, before ripping it out again as he fell past me onto the bloody floor.

The porter came rushing in and froze two steps into the doorway. His eyes wide and his mouth open. He stared at his dazed, naked, bloody mistress pulling herself to her feet.

"Help me," I said to him, or tried to, as the blood filled my throat and I coughed.

He had a sword in his hand. The porter's face changed from horror to fury, and, seeing I was so terribly wounded, rushed at me to finish me off.

Instead, I knocked his blade aside, grabbed him, slit his throat and drank his blood as his heels drummed on the floor. He was simply doing his duty but I wanted to live, and so he had to die.

My wound burned as it knitted together, the lancing pain like being run through again, but the pain went away and I was healed. The blood covering half my body was already beginning to dry.

"Why?" I said to Cecilia, pushing her to the floor again before she could regain her feet. "Why did you do this?"

She sneered, her beautiful face twisted in contempt.

"Why, Richard? *Why?* To protect ourselves."

"You and Eustace?" I pointed with my sword to his body.

She laughed a bitter laugh. "You think yourself so wise and yet you are a fool."

"Who, then? Geoffrey de Charny? You are his?"

She shook her head. "You know nothing at all."

"I know that my brother William made you. He made Geoffrey de Charny and his two squires. That brute Eustace there. So many of you under my nose. By God, you sent that big filthy bastard to kill me in the stews."

"No, Richard. Not I. We were not supposed to kill you. Only to discover the others that you had gifted immortal life. That arrogant merchant, Stephen Poole. Others, though, we suspected. The woman who travels to Bristol. Other soldiers. But my dear Humphrey could not contain his jealousy and he sent Jacob to kill you. I warned him that you would not fall so easily."

"Sir Humphrey? Of course, it had to be your brother."

She grinned. "My *brother*. Ha! I never met him until my lord William brought us together. In time, my Humphrey and I fell in love. We have often lived openly together as husband and wife. For many decades. And at other times we pose as siblings so that we both may marry into wealth or position." She laughed, suddenly, flicking her unbound hair. "I had you dangling, did I not? And yet you refused to marry me for so long. A shame. We could have lived together. Shared a bed together. For years." Rising up on her knees, she opened her arms wide, displaying her nakedness. "It could have been delightful, sharing each other all this time, dear Richard, if only you had not been so bull-headed about it." Her eyes were wide and sorrowful. Her skin, pale and perfect.

"Why?" I asked. "Why, why? Only to now murder me?"

"Oh," she said, tilting her head. "I am so sorry for that. But Humphrey said that you had to be stopped before you undid everything we have worked so hard for. And you also had to be punished for murdering Geoffrey. He was the best of us, so Humphrey liked to say. If you ask me, Geoffrey was the most tiresome bore this past hundred years. Always wittering on about honour and jousting and such. But I did not want to kill you, Richard. I do have such affection for you."

"What were you planning?" I asked. "For what purpose did William make you? Why did he bring you all together?"

"Oh, they do not tell me such things. I am afraid I would not know."

"Do not play the silly maid with me, Cecilia. I know you well enough to know that you are not a simpleton."

She smiled and sat back, still kneeling. "You are so kind."

"You are trying to control the Crown of France, are you not? You were behind the plan to kill King John and take power through controlling the Dauphin? I have put a stop to all that."

She sighed. "Yes, you are so very clever, Richard."

"But your brother. That is, Sir Humphrey. What is he…" I trailed off. "Sir Humphrey is Prince Edward's man. Or pretending to be." I recalled how the Prince had changed over the years, turning from valiant golden prince into a darker, meaner spirit. Surely that was in part due to Ingham, whispering in his ear for a decade. "Is he going to kill King Edward?"

She laughed. "I may not have killed you. But I have delayed you. Humphrey has already sailed with the King and you will not have time to stop him. When the King falls, Prince Edward will rule. And through him, us. Other plans shall have to be made for France. King John remains a prisoner in England, does he not? Humphrey shall find a way, he always does. And soon, our lord will return at the head of a great army and the crowns of England and France will be his. And then we shall rule all Christendom for eternity."

I scoffed. "Once you have served his purposes, William will discard you. He will rule alone and you shall have nothing."

"No!" she said, rising up onto her knees again, her bare chest thrust out before her. She jabbed a finger at me and spoke with such passion that she quivered. "He swore his undying love for me. For *me*! I shall be at his side, ruling as his queen. As the Empress of Christendom."

"You and William—" I began.

She leapt to her feet, snatched a dagger from Eustace's corpse and stabbed up at my groin with a scream of fury.

It gored the inside of my thigh even as I twisted away, jumped back, and brought my sword down on her neck.

She fell, her head almost entirely severed.

I dropped to my knees beside her and held her as she died. The blue of her eyes dimmed and her eyelids fluttered closed. Her hand lifted toward my cheek only to fall before she reached me.

Chasing out the servants from her home, I put her chamber to fire so as to burn the bodies. No doubt the servants would be raising the hue and cry to have me captured and tried for murder. Two of the deaths were matters of self-defence but I was certainly guilty of the murder of the porter and so the name and persona of Richard of Hawkedon would have to be abandoned.

I rode south to find Rob and Walt.

We had to find passage to France, join our army on campaign, and save King Edward's life before he was assassinated by the immortal Sir Humphrey Ingham.

***

By the time we caught up with the army, Edward's campaign was in full effect. He wanted to take Paris for England or at the least cause so much destruction and terror that the French would finally seek terms.

Hundreds of ships crossed back and forth across the Channel, taking vast quantities of supplies to the army and I had to pay a great sum to get one to find room for us. In Calais I paid a fortune for a few good horses and we hurried on. All the while I prayed Edward yet lived. The spring had been remarkably warm and dry but it was after Easter by the time we rode south in the wake of the devastation.

Riding those long miles, I tried not to think of Cecilia but I kept going over it all. Recalling all the little things over the years that should have alerted me. Her childlessness in itself was not enough but her continued youthful beauty as the years went by certainly should have been. I was simply infatuated with her. With who she pretended to be, that was. Perhaps it was only ever blind lust. I wondered if anything she had said and done had ever been true.

She had said I thought of myself as wise. But that had never been so. It was clear that she did not know me as well as she thought. And that made me feel better. I may have had a false idea of her but clearly she had one of me also.

I told myself that I had thrown off the betrayal. And yet I found that it was on my mind for a considerable time after the anger turned to melancholy.

Our army was unopposed and the English had burned villages and towns all around Paris to the south. Places like Orly, Longjumeau, Montlhery. The great army marched up to the walls of Paris and cut it off from the south. Our garrisons across northern France cut it off from the north. Inside, food shortages and subsequent price rises caused the population to panic. Edward had forced displaced people from the surrounding villages, towns, and suburbs into Paris and all those within the walls knew that in their future lied starvation. Smoke from the burning homes and villages drifted across the city and flames could be seen coming ever closer as the English army marched back and forth outside the walls, turning the rich suburban homes into charred timbers and ash. All the while, English trumpets blew and the kettle drums sounded.

The Parisians were too afraid, or too wily, to leave the safety of the walls.

It did bring the French diplomats into urgent negotiations, but the obstinate fools delayed and delayed and our army suffered from the usual maladies. And so the King decided to reposition the army, moving west away from the city and then to the north.

That was where we found them.

By the town of Galardon, with the towers of Chartres Cathedral silhouetted against the swirling grey sky in the distance across a vast open plain. The weather had finally turned and dark clouds gathered overhead. Beneath, our enormous, filthy army spread in shadow across mile after mile of flat French countryside.

The land burned beyond and the men were miserable because everything had been picked clean a thousand times over and there was nothing left to steal.

"How we going to find him?" Walt asked as we stared at the trudging lines of horses and men and banners held aloft waving in the growing wind. "Find him, that is, without giving the game away."

I knew he was thinking of our search for the black knight and how our actions there led to Thomas and Hugh being killed.

"And when we do find him," Rob said, while I recalled it. "How do you mean to apprehend him without men stopping us?"

"We have no time for cleverness or subtleties," I said, drawing my sword and raising my voice above the wind. "I will ride up to Ingham and murder him. Then we shall flee and stay away from the English until all living are now dead."

Rob hung his head and said nothing.

Large blobs of rain began to fall, here and there, pinging loudly when they hit steel or drumming on the dry earth.

I raised my voice and called out. "Where is Sir Humphrey Ingham?"

A sergeant rode over to us, looking me up and down. I was dressed well enough but I had left my armour back in England. We all had.

"Can I help you, sir?"

"I seek a man. A knight named Sir Humphrey Ingham."

He looked at my naked sword and the fury on my face. "If he has angered you, sir, you must take your disagreement to the King."

I snarled. "I will cut off his damned traitorous head."

In the distance, thunder rumbled.

"A traitor? Sir Humphrey? Surely not, sir?"

I scoffed. "He is Brutus. He is Ganelon. He is Judas. The King himself is in danger. Where is Ingham?"

"But..." he stammered. "He is with the King, last I saw."

"Where, man?"

He raised his hand and pointed south. A cluster of banners whipped and twisted in the far distance and one of them looked like the King's own arms.

I spurred my horse and raced forward through the men with Walt and Rob riding as well as they could behind me. It would not do to get too far ahead of them, so I slowed.

The rain came down harder and harder until the heavens opened and the rain came down in sheets. Men all around us covered their heads with whatever they had and trudged on.

"There is the King!" I shouted to my men, pointing with my sword.

King Edward and his lords came on in a hurry, no doubt hoping to reach some sort of shelter miles beyond, or at least outrun the sudden storm.

The rain gusted into my face like a thousand tiny whips. The ground turned to mud and the rain ran across the surface like a river. My horse slowed to a walk, lifting his hooves up high and stepping through the morass.

"Get on, will you," I shouted at him, raking my spurs on him.

Lighting flashed overhead and almost at once thunder sounded, powerfully enough to be felt through the earth. The men all around me hunched and fought their way onward through the storm. There was no shelter to be had anywhere for miles around and so all they could do was go on.

The rain, already as heavy as any I had ever seen anywhere in the world, suddenly got heavier. My horse would not move, so I dismounted and he jumped away through the muck. Peering behind me, I saw Walt helping Rob to his feet. One or both of them had been thrown from their mounts.

"Come on," I said, fearing that I would lose the King's men, who were so close.

I lifted my knees high and fought through the liquifying mud. Soldiers were shouting at each other in fear.

As the rain eased off slightly, I caught sight of the King and his men, dismounted and fighting to hold on to their panicking horses. I thought I could see Ingham there by the King's side but it was so hard to see.

It suddenly turned cold. Bitterly cold, like the deepest winter had descended.

"What is this?" Walt shouted in my ear. His eyes were wild. Shivering violently, he and Rob clung to each other like drowning men.

I had no answer for what it was. Never in my long life had I known anything like it. Underfoot, the flowing water drained away but the mud began to freeze, even as we walked through it.

Men wailed all around, fighting their horses, fighting to hold on to supplies as the wind whipped up and blew away blankets, sheets, clothes.

The King's men clustered around him, I hoped protecting his royal person from the elements. Ingham was there amongst them. I could see him.

"Stop!" I shouted. "Edward! Beware!"

I thought, perhaps, that Ingham turned and looked in my direction. But my voice was carried away by the hurricane and the temperature dropped further, turning the ground to ice. Men were blown off their feet and some rolled along the ground.

Rob got his leg stuck and together with Walt we pulled him out before the ground turned as hard as iron.

"Hurry, now," I shouted in their ears and they nodded, drawing their swords.

As we pushed through the wind, the rain turned to hailstones. The smallest of which was the size of an acorn and most were the size of a fist.

Men fell in their scores as they were struck by the storm of hail. A cacophony rose above the roaring of the wind to become deafening as the deluge of stones struck helms and armour for miles around. Men cried out in pain and terror. Horses ran in wild panic or lay down on the ground in despair and agony.

Soldiers fell down dead or insensible from the impacts. The King's men, many covering him with their bodies, dropped under the assault. Felled by enormous lumps of ice or collapsing from the relentless driving impact from thousands of smaller ones, knights and lords crawled through the crunching ice underfoot into hollows.

Leaning against the driving wind, I struggled on, step by step. I passed two knights huddled against the belly of a dead horse that lay on its side, one leg jerking in the air.

Other men struggled on, bent double, headed across the plain as if there could be salvation elsewhere if only they could reach it.

Two of Edward's bodyguards held the King between them, making off through the ice and wind. The others had fallen behind or were knocked insensible all about us.

Behind Edward, Sir Humphrey Ingham stalked forward.

He was making better headway than the King and his men, gaining on them with every step.

In his right hand, he held a long, thin dagger.

I roared a warning but my voice was whipped away as soon as it was spoken.

Pushing forward, fighting the wind, I forced one leg forward and another, lifting my knees up and down with my watery eyes on the ground.

I was so close.

When I looked up, Ingham was an arm's length behind the King. He reached out with his left hand to grasp Edward on the shoulder. His right was pulled back with the dagger in his hand.

"Ingham!" I shouted with everything I had.

He half turned in surprise and with that moment's hesitation, I lunged forward and stuck my blade into his leg. It hit his armour but it was enough to trip him. I stumbled forward and dropped down on him.

Ingham grasped the blade of my sword and ripped it from my grasp, throwing it behind him.

I locked my knees either side of Ingham and lifted his visor with one hand while I drew my dagger.

He stabbed me in the body, just beneath the ribs. God, it hurt. The dagger was long, and sharp as Satan.

With my free arm, I trapped his arm and blade inside my body, and I stabbed him in the face with my own blade.

The King was shouting something. His bodyguards came forward.

I stabbed Ingham again, over and over.

My men pulled me away.

Edward was there, pushing his two bodyguards away from him. The hail was easing off, turning to sleet. And the wind was no longer strong enough to blow a man to the ground.

"Richard!" the King shouted.

"Ingham, sire," I said, wincing. It hurt to speak. "He was going to kill you."

Edward looked at the body and then back at me.

He nodded once.

"I saw the blade," the King said, scowling and shaking his head in wonder. He broke off. "You are hurt."

"All is well, Your Grace," I said, clapping him on the shoulder. "All is well." Raising my voice, I waved over his bodyguards. "Get him somewhere safe, will you."

"Why?" the King said. "Why would Ingham do this?"

"He was paid by the Dauphin's men," I said, lying easily. I had rehearsed my accusations. "Paid to assassinate you. I discovered the plot and came to warn you."

"God love you, Richard," the King said as they tugged him back toward safety.

"Come on," I said to Rob and Walt, as the storm passed. "It is over."

2 4

The Death of the King

"THE ARMY WAS FINISHED after that," I said to Stephen, weeks later, in London. "And Edward's resolve to continue the war must have crumbled."

We sat in the hall together for what we knew would be the last time for a generation, at least.

"I cannot fathom it," Stephen said, shaking his head. "How can a storm be so powerful?"

"God can do as He pleases," I said. "And He decided to do what the French could not."

All told, we lost a thousand men to the storm and six thousand horses. There was never a storm like it in all my days, before or since. It was undoubtedly a sign from God that He wished Edward to end his war and so that was what Edward did.

The Treaty of Bretigny brought the war to an end. He agreed to drop his claim to the throne of France. And in return, the French recognised all that Edward and the English Crown had won in the war.

Edward III obtained, besides Guyenne and Gascony, Poitou, Saintonge and Aunis, Agenais, Périgord, Limousin, Quercy, Bigorre, the countship of Gaure, Angoumois, Rouergue, Montreuil-sur-Mer, Ponthieu, Calais, Sangatte, Ham and the countship of Guines.

What is more, these lands were to be held free and clear, without doing homage for them.

After twenty years of war against the mightiest kingdom in Christendom, King Edward III had established a truly mighty empire.

My own quest was also over.

It had taken far too long and I had almost destroyed us entirely. My decisions had led to the deaths of my brothers Thomas, John, and Hugh.

But we had uncovered the whole nest of snakes in the end. We had, perhaps, saved the lives of two kings and disrupted my brother's plans for the domination of two nations.

Decades before, William had given the Gift to a number of French and English knights and left them with instructions on how to prepare for his return. I had been looking for them for so long and now, it was over. It was time to leave England and hide elsewhere for a few decades.

Eva would stay in London for a few years to manage the trade and the information network, posing as Stephen's widow.

Stephen would move to Bristol and pretend to be Eva's steward, taking care of things there. We would maintain correspondence and all would watch and listen for signs of William's return.

I kissed Eva and embraced my brothers in the hall of the London house and went on my way.

England, on top of the world for a moment, did not fare well.

Prince Edward administered the lands of Gascony and all France, ruling like a king. But he became embroiled in the knotty and interminable web of shifting alliances between all the rulers in that part of the world, from Castile and Aragon to Poitiers and Bordeaux. He fought in dozens of battles where generally he won. And he wrestled in diplomacy with hundreds of lords where generally he failed.

And fate turned against our prince.

In 1367, when Edward was in his prime at thirty-seven years old, he was on campaign in the disgusting heat of a Spanish summer when his entire army fell to the bloody flux and other common maladies. The Prince was himself afflicted so terribly that he never fully recovered. His body went into a long and painful decline.

Some men whispered that it was divine punishment for his black dealings with this lord or that. Others thought he had been poisoned and it had rotted his body from the inside.

Over the coming years, he was stricken with dropsy so that his limbs and body would swell to enormous size. He could not even ride and had to be carried in a litter here and there. A shameful and emasculating fate.

One by one, his great friends and allies, like the capable soldier John Chandos, died.

In 1370, Edward's eldest boy, another Edward who was just five years old, died from a resurgence of the Black Death.

The pestilence would return every few years and take more from our people. Mostly children, and so each generation was aggrieved in their hearts beyond all recovery.

It was the death of his eldest son and heir, on top of his own endless physical agonies, that broke the Prince's will. There was another son, Richard, who would one day become King of England. But a man can only bear so much pain and, when he was back home in

England for his boy's funeral, Edward's flux returned and drained him of his will.

Bloated, pale, and weak, our Golden Prince died in 1376 aged forty-five.

King Edward would make it just one more year before himself succumbing to age and the ravages of grief.

He was never the same after the storm. After the peace he had won. All his life, he had fought for victory and when he achieved it, he found himself broken by the effort.

His boundless energy and enthusiasm were gone. Used up in the fight. Perhaps it was the toll of decades of physical exhaustion and from being thumped about the head too many times in battle. God knows, that seemed to do for the wits of many a knight I have known.

After the peace, he passed much of the leadership of the realm onto his son and even though the Prince of Wales had struggled with international diplomacy in a way that the King never had, old Edward left him to it.

Queen Philippa, who had brought forth from her womb thirteen princes and princesses for England, died in Windsor in 1369 and the loss brought Edward very low indeed. He had loved her dearly.

His health failed him more and more and by the summer of 1377, he was never out of his bed. The King's mind had long been failing but his wits were by then almost gone. His days were numbered and he would soon depart for Heaven.

My own heart was breaking at the news coming from England of the King's demise. It was a risk, perhaps, but one I could not resist.

I went to see my king one last time.

***

Stephen's wealth, connections, and well-placed agents bought the necessary access to the palace at Richmond and, after waiting all day, I was shown by one of Stephen's men into the King's bedchamber.

The smell was appalling and his servants all had cloths tied across their faces.

"Who is that lurking there?" the King said. His voice, once so powerful that in a single breath it could move the hearts of a thousand knights, had become the rasping whisper of a dying old man.

"It is Richard of Hawkedon, Your Grace," I said, coming forward. "I thought you asleep."

"Asleep? No, no. I never sleep. Never get enough. Too much to do. Come here, man."

I went forward and bowed, before taking a knee beside him.

He frowned. "Is that you, Richard?"

"It is, Your Grace. I came to speak with you."

"Well? What is it you have to say?" his eyes flicked up around the room. "Where are we? Is this... Villeneuve?"

"This is Richmond, Edward. We have not been at Villeneuve for twenty years. Twenty-five, perhaps. That was where the lords of Calais surrendered their town to you. After we beat the French at Crecy."

"It seems like another life," Edward whispered. The corners of his mouth twitched and he lifted a skeletal hand toward my face before letting it fall back to the bed. "Another life for me. But perhaps not for you, Richard. How is it that you are unchanged from that day to this? They always told me you were not one of us and now I see how right they were. Or have I truly lost my mind after all? You are an impostor, perhaps. His son, or grandson, pretending to be my friend."

"They were right," I admitted. "And yet I am the same man who was at your side that night in Nottingham when you were newly our king."

"Do you recall it as I do, I wonder?"

He was testing me and his mind had degenerated so far that I am sure that he believed he was doing so with subtle cunning.

"I recall it clearly, Edward," I said. "You were all so young. The lords around you were loyal but they needed a little encouragement and the belief that they could help you destroy Mortimer. And I watched from the edges as you slowly grew to become the man I knew you could be. After you married Philippa, you changed. Marriage often does that to a man but the stakes were so much higher for you than for ordinary men."

"Oh," he muttered, clutching at his sheets. "Dear Philippa. Gentle, compassionate Philippa. She was stronger than iron, you know. She would have had Mortimer's throat slit in the night if it meant being done with him."

I smiled at the thought. "I admit, sire, that for some time I planned to murder Roger Mortimer myself. My friends convinced me that it would destabilise the kingdom and of course they were right. But I kept a close eye on Mortimer and his bodyguards. Your mind may be going, Edward, but no doubt you recall the humiliation of the Great Council in Nottingham where Mortimer called you untrustworthy and accused your men of plotting against him." My voice shook as I spoke and tears pricked my eyes. "You were the *King* and he spoke in such a way. The outrage could not stand and it was my friend Thomas who literally held me back from storming to Mortimer's chambers that very night and delivering to you his head."

Edward laughed at that. A laugh that ended in a cough. "Your friend had good sense. You talked me into taking action, finally."

"You did not require much persuasion, Edward."

He smiled. "No."

"On the morning of the fateful day, I told you of my plan and you merely nodded. I was proud of you. Later, I gathered twenty-two of your companions and brought them to the culvert outside, below the castle, which you unlocked for us with your own hand."

"Who were our companions that night, Richard?"

"Let me see. Montagu, Ufford, John Neville. John Moleyns was still there. The three Bohun brothers. Humps was perhaps twenty-one and Ned and William were not yet twenty."

"Steadfast fellows," Edward said. "Thank God for those men."

"Thank God for those tunnels beneath Nottingham and for your courage. Our companions were in a very high state but you were the embodiment of calm and your steadiness in turn calmed them. It was quiet and we saw few servants but those we swiftly subdued. The garrison commander was loyal to you and so we were not challenged until we entered your mother's apartments."

"My mother," he muttered, shaking his head. "Do you recall what she cried?"

"Your mother beseeched you most fervently. Fair son, she called, have pity on gentle Mortimer."

Edward nodded in confirmation, though clearly it pained him to recall it and so I continued.

"Mortimer was in a chamber adjacent to hers and when I threw open his door, his men cried murder and attacked me. Two of them, I killed, though there were others I merely wounded. Mortimer was quick to give himself up rather than fight. As much as I wanted to paint the walls with traitor's blood, I knew it would be better for you if I restrained myself."

Edward chuckled in his throat. "Two dead and half a dozen wounded is my Richard when he restrains himself," he said.

"I continued to restrain myself, if you recall. As the sun came up, we went out into the town and took all of Mortimer's supporters lodged there into our custody. And soon, Mortimer received the justice that he deserved. I rejoiced at the sight of him dangling at the end of that rope. It pleases me still."

"So long ago," he sighed, "and yet also no more than a blink of the eye." He squinted at me. "Do you never grow old, Richard?"

"Not so far."

"What *are* you, Richard?"

A dozen thoughts crossed my mind.

I am a blood-drinking immortal. I am the progeny of a mighty ancient conqueror whom someday I must kill. I am the bastard son of a bastard son. I am cousin to Alexander and to Caesar. I am a murderer. A failure. A fool.

"I am a knight, my lord. An English knight." I smiled. "A very old one."

He narrowed his eyes. "How old?"

"I have lived over two hundred years."

"Is this madness?" he asked, an edge of horror creeping into his voice. "Is it my madness?"

I took his hand. "Not this, my lord. Strange beyond reason and yet it is truth."

He sighed and closed his eyes, so that I thought he was asleep. But he opened them and spoke earnestly. "Will you look after my son? See he makes a good king, will you? I think perhaps he does not know how much he needs the love of the people and the loyalty of the lords. Help him to know, will you, Richard?"

He had forgotten his son was dead. It would be the King's grandson, Richard of Bordeaux, who would take the Crown. I did not have the heart to correct him.

"I will, Your Grace."

He smiled and lay back.

It was a lie in more ways than one. I could not stay in England to watch over the young king to be.

"I failed, did I not?" he asked.

In many ways, perhaps he had. But he had done more, been more, than most men who ever lived.

"Failed? How can you say such a thing? You defeated France, my lord. Again and again."

"God wanted me to stop," he muttered.

"That He did. But He also helped you capture the King of France."

"Oh yes." His tone was one of surprise and he chuckled to recall it and I saw the merest hint of the energetic young man I had first known. "But that was not God but you, Richard, if my memory does not fail me." He closed his eyes and his voice fell to a whisper. "You gave me France."

I bowed my head. "I have lived a long time. Served many kings. You were a king that England deserved. And it has been an honour to serve you, Edward."

Whether he heard me before he slept, I do not know, for I was escorted from the chamber.

Three days later, the King was dead.

***

After leaving England, I went to Castile but there were too many Englishmen there, fighting in free companies under veteran captains for this lord or that, and so I went to Italy.

I found the same there, only more so. Thousands of English soldiers in dozens of companies fighting for one city against another. Some companies rose and others fell. I was welcomed for my skill at arms in any of them but I had had enough of the base, mercenary nature of their endless squabbling. And so, I went further east for a while before eventually returning through the Italian wars to England.

Walt was beside me through all of it. He was proud to call himself Sir Walter of Hartest and he strove always to live with the honour of a knight. The fact that he failed more often than he succeeded could not be held against him, as all knights struggled so whether they were a peasant or a prince.

The code of chivalry was ever an ideal to reach for, and to sometimes fall short, rather than a standard to live by.

In truth, I could well have done without Walt's constant stream of unsought opinions but not without his steadfast companionship.

Rob Hawthorn spent as much time as he could with his family until the talk of his agelessness grew to endanger the legacy of his good name.

It broke Rob's heart to leave them but he had done his duty by making strong sons and daughters and had established a robust family line that would continue on down the centuries without him. His son, Dick, was a man grown by then and ready to inherit. Stephen helped Rob make a faked death by reporting the sinking of a ship that did not exist and so the son took over Rob's land and became the head of his family. As is right and proper.

When Rob left England to join us in Italy, he left a kingdom in upheaval.

Richard II appeared at first to be another fine king in the making. When he was just a boy, he took a personal role in quelling the terrifying rebellion of the commoners of Essex and Kent. In 1381, the ungrateful masses of those Godforsaken counties stormed London, killing and robbing like crazed savages. Only the physical presence and the wise and goodly words of the young king served to calm them. After the fools were disbursed, they were rounded up and quite rightly sorted out once and for all. Sadly, this early success may have been Richard's finest hour.

He lost his crown to his cousin, Henry Bolingbroke, who was a truly great knight in his youth and a rather mediocre king. But he fathered Henry V who took the throne shortly before I returned to England.

Henry V was, perhaps, an even greater king than Edward III. I was proud to serve him, though I was careful this time to avoid becoming his friend and companion.

I resolved to live and to fight like a knight but I could support the King from afar. This I did through my personal strength of arms, and those of my knights Sir Robert and Sir Walter, and through funding King Henry's campaign with loans from the coffers of the White Dagger.

We fought France again, of course. And again, we thrashed them so completely that it shook the French to their souls.

During the Battle of Agincourt, our English steadfast archers fought like bloody heroes. They also, by order of the King, slaughtered a great mass of the captured French nobility, which much increased the numbers felled on the field.

It seemed as though England was poised to subjugate all of France, for the French Crown was promised to Henry's son and heir, who ruled as Henry VI.

But tragedy struck. The victorious Henry V was in his prime, the most celebrated man in Christendom and the most magnificent King of England who ever was, when he was destroyed by dysentery. Surely, the most ignominious way to meet one's end.

Henry VI was just a boy when he inherited and, without the hero king, England's nobles could not keep their hands around France's throat for long. And when he grew to manhood, Henry VI was both weak and mad.

Dear old England suffered.

All through our weakest times, I fretted for us, as I knew that my brother would one day return to Christendom, and I feared that it would be at the head of a great army seeking to conquer it.

As it turned out, I was quite right about both his return and the army he was leading.

But it was decades more before my brother made his traitorous move.

We kept a close eye on the Black Forest but my grandfather and his sons lived quietly, ruling through fear over the villages nestling in the valleys around them. All it cost those people was the sacrifice of a lovely young woman every few years to the monster that lived in the woods and they could pretend to the outside world that all was well. One day, I would pray, one day, Lord, I will put Priskos and his sons to the sword. But I would have to grow far stronger, and I would have to defeat William first.

For the longest time, I believed that we had routed out William's nest of immortals. We could find no more. Not in France or England, or Italy or Spain. Every trail led nowhere.

And then, after years of searching, we finally uncovered another one of William's spawn in France. One we had missed. One that I had overlooked with my own eyes. A man lurking and biding his time in one guise or another for decades and centuries until his evil could be contained no longer.

When I finally found him, he had made himself into one of the great nobles of his time. A Marshal of France and a hero of the battles that threw the English out of his lands forever.

A man so depraved he fashioned a raving mad peasant child called Joan into a parody of a soldier and set her on a path that led to her appalling death, screaming and bound as the fire destroyed her flesh.

A monster with a heart so dark that he consumed children like capons, bathing in their blood even as they screamed their last.

A heretic who called upon the power Satan and all the demons of Hell in the towers and dungeons of his fortress home.

But that is a tale for another time.

VAMPIRE

HERETIC

The Immortal Knight Chronicles
Book 5

Richard of Ashbury
and the mass murderer Gilles de Rais
1429 - 1440

1

The Bishop of Nantes

April 1440

THERE WAS NEVER in all my life a story more depraved and hideous than that of Gilles de Rais. For all the horrific, evil deeds that I have both witnessed and myself committed over eight centuries, it causes even me to shudder to relate the crimes of that great Marshal of France.

It was a dark time for England.

Our King was Henry VI, a young man who had been gifted the crown of France by the military successes of his father and who seemed determined to piss it all away. He was timid, soft in the heart and in the head, weak-willed and cowardly as a man and a king and sought only peace instead of victory.

And so we lost.

Before his majority, England had been ruled by a gaggle of lords who were the fading echoes of their mighty fathers. Administrators in their hearts, the only fighting that they excelled at was the squabbling of the court and in battle they were hesitant and had the alarming tendency to flee when defeat reared her head.

The series of wars that we had waged against France for over a hundred years was limping toward a miserable end. After the soaring, magnificent glories of Crecy, Poitiers, Agincourt, and Verneuil we were brought crashing to earth by the ignominious defeats at

Orléans, and Patay.

We were undone by many things but principle among them was the divinely inspired leadership of Joan the Maiden of Orléans.

Those military defeats weighed heavily on me and the knowledge that the figurehead of our destruction had ultimately been burned at the stake for heresy brought me little comfort. I was heartsick and disillusioned at the collapse of our fortunes and had spent years in London, miserable and unable to summon the will required to return to France before it was lost forever.

It was nine years after Joan's execution, in early April 1440, that I received a hastily-written letter from Stephen Gosset begging me to join him in Brittany.

Richard, I pray this letter finds you in better spirits than when we last spoke. There are rumours here of a familiar nature and it is imperative that you join me in Nantes immediately. The subject of said rumours is a man known to you and is one of remarkable power and thus I implore that you come attended by our strongest comrades. As always, our business in London can continue to be maintained by the Lady of the house. I beg you, Richard. Hurry.

The scrawl was barely recognisable as Stephen's, though it most assuredly was, and his usual care to encode the business of our Order had been abandoned for open clumsy innuendo. It was not even signed.

"What do you make of this?" I asked Eva, who was the Lady that Stephen had referred to.

"That you shall shortly have some bloody business to attend to," she replied. "And I will be able to run our affairs here in peace without your glumness seeping from the walls."

I had found little to fulfil me in the running of our estates and managing trade. I had no aptitude for it. Nor did I enjoy the gathering of political and commercial information by the management of our agents and preferred to travel to see events for myself, whether it was to Scotland or Ireland or further afield. Even so, the concerns and passions of the people engaged in the local and regional events seemed so petty and transient, no matter how deeply felt they were for those involved.

So Eva's accusation of glumness was true, and I had been out of sorts for some time. My men liked to joke that all I needed was a battle to wage and a war to win but I had been fighting those for so long and all for nought. What did it matter whether this king or that sat on the French throne? They would all be dead soon enough, and the lords that supported them and the men who died fighting for them, and so what was the use in fighting?

But on reading Stephen's letter, I felt an ember deep within me begin to burn once more. Could it be true, I wondered, that Stephen had uncovered an immortal in Brittany? And a powerful immortal at that. Scanning the words again and again, I felt the stirring of my true purpose once more.

I quickly summoned back to London Walter and Rob, engaged three trusted young valets, and arranged for our journey across the Channel to Nantes in Brittany, where Stephen was currently employed.

On his most recent period away from England, Stephen had fulfilled an old ambition by attending the College of Sorbonne in Paris to study theology and law and thence had become a lawyer for the Church. His intellectual excellence, enhanced through his unnatural long life, had enabled his swift progression through the institution. Despite his repeated insistence to his masters that he lacked any professional ambition, he soon found himself so well regarded that he was able to apply for and was granted a position in the episcopal see of Nantes.

Why would such a brilliant young man, they asked him, seek to bury himself so far from Paris, which was the centre of learning for all the Earth? Of all the great lords of the Church that you could serve, why request the service of the Bishop of Nantes?

Stephen had made his typically smooth excuses and they in turn had waived him off as another fool who would rather never reach his potential than to fail in the attempt.

But it was not the Bishop himself that attracted Stephen, nor the lowly position as episcopal notary, but instead was whispered rumours that had travelled all the way from the distant wastelands of Brittany to the grand halls of Paris. Rumours that hinted at a great and bloody evil. Some months after his curious relocation to Nantes, Stephen sent his scrawled letter.

One line in that letter was ever on my mind during the journey and I wondered what it might mean and who it might refer to.

The subject of said rumours is a man known to you and is one of remarkable power.

"Damn you, Stephen," I muttered on the dockside in London. "Why must he speak in unanswerable riddles?"

At my side, Walt shrugged. "Likes being clever, don't he."

We crossed from London to Nantes by ship, travelling along the southern coast of England across to the northern coast of Normandy and then following that dangerous, craggy coast around headland after headland in choppy dark seas until finally we reached Saint Nazaire in the mouth of the Loire. From there we travelled upriver to the great city of Nantes.

"Strange," Walter said as we passed through that country. "Strange to be back here again."

We stood at the rail of the boat as it sailed up river on the flood tide, pushed by a stiff westerly wind. It was cold and spring seemed delayed, as if the land lacked the strength to throw off the remains of winter.

"Is it strange?" Rob asked, wistfully. "Seems fitting, to me. We brought much evil to these parts."

"Wonder if they remember us," Walt said. "If they remember the White Dagger Company and that bloody banner we fought under."

Rob nodded. "A field of red with yellow flames beneath rising up to touch the white dagger in the centre. Who could forget it."

"It was not evil we brought but justice," I said. "And all who lived then are long dead, as are their grandchildren. Whatever strangeness you feel comes not from the land but from your own imaginations. Pull yourselves together."

They said nothing in response which spoke volumes about their true thoughts. And the truth was I felt disquieted myself. Not so much by memories of the distant past when I had hunted Brittany and Poitou for the black knight Geoffrey de Charny but by more recent ones.

Our disastrous losses to the French a few years before had shaken me to such an extent that I was not the same man as I had been. It seemed so unnatural that our veteran army had been defeated by a mad young woman still in her maidenhood. An unholy reversal of the true order of things and it was simply the final insult for our nation, which seemed to me to be in sharp decline.

The Loire, up which we sailed was the great river of France, stretching more than six hundred miles from the central highlands in the south, up and across the land to the west coast and its waters fed the richest valley in Christendom. The very same river had formed the limit of the English dominion in the war, making a great front line upon which our armies had pressed for years.

It was the great bastion on that river, the city of Orléans, that we had needed to crush for us to become masters of all France. On the Loire was it that the French armies led by that mad young woman Joan of Lorraine had instead defeated us time and again, earning herself the name the Maiden of Orléans.

And it was where my own weakness and indecision had led to the slaughter of thousands of magnificent English bowmen.

But Orléans was halfway across France to the east and there was nothing to be done about the war any more. Through treaties wrangled and petty sieges conducted, King Charles VII was carefully and inevitably winning back his entire kingdom from the English and Henry VI was gladly giving it to him. Order had finally been imposed on the countryside and the bandits and thieves, the bands of *routiers*, and rampaging free companies driven out by forces loyal to the king.

Nantes was the picture of peace as we moored in the city on the 15th May 1440. The grandest buildings were of the typical Loire sandstone; either grey-white or yellowed-cream depending on the way the sun fell on the walls or beautifully carved columns and reliefs of the towers and facades. Still being built and covered in scaffolding, the cathedral was already grand and well-proportioned and perfection itself without being ostentatious. At first glance, the same could have been said for the city as a whole, although there was much in dire need of repair when we got into it. A large portion of Nantes had been reduced by a terrible fire and the acres of blackened timber, jutting up at all angles like the limbs of burned corpses, were yet being cleared.

Thinking of the urgency expressed in his letter, we did not pause even to secure lodgings in the city but went straight to the cathedral and asked after the Bishop's notary Stephen le Viel, which was the pseudonym he was using. It seemed as though we were expected and while Walter, Rob and our servants waited below, I was shown up almost directly to an antechamber and bidden to wait before the porter left by a different door to the one in which we had entered.

I sat waiting in the antechamber, listening to the hustle in the hall beyond and the shouts of the builders working on the cathedral outside. The decoration all around me was quite beautiful and even the tiles on the floor were bright and shining reds and greens, glistening in their rich glaze.

"Richard!" Stephen cried, flinging the door open and striding toward me. "How quickly you have come."

His clothes were rich and his hair cut into a fashionable length beneath his cap and he seemed rather fat and happy.

We embraced and I held him at arm's length. "You insisted upon urgency and so here I am. What is it that you believe you have uncovered in this damned duchy?"

He glanced over his shoulder into the hall from where he had emerged and, taking me by the elbow, pulled me away and lowered his voice.

"Rumours of children going missing from lands to the south of this city, about twenty miles away, right across a great swathe of countryside."

I sighed, feeling the ember of excitement fading fast. "Is that it? Missing children again, Stephen? How many times over the years have we followed rumours such as this, only to find the most mundane of causes? They are almost always found drowned in some overgrown pond or wash up miles downriver. It has never once been an immortal."

All while I spoke, he flapped his hands at me to lower my voice and he hissed at me. "It is *dozens*, Richard."

That gave me pause. "Dozens? Are you certain?"

He looked me in the eye. "Scores, sir. Perhaps even more. Scores of children gone missing, never to return."

I pursed my lips. "And you think an immortal is the cause? Why so? Why not slavers, taking them off the coast and from raids inland? Probably the damned Moors again."

He opened his mouth to answer but a powerful voice rang out from the hall beyond where we stood.

"Stephen? Is it your man or not? Where have you gone, Stephen? Why are you always vanishing when I need you, Stephen?"

My friend straightened up and whipped around and raised his voice. "Yes indeed, Milord Bishop. We are coming now, Your Grace." He rolled his eyes at me and lowered his voice. "Quickly, Richard. I have told the Bishop that you are a faithful man who has conducted many investigations of a secular nature for various lords over the years, especially in Normandy. Only by telling the Bishop this has he allowed me to bring you here to be engaged in a secret but official capacity to investigate these rumours."

I nodded slowly. "I am a faithful man, am I? Faithful to whom?"

Stephen swallowed, his face growing pale. "Why, to me, Richard. It was the only way to get them to trust you enough to bring you in."

"I see."

The voice from the chamber rose again. "Stephen! I hear you hissing out there like a pair of old maids. My patience grows thin, sir."

Stephen, as outwardly subservient to authority as ever, turned on his heel and strode into the chamber with his head bowed and I followed.

The Bishop's audience hall was sumptuously decorated with wood panelling and fine carvings covered in gold leaf and painted in rich vermilion and indigo. Elegantly proportioned windows filled one wall, overlooking a portion of the cathedral that was covered by scaffolding swarming with builders.

At the top of the chamber the Bishop sat on his throne, which was quite tasteful, as far as thrones go, and it was positioned behind a long table where clerks and priests examined papers filled with tabulated texts and calculations, and architectural drawings. None of the other men paid us any attention at all as we approached the great lord who was Bishop of Nantes.

"My apologies, Milord Bishop," Stephen said as we drew near. "It is indeed my man who has come, finally, from his recent work in Normandy. Please allow me to introduce—"

"Fine, fine," the Bishop said. He was a tall, fat man with a rather kindly face. Some Bishops, grasping and ambitious as they often were, aroused in me nothing but immediate and lasting contempt. But I must say that the Bishop of Nantes did not. His manner was rushed but his tone was not overly rude. "So, you have experience with this sort of thing, do you?"

I glanced at Stephen. "I have some experience with the investigation of certain dark crimes, Your Grace. Only, if you will permit me to say, I am afraid I do not yet know what you mean by this sort of thing."

The Bishop pursed his full lips. "No, indeed. Well said, sir. We must reserve our judgement until the facts are established. But this business with le Ferron is cause for concern enough."

"Le Ferron?" I said, addressing Stephen.

The Bishop nodded to Stephen, who turned to me. "Two days ago, at Pentecost, a priest named le Ferron was seized. Dragged from his church before the parishioners and thrown into a black dungeon. Le Ferron and his brother are noblemen and vassals of Duke Jean, the Lord of Brittany, and so this is a grave crime against the Duke that must be answered for."

"Bah," the Bishop said. "The Duke will order the release of le Ferron and if he has any sense, the Marshal will give him up."

"The Marshal?" I asked. "What Marshal?"

The Bishop raised his eyebrows at Stephen. "You did not inform your man of the subject of his investigations?"

Stephen made a little bow. "I thought it best not to put such a thing in writing and was a moment ago about to explain it to Richard before you requested that we attend to you, my lord." Stephen fixed me with a warning look before explaining. "The man who has broken the Duke's peace is also the subject of our investigation in the missing children. He is Gilles, Comte de Brienne, Lord of Tiffauges, Laval, Pouzages, and Machecoul, the Baron de Rais, Marshal of France and Lieutenant-General of Brittany."

I believe that my mouth gaped open like an imbecile's for a moment but swiftly I found my jaw clenched in quivering rage.

The name was known to me. It was one I had not heard for almost a decade but a name that had often been spoken in the past along with that of another. For Gilles de Rais had been the closest companion to and steadfast captain of the Maiden of Orléans. And I had always suspected that it was he who had been the architect of her victories. It was he, surely, whispering in her ear, who had directed the French to victory and not the divine voice of God's angels in her head, as she had claimed. For why should God send angels to aid the French and not the English?

It was not only I that held these same suspicions about Gilles de Rais, for he had been rewarded with high honours. Indeed, Gilles was one of only four lords granted the honour of bringing the Holy Ampoule from the Abbey of Saint-Remy to Notre-Dame de Reims for the consecration of Charles VII as King of France. It was at the coronation that Gilles was also made Marshal of France in recognition of his superb generalship in the campaigns. His appointment as Lieutenant-General of Brittany also meant that he was the King's representative in the region, similar in some ways perhaps to the sheriffs of English counties. These were the highest possible appointments that could have been made for a young military leader.

In contrast, Charles had soon tired of and discarded the poor mad girl before she was captured, tried and burned to death. And the newly feted Gilles de Rais had callously abandoned his former companion to her fate.

"Gilles de Rais?" I asked Stephen. "Did you say that this killer of children is Gilles de Rais?"

"Yes," Stephen said, watching me closely. "Almost certainly."

"Now, now," the Bishop said, chiding Stephen. "We have nought but unsubstantiated rumour about murders and witchcraft. I must stress that currently all of these horrid claims are nothing more than hearsay. Come now, you men, we all know how village folk like to gossip about their betters and there is not a single body nor bloody blade to add credence to this talk. They *say* that children have disappeared but have they truly? And if they have gone then who has taken them? And what then was their true fate? Do you know, Stephen?"

"No, Milord Bishop."

He nodded his big head sagely. "This is why we must have *evidence* before anything can be done. Evidence, do you see? Stephen here has my written authority to travel from place to place and take depositions from anyone who is willing to provide them. But this investigation must be conducted in full secrecy, do you hear me? None of this shall get back to my cousin the Duke until we are certain that crimes have been committed. And of course, we certainly do not wish to alarm the Baron de Rais himself, do we." He broke off, looking me up and down. "You have the bearing of a capable man but I warn you. Do not alarm the Marshal or any of his men. He maintains a personal army of two hundred superbly equipped veteran soldiers, mounted on the finest horses and if you go blundering about then you will end up thrown in one of his dungeons just as le Ferron has. We do not have a force capable of resisting them in Nantes, and even my cousin's personal guard is not so large as that. Do you understand?"

"The Marshal maintains a personal army of two hundred mounted veterans?" I asked. "Men who fought against the English?"

Stephen shot me a look.

"Why certainly, Master Richard. And you are quite right to be fearful as these are men who are not to be trifled with and neither is the Marshal. If we go making unsubstantiated rumours then the King himself may intervene and take steps to protect his man from proper justice." The Bishop cleared his throat. "Assuming he is guilty, of course. Bring me evidence, sirs, *evidence*. We must have blood and bones, God forgive me for speaking it, the blood and bones of these innocent children and also sworn statements from witnesses to murders and witchcraft or else we have nothing at all. Now, God be with you."

2

A Cursed Land

May 1440

STEPHEN KNEW THE way south from Nantes to the lands around Tiffauges Castle and we rode out together, we four immortals and our servants, across the Loire and out into the wilderness beyond.

Most of the Loire Valley, hundreds of miles of it, provided fertile soil and a delightful climate for producing abundant crops, healthy people, and wealthy lords. But south of Nantes, it was rather different.

It was an area where met three regions of France; Brittany, Poitou, and Anjou and it was a broken country. The land itself looked like it had long ago been smashed, shattered, and wrecked, perhaps at the dawn of time or during some great catastrophe. All hard earth, thin rivers, or dank marsh, with scattered fragmented jumbles of grey rock and the people were sullen, scrawny, and bitter and the lords were few and far between. There was not enough wealth in the land itself to sustain many knights or gentlemen but there were prosperous commoners who carried on trade up and down the Loire.

Those people that we saw as we trotted through their villages either hid from us or cast unfriendly glances in our direction. I made sure to wave, smile, and call out greetings but not one gesture was returned in kind.

We were dressed in ordinary clothes, as a reasonably wealthy townsman might wear. All of us but Stephen wore a sturdy, padded doublet beneath those clothes but these were thinner than the gambesons we would wear beneath plate and mail armour during warfare. Thick enough to protect from a slashing cut and would perhaps serve to resist the thrust of a dagger but little more and I knew we would have to avoid full combat at all costs, especially if the Marshal's small army was properly equipped for war. We did not even have steel helms to put on, should a battle threaten.

Likewise, our horses were well bred and rode wonderfully but they were not trained for battle and so we could not hope to fight from them. Wherever we went and whatever we did, we would have to avoid combat wherever possible.

In spite of the poor weather, bleak landscape, and unfriendly welcome, I felt reinvigorated by the ride. Once more, I felt wrapped in the comforting cloak of purpose.

By the end of the day, we drew near to our destination and we slowed to a stop as the battlements appeared on the horizon. Our horses were tired, and I was wary of alerting even a fraction of the Marshal's personal army to our presence.

The castle itself was a substantial fortress. Standing on a massive outcrop overlooking two ravines through which ran the rivers Crume and Sevre. Towers of differing heights jutted up over thick walls, silhouetted against the sky.

"Have we not been here before?" I asked Walt. "I look upon those walls and it feels somewhat familiar."

He nodded, pursing his lips as he recalled it, but Rob answered in his stead. "Came through this way a few times when we was looking for the black knight and when we was trying to bring Jean de Clermont out from hiding. Our lads needed somewhere to spend the winter, probably, what was it, ninety years ago now? By God, that's a long time. We talked about taking this place with our company of fifty men."

"Well," Walt said, "*you* talked about it, Richard."

Looking at the imposing fortress, I scoffed at the notion. "I must have been mad."

Walt laughed, as did Stephen.

"It has been much added to in the years since," Rob said, appraising the place. "More towers, new walls. Higher than before. We would need an army to take it now. Five hundred, perhaps."

"Five thousand, more like," Walt said. "And a score of cannon."

But we were not going to take the castle. Not with an army or in any other way. Gilles de Rais was said to not be in residence and instead he was at another of his many castles, in Machecoul, thirty miles west toward the sea. When a lord was not present, with his court and household, a castle would be almost entirely empty. Perhaps a caretaker or two to guard against burglars and squatters, and to fix a leaking roof to stop the place falling into ruin before the lord returned. But we could not be certain that Tiffauges was not also guarded by members of the Marshal's army. It seemed unlikely to me but Stephen claimed the villagers believed those soldiers and the Marshal's men resided in the empty castles. I had not believed it but smoke drifted from within and from one of the towers and so it was not worth the risk.

Instead, we wanted to speak to the people in the villages subject to Gilles de Rais. And we had one specific man in mind.

"Come," I said to Stephen, "let us find this village of Tilleuls and get a statement from this physician of yours."

All about the landscape was bleak and wind-blasted. Underfoot, the ground was stony and the soil so thin that the trees grew stunted and were bent over by the endless winds. Water pooled here and there in hollows, their surface choked by weeds and green slime. Above us the sky was low and dark, like a roof of broken slate.

"Best wrap up your bow," I said to Rob. "You look like an Englishman."

"Plenty of bows like this in France," Rob objected. "In Brittany, too. Not just hunters but soldiers, too. Some of them. Levies, mainly, when raised from the country."

"I'd rather you did not look like an Englishman or a poacher or do anything that might make the commoners mistrust us. You will unstring and sheath your bow and hide the arrows. From the first moment we make ourselves known to the people of these lands we must be beyond reproach. We will pay for everything we use, and we shall pay handsomely. We will be courteous even when treated rudely. Do you hear me, Walt?"

He affected outrage. "Why do you single me out?"

"Do you hear me, Walt?"

"Yes, Richard."

"And we are all from Normandy. Even Walt."

"That's right," Rob said. "And if anyone asks, we just say his mother was ravished by an Englishman."

"Don't you mean a Welshman?" Stephen said.

"Oh, charming," Walt said. "Even my dear old friend Stephen Gossett is having a dig at poor old Walt, who never did his friends no harm in his life and then this is how they treat him in his turn."

"That is enough, now," I said, seeing the roofs of houses up ahead for just a moment as we went over a rise in the road. "We must present ourselves as trustworthy men who can be relied upon to get the evidence needed to arrest their lord and to put him on trial."

"Why can we not just kill him?" Walt asked as our party picked our way along the narrow tracks toward the village. "Just ambush him, cut off his head and be done with it."

Stephen sighed elaborately. "He may be both mortal and innocent, Walter. We cannot murder an innocent man."

"Innocent?" Walt said. "Of course he done it. People don't talk about things like that if it ain't true. And if he has done things that that, like what they say he done, then he has to be immortal. Don't he?"

"Not necessarily," Stephen said, sniffing and lifting his nose up. "Immortals do not have a monopoly on violence."

"But if he is guilty of murdering children," Rob said, speaking slowly and frowning. "Why do we not just kill him anyway? Whether he's been drinking their blood or not?

Mortal or immortal, he will deserve death."

Stephen lifted a finger up and took the kind of breath he often took before launching into a pompous lecture.

I hurriedly spoke before he could get started. "Because our Order exists to kill William's immortals. Not to assassinate common murderers for the sake of it. If he has committed crimes, then the Bishop and the Duke must be the ones to pass judgement. Only if he is an immortal is it our duty to put an end to him."

Stephen and Rob nodded in agreement.

"You're saying we first have to find out if he is a killer and then also find out if he is an immortal before we can do anything?" Walt said. "Be easier if we just take him, that's all I'm saying. It's what we done before. Take him, cut his flesh and have him confess that is guilty and a spawn of William de Ferrers before we slay him. Like we done before."

"That was different," I said. "That was war. There is no war here. And the easier route is not often the right one to follow. We must act rightly for we are knights, we three, and Stephen is a moral man, are you not, Stephen? Despite once being a monk and now being a lawyer."

My words drew laughter from all three but they quickly fell silent and I hoped they would think on what I had said. Even so, I was not feeling so confident about doing the right thing myself.

Gilles de Rais had been one of the architects in the downfall of the English armies and the revelation that he may have been an immortal the entire time brought the whole conflict since Orléans back into relief. He was at Joan of Lorraine's side during every battle and thus it was he who had been whispering stratagems into her ear.

Our defeat suddenly made sense to me. And I had an opportunity to put it right, to take revenge for the losses we had suffered.

But perhaps Gilles was not an immortal. Perhaps it was my desire for him to be so that coloured my thinking and twisted my thoughts.

And if he was not an immortal then was he a man capable of murdering children? Dozens of them at that, so Stephen had suggested. Dozens or even scores.

Whether Gilles was good or evil seemed to rest on whether the Maiden of Orléans had herself been divinely inspired or heretical. Had she been practising witchcraft all those years ago when she led armies while dressed as a knight? Had she drawn from the power of evil? If so, then it seemed likely that Gilles was also evil.

Or had she truly been divinely inspired, following the directions of angels and God above? For if that was true, as the French yet claimed, then how could Gilles be either evil or immortal?

I had no answers but I hoped to find some amongst the commoners of the region and first of all from the people of Tilleuls.

"Here we are," Stephen said as we rode into the centre of the village.

There was a stone church, quite plain but in good repair, and a group of good houses around the large central square, built tall and with tiled roofs. The gardens were well-kept, and the stink of the middens and cesspits was not as foul as in many such places. In fact, it was as fine a village as I had seen in the area.

When we approached there were children playing a game of some sort in the middle of the village before the church but before we came close they scattered beyond the building and into the houses. In the silence after the children's voices stopped, all I could hear was the sounds of our horses breathing and their hooves echoing from the walls of the church and the houses all around.

A movement caught my eye and I turned to see a pair of shutters slam closed in the upper window of the house there. Almost at the same time I heard a door bang shut on the other side of the church and there was the scraping of a bar being pushed into place behind it.

The wind blew up a swirl of dust beneath us.

"We mean no harm!" Stephen bellowed suddenly, right behind me.

I almost jumped out of my skin and my horse sprang forward in surprise.

"For God's sake, Stephen," I said as I reigned my horse in. "Do you think that will bring them running with jugs of wine and a platter of almond tarts?" He began to answer but I did not let him do so. "Get off your bloody horse and lead us to the house of your potential witness."

Sheepishly, he pointed to the grandest house in the village. A two-storey place with an attractive tiled roof and windows with sound panes of glass in them. "The physician's house."

"Watch the approaches at both ends of the village," I said to Walt and Rob. "Do not let the servants wander. Be respectful to all the folk here but remember also that any of them may be in league with the Marshal."

Both men nodded and moved to instruct the valets. I noted that Rob checked his bow in its sheath and loosened the cover on his quiver.

Stephen was speaking through the closed front door of the physician's house as I approached. He turned and his face was one of despair.

"The physician is away," Stephen said. "And they will not admit us."

I sighed, for it suddenly seemed obvious that he would not be there, for physicians who do not reside in large towns travel all over visiting the sick. "Where is he? Do not tell me he has returned to Nantes? We could have stayed and met him there."

Stephen jerked his head at the door. "The woman there will not say."

"Is there no other within who will help us?"

Stephen shrugged and stroked his chin. "To speak plainly, Richard, I was doubtful whether even a man as learned and decent as the Master Mousillon here would speak to me in an official capacity. His servants would certainly lack the courage to do so."

"You are the one who lacks courage," I said and stepped up to the door before banging on it with my palm. "We are on official business, madame. Is the lady of the house within?"

There was a pause before a soft voice answered. "This is she."

"Please would you open the door but a little, madame, so I may state my business? We have come as previously agreed with Master Pierre Mousillon, some weeks ago now. Perhaps you already know of why we come but I must say that we come from Nantes on peaceful, legitimate business, and not from Tiffauges or Machecoul or any other such place."

After a moment, the lock turned and the door opened a little.

"Thank you, Madame," I said, "I appreciate the—"

My tongue stuck to the roof of my mouth as I laid eyes on a beautiful young woman who was not more than twenty years old. Perhaps she was a servant or perhaps Master Mousillon had got himself an especially lovely young wife, but I suspected she was a daughter.

"Ah," I said, softening my tone and lowering my voice, "my apologies, mademoiselle, I believed I was speaking to the lady of the house. Is your mother present?"

"My father is Pierre Mousillon," she said, in the most delightfully high, clear and yet warm and steady voice. "I am the mistress here. Now, my father is away and will not return for some time. Please, sir, I beg that you leave me be."

"A moment, if you please," I said, placing my hand gently on the door frame and leaning forward. "I shall certainly do whatever you wish but perhaps you can help me before I go?" She paused, looking up at me. I snatched off my hat and clutched it in my fist. "You see, mademoiselle, we have come about the boy. His name is Jamet. Forgive me but he is your brother, is that correct?"

She breathed in and held up her chin, her eyes shining. "He was."

"I see. And as I understand it, young Jamet Mousillon disappeared last year and I am here to discover what occurred and also to see justice done."

"Justice?" She hesitated, peering at me through her fierce eyes. "And who are you?"

"My name is Richard. This is my friend Stephen. He is a lawyer but try not to judge him too harshly, for he is not so bad, as far as members of his profession are concerned. Stephen here is the one your father spoke to in Nantes, about your brother."

She peered at Stephen, fixing him with a fierce gaze. "What did my father say to you in Nantes?"

Stephen swallowed, bewitched by her beauty and disconcerted by her directness. "That he could no longer keep silent about what all in these parts know. He provided me with the particulars of his own tragic case and outlined many others. When we parted, we agreed that if I could get others to swear a witness statement, he would do also."

The young woman lifted her chin and unflinchingly fired her next question at him. "Where was it, precisely, that you met my father?"

"My lord the Bishop of Nantes had taken ill, and your father was the third physician called, as the other two only caused the Bishop's condition to worsen. After your father had administered his treatments, I asked him if he knew anything of the rumours in the area in which he lived. I admitted that I was keen to find a legal resolution to these concerns, no matter the social standing of the potential criminals involved. I believe I said I would prosecute the King himself, if he was the culprit. It was then that your father told about little Jamet. He was receptive to speaking further and so I said I would attend him here, as soon as I was able."

The young woman nodded once, confirming this was correct. "You are late. You said you would come by the end of last week, sir, but you did not and my father had to leave."

"I am at fault," I said. "As Stephen had to wait for me to arrive in Nantes."

"Neither of you are Breton," she said, prompting us.

"I am from Normandy and Stephen comes from Paris," I said. Small, necessary lies such as these came so easily to me by then that they were undetectable as such. Deceit is a skill and just like any other it may be improved through rigorous practice. "And this is why those in authority here have engaged us to make these enquiries. Because we are uncorrupted by any taint that might have crept into local men. May we come in to speak with you, please? It would be just for a few moments and then we will return at a time convenient for your good father."

She glanced over her shoulder, took a deep breath, nodded once and stepped back, opening the door wide.

Inside, the house was dark. An old man, a servant, stood in the back of the room with his hand on the pommel of a short sword that he held, sheathed, but ready. He was withered and bony but his eyes were unwavering and I recognised in him a man willing to do violence. That was more important in a bodyguard than physical strength. I nodded to him in greeting but he gave no response.

The house was sparsely furnished but what furniture there was spoke of a certain wealth. The fireplace crackled with warmth and every surface appeared clean and the home was well cared for.

She invited us to sit at the dining table which dominated one side of the main room, which we did, though she herself remained standing with the old servant behind her.

"Now, to get started," Stephen said, opening his satchel and pulling out a sheaf of parchment, an inkpot, and a pen, setting them each in turn upon the table. "Might I have your name, mademoiselle?"

She scowled and glanced around at the old man before looking at Stephen again with irritation and considerable nervousness.

"For God's sake, Stephen," I said. "Put your lawyer's tackle away, man."

"I have no desire to have my words recorded, sir," the woman said.

"No, indeed," I said. "Is that not so, Stephen?"

He shoved his things back in his bag and lowered his head. "My apologies."

I leaned forward, planting my hands flat on her table. "Please understand that Stephen is entirely unused to the company of decent people, for he spends all of his waking hours amongst dusty law books and dustier old priests."

She smiled, not because my jest was amusing but because she appreciated my attempt at levity. "No apology is required, sirs. My name is Ameline Mousillon."

"Thank you, Ameline," I replied. "We do not wish to pry into your particular tragedy, unless you wish to tell us of it, but we would greatly like to hear about what it is that goes on in these parts. You see, we know of rumours but because we are outsiders and completely new to this land, we have very little in the way of facts."

"None at all," Stephen muttered, before wiping his mouth, for the woman's beauty had quite stoppered up his lips.

Ameline took a breath. "What is it that you wish to know, sir?" The servant behind her hissed a warning I did not catch but she turned on him. "Oh, enough, Paillart. Do you not think we have had our fill of keeping silent? I think you will find that it is the prolonged silence of too many souls in these parts that has allowed the evil to grow as it has." Her cheeks became flushed as she spoke and she ended with a tight clearing of her throat. She pulled out a stool and sat at the table opposite us and took a moment to compose herself before continuing.

"I do not know when it began. It was some years ago, perhaps four or five years. I do not know for certain and I am unsure if anyone does. Children going missing. It was only one or two, I suppose, from each village. One or two per year, perhaps. And each village knows mainly of itself, of course." She cleared her throat again. "Paillart, could you bring me some water, please?"

With a glare at me and Stephen, he left the room for the rear of the house.

"Speaking to us about these things shows remarkable decency and bravery, Ameline," I said, softly. "Please, do go on. Can you give us the names of the missing children?"

Ameline bit her lip and hesitated before shaking her head. "Their mothers and fathers would not wish me to. They would not speak with you."

"You are speaking with us," I pointed out.

She smiled. "I am not as they are."

"Oh? How so?"

"We are foreigners, you see. My family, we came here fourteen years ago from Poitiers. We are outsiders and always will be."

"You and your father," I said, "and your brother?"

"My mother also and my sister. They died. My sister before Jamet and my mother soon after. It was a fever but my father could do nothing for her. The villagers say she died from a broken heart but of course that is mere superstition."

The servant Paillart returned and placed a cup of water in front of Ameline. He did not bring any for us and Ameline did not offer us any either. She was yet unsure about us and remained nervous. She wanted us gone and I sensed she might throw us out at any moment.

I sat back and looked at her again. "Were you in receipt of an education, Ameline?"

"I can write in French and Latin," she said, surprised by my question but proud enough of her accomplishments to speak of them. "And I manage the household finances and my father's business."

"You have books here?" I asked by way of conversation.

She frowned. "Only my mother's book of hours. It brings me great comfort."

I nodded, smiling. "May I ask why your father remains in this place? Why not move to Nantes or back to Poitiers?"

She coloured and lowered her head. "We live here."

"Of course, of course. Tell me, does your father have much business at the castle? At Tiffauges?"

The name of the place was like a jolt through Ameline and Paillart both and I thought that we would be asked to leave immediately. But the moment passed.

"On occasion, my father has been called on to attend to a member of the Marshal's household," Ameline said. "But the Marshal has other physicians, thanks to God."

Sensing I was on dangerous ground, I spoke softly. "I wonder if I wanted to speak to a servant of that place, who might I speak to?"

From behind her came a gravelly, Breton's growl. "Say nothing, my lady." Paillart stepped forward behind Ameline. "These men must go."

I looked at him and spoke in a low but firm voice. "We are here for justice, Master Paillart. We are here for Jamet and for all the other boys and the girls who have had no justice. Mademoiselle, I know you are afraid and I am sure you are right to be. But look at me. Look closely at me. I say again that I am here for justice. And I am not afraid."

Ameline sat up and seemed about to speak but Paillart got there first. "Then you are a fool. Mistress, these men must leave. They have been here too long. Your father would wish them to leave, Mistress."

I stood and dragged Stephen to his feet. "Of course, we shall take our leave. Thank you for speaking with us, Ameline. We shall, I think, be staying at the inn north of here, in Mortagne. When your father returns, we shall speak with him then. And I hope that I shall see you again, also."

She smiled. "My thanks, sir. I hope for that, also."

As we walked through the quiet village to our horses, the evening sunlight broke through the low layer of clouds and I slowed to savour the feeling of warmth on my face.

Stephen looked up at me, shaking his head. "Why must you seduce every pretty young woman you meet, Richard?"

"Seduce?" I said. "You mistake courtesy for seduction, sir."

"Hmm," he said. "Your courtesy is so forward it is enough to make a whore blush."

"Do stop acting the old maid, Stephen. Why are you in such a foul mood?"

Our pages brought our horses and held them ready. In the distance, I saw Rob at one end of the village and Walt at the other. They both reported, through gesture, that all was well. The daylight would soon be gone.

"I am in no foul mood," Stephen replied. "But if I were, it would be because we have wasted our time coming here."

I swung myself into the saddle and looked to the north. "Oh, I would not call it wasted."

"Yes, and we both know why. But we have nothing to do now but wait for Pierre Mousillon to return, and who knows how long that will be."

"No, there is much to be done. Let us return to the inn at Mortagne. We may begin asking the locals for what information they are willing to give. And, if at all possible, I will go to Castle Tiffauges."

"What? You are mad. The Marshal is not there, so why would you go?"

"Someone may be there. A servant, at least, who might be willing to reveal his master's secrets."

"Richard, you agreed to conduct yourself in accordance with the law. If you go around torturing people for information, it risks invalidating all of our—"

"Keep your hose on, Stephen. I said nothing of torture." I patted the purse on my belt. "I mean to obtain information by way of bribery."

"We must be careful," he argued. "The poor commoners of this land have been much abused by their lord."

"So it seems, at least," I pointed out.

"Whatever the truth of it, you must admit that something terrible has been going on here. The people are mightily oppressed and have absolutely no legal recourse to do anything about it."

"Of course not," I said. "Why would they have?"

"But do you not see how powerless it makes them? How utterly at the mercy of their lord they are?"

"That is the proper way of things," I pointed out and not for the first time.

"Their collective will is close to being crushed and so we must tread carefully and not go barrelling about with random questions and so risk ruining our investigation before it begins."

"Do not concern yourself, Stephen. One way or another, we shall learn what we need to know. And then we shall have our revenge on Gilles de Rais."

"Revenge?" he said, aghast. "What do you mean revenge? This must be about justice, not revenge. Richard?"

I ignored him and rode north to find the inn at Mortagne.

That night, I lay awake, looking up at the gloomy beams and ceiling above my bed, thinking back with deep dread and clinging regret to eleven years earlier. It had started at the battle that ultimately brought me into conflict with the mad girl Joan of Lorraine and her captain Gilles de Rais.

3

The Battle of the Herrings

February 1429

THE ENGLISH AND BURGUNDIAN armies were besieging the great city of Orléans. It was a cold February in 1429 when I joined a supply column heading south from Paris to our forts ringing the walls of Orléans, bringing three hundred carts and wagons laden with arrows, cannons, cannonballs, and barrels of herring. The tons of preserved fish were because Lent was approaching and even on campaign the proper fast was attempted to the best of our ability.

There were a mere fifteen hundred men in our supply column. We were led by Sir John Fastolf and I was posing as a common man at arms, though a well-respected and well-equipped one. The only authority I commanded was that which was expressed naturally by my manner and bearing and I was contented to quietly follow Fastolf, who appeared to be a competent captain.

I had known some of his ancestors over the decades. The Fastolfs hailed from Norfolk and ruled over boggy coastal lands quite competently and every so often a son would rise to prominence as a bishop or a sheriff. A perfectly conventional English noble family. The kind of family that quietly and dutifully served its king and its people and thusly made England into the magnificent kingdom it was.

By 1429, Sir John was getting on a bit. Almost fifty, he had married a wealthy older widow, passing up the opportunity for sons in exchange for fortune and now held a series of rather splendid estates all over England.

I had seen him conduct himself well during the siege of Harfleur, fourteen years earlier but he had been wounded and sent home and so had missed the bloody glory that was the battle of Agincourt. All men who had been abed in England thought themselves accursed that they were not at Agincourt and no man thought it more keenly than Sir John Fastolf. Though I was a nobody, a poor man-at-arms with inexplicably fine armour, I had been there and Sir John, I am certain, held it against me.

The relief column that he led seemed to be protected well enough. Our eventual defeat at the hands of the French was yet many months away and it seemed to me, and to many of those fighting on both sides, that an ultimate English victory was almost inevitable.

Why was I fighting there at all? It was a question I asked myself even at the time and more so ever since, for my duty was to the Order of the White Dagger and not to the King of England.

And yet, we had come so close to taking the crown of France for the English king but after Henry V's untimely death, it was in danger of being snatched away.

And so I fought because I was an Englishman, first and foremost and also because we had uncovered no more immortals after the nest of them we had cleared out almost ninety years before.

That was why I found myself fighting once more with the English army against the French. Not as a lord, because I wished to keep out of the politics and the endless questions and plots of the nobility and because I believed it would be easier, simpler, to fight as a common man-at-arms.

I was wrong. Utterly and idiotically wrong to think such a thing but I did not know it yet.

In those days, there were spies everywhere. The front line of the war, that is the extent of English control from the north coast and Paris, was the Loire River but it was far from a solid barrier. Indeed, it could hardly have been more porous to enemy incursions and our coming was well noted. Indeed, it was essentially impossible to hide our coming across the featureless plain as we approached our siege works, far beyond the horizon to the south.

I was in the vanguard at the front of the long wagon train but had sent Rob and Walt further ahead to watch for ambushes. Vigilance was our only defence at being caught out in the open.

Both men came back, riding hard, to our convoy, their horses breathing heavy.

"Enemies, Sir Richard," Rob called to me from the saddle.

He had been knighted on the field of Poitiers, as had Walter, and all three of us were posing as mortal men-at-arms fighting for the pay and for the promise of spoils and ransoms. Yet, old habits die hard and especially when feelings are high and battle may be near.

"How far?" I replied. "How many?"

"Thousands."

Sir John Fastolf rode up with his retinue behind him. "What is this you say, man?" he cried. "Thousands of French? I doubt that."

He turned to the knight at his side. "Send someone credible to the south, Hugh, see what this is all about."

A few moments later and two riders trotted off.

"Sir John," I said from my horse. "Perhaps we should bring the men in to make a defensible line here?"

"Here?" Fastolf looked around at the flat plain. "There is nowhere to make a defence. Besides, our supplies are needed by the army. No, no, we shall continue onward, I think."

"But sir!" Walter called. "There are thousands of mounted men-at-arms not three miles southward. Coming this way, sir."

Fastolf hesitated. I knew he doubted my men's judgement but if they were right then an enemy force of such a size and strength would mean the death of us. Our three hundred wagons were spread out over a vast area and our mounted men and archers would be unable to protect them.

"Order a halt," Fastolf commanded. "We shall wait here until we can confirm this rumour."

"Most likely it is our own men, sir," Sir Hugh said to his friend and commander. "Our own men come out from the forts to meet us. Escort us in."

"No, my lord," Rob blurted. "Forgive me, sir, but the enemy had banners unfurled and the ones I recognised were French."

"And Scots," Walter added. "Bloody treacherous Scots, hundreds of the bastards. No doubts about that, sirs."

I kept silent, watching Fastolf's face crease into frustration. The wagons creaked to a stop behind us and the men drifted forward to see what was occurring.

In little time, the two men who had trotted off came charging back in full gallop. Before they even came close, Fastolf was calling out orders to prepare for battle.

"We shall make for that hillock," Fastolf said, pointing with outstretched finger. "And prepare stakes."

"What about the wagons, sir?" one of his men said.

"We must leave them," Fastolf said. "It is regrettable but we cannot defend so many and they would take too long to traverse to our defensive position upon the hill."

Walt and Rob glared at me, for the hillock was low and small and entirely unsuitable. And indeed I felt compelled to speak up.

"Sir John?" I said, drawing sharp looks from his men. "Might we not draw the wagons up here? If we make a wagon park where we stand, forming a great square or circle or any shape that creates a perimeter, then we may bring the men and horses safely within. Our brave archers may then shoot the enemy at will. We shall be unassailable."

"How dare you, sir!" Hugh cried. "Do not question your captain again. Sir John has spoken and it is our duty to follow his commands. When he says—"

Fastolf held up his hand. "Peace, Hugh, I beg you. Peace." Sir Hugh fell silent and glared at me while Fastolf, to his great credit, continued. "Richard's suggestion has merit. Command the drivers to bring the wagons up into a perimeter. And have the archers plant their stakes beyond."

His men gaped in astonishment for a long moment until one of them began shouting commands. Soon, they all followed and our great convoy of three hundred wagons and carts, was arranged into a rough and large fort, where the walls were wagons. It was conducted swiftly but only with much shouting and cursing and with such great clanking of wheels and chains and neighing of horses that any enemy within ten miles would have thought we were having a battle all by ourselves. The archers were commanded to plant their long wooden stakes on the outside of the wagons, most at the front and others on the flanks, so that the enemy horsemen could not charge close and push their way through by weight of horse.

"Thousands, was it?" I asked Walt and Rob, as we watched the madness behind us.

They exchanged a look. "We're in for a rare scrap, Richard," Rob said.

"Don't really think this will work, do you?" Walt asked, nodding at the chaotic mass of wood and wheels being shifted into position.

"It was a proven tactic employed in open country by the people of the grasslands against the Mongols," I said.

Rob scratched his head under the rim of his helm. "I thought no one ever defeated the Mongols in battle?"

"The French are not the Mongols," I pointed out.

Even as we drew the last of the wagons into position at the rear, our enemy came into sight through the woods and hedgerows up ahead. First, it was scattered groups of horsemen emerging from the shadows beneath the bare trees to watch us and our strange behaviour. But very quickly the main force followed, already deployed into a broad front and flying their banners and with lances held high. They had horsemen, infantry, and crossbowmen, and their colours were bright and their armour shining in the late winter sun.

"Should we perhaps retire to within our wagon fortress, Richard?" Rob suggested.

"I think perhaps we should."

Their forces were commanded by Jean, known as the Bastard of Orléans on account that he was the illegitimate son of the old Duke of Orléans. The Duke was long dead but he had been the second son of the old King of France and so Jean the Bastard had royal blood and was first cousin to the Dauphin.

And the French were indeed supported, as Walt had claimed, by a powerful contingent from our old enemy, the cunning Scots. They were led by a superb soldier named Sir John Stewart of Darnley. He was a wily old sod who had fought and won a dozen battles in France against the English over the previous decade.

"It would be pleasing to me," I said to Walter and Rob as we watched them approach from atop barrels of dried herring on the back of a wagon, "if we could put an end to Sir John Stewart."

Rob nodded and caressed the side of his bow stave. "I'll put an arrow in his eye if I can, Richard."

More and more companies emerged and took position a mile away. The mounted men alone outnumbered us and there were thousands of spear-armed infantry and crossbowmen in formations

"They're taking their sweet time," Walter grumbled, leaning on his poleaxe.

"They are right to be afraid of us," I said, looking over my shoulder at our archers. "We shall pick them apart and drive them away."

Rob grinned. "Another Agincourt."

Walt scoffed. "You're always calling everything another Agincourt, Rob. You said that after Verneuil, five years ago."

Rob's grin fell into a scowl. "Well, it's true, ain't it?"

Walter ignored him, squinting into the distance. He tensed.

"What is it?" I prompted.

"Those wagons," he pointed them out amongst the colourful pageantry of the men-at-arms. "See that. And there. Also there. They're carrying cannons, Richard. Are they preparing them to use against us?"

It was already cold and yet I felt a sudden shiver of fear. "Warn Fastolf," I said to Rob, who raised an eyebrow. "No, no. I shall do it myself."

"You see!" his man Sir Hugh cried when I relayed the warning. "We shall be blasted into pieces. We should have abandoned the wagons. Sir John? We must retire to a more favourable position. The hillock yonder, as you first ordered earlier this day. Shall I relay your order to the men?"

Fastolf glared at me while his man was speaking. "It is too late now, Hugh. If we leave the protection of the wagons, they shall run us down. We are vastly outnumbered, are we not? How many are there?"

"A thousand, my lord," one of his knights said, shrugging. "Perhaps a little more."

The others in his retinue nodded.

"They are four thousand," I said. "See for yourself. Count the banners, my lords. There are five hundred Scots alone, you can see it with your own eyes. My lord Sir John is right. There is no leaving this place now so we must weather the storm. Have no fear. These cannons are barely capable of hitting a castle wall, let alone striking us here. We must sit and listen to them blasting their filthy, stinking smoke at us for half a day until they run out of gunpowder and cannonballs and then we can be on our way to Orléans and reach the forts, God willing, by nightfall."

The first of their cannons fired and the ball flew just over the front row of our wagons, killed two horses and smashed a wagon at the rear that was still being eased into position. It exploded into a shower of splinters and its cargo of arrows was tossed into the air like sparks from a bonfire. Men ran screaming and pages fought to control the panicking horses.

"Get out of my sight," Fastolf said to me.

I returned through our soldiers and archers to Rob and Walt who were cowering against a wheel of the wagon we had been standing on.

"Did you warn him about the cannons, sir?" Walt asked.

I looked down and sighed. "I do not think that wheel will serve to protect you, men."

Another cannon fired and the ball ripped through the air over our heads with that sound that I would come to know so well over the coming centuries. It landed unseen beyond our wagon fortress but other than being a few feet too high was right on target.

"I think I may have understated their effectiveness a little," I admitted, crouching down beside Rob and Walt.

Another cannon sounded and a ball bounced in front of our position before crashing through a wagon at the right flank of our fortress. It took off a wheel and the whole thing collapsed, spilling its barrels of herring outward onto the archers' stakes beyond in a mound of dried fish.

Our men were shouting continuously now, yelling at each other in their fear. Many sat on the ground and hunched over with their hands over their heads. Some already lay stretched on their faces which was certainly the most sensible but also least dignified form of repose one can effect.

The bombardment continued for some time but after their first successes, their balls went too high or too wide just as many times as they hit us. In those early days, the practice of field artillery was hampered by the inconsistency of supplies, as it was by the lack of expertise. Gunpowder was variable in quality, as were cannonballs and the cannons themselves. Each one had its own unique issues that had to be adjusted for and with repeated firings the barrels grew hotter, expanded and were in danger of breaking or even exploding. I would not see the science of cannon artillery reach its peak until I fought against the armies of Napoleon almost four hundred years later.

We took casualties but not so many that our men dissolved in panic. Indeed, the more we took, the more the men-at-arms and archers grumbled about their inaction. They wanted to ride out and take the battle to the enemy. A natural reaction but to act upon it would have been foolhardy in the extreme.

"I believe their rate of firing has slowed," Rob said from where he sat, leaning back on the wheel of our wagon and sharpening his arrowheads one by one. His fingers were white from the cold.

"I believe you are right," I said, grasping the side of the wagon to pull myself up. I poked my head up over the top of the barrels. "Well, would you look at the mad bastards."

Walt and Rob scrambled up beside me as the cannons fell silent and we heard the familiar sound of kettle drums beating and war pipes droning.

"The Scots are attacking," Walt stated. "But not the French."

I laughed because it was true and because it might just mean we would not be pounded into dust after all.

Hundreds of Scots came forward on foot, clutching their weapons and cheering themselves on with the banners waving above them.

"Archers!" I shouted. "Archers, stand and come forward. String your bows, you blessed bastards. The Scots are crying to be filled with English arrows once more. Come on, up you lucky bunch of bastards. Now is your time for glory."

In my excitement I had forgotten my lack of formal position and yet the men responded. They were professional enough to need little encouragement at such times and their captains organised them efficiently. As soon as the five hundred Scots were in range, our shooting began.

The poor Scots fell. Our arrows smashed into them and many of the mad sods were wearing inadequate armour which our arrows easily pierced. Still, they came on like the wrathful devils they were and when they came close to our stakes, our archers climbed on the wagons to shoot down into them.

Their success in reaching us must have encouraged the French for then their mounted men-at-arms came across the plain to crush us with their horses and steel.

We had thousands and thousands of arrows on our wagons and so our archers did not hold back but instead shot and shot at the Scots and the French as they charged us. Our arrows alone were enough to drive off the French who fled back to their lines.

The Scots, though, were filled with a murderous rage that the French did not feel and they pushed forward again and again. Their final assault reached the walls of our wagons and many of them clambered up the sides before they were struck down.

Thousands of French men-at-arms held in the rear and watched their allies being killed.

Was it a ruse to draw us out? It likely was but then the French were ever filled with terror of the English archers and so I suspected that they were genuinely frozen in inaction.

"Bring the horses," I commanded our pages, raising my voice so that other men would hear. "Bring the horses up and move aside that wagon on the flank there."

Other knights wondered aloud what we were up to and I answered, again speaking so that scores would hear my words.

"We shall ride out. Do you hear? We shall ride out and come at the Scots from the rear. If they do not flee, they will be killed to a man."

No order was given, as far as I know, and yet a hundred men and then a hundred more streamed out of our fort on the flank. We came at the Scots just as I said and ran them down. Those few captains of theirs who were mounted chose not to flee and to instead die with their men.

I aimed for the banner of Sir John Stewart of Darnley and charged him alone on my tired horse. It was a hard fight, but I brought him down and quickly dismounted. I strode forward and shouted that he was to surrender himself to me. Instead, he rolled onto his feet and rushed me with his poleaxe and I drove my sword point through his visor as I bore him to the ground.

"The French come!"

At the cries of warning, I leapt back atop my horse and prepared to meet the attack.

Our lines formed as the French approached and I found Walt at my side once more, riding a horse that was not his. He opened his visor to lick an enemy's blood from his steel gauntlets before closing it again. His face had been contorted into a wide grin.

Our enemies were led by the Bastard of Orléans himself but as the great wall of steel that was the French came close to us, a massive volley was loosed upon them from hundreds of English archers standing on the backs of the wagons. Another volley smashed into them and the French approach was halted. Horses fell as another volley crashed in a great cacophony of clanging iron against steel and then a volley of English jeering went up as the French turned and fled.

"Did you see?" Walt shouted. "The Bastard of Orléans fell!"

We would later discover that the cousin of the Dauphin had been merely wounded but the sudden shock of it, on top of the total slaughter of the Scots, was enough to drive the French from the field.

As our convoy unwound itself and continued toward Orléans, the archers and the men were thrilled by our unlikely victory. All knew how it was my defensive strategy that had saved us from being caught in the open, and they knew it was my tactical decision to counterattack. I was feted and I felt good about their praise, for I have always been vain.

But as we rode, Sir John Fastolf glared at me with hostility. He would claim the victory as his own, of course, but the men would know the truth. And he would know it himself in his heart. I had made an enemy of Sir John and it would come back to haunt me in the defeats to come. My decisions that day may have won a battle but they also may have lost us the war.

In fact, we should have lost the battle, if only the French had acted decisively. If the French had continued their barrage of cannon and so blasted holes in our defences, they could have charged in and slaughtered us. If they had brought forward their hundreds of crossbowmen first, they would have softened us up further. But the Scots could not control themselves, as usual, and the French had lacked the will to finish us off. Ever since the days of Edward III, the English armies had been protected by an invisible cloak of invincibility. It was a cloak that existed in the hearts of Frenchman and Englishman alike and that magic had turned dozens of battles that should have been English defeats into English victories.

But it would not last for much longer.

For unknown to me, or to any of us, that very day in a place far to the east, a young girl was begging for permission to meet the Dauphin. Claiming to hear the voices of angels commanded by God, Joan of Lorraine swore in front of witnesses that the Dauphin's arms had that day suffered a great reverse near Orléans.

When news of the victory that I had wrought reached the court of the Dauphin, the girl Joan was finally invited to his presence.

After convincing him that she was indeed divinely inspired, she was given leave to lead an army to the city of Orléans and so defeat the English.

At her side as she approached the city was a nobleman from Brittany named Gilles de

Rais.

4

Castle Tiffauges

May 1440

"THIS IS A TERRIBLE idea," Stephen said as we approached the gatehouse of Castle Tiffauges. "The priest will not be within."

Rob and Walt rode behind us in silence, prepared to do violence, should it come to it. Rob had even strung his bow in preparation and held it low and ready. Our three valets rode behind them as I hoped that a larger party would make a grander impression on whoever I found within the castle.

One of the Marshal's servants was a priest who I had two interesting pieces of information about in the few days since arriving. Firstly, he had stayed his master's hand when a fellow priest was threatened with murder, and second, it seemed he had attempted to flee from his master's service some months before. I believed that he might possibly be an unwilling participant in whatever was going on in the castles and manors of the Marshal. And if that was true then perhaps he would be willing to make a statement himself. Or at the very least, perhaps he would provide information on the other servants, such as who they were, what they were up to, and where they might be found.

My men disagreed.

"You did not have to come, Stephen," I replied, leaning forward to pat my nervous horse's neck. "If you truly think this such a terrible idea."

"I am not one to shy away from danger," Stephen said, clutching his satchel to his chest and hunching over in the saddle, his face pale beneath his hat.

"And the priest is here," I said. "The Marshal's choir remains in this castle to practice their singing, day and night, and so the priest will be here, also."

"Hmm," Stephen said, for although we had this information from more than one local, he suspected half of what was spoken was rumour. "It is whether the Marshal's soldiers are here that concerns me."

It concerned me, too, but I was never going to admit it. "We are not going to assault the place, Stephen. Why would the soldiers bother us, even if they are here?"

The castle was powerful indeed and commanding, built with enormous blocks of sandstone and tiny, narrow windows dotting the towers and the curtain walls. The strength of the place bore down on us evermore the closer we got.

"What is with this damned weather?" Stephen complained, rubbing warmth into his arms as he rode. "The calendar approaches summer and yet winter's cold has not passed. Will it never be spring?"

"Cursed land, ain't it," Walt called from behind.

"Don't be ridiculous," Stephen said.

The ramp up to the gate tapered until it constricted to the width of a cart or two horses riding abreast. Attacking the place would indeed take an army and I forced down the nervousness rising in my throat.

"The Marshal is not in residence," I said aloud. "Other than the choir and our priest, the place is practically empty."

"Who are trying to convince?" Stephen said as we came to the gatehouse. "Me or yourself?"

The outer gate was open and the portcullis up in the darkness of the ceiling above when we passed into the gatehouse. A castle's gate was rarely closed, whether the lord was in residence or not, for few men would be desperate or fool enough to attempt theft or mischief when they knew that retribution would be swift and terrible. Even so, I half expected the inner and outer doors to magically slam shut but we rode into the courtyard inside the gate, the hooves from our horses loud on the cobbles and echoing from the four walls. Looking up, the windows all around were black like the narrowed eyes of a snarling wolf.

An old porter came out striding from a side door, still chewing something and wiping his greasy hands on his apron as he came forward.

"The lord is away," he said. "What business have you here?"

"I have come to see the priest," I said, confidently. "Please take me to him."

"Priest?" the porter said, scratching his nose. "What priest? Who are you, sirs?"

"We serve the same master, you and I," I said, lying. "And so I need not answer to you. Bring me to the priest, or our master shall be sore disappointed."

He squinted at me and I felt certain he was about to summon guards. From what I had heard about the strange goings on at Castle Tiffauges, the rumours of comings and goings in the darkness, I had hoped to bluff my way in with vague assurances.

"I will have your name before I let you within," the porter said, finally, before pointing to me. "And you shall come alone, without your men. Not a one of them. And you shall come unarmed."

"My name is Le Cheminant," I said, which meant the Traveller. It was as good a false name as any and it was not an inaccurate moniker to assume. "And I agree to your terms."

My men grumbled at me as I dismounted.

"You must not enter this place unarmed and alone," Stephen muttered, rushing over and grabbing my arm before I went in.

"Stay here and do whatever Rob and Walt tell you to do," I replied as I removed my weapons and handed them to my valet.

Stephen was outraged because he was far more ancient than they and had been my companion for longer, and he considered himself to be above them in every sense. However, he was naive to physical dangers in a way that my soldiers were not.

Walt and Rob moved to take positions by the outer gateway and also by the door I was to enter by, so that they could watch for approaches and warn me and also so that they could quickly come to my aid, should I require it. All this was done without words and even without much in the way of glances.

"Le Cheminant, is it?" the porter said, frowning. "My name is Miton. I shall escort you to the chapel. Dominus Blanchet will be there or in his quarters."

"Very well, Miton. Lead the way."

While the exterior of the castle was severe and brutal, the interior was remarkably different. In my experience, castles were poor places to live. They were always cold, the chambers small, and it was ever dark and smoky. What is more, when the lord was not in residence, a castle would be quiet and miserable. Tapestries would be taken down from walls. Rooms, towers, entire wings would be closed up. Fires would not be lit. The caretakers would keep to their own quarters most of the time and the rest of the place would be left to the spiders.

But not Castle Tiffauges.

It was like walking into a dreamland. Ornate decoration adorned every wall and surface in a riot of blue, red, and yellow painted patterns, and intricate carving embellished with gold and silver leaf bordered every doorframe. Open courtyards resounded with the tinkling of beautifully carved marble fountains and passing from one wing to another I found every chamber lit with wax candles in silver holders and enamelled oil lamps, even in rooms with no people within. Servants walked to and fro, going about their business. I saw a priest in his full raiment hurrying along with a young servant behind him carrying a handful of books and I expected that the porter would call out to him that he had a visitor. Instead, he said nothing and we continued on and I realised this meant there was more than one priest in residence. Four soldiers lounged in a small inner courtyard drinking wine and playing dice. They glanced at me as I passed but made no move to stop me. Manic laughter echoed from a tower window. The castle was full of life. I found it profoundly disturbing.

I wanted to ask Miton the porter, strutting along beside me, to confirm that Gilles de Rais was not in residence but he was suspicious enough of me so I held my tongue.

"When is our master due to return?" I said instead, thinking I was being cunning.

"You don't know?" he said, squinting up at me. He shrugged, flinging his arms out. "But who knows with him? He comes, he goes. No warning. One day he's in Machecoul, the next he's here. Then he's off again, God alone knows where." Miton shook his head and broke off muttering.

"Were you a soldier, Miton?" I asked him suddenly.

He glanced up. "Course I was."

"Did you serve with our lord? At Orléans?"

He sniffed. "I was there."

"Did you see her?" I asked. "The Maiden?"

Miton jerked to a stop. His face clouded in darkness, glancing around us but no one was near. "Speak not of her." His hand was on the hilt of his sword. "Speak not of her in this place."

I raised my hands. "I apologise, sir. I shall not speak of it again."

Miton hesitated and nodded, striding past me in his jerky gait. I hurried after him, wondering at the reasons for his outburst. Was it moral outrage? Or fear? Did he have deep love for the Maiden or did he regard her as a heretic?

Clearly, I would get no more from him on the matter.

Distant singing echoed through the castle and it grew stronger as we entered the most distant wing, resonating from the walls of the chapel there. There must have been dozens of choristers and the sound was like Heaven had come down to Earth.

Inside, the chapel was lit by hundreds of tall wax candles, illuminating the golden rails, golden crucifixes and candle holders and the vivid colours of the painted statues seemed to glow with inner light. The boys of the choir had fallen silent and were making their way from the chapel when I entered. It seemed as though the walls yet echoed with their beautiful song. One or two of them eyed me warily and it seemed as though those ones pushed forward through their fellows to get away from me more swiftly.

"There." Miton stabbed his finger at the priest. "Do not leave this chapel. I will wait until you are done."

The priest wore his full priestly vestment. A bright white alb showing at the wrists and the hem at his knees, long amice around his shoulders, an embroidered maniple of thick silk and golden thread draped over his left arm, a crimson stole hanging around his neck and heavy and intricately embroidered chasuble. He was a small man of about forty years with an open, kind face. When I drew closer, though, I saw his eyes were filled with a profound fear and he shook beneath his robes.

"Is this it?" he asked me in a small voice. "Is it time?"

"Time for what?" I asked, brightly. He simply stared at me, confusion playing in his eyes. "My name is Le Cheminant. Are you Dominus Eustace Blanchet?"

He blinked and spoke warily. "Yes, that is who I am."

"How delightful to meet you, brother. I hoped to speak with you about what happened at the church during Pentecost."

Blanchet's eyes flicked around all over the chapel and finding that we were alone, turned back to me. "Why? Who are you?"

"I told you my name. Allow me to tell you something else. The Marshal went with armed men to the church at Saint-Étienne-de-Mer-Morte during the Pentecost Mass. He and his soldiers entered with their weapons drawn. The Marshal bore an axe in his hand and he seized the priest, threatening him bodily, forcing him to his knees. And then you, Gilles de Rais' personal priest, came to the rescue of the threatened man and stayed the Marshal's hand. You saved the priest le Ferron from a bloody death at his own altar and instead the Marshal dragged him off to the dungeons of Machecoul where he remains. Is this all true, brother?"

He looked around again, eyes flicking about. "Where did you hear such a thing?"

"Brother, there were scores of witnesses. A certain number of them were willing to give an account to agents of the episcopal and secular authorities."

Blanchet's eyes bulged and he swallowed twice before he could speak. "You come from the Bishop?"

As I was under strict orders not to reveal the Bishop's investigation, I could not confirm it outright. "I did not say that."

He shook his head in frustration. "What are you saying, sir? Are you threatening me?"

I sighed and lowered my voice. "Brother, after I heard how you had saved that priest's life, I asked after you. I asked about you in Nantes and in other places. What I heard was that you are somewhat newly come into the Baron's service from elsewhere in Brittany, by way of the Order of Saint Benedict. What is more, I heard that you lived for a week or two in a village a few miles north of here, at the inn at Mortagne. You know what the innkeeper, Bouchard-Menard, told me? He told me that you were then brought back here by servants of the Marshal. Brought back against your will, so he told me, shouting at the men to leave you be while they carried you out of your room at the inn, tied up and bundled onto a cart and dragged back to Tiffauges in the dark of the night."

He swallowed and looked down, no doubt greatly ashamed.

"Now, a man like that," I continued, "a man who attempted to flee this place, and a man of God who risked his life by defying the will of his master to save the life of a priest, well, that is a man I wished to speak with, Dominus Eustache. Despite what my friends urged me, I believe you may be willing to speak to me in turn about certain things. Things that are said to happen in Tiffauges and Machecoul and other accursed places. Do not be so afraid, Dom Eustache. The Baron will never know that we spoke, you and I."

Blanchet coughed and whispered. "He knows everything." Then he crossed himself and then crossed himself again. "I will deny speaking to you."

"Very good," I said, clapping him on the shoulder. "I will deny it also. And so as far as the world is concerned, we never spoke at all. All I want is to know from you, brother, is what happens here."

He looked down at the floor and spoke so softly I could barely hear him. "I do not know what you refer to, sir."

"Oh, you know. What happens to the little boys that are brought here in the night? What is done to them? And who is it that does it?"

Blanchet shook his head. "I do not know all that happens. In truth, I know nothing at all."

"You know enough to be afraid."

"No, no. I am happy here. I am blessed."

"I shall tell you what I think," I said, leaning in and lowering my voice. "I think you did not know the nature of your lord until it was too late to flee. But you are still a decent man and that is what drove you to save the priest on Pentecost. And so I think that you, as a decent man, will want to unburden yourself and help me to save others who might yet be saved."

He took a sharp breath and let it out slowly, glancing up at me once before replying. "He is violent. He drinks, now. Always. I was so blind, at first. Like a fool, I believed that because he was rich and powerful and devout that he was a good man. And I did not know that I was a prisoner until I fled and they brought me back. But nothing can be done. Whatever you are doing, whoever you are from, even if you are from the Bishop, nothing can be done. He is too powerful."

"Your lord holds his Barony from the Duke. And there is the King, who made him Marshal by royal command and can unmake him in turn. The Church is perhaps even more powerful than them both, and the noble Bishop of Nantes is the cousin of Duke Jean and what happens if they decide to work in concert, brother? No man is too powerful to escape his crimes, even on Earth, if there is a will to do something about it."

His eyes narrowed. "And is there such a will, sir?"

I had been commanded, on pain of terrible repercussions, to keep the investigation secret. The Bishop wanted no hint of an investigation to get back to Gilles de Rais, for what I imagined was a variety of reasons. And so I forced myself to hold my tongue.

"Listen, brother." I placed my hand on his shoulder and leaned in close. "Even the Marshal must know his actions will have consequences. He has abducted and imprisoned a vassal of the Duke, this priest le Ferron whose elder brother is also a powerful lord. Questions are being asked. But all the answers I want from you are about these other servants of your master. Who are these men who do his bidding? Who are the men who brought you back when you attempted to flee?"

"Very well. But you heard nothing from me, do you understand?" Blanchet looked around again. "The worst of them is Henriet Griart. An ugly man. Strong, fat. Sour. Not yet thirty years old. Just as bad is the one they call Poitou. His true name is Etienne Corrillaut but everyone calls him Poitou, I assume because he is from there. He is younger but balding on the top of his head at the front. His body is as thin as a stick but somehow his grip is like iron, strong enough to bruise me for weeks with no more than a grasp of his hand. He laughs often, at nothing. They are commoners who serve our lord as valets but they do whatever the Marshal wills."

"What does he command them to do?"

"I do not know, whatever the Marshal wills. And my lord also has two other servants who seem more like companions. Gentleman, I believe though I do not know what they are but they call the Marshal their cousin. One is named Sillé, a big man, older, and he perhaps rules over the others. He often carries a coil of rope that he uses to whip his horse but he carries it with him everywhere he goes and even hangs it on his belt when he sits down to eat. One other is Milord Roger de Briqueville, who is a knight. Tall and dark, like the Marshal. He is always drunk on brandy wine, just like the Marshal. He smiles and speaks well, like a lord, but he is frightening. There is a darkness behind his eyes. All these men go where my lord goes but they also do his bidding elsewhere. He sends them hunting but I never see them return with any prey."

Henriet, Poitou, Sillé, Briqueville. Hunters, are you? Soon, you shall all become the prey.

"What of this cleric I have heard so much rumour about? The sorcerer."

Blanchet's eyes almost popped out. "Prelati the Florentine. He is an alchemist but yes, they say he practices magic. He is always with de Rais now or else in his tower. Rarely seen."

"The rumours are that this Prelati summons demons for the Marshal."

"I know nothing of all that. It is probably peasant rumours, you know how the common folk like to gossip about such things. Prelati came here after me but what brought him and what he does, I do not know. Whatever it is, I believe he is a fraud."

"What brought *you* here?"

Blanchet sagged and held a hand over his eyes. "I was in Orléans."

"For the siege? Truly, brother?"

"No, no. Not for the siege, no. Sadly, I did not see the glory of the Maid. I mean after, when peace had come. I saw the Baron's pageant play."

I had heard of this extraordinary event but I still barely believed it was true. And if it was true, what did that say about whether Gilles de Rais was a mortal or not?

"Tell me about the pageant play, brother."

Blanchet took a deep breath and his eyes focused through me into the past. "It was years ago. Perhaps five years. It was a play but that is hardly the word to describe it. It was a festival. It began each day at dawn and ran all the way through until darkness fell. It was performed by a hundred and fifty people, each with spoken lines. And there were five hundred non-speaking parts. Twenty-thousand lines of verse. Twenty-thousand, sir! It was a re-enactment of the entire siege, you see. The expense of it cannot be calculated. No man in the history of the world has spent so much of his fortune on such a thing. For each performance, entirely new costumes were provided. Do you understand? At the end of the day, the costumes were thrown off, sold, tossed into the Loire, thrown on fires. And each morning over six hundred identical costumes were handed out to the players again. And, you must understand, these were not cheap costumes but true clothing. Robes that a lord would have been proud to wear, made from the finest cloth and embroidered and patterned and dyed with the utmost care. Even those who were dressed in the rags of the defeated English were made of fine, thick cloth and cut into jagged edges as if they were torn and dirtied. It was a wonder, a true wonder. The play began with the vile English making their plans in London, and at the climax there was the Maiden's victory. In between was her journey, and her battles against the enemy as she destroyed their forts one after the other. You saw her wounded and carried off. You saw her stand when others fled, and by her example, turn the tide of the battle. It was glorious. So many stages, all open to the air. Indeed, at times there would be simultaneous scenes being acted on two or three. On one, Joan would be haranguing the commanders to act while across the city the players would be acting out a raging battle. The crowd surged from one stage to another, following the action. And the wine, sir. You cannot imagine how the wine flowed. Barrels of fine vintages rolled out for every performance, all day, and every person in the crowd was filled with the wine. All free, of course. All rooms in the city were paid for by the Marshal. Enough wine and bread and meat to feed thousands, every single day. They say it cost eighty thousand gold crowns."

"A fortune," I said. "Enough to buy a duchy. And this disgusting display of opulence so impressed you that you sought service with the Marshal?"

He looked at me with surprise. "Because it was all for *her*. For her memory. To put right the lies they told about her. The Marshal wrote the play himself, all twenty-thousand lines of verse. To tell you the truth, as poetry goes it was not inspired. But it did not need to be when the tale itself was inspiration enough. You see, he told, and they showed, Joan tending to her work in her village when she had her vision that commanded her to go to the Dauphin. It showed her interview with the Dauphin, when she inspired him into believing in her. It even showed her return to the city after the great final victory against the vile invaders at Patay. It was for the glory of Joan. She was the heart of it. As she was in life. And at her side throughout it all was her most faithful captain, her brave and loyal bodyguard, the devoted soldier Gilles de Rais. And that is why I came to serve him. Because he served her. And she is here no longer, because the English burned her, and so I came. God forgive me, I came to this evil place. But I did it for *her*."

I placed my hand on his shoulder, for I believed I knew a good man when I saw one, and he seemed to be suffering greatly. Taking my leave, I swore I would not bother him again and reaffirmed that if anyone asked, I would deny ever having spoken to him.

"I swear to you, Dominus Blanchet, that one way or another, this will all be over soon."

"God bless you," he said, and went away shaking.

I went out to find the porter and told him my business was concluded.

Miton shrugged. "Thought you might have him with you."

I nodded. "You thought I was here to murder Blanchet. Yes. Of course you did. Not today, Miton."

He shrugged again and led me out through the decadent, beautiful interior of the castle. Before I left, I heard the distant sound of the choir starting up again and I thought about what the priest had told me.

Henriet, Poitou, Sillé, Briqueville. And Prelati the alchemist.

I had their names, their descriptions, and I knew they roamed the countryside hunting for prey and I meant to pick them off one by one.

In fact, I was to find that the damned porter or some other bastard told those very same men about a prying visitor calling himself Le Cheminant. And I would find out that, while I was searching for them, they were coming for me.

Two days after my visit, with his entire household, Gilles de Rais returned to Castle Tiffauges.

5

Abduction

June 1440

TIFFAUGES WAS A distant silhouette against the bone-white sky. I crept forward toward a cluster of jagged black rocks and behind wind-blasted scrub and sedge so the position was shielded from the main track heading northeast or southwest. There was also a good view on the track into Tiffauges village.

I whistled a couple of short trills, like a blackbird, and after a moment the replying tune came from deep in the rocks. I crawled forward and settled in next to Walt.

"Bring any wine, Richard?"

"You will find barrels of the stuff back at the inn."

"Bloody chilly again, is it not? Did you not bring any wine for yourself? Miserable cloud and damp all day long but it's clearing up now so it'll get real cold tonight, real cold and you'll wish you had it."

"Drinking wine on watch is utterly foolish. Once a man gets comfortable, he may as well give up and go to bed, for sleep is certain."

"Oh yes, is that so?" Walt said, looking me up and down. "Why you got that nice fur-lined cloak with you, then?"

I laughed. "What happened today?"

Walt's face grew serious. "Thought you might have heard tell of it at the inn by now. He's come back. Our lord of Rais."

"Dear God. When? What did you see?"

"Started early on. Stream of riders coming in, one or two at a time from the west. About the middle of the day came about fifty soldiers, all in their finery. Shining armour like each one of them was a prince, with pennants on their lances and streamers on the horses' tales."

"Yes, the Marshal has a penchant for ostentation."

Walt raised his eyebrows. "Does he, by God? These debauched barons, eh. Well, like I was saying, they were all done up fancy but they rode smartly, too. Like they was parading before a king, only there was no one to see them but I. They came up the road, tight together, two-by-two and nose to tail. Pages and squires came up behind and they was not far off in neatness, neither."

"Fifty soldiers, you say?"

"First group was fifty or so. Then came up the lord himself, riding in a party with fine horses. I swear to you, each horse was a walking fortune. Beautiful creatures, they was. His lordship rode beneath an unfurled banner in black and gold, great big thing like a war standard. Behind him was men playing trumpets and banging drums as they rode. And up after came more soldiers. Seventy, maybe. Same as the first lot. Fanciest fighting men you ever saw, all trotting on powerful big war horses. Later on comes wagon after wagon, some full of servants, most of them with barrels and sacks. Few people still coming in, here and there."

"By God, that is a large household."

"If I hadn't known better, I'd have sworn it was a king coming home from war. Or going off to one."

"Anything since then?"

"Nothing much and I doubt you'll see anything now. They just arrived after a day or two on the hoof so they'll all be pissed up by sundown. Might as well come back to the inn and sleep in your bed, sir, not sit in this dank hole and shiver in the dark for no reason."

"I appreciate your concern but one never knows what might occur. If the Marshal or any of his men are in fact immortals then they may sneak out for blood. We must remain vigilant. Besides, I already slept today in preparation. No, you get back and get yourself to rest. It will be your watch again on the morrow."

"All right, I will go get my head down after a flagon or two of ale and a bit of that boiled beef, if they have it still. But you just promise me you ain't going to go in there and fight all them soldiers. Not without me and Rob, at least."

I laughed. "Have no fear of that. We seek only to nab a servant for questioning. Nothing more."

"If you say so, sir. Good luck. God bless."

After he scrambled away toward the horses behind the hillock, I noticed the sounds of the place. The ceaseless wind rustling through the clumps of grass and whistling between gaps in the rocks. Buzzards wheeled overhead and already I could hear an owl screeching in the distance. Rooks cawed as they headed for their roosts, their black shapes sliding across the darkening sky. Goats cried their misery to each other across the plain. I pulled my fur-lined cloak closer about me and settled down further. It was sheltered from the worst of the wind but the rocks under me and at my back leeched the heat from my body even through the furs.

"Should have brought some bloody wine," I muttered to myself as the light faded. The moon was almost full and I prayed that the clouds would indeed blow right away before it rose, else I would be able to see nothing at all.

Stephen had complained about my strategy. He believed the best way to obtain the evidence we needed was a thorough questioning of the people from every village, hamlet, and farmhouse in the region and to do it thoroughly he needed my help, and Walt's and Rob's.

"They shall never speak to us," I had said. "My way is better. Swifter."

"How can it be swifter if all you do is huddle in the rocks and do nothing, day after day? At least by speaking to the people I am making progress of sorts. Collecting names."

"Hearsay from peasants," I said, scoffing.

"There is often truth hidden in rumour," he said. "And they are not peasants, Richard, as you would know if you bothered to speak to any of them."

"I have spoken to many of these good people," I said.

"Yes, to the physician's pretty daughter and to the innkeeper, while he brought your wine. What a dogged pursuit of the truth you have committed to, sir. If you would but listen to the stories of those who have suffered, you would be moved to act on their behalf."

"What do you think I am doing here?" I snapped. "Am I not taking action?"

"You mean to go charging in, as you always do. As you already have done, in fact and now you mean to do more. Illegally abducting a servant, Richard? It may undo our standing with the Bishop and the Duke and with the good folk of these parts. They have suffered for so long with no legal recourse. Despite having been so abused for so long, they are yet powerless to defend themselves but now we are here and we can represent them but first we must listen to what they have to say."

I had no interest in hearing them complain for days on end and I believed that I knew enough.

"For years they have able to submit a petition to their Duke," I pointed out. "And to the King. If they have not done so then that is their own fault."

"They are rightly terrified of repercussions!" Stephen said, almost wailing. "They are being preyed upon by the man who should be protecting them. Does it not outrage you, Richard?"

"I am here, am I not?" I countered. "I will find out if he is an immortal and slay him if he is. Otherwise, these people's troubles are their own. Now, while you go about listening to these peasants gnashing their teeth, I am going to illegally abduct one of his servants, beat the truth from him, and then we shall know what is really going on here."

Recalling it again, I realised that I had spoken with unnecessary heartlessness. But

Stephen always did have the propensity to nag like an old maid when the common folk were concerned.

Before the last of the day's light was completely gone, I caught movement at the base of the castle. A wagon came down the slope from the gatehouse and then went on rumbling and bumping along the track to the east. A lantern held aloft helped to show that two men sat up on it side by side, driving the single horse. It was a long way from my hiding place and they were wrapped up in cloaks and hoods but I fancied that one of the men was thin while the other was broad.

Could it be the valets Henriet and Poitou that Blanchet had told me about? It was surely wishful thinking on my part but I could not allow the opportunity to be missed. Keeping low, I slid back from the rocks and ran, stooped in half, behind the hillock to my horse. I had left him saddled so that he would be ready for just such an eventuality, the poor creature, and so I mounted him and headed out for the track. Night was falling fast and I had already lost sight of the wagon for some time.

My black horse was concerned by the strangeness of it all and went very slowly indeed until the moon came out. More clouds blew away until the world was illuminated once more and my horse picked up his pace. Following the track east, crossing the old stone bridge over the river, I thought I had likely missed the wagon. Perhaps it had turned for some house along the way. But then I saw the lantern glinting in the distance and I knew it was yet heading east. I thought it unlikely that they could see me on my dark horse but still I kept well away rather than scare them into flight before I could spring an ambush somewhere.

After a couple of miles they edged to the northeast, further from the river. I knew there were houses out there in the dark. Single dwellings, hamlets with three or four families, and larger villages, and I could smell the smoke from their fires and occasionally saw a flash of light from lamps through the edges of shuttered windows. But the wagon rumbled on by them all, deeper into the night. Every so often I stopped to listen, straining to hear over the wind. Once or twice I fancied I heard voices and perhaps a bark of laughter. Always the noise of the wagon banging over ruts and squeaking off in the distance continued and so did I.

The wagon stopped. Its lantern illuminated the driver and his passenger as they sat motionless. There was nothing in sight, not in any direction. Nothing but fields and plains edged in silver and shadow.

A light flashed in the east. A faint yellow glow winking on and off.

The wagon rumbled into life again, turning from the main track to head toward the light. Going slower than ever, I urged my horse forward. He was nervous but well-bred and he trusted me enough to obey after a moment's hesitation.

A house loomed in the dark, the moonlight showing a reed-thatched roof and another wagon sitting outside. Far beyond, squared lines and woodsmoke suggested a village of a few houses. I stopped and waited as the wagon creaked to a stop and the men called out a greeting. Another man emerged from the house, throwing a streak of yellow light across the scene, and muttered words were exchanged. A fourth man stomped out with a bundle over his shoulder which he threw into the flat back of the wagon I had followed.

That bundle was a boy, his limbs bound in some way and his head and shoulders covered in sackcloth.

He cried out as they tossed him down on the timber floor of the wagon and one of the men thumped the lad in the belly to shut him up. Another man jumped into the wagon and crouched by the boy.

I removed my cloak, rolled and tied it to my panniers, climbed into my saddle, and checked to ensure my sword and daggers were where they should be.

My intention had been to take and interrogate a single servant. If I intervened while there were four men, possibly more within the house, that made it highly unlikely I would be able to complete my mission. Alerting them to my presence would make taking them another night all the more difficult, perhaps impossible if they kept within the castle.

But of course, I could not allow them to take the lad to Gilles de Rais. He would go through the gates in the darkness and never see the light of day again and so it mattered not one bit what the consequences of saving his life might be. I resolved to take them on the road before they returned, perhaps while they crossed the bridge so that they could not easily flee. I would surprise them, bind them, question them and finally free the boy and take him back to his mother and his father, wherever they might be.

The boy cried out and I saw the men were pulling down his hose from beneath the sacking. One of the men stood over him, loosening his own doublet, pulling out his shirt tails, and undoing his belt.

Resolving to ride in, snatch the boy up, and ride away before they could react, I spurred my horse and he jumped forward, startled by my sudden command and tossing his head in protest. He was a good horse but I was asking too much of him to race toward that scene as if he was trained in war. Instead, he swerved away and snorted, stamping his foot on the stony ground. In the time it took to wrestle him back under my control, the men were alert to my presence.

"Who goes there?" an angry voice called out.

"Show yourself!"

I rode toward the light and stopped at the edge of it. "I am a simple traveller," I said, speaking slowly but clearly.

They had their hands on their daggers and two of them wore short swords on their hips. The boy squirmed on the back of the wagon.

"You alone?" the one standing over him said. He was thin, with a pinched, ratty face.

"Course he is," the fat one said, standing at the rear of the wagon with one hand on the boy's bound ankle.

"Get off your horse," a third man said from behind them. "Get off it and come here."

I laughed. "Why would I do that?"

"If you don't," the fat man said. "We'll make you."

A fourth man edged around to my flank in the shadows, attempting to be silent.

"I think what I shall do is ride immediately to the authorities and tell them I have witnessed an appalling crime."

They stared at the boy and back at me.

The fat one recovered his wits first. "Crime? What crime? Ain't no crime. We're just returning this boy to his father."

"He run away," the thin one said, grinning.

"What is his name?" I asked. The fourth man edged further to my flank and I lost sight of him. "For that matter, what are your names, sirs?"

They laughed, first one and then all three of them chuckled.

"Don't you worry what our names is," the fat one said.

"Oh, but I do worry. Let me see if I can guess them, shall I?" I pointed at the skinny man clutching the bunched-up tails of his shirt in one fist. "You are the one known as Poitou." He gaped at me and I pointed at the fat one. "And you are called Henriet Griart." The two men looked at each other and back at me while I pointed at the third man. "I do not know your name, nor the name of the oaf stumbling around in the dark there, but I will have them soon enough. For now, simply hand the boy over to me and I will say no more about it."

They overcame their confusion rather rapidly when they knew what it was that I wanted and Henriet smirked and grasped the boy's leg harder, digging his fingers in. The boy whimpered and writhed.

Poitou grinned as he stuffed his shirt back into his hose. "He ain't for you," he said.

"Ah, I see," I replied. "He is for your master, is that what you mean?"

Poitou giggled. "Who's to say where he ends up, whether it's with the master or—"

"Shut up, you fool!" Henriet snapped.

The man creeping in the dark scraped his foot and I realised he was closer than I expected and I turned as he rushed toward me. He was coming to grasp my horse's bridle or reins to stop me fleeing while the others pounced on me.

I kicked out at him, connecting with his shoulder hard enough to send him sprawling with a shout. The others wasted no time in drawing their weapons and so I pulled my sword and rode forward, turning to come around the wagons. I passed by the first and into the light of the house where a fifth man rushed out with his sword drawn, screaming blue murder. It surprised me, I will admit, and frightened my horse. He came close enough to slash his blade down the back of my calf and I turned and speared the tip of my sword down into his throat. He dropped his blade and wheeled away clutching at the blood gushing from his neck and I knew that I had caused a mortal blow.

I turned to see Poitou jump from one wagon to the other, falling on his face as he landed. It was too great a distance for a mortal man to leap and I knew in that moment that he was an immortal. Rushing to kill him quickly, I found another man coming with his dagger drawn.

"He's killed Ysaac!" he cried. "He's killed him!"

"I'll kill the bloody lot of you," I shouted, and I leaned down and ran the man through his chest.

He fell to his knees and I swung my sword up to block a wild blow from Poitou, standing on the back of the second wagon. The swords rang and my arm was jarred from the impact. He was untrained but immensely strong and I was surprised that neither blade was damaged. I threw his sword back and stabbed him in the belly. He wailed and fell back, scrambling away. His wound could not have been deep but being stabbed in the guts is rarely a pleasant experience. I looked for the other two.

"Stop!" Henriet shouted.

He stood on the rear of the other wagon with the boy standing before him. The poor lad was about eleven years old or so. His face swollen and bloody and his hands bound. Henriet had one fat arm wrapped tight around the boy and he held his dagger to the lad's cheek.

"If you don't stop right there," Henriet said, "I cut his face off his head and eat it in front of you."

"And if you harm him," I said, forcing myself to be calm, "then I shall certainly murder every one of you."

Henriet grinned, his teeth brown and black in the lamplight. "You want him, do you, you bastard? You want this? Do you? Eh?" He took his blade and sliced into the boy's arm, a long, wicked, twisting cut down the inside of his elbow. The boy cried out in anguish and his legs gave out, though he was held where he was by the massive arm coiled about him.

"Enough," I said, my voice coming out as a growl. "Hand him over."

Henriet grinned and shoved the lad off the wagon. Wrists and ankles bound as they were, he fell on his face in the dirt, landing hard. He lay motionless in shadow.

"Best take him and go," Henriet said. "Before he leaks himself to death."

I rode to the wagon but Henriet must have guessed my intentions, or else he was a naturally mistrustful soul, for he jumped from the far side and loped off into the darkness. The other man likewise scampered away.

"Henriet?" Poitou wailed. "Samuel? He's killed me, he's killed me, he has. My guts be pierced. Henriet? I need blood, Henriet. Samuel, you come back here, you filthy bastard."

Jumping from my saddle, I stooped to pick up the boy. He was unconscious and drenched with blood from his wound and soaked from pissing himself. It seemed likely that he would die but while there was breath in him there was hope, and so I flung him over my shoulder, mounted and eased him into position in front of me on the saddle, holding him upright.

After a mile or so, I stopped to wrap my cloak around the lad. He was cold to the touch and his head bounced around alarmingly as I rode. The horse was tired after his exertions that night and I begged him, over and over, to have strength and keep riding.

There was a physician, Pierre Mousillon, in the village of Tilleuls. I prayed that this time he would be home and that the boy would still be alive when I reached it.

Through the moonlit landscape, I rode.

"Hold on, there, son," I said, over and over into his ear. "Just hold on."

6

The Physician's Daughter

June 1440

I BANGED MY FIST against the door again. "Please! I need help!"

The boy in my arms was soaked with blood and his skin was cold to the touch. He seemed dead already but there was the faintest whisper of breath coming from his nose and so there was still hope. But there would not be for long.

"Please, I need the physician," I called through the door. "I need Pierre Mousillon, the physician."

Shutters banged open on the floor above the front door, spilling wan yellow into the blue-grey night. "Begone!" the voice called, harsh and urgent.

I backed up, carrying the boy. "Who is that? Are you the servant? I need your master."

"Be off with you, I say," the servant hissed.

"I met you, sir. My name is Richard. Let me see, your name is Paillart, is it not? You were present when I met with your mistress."

"What's that to me? You need a physician, you got to go to Nantes."

Other houses in the village behind me opened their shutters at the commotion and the church door creaked open. Yet no one came to help.

I shifted the lad, lifted him slightly so the light fell on his face. "For the love of God, man. Look, see here? I have a boy. See this boy in my arms? He is dying, Paillart."

The servant was pushed aside by the young woman, Ameline. She held a lamp out of the window and peered down, her hair free and lit up like a halo.

"Open the door, Paillart," she said.

He stayed where he was. "It's a ruse, Ameline. A ruse. He's no good, that one, I can smell it on him as clear as—"

"Open the door," she commanded.

Grumbling, he moved off into the house.

"Thank you, my good woman," I said. "The boy is in need of—"

"If this is a ruse, I shall gut you myself," she said, and brandished a long knife.

"I understand."

The door was unbarred and opened.

"I'm watching you," Paillart said, pointing at me with his drawn sword.

"Out of the way, man," I said and I strode into the dark house.

"Put him on the table," Ameline ordered me and I obeyed, laying the boy gently down upon the dining table as she cleared away the surface. "Light all the lamps and bring them here," the woman ordered her servant. "Candles, too. I must have light."

"Forgive me, good woman," I said. "Is your father not yet at home?"

"He is home," she said, her eyes fixed on the boy as she peered into his face. "Yet he will not be roused until morning and if we could rouse him, I fear he would be insensible."

"Ah," I said, my heart sinking. "Is there anything you can do for him?"

"What happened?" she asked. "Where is this blood coming from?"

"His arm. A cut, see, here? There was a group of men who—"

"Cut away his clothing, all from his upper body," she ordered, then raised her voice. "Paillart, we must have clean water immediately and then hot water as soon as you can."

The servant came in with two lamps and a bundle of candles in his arms, speaking rapidly. "Yes, mistress. Lighting the lamps, cold water, then hot. Anything else?"

"The boiled cloth, my father's physic bag, and the needle and thread."

"At once, miss."

She pointed at me. "Take this one with you." She glanced at me. "If you wish to save this boy's life, you will follow Paillart's orders."

I nodded. "I will."

"And take off your belt. I need it."

While Ameline worked on the boy, I did as I was instructed and lit and tended the fire, and fetched and boiled water. When I was called back in, I found the room filled with light and the delightful smell of fresh blood. The boy was on the table, his upper body bared. He groaned, a low, mournful cry and twisted where he lay. My belt was tied about his upper arm just below the shoulder and Ameline was sewing together both sides of the long gash down the inside of his arm.

"Out of my light!" she snapped, and I stepped aside. "Hold him down."

"He lives," I said, placing my hands on the boy's chest. His skin was cold and damp. "By God, you have the skills of an army surgeon."

She blew a strand of hair away from her face as she worked, concentrating closely. "I think that he will die," she whispered. "And so we must pray to God."

Paillart came in. "The bandages, mistress. Clean and new."

"Out of my light!" she barked at him. She wrapped his wound up with practised skill and slowly loosened my belt before handing it back to me. "I apologise. I fear it is quite covered in blood."

"It is not the first time," I said softly as I tied it around my waist. "What now?"

"Now, we will see if he survives to see sunrise. Paillart, carry him to my bed, will you, please?"

"Oh, no, mistress. Dear me, no. Your own bed, mistress? I will not hear of it."

"Do as I say."

"Let it by my bed, Ameline. Don't sully your good clean bed with the filth of this peasant, I beg thee."

"It is because my bed is good and clean that the boy shall have use of it. Now, you will do as I command."

He sighed and scooped the boy up with a profound gentleness and bore him toward the stairs, whispering kind words as he did so. "There now, lad. You'll be alright now, you will. You just rest, son, and you'll be right as rain, you will."

Ameline stood and stretched her back, her hair falling about her face with the light falling on her from every angle and her dress straining at her chest. Her hands were bloody up to the elbows. She looked really quite wonderful.

"I will wash, now," she said.

"Thank you," I said. "For saving him."

"He is not saved."

"For doing what you have done, then," I said. "You were magnificent."

She scoffed, and yawned. "He will need watching," she said. "In case he takes a turn."

"I will watch him," I replied. "If you do not mind it."

She eyed me. "Who is this boy to you?"

"Nothing," I said. "I do not even know his name. There were men from the castle. I followed them. They met more men, at a house a few miles east of here across the river. They handed over that boy, who I assume was bound for the castle. I stopped them but they hurt the boy. I wanted to finish them all off but he was dying. I had to get him help."

Paillart returned, stomping down the stairs and into the parlour. "What's that he says? He assaulted the lord's men?"

"I stopped them from taking this boy, yes," I said to him.

"That's trouble, that is, miss. That's trouble, and trouble for you and for your father."

Ameline said nothing but regarded me with a strange look in her eye.

"I want no harm to come to you," I said to her. "No one will know I brought the boy here."

Paillart scoffed. "No one will know? You daft sod. Everyone will know, and know already. You've done it now, so you have."

"Whatever I have done, I have done with good intentions and for good reason. I will let no harm come to you, my lady." I looked at her servant. "And I will kill every man in that castle if I have to."

"Paillart," Ameline said. "Escort Richard to my room so that he may keep watch on the boy. Then go spread word that a boy has been found."

"Go?" he spluttered. "And leave you alone with him?" He jabbed a finger at me.

"Father will wake soon enough," she said, unconcerned. "And you must find the boy's mother and father and have them come. Before it is too late. Go and find who has lost a son about his age in the last day or two. Other servants in the village may ride out also to let the boys' parents know so that they can be here for his end, if that is what God wills. We must do that for them, at the least."

I sat alone in the bedchamber, on a low stool, watching the boy breathing beneath the sheets. Every breath in seemed a miracle, and every breath out seemed as though it would be his last. The lamplight played across his grey face, making it seem as though he twitched and grimaced where in fact he lay as if he was dead. The only sign was that breath in and the shuddering breath out. Over and over. In and out. I grew tired and my head nodded.

"Here," Ameline said, nudging me with her knee and handing me hot wine. Grey light shone at the edges of the shutters. I must have fallen asleep. In fear, I looked at my charge.

The boy yet breathed.

"God bless you," I said as I took the warm cup in both my hands and breathed in the spices. "Some watchman I turned out to be," I said. "My apologies."

"It is well," she said softly, and placed a stool beside mine. She had her hair tucked away beneath a simple cap. "He has passed the most dangerous hour. And you had a long night, full of adventure."

I smiled into my cup. "Not compared to some nights I have had, my lady."

"You must call me Ameline, sir. Your work must be quite remarkable, if saving a boy's life is not a thing out of the ordinary."

"I snatched him away from danger but it was you who saved him, if saved he is."

She looked at me, a slight smile on her lips. "Unless you wish to argue further, sir, shall we agree that we both saved him?"

I smiled and nodded. "Let us so agree it. And you must call me Richard."

She flashed a quick smile at me and looked once more to the boy. We shared a quiet, companionable silence while we sipped our hot spiced wine. It roused me.

"But you are wounded, Richard," she said, looking at my leg.

"I am?" The hosen over my calf was torn and drenched in dried blood. I recalled that the man who had sneaked up on me in the darkness had cut me there. "Oh yes. Well, I am sure all is well now."

"But your wound must be cleaned before the corruption begins." She moved to one knee and reached for my leg, poking a finger into the sliced fabric to look beneath.

I had little doubt that the wound had already healed and so shifted my leg away. "A scratch on a branch, nothing more. The blood is not mine."

"Is that so?" she asked, disbelieving me. The sharp tear was clearly caused by a blade and the wool was dark and stiff all around where my blood had gushed out. "Very well." She sat back and frowned.

I thought perhaps she had noticed there was no wound to be seen on my flesh and I spoke quickly to distract her from what that might mean.

"Is what your servant said true?" I asked. "That I have caused you danger by coming here?"

She reached out a hand and grasped mine firmly where it rested on my knee. "I am thankful that you came here. I would not have had you go anywhere else. Whatever the consequences, that shall remain the way that I feel."

I squeezed her hand back and she let it linger on my knee for a moment before withdrawing it.

"How much like Jamet he looks," Ameline said softly, tilting her head to regard the sleeping boy. "If only someone could have saved him as you did this one."

"Forgive me but he was taken in this manner? By men in the night?"

She sighed. "We told him. We all told him. Never go off with anyone. Never, not for anything. Stay within sight of the church at all times, never once lose sight of it. I wonder what cunning they employed to get him away. They said it was La Meffraye who took him."

"The Terror," I said. That was *La Meffraye* in the Breton dialect.

"That is what they call them," she said. "And they are well named. The old woman from the castle who wanders from village to village with her evil familiar at her side, tempting the children away with her sweets and promises and dark magic. But no one knows what happened with Jamet, not truly. Perhaps it was not La Meffraye after all and instead it was the men, and they snatched him up in a sack. Not knowing how it occurred is perhaps the most awful part. Is that appallingly selfish of me? How conceited I must sound."

"Not at all," I said, as gently as I could. "Surely, nothing could be further from the truth."

"Ever since my brother and my mother, my father is almost never at home. He attends to the sick for miles all around. When he does come home, he does not stay. When he is here, he drowns himself in brandy wine. I think that his heart cannot bear it."

"I can understand such actions," I said. "People stay away from pain, like an animal fleeing attack, or a child flinching from a hot candle. But we are also drawn to places where we once felt strength and love. And no doubt that is why he returns to his home. To you."

She scoffed, though there was a surprising lack of bitterness in it. "Strength and love, or even to the illusion of such things. As can be found in a bottle of brandy wine."

No matter the pain her father felt, he had a duty to his daughter, the only member of his family still alive. Despite all her evident ability and the strength in her heart, she needed him.

"Perhaps, in time, he will find the strength to be your father once more."

She sighed at that, almost gasping at the sudden emotion of it. "Forgive me," she whispered. "I do not know why I burden you with such nonsense."

Ameline had lost her brother, and the grief had taken her mother in turn. And her father's misery had driven him away while only she remained, all alone with no one but a grizzled old servant for company. And no one to share herself with.

I reached out and took her hand. "It is no burden. But if it was, I would bear it gladly if it meant easing yours."

Our eyes met and her look was unwavering, latching onto mine with a fierce scrutiny. I could have drowned myself in her eyes but I sensed it was she who was drowning and she saw in me the strength that she needed to pull herself free.

A loud voice burst in on us, filling the room with outraged surprise.

"What is the meaning of this?"

Her father loomed in the doorway, his hair wild and shirttails flapping. His eyes were red and unfocused as he blinked all around, leaning on the wall. I could smell the drink on him from across the room.

Ameline snatched her hand away and jumped to her feet. I stayed seated.

"Father. It is nothing. This good and decent man brought the child in the night, grievously wounded and in need of a surgeon." She lowered her voice. "And so I attended to the boy myself."

The father's outrage dwindled into shame and he hung his head. "Ah. I see. Well, get off with you, now, girl and fetch my water. Where is Paillart, for the love of God?"

"Gone to send word to the boy's family to come and collect him," Ameline said. "He will be back soon."

Her father stuck a finger in his ear and wiggled it around. "Well, what is all that blasted commotion that roused me? Is it Sunday already?"

As he said it, I noted the swell of voices outside, several of them, speaking softly but incessantly and growing all the while in volume. It did indeed sound like folk gathering for Mass at the church across the square.

"It is not Sunday, father," Ameline said and crossed to the window. She pushed open the shutters and then stepped smartly back, crossing herself in the morning light.

I stood and looked out, edging forward to lean on the sill.

There were a dozen people outside, men and women both, drifting closer to the house from all directions. Some led horses behind them. When they saw me at the window, the men pulled off their hats. Beyond the group directly below, more people approached in ones and twos from both sides of the street. Horses clopped in at the edge of the village.

"God bless you, sir," one of the men said. "I heard you found a boy in the night and we was wondering, me and my wife, if it's our little Michel?"

Another man shuffled forward and bowed, before looking up. There were tears in his eyes. "Is it my Jean, sir?" he sobbed, sucking in a great big gulp of air. "Is it my fine boy,

Jean?" He sank to his knees and held up his hands in supplication.

All at once, they all began speaking, asking questions, begging me for answers.

"Dear God," I said, turning to Ameline. "We must go down to them."

7

Oaths Sworn

June 1440

MY ARRIVAL THE NIGHT before had woken the whole village and Paillart had told them what had occurred and to send word out to the neighbours. And so word had spread as quickly as lightning and parents from all around had come in as quickly as they were able to in the mad hope that it was their child who had been found, even if theirs had disappeared months or years past.

Their hopes were quickly dashed, of course.

The boy's parents were an old couple from just a few miles to the east, the father a cartwright named Pierre le Charron. Their boy was named Guillaime and had been missing for two days.

Both fell to their knees by the bed and wept and thanked God. I turned to leave but the mother cried out.

"You saved him, sir. You saved my sweet boy. God love you, sir, God keep you and watch over you."

Their gratitude was almost more than I could bear but far worse was the sight of the other parents outside turning to leave when the boy's name and parentage was confirmed. It was heart-breaking to see their hopes crumble but I had an idea that I might have caught them at just the right moment. At least, perhaps, it was worth a try.

"Wait, please," I called out. "I beg you."

After much cajoling and pleading, I had them come into the church. The priest was wizened and sickly but kind enough to allow the use of his nave, though he was suspicious of my intentions. They all were.

The sun had come out stronger that morning and the light shone through the narrow windows high up on the walls of the nave and poured in through the open door, along with the faint smell of spring.

Standing by the altar, I noted that the parents were angry and fearful. They did not know me and so they did not trust me but I had won a certain level of renown from my rescue of young Guillaime and they came in, clutching their hats and hoods to their chests and crossing themselves. It was a small church and was soon filled with scores of local people, from Tilleuls and the neighbouring villages. Their anger and disappointment were palpable but the fact that they came at all suggested something else.

It suggested that they felt some hope.

Perhaps, I thought, I was imagining it. That it was wishful thinking on my part. But they were there and they stood to listen to me address them.

I could bellow words of inspiration at a company of unruly soldiers before battle but standing before the eyes of those grieving families I found my words dried in my mouth.

"Thank you, all." I coughed and cleared my throat. "I am sorry that I rescued just one boy last night. I wish that I had found and brought back all of them. But I suspect that is not to be. What is worse, I suspect that can never be. You know in your hearts that this is true." At this, I saw many heads drop and many sighs sounded. I glanced over to catch the eye of Ameline, who returned my look. She nodded, a tight, determined set to her lips. "You all have suffered. For many years, you have suffered, and you have had no justice. And no hope of justice. Until now." At that, a few heads lifted. "Some of you may know me, or my colleagues. We have come from Nantes with orders to take sworn statements from those who would bear witness against the man who has committed these crimes against you."

"It is not a man," a voice called out. "But a monster."

Many called out their agreement.

"A monster, yes, indeed," I said. "A monster who is served by monsters. But they must be arrested and tried as men, in court, and when they are found guilty they will be hanged."

"That's too good for them," a woman shouted. "They need to be burned!"

This brought another chorus of agreement.

"I wish it also," I said. "But there will be no trial." I looked around, letting my words echo.

They muttered in confusion and I let them feel baffled for a moment.

"There will be no hanging. And none will burn." They stared back at me in disbelief for offering hope before snatching it away. "There will be no justice at all for those you have lost until the good people of these lands come together and bear witness to these crimes." They began muttering to each other again. "All those who lost their children, I ask that you make your sworn statement. A statement sworn with your names and entered into the records of the official investigation. Once we have enough of these statements, a warrant will be issued and the criminals will be arrested."

"That will never be done!" a man cried out.

"You ask us to risk all," another said. "Add our names? Accusing *him*, in public? It will be the end of us, sir. The end!"

A woman wailed. "We have other children. Who will care for them when we ourselves are carried off?"

They erupted into endless objections.

"Who are you, sir?" someone called out, and then repeated until the others quietened. "Who even are you to come here and speak thusly to us? Where do you come from? Who do you serve?"

Another man answered. "Pipe down, Gerard. You know he saved Pierre le Charron's boy? Give him his due."

"He saved one boy and I'm supposed to bow down at his feet? I ask it again, who do you serve, sir?"

I held up my hands. "It is a fair question." The muttering died down. "I say, it is a fair question. You do not know me. We have arrived in your midst and we are asking the world. Now, I will tell you. But before I tell you, I ask you to listen. We were brought here, myself and the lawyer Stephen who some of you have met, along with our men who have gone with us to guard us. We were brought here under the strictest orders not to reveal the full nature of our employment to anyone because to do so would risk the success of the investigation itself." They grumbled but I held up my hands. "Have I not said I will tell you?" When they calmed themselves I continued. "And I will tell you because I trust you. I trust that you will today do what is necessary and you will add your voices together with such force so that nothing can stand in your way, no matter what the monster Gilles de Rais hears about it. So, I will tell you. It is the Bishop of Nantes who directs this investigation. It is he, along with his dear friend, Milord Jean the Duke of Brittany, who will issue the warrant for the Baron de Rais' arrest. It is the Bishop of Nantes who will sit in judgement of his crimes. Our demonic Baron de Rais will be finished. And this will happen. But only after each of you sits down with me and my lawyer to make your sworn deposition." I waited for them to digest what I had said. "Now. Who here is willing to step forward?"

Silence.

Feet shuffled on the floor and people glanced left and right. At the back, I saw someone duck out and then another two, and I was certain the trickle would turn to a flood and I would be left standing alone with the priest. Assuming he stayed.

I sighed. It had been worth a try but I was expecting too much from them. They had been subjugated by terror for years and now I was asking them to throw off their caution for a stranger's promise. It was too much.

"I will do it."

Turning, I found the one who had spoken and stepped forward.

"Ameline Moussillon," I said and bowed my head. "Truly? You wish to make a sworn statement? Are you certain?"

Her gaze did not waver. "I am."

"Well, then, mademoiselle, you have my sincere thanks."

"No," she said. "It is I am who am thankful. You have come and you have shown through your actions that you mean what you say. Because you are here, you have saved Guillaime le Charron from a fate he would have shared with my dear brother. His name was Jamet and he was taken and I know in my heart that he is dead now. He was murdered. Murdered, like so many others, by the Marshal. He was murdered by the Baron Gilles de Rais of Tiffauges. We all know it but none of us can speak it aloud. Well, I shall speak it. I shall swear it, in writing, and I shall speak the words in a court or anywhere else required of me so that the Marshal is punished for his crimes. You have my word."

I nodded to her, struck dumb by her bravery.

Beside Ameline, her father stood looking down at his daughter, leaning on his stick. He seemed astonished and horrified in equal measure and I was sure he would berate her and order her to know her place and send her away. The physician looked around at the villagers, who all were staring at him also, waiting to see him quash his daughter's reckless courage.

Drawing himself upright, he hobbled forward half a step. And then a step further. Lifting his chin, he looked around at the entire congregation.

"Some weeks ago, I went to see the Bishop of Nantes. He sent some scrawny little episcopal lawyer to speak to me in his stead. I told that young man I wished to make a statement. To give evidence. To bear witness to the crimes and to name the criminal. But my courage failed me. I did not make the statement." He cleared his throat while the villagers muttered in surprise. "But I will do so now. My daughter has shown me today what courage is. And for that, I am grateful. So yes, sir, I will make a sworn deposition. I will do it, yes. I will do it."

As he stepped back, he wiped his eyes with his spare hand before wrapping that arm around Ameline's shoulders. She patted his hand and glanced at me.

That was all it took for more of them to step forward and offer their support. At some point during the meeting, Walt appeared and he came forward while people were giving me their names.

"You had an eventful night then, I take it?" he said, grinning and jerking a hand over his shoulder. "By the way, I just see someone hanging around that I reckon you might—"

"Find Stephen," I snapped. "Get him here immediately before they change their minds."

I was right glad that morning by what had transpired. With a mountain of witness statements, it seemed certain to me that the Bishop and the Duke would have to act in issuing the arrest warrant for Giles. And then even his private army of two hundred expert soldiers could not save him.

But it would not be so simple.

And what is more, there was someone else watching from the shadows that morning in the church in Tilleuls.

Someone small and hooded and all-but unnoticed, keeping expertly to the darkness, who would soon scurry back to Castle Tiffauges and report on everything that had transpired.

If only I had given Walt a moment to speak, we might have avoided so much of what later occurred. But such is the way of things and sometimes all we can do is regret terrible events and missed opportunities. And to move on from regret we must somehow come to terms with what happened and our part in it.

My regrets, my guilt and my sense of failure, stemmed from the day the Maiden of Lorraine arrived at Orléans and began undoing all that had taken a century of war to achieve.

8

The Maiden at Orléans

April 1429

IN MAY 1429, ELEVEN years earlier, we were with the English army outside of Orléans. Our siege around the city was not one of continuous trench lines ringing the walls. We never had anywhere near enough men to undertake such works nor could we have hoped to man them, even with the army of Burgundy in support. Instead, we had constructed a series of small forts that covered strategic approaches. We had seven strongholds on the north bank and four on the south and one on an island in the river.

From the start, we had meant to assault the city from the south across the bridge that led into the middle of the city but the garrison had defended well and we had fallen into a strategy of grinding them down over weeks, months, and years.

I was not there but I heard well from the grumbling of the soldiers that building the series of forts, the siege outworks had been bloody difficult. The garrison sallied out endlessly to assault our men and tear down what we had made whenever they could drive us off. But our men were veterans of such warfare and could not be resisted for long. Because we did not have enough men to stop the flow of enemies entirely, they could still get some supplies in and men out but that could not be helped.

On the south bank, covering the bridge into the city, we had a huge defensive complex, made up of linked forts. Guarding the approach to the bridge from the east was a fort, while to the west of the bridge complex was another fort which also guarded the bridge to the island of Charlemagne, which had yet another fort to protect it.

On the north bank, to the west of the city, was the great fort of St. Laurent, the largest of them and where the commanders resided. I made sure that was where me and my men lived also, to be close to the heart of the English command.

In hindsight, I should have tried to take effective command of one of the other forts instead.

North of that, ringing the city were a series of others that guarded the approaches. These were wittily named, London, Rouen, and Paris, because they sat across the roads that led ultimately to those places. The massive forest that supplied the city's wood and charcoal lay to the northeast and we had no forts there but we moved freely there in force. Far to the east, about a mile from the city, we had our final fort named St. Loup. This covered any approaches from upriver, however, it was almost totally isolated from the rest of the forts and would struggle to receive reinforcements, should it be attacked.

And attacked it was. But not yet. Not until *she* arrived.

"It's only a matter of time before the garrison surrender," men told me when I arrived at the forts with the supply convoy and our remaining barrels of herrings.

"Is that so?" I asked them, after touring the forts myself. "What makes you so certain, friends?"

"The Earl of Shrewsbury Sir John Talbot is in command now," they said, "and he knows his business well enough, does he not?"

"I suppose he does," I replied.

"Mark my words, lads," one old soldier named Simon cried out. "I been doing this for close to thirty years, now, so I have. I know my business even better than Shrewsbury and I know that the city will certainly fall by this coming summer."

"Perhaps even before the end of spring," another soldier said.

"Any day now," another claimed.

"Summer," Old Simon said to me. "Mark my words, you lads, mark my words. We'll be in there, raking the silver and gems into our purses, by the end of summer."

"The fall of the city is not the objective of our efforts," I said to them. In return, they scratched their chins and frowned. "It is the gateway to the south, is it not? You men surely know that when Orléans falls, it will secure the northern half of France above the Loire for the English and will so open the way for us to assault and crush the forces of the Dauphin Charles in the south."

"Course, that be true enough, and all," Old Simon allowed. "But first, they'll surrender and we'll get rich. Right, lads?"

They cheered his witless confidence but even a fool could see that the stakes could hardly have been higher, especially for the French in general and for the Dauphin Charles in particular.

It was not only the general soldiery who were convinced that they need do nothing other than sit on their arses for a few months to achieve victory. Indeed, how confident were the lords of England also that Orléans would fall, and how resigned the city's denizens and leaders were to that very thing.

In March, the Bastard of Orléans offered to surrender Orléans to Burgundy. The terms were incredibly generous. Humiliating, even. The enemy proposed that Burgundy would be able to appoint the city's governors and half the city's taxes would go to the English. The other half would go for the ransom of the imprisoned Duke of Orléans, they would pay ten thousand gold crowns to Bedford for war expenses, and the English would be allowed to pass through the city, and so our army could assault the Dauphin and win all of France for England, forever. All of this, France itself on a platter, in return for lifting the siege and handing the city to the Burgundians.

The regent, Henry V's brother, the Duke of Bedford said no.

He was convinced that the city was about to fall anyway and so he would have all the plunder and possession of it for the English. Why on earth, I am sure he thought, would he hand it over to the damned Burgundians?

Not only was the opportunity thrown away, it naturally annoyed the Burgundians so much that they took their army away from Orléans.

While all this was occurring, we began to hear hints about a witch who was coming from the east.

I did not know this at the time, but it seems that vague prophecies had been circulating in France concerning an armoured maiden soldier who would rescue France from destruction by feat of arms. Many of these prophecies foretold that the armoured maiden would come from the borders of Lorraine.

It just so happened that this witch was coming from Domrémy, on the borders of Lorraine.

"It's nought but a barrel-load of arse pimples," Walt said, spitting.

It was finally a warm day and we sat on fresh grass with the sun on our backs supping beer with a few hours to spare in between our duties. I would rather have enjoyed the day in silence but soldiers are the world's greatest gossipers, save old women and new mothers.

"Perhaps it is the truth," I replied.

Walt scoffed. "What, some little girl marching with soldiers, dressed as a page boy, is going to save France?"

Rob looked up at the sky, as if seeking inspiration. "They say she is no longer dressed as a page but now wears full plate armour and helm. Just as it is foretold in the prophecy."

"Prophecy," Walt said, spitting again.

"I suppose it does seem rather unlikely," I allowed.

"Do you believe in prophecy, sir?" Rob said. "That events is preordained by God?"

"I have been assured by a number of priests and monks, including dear Stephen, that mankind is given free will, to make what choices we will. If this is the case, how can there exist such a thing as predestined actions?"

Rob frowned. "Can't God do what He wants?"

"I am sure He can. I believe this is what we would call a miracle."

"This whore from Lorraine ain't a miracle," Walt said. "Some cunning sod has tarted up his little piece in fancy armour and is dragging her here hoping we take fright and run away. Won't work, Richard. Look around you. Look at the miserable, hard-faced bastards we have here. All they want is to get inside them walls over there, finally, and have at the wine and the women therein. Ain't no sodding witch going to turn these sons of war from them there walls, no, sir. You wait and see."

I thought he was probably quite right about all of that.

We soon knew, as did the citizens of Orléans, that this maiden from Lorraine had been brought before the Dauphin himself. Reports were confused but by the end of March we heard that she was marching in a suit of plate armour, mounted on a warhorse, flying her own banner while attended by pages, heralds, servants, and high-born knights serving as her bodyguard.

It was fantastical. We could not quite credit the rumours we were hearing.

And then her first letters arrived addressed to our commanders.

Begone, or I will make you go.

The missives were signed, *La Pucelle*, which meant the Maiden.

It was all so strange. A peasant girl, by all accounts, addressing great lords and giving them ultimatums. The men jeered and cursed her and mocked the French for falling for the ruse. But underneath it all, I sensed a disquiet among the English. Perhaps it was only I who felt such anxiety but, knowing what later occurred, I do not believe I was mistaken in noting the rising apprehension.

At the end of April, a messenger arrived at the fort of St. Laurent, his horse shuddering and the man himself sweating. I rushed over to the commander's position in the hope that I would hear of what was occurring.

"My lord," he said to Sir John Talbot, speaking with all urgency. "A great supply column approaches from Blois. From the south, on the other side of the Loire."

"Indeed?" Talbot cried and turned to his men with a smile on his face. "We shall send word to the bastilles guarding the bridge to intercept them."

His knights smiled also, for if we stopped the convoy, as we had done to many others, it would mean additional supplies for the men and quite possibly additional wealth for the lords.

"Begging your pardon, my lord," the messenger said, catching his breath. "I must also report that the convoy is escorted by five hundred soldiers."

The grin fell from Talbot's face. "Five hundred? Are you certain, man?"

"It is five hundred, my lord, at the least."

"And..." the messenger continued, then paused.

"And?" Talbot cried. "Out with it, man."

"And they say that the Maiden of Lorraine is with them, my lord. The Maiden what has been sending letters, I mean, my lord. The Maiden who they say is beloved by God and who is destined to—"

"We know what damned maiden you speak of," Sir John Fastolf snapped. "Be silent."

"By God," Talbot muttered, turning to his men. "We shall allow this convoy to pass. It is a shame but it cannot be helped. On the next occasion, assuming they are not so well defended, we shall take the supplies."

"Are you mad?"

They turned to me as one and I realised I had spoken aloud without thinking.

"Hold your tongue, sir!" Sir John Fastolf roared. "How dare you?"

I stepped forward toward the group of outraged lords and addressed Talbot, the Earl of Shrewsbury, directly. "Forgive me, my lord. But surely we must make every effort to stop these supplies entering the city? It otherwise might extend the siege beyond the summer and into the winter and who knows what might occur if we tarry here another year?"

"Tarry?" Fastolf said. "Control yourself, sir, or I shall have you removed from my presence."

Talbot was quiet, though, as he regarded me and when he spoke it was with condescension. "Our only soldiers on that side of the river are the ones manning the bastilles that guard the bridge. If I order the men out of those forts, the garrison from the city will assault the bridge and with no men to defend them, we will lose them. What is more, taking such action is unnecessary, because there will be no way for this convoy to cross the river and so they will retreat, just as so many other convoys have done in previous months. Now, young man, I know it may be difficult for you to understand but this is the best course of action. You, Richard, are an able commander of a small company and carry out your duties guarding the perimeter and escorting messengers perfectly well. But you will allow your betters to dictate matters of strategy, will you not? You are dismissed, sir."

I scoffed and looked at him, at Fastolf, and at the furious knights all around them.

"Thank you, my lord," I said, bowing.

Later that day, the supply column came at the city from the south just as the messenger had warned. Unable to approach our forts at the bridge, they instead made to cross the river by boat opposite our fort of Saint-Loup on the north bank.

And from afar we watched upriver and heard reports as they came in. While French skirmishers kept the garrison of Saint-Loup on the north bank contained, a fleet of boats from Orléans sailed down to the landing to pick up the supplies, and the soldiers, and the Maiden.

"You must stop them, my lords," I urged Talbot and Fastolf. We watched the events from afar, on the north bank. "There is yet time to stop them before they embark."

"Remove this man," Talbot muttered, watching the fleet sail upstream to where the small army and the wagons waited as the sky darkened toward nightfall.

No one moved to do so but I fell silent. They would not listen to reason.

Walt edged forward at my elbow. "Do you see the Maiden, sir?" he whispered.

"Do not be absurd," I said. "I can hardly make out one man from another at this distance."

"I can't see her, neither," he grumbled.

"The winds blows east," someone nearby said, with excitement in his voice. "And so they will not so readily return to the city against the wind."

There were murmurs as the men all around concurred. Some even went so far as to celebrate the fact that the supplies would remain stranded on the south bank as night fell.

"Perhaps a limited number of companies might raid the convoy in the night," Fastolf suggested to Talbot. "Take some for ourselves and help drive them off."

Talbot nodded. "Raise the signal before dark," he ordered.

But then one of Joan's reputed miracles occurred. The wind which had brought the boats upriver suddenly reversed itself, allowing them to sail back to Orléans smoothly under the cover of darkness and there was not a thing we could do about it.

It was no miracle, of course. The wind often changes as night falls, and though no man can say why it does, all men know that it is the most natural thing in all the world. No man alive has not noted the fact of it and yet the French were convinced that the Maiden had intervened with her prayers and then God had answered.

Either way, the long-awaited Joan of Lorraine had arrived.

The people of the city celebrated the arrival of the prophesied Maiden, who was destined, so they said, to save them all.

"It's a barrel load of arse-pimples," Walt said again as we watched the boats of the convoy, little more than black shapes moving on the black water, heading up to the landing places at the city walls. "All that stuff about the Maiden. Ain't it, Richard?"

"Certainly, it is," I replied, the dark shapes bobbing in the distance becoming lost in coal-black shadow.

Only later would I discover that sitting hunched down beside the young woman in the bottom of one of those river boats as it landed in Orléans, was a nobleman in the finest armour, named Baron Gilles de Rais.

None of us could know at the time but it was the beginning of the end for the English in France.

9

Illumination

July 1440

"THIS IS NOT enough," the Bishop said, looking at the list of named witness depositions. He rolled it back up and tossed it onto the desk in his audience chamber.

Stephen and I exchanged a look.

We had taken more than three weeks to record almost thirty sworn statements from bereaved parents and other local people who felt brave enough to go through with it. Each one had taken time to locate and Stephen recorded their words. Some had changed their minds and refused to speak to us after all and we had crossed back and forth from Cholet to Challans, fifty miles from east to west, and twenty north to south. A vast area and we had run ourselves ragged. Our valets especially were exhausted. But I had driven my men hard, day after day, because those statements were the means of bringing Gilles de Rais to justice whether he was an immortal or human.

"Not enough?" I said, incredulous. "What in the name of God do you mean not enough? We did precisely as you wanted and now you say to us that it is not enough?"

The Bishop stared in astonishment and his clerks and servants muttered behind him. "How dare you, sir? How dare you speak to me in this fashion? I will have your apology, sir, or I will have your damned head on a pike."

I scoffed. "If you are going back on your word, my lord, then I will end this in the way I am used to."

"What in the world do you mean by that? If you are not careful, I will have you dragged from here and thrown in gaol."

The two guards at the back of the room stepped forward, ready to do the Bishop's bidding.

"Richard," Stephen said, warning me.

I smiled at the Bishop. "You may certainly try."

He scowled, his fat cheeks wobbling. He certainly had the authority to have me treated very badly, if he so wished. But after two and a half centuries of immortality, I was capable of quickly and accurately judging a man's character. And the Bishop, though he blustered, was at heart a kind and decent man and I knew I could face him down.

"You say these are not enough, my lord?" Stephen said, stepping forward to pick up our list. "I suppose we could find a few more who are willing to make their sworn statements but it was something like a miracle that we have secured so many as this."

"No," the Bishop said. "I am sorry, Stephen. Depositions from peasants are not enough for us to issue a warrant for the Baron's arrest."

Stephen and I turned to look at each other in shock.

"Your pardon, Milord Bishop," Stephen said, "but we followed your orders. You told us this was what you needed."

"I did," the Bishop replied. "And I have since spoken to the Duke. He is unwilling to act on this basis alone."

"Unwilling?" I said, still speaking with too much passion. "So he may be persuaded to change his mind?"

The Bishop looked me up and down, as if suddenly recalling that I existed. It seemed as though he would pretend I had not spoken but then he deigned to reply. "I misspoke. He will absolutely not issue a warrant based on the depositions of peasants, no matter how many of them there are."

"They are not *peasants*," I said, snatching the roll of names from Stephen's hand and brandishing it like a weapon. "Less than half are labourers, as you can see for yourself from the professions listed by the names. You have builders, embroiderers, fullers, carders, butchers, spinners, a cartwright, roofers, coopers, a herbier, potters, millers, a boat builder, and a physician, for God's sake." The Bishop had his hands up, palms facing me, to shut me up. "These are good and decent people who have bravely taken a stand for each other and for the sake of justice. I gave them my word that action would be taken if they spoke up. I gave my word that justice would be done."

The Bishop sighed. "You should not have done that."

He was right. I should not have done such a foolish thing. I had been caught up in the moment in the church and had wanted to give those desperate people the hope that they deserved. It was not even hope for the lives of their children but it was at least the hope that justice would be done and their murderers punished.

Right he may have been but still I was angry and ready to break the Bishop's writing

316

desk over his head.

Stephen stepped to my side and placed his fingers on my arm. "Our intentions were good, Milord Bishop. Whatever we have done, we have acted only on your instruction."

"Oh?" he said, darkness clouding his expression. "Was it my instruction that led you to assault the Baron's servants?"

I snapped at him. "They would have killed that boy if I had not acted."

"It is a shame you could not have seized one of the servants. Perhaps if you had done so, we could have used him."

"Seized one?" I said. "What do you mean, seized one? It was all I could do to get the boy to safety before he perished in my arms, Bishop. And as for seizing one, I would have killed the bloody lot of them if I had the—"

Stephen grabbed my wrist to shut me up and spoke over me. "If we had one of the servants in our possession, my lord, if we had one and brought him to you. Would that be enough to have the warrant issued?"

The Bishop pursed his lips. "It might... if the servant was to make a deposition that directly accused the Marshal of specific capital crimes. The servant would have to describe the Marshal committing murder and conducting heretical acts. Yes, that would be enough to persuade the Duke to issue an arrest warrant." He sat back in his enormous, ornate chair. "But I fear you have by your actions quite ruined any chance of that. They will not venture from their castle now, I am sure."

"They will come out, alright," I said. "They have a need for blood that they will not be able to deny for long. And if they do not, well, I will simply storm the castle and tear the place down around them."

The Bishop sat upright and banged a palm on the table. "You will commit no crimes, sir, or I shall have you dismissed at once from my service. Do you understand?"

I stepped forward and leaned down. "I will bring you one of his men. You will get a confession out of him and issue the warrant. Do we agree?"

He spluttered. "I do not make deals with underlings, sir. You do as I command, do you understand?"

"Do we agree, Milord Bishop?"

He glared at me, no doubt expecting that the authority of his office would intimidate me into submission. When it did not work, he sighed and leaned back again. "Yes, yes. Bring one here to Nantes. I will speak with the Inquisition and we shall do the rest."

Stephen bowed and pulled me back. "Very well, Milord Bishop. We shall do so at once."

He pulled at me again and I stepped back, bowing before I left.

"That bastard," I said as we left the Bishop's palace and stepped out into a steady rain. "That lying, treacherous bastard."

Stephen glanced over his shoulder to check no one was in earshot and moved away across the courtyard, heading toward the gatehouse. "He has his hands tied as much as we do. His legal authority does not extend to arresting the Baron alone. Gilles de Rais is the

Duke's vassal and so the Bishop must satisfy the Duke's requirements."

I stared at him. "Yes, I know that, Stephen. Still, he could have forced the matter and he would have done if he had a spine running through his body instead of a lump of wet cheese."

"So, how do we find one of the servants?" he asked, grimacing at the sky and pulling up his hood.

"Let us speak to the others."

Walt and Rob were waiting at our inn near the centre of the town and we found them with our valets drinking wine in the public rooms downstairs.

"Are we all set then, Richard?" Rob asked brightly as Stephen and I sat down, shedding rainwater from our clothes.

Walt elbowed Rob. "Look at them, Rob. You reckon those are happy faces? What's gone wrong now, Richard?"

"We need to kidnap one of those servants and bring them back here."

Our valets hung their heads, for no doubt they were enjoying their time in Nantes and were hoping they would not have to return to the wilderness near Tiffauges.

Rob and Walt looked at each other, then grinned.

"Can't we just murder the bastards?" Walt asked, swirling the wine in his cup and squinting into it.

"Not all of them. We must return to the castle and grab one of the men when they leave."

Stephen leaned in. "I would agree with one thing the Bishop said. They will surely be too alert to leave their castle undefended, following your recent brush with them. They know we are watching and so they will be ready for us."

"He's got a point there, Richard," Walt said, raising his hand for the servant to bring him more wine.

"Two hundred soldiers in plate armour," Rob said. "The Marshal's got to be using them for something."

I drummed my fingers on the table. "I would not be so certain of that. The Marshal spends money even faster than does Walt." My men laughed at Walt's wounded expression. "Those soldiers are pretty as a picture, are they not? With their polished steel and bright pennants and fancy riding in formation but I saw a few when I went to see the priest. Drinking, dicing, lounging about and totally unconcerned with the sight of me, a stranger, in their midst. I have not heard of these soldiers harming any villagers, have you? Not in any of the depositions we have taken. No, I am quite convinced that it is for show, I tell you. To impress upon his people that their lord is a great man. He acts like a king, you said it yourself, Walt. These soldiers are how he dominates his people but by overt demonstration of his wealth, not through strength of arms."

Rob nodded slowly, pursing his lips. "Sounds like a most favourable employment. I wonder how much is their daily pay?"

"More than Richard pays, I bet," Walt said and they laughed, clashing their cups together.

"Very amusing." I turned to the valets. "Prepare our belongings and see to the horses. We will leave today. Now, please." They knocked back their wines and stood to obey my commands and I waited until they were out of earshot before continuing. "It seems clear to me that Gilles de Rais and at least some of his men are surviving on the blood of these children. Certainly, the scrawny one called Poitou and the fat one called Henriet. Perhaps they are bleeding their living servants, as we do, but consider how many children that have disappeared over the years. How many would you say, Stephen?"

He sighed and shifted in his seat. "Very difficult to calculate such a figure. Based on the depositions we have taken, it is certainly over one hundred. Extrapolating over the years since the first ones disappeared and over the number of villages within his lands, I believe, although I cannot prove, that it is over four hundred children."

"Dear God," Rob said, crossing himself. "Four hundred murdered children from these accursed lands."

"Perhaps many more," I said. "It could be thousands. Who can say how far afield they have travelled over the last few years?"

"Dirty bloody bastards," Walt said, downing his wine and slamming his cup on the table. "Let's go find them."

***

I did not wish to be without either Walt or Rob the next time I had a run in with the Marshal's servants and so we took turns on watch in the same place as before. The jagged rock formation on the plain north of Castle Tiffauges provided enough cover for us all but we could not move around without showing ourselves, should anyone be watching for us. While I slept in the daytime, wrapped in my cloak and wedged in the pile of rocks, Walt stood watch, peering through the light brush and sheltering from the sun beneath his wide-brimmed hat. Rob took over in the evening and first part of the night, while I took the later watch until dawn.

Stephen and our valets were safe back at our inn at Mortagne, not too far away. If we were forced to wait more than a couple of days, I knew I would have to send Rob and Walt back to get their supply of blood before they degenerated into the blood sickness.

The first day, we saw nothing but ordinary castle business. Supplies of wood and fresh food were trundled up through the gates. During the night, I was sure I would see the servants slinking out to find another child to feed on but the night was still and silent and none emerged and I settled down at dawn, feeling irritated and spoiling for a fight.

In the morning of the second day, Walt shook us both awake and we crawled forward while he jabbed his finger at the castle. Peeking over the top of the rocks, I watched as around three score of the Baron's soldiers rode out of the gate in their exquisite armour on their powerful, shining horses.

"They've spotted us," Rob said, sending a chill through me. He grabbed his bow and slipped an arrow out of his bag.

But the great mass of soldiers turned their magnificent beasts onto the main track and headed west, throwing up a cloud of dust into the morning sun.

"The Baron's escaping," Walt said, peering out from his hat. "Sneaky bloody bastard."

"Shall I get the horses?" Rob asked, tugging his hood closer about his face.

"The Marshal's banner is not flying over them," I said. "He is going nowhere. It is just the soldiers."

"Could be a trick?" Walt said. "Keep his banner over the castle here while he flees with his soldiers?"

"Could be," I said. "And yet he seems like a man obsessed with declaring his own position to the world. I do not believe he would skulk away anywhere in such a way."

"You might be wrong," Walt said. "Maybe I should follow those lads, just in case."

"No, it does not matter what they are up to. Even if the Marshal is with them, we do not want him. We want one of his men, that is all."

"That must be a quarter of his strength," Rob said as the riders thundered away. "More, even. Why would he send so many men away?"

"To the west is his other favourite castle at Machecoul. They must be headed there for some reason. To protect the prisoners that he is keeping there, no doubt, the priest le Ferron and the men the Duke sent to bargain for his release."

"There are soldiers enough at Machecoul already," Rob said.

I sighed, because I did not have any answers though I needed to pretend certainty. "Some other important reason, then."

"What could be so important?" Walt asked.

I snapped at them. "Whatever they are doing, it is of no concern. We will stay here and remain focused on finding a single servant to take. Wake us if you see any such man emerging, otherwise I am returning to sleep."

It was almost dark when Rob shook me awake and hissed in my ear. "They are coming out, sir. The servants are coming out. A wagon with four men. Heading east."

I crept to the top of the rocks and watched the light of a lantern bobbing along the road as the wagon banged and squeaked

"Just as last time," I said. "Well done, Rob."

We scrambled for our horses and followed the wagon at the longest distance we could. There was not much cover in the landscape and much of it was flat. But we had experience scouting enemies from horseback and keeping a constant watch on one's target is not necessary, especially when they are driving a wagon along a track. However, the sun soon set and the moon was waning. With the sporadic cloud cover it became very dark indeed and I had to rely on my men's enhanced night sight. If I was right and Gilles de Rais' men were revenants, created by ingesting his blood, then their vision would likely be even better than

Walt and Rob's but I prayed we would not be spotted before we could close the distance and attack them.

The wagon soon stopped by a large farmhouse. We saw it in the distance, as light from inside spilled out from the open windows on the top floor, as if the very building was a beacon.

"Not exactly ashamed of themselves, are they?" Rob muttered as we observed from afar.

"The people are so cowed that they do not care who sees," I said. "But they shall find their confidence is misplaced tonight."

"Ain't going to be easy, Richard," Walt said. "Forcing our way inside that place with four of them in there."

"What do you want to do?" Rob asked me.

"We will ride up fast," I said. "Go through the front door and grab the closest or the smallest or the quietest man. We will truss him up and throw him over the spare horse. If the others resist, we will kill them."

Rob cleared his throat. "Stephen said we should try not to murder anyone."

"We'll murder the lot of them if need be," I said. "Come on, let it be done."

Quickly, we divested ourselves of our cloaks and stowed them and other unnecessary items on the horses and prepared our weapons. We rode up to the house. It must have belonged to a wealthy franklin and the outer walls on both the ground floor and the one above were covered in pale blue painted plaster between the timbers of the building's frame. The shutters were thrown open to the night and the lamps within threw yellow light from all four windows.

If anyone happened to look out of those windows as we approached, they would have seen us illuminated in the glow. They had even left the lamp alight on the wagon outside. The horse stomped his foot and snorted at ours as we approached, and Rob hushed him after we dismounted and threw our horses' reins around parts of the wagon.

Steeling myself, I lifted the latch and threw open the front door with my dagger in hand. The room was empty.

On the ground floor was two rooms. One large and one small and I stood in the larger of them, occupied by a table with two lit lamps and five good candles throwing out light, a pair of benches, and a large hearth and chimney at the far end. A small fire burned in the hearth, rapidly going out. Stairs at the rear, by the back door, led to the floor above.

Otherwise it was quiet.

I nodded at the stairs and we rushed to the rear and charged up to the next storey, ready to fall upon the Marshal's servants.

There was no one upstairs in either bedchamber. Again, those rooms were lit with multiple lamps, stood on the bed frame, on a storage chest, and others placed on the floor by the open shutters.

We looked at each other blankly but I was beginning to feel a twisting in my guts.

"Maybe they went out the back way," Walt said.

"That must be it," I said.

"There was a cellar," Rob blurted out.

We clattered down the stairs and Rob pulled back the hatch in the floor by the back door. The hinges creaked and so, any remaining chance at surprise gone, I jumped down the steep steps into the cellar.

It was empty. Again, they had lit the cellar with a lamp but there was nothing within other than barrels on one side and sacks of dry goods on the other.

"What's with all the bloody lamps?" Walt muttered.

"There must be a passage from here," Rob suggested. "A passage leading away underground to some secret place where they bring the children t0—"

"Oh, don't be a plum, Rob, for God's sake," Walt snapped. "They done sold us a duck, have they not?"

"We must flee," I said. "Immediately."

Even as I spoke, there came the sound of hooves drumming outside. A sound that grew and grew until it seemed as though an entire army was charging up on us.

"Dear God," I said. "Up, up!"

We charged back up the steps and I threw open the front door to see dozens of the Marshal's soldiers swarming outside in their steel armour with their weapons drawn, glinting in the lamplight. Our terrified horses were already surrounded, with soldiers grasping their reins, and there was no way through.

I slammed the door shut, swung down the bar, and turned to my men. "They outwitted us, the bastards." We drew our swords and looked at each other.

"Worth trying to talk our way out?" Rob suggested, as the shouts of the soldiers grew.

I almost laughed and he hung his head. Each of us knew that we faced what might prove an insurmountable challenge and I felt death's presence lurking near. "Bar the door," I snapped at Walt. "Let us be away through the back."

The men outside called orders to each other, and many laughed as they did so, for they believed bringing us down would be no more than sport.

By the time I ran through the back door, there were already a dozen mounted soldiers riding down the wattle fences surrounding the kitchen garden. They charged at us with their swords and maces raised and I pushed Rob back inside and shut the door behind us. We dragged the table across the room and pushed it against the rear door, then threw a bench and a chest against it.

Walt backed away from the door as the soldiers tried to force it open.

"The windows," I said, nodding at the nearest one. There was one in each room, on the south side like the front door, and each large enough for a man to climb through. Sure enough, a helmeted head poked through the one I had indicated as the soldier it belonged to tried to climb in. Walt grabbed the man's helm and twisted it off. His shocked face looked up as I cleaved his skull in two with my sword and pushed his twitching body back outside again where his comrades cried out in anger.

A crash from the smaller room next door alerted us to more men climbing in through there and I left Walt to guard the window while Rob and I went to deal with the intruders.

Three men were already within and helping a fourth in through the window. All were armoured in steel and with helms down. There would be no breaking through such fine armour and our only chance was in slipping our blades into the gaps between pieces. I knew from experience that seeing through such helms as they wore would be difficult and I rushed them before they noticed my approach. One man I threw back off his feet into the shelves against the wall and the next man I wrestled off his feet. Rob, with his archer's strength enhanced by his immortality, pushed one man back out of the window and then pitched another one off his feet right out after him. We fell on the downed men, flipped open their visors and ran them through their terrified faces.

Walt shouted a warning from the other room and I ran back to find him grappling with an armoured soldier while another pulled himself through the window. Blood soaked one of Walt's arms.

Guiding the point of my sword with my free hand, I slipped the blade under the soldier's aventail and speared him through the back of the neck and he fell straight down. Together with Walt, we forced the other man back from the window.

Both the front and back door resounded with hammering while outside the soldiers shouted orders to each other. The furniture across the back door shifted as the men pushed and shoved and heaved their way through.

Rob came running back from the other room with a group of soldiers after him that I checked with a wild cry and the swinging of my sword. But they were not to be held at bay for long, not by an unarmoured opponent, and they rushed us with full-throated cries of their own. I grabbed the arm of the first one and heaved and swung him across the room with considerable force and he crashed into one of the lamps, knocking it to the floor where it broke and threw oil across the floor, which burst into flame.

Never one to miss an opportunity for destruction, Walt grasped the other lamp and threw it at the feet of the attacking soldiers. The flames flashed up and drove them back.

At the back door, the soldiers finally pushed their way in and we found ourselves heavily outnumbered and attacked from both sides.

"Up!" I ordered, and we bundled our way up the stairs.

From there, we held them off at the top. A few brave souls rushed us and we seized each of them in turn and killed them, one after the other, and threw the bodies back down the steps. We held them for long enough that the flames spread in the room below, catching on the furniture and the beams in the walls and floor, driving them away from the base of the stairs.

They clambered in through the windows upstairs and I killed them as they came in. One man I smote with a single blow through his helm and I quickly sawed his head clean off and threw it down to the men below, shouting at them to come and share the same fate.

All three of us were wounded and bleeding and the next man I tore off his helm and sank my teeth into his face and savaged his cheek. He screamed like a woman and I held him in the window before tearing off half of his face in a jagged big streak and throwing him down to his fellows. I sucked the blood from the chunk of flesh and tossed it out with the blood streaming down my chin. The fire below flickered out of the building to shine on me and the heat was growing with every moment.

"Come and die!" I shouted through the smoke and flame. "Come and die, cowards, and I will drink your blood! I will feast on your flesh and wear your skin. I will devour your souls. Come and die! Come and die!"

Instead, they remounted their horses and rode away into the darkness, their collective will shattered by the horror that we had sown.

We had killed a score of them and wounded more so their trap had failed. But so had our plan to lure them out and seize them. Instead, they had outwitted us and played me for a fool. We had our lives, to be sure, but we had nothing else.

Bloodied, battered, and coughing out smoke, we calmed and mounted our horses and slipped carefully through the darkness to our inn as the sun turned the sky red in the east.

There would be no warrant for the arrest of Gilles de Rais.

1 0

Summoning Demons

August 1440

"RICHARD!" STEPHEN THREW open the door to my bedchamber before dawn and I sat bolt upright, heart racing, and grabbed my sword from beside the bed.

"What is it?" I asked, grasping one of the bedposts in one hand as my head swam, brandishing my sword in the other.

"Another child has been taken."

"Dear God. We must act swiftly. What has happened?"

"We had a local man ride through the night to tell us," Stephen said. "Bone tired and his horse will never be the same."

"I hope you paid him well for bringing us the news."

For weeks, we had spread word everywhere we travelled to take depositions, that we would pay handsomely for immediate news of lost children. We stipulated that it must be genuine information and it must get to us swiftly, so that we might catch the servants in the act. Perhaps yet on the road.

"Of course, I tried, but he would accept no payment, saying he was cousin to the missing boy's mother. He said the blacksmith in Saint-Georges-Montaigu had lost his son. The father is named Jean le Fevre, his son they call Little Jean, aged about twelve or so."

"Where is the rider now?"

"Drinking spiced wine in the public rooms below."

"I must speak with him."

"You suspect a trap?"

"Trust me, Stephen, if you had been with us in that burning house last week, you would suspect it also."

I shouted for the valets to prepare our gear and the horses. Walt and Rob stumbled, bleary-eyed, from their rooms and came down with us to speak to the rider. He was younger than I had expected, little more than a boy himself and just a little, narrow-shouldered thing, he was.

"You can save Little Jean, can't you, sire?" he said, jumping to his feet as we approached. He swayed on tired legs and Rob helped him to sit once more on the bench. The innkeeper, Bouchard-Menard, lit a candle on the table and I watched the young man's face as he spoke it all again. His cousin's boy went on an errand and did not return. Little Jean had ever been a dutiful boy and had never tarried before.

"He is twelve, you say?" I prompted, looking at Stephen.

"Twelve years, yes, my lord, or perhaps eleven. Thereabouts."

It was the most common age, Stephen had found, when collating the many witness statements. Almost all of those lost were boys aged between eight and fourteen and most of them were aged twelve.

"It seems," Stephen had said, "that even demons have preferential tastes."

"Thank you," I said to the exhausted young man. "For bringing this to us so swiftly. You must rest. The good innkeeper here will take care of you until you have strength enough to return home. We shall do everything we can to find young Jean."

"Believe him, then?" Walt asked a little while later as we made for the stables.

"Don't you?" Rob asked, hoisting his arrow bag onto his shoulder.

Walt shrugged. "I suppose he's too simple-minded to make a good liar."

Rob grinned at him. "Takes one to know one, eh?"

Despite himself, Walt laughed. "A truer word never was spoken, sir."

I laughed also but then shook myself. "We shall have fewer jests and more alacrity," I reminded them. "A boy's life is in peril."

All of us together, along with Stephen and the valets, hurriedly rode south, beyond the immediate environs of Castle Tiffauges, toward the village of Saint-Georges from where the boy had vanished. Something about the abduction had brought the reality of it into sharp relief that morning and I was filled with emotion. He had been taken the day before, perhaps only half a day since he was a happy young lad going about his business. And I knew that he might be suffering even as we rushed to his aid. Suffering by having his blood drained from his body and who knew what other horrors being inflicted at the same time. Baron Gilles de Rais had created those horrors, he had made his servants into blood-mad revenants and the whole nest of the bastards had been growing fat on the children of the lands he was supposed to be protecting.

"I will kill him," I said to myself as I rode, twisting the reins in my hands. "I will damned well murder him and every bloody one of them."

It took half the day to get to Saint-Georges-Montaigu. By the calendar it was the height of summer but it had never really begun on the ground. The crops were stunted and the best that could be hoped for was a miserable harvest and at the worst, the rain and damp would continue and there would be no harvest at all. If that happened, and they could not import grain from elsewhere, people would starve.

And while the crops remained stunted, the weeds grew amongst them as wild as ever, winding their way between the stalks of wheat to choke them until they were torn out by hoe and by hand. People laboured in the fields as hard as they ever did but their hearts were sick with the thought that their efforts might be for nought.

Saint-Georges-Montaigu was a decent-looking village on the side of a small, low valley, with buildings of stone and a fine, if small church.

The people there were out in the street as we rode up and many recognised us from our traipsing back and forth collecting witness statements. Some, I thought, had even been in the church when I had promised them justice and two of them I recognised as they had provided sworn statements about their own stolen children.

I had expected that these people would be anxious and afraid. In fact, they were furious.

The men and women gathered outside the church swarmed us even before we could dismount. Our valets were frightened. And not just the valets.

Walt muttered a warning. "How about we ride right through them?"

I did not want to hurt them in an effort to get away but it certainly seemed that they wished to inflict harm on us.

"You promised us!" the blacksmith swore as he stomped toward me, waving a wide-bladed short sword over his head. "You stood before us and gave your word. And now this!"

"Aye, Richard," Rob said. "Let's ride on through."

"It would be sensible to do so," Stephen said.

The crowd called out curses and named me as a betrayer.

"False!" a woman cried. "He is false!"

Mobs are perhaps the most dangerous thing in the world and it is always prudent to flee from them as you would flee from a bear or a rabid dog. Instead, while my men hissed and swore at me, I dismounted and went to the blacksmith with my hands spread wide. I hoped he would not behead me.

"I came to you," I said. "I came as soon as I heard. I came to help. Help you, I say, help to find Little Jean."

"Help?" the boy's father said, eyes bulging. A tall man, and lean, he seemed half skeleton in his anguish. "It is too late for your *help*, sir. You must go, before I do something I regret."

"When did they take him?" I asked them.

"Yesterday," a woman said beside me. "In the full light of day."

"What happened?" I asked the crowd. "Where was he?" I asked the blacksmith. "The rider who came to us said your boy's name is Jean? What happened to Little Jean?"

The man seemed to suddenly deflate and his shoulders slumped. "I cannot keep him in my sight every hour. I cannot. I have business. He was sent to fetch the charcoal in the morning. And he..."

When he could not find the words, the women clinging to him filled in the details.

"He never returned with the charcoal, sir."

"But he was seen, he was."

"Seen with *them*."

I grabbed the woman who had spoken. "His servants? The ones they call Henriet, Poitou? Sillé? Roger de Briqueville?"

They replied all in a jumble, half speaking over each other.

"No, no. No, sir."

"It was her."

"Her and her familiar."

"The old woman and the young."

"La Meffraye and her girl."

"La Meffraye's granddaughter, a little demon spawn."

"She teases the boys in, so she does, with smiles and sweets and promises."

"We told them not to listen but..."

"They was seen, leading him away by the hand towards *his place*."

I turned to the one who had spoken last. "To Castle Tiffauges?"

They crossed themselves as they nodded in confirmation.

"Why did these witnesses not stop them?" I asked.

"It was from far away," one woman said.

"They was children themselves, sir," another said. "They was afraid."

I could certainly understand that. "You say that Jean was taken by La Meffraye and this young girl who assists her and they led him away by hand. You mean they travelled on foot from here to Tiffauges? No horses or carts?"

"They walk always, La Meffraye and her familiar," a woman said, to much nodding from the others. "Horses and other beasts will not allow them near."

"Smell the demon blood," another confirmed.

I had to hold up my hands and raise my voice to speak over their peasant nonsense.

"I shall go to Tiffauges at once," I said. "If Jean lives, I shall bring him back."

They stared at me like I was mad, silence settling over the crowd at last.

"You?" the Jean the blacksmith said, breaking the spell. "You alone?"

"Me and my men," I said, jerking my finger over my shoulder. "It will not be the first time we have stormed a castle."

Shaking their heads, they wept and cried, for they knew then that I had lost my mind and that there was no hope for Little Jean le Fevre.

"Leave, leave," the women said, pushing me. "Be gone."

"Not only will I find your boy," I said. "But I shall kill Gilles de Rais and his hellish servants when I do it."

It only made them wail louder and heave against me. I stepped back toward my men as the crowd surged forward.

"You are a liar," his father said, his face contorted in anguish and his voice breaking and raising to a wail as he ranted. "A liar and a deceiver. You gave us hope and then you snatched it away. Go! Never show your face here again or I swear I shall murder you myself and the law be damned."

Swinging myself into the saddle and turning my frightened horse around, I looked back at the crowd.

"I will return. With your boy or with his murderer's head."

We rode away, with their angry shouts and curses ringing in my ears.

***

Gilles de Rais was not at Castle Tiffauges.

For the first time since he had arrived there, his banner was not hanging over the battlements of the tallest tower.

We took our usual position a mile away across the plain in our rocks by the hillock.

"Gates are shut," Rob said, unnecessarily nodding at the castle. "Portcullis down. No banner. That's that, then."

"Doesn't mean he's gone," Walt pointed out. "Could just be pretending. Skulking inside."

I still thought that was not the Marshal's way of doing things but then I had been recently outwitted to such an extent that it had almost cost us our lives. So I said nothing about that.

"Ride to the village," I said to Rob, jerking my finger northward. "Find out if they saw him leave. Saw his person, that is."

While we waited for his return, the rest of us sat in our saddles and watched the great mass of the castle, squatting like a great stone beast upon its rock.

"If the Baron *has* fled," Stephen asked, "surely the boy is not within."

"Perhaps Jean was taken for the benefit of revenant servants who yet remain. See, the smoke rises from that tower."

Stephen covered his eyes with his hand and slumped against the rocks. "You promised those poor people that you would bring back their boy. You swore you would storm that fortress, Richard."

"I did," I said. "And I stand by it."

Stephen scoffed and for once, Walt seemed to agree with him.

"Come on, sir. Can't fight our way into that, anyway, can we," Walt said, chewing on a piece of sausage. "Not a hope."

"Some of the walls are old." I gestured. "See, on the northwest tower? And on the eastern wall."

Walt stopped chewing. "Was hoping you hadn't noticed."

"How could I not? The mortar is crumbling and lichen growing on them. They may not have been repaired in all the years since they were built."

"Probably still younger than you, though."

I grunted. "Probably."

Stephen glanced between us. "Surely, you do not intend to scale those walls? But you would need ladders. Or ropes and iron stakes, at the very least, hammered into the gaps between the stones and the rope wrapped around them."

Walt snorted a laugh. "That'd be nice."

"If we are to save the boy, we cannot delay."

Stephen's expression plainly suggested that he considered the boy long dead. But he had sense enough to not say so aloud in my hearing.

After some time, Rob came galloping back and came running forward, hunched over at the waist. "He is gone. East, on the road to Machecoul. Yesterday at dawn, he left with his army, flying his banner aloft."

"Dawn yesterday," I said. "Before Little Jean was taken by La Meffraye and her girl. Perhaps there is hope after all. See for yourselves, it is as I said. Smoke from more than one fire rises from within the walls. There is life there. If it is as the last time I was there, it could be fifty or a hundred men within. One or more of them requiring blood."

Stephen rubbed his eyes and summoned courage enough to confront me. "Surely, Richard, you know there is no hope. If Gilles de Rais has indeed gone, I will agree that perhaps his servants are still within. But if that is true then they would have had the boy all last night and all the hours so far today. If they use boys for the purposes which we suspect, the poor lad is surely drained white and long dead by now."

"All the same," I said, speaking slowly and keeping my voice as low and steady as I could. "I am going to find him. If he died within, his murderers are still there. And it is they who will be drained white and dead before long. You stay here, Stephen. Hold the horses."

"I will send the servants home," he said, jerking his head to them.

"No. They stay with you at this position. We may need them."

He realised I meant that we may need their blood if we are injured in the attempt on the castle. "Very well. God be with you all."

"Fortune favours the bold, Stephen," I said.

As I spoke it, I thought of the disasters at Orléans and the lost battles afterwards. Joan the Maiden had been bold and she had been so favoured by fate. But had it ever truly been Joan or was it Gilles de Rais who had been the bold one? Inspiring the French with his cunning employment of a prophecy about the Maiden saving France.

"I believe those were Pliny the Elder's last words," Stephen said.

"Truly?" I asked. "I take it he was a great knight?"

"Well, Stephen began, furrowing his brow. "I believe he was a soldier in his youth."

"Fine words," I said.

"Load of nonsense," Walt said. "Boldness gets you killed. Fortune favours the cautious, more like."

"And will those be your final words, Walt?" I said.

Walt wiped his mouth. "I'm going to live forever, Richard. You ain't never going to shut me up."

We laughed together and Stephen stared at us, confused. He did not understand that soldiers must make jests at such times. We were about to risk our lives in a perilous stratagem and a man either laughs at fate or is crushed by the fear of what may come. Indeed, I have come to understand in centuries since that the ancient aphorism should mean that fortune favours the bold *in spirit*, not necessarily in deed. Although, if you have one, you tend to find yourself risking the other.

"It is not too late to return to the inn," Stephen said. "Or even to Nantes, to reconsider our strategy. You promised the villagers, the blacksmith, yes. But you need not abide by it in these circumstances."

"Stephen, I am disappointed in you. We must go. We are knights, we three, and we have sworn to protect the innocent."

We stripped ourselves of whatever we did not need and walked through the wind-blasted clumps of sedge and scrub toward the castle. It was late in the day and the shadows were long. Night would soon fall but in the meantime if anyone was keeping a close watch of the approach, we would be seen.

But none came and we closed with the castle without any warning cry or trumpet or bell sounding and without soldiers coming to stop us. I almost hoped for it, and prayed a group of horsemen would ride us down. For we could kill them and take their horses and ride in through the gates instead of risking our necks in a mad climb.

And it was mad. The closer we got, the more absurd it seemed. The lowest wall, on the east, was atop a thirty feet high rockface and the wall itself was another forty feet above that. A fall of such a height was not survivable by a mortal man and would perhaps even be enough to dash one of us to pieces.

With a chill, I recalled the story about Joan the Maiden. When she had been captured and held by the Burgundians in Castle Beaurevoir in the north, she leapt from a tower and fell seventy feet. Somehow, she did not die. It was one of the key pieces of evidence that led me to believe Gilles de Rais had made the girl into a revenant by forcing her to ingest his own blood, for how could a mortal girl survive such a height?

I looked up at the wall, impossibly high overhead, and imagined the fall from the top. They said Joan lay crippled at the bottom and was unable to walk but then somehow she recovered in a few days and was soon as fit as she ever was.

And so it was impossible to avoid concluding that she had either been a revenant or she had truly been blessed by God's own hand. And if it was the latter then what did that mean for God's judgement of England?

Walt nudged me. "Come on, don't just stand there gawking. It ain't going to get any lower."

And we climbed.

Hand over hand, clinging to the crumbling facing stones. The blocks were almost half a man's height and so it was a stretch each time to reach up a hand and drag up a foot. Searching always for a secure hold, enough to bear my weight.

My hands were soon raw and my knees scraped bloody.

Joan was ever on my mind. Surely, she had been given blood after her fall. Or perhaps she had taken it from someone against their will. But I could not imagine such a thing would not have been reported at the time. Joan of Arc, savaging the neck of one of her gaolers?

They said that she had landed on the muddy ground of the drained moat but even so, it was not possible to fall the height of seven floors and make a swift recovery. If I were to fall from the wall, I thought, I would have no moat, drained or otherwise, but a steep ravine with hard stones and a rock floor. A fall onto a stone would crack my skull open like an egg and my brains would be dashed out.

My foot slipped and I grasped a handhold, missed it and my fingers slid down the side of a block before I could arrest my fall. I lost the nails from both middle fingers of my left hand and I had to stop and clutch at the wall, shaking, with tears running down my face from the pain. I have been stabbed, sliced, and shot with arrows and balls and bullets more times than I can recall, and I have even been set on fire, but there is a particular agony to losing one's fingernails. Especially when dangling on the side of a castle wall.

Rob was far above me and Walt, much closer, looked down and cried out, alarmed. I hissed at him to keep going and forced myself up. It would not do to be so outdone by my men and I hurried up and up, being driven by the pain and the blood and the anger that Gilles de Rais had defeated me, had defeated England. His old castle wall would not defeat me.

I pulled myself up over the battlements at the top soon after Rob and ahead of Walt. We sat on the other side, breathing deeply. It was almost completely dark in the shadow of the battlements and the sky above was dark blue on its way to black.

"We should have tried," Walt said, "knocking on the front door."

"Come," I said, pointing to the doorway that led from the covered parapet walk along the wall into the nearest tower. "Let us go down."

Rob nodded and drew his sword.

"Put it away," I said, to confused looks. "Almost every soul within is a servant. I would avoid starting a mass panic, which we will surely cause if we charge in like soldiers."

Walt scratched his head. "Can't we just kill them all?"

"We're not killing anyone unless they are a revenant," I said. "Knights cannot slaughter at will, like barbarians, our oaths will not allow it. Our oath to the Order of the White Dagger is to kill the spawn of William de Ferrers."

332

"Yes," Rob said, sliding his blade back through his belt ring. "You are right, of course."

Walt shrugged. "If you say so. What if we're in danger?"

"Defence of one's self and one's companions is a separate matter. If anyone attempts to harm us, we will kill them as usual."

"Oh," Walt said, brightening. "That's alright, then."

The castle was lit up all over, just as it had been on my first visit. Empty stairwells and chambers were lit with beeswax candles and lamps in the walls and fires burned in rooms with no people. Even if Gilles had been present, it would have been a mad waste of money. Who was the display for? The servants? It was they who were employed in all the cutting and fetching of wood and lighting and refilling of lamps, all day and all night. Who was it supposed to impress? All I could think was that it was for God, for who else would be watching? Perhaps it was some strange expression of guilt that he felt for his crimes, I thought, or perhaps I was assuming that he was a man and not a demon in human flesh, for if he felt guilt at all then why would he continue as he had?

On the ground floor we found two servants carrying empty serving trays and they froze in surprise when they saw us approaching.

"Where is La Meffraye?" I asked them.

"Eh?" they asked, both gormless.

"The woman," I snapped. "The old woman servant."

"Old woman?"

"Come on, man," Walt said, grasping a fistful of the man's clothes at his chest. "Can't be many women servants here."

"Yeah there's the old one and the young one," he said, eyes flicking between us. "But we ain't allowed to speak to them, nor even to go near them, sir, not for no reason at all, sir."

"Specially the young one," the other man said, glumly.

"Quite right, too," I said. "Now, where can I find their quarters?"

They blew out of pursed lips. "Can't be saying, my lord. Can't be saying. Not allowed, is all. Not on our lives."

I grabbed the free one by the neck. "It'll be your damned life if you don't tell me where they are!"

He gulped and pointed a shaking hand. "You go down by the lower hall, through the outer yard, past the guardhouse toward the chapel but then you gots to go through—"

"Take me there!" I said and shoved them both forward, tossing their trays to the floor. "Now! Faster!"

They all but ran through the castle and we hurried after them.

"Thought we weren't hurting no one innocent," Walt observed behind me.

Other servants we saw drew back in confusion to allow us to pass until we came out into a vast courtyard.

"That tower?" I asked the servants, pointing to the nearest one, which had smoke drifting from the chimney.

"Oh, no, sir!" they said. "We ain't allowed in there, sir. That's the magician's tower."

I turned on them. "The what?"

"The magician's tower. The sorcerer."

His idiot companion shook his head. "Alchemist, my lord. He's the master's alchemist."

"What goes on there?"

They both turned white. "Can't say, my lord."

"Forbidden."

"Not to go near."

"Not never."

I drew my dagger and forced the nearest one to his knees, placing the edge of my blade against his throat. "Do they take the children in there?"

The servant pissed himself and wept, tears welling and quickly spilling down his cheeks. "Yes," he whispered. "Yes."

Throwing the servants down, we raced toward the base of the tower and threw open the door. I took the stairs two at a time and wound up and around to the first chamber, which was lit up and had a table with the remains of a recent meal but no one else. There were noises above. A man's voice echoing through the floor. Up and round and up again until I threw open the door to the room where the noises came from and there I froze in horror.

Before me was an unholy scene.

A man in white robes with his hands outstretched stood in the centre of a five-sided star painted on the wooden floor. At each point burned large candles and there were bowls of blood beside them. At the feet of the white-robed man was a naked boy, whose arms and belly had been crossed with cuts, bleeding freely. He writhed against his bonds but his mouth and eyes were wrapped with black velvet cloth and a well-dressed brute held him down by the shoulders, leering at his victim as he did so.

Across the room at the slit window, looking out at the night, stood the third and final man. He was tall, wearing very fine clothes, as a rich lord might wear.

They all turned as I burst in, their eyes filled with surprise and fear turning quickly to anger.

The alchemist jabbed his finger at me. "Begone from this place! I shall cast you out with the power of the demon Barron, with the power of Satan, with the power of—"

I rushed him and drove my fist into his guts with such force that he was lifted from his feet and driven back before collapsing into a ball, his white robes settling around him.

The man on his knees leapt up and backed away, holding his dagger back by his hip, ready to drive it into me. On his belt hung a coil of rope, such as a herdsman wore. "You made a mistake," he growled, lip curling into a malicious grin. "The last mistake you will ever make."

He darted at me with incredible speed. Immortal speed. His dagger flashed low and then up toward my neck, twisting and flicking the blade like an expert cutthroat.

334

I leaned away, grasped his wrist and whipped my sword down to take his arm clean off at the elbow. I tossed his forearm, somehow still clutching the dagger, over my shoulder. He wailed and fell, clutching the stump of his ruined arm and scurrying back on his arse toward the wall while blood gushed from his terrible wound.

The third man had not moved from his spot by the window. There was a short sword at his side with an ornate hilt, in a scabbard decorated with gold.

"Are you *him*?" I said, stepping slowly toward the window. My toe kicked over a bowl of blood on the floor and it splashed across the floor in a dark, shining fan. "Answer me."

He faltered, shaking, looking at me and at my men behind me. "I am... I am Sir Roger de Briqueville."

"You are him," I said, drawing closer still. "You are the Marshal. Do not lie to me."

"No," he said, raising his chin and holding my gaze. "You are mistaken. You will not find him here."

I stopped. For some reason, I believed him. "Where is Gilles de Rais?"

Briqueville hesitated. "Not here." I tilted my head and he hurried on. "That is to say, sir, that he has relocated temporarily to his castle at Machecoul, to better protect his noble prisoners."

"He knows the Duke is coming for him?"

"Ah, yes. Indeed, he does. At least, he suspects that it is so."

I looked around to see that Rob had scooped up the boy, Little Jean, in a cloak he had found somewhere and was removing the blindfold and bonds, all the while whispering gentle things to him. Walt stood over our other two prisoners with his sword drawn. I knew it would be taking every ounce of self-control he had to resist murdering them both.

"You are an immortal?" I asked Roger de Briqueville.

He glanced at the man with the dismembered arm before drawing his eyes back to me. "I know not of what you speak."

I sighed. "It is a shame that you are not honest with me. All your deceit means for me is torture for you, sir. You should know that I will take off your fingers and your eyelids and your ears and at some point as your body is taken from you, piece by piece, you will tell me it all anyway. So why not avoid the bloody and agonising part and simply tell it all now?"

Walt spoke over his shoulder. "Seems a shame. Maybe we should do it anyway? I'll do it."

"Perhaps you are right," I said. "I would enjoy seeing justice done."

"Please," Briqueville said, his calm demeanour beginning to waver. "I am an innocent man. A mortal man."

"Be silent, Roger," the one with the missing arm said through gritted teeth.

I turned to regard him. He was a well-built man of forty or so, with a big jaw and a low brow like a shelf over dark eyes.

"And who are you?" I asked him.

He spat at my feet. "You will soon die. All of you will die."

"Who is he?" I asked Roger de Briqueville.

"Sillé," he said. "His name is Sillé."

"Ah!" I said, brightly. "I have heard of you. Yes indeed, you are one of Gilles de Rais' most faithful servants. You are one of those men who journeys out into the villages and homes for a hundred miles east and west to bring home young boys and sometimes girls, using your rope there to bind them up. You bring them back here and your master drinks their blood and murders them. And so do your comrades, the servants Poitou and Henriet. I have met them, sir. I saw how their strength and speed were much increased. I know what they are. And I know what you are, too."

"And we know what *you* are!" Sillé said. "A traitor and a betrayer of the true master!"

"The *true* master?" I wondered if he meant my brother William, who was perhaps considered by these servants as the master of Gilles de Rais. "Tell me about the true master."

Sillé scoffed.

Walt laughed his mirthless laugh. "Seems like we got another one who cares nought for his fingers and his eyelids, Richard."

I nodded. A whimpering behind me brought my attention and I spoke over my shoulder without taking my eyes away from the captured men. "How is the boy, Rob?"

"Freezing, exhausted. Cuts ain't deep, though. Reckon he'll be right as rain, God willing."

The alchemist groaned and shuddered and crawled to the wall. I wondered if I had fatally ruptured his entrails. "Are you one of the blood drinkers?" I asked him. "I know who you are. You are Prelati the Florentine alchemist and sorcerer. Did the Marshal give you his blood to drink?"

Prelati looked at me with tears in his eyes. "No."

"Is he telling the truth, Roger?" I asked. "Or are you all three here for the boy's blood?"

"No, by God," Briqueville said. "Not I. I would never stoop so low. It makes a man's seed dry and I have a noble name to pass on. I will take a wife and make a son and that will be the only everlasting life for me."

I resisted the urge to explain to him that he would hang before he made a son and merely nodded. "What of these others?"

Sillé, clutching his stump to his chest, roared at him. "You are a betrayer! The master will cut your heart out. You will burn in Hell."

"Can I shut him up, sir?" Walt asked.

"Please do."

Walt kicked Sillé in the belly, then he aimed a second kick in the man's face which drove the back of his skull into the wall with an awful, wet crunch. He fell unconscious, his chest soaked with the blood from his wound and the arm itself now flung out and leaking everywhere. Sillé was not long for the world.

"Well?" I asked Briqueville.

"He is one," he said, pointing to Sillé. "He and Poitou and Henriet."

"Oh? Not Prelati? And you truly expect me to believe that you are not one either?"

He shook his head. "Never. It is evil."

"And yet you are willing to partake in child murder," I said, confused. "How can you speak of evil?"

He lowered his gaze. "I never killed a child with my own hand and I never knew what this place was until it was too late. You see, I was deceived, sir. Snared. I wished to flee but was trapped from fear of my lord, who would never let me go nor let me live if I fled."

It sounded so similar to the excuses of the priest Dominus Eustache Blanchet that it made me doubt not only Briqueville's words but the priest's also.

I sighed. "And what about you, Prelati? Let me guess. You are a victim, also and were forced against your will to sacrifice children and summon demons?"

On his hands and knees, he crawled forward along the floor toward me, knocking over a candle that rolled into a pool of blood and was extinguished. "You are as he is, are you not? The master is afraid of you, my lord. He knows you. From a long time ago, he knows you. A century ago, he said, confiding in me one dark night. You are an ancient one, of great power. Greater even than the true master and your blood will make me more powerful than the others. Please, please, my lord, hear my words and know that they are spoken from the depths of my heart. I beg you. I will serve you. I will serve your every whim. I can perform transmutation if only you provide the materials and I can make you rich, my lord. Richer than any king since Croesus. All I ask in return is that you make me one of you, like your good men here. Give me your blood this night and I will create mountains of gold and I will summon demons to serve your every whim for millennia, until the Last Judgement."

He fell upon my legs, grasping them and reaching up with one hand. With my knee, I struck him in the face and he fell back, wailing, spilling another bowl of blood across the floor and further soaking his white robes.

"I would never give the Gift to a creature as pathetic and useless as you. And it seems that even Gilles de Rais, who gave his own blood to odious, witless fools like Poitou and Henriet, thought you unworthy of it."

Prelati wailed and covered his face with his robes as he scuttled away on his side toward the wall, like a wounded spider.

Sillé stirred and pulled himself upright, clutching his arm once more. His face was grey and his eyes glazed.

"Sir?" Rob said. "We should get the lad away, now."

He was right and not only for the boy's sake. For all I knew, there could be half a hundred soldiers gathering outside the tower, alerted by servants.

"Sillé?" I asked him. "Do you deny that you were changed by ingesting your master's blood?"

He lifted his chin. "Why would I deny such a thing? I am honoured by the blessing. I am brought closer to God by the gift of the blood and I have done their bidding. Such an honour can never be taken from me, not by you and not by death."

"My Order is sworn to unmake all beasts such as you, Sillé." I showed him the blade of my sword. "Kneel, and prepare for your death."

He tried to spit but his mouth was too dry. "You will never unmake the master."

"Lean forward," I commanded, and struck his head from his body with a single stroke. His head rolled toward Prelati, who thrashed it away by kicking his legs, and scurried back across the room.

"Your turn," I said to Briqueville.

He tore his gaze away from the headless corpse twitching within the pentagram. "I swear to you that I am not what he was. I swear it."

"You certainly deserve death anyway for the crimes you have done."

"I do," he said, sobbing. "I do."

"Your only hope," I said, "is to submit a full confession of those crimes and the crimes of your master to the Bishop of Nantes and the Duke of Brittany."

He cried out and sank to his knees. "I will. I will do it. I will."

"Give me your sword," I ordered, and Walt moved to my side in case Briqueville attempted to use it on me instead of surrendering it.

Behind me, a door banged and I jumped about to see Prelati fleeing through a door, his robes billowing out behind him.

"Sneaky bastard!" Walt cried and ran after him.

But I called Walt back. "We have tarried too long as it is. The murdering sorcerer will get what is coming to him but now we must get the boy to safety and drag Briqueville to Nantes."

I looked down at Little Jean as Rob held him like a baby in his arms. The boy was deathly pale and shivering, eyes flicking about beneath their lids.

"All will be well now, son," Rob said to him. "All will be well."

***

There were no soldiers waiting for us, and the servants I had accosted earlier had long fled, along with every other soul in the place, or so it seemed. Once we made our way through unchallenged, we roused the porter and ordered him to open the gates.

"These men are good friends, Miton," Briqueville said. "Let us out at once."

"In the dark?" Miton said. "Anyway, how'd they get in?"

"You know me, do you not?" I said to him.

Miton's face clouded. "You said you was one of my lord's men but you was a liar. I should never have let you in before."

"Oh, but I am a faithful servant, am I not, Roger?"

"Indeed he is, Miton. Would I be in his company if it were not so?"

Miton eyed the injured boy in Rob's arms and hesitated. My patience long gone, I grasped Miton and lifted him against the wall. "Open the damned gate. Now."

Stephen and my servants met us on the plain and we rode away from the evil place, though it left a filthy stain in my soul. I felt contaminated by the evil and executing one servant and taking another had only served to deepen the feeling that no amount of killing could undo the malevolence that had been done.

At least we had recovered the child while breath remained in his body. We brought him at once to Tilleuls where the physician Pierre Moussillon treated the boy's wounds and put him to bed. Ameline and her servant Paillart had opened the door willingly, this time, and managed to rouse the old man.

"Your father is in good health," I said softly to Ameline, by which I meant that he was not pissed as a newt. "I had thought you alone would be capable of attending to the boy."

"Yes," she said, smiling. "He has been entirely himself these past three days. I think you have given him some hope, perhaps. Not for Jamet, of course, but for the people here. It is like a curse is being lifted."

"Surely, that is not my doing," I said, smiling at her.

Seeing Ameline's face smile at me in return made me feel as if I was at home.

"You saved another one, sir," she whispered to me. "Surely, you are working miracles."

"I wish only that I could have come last year," I replied.

She took a deep breath and placed her hand on my arm, looking up at me through her lashes. "I wonder, now that you have come, whether you put any consideration in staying longer."

I was saved from having to answer by her father bellowing for her from upstairs and she went to attend to him. The servant Paillart came in with an armful of wood which he dumped by the hearth and began tending to the fire.

"I hope you ain't playing on her heartstrings," he muttered with his back to me. "She be an honourable girl, who deserves to be treated so."

My instinct was to tell him to mind his own damned business but I sensed no malice in his words. It was more like an old soldier offering advice to the younger man he perceived me to be.

"I will not dishonour her," I said, softly.

He peered at me over his shoulder, as if wondering if I meant I would not lay with her or if I meant that I intended to marry her. In truth, I wished I could have either, or both, but such a thing could surely never be.

The next day, Jean le Fevre came to claim his son. He fell to his knees at his boy's bedside and his happy weeping sounded through the house. When he came down, his throat was too tight to speak and all he could manage was to shake my hand with both of his while he looked me in the eye, tears flowing from his.

"You must rest longer," Ameline said. "Stay and eat with us. I know my father would like it."

"Nothing would give me greater joy," I said. "But we have rested the night through and now I must get the prisoner to Nantes. With his confession, we can take Gilles de Rais and truly put an end to this nightmare."

Poor Ameline. Her nightmare was far from over.

Two weeks later, on Tuesday 13th September 1440, we went to arrest Gilles de Rais.

11

The Arrest of Gilles

September 1440

WE RODE SOUTH UNDER the black banners of the Bishop of Nantes, for it was on his authority that we finally acted, in partnership with Jean the Duke of Brittany.

Roger de Briqueville had confessed all.

I was not present for his questioning but I am told the words spilled from his mouth faster than the Inquisition could record them. He told a tale of continual murders, depravity and sinful lusts, and worse even than all that he told of heretical acts of worship and demon summoning and the invocation of Satan himself. And all throughout Briqueville's long, desperate confessions he named the deviant, the criminal, the heretic, as his lord Gilles de Rais.

It was to Castle Tiffauges once again that we rode. The Marshal had returned to his most favoured home and fortress just days before from Machecoul. The Bishop believed he was attempting to confuse us as to his true whereabouts but we had enough agents by then watching his nests and reporting back to Nantes to know where he was at all times.

And yet to me it seemed less like a cunning ploy and more like desperation. It rang of the frantic oscillations of a beast caught in trap that it does not understand. We were coming for him and he did not know what to do about it.

Our company was a large one, almost eighty men. Some were soldiers, all were armed, although Stephen and the other lawyers were armed with writ and warrant rather than brigandine and blade.

"It is not enough!" I had said to the Bishop. "His personal army is two hundred strong. Less a score or two, perhaps. They will outmatch us in number and in skill."

"God will protect you," the Bishop had insisted, raising a soft, fat palm to the sky. "And anyway, there are no more men."

"The Duke can raise thousands," I replied.

"And if you find that thousands are required," the Bishop said, "then he will raise them."

"That will be marvellous for you and the Duke, my lord, but in the meantime me and my men will be long dead."

"I have every confidence in you all."

We purchased what additional armour we could from the best merchant in Nantes. I found a new coat of plates in Nantes made from the finest steel plates riveted between two layers of thick linen. Somehow, he knew that we were associated with the Bishop in some way and constantly attempted to entice us into purchasing absurdly overpriced nonsense instead of the robust forms we required.

"That piece is of course excellent," the armour merchant said as I tapped the rivets and plates all over with my knife. "But it is rather heavy and unrefined. For a man of your obvious taste and means, I would recommend this remarkable item newly arrived from the armourer in Milan. The steel is lighter and the outer layer is this splendid red velvet and the rivets are well gilded, as you can see."

"I would rather suffer the extra weight for the added protection of the thicker steel," I said. Rob was rapping his knuckles against a series of helms behind me and I had to raise my voice. "And the Milanese piece is hideously gaudy."

"I'll take it," Walt said, grinning.

"No you bloody well will not," I said. "I will not have you at my side all tarted up like a whore on May Day. You shall have that coat of jacks from Nuremberg and you shall be grateful, sir."

I got for myself an open-faced sallet which left my face exposed but would enable me to see, while Walt and Rob made do with a pair of old bascinets that had the long, pointed skulls which had been popular thirty or forty years earlier.

"I always liked these," Rob said, grinning at the helm that he held in his hands.

"Only because they add four inches to your height," Walt grumbled.

For all our new armour and dozens of companions, approaching Tiffauges across the plain that September day, I found my heart was in my mouth. If our company of soldiers, palace guards, bailiffs and lawyers clashed with the Marshal's army, our side would collapse and flee, and they would be cut down.

"Wait here while we go on ahead," I said to Labbe, the Duke's captain of arms, who was in command of our troops.

"It is I who must serve the warrant," Captain Labbe replied. "Personally."

"You will serve nothing if you are lying dead on the field," I replied and galloped off with my men, Stephen included.

"I been thinking," Walt said as we approached, slowing our horses to a walk. "Has anyone considered that this Marshal, the Baron Gilles de Rais, might be your brother William in disguise?"

The wind grew colder every day and it cut into every inch of exposed skin and between gaps in my armour. It was turning to autumn without ever being summer and the crops all around were stunted and diseased and I knew none of the sheep and goats scattering at our approach would live to see Christmas.

"Of course I have considered it," I said. "But I saw the Marshal in battle, at Orléans and at Patay. It was at a distance but I would have recognised my brother even so. It is not him."

"Besides," Stephen said. "William promised to leave Christendom for two hundred years and it has been merely a hundred and fifty."

"A hundred and eighty years," I said, correcting him. "And I never believed he would commit to the letter of the agreement. I have often doubted whether he would keep to the spirit of it either, come to that, and yet he seems to have done so. We have had no word of him ever since."

"Perhaps he died," Rob said. "In the East."

"Perhaps," I admitted. "Though I somehow doubt that we will be so blessed. He will return one day soon and when he does, we shall kill him. But first we will take this lord and if he is one of William's, we shall see him destroyed."

I spoke with complete confidence but I still wondered if it could be true. Certainly, I would not put such a thing past William. He could certainly have taken the identity of one of his immortals and then ruled the land in his name. The depths of depravity had the ring of William's evil to it. Indeed, the first horror that I had seen him inflict was when he murdered my half-brother's little children and consumed parts of them.

Will I soon see William again? I wondered. *Is he almost within my grasp once more?*

There was no army drawn up and waiting on the plain before Tiffauges. There was no one at all, in fact, and the gateway to the castle was fully open and the Marshal's gold and black banner hung from the tallest tower, declaring to the world that he resided within.

"That's a trap," Walt said, pointing up at it.

"Nonsense," I said.

"Got to agree with Walt, Richard," Rob said. "Too good to be true, ain't it?"

"I think not," I replied, though I could never have explained why. It was merely a feeling that Gilles had given himself up.

"But where's his army?" Rob insisted. "Waiting within?"

"Perhaps he has dismissed them entirely."

"Why in the name of Jesus Christ and all His saints would he go ahead and do something as stupid as all that?" Walt said. "Don't make any sense."

"What about this man's actions makes sense, Walt? Nothing he has done has any reason to it. His magnificent play in Orléans that was so lavish it almost ruined him. The needless murdering of this great host of children when he could have quietly supped on living men's blood, undiscovered and safe for centuries more. Charging from one castle to another with no pattern nor reason. They are the acts of a man who has lost his mind and lost his will besides. He seems already defeated, does he not?"

From the corner of my eye, I saw Rob and Walt raise their eyebrows at each other.

"Whatever you say, Richard. After you, then."

I cleared my throat. "Perhaps we will allow the Duke's captain of arms to go in first."

In spite of my confident words, I was still on edge as our party approached the gate. We all watched the narrow slits of the windows in the towers flanking the gatehouse and in the walls. Every loud clop of a hoof on the cobbles caused me to flinch, expecting a crossbow bolt to come shooting down right after. I watched Captain Labbe's men file in through the gate passage and half expected boiling water to be dumped down on them through the murder holes or for the Marshal's soldiers to rush out from the courtyard.

But all was quiet.

In the courtyard, with the walls and towers now on all sides, I wished that I had a shield to raise over my head because surely it was the most perfect spot on earth from which to murder a company of men.

And yet the stable hands took our horses and we were shown in through the main door by the porter as if we were expected and escorted through the castle to the main hall.

"I bloody well knew it, you lying sod," Miton the porter said to me, wagging his finger in my face before strutting off. No servants scattered from our path and the place was no longer illuminated throughout as it had been.

"Where is everyone, Miton?" I asked the porter.

"Dismissed," he said, miserable. "Dismissed and sent home, never to return."

"What of the soldiers?" I asked. Just behind us, Captain Labbe and his soldiers listened closely for Miton's reply.

"Dismissed also," he said, shaking his head.

"He lies," Captain Labbe said. "They are here, lying in wait to protect their master, are they not?"

"If they are then no one's told me nothing about it," Miton said, glumly.

I did not know what to think. It certainly seemed as though the Marshal was capitulating but that may have been part of the ruse.

"Make ready," I said to my men. "String your bow, Rob, and have a good arrow ready."

Miton paused by an enormous set of doors and spoke before heaving one of them open and stepping aside. "My lord the Baron of Rais awaits you, sirs, in the lower hall."

The lower hall was very grand in scale but quite spare in decoration. The floor was paved in stone but it was rather rough and no rushes had been spread. The walls had sconces for suspending tapestries and yet the walls were bare. Open doors on both flanks and a gallery showed just darkness beyond and I wondered what was lurking there.

344

But we filed in and spread out and approached the far end.

For there he was. Finally, I saw him in person.

It was not William.

Gilles de Rais stood raised above us all on the dais at the top of the hall, dressed in a magnificent black and gold samite robe, with long sleeves and an elaborately embroidered hat upon his head, woven with bands of red silk and cloth of gold. The Marshal was tall and slim, with wide shoulders and black hair. At his hip, he wore a sword with silver inlay encrusted around the hilt in chevrons and knots, and the scabbard was covered in shining black silk with rubies around the top and a line of them all the way down to the point, like shining droplets of blood.

Rarely have I seen kings so majestically attired.

His face, though, was drawn and miserable. Around his eyes, his skin was pink and raw as if he had been awake for days. Those eyes cast around over us as we trooped in and advanced on him up the hall.

By the Marshal's side were his servants Poitou, Henriet, the priest Blanchet who I had met weeks before, and the sorcerer-alchemist Prelati, who had fled from us when we had rescued the boy. They each of them looked terrified, and well they might, for we were two score angry soldiers and bailiffs bearing down on them and their master, it seemed, was offering them no protection.

"Gentlemen," the Marshal said, his voice remarkably loud and clear and commanding. A magnificent voice, truth be told, and one used to being obeyed. "No need to be so fearful. You may approach and state your business without threat or hindrance."

Other than Stephen, who was at the forefront, my men and I kept somewhat back and to one side, watching the doors for sudden assault. It was again a most perfect place for the Marshal's soldiers to ambush us from all sides, surrounding us with their greater numbers before cutting us to pieces. Above, the gallery was dark and I imagined a score of crossbowmen hiding up there, crouched with their bows ready.

I nudged Rob and nodded at the gallery. "Use the door and find a way up that gallery. If it is clear, keep watch on us with your bow. If not, raise the alarm. Walt, go with him."

They slipped across the hall and through the door.

As my men left, the captain at arms stepped up to the base of the Marshal's dais, pulled off his armet and lifted his chin before raising his voice so that it echoed even from the shadowed timbers of the ceiling far above.

"My name is Jean Labbe, Captain of Arms for Jean V, the Duke of Brittany. I come to deliver this warrant to you, my lord."

He glanced behind him and beckoned Stephen forward.

Stephen wore only robes and was practically unarmed and so when he stepped in front to become the foremost of our party, I was unsurprised to hear his voice wavering slightly as he spoke. Still, his voice was clear and loud and none in the hall would have missed a word.

"We, Jean Labbe, captain, acting in the name of my lord Jean V, the Duke of Brittany, and Stephen le Viel, lawyer, acting in the name of Jean de Malestroit the Bishop of Nantes, do hereby enjoin upon Gilles, Comte de Brienne, Lord of Tiffauges, Machecoul, Pouzages, and so on, the Baron de Rais, Marshal of France, and Lieutenant-General of Brittany, to grant us immediate access to his castle, whichever castle that may be, and to surrender himself to us as prisoner so that he may answer according to due process of the law to the triple charge of murder, and of witchcraft, and of sodomy, which is laid against him this day, the thirteenth of September in the year 1440, by the order of the Duke of Brittany and the Bishop of Nantes."

Stephen's voice echoed in the silent chamber.

All eyes were on Gilles de Rais. This man had been committing his crimes for years. Many of them in my company had friends or family who had lost sons or daughters. But still, it had only ever been whispered of in the darkness, about kitchen tables after children were abed, and in the dark corners of alehouses. All those who whispered had known that the Marshal was beyond the reach of the law. It did not apply to such men. The distance was too great between the ordinary folk and the lords above them. Only when one lord crossed another, or acted against the king, would they find themselves in trouble.

But there it was. The long-awaited warrant read aloud in the demon's presence, and the crimes named not in the darkness but in the full light of day.

The Marshal seemed to hardly react at all. I seemed to detect a small sagging in his stance, as if he had breathed all the air from his chest and but had not yet decided to breathe in once more.

Beside and behind him, however, the servants reacted. The priest, Blanchet, crossed himself repeatedly and prayed under his breath. Prelati the Florentine alchemist held his hands up to God as if beseeching him directly and personally, wailing softly in his mother tongue and in Latin. His Italian theatrics were quite repellent in their falsity. The scrawny monster Poitou sneered at me, glaring at me out of everyone in the crowd, because he knew that I was the main instrument in his destruction. His fingers grazed the dagger at his hip and I watched, ready in case he decided to throw it at me. Henriet hugged his arms about his fat body and rubbed himself up and down, as if trying to comfort his flesh.

"I deny the charges," the Marshal said smoothly, his eyes narrowing.

"Of course you do, my lord," Stephen replied, looking up at him. "And you may defend yourself against them in court."

Gilles grinned at him before looking up and fixing me with the full force of his gaze. "I knew you would come for me again, one day. I knew it. And now it is that day. The day that I have imagined. For many years, I feared you would creep into my chamber and slit my throat as I slept, or perhaps you and your companions would assault me as I travelled or besiege my castles. Never did I imagine this." He laughed. "Writs and warrants? Surely, all this does not become the likes of you, sir."

The men in the hall were confused and I am sure that they assumed the Marshal was speaking to Stephen or to Captain Labbe.

"I only wish I had come sooner," I said, drawing surprised looks from everyone in the hall. "And seen to your end before all this."

"A shame for you, then, that I shall be free and safe once more," the Marshal said. "In time."

We stared at him, all of us confused by his mad confidence.

"Surely, my lord Marshal," I said, "you understand that this warrant spells your imminent death? You are to be taken into custody and then you shall stand trial for your crimes and they are crimes that you cannot escape from, even if you deny them. No, you cannot wriggle free of this, sir. Not for all your wealth."

He grinned again, pulling the pale skin of his face tight over the bones of his skull. "You have no conception of my *rights* as Marshal of France. The King himself will intervene to free me, by his command. Oh, you shall see it happen, sir, yes you shall. You know, do you not, that the Duke and his cousin the Bishop, stand in opposition to our King, who loves me dearly?"

I was astonished and felt a knot of disquiet forming in my guts. The politics of the French court were a special kind of insanity and for all I knew, he spoke the truth and the King of France would personally ride in and free his beloved Marshal with his own hand.

But we had a duty to perform and I said as much. "Even if all that you say is true, my lord, you shall still come with us, now."

"Shall I, indeed?"

I could not help but glance up to the gallery. To my relief, I saw Rob and Walt's faces up there, looking down. I always felt better knowing Rob's bow was in his hand.

"Us, is it?" the Marshal said, a knowing smile on his face. "You say us, as if you yourself have not engineered this entire sham."

The Duke's and the Bishop's men looked at me in even more confusion.

"You have it wrong," I replied. "It is no sham. The lords and the people of this land have long recognised you as a monster and finally they have moved to end your crimes. I have done nothing but facilitate them and am here now to protect these men, should you, in your madness, decide to resist by force."

"Ha!" he cried, dramatically throwing his hands into the air. Many of the men flinched. "And you would stop me, would you?"

"You know that I would," I replied.

And yet, I was far from certain. The Marshal was certainly quite ancient himself, having survived two centuries or more as an immortal and had clearly been gorging himself on far more blood than I had in that time. His strength could have been greater than mine, and he was an experienced soldier and a knight. He had defeated me once before, when he commanded the forces that had slaughtered mine.

"If you are so strong, sir," he said, smiling a knowing smile, "then why did you not save your people when you had the chance? Did you men know that there is an Englishman in your midst? They all are. All of his men, also. As English as King Henry."

"Nonsense," I said, not daring to catch the eye of Captain Labbe or the others. "We are Normans. Now, hand over your sword to the Captain, give yourself up into his custody, and let us be done with this."

"Me alone?" he spoke lightly, as if it were a small thing. But he seemed tense as he waited for the response.

Stephen spoke up. "The warrant names also as your accomplices Etienne Corrillaut the one they call Poitou, Henriet Griart, Prelati the Florentine, and Dominus Eustache Blanchet. Also, the woman they call La Meffraye."

Casually, he nodded, and yet it was as though that great tension had gone out of him. "Oh, very well. If you insist." Sighing, as if it were little more than an irritation, he unbuckled his sword and held it so that Captain Labbe could take the hilt. I expected the Marshal to suddenly spin it about, whip the blade free, and begin cutting his way through the mortals. Or still I was ready for the hidden soldiers of his army to descend upon us from all sides and so free their master.

But the sword was taken.

Gilles stepped down from the dais and Captain Labbe's soldiers surrounded him, ready to escort him from his own hall. I could imagine the sense of unreality that those soldiers felt. It was unheard of, literally an unknown event, for commoners to arrest a noble of anything like the Marshal's standing. He was a great baron and rich beyond any commoner's conception. For all Stephen's whining over the years that the common folk needed the legal means to challenge their overlords, in his heart every man knows the powerful are supposed to rule over the weak and to witness something different is to see the natural order being undone before one's very eyes. The profundity of the moment seized every soul present, of that I am certain.

Up at the top of the hall, the Marshal's men became greatly anguished and Henriet and Poitou, I am sure, strained to resist their arrest. They could certainly have killed the bailiffs, if they chose. A handful of them, at least. Perhaps they feared me and my men and knew they would ultimately fail. Or perhaps some other reason stayed their hands.

Henriet, eyes darting around the room, jerked into action and cried out.

"I cannot, my lord! I cannot do it! Forgive me!"

Even as he spoke, he drew his knife and began to saw at his own throat. I was already rushing forward before he acted and managed to grasp his wrist and pull his hand away from his throat so that only a little blood was spilled and before he was able to cut through the great veins. He was stronger than any normal man, of course, but I was stronger still. As I held him, the bailiffs prised the blade from his hand before he could do himself mortal damage. We clapped the irons on him while he wept in despair.

"Why did you stop him?" Rob muttered, coming down with Walt as the bailiffs rounded all the Marshal's servants up and prepared them for the journey.

Walt nudged Rob in the ribs. "You want him to get tortured to death, that's it, ain't it,

Richard?"

Rob ignored him and looked at me strangely. "Are you perhaps not taking this legal approach a little too far?"

Why had I stopped his attempt at self-murder? Partly, yes, I wanted him to suffer before he died but there was something else nagging at me. His cry to his master that he could not do *it*. Clearly, he meant that he could not give himself up but the way he spoke it, intoned the word *it*, seemed to suggest it was something he and the Marshal had discussed before our appearance. Had Henriet agreed to give himself up peacefully, only to give in to despair? Or was there something more to it? Was there something else he had promised?

"I want him to confess, that is all," I said. "And so condemn his master with his words. He cannot do that if he is dead."

"As long as he dies eventually," Rob said.

We took them all back to Nantes where they were to be tried. All the lands we rode through belonged to the Marshal. Every field, every village, tree, and beast were his. His lands stretched for miles beyond the horizon to the east and to the west and brought him vast incomes that made him fabulously rich. Yet, he had not fought to protect them. There were over a hundred soldiers in his private army and yet he had not used them. In fact, he had perhaps even dismissed them from his service. Why had he given himself up?

He sat straight-backed in his saddle, wrapped in his gorgeous sable cloak with his head held high beneath his hat, as if he were simply out for a ride. As if he were perfectly content with his life and with where he was in that moment.

I felt that disquiet again, that I was missing something obvious, something before my eyes and yet I had not the wit to make note of it.

But were his actions so suspicious? Very little he had done for some time made any sense, so it seemed likely that the man had simply lost his mind and could not accept that he would soon hang for his crimes.

Either way, I was sure, riding behind the arrested men in grim silence, that it was over. That not the King nor God Himself could now save Gilles de Rais from his fate.

He was the man responsible for our defeats nine years before, at Orléans, but soon I would make amends.

1 2

Siege of Orléans

May 1429

WE HAD NO IDEA of the danger we were in. After Joan came to the city of Orléans in April 1429, we still thought it was laughable. There was some nonsensical old myth, some confused prophecy, that said a maiden would drive away the enemies of France. It seemed to be utter nonsense.

Inside Orléans, Joan acted like a holy woman or even like royalty, parading herself around the streets of the city handing out food to the people as if she had arranged and brought it herself, rather than simply accompanied a convoy that was coming anyway. But the people did not care. And the garrison received their long-awaited salaries that the King had sent. But Joan, with her natural cunning, made sure they believed that it was her who had been responsible for the issuing of the coins.

She began sending messengers to each of our forts, demanding our departure. These messengers were cursed and jeered by all. Some of the commanders of the forts threatened to kill the messengers, accusing them of being emissaries of a witch, and they were driven off.

Unbeknownst to us at the time, Joan was even engaging in discussions of tactics with the lords in Orléans. According to what I heard later, she urged nothing but direct and immediate assaults on all of our forts, one after the other or even all at once. Those commanders would not hear of it. The French had not properly attacked the English for decades and they were afraid to do so. Most had never participated in an assault. Their most recent attempt, at the Battle of the Herrings, had once again resulted in their defeat. They knew, in their bones, that attacking the English, when we were prepared and ready, with stakes and archers, would always end in failure. It had been that way since Crecy, since Poitiers, since Agincourt.

And yet, somehow, Joan's utter conviction was infecting even those weak men. Her assertion was that all the French had to do was try an assault to be successful. Her madness poured out of her and into them.

One of the commanders left the city in the night and ran for the forest, along with a sizable bodyguard. They were spotted and I was ordered by Talbot to chase after him and to stop him. I took Rob, Walt, and a score of other veterans on good horses and with spares and set off. We tracked them down river toward Blois, but they had too long a lead and we could not catch them before they reached the city.

When we returned, I discovered that the Maiden had come out of the city and personally surveyed our fortifications.

"She was dressed in full harness!" the men told me. "Shining polished armour, all over. Like a man!"

"What did she look like?" I asked them.

"Ah, she was hideous," Old Simon assured me. "Like a deformed dwarf, she was."

"You are mad!" another said. "She was tall, with long, flowing blonde hair."

"She wore a cap the entire time," another man said, cursing the others for their ignorance. "But one could see she was a great beauty."

Half the men howled in derision.

"Nonsense," Old Simon roared. "She was pinched in the face, with a turned-up nose like a fat skeleton."

None of us could understand it and Walt and Rob put it down to the typical ignorance and argumentative nature of the English soldier on a long campaign. But I felt some disquiet. How could they have seen such different things? It hinted to me of some vague unnaturalness. Perhaps, I thought, she was a witch after all. And I was not the only one.

Seeking clarification, something solid I could cling to, I asked Talbot what she had looked like, seeing as he had exchanged shouted words with her over the palisades.

"What do you care what the witch looks like?" Talbot snapped when I asked him. "Who are you to ask me such a thing? Mind your duties, man, or I will have you shipped back to England in chains!"

I knew he did not like me and was threatened by my expertise, but I was shocked by his open hostility.

Rob attempted to explain it. "You don't know your place, Richard." He hurried on, when he saw my expression. "That is, your place as he sees it. You have no lofty position here, you are merely a lowly captain with a handful of men. You have no land, no income. And so the likes of Lord Talbot ain't ever going to listen to you."

Walt gestured at me with the nub end of a loaf of dry bread. "And you scare the wits out of most men, sir. Give men the jitters, so you do. You have a right nasty look in your eye, half the time."

"I do not," I said, offended. "I am the most civil man in the world."

They glanced at each other and said nothing.

A couple of days later, our scouts rushed in to warn us that a reinforcement convoy was coming up from Blois in the southwest. And somehow, there were other convoys converging on us from Montargis and Gien. It was early in the morning of the 4th May when the Blois convoy approached on the north side of the city, close to the fort of St. Laurent.

"We must meet them," I urged Talbot. "Form up and stop them outside the fort."

"Be silent," Talbot snapped. "Someone silence that man, there!"

No one moved to silence me but I held my tongue for a moment while Talbot stared out at the enemy forces.

"They are too many," he said. "If we pull men out from the forts, the garrison in the city will rush out and take us at the rear."

I suppose it was a sensible precaution. But war is not a sensible business. It cannot be undertaken successfully without taking risks. Talbot was more afeared of losing the forts than he was of allowing the enemy to go unchallenged in their approach of the city.

The best commanders understand that battles are won in men's minds as well as in the force of arms. More so, in my experience, and as the English would soon discover. Sadly, Talbot was not one of the best commanders. And as we stood down and watched the French reinforcements riding between our forts and heading into the city, I saw *her* for the first time.

For Joan the Maiden rode out to escort the convoy in.

She seemed small to me, although she was mounted on an enormous destrier. She wore a helm with a closed visor and held aloft a great banner flapping and snapping in the wind overhead. That banner was one I would come to know and to hate by sight. A great white banner sprinkled with fleur-de-lys all over. On one side was depicted the figure of Our Lord in Glory, holding the world and giving His benediction to a lily, held by one of two angels kneeling on each side with the words Jesus Maria besides. On the other side of the banner was the figure of Our Lady and a shield with the arms of France supported by two angels.

But that day, Joan and her banner were far away and hidden, on and off, by the mass of men around her.

"She ain't all that," Walt observed. "They just strapped a harness around some little harlot from Lorraine. She ain't even got a weapon, has she, what's she going to do with that banner?"

"Her presence is the weapon," I said, seeing how the French soldiers swarmed her and cheered her very presence.

"Eh?" Walt asked. "How's that then?"

I said nothing in reply as the enemy paraded in through the walls to Orléans, cheering and singing.

Watching Talbot, he seemed pleased to have avoided a battle but he was too ignorant to know he had just suffered a defeat. And it would not be the last suffered that day.

***

It was no later than midday when the enemy launched an assault on the fort of St. Loup. That was the most easterly and the most isolated of all of our forts. The fort was there to ward against supplies arriving from the east by land and by river and that was the exact reason the French decided to take it.

Provisions convoys were coming from that direction and our four hundred men in the fort there would have stopped them.

Defending is all very well, and it makes men feel secure and it is simple for less experienced troops to know what to do.

But in such a siege situation, where our forces were divided into groups, it was possible for the enemy to overwhelm a single defence point. Talbot and the other commanders were complacent but they were not incompetent. Most of the forts on the north bank of the river were close enough to support each other and St. Loup was the only fort that was too far to receive such reinforcement.

And so our four hundred men in St. Loup found themselves suddenly assaulted by almost two thousand French soldiers.

"We must relieve them," I shouted at Talbot, who seemed stunned by the moment. Fastolf was speaking in his ear and he turned on me as I approached.

"Be quiet," Fastolf snapped. "Of course we must. But we cannot risk the other forts falling."

"Risk?" I said to Fastolf. "This is an opportunity, sir. Look at them, out the walls. Their backs are to us. Mount the cavalry, pin them in place, and bring up the men on foot."

"Do not think to teach me my business," Fastolf snapped. "You are not in possession of the facts." He pointed at the attack. "Our scouts tell us that French reinforcements are converging on St. Loup from the east, coming in from Montargis and Gien. It is our garrison who are pinned in place."

"That is grim news indeed, sir. But all the more reason for us to commit now."

Fastolf chewed his lip and looked to Talbot, who was in command. "My lord?"

I held my breath.

"Send word. Order the garrison of Paris to attack the French."

When he said Paris, he was using the vernacular name for the fort of Saint Pouair which was the closest to St. Loup.

"Is that it?" I blurted out. "One garrison? My lord, if we bring out every garrison, we can wipe out the French and end the siege by the end of the day!"

"Remove yourself from my presence, sir. If you wish to throw your life away, feel free to charge headlong into death."

I pulled my helm on my head and shouted at Talbot. "It will not be the first time!"

With Walt and Rob and a few brave souls who felt as we did, we rode out of St. Laurent around to the northeast to join the garrison. In truth, it was hopeless. In the wasteland north of the city, we three hundred men assaulted two thousand French.

And we were thrown back. Again and again. At one point we came close to coming around their flank to the north but a sortie from the French blocked us.

By nightfall, St. Loup fell.

We lost a hundred and fifty soldiers and forty were taken prisoner. Some of the English defenders of St. Loup were captured in the ruins of a nearby church. The rumour was that their lives were only spared at the saintly Joan's request. The thought made me sick to my stomach.

When St. Loup fell, our purpose for assaulting them was over and so we retired our northern assault and trudged back into our forts as night fell. It was not an unrecoverable failure but already I sensed the momentum turning in favour of the French.

"We must take the fort back," I said to my men. "Take it tonight. Or at first light. Before it is too late."

"You reckon Talbot will listen?" Rob asked.

I slumped. "No."

The next day, there was no French attack. Whether it was the fact it was the Feast of the Ascension or if they needed to rest their men after the assault the day before, they took no action. It was the perfect opportunity for us to regain the initiative.

Instead, we sat in our forts and fretted.

In the morning, the French crossed the river from Orléans on boats and barges and by a makeshift pontoon bridge. I watched from the north bank along with hundreds of others. They came out in a great mass of soldiers and armed citizenry but of course our garrisons on the south bank were waiting for them. It was a hard-fought struggle and the French were forced back.

Joan was wounded in the counter-attack. Panic set in amongst the French and they retreated back to the river, dragging Joan back with them. Seeing the witch on the run and her spell broken, our garrison burst out to give chase as the men fled.

I did not see what happened next because the city walls hid the events from us but we all heard the story soon after. With the French in full flight, Joan, at the rear, stopped. Standing completely alone as hundreds of furious English soldiers charged her, she turned around on them, raised her holy standard, stamped the foot of the pole upon the earth and cried out.

"In the name of God!"

For some reason, this was enough to check the English pursuit. Why they did this is difficult to understand and many said that she used magic on them, either from her spell or by some magic inherent to her person. Whatever the reason and whatever really happened, it was enough to send the English back to the safety of our fort on the south bank and the fleeing French troops turned around and rallied about her.

At her side through it all, Gilles de Rais persuaded Joan to immediately resume the assault which he led in person.

His military brilliance with Joan the Maiden providing the inspiration, their attack carried the day.

With the Augustins fort in French hands, our Tourelle's garrison was blockaded. That same night, what remained of our garrison at St. Privé evacuated their outwork and went north of the river to join our strongest garrison, where I was, in St. Laurent. The last garrison on the south bank Glasdale was therefore isolated but there were eight hundred good men ready to throw back whatever came their way.

Despite her wound, Joan rallied the cities within the city and they joined the attack the next day. They bombarded our men for all hours and attempted to undermine the walls of the fort and setting fire to whatever they could. And still our experienced men were unconcerned.

All of a sudden, La Pucelle appeared with her great white banner held aloft and charged the front walls of our fort herself. As she charged by the cowering French soldiers, she grabbed a ladder and threw it up against the wall, calling out to them as she went.

"All is yours! Go in! Go in!"

The French were much stirred in their hearts and they rushed in after her, throwing up dozens of ladders to storm the walls alongside her.

One of our brave archers shot Joan with an arrow.

She was spitted between the neck and shoulder with a yard-long, thumb-thick arrow with its wicked iron point. She was thrown down from the wall and carried away. Our men knew they had won when the French assault faltered and fell back. Everyone knew that such a wound was fatal. There was no way that a man could survive such a terrible blow and the word quickly spread, even across the river, that Joan the Maiden was dead.

We celebrated in every fort and felt that the tide had turned back in our favour.

And then she emerged from the city. She was walking, leaning on her companion Gilles de Rais.

"Take heart, good soldiers of France," she called out. "Take heart and feel good cheer, for God knows that a final assault will carry the day."

We heard the cheering from a mile away and they renewed their attack like the Devil himself was at their heels. Our men fled and the fort, burning all over, fell just before night came.

It was a true disaster. In all the assaults, we had lost a thousand men and six hundred had been taken prisoner. With the south bank of the Loire lost, there was no point in holding the north bank because the city could be resupplied from the south until Judgement Day.

And so, just a week after Joan's arrival, the siege was over.

Lord John Talbot ordered us to demolish our forts and siege works and we drew up our army.

The French came out and drew up before us to the west of the city.

"Attack," I urged Talbot and the other commanders. "We can undo all that has been done if we just attack them. Our soldiers are better than theirs."

Talbot's eyes were fixed on the white banner of Joan the Maiden.

"They will attack us," Walt said. "Look at them. Roaring for it."

For a time, it seemed as though he was right but in the end they simply stood watching us for an hour and Talbot ordered us to retreat. The enemy were so close, I was certain they would fall upon our rear and rip us to pieces. But they were still afraid of us and they let us slink away.

The last thing I saw before I rode over the hill through the trees was Joan's banner flying over the massed French army.

Beside hers flew the golden and black banner of Gilles de Rais, but I thought nothing of that at the time. It was just one more banner amongst dozens.

It need not have meant the end of the English war on the French but their aggressive use of artillery and frontal assaults influenced French tactics for the rest of the conflict.

Joan and Gilles were far from done with us.

1 3

The Trial Begins
September 1440

THE TRIAL BEGAN IN the great hall of the castle, arranged carefully to conduct a tribunal. What a grand hall it was, with enormous, modern windows with glass panes so that the lofty interior was filled with light all the way to the rafters and beautifully carved ceiling high above. At the head of the hall on a high dais almost the width of the hall, was the chief officiating judge, the Bishop of Nantes in his purple robes. Directly behind him and above him, on a table covered in white cloth, was a great, golden crucifix, encrusted with rubies and emeralds and sapphires. Beside the Bishop of Nantes were his fellow assessors, the Bishops of Le Mans, Saint Brieuc, and Saint-Lo, along with the Chief Inquisitor of Nantes and other assessors I did not know. Serving them and the court were the typical functionaries in their gowns and caps, hunched over their tables with quill in hand to record every word spoken during the proceedings.

Also there, at one side of the hall below the judges, was the public prosecutor in his gown, my dear comrade Stephen Gosset, going by the name Stephen le Viel. He appeared composed but I knew him well enough to know by the set of his head and the way he held his shoulders that he was nervous. And why would he not be? For the hall was filled with members of the public, many of them the families of the victims of Gilles de Rais.

On the opposite side of the hall to Stephen, was the witness stand and beside it a huge iron cage with a bench along the rear. Empty, for the time being.

And between the judges and the public, also empty, was the huge chair reserved for the accused himself. He would be seated with his back to the public, facing the Bishops.

I sat near to Stephen, at the front of the public gallery, where I would be able to look across and see the side of the Marshal's face during his trial. I wondered how long it would take for the tales of the blood drinking to come out. My men, including Stephen, fretted somewhat that our secrets would be revealed yet I was not concerned. No one would believe in the blood magic and instead it would serve only to emphasise the satanic nature of the crimes and the men who committed them. Whatever accusations Gilles made against me and my men, we could throw off, I was sure of it and Stephen was prepared with clever responses.

The Marshal had been provided with a small suite of rooms in the castle of Nantes where he was awarded all the customary privileges of a nobleman who had yet to be proved guilty of any crime. It was disgusting, of course, but that was simply the way it was and there was no chance of having him clapped in irons in a dank dungeon cell.

"Do you reckon they'll declare him innocent in the end?" Walt had said, on hearing that the Marshal was held in such comfort.

"Of course not," I replied. "Already they have an enormous amount of evidence and the Inquisitors will obtain more from the servants. Do not concern yourself."

But I was concerned. I told myself that, if the people of his lands were denied proper legal justice, I would simply find Gilles de Rais and cut off his head. The same went for his servants, those that were revenants and perhaps even those who were not. Though they were guarded by soldiers of the Duke and the Bishop, I was sure I would be able to find a way.

In many ways of course I would have preferred to do the deed myself but it was important that I stay my hand unless there was no other choice. There were thousands of good men and women, fathers and mothers, brothers and sisters, who needed to watch their master hang before them for the monstrous evil he had done to them if they were to have any hope of satisfaction. I knew this because they told me. They had come to see the trial in their hundreds, from miles all around, and the inns of Nantes were full to bursting and I met with them before the trial

"I got to see him hang," some said. "With my own eyes."

Others had similar reasons. "And he needs to see *us* before he dies. To know it was us what did for him."

"He must burn," others replied. "Burn and be destroyed so that come what may he has no body to use on the Day of Judgement."

For their sakes, I hoped the trial would prove swift and satisfying.

Certainly, I had high hopes, for the Inquisitor of Nantes would personally apply their tried and tested methods to extract the necessary confessions from the accused persons.

Back in 1252, Pope Innocent had issued a papal bull authorising torture for the express purpose of obtaining a confession. The accused was first *threatened* with torture in the hope and expectation that the threat itself would elicit a confession. And it certainly was enough for many people, as I have often found in far less formal and less legal circumstances. If the threats failed, the Inquisitors would bring the accused to the torture chamber and show them the instruments to be used. It was oftentimes at this moment that the accused would decide to speak and in practice, many in the Inquisition moved immediately to this step because it was more efficient that way.

"Men are afraid of pain," I said to Stephen as we watched the Inquisitors preparing their assigned room in Nantes while the tribunals were likewise being set up in the halls. "It is a simple thing to frighten them into speaking to avoid it."

"Oh, no," Stephen said. "That is not it at all, Richard. It is far more deeply and accurately reasoned that that."

I sighed. "I suppose I would have to spend years in Paris listening to doctors of theology explain it to me before I could hope to understand."

"No, no, it is perfectly straightforward. You see, the Inquisition knows that deception, the lies themselves reside in our tongues but the *truth* lives within the flesh. It is the body that is required to be examined in order to extract the truth from it. Lies, spoken by free tongues, are ephemeral and meaningless. Flesh and blood, however, cannot be denied."

"I suppose so," I allowed. "Still, these Inquisitors must enjoy hurting people."

"In fact they often do not need to touch a person at all. And when they do, it is done with the utmost reason and care. They inflict pain only to draw out the truth, nothing more."

"Come, Stephen," I said, lowering my voice lest they overhear me, "look at them. I have seen men with eyes like that in every army I have fought in and against. They love twisting the knife."

"You see a man like that every time you look in a mirror, you mean," he said, tutting. "They are learned men, practising the application of perfectly clear reasoning. Only through torture can we satisfy the demand for truth because it is so deeply hidden in the flesh. Hidden so deeply that the accused may not even be aware of it until it is drawn out. And how can truth be drawn from flesh, like water drawn from a well, or like a knife drawn from flesh? Pain, Richard. Pain is the conduit for truth, as I am sure you well know. It is distillation of the pure substance, that is to say truth itself which is another way of saying nature itself or God, if you like, lodged in the impure flesh. Pain betrays the truth by exposing it to view through the sounds and gestures it produces. Pain causes the accused to speak involuntarily, without his own volition, and so what emerges is uncorrupted by the lies of the tongue and the wits of a man."

"I am no expert of course but this theoretical complexity has the whiff of the alchemical, do you not think it so?"

"No, I do not think it so."

However, seeing the Inquisitors at their business, it was clear enough that the ones before us at least took no joy in their work. It was simply that. Work.

While they began to organise the evidence, the trial itself was begun.

Rather, it was two trials, running in concert with one another. The ecumenical tribunal was presided over by the Bishop of Nantes, and the civil court was presided over by Chief Justice Pierre de l'Hospital, Chancellor of Brittany. The Bishop's court would try the man Gilles de Rais for satanism, heresy, unnatural vice, sacrilege, and the violation of ecclesiastical privilege. The civil tribunal would deal with the charges of murder and of rebellion against the authority of the Baron's liege lord, Jean V the Duke of Brittany. Although one might assume the civil court would have precedence due to the utmost seriousness of the crimes of murder and rebellion, in fact it was the ecclesiastical court that would lead matters. For one thing, it was under the Bishop's authority that most of the investigations had taken place, led by Stephen's guile and my rather brute force approach. And for another, what more serious crime could there be in Heaven and earth than heresy?

"Are you well prepared, Stephen?" I asked him, while the hall was filling with officers of the court and members of the public. It was noisy with talk and the scuffing of feet. Stephen sat at his table to one side of the hall near to the front. "Chief Prosecutor, eh?" I said to him. "The Bishop certainly has faith in you."

Stephen sniffed. "As well he might, sir. I have prepared the arguments carefully and have full confidence in them."

"Then why do you look so nervous?" I asked, grinning.

"I am not nervous, Richard," he said, primly. "I am merely concentrating on my arguments regarding the charge of sodomy."

"Why?" I laughed. "Briqueville stated he witnessed the acts himself. Many acts, in fact."

He lowered his voice and leaned in. "That is just it. We cannot enter Briqueville's statements into the record of evidence. He confessed fully only on those terms and the terms are being agreed to due to the fact that he's a damned noble."

"Barely," I scoffed. "But what does it matter? You can skewer him with the charge of heresy alone."

He ignored me and muttered almost to himself. "We can but hope the other servants confess to this charge also. Only then will his conviction in the ecclesiastical tribunal be unquestionable."

"Surely, you cannot mean that sodomy is a greater crime than witchcraft? Than heresy?"

"Well," Stephen said. "Sodomy is a form of heresy, in the eyes of the Church. Perhaps the greatest form."

"What nonsense."

He tilted his head. "Why do you think it is a crime at all?"

"Well," I said. "It is unnatural, I suppose. Not that it stops men who feel compelled to do the deed."

Stephen all-but wagged a finger at me. "No one is compelled to sin. We each make the choice of whether to sin or not."

I sighed. "You have never been on campaign, have you, Stephen. There is often a man or two out of every hundred who do not mind sharing a bedroll and who venture alone together into the woods every once in a while. No harm in it, truth be told, as long as it does not interfere with a man's duty."

"How can you say such a thing?"

I was surprised at his vehemence, especially as I had often wondered whether Stephen engaged in an occasional sodomising himself. He liked women, that much I knew, but there was always the whiff of the degenerate about him.

"Come, Stephen, you are not innocent of these matters. You were a monk, for God's sake. Half the lads in the priory are there because they prefer the warmth of a hairy backside to the smoothness of a woman."

"How can you joke about such things? The law is very clear. Sodomy is a deliberate sin against God. It is an act of defiance against God's law. An act of rebellion, if you will, even more serious than rebellion against one's earthly lord."

"And yet all sins are acts against God, are they not?" I was proud of myself for recalling that one from my youth. I had such lessons beaten into me quite thoroughly.

"Yes, yes, but this base self-gratification is against Nature itself. It is wholly avoidable and so it is especially malicious. You see, a man's soul and his body are provided by God and so both are inherently good, as God is. But of course because of original sin, our bodies are also corrupted to one extent or another, and it is these lower, base parts that drag the goodness of our souls down to Hell. And it is our soul that restrains our base urges and leads us to salvation. And so the act is a sin against Nature and also a sin against the grace of God. There is no act which is so sinful, so against God, than sodomy."

"Not even murder?"

"Well," Stephen said, shifting in his seat. "It would be a bad Christian who considers a crime against the soul as lesser than a crime against the body, would it not?"

Exasperated, I sighed. "I do not know, Stephen. It seems to me that you can apply too much reason by far to such things. Of course murder is worse than arse thumping, man. What are you talking about? You have too much time at the college of the Sorbonne, that is what I think. You need to get back to the depravity of London, where you belong." I shook my head in wonder at his holy nonsense.

It was not that I necessarily disagreed with him but one does not need reason to know whether something is right or wrong. We feel the truth of it in our guts and then afterwards apply reason to one degree or another in order to justify our feelings. And for all their clever words and arguments, all moral philosophy is no more than this. Whether they be noble and courageous as Socrates and Nietzsche, or depraved and deluded as Sartre and Marx, their life's work is simply the elucidation of and justification for feelings that emerged unbidden and uncontrolled from their guts, heart, and balls.

Stephen frowned. "If only you would consider continuing your formal education, Richard. It might serve to help our greater cause if you were able to understand the nuances of—"

I was about to explain the nuances of my fist to his face when the crowd's hubbub grew suddenly in volume and emotion and I turned to see the Marshal's servants being led into the iron cage by the witness stand.

The priest Blanchet, the alchemist Prelati, and the two revenants, Poitou and Henriet. Both of these last two looked very ill indeed. Green and pale in complexion, and weak and gaunt. The lack of blood was turning them into beasts. I wondered if they would turn on the mortal priests inside the cage and savage them in full view of everyone, bishops and butchers both.

What a noise the people made. First one man shouted a curse, and then more began jeering and calling down the fury and the hand of God, until the place was in an uproar. The Bishop ordered them to be quiet and had the court bailiffs march into the public galleries and threaten and shove the people down.

"I will have silence or I will have every one of you removed for the duration of the trial!" the Bishop said, in a surprisingly powerful voice that echoed down from the ceiling, as if the Lord Himself had spoken.

The fear of missing the tribunal drove them to control themselves.

I wondered how they would react when the Marshal was brought in.

"Call the accused to appear before us," the Bishop said to the Clerk of the Court.

"Call Messire Gilles de Rais to appear before the court!" cried out the Clerk.

And the public, rising in a great wave, muttered and cried out and then roared, as the Marshal himself marched in from the side of the hall with four soldiers escorting him. He was dressed in red and black velvet, with red velvet boots and a red silk sash across his body. Though the crowd were baying for his blood, he did not so much as glance their way and instead wore a small smirk on his face as he stopped in front of his ornate chair and turned to the array of bishops, thus showing his back to the audience.

The Clerk was shouting down the public and the bailiffs were shoving the crowd back. The Bishop raised his hand and the thunderous look on his face was enough to remind them of his earlier threat to expel the lot of them and they managed to calm down.

When it was quieter, the Bishop of Nantes nodded to Stephen who got to his feet and cleared his throat. A hush descended and it seemed as though everyone stopped breathing, or perhaps that was me alone.

"Thank you, Milord Bishop. If it pleases the court, I shall now read the charges against the accused and enter them into record. Messire Gilles de Rais is indicted for witchcraft, sodomy, and heresy." He crossed the hall and handed a sheath of parchment to the Bishop and moved back to his place.

"Messire de Rais," the Bishop said. "Have you anything to say in response to the grave charges levelled against you in this court?"

The Marshal bowed low before standing upright and thrusting forward his chin. "I have full confidence that I shall unequivocally prove my perfect innocence to the court in no time at all."

Behind me, the public growled at the preposterousness of his statement and no doubt many were shocked at the brazenness of the lie that he was innocent.

The Bishop sighed, for his life would have been much the easier if the Marshal had crumbled and admitted his guilt but of course that was hardly expected. "No doubt, Messire de Rais, you will therefore require the services of a counsel for your defence of these charges?"

Gilles grinned. "Oh, no, my lord. Why would an innocent man need to rely on a lawyer's tricks when the simple truth will do perfectly well?" This drew hisses and noises of revulsion. The smirk on his face only grew. It dawned on me that the Marshal knew he was doomed and was simply enjoying tormenting and outraging the public behind him. "You see, my lord, I am a perfect Christian in every regard. A perfect Christian, I say, and nothing will give me greater joy than to prove this to the court."

The crowd surged forward and someone threw a fist-sized hunk of cheese at the Marshal, which missed, and then from another angle came a walking stick, hurled with considerable force. It clanged off the back of the Marshal's ornate chair and clattered along the floor.

The public were soon cleared from the court by the bailiffs and though they were mad with anger, they were still rightly afraid of the Bishop, who was only a couple of steps removed from God Himself.

"Because the charges include heresy," the Bishop said when they were gone, "I must seek assistance from a representative of the Holy Office in determining the truth of this case. Therefore, I will formally request the services of the Inquisition."

The Chief Inquisitor nodded. "Yes, Milord Bishop. Messire de Rais will be brought before the Inquisition."

I watched the Marshal as his sardonic grin fell from his face. He swallowed, as if a great stone had appeared at the back of his throat.

"Let it be thus recorded," intoned the Bishop, "that Messire de Rais will appear before the Inquisitor of Nantes of the Dominican Order. Oh, I should say that the accused has the right to object to this, if you do so wish, my lord?"

The Marshal forced the grin back onto his face. "Object? Why should I object, my lord? As I am entirely innocent of the charges, why, I welcome the questions of the good brothers of the Inquisition." He swallowed again.

"Very well," the Bishop said. "Now, you have the opportunity to name your enemies. For we shall summon witnesses to testify and so you may register with the court those who would have cause to do you harm with their words."

At this, the Marshal faltered. No doubt, he sensed that he was in some sort of legal danger in that moment but he did not have the understanding of the procedure to head it off. If he had but taken counsel, they would have told him to name each and every one of his servants that he could, and also to name every one of his subjects. For then their testimonies would be formally doubted by the court. But Gilles merely grinned and attempted to bluff his way through with the mad assertion that he was innocent.

"But, Milord Bishop, I have no enemies to name." The Marshal frowned and cleared his throat. "Except, there is one who has betrayed me. A knight in my service, and a friend, who I fear has quite gone mad and fled from me some days ago. I know not to what ends his actions were taken but I fear he means me no good. His name is Roger de Briqueville."

I swore under my breath. By so naming the man, the Marshal had ruled out the secret testimony already sworn. The testimony that had spoken of murder, sorcery and demon-summoning, or heresy and sodomy. The testimony that the charges themselves were based on.

The Bishop's face fell. "Very well. The name shall be entered into the record that the testimony of Roger de Briqueville will be understood to be *recusationes divinatrices*, and any such testimony will be treated with the gravest suspicion of prejudice. We shall now adjourn this meeting to allow other witnesses to be heard."

At this, the Marshal turned and looked directly at me with a glint in his eye for a long moment before he was escorted out.

"I suppose this means I will have to find a way into his chamber after all," I said to Stephen as the bishops filed out. "I should have done so when first we came to Brittany and saved us from all this legal bloody nonsense. What was I thinking?"

"No, no. Do not be overly concerned," Stephen said. "Now, we let the Inquisition do their work. They shall find the truth by drawing it from the flesh of the monster's servants."

14

The Question Extraordinary

October 1440

BEING IN THE PRESENCE of the deceitful, child-sacrificing sorcerer turned my stomach. Watching Prelati as he was brought into the chamber for Questioning by the Inquisition, it seemed clearer than ever that I should have sought simply to execute all of them instead of allowing any to live a moment longer than necessary. As well as the monks of the Inquisition, and their clerks, two guards watched proceedings. Stephen and I stood at the rear, behind the prisoner, and observed in silence.

They strapped him, hands and feet stretched out and bound to the rack in the centre of the room. Within his sight was the array of all the other equipment that would be employed, should he prove unwilling to cooperate. His bonds were tightened and the mechanism employed only until it was taut. Prelati was not suffering any pain. Not yet. They would, however, use whatever torsion proved necessary to elicit answers.

The Inquisitors need not have worried, for he was a man willing to say anything if it meant surviving.

"Francois Prelati, cleric, examined and interrogated for deposition," the Inquisitor said. "He has previously stated that he originally came from the diocese of Lucca in Italy and received his clerical tonsure from the Bishop of Arezzo. He has studied poetry, geomancy, and other sciences and arts, in particular alchemy. He is aged twenty-three or thereabouts, to the best of his belief." The inquisitor looked down at Prelati. "This is correct?"

"It is," Prelati said. He appeared composed and radiated openness, as if he was willing to tell all and tell it gladly.

The Inquisitor read from a list of prepared questions in a manner that suggested he was almost entirely uninterested in the answers. "Tell me how you came into the household of the Baron de Rais."

"I was staying in Florence, about two years ago, with the Bishop of Mondovi when a certain Milord Eustache Blanchet, a priest, came to me, who made my acquaintance through the mediation of a certain master from Montepulciano. Blanchet and I, as well as Nicolas de Medici, saw each other frequently for a time, eating and drinking together, and doing other things. And one day Blanchet asked me if I knew how to practice the art of alchemy and of the invocation of demons. And I said yes."

"You said yes," the Inquisitor repeated. "But were your words the *truth*? Did you know of these things?"

"Oh, yes," Prelati said, licking his lips. "Most assuredly. I had studied these things both extensively."

The pen scratched away, taking it all down. "What then?"

"Blanchet asked if I wanted to come to France. He said there lived a great man named Lord de Rais, who much desired to have about him a man learned and skilled in the said arts and that if I went there, I would receive generous accommodations. And so I came, bringing my books on alchemy and invocations. First, we went to the Marshal's grand house in Orléans but he was not there. When we got to the border of Brittany, there came four men to meet us. Henriet Griart, Poitou, Sillé and Roger de Briqueville." That last name would be changed in the official record to say simply *and another.* "They all together brought me back to Tiffauges to meet Milord de Rais."

"What happened at this meeting?"

"The Baron presented me with a book, bound in black leather. Part paper, part parchment, having letters, titles and rubrics all in red ink."

"You are certain it was ink?" the Inquisitor looked up. "And not blood?"

"I am certain of nothing. The writing was in the colour of red. This is all I can attest to."

"Continue."

"After asking my opinions on various elements of the content, Gilles asked me to try out and test them, particularly the invocations. And I agreed. So one night soon after, in the large lower hall of the castle at Tiffauges, the lord and the others that I have spoken of, took candles and other things along with the black book with red ink. Using the tip of a sword, I drew several circles comprising characters and signs in the manner of the armoires, in the composition and drawing of which I was helped by Sillé, Henriet Griart, and Poitou, as well as Blanchet."

"The priest Blanchet participated in the invocations?"

"Actively," Prelati said, his eyes shining. "Until my lord sent them all out so that it was just Gilles and myself in the hall. We placed ourselves in the middle of the circles. I drew more characters on the floor with a burning coal from an earthen pot, upon which coals I poured some magnetic dust, commonly called magnetite, and incense, myrrh, aloes, whence a sweet smoke arose. And we remained in the same place for two hours, variously standing, sitting, and on our knees, in order to worship the demons when they appeared, and to make sacrifices to them, invoking the demons and working hard to conjure them effectively. We took turns reading from the book, waiting for the invoked demon to appear. But nothing appeared that time."

"This book with the red ink gives instructions on raising demons?"

"Not that alone. But yes. The book says that demons have the power to reveal hidden treasures, teach philosophy, and guide those who act."

"Tell us," the Inquisitor said, "by what words do you summon these demons, precisely?"

"One invocation goes thusly." Prelati's voice took on a commanding, powerful timbre. "I conjure you, Barron, which is the name of the demon, I summon you, Barron, Satan, Belial, Beelzebub, by the Father, Son, and Holy Ghost, by the Virgin Mary and all the saints, to appear here in person to speak with us and do our will."

At this, everyone present crossed himself and most looked all around the chamber as if expecting a demon to jump out.

I was half hoping that it would. We collectively let out a breath and the questioning continued.

"What other methods did you and the lord of Rais employ in order to summon a demon?"

"Many things. We used a stone named diadochite, and we used a certain variety of crested bird. We did attempt to summon the demon in many places, inside and outside of the castle."

"Did you use murdered children for these rituals?"

This was the question I had been waiting for. Would he confess to the crimes that he had committed and so condemn his master with his words? Or would he attempt to deny it and so face the Question Extraordinary.

Prelati swallowed and cleared his throat a number of times. The Inquisitor waited patiently. "The servant named Poitou told me that the room given to me in the tower for the invocations and for my alchemical work was the same room in which our master Lord de Rais had killed young boys, or caused them to be killed. And also that Gilles had slaughtered boys in my personal chamber before it was given to me, and he killed boys in all the places where I worked."

"Why did he do this?"

"Poitou told me that the children's blood and members were offered to demons."

"You claim you did not take part in these crimes yourself, and were not witness to any of them?"

"That is correct."

I scoffed, loudly. "Ha!"

The Inquisitor and everyone else turned to me.

"Say nothing," Stephen whispered. "Or you endanger the evidence."

I cared little for proper legal procedure but as I was in attendance only by courtesy, and as I wanted to hear it all spoken, I held my tongue. I even bowed my head to the Inquisitor for a moment.

He returned to the questioning. "You heard only rumours of murders done in places of your work, before and after your work was done, while you were elsewhere?"

"That is correct."

It was absurd. I had witnessed his murderous crimes myself. Only through my intervention had a boy's life been saved. Prelati was not only aware, had not only witnessed, but had been a willing participant in child murder for the purposes of raising demons.

"In fact," the Inquisitor said. "The other accused have given sworn initial statements that claim you were witness to the victims of murder, at the very least. They claim that you saw physical remains with your own eyes. Now, we will of course put you to the Question to discover the truth. Unless you would care to correct your statement first?"

Prelati glanced at the mechanism of the rack and winced. "Yes. Yes. Once, I entered Sillé's chambers and he had the body of a very small child laid out on his floor. It had been opened down the front."

"What of the Lord de Rais?"

"Yes. Once, he brought to me the hand, heart, eyes, and blood of a young boy, all kept in a glass. And he gave this glass to me so that I could offer the remains to the demon when he was summoned."

"And who murdered that child?"

"I do not know. I did not ask and was not told. I assumed the Baron had caused it by his own hand or had caused one of his men to do so."

"What then of the parts?"

"They were used as the offering in the proper ritual. No demon was forthcoming in this instance, however."

"What happened to the parts and the blood after the failed ritual?"

He cleared his throat. "The parts were burned in the grate."

The Inquisitors paused for a few moments of whispered conversations between them before taking their positions once more. All but one servant who moved to the rack and began turning the crank at the head of it which began tightening the ropes.

"My lords," Prelati said, his voice quivering. "Sirs, brothers. I have freely answered every question that you have put to me."

"Oh, you have indeed," the Inquisitor said, smiling pleasantly. "And now we shall ask every question once more but this time we shall elicit the answers from your flesh as well as from your tongue." He nodded at the servant who rotated the crank. The machine turned and Prelati gasped and groaned as the ropes pulled at him. "Now, tell me how you came into the household of the Baron de Rais."

For a time, I revelled in Prelati's agony but his answers remained remarkably consistent, as far as I could tell. But the Inquisition would ask and ask again, searching for inconsistencies that they could then tug at like loose threads.

When they resolved to further check the truth by pouring water from a funnel into his mouth until he almost drowned, over and over again between each question, I stood and let myself out, unable to listen any longer to the depravities and the crimes and the weeping of the tormented.

"He lies so easily," I said to Stephen during the recess for lunch in our inn across from the cathedral. "Even with all the pain, he excludes the blood drinking without cracks appearing in his tale. He tells just enough truth to appear to be telling all but not so much that he might yet hope to avoid a sentence of death. Sneaky bloody bastard."

"You called him a charlatan," Stephen pointed out, gesturing with his cup of wine. "And such men make their way through expertise in deception. Besides, it suits our purposes that no tales of blood emerge in the trial." He lowered his voice and leaned across the table. "Already I have undertaken to alter statements and omit evidence. If any of them speak of blood drinking and we cannot cover it up, well..."

"Yes, yes," I said. "Even if they speak of it publicly, none shall think it truth, of course. It will be just one more vile part in the madness, rather than the cause of it all."

"Is it the cause of it all? The blood? Do you believe that, Richard?"

"I do not know. Perhaps it is. What else could it be? These acts are not natural. They are the furthest thing from nature as can be. Which seems rather similar to us, does it not?"

"Far from nature?" Stephen asked, sighing. "I suppose it is so. And yet we others have not succumbed to depravity and evil. Not even Walt. Something else caused Milord de Rais to take this path. He was evil already, in his heart, and it was only the wealth he accumulated that allowed him the means to enact it in the world."

"He made pacts with Satan. With demons. Prelati said so. I saw the rituals with my own eyes."

Stephen crossed himself. "I will not believe anything that Prelati creature says. Even when racked, or given the water questions. But I agree that the Marshal's actions are evil. They are Satanic. But were these acts done with Satan's hand? Or a man's?"

I gulped down the rest of my wine. "I do not know where the strength of our blood comes from. My grandfather claims his mother lay with a god. The sky god, he called him. What if, in his pagan babblings, he and his barbarian mother confused this god with Satan himself? Walking the earth, mating with a human woman?"

Stephen crossed himself again. "That cannot be, sir."

"Why?"

"Because..." He sighed in frustration. "Because you are not evil. Nor am I. Nor Eva. Do you consider Eva to be evil?"

"She is no saint," I said. "You have not seen all the things she has done in her time."

"But is she evil?"

"No," I admitted.

"That is right," Stephen said. "And even if William is, and Priskos and his sons are, the ultimate origin of this power cannot be from the loins of Satan. For nothing so evil could become good."

"What makes you think we are *good*? We drink blood. Human blood. If you had to decide if such a thing was either good or evil, which would you choose?"

"Why must it be one or the other, Richard?"

"You know why. You yourself told me what it means to be orthodox or heretical. A thing is either natural, and so from God, or unnatural and so is evil. I ask you, how can drinking human blood be natural?"

"We *do* good, Richard. Good deeds, good acts. You saved the lives of children who would certainly have died otherwise. We put a stop to all this. Yes, we were late, but if not for us taking action, how much longer would this have gone on for? What would the world be like if we had not with our actions stopped such evil as we have found? Come now, we must return for the deposition of the priest Blanchet."

I scoffed. "That lying sack of horse dung. When I first found him, he had the balls to beg ignorance. Swore to my face he knew nothing. We shall see what he has to say with the rack threatening. I would not be surprised if he was a damned revenant this entire time. How can we catch him out?"

"I do not see how we can, not during the questioning. You are certain Prelati is human?"

I shrugged. "He begged to be turned into an immortal. It appeared genuine. And if he was deceiving me then and is doing so now, well, what does it matter if he ultimately burns either way? For surely he has condemned himself with his own words."

"I pray it is so. Summoning demons with children's body parts..." He closed his eyes and slowly shook his head at the wonder of it. "Humans do not need your family's blood to do evil, Richard."

I nodded. "True enough. Very well, then. Let us hear from this Blanchet, shall we?"

***

The monkish priest, Dominus Eustache Blanchet, was a different man entirely to Prelati. He was brought in, hunched over and close to weeping, with all the appearance of being a broken man. He said please and thank you to the Inquisitors as they made him ready for the Question. He was strapped into place upon the rack, as Prelati had been, but Blanchet shook in his bonds even before the machine was tightened.

"I came from Mountauban in the parish of Saint-Eloi, in the diocese of Saint-Malo, originally. I was born about forty years ago, to the best of my belief. After my years in orders, I came into the service of the Baron. About five years ago, I would say."

The Inquisitor looked down his list of questions. "A previous witness, Francois Prelati, claims that it was you who fetched him from Florence. Is that the case?"

"It is."

"And did you know when you set out that he was a demon summoner?"

Blanchet licked his lips. "And an alchemist, yes. Summoning of demons is not forbidden by the Church."

The Inquisitor paused to look up from his notes. "It is if done in a heretical manner, brother."

He swallowed and then swallowed again. "Of course. Which is why I ensured Prelati was properly educated in the matter, as well as in alchemy. He came well recommended by Nicolas de Medici and on discussion with Prelati, I concluded that he had the necessary skills to conduct the processes my lord wished to undertake."

"And which processes were these?"

"Why, to create gold."

"And?" The Inquisitor looked up and waited.

"All was to create gold, sir," he licked his lips. "That was the purpose of everything, to the best of my belief. Prelati had knowledge of the Philosopher's Stone and other special substances necessary for such works."

"Did the summoning of demons not disturb you, brother? Did the notion not alert you to the danger of heresy?"

"Oh no, sir. That is, I am ever vigilant where heresy is concerned, my lord. Only, I knew that Francis, I mean that is to say Prelati, was a qualified cleric and the demons were only to be summoned for the purposes of the transmutation from base matter into gold. And they would never enter any agreement with Satan in order to complete the summoning and so it was only sorcery and not witchcraft. It would be entirely orthodox, you see, sir, and the demon would be employed only for transmutation. Not for any other purposes. I would never commit heresy. Never."

The words were scratched into the records and the Inquisitor looked up at Blanchet. "And how would the demons help? What would they do? Please explain it precisely."

Blanchet swallowed. "I am afraid that is outside the realms of my expertise, brother."

The Inquisitor inclined his head. "Ah, is that a fact? So you, in fact, were not completely confident that the activities would not be heretical?"

Blanchet frowned, unable to see where he had erred. "I had every confidence in Prelati's expertise. He came highly recommended. Highly recommended."

"Hmmm," the Inquisitor said as the priests words were considered. "And you later took part in these ceremonies to summon demons?"

"Oh, no, sir."

"We have sworn testimony that you were in attendance. Where there is disagreement in testimonies then all parties must be put to the Question." The Inquisitor nodded at the servant who moved to the mechanism of the rack.

Blanchet shook and spoke quickly. "That is, I should have been clear, sir, I should have been clear when I spoke that I was in fact in attendance at one or two of these conjurations but when events turned somewhat heretical, or rather they had a potentially heretical nature, I naturally removed myself from the hall and from the tower immediately and did not return."

For a moment, the only sounds were the scratching of pens on parchment and the shaking, laboured breathing of Dominus Eustache Blanchet. I fancied I could almost hear the sweat running down his face. Was he simply nervous, I wondered, or was he in shaking need of human blood?

"During these conjurations, before you removed yourself of course, did you hear Gilles de Rais call upon Satan?"

The Inquisitor waited.

Blanchet gulped and glanced across the room at me before looking down before speaking in a quiet voice. "Yes."

"What did he say, precisely?"

"It was not when I was in attendance, but I happened to overhear them speak. Prelati and my lord, I should say Milord de Rais. They entered into Prelati's tower together and I fear I followed them at a distance."

"Why did you do such a thing?"

Blanchet's words tumbled from his dry lips. "By this time, I was growing suspicious. Because, you see, I had seen Prelati making his grant experiments at alchemy only the one time when he first arrived. Ever since then it had been all secrets and conjuring and smoke in the night. And so I followed. I heard Prelati call out the words and my lord repeat them."

"What words were these?" The Inquisitor looked up. "Precisely."

Blanchet sobbed momentarily but when the servant reached for the mechanism, he forced the words out. "Come, Satan. And then they said it again, more forcefully. Come, they said. And finally, they said come, Satan, come to our aid."

The Inquisitor was silent for so long that Blanchet lifted his head as far as he was able in order to see what was happening.

"Did you confront them?" the Inquisitor asked.

Blanchet dropped his head back on the rack. "I did not."

"Did you go to the Bishop with this knowledge?"

"I intended to. I got as far as Mortagne, at an inn. But I was afraid, God forgive me. I was afraid if I spoke of what my lord had done then he would kill me. As soon as I left, he sent men to bring me back."

"Oh? The innkeeper, Bouchard-Menard, has sworn in a statement that you stayed with him for seven weeks. Is that not the case?"

"Seven weeks, was it? Yes, that is right. My lord sent Poitou to threaten me. I resisted. Afraid to return and face murder but afraid to go on to Poitiers or elsewhere to swear to what I had told. And they sent Henriet. His threats were terrible. My lord wrote me letters, begging me to return. His words were honey but I knew his intent was poison. I failed in my duty to the Church, to my Bishop and to God, I know that. It was fear. I have sinned and for that I seek forgiveness."

"And yet you returned to the Baron's service. Why?"

Blanchet sobbed once more. "They brought me back. In the night. With a sack over my head. Threw me in the back of a wagon, all trussed up, and they swore they were going to hang me that very night. I begged them not to. Whether they meant only to frighten me or if they had a change of heart, I do not know, but they brought me back to Tiffauges and I knew from then on that I was a prisoner. To leave would have been my death."

"Why were you so certain? Were you told this?"

"It was implied." He gasped. "I knew."

"Because your knowledge of the summoning might have led to excommunication for the Baron? Was that all you knew? All you wished to tell?"

Blanchet banged the back of his head on the rack, his face screwed tight. "I knew also of murders. Murders of children. Oh God. Please forgive me."

"You witnessed murders?"

"No, thank God. But I heard. Over time, I heard from Poitou and from Henriet. At first, they hid it all from me and then over time, over the months and the years, they would tell me things openly. They delighted in my misery and terror at hearing such things spoken. I believed them to be malicious fabrications meant only to terrorise me but slowly I realised it was truth."

"They confessed to murders? What murders did they confess to, brother?"

"I asked where Francis' page had gone. That is, Prelati's page. He brushed me off. But other pages had disappeared also, the nephew of one of the soldiers, and the son of a pastry chef employed at the castle. All around fifteen years old. All quite close together. It was Poitou who turned on me one night, quite drunk, and said that he had killed them all. He and Henriet and my lord Gilles de Rais. They had, forgive me, they had buggered them and murdered them. I was shocked, brothers, shocked, I swear it. Poitou is such a grubby creature, I gave it little enough credence. But then I noticed a number of other rumours."

"What rumours were these?"

"One was that several old women detained in the prisons of my lord the Duke of Brittany, in Nantes, whose names I do not know, led children to Machecoul and Tiffauges, and delivered them to Henriet and Poitou, who killed them."

"Why would they do that?" the Inquisitor asked.

Blood, I answered in my mind.

"I do not know the reason," Blanchet said, closing his eyes.

"You say there were several old women. Are you certain it was not a single old woman and her granddaughter?"

"You speak of course of Perrine Martin, who they call La Meffraye. She is a terror, that is true. I have seen her and her granddaughter bringing back children, little ones. When I was innocent, naive and unsuspecting, I saw nothing untoward in it. Two servants, one old and one young, going to fetch a new boy for the stable or the kitchen. Somehow, I did not notice there were never child servants in the castle. Not one. Those little children all disappeared but I thought that they were servants and so I did not notice. Not for a long time."

"What about the choir boys?" I called out.

The Inquisitor scowled at me but turned back to Blanchet. "Tell me about these choir boys."

Blanchet swallowed furiously before he answered. "Messire de Rais would procure the very best boys from the elite choirs of France and Italy. He paid their parents fortunes if they would send their brilliant boys to Tiffauges. To some he offered grand estates. He was obsessed with creating the greatest choir that ever existed and it seems to me that he did that very thing. But there was none to listen to the choir but us servants and once in a great while the master also."

"Did these boys ever disappear?" the Inquisitor asked. Many of the choir boys had provided sworn statements already and so it was an opportunity perhaps to catch Blanchet in a lie.

"Some left," Blanchet said. "But there always seemed to be good reason. When I think of it now, it seems clear that some of the prettiest ones were taken and... slain. And yet as with the servant children, I did not think much of it until later. May God forgive me, if only I had noticed there were no servant children present."

"No children but one," the Inquisitor said. "Madame Martin's granddaughter."

"Well, they need her to get the others," Blanchet said. "They told me that she forms part of her grandmother's bait, along with the sweet treats and sweeter promises, and so Poitou and Henriet never go near her. Just leave her and La Meffraye to their business. The girl is old enough to be wise and imposing to very small children, and of course she is common as they are. And they trust her when she tells them what her grandmother says is true. She takes their hands and leads them through the castle gates and—"

He broke off, sobbing.

It was quite a remarkable act.

"Thank you for your cooperation, brother," the Inquisitor said, pleasantly. "And now we shall ask these questions again, this time seeking answers from your flesh as well as from your tongue."

***

During the adjournment of the tribunal, Gilles de Rais asked for and was given permission to hear Mass. It was quite extraordinary that he was allowed such a thing but then he was still a powerful noble and had not yet been convicted of anything. Still, it made my skin crawl.

And while the ecclesiastical court was gathering evidence, the civil court met to consider the charges of murder and rebellion in a hall very near to ours. The Inquisition led the examination of the witness on behalf of both courts. And again, Gilles de Rais had declined the offer of counsel for his defence.

It reminded me that Joan of Arc had also decided to reject the offer of counsel in her trial, nine years earlier. It was an extravagant display of the arrogance that both she and Gilles shared. Perhaps it was not arrogance but ostentation. A kind of elaborate, theatrical gesture that was intended to show their contempt of the courts who deigned to try them. In the Marshal's case, it was not so surprising an attitude from one of the most celebrated and the richest men in France. And Joan had considered herself instructed by the agents of God, which is to say that God spoke to her almost directly, choosing her as the vessel for His divine will to be enacted upon the earth. It is difficult to imagine a greater arrogance than that, whether she was lying or mad.

We heard that the old woman, La Meffraye, had been captured attempting to flee, alone, toward Normandy and was then returned to Nantes. I doubted she was gifted with immortality but I intended to speak to her, also, just as soon as I had seen the torture of the servants. They were still looking for the granddaughter, but I doubt anyone was looking very hard. Children, even grown ones like the granddaughter, were subject to obeying the will of their elders and even La Meffraye was not looked upon with any real malice. There was a sense that the old woman was merely obeying her master's commands. Personally, I would still have the evil old witch hanged, and the granddaughter with her, but if they were mortals then it was not really my business.

The evidence was gathered not only from the accused's conspirators and accomplices but by the villagers and other victims. There were the sworn testimonies we had already taken in their scores but the Inquisitors wished to speak directly to a select few, who told their sad stories while the Inquisition scratched down their words.

I was present at the questioning of a distraught Perinne Rondeau of Machecoul.

"We came to Machecoul on account of my husband Clement was looking for work and we heard there was work there," she said, speaking quickly and wiping her nose with a filthy handkerchief after every sentence. "But my husband got sick, terrible sick, which caused us extreme unction and we thought sure he was going to die, thought it for a long time. And it was then when the Master Francis came to see us."

"Master Francis Prelati?" the Inquisitor asked.

"Just so, Milord," Perinne said. "And he came with a priest called Dom Eustache, who both of them asked to lodge in our room upstairs. Well, we had no choice, did we, on account of needing the income from letting it and on account of that we knew they both were in the service of the Marshal, and we can't be saying no to men such as them. It were strange, though, that they both slept in the same room together and also together with their pages, the two men and the two boys all together in the room. Master Francis and Dom Eustache went out often to dinner, back to the castle or elsewhere, as it suited them. It was one day when my husband was so very ill, my tears and crying at his illness was causing him such great distress that I took myself into the chamber upstairs. The pages let me in and they just lay on their pallets and I lay upon the bed, weeping to myself that I was soon to be a widow. When my lodgers returned, they were very irritated to find I had been allowed in and, showering me with the most filthy and vile insults, they did carry me, one by my feet and the other by my shoulders, to the staircase, telling me they was going to throw me down it from the top to the bottom. With this very thing in mind, Francis kicked me in the lower back with terrible force and I would have fallen had not the nurse caught me by my dress and arrested my fall. Together, me and the nurse fled until the men had fallen asleep."

"So, they assaulted you most terribly," the Inquisitor said. "You earlier indicated that you suspected the murder of a child?"

"Just so, Milord. It was soon after when I heard Francis say to Dom Eustache that he had found a beautiful page for him from around Dieppe, about whom Francis said he was extremely delighted. And so it was that a young, very beautiful child, saying he was from the Dieppe region and that he was of a good family, came to stay with Francis. And he stayed there for fifteen days, thereabouts. Then he weren't there any more. I was shocked and asked Francis what had become of the boy and he said that the boy had cheated him royally and that he had taken off with two crowns. I felt very strongly that he was lying, Milord."

"Is that all you have to say?"

"Only that Master Francis and Dom Eustache afterwards went to stay in a different house. I was right relieved they had gone, for no money is worth housing evil under your roof. But they went to stay in a small house in Machecoul, where a man named Perrot Cahu lived until they threw him out, stealing from him the keys to the house. That house, Milord, is far from all the other houses. An isolated place, on an outside street with a well at the entrance and in this small house was where Francis and Eustache lived from then on. And at times, the Lord Gilles de Rais was seen at night going into this place."

"Did you see him with your own eyes?"

"No, Milord, but the village seen him, if you catch my drift."

The Inquisitor called in Jean Labbe the Captain of Arms and requested that he accompany Perinne Rondeau back to the house of which she spoke and to investigate the place.

It was two days later when I heard that they had found physical remains. There were ashes removed from the house of Perrot Cahu, ashes with the bones of children in them, and the small shirt of a bloody child that stank so horribly that Madame Rondeau was violently sick at the sight of it.

The fates of Francois Prelati and Dominus Eustache Blanchet were surely sealed.

Taking supper at the inn, I drank heavily.

"He was lying throughout. They both were. Very carefully, very cleverly, admitting to only so much that they might hope to avoid the rope."

"The bloody vest of the child in their house surely puts paid to that," Stephen said.

"I will take your word for it and I pray that it does. But do you think that was true, what

Blanchet said in his confession?" I asked. "That there were women at the prison bringing children to Gilles?"

Stephen chewed his mutton while pondering it. "Quite possibly. This makes you very concerned?"

"It makes me wonder how many other bloody things we missed. Other men bringing children to the Marshal and the servants. How many of his agents are there out there still? How many of them are revenants that I must slay?"

Stephen smirked. "I doubt he turned a gaggle of old women into revenants, Richard."

"No? How do we know? He might have a whole army of hunchback old nags and filthy little girls out there in the wastes as we speak."

Stephen sniggered and, after resisting, I laughed with him before sitting back and rubbing my eyes.

"You should get some rest, Richard. Tomorrow shall be extremely unpleasant."

In the morning we would hear the depositions of Gilles valets, accomplices and immortals, the servants Henriet Griart and Poitou.

"If I get through the day before murdering both of them it will be a miracle."

1 5

Evil Confessions

October 1440

THE INQUISITION WERE remarkably professional. Even when confronted with men of pure evil, they applied what they considered to be the minimum agony required. As much as I have always enjoyed punishing the wicked and hurting bad people, I would not have done such a fine job. I would certainly have cranked that rack around until limbs were ripped from their sockets.

I was certain when they began their interrogations that the Marshal's two servants were revenants and so I felt like slitting their throats before they had even finished answering the first questions. But it was their statements which would serve to thoroughly convict Gilles de Rais and so I did my duty and resisted. Every urge, I fought down, as much as I shook to still myself.

The skinny young creature was lifted onto the rack and tied in place. He settled down and relaxed as if it was pleasant for him to do so.

When the Inquisitor began the questions, I held my fist over my mouth and listened.

"My name is Etienne Corrillaut but people call me Poitou. I was from Pouzauges. I reckon I'm about twenty-two by now, best as I can make it out. They brought me to Machecoul to be a page for my lord. I served as a page for many a year. Just doing my duty, as always, was good Poitou."

"What duties did you do with regards to murder?" the Inquisitor asked.

"Well, sire, it was me, Sillé, and Henriet what would find and lead children to Gilles de Rais, the accused person in this trial, sire, lead them to his room so we did. Many boys and girls on whom to practice his normal activities, as it were, sire."

"How many children did you personally find and escort to the rooms of your lord?"

"Oh, can't rightly say, sir."

"How many? Was it three? Four? Forty?"

"Oh, yes. Probably forty, sire."

The Inquisitor sighed. "Can you count?"

"Yes, most assuredly I can count. It was forty, sire, thereabouts. Up to forty, I would say."

Everyone in the room knew he was lying but it hardly mattered for the sake of the trial and the Inquisitor continued.

"What did Gilles de Rais do with these children?"

"Well, like I say, sir. He would tell them they was delightful to look at and so on and so forth and he would tell them they had nought to fear and he would say he was going to get them dressed in the finest clothes and take them to meet the King and all sorts. And then he would kill them."

"What method would he use?"

Poitou closed his eyes, a small smile on the corners of his mouth. "Sometimes he would throttle them with his own hand, especially if they was a noisy sort. Sometimes he'd have them suspended by the neck with ropes or cords, on a peg or small hook what he had in his rooms. Then he let them down ofttimes and would say again that he was only having fun with them. But then he would break their necks with a cudgel, slit their throats, or open their bellies, or just straight up remove their heads right away."

The Inquisitor took a sip of wine and a deep breath before continuing. "And did he practice his lascivious lusts upon them?"

"Oh yes, sire, but not usually until they was dead, sire. Or very nearly."

"What was your role in this? Yours and the other servants."

"Me, Henriet, and Sillé, would help hold them down, or string them up, and we'd gather up the blood in jars and cups and burn the bodies in the fire. Roger would join my lord in his debaucheries at times but he often just watched and drank wine. And..." he trailed off, looking left and right. He was hiding something but after what he had said, it was almost inconceivable that it could be anything worse."

"You will now give me specific details. You will provide the names of the victims and approximate times. As many as you can recall."

While Poitou began naming children he had taken, I stood and let myself out of the chamber. I found my hands were shaking. It was all I could do to stop myself from going back in, killing Poitou, then finding Gilles and all his other servants and cutting them into pieces.

But I knew that justice would be done. Each had confessed to mortal crimes. Each would soon face death and though it would be swifter and kinder than they deserved, at least it would be done. And the parents of the children would see proper justice being done under the law and I should not deprive them of that.

After two more hours, Stephen emerged, white as a linen tablecloth and shaking all over.

"Such evil," he muttered into his hot spiced wine. "How could they do it?"

"He is a revenant," I said.

"Are you truly certain?" Stephen asked.

"Did you not see his sickly pallor in there?"

"Some men have such a look," Stephen said. "He has been in prison for days. Surely, without blood he would be in a far worse state. Or likely dead."

"True," I admitted. "But I doubt it. I saw the way he moved that night, leaping further than a mortal man can. Either way, he is not long for the world. And I do not think I shall join you for the deposition of Henriet. It will be much the same as Poitou's, I expect, and enough to see him hanged."

"And so it will be just me in there with the Inquisitors and clerks of the court," Stephen said, running his hands over his face. "Listening to more of that. I cannot take it alone, Richard. At least if you are there, I will know you suffer with me, for a burden shared is a burden halved, is that not the case?"

"Suffer alone you must, for I have other business to attend to."

He peered at me. "What other business?"

"The old woman, La Meffraye. She is here and I will speak with her before she, too, is hanged. She is the one who took Ameline's brother. I will have from her what happened to the boy and then ride to the village. At least I can give Ameline that, if nothing else."

Stephen pursed his lips. "Well, enjoy your visit to your young lady, Richard." He planted his hands on the table and stood. "I am going to spend many hours recording accounts of the worst murders ever committed, given by the fiend himself. Good day."

***

They let me into her cell. It was bitterly cold within, and dim with the only light coming from a slit of a window high above. It reeked of piss and mould and the stench made me angry just to be in its presence.

I held a lantern in my hand and stood over her as she sat on the stool they had provided for her.

"I know you," she said, giggling. "You're the one they was afraid of."

"Are you a madwoman?" I asked her.

She shrugged. "Who's to say who's anything, my lord? Maybe I am mad and maybe it's you what is mad? Who's to say?"

"I will say," I said. "And you certainly sound mad to me. Now, tell me, woman. How were you recruited to undertake this work?"

She grinned up at me with her hideous, wrinkled face, and brushed her filthy grey hair away from her face. The rotten creature had a number of teeth missing and the ones that remained were either yellow or brown. "Recruited, sire?"

"How did you first come into the Baron's service?"

"Oh, I see now, sire. Yes, I see." She crossed her arms over her bosom. "Well, I don't rightly know. Long time ago now, so it was."

"Indeed? Was it before he was calling himself Gilles de Rais?"

She glanced sharply up at me. "What you mean when you say that?"

"Only that the Baron is far older than he appears and has likely posed in many guises this last century or two. Who was he posing as before?"

She looked away. "Don't know what you mean, sire."

"Well then, let me tell you what I mean. It is my sworn duty to slay all men who are like your master the Baron de Rais. All who live on, ageless, staying youthful by drinking blood. All men like him, and all women, also."

The old woman gaped at me. "Right then, well you best be off doing that then." She pointed at the open door behind me. "Go on."

I smiled. "I shall. Once I determine if you are likewise one of them or not."

She gasped. "Me, sire? But I ain't like *them*, sire. Don't tar me with that brush. I am a humble and obedient servant, so help me. Always have been."

"If you do not convince me thoroughly, I am afraid I shall have to gut you here and now."

"All I ever done is follow the commands of my lord. Just a girl, I was, when he first sent me off for him."

"Oh? When was this? What year?"

"Don't know. What year is it now? I was a girl and he was going by the name Jean de Craon. He had these folk pretending to be his family, but they weren't truly. They come and go, some living and others dying. Later on, he sent me to find little boys. Handsome little boys who weren't afraid, is what he wanted. I brought a few but he never seemed happy until there was this one little lad I brought and my lord said he was the one. Charming little fellow, he was. Bright and full of beans and my lord gave him an education. Called him Gilles. Called him his grandson and showed him off while he grew. My lord told folk young Gilles had gone away and he himself hid in his castle, dismissed servants and friends until one day my lord died, almost unnoticed. And this boy Gilles inherited everything. But when he came back home to claim it..."

She broke off, covering her mouth and looking down.

"Go on."

"When the boy Gilles come back I saw at once it was in fact my lord Jean de Craon. Somehow, it was him, unaged and same as he ever was but pretending to be named Gilles. And he sent me to work, luring in the boys and sometimes the girls. I was told that the children could be boys or girls but that for preference they should have fair hair and be clean-limbed. The Sire de Rais liked best for children to be between eight and twelve years old but there were a few that was younger and some that were older. Youngest one I found was about seven, and his brother was fifteen, he came along with me, too. And that's all there is to it. I ain't one of them. Not me, my lord. I'm a loyal servant, that's what I am and nothing more, so help me."

"What of your own family?"

"What family?"

"Have you not had children of your own?"

"Oh. A few. They ain't got nothing to do with it, you leave them out of it, do you hear?"

"So they are yet living?"

She wrinkled her nose. "I ain't offered one of my own up to him, for God's sake. How could you say such a thing, sire?"

"No, quite right, that would be monstrous. But you were complicit in scores of murders. Hundreds, perhaps. And so you will soon die by hanging on the orders of the court."

She screwed up her face. "Only following what my lord ordered me to do. All I am is a humble servant. Most humble."

"Tell me, do you remember a child named Jamet Mousillon? The son of a physician?"

She wrinkled her nose. "Why you want to know about him? Why is he special?"

"What happened to him? I am sure he was killed eventually but how did you take him?"

"So many boys. Can't recall them all."

"No? And yet I recall that you worked often with your granddaughter. A girl old enough to be charged with the same crimes as you and yet so far she has evaded justice. An oversight that I can easily put right."

"No!" She scurried forward. "No, sire. Not her. You stay away from her. My family must be safe. My dear girls, my dear boys. You'll not go near her if you know what's good for you. Hear me, do you?"

"I am not sure I do. Why should I not seek justice? Perhaps it was your granddaughter who enticed away young Jamet from his village?"

Her face drained of colour. "No, no. It was me. It was all my doing, I swear it."

"Tell it, then. How did you get a learned young boy to obey you? What magic did you employ?"

"No magic. It was a simple enough thing. Simple as any. He was on his lonesome, tossing stones into the pond. The little ones just want the attention of a kindly person. I asked him all about himself, usual questions, and they love to tell it all. All about themselves and what's on their minds and the battles they been fighting with one child or another or with their mother or father. Don't recall what he said in this instance. I asked him if he would like some sugar cakes and he said yes and off we went."

"Why on earth would he follow you all the way back to the castle?"

"Don't know why they do it, truth be told? Ain't got no fear in them. Even when they been told to watch out for me, to watch out for La Meffraye, they just come along. Hop straight into my hand like a little bird what never seen man before. Innocent little lambs they are with no notion of danger. Can't imagine the evil, sire. Ain't in them. Then I gives him by the hand to Poitou and he leads the lad away into my lord's chambers. And that be that."

"Dear God Almighty. Your heartlessness is overwhelming. At least there is some comfort in knowing that you will hang for the evil that is in you."

She let out a juddering sigh. "As long as my family goes on, I can die satisfied I did my duty."

I was appalled by her hypocrisy at the time but later I realised she was behaving naturally. We all chose our own offspring, our own family, over the rest of the world. If we do not do so, in fact, it is we who are acting against nature. And to act against nature is to sin.

Overcome by her witless evil, I suddenly wanted to be done with it. All the endless questioning and feet dragging. The absurd denials by Gilles de Rais, or whatever his true name was, were simply drawing out the farcical trial. All the Dominicans from the Inquisition, all the bishops and the lawyers, all poking away to uncover a truth they would never find or not comprehend if they did. And, I was realising, I would never know it myself. None of his followers knew enough to fill in the gaps.

Returning to the chamber, I found Stephen sitting on a stone bench with his head in his hands.

"Is the Inquisition done with Henriet Griart?"

Speaking from within the shield of his own hands, Stephen groaned. "I am done with being a lawyer."

"Good," I said, sitting beside him and clapping a hand on his back. "It is a calling for scoundrels and knaves. Though I must say, you seemed quite suited to it."

He laughed a little and sat up. "The things they did, Richard. I shall have to live now for the rest of my life knowing that men are capable of such things. And if men can act in such a way, what then can it be like in the bottom level of Hell?"

"You will never know. But those men will. And their master, too. Listen, Stephen. Get me into his quarters. Tonight."

"Who? De Rais? You mean to kill him? After all this?"

"No, no," I said, though I half expected that I would. "Soon, after all these statements are read to the court, he will be sentenced and executed. And I will never know where he came from. What my brother told him."

And I will never know about her. Was she one of us? Was she a military genius who outwitted me on the battlefields of Orléans and Patay? Or was she just another poor victim of this monster?

"I shall have to use every favour I have yet to call in," Stephen said. "He is well guarded and I may be rebuffed."

"You must overcome their doubts. Tell them that you are prosecuting the crimes on behalf of the common people, who are too weak to do it themselves."

He glanced at me with a dark look in his eye. "You continue to sneer at the common people as if you were not one of them yourself."

"What do you mean by such a remark?"

"Nothing, sir. I am tired, that is all."

"You say I am a commoner myself?" I pondered it for a moment. "I take it you say so because my natural father Earl de Ferrers was in fact a bastard son of Priskos? No, you are right, that is a fair observation. And yet my mother was nobly born, to a proper English lineage. And one might say, considering that Priskos spawned such men as Alexander and Caesar, that my blood is as noble as it comes."

"All I mean, Richard, is that your blood might be noble but you are one no longer. A nobleman lives as one, holding land for his lord, and is recognised as one by commoner and by his peers and his king. But you spend all your time amongst commoners, all men see you as one, and your king does not know you. As far as the law is concerned, you are a commoner."

"I do not know about that," I said. "But I suppose you are right enough." Even as I said it, I knew it was not the whole truth. The law applies to all men but it was never written with a man such as me in mind. Perhaps I was a lord no longer but I could not see myself as a commoner either. I was a knight in my heart but an immortal in my blood and what that made me as a whole, I did not know. "But I must speak with Gilles de Rais tonight. You can make it happen, I know you can."

"If we are discovered, it could end badly."

"Stephen, if it goes badly, I shall simply have to kill them all and we will have to escape before they catch us."

He sighed. "Hardly the virtuous path."

"We have done such sinful and illegal things before, have we not? At the least, I know I have done and will gladly do so again, if need be. Come, now. Take me to Gilles de Rais."

Gilles de Rais had been in command of the forces that crushed us at the climax of the Loire campaign eleven years earlier and on my way to speak to him, face to face, I could not get that final battle from my mind.

16

The Battle of Patay

June 1429

AFTER WE ABANDONED the Siege of Orléans on 8 May 1429, our armies withdrew to our nearby garrisons all along the Loire. We were split into smaller groups and companies and distributed fairly in this fortress or that. I was commanded to join the garrison at Meung-sur-Loire, not much more than ten miles away from Orléans, downriver to the southwest.

It had been an enormous setback, there was no doubt about that. But equally, it was not an unrecoverable military disaster. We still had thousands of superbly equipped and supplied veteran soldiers holding well-fortified positions in towns that were large enough to support us on both sides of Orléans up and down the river.

Still, there was something indefinable in the air. A vague sense of disquiet over and above that which might be expected from such a setback.

"Bunch of whiners," Walt said about our fellow garrison troops, who grumbled about being defeated weeks before.

"Ain't used to defeat, are we," Rob said. "They'll get over it and then we'll charge back in and finish them off. Right, Richard?"

I did not answer, because I was as disquieted as anyone. Though, I did not make my feelings known and as much as I could, I kept my concerns to myself and instead focused my attention on the defences and getting to know the men that I found myself garrisoned with.

They were good men. About five hundred had been in the forts around Orléans and the other eight hundred had been established there before our evacuation. Our defences at Meung-sur-Loire consisted of three components. The walled town, the fortification guarding the bridge over the Loire, and a large walled castle just outside of the town. The castle was small but well-made and served as the headquarters for our commander the Earl of Shrewsbury John Talbot. I did my best to keep out of his way.

We bedded in and waited for our reinforcements to arrive. Word had been sent that Sir John Fastolf was on his way from Paris with a reinforcing army of several thousand, headed for the Loire River valley.

Once they arrived, we might actually attack the French again or perhaps we would continue to wait for them to come and attack us. A surprising number of our soldiers did not believe that the French would follow up on their victory, for they had conducted only defensive campaigns for decades and as the days turned to weeks, it seemed ever more likely that they were right. The French forces held at Orléans, as if they had no idea what to do next.

As the atmosphere of indecision settled over us, I increasingly wondered why I was there at all. I was doing nothing at all for the English cause in France, and I was certainly not acting to further the aims of the Order.

"We can't leave, Richard," Rob said beside me from the top of the walls of the town, where I had raised the question with my men. "Can't leave our friends to their fate."

"Can't we?" Walt asked. "What good we doing sitting here on our arses?"

It had been a month since fleeing Orléans and we wondered if we would pass the whole summer without fighting again. Many soldiers are happy with avoiding battle. But not me and not my men.

"You are right," I admitted. "I should have made myself a lord. Going about in war as a commoner is no use at all. It seems that no lord these days cares one whit whether a man has ability if he is not a gentleman of some description. It was foolish of me to think that my inherent nobility, and my knightly qualities, would shine through and overcome the limitations of my apparent station. If I was a lord in this moment then I could do something about all of this but instead my presence simply angers them."

"When you made us knights," Rob said, "we knew we would rarely be recognised as such. But you told us that we would be knights in our hearts and so we have been from that day to this. And you have fought, as we have, for free companies and captains, from Athens to Avila, and never were we regarded by our companions as knights or nobles but we knew in our hearts that we must act with knightly virtue in all things. And so we did, come what may."

"Yes, yes," I said. "And so we will continue to do. But this is different. Our companions are Englishmen, fighting for the King of England. And even if he is a useless boy and his lords are witless cowards, they are the lords of England. I had expected that they would respond to my suggestions more favourably rather than to dismiss me as a useless commoner."

"Talbot hates your guts, alright," Walt said, grinning.

"Fastolf and all," Rob added. "When he gets back here, you'll be getting it in both ears."

"I do already from you two damned jesters."

Walt shook his head. "Perhaps if, instead of making yourself a lord, you should have pretended to be an obedient soldier, Richard."

"Aye," Rob said. "That's what makes the lords angry. Choose one or the other. You can't be both."

"Yes, yes, very amusing, I am sure."

"True though, ain't it," Walt said.

In the distance, a group of horsemen rode hard toward the town. Dust kicked up behind them and even from so far away I could see that their horses were struggling and the men were agitated.

"That our men?" Walt asked, squinting.

Rob nodded. "They were watching Orléans. Look at the state of them. Must have been galloping all the way."

"Only one reason to ride like that," Walt observed.

"Yes," I said. "The French are coming."

The French army came up quickly and in great numbers. We had been expecting a siege of the town and castle but instead they threw all their numbers at the fortified bridge over the Loire and took it by storm inside of a single day.

Joan of Arc controlled a force that included captains Jean d'Orléans, Gilles de Rais, Jean Poton de Xaintrailles, and La Hire. The French had five thousand soldiers. Bypassing the city and the castle, they staged a frontal assault on the bridge fortifications, conquered it in one day, and installed a garrison. Immediately they had cut off our ability to move south of the Loire.

Still, we expected that they would invest Meung-sur-Loire but instead they marched on without attacking town or castle and turned to march to Beaugency just five miles away downriver and put it under siege.

At the same time, another French army assaulted and defeated our garrison at Jargeau on the other side of Orléans which was commanded by Suffolk, William de la Pole. Their defences were good and there were seven hundred men under his command. Somehow, the French simply overwhelmed them and there was another fortress lost. We suffered heavy losses and Suffolk was captured.

Unlike Meung-sur-Loire, the main stronghold at Beaugency was inside the city walls, forming an imposing rectangular citadel. By the time the French had assaulted the walls a couple of times, our soldiers abandoned the town and retreated into the castle. The French brought up their cannons and bombarded the castle with artillery fire. That evening, with the cannons still firing at the walls and towers of the castle, the French received more reinforcements from the east.

Hearing news of an English relief force approaching from Paris under Sir John Fastolf, d'Alençon negotiated the English surrender and granted them safe conduct out of Beaugency.

Our long-awaited reinforcement army under Sir John Fastolf, which had set off from Paris following the defeat at Orléans, now joined forces with survivors of the besieging army under Lord Talbot and Lord Scales at Meung-sur-Loire.

"We must launch an assault on the French now, my lords. We must."

"Why do you insist on speaking when we care nothing for your opinions?"

"If we do not stop this wave of assaults now then we will not do so at all. They will roll over us all the way to Paris."

"Do not be absurd, man," Fastolf snapped. "We cannot risk a pitched battle against a foe who so outnumbers us."

"Why not?" I said. "Overall numbers matter only in the minds of the soldiers. What is important is how many soldiers we can bring to bear at any one time."

"We must retreat back to Paris," Fastolf said.

"No, we cannot abandon the remaining garrisons to their fate," Talbot argued. I thought that he was coming around to my way of thinking but that was too much to hope. "We must find another town to take and hold. If we can encourage the French to besiege us, we can split their forces and assault them in turn, perhaps in spring next year."

"That is madness," I said. "We would then be crushed in turn."

"You are not part of this conference and you will now leave."

There was nothing left to do but follow Fastolf's plan to retreat towards Paris.

Our forces were in constant contact and so when we marched away northward, the French set off immediately after us.

We were in the lead and had half a day on them, so it should have been a simple thing to outmarch the enemy. We had done so many times before. Yet again, though, it was down to a matter of will. Ours was perhaps not broken but it was subdued. Even though we knew the enemy was after us, it seemed that the men trudged in weary defeat rather than raced away for the sake of their lives. We had not gone fifteen miles when they caught up with us near to the village of Patay.

That little village was one I knew well enough, for it was just a day's ride north from Orléans and our patrols had gone around it and through it a dozen times.

"That city is cursed," Walt said, spitting, as the enemy horsemen massed through trees and hedgerows to the south. "Why can we not win when we are near it?"

"Not the city, is it," Rob said, stringing his bow. "It's the witch."

"Can it be true?" Walt asked. "Is she using magic?"

I thought she probably was.

"No," I said. "Her presence has put the wind up them, that is all. It will take one sharp defeat for the French to return to their craven ways, mark my words."

"Form up," came the orders relayed from Fastolf.

In this battle, we employed the same methods we used in the victories at Crécy in 1346 and Agincourt in 1415, deploying an army composed predominantly of longbowmen behind a barrier of sharpened stakes driven into the ground to obstruct any attack by cavalry.

This time, however, it would not go so well.

"The French are coming. They be right on our heels, sir." Rob said. "We won't make it to a better position."

"Where is Talbot?" I asked the fleeing archers around me. "Where are the lords?"

"Ahead," they said. "Far up ahead. Not here."

"Got to do something, sir," Walt said. "Look, there. Riders gathering."

"Listen to me," I shouted. "Pass the word. Fill the trees by the road and prepare to ambush the enemy as they pass. They will not charge us in the trees. Pass the word."

Wonderful men, they were. Proper soldiers. The senior men chivvied the new lads and together they took positions along three hundred yards at the edge of the woodland and made ready for the mounted men-at-arms to approach along the road below. They were tense. We all were. But we had plenty of arrows and stood a good chance of driving the enemy vanguard away with heavy casualties and by then our own soldiers would hopefully return and deter the rest of the French army.

Talbot and his knights rode back toward us. They were just a score but dozens more came behind him.

"Thank God," Rob muttered.

"About bloody time," Walt said.

When Talbot approached, he began issuing commands all along the line and our archers began trudging down the hill toward the road.

"What in the hell are you doing?" I shouted, riding toward him.

"We must block the road," Talbot called, irritated by my question and yet answering all the same and indicating the position with his sword. "Archers to redeploy. Five hundred of them will hold the road with the remaining men to shoot from the flank."

"There is no time," I said. "The French are there. You can see them, my lord, with your own eyes."

"A handful of scouts, nothing more. There is time." He turned from me and took position on the road, as did his knights and the other mounted men until there were perhaps three hundred of them.

It was then that I realised just how mad I had been in making war as a commoner, without any significant official position. It was true that every decade it became more difficult to buy my way into the nobility and yet I could have done it, had Stephen and Eva prepared my lineages properly beforehand. And yet in my arrogance I had thought my natural leadership qualities would overcome all social distinction during battle. Men would follow me, that had proved true enough, but lords would not step aside for me. How could I have been so utterly foolish? The coming disaster was Talbot's making but it was mine also.

Mine even more so, for I should have known better.

"Where's the rest of the bloody army?" Walt cried. "What are they doing?"

"They are coming back, there, do you see? Banners and pennants above the hedgerow, coming this way."

"Make ready!" the cry went up all along the line and my heart sank.

French men-at-arms appeared in their dozens and formed up, until they were hundreds.

Joan the Maiden was at the rear, her great white banner with the fleur-de-lys and the angels held aloft like a beacon, drawing in ever more French warriors, desperate to fight for the Maiden of Orléans and so for God. I understood then why the French were so revitalised. What it was that had possessed them. It was not simply courage and a new belief that they could win against us, finally. Joan had filled the French with the zeal of a holy war and they were become weapons of God to drive out the heretical English invader once and for all. Our presence upon French soil was sacrilege that would be cleansed only with our blood.

Our archers were halfway down the hill and spread out in no formation at all and almost none had planted their stakes in the ground to deter attack.

It took just a few moments for the hundreds of French to become a thousand and then so many that I lost count. Among them, I recalled later when it had meaning for me, was the black and gold banner of Gilles de Rais. Indeed, it was he who was commanding the forces of the vanguard and urging them on with great passion.

I could see what was going to happen. We all could.

"Shoot!" I called to the archers. "Get arrows into them. Shoot, now."

It was a mad hope perhaps but I thought we could scare them away by showing we were waiting in the woods, coming out of the trees to shoot at them. But the French knights saw English archers scattered and unprepared and nothing was going to turn them from such a thing. It was the kind of thing a mounted soldier lived for. Something dreamed about but hardly realised.

They came at us in a great mass of horse and steel, with lances and axes and swords. Our archers shot what arrows they could but they were so many that they ran right over the scattered archers, cutting them down with such ease. I saw Old Simon amongst them, raging even as they hacked him to pieces. Around me, the archers cried out in anger at the sight of their brothers down on the road being so destroyed but still they turned and filed away through the trees.

"Stop, wait. Keep shooting!" I shouted. Walt and Rob attempted to stop them but they knew the battle was lost, even before I did.

"Fastolf has come," Rob said, pointing with his bow down to the road. "A counter charge could hold them."

When Fastolf and his mass of knights instead turned and fled, it was as though I saw England dying. Where were the great men of the past who would have ridden to their deaths? For glory, even if nothing else?

"All is lost, Richard," Rob said.

"There must be something..." I muttered.

"It's over, sir," Walt cried. "It's over."

Before I pulled back through the trees with the archers, I saw Talbot and his knights riding hard, northward. Away from the battle. Away from the dying archers Talbot had sent to their deaths with his idiotic command. Talbot rode on by the rest of our army, who were spread out along the road coming to relieve archers who had already fallen, and Fastolf rode with him, escaping with their lives but leaving their honour trampled in the dirt.

The French vanguard slaughtered our archers and continued on until they smashed into our main force who were not deployed. It was not two armies fighting but knights against men. It was not battle but murder and Englishmen died in their thousands as we fled from the slaughter and were picked off one by one.

Out of our army of five thousand, we lost more than two thousand that day. Most of them were our archers. The French lost almost no one.

Fastolf escaped all the way back to Paris but Talbot was captured. Talbot actually had the gall to accuse Fastolf of deserting his comrades in the face of the enemy, a charge which he pursued vigorously once he had negotiated his release from French captivity. Fastolf hotly denied the charge and was eventually cleared of the charge by a special chapter of the Order of the Garter but everyone knew the truth. Every soldier of England. His name will forever be tainted, as rightly it should. Talbot, though deserves as much blame as anyone. But so do I. It was in my power to make myself a lord and so lead an army to victory but instead I was playing at being a soldier and it cost those brave men their lives and ultimately it cost England the throne of France.

The destruction of our army and the loss of veteran commanders had immediate and terrible consequences for our strategic and political position in France. It was a loss from which we would never recover. We were disorganised and frightened and over the following weeks the French swiftly regained swathes of territory to the south, east and north of Paris, filled with an energy that they had not possessed for a hundred years.

The French marched to Reims and there the Dauphin was crowned as King Charles VII of France on 17 July.

We knew the country so well and had been routiers and bandits for long that we slipped through the worst of it and smashed through the rest, until we made it back to Paris. We brought thirty-four archers with us, as well as a few pages and servants. It was a measly number and half of what we started with but those men were forever grateful to me for getting them home. So grateful that they stuck with us when we set out to fight the enemy once more. This time, I was determined to defeat the one who was responsible for the disaster.

I swore that I would find and kill Joan the Maiden.

17

Gilles' Confession
October 1440

STEPHEN ARRANGED IT so that I was let into Gilles' chambers in the dark of the night. We were able to lean on enough people to gain access but it was far from officially sanctioned and Stephen kept watch from the other side of the chamber door while I went in. He seemed convinced that we would be discovered and rousted out at any moment.

"Are you going to kill him?" Stephen had asked a dozen times on the way to his quarters.

"No, no, certainly not," I said. "Most probably."

Stephen grabbed my arm. "We shall have to flee immediately if you do."

"I will restrain myself." After I spoke, I pulled away my arm away.

"Why do this at all, then? Merely to satisfy your curiosity? You risk spoiling the entire trial."

What could I say? That I wished to face the man who had defeated us on the battlefield? That I also needed to understand what had turned him into the monster that he was and whether such a degeneration was something that might lie in store for me or for my men?

"I simply must, that is all. I must."

When I closed the door behind me and stepped within, I was still not certain if I would do the deed. A murdered Gilles would leave the bereaved families without the sense that justice had been done. There would be many who would say he had been innocent of the charges and where would that leave the people? I would have to kill Poitou and Henriet, also, although I was dearly looking forward to that.

But I was so curious. I wanted to speak to him and find out *why*. To find out what he knew of William.

Perhaps these were excuses I told myself while yet knowing deep down that I was there to cut out his heart and feed it to him.

He stood across the other side of the room, watching me enter. An imposing figure in his own hall and in the courtroom, seeing him standing close made his stature and bearing even more impressive. Broad at the shoulder, tall, and slim, he looked like a man of immense strength and also gracefulness. Dressed in black velvet with silver embroidery, he looked like a starry night or a pot of black ink spilled across a desk reflecting candlelight. His hair was as black as the midnight outside the window.

"So," he said, holding his palms out by his side. "You have come at last." His voice was level and self-assured.

"How do you know me?" I asked him.

He raised one eyebrow and peered at my face. "Do you not know *me*, sir?" he replied. "You do not recognise me?"

"Certainly, I do. But I do not know from where. Or from when. Was it long ago?"

His shoulders slumped. "Long enough. As for where, why, it was here."

"Nantes?"

He seemed disappointed. "I suppose you have lived so long and done so much that it was an event of little significance to you. But it was near Tiffauges, a little less than a hundred years ago. Even then, I was the lord of Tiffauges, having taken it from another. But the castle was smaller then, and the lands about a little different. There is a hill, now bare and wind blasted and cropped close by the sheep but once the place was covered by a woodland. It was there where you ambushed me and my men. I called myself Charles de Coussey. You were looking for a knight who fought under a black banner. One of us."

"By God, I think I do recall it. I lost most of my company." That was the battle where Rob had been almost killed before I turned him and the other survivors into immortals.

"I very nearly defeated you," he said, smiling. "Though, you killed my horse and put your heel through my face. I had never known strength like yours and it terrified me, certain that all my efforts were to be undone. But I played the mortal and told you what you wanted to know about and you ransomed me back to my men, thank God. I knew at once who you were. You are my lord's evil brother, who he had warned me about so many years before."

"Your lord? Your lord is William," I said. "He told you that I was evil?" I scoffed at the audacity of it. "And William turned you into an immortal and he commanded you to become powerful and rich and to wait for his return?"

"Just so," he said. "I was nothing when he found me, nothing. Not even a knight. My father was a carpenter, though I always liked to fight and I knew I would be a soldier one day. And then my lord found me and raised me up."

"Well, I must say that you have done well to raise yourself up. Another generation or two and you might have made yourself into a duke and one day even a king."

His lip trembled. "It was a long road from my beginnings to here."

"My brother chose you well, that much is clear. You have done remarkably well and to have done it alone, without others like you to help you. But then you went mad. You began murdering children, and delighting in their deaths, and practising perversions upon them."

He took a shaky breath. "Yes."

"Why?" I asked him. "Why have you done this?"

"You ask why?" he said. "My lord promised to return but it has been two hundred years! He has abandoned us, sir. It is clear that he meant never to return. And so what was I to do with my wealth? With my power? I was ready ten years ago, twenty. But now I know that it will never be. All that effort wasted. All the deaths, for nothing."

"But why the children, man?"

He shrugged. "Surely, you know the power in the blood of a child? It is powerful and pure. It gives us great strength, greater than a grown man can give. You have felt it."

"I have not felt it, nor will I ever."

"You pretend to some great morality? You, who are the incarnation of evil, like my master, your brother? Surely, you know that you are no different to me. How many have you murdered in your life? Hundreds? Thousands? There is no greater killer in all the days since Adam was thrown from the Garden than you, sir, and you look down on me for taking the lives of a few worthless peasant children?"

"Your evil will soon be ended. The lords of this land have finally done their duty to end you, and so they will."

He tilted his head, a small frown on his face. "The lords of this land are doing their duty? But, what on earth do you mean, sir?"

I scoffed. "The Bishop of Nantes has pushed for this investigation. And the Duke of Brittany also. The people could do nothing and that was what you counted on in order to carry out such an evil campaign of horror but your betters have done their duty."

Gilles' smile grew until he laughed. "You are more ancient and more powerful than I will ever be and yet you have a strange innocence about you. A guilelessness like that of a child... no, not quite. Not in all things. Only where lords and princes are concerned. It is a failing one sees in men cursed by noble birth such as yourself where you believe that the nobility are at their heart good and decent and virtuous yet the common man is base and petty and sinful. Well, let me tell you that I have been both commoner and noble and I see that there is no difference between the two."

"Utter nonsense," I said. "You are quite mad."

"Why, then, has our Duke acted to stage this trial now, sir? Why has his cousin the Bishop of Nantes acted on his behalf now?"

"Because I gathered the necessary evidence," I said, feeling uncertain.

"Indeed? And this could not have been done in the years gone by?"

"Why then?" I said, sharply.

"I am the vassal of Duke Jean of Brittany. And if I should be convicted of a capital crime, why, all my earthly property will become his. All of my castles, manors, my mills, villages, my libraries, and all my possessions. You should have no doubt that his first cousin and dear friend the Bishop will receive a considerable fraction of the total."

"You ascribe base motivations to those who are doing no more than their duty," I said. "You speak as though you are an innocent man being persecuted instead of a monster being dealt justice. I had hoped that there would be some secret to be revealed but now I see that you are nothing. For all your achievements, for all the wealth and power you hoarded, you are an empty vessel and when you are gone nothing will be different except that the children of these lands will be safe, finally."

He snorted. "You are nothing like your brother. He was wise beyond measure and learned in the arts and poetry and history and in the faith. A demon in human form and evil to his core, yes, but he was wise as God Himself. Yet you know nothing at all. You think these children will be safe, now, when I am gone? What world is it that you are from, sir? Do you believe that we live in Heaven already or do you understand that the earth we walk upon is already Hell itself?"

"You speak so lightly of Hell but soon you will go there. Perhaps you will meet that poor girl you sent there by your actions, the poor mad girl Joan of Lorraine, who you used for your earthly gain only to abandon and then see sent to the eternal flames when she burned at the stake."

He whipped around, eyes bulging, and he roared in my face. "Do not speak of her!"

Every inch of him shook as he stood with his fists raised. He was undoubtedly strong after so many years drinking vast amounts of blood every day and perhaps he was even stronger than I was. Still, he resisted attacking me and I resisted striking him.

Letting out a growl, he turned back and stalked away with his fists clenched at his sides.

"I will speak of what I like," I said, though I said it softly. "And I may even have you tortured so that you would speak the truth to me about her."

That brought him about again with fear in his eyes. Fear of the pain? Or of something else? The pain was enough, God knows.

"I will not have her good name sullied by doubters such as you."

"Her good name?" I said, incredulous. "She was burned as a heretic, sir, and she has no good name."

It seemed for a long moment that he was going to assault me after all but something passed behind his eyes and a forced casualness descended over him. "Even you must know her trial was a nonsense. An assassination by legal means."

"Must I? What about it was a nonsense?"

"Everything about it, from start to finish. It was theatre, played to convince the masses that her brilliance was not only over but that it had always been false. I am astonished that you lack the wit to see that."

"Why do you not convince me?"

He shrugged, suddenly affecting a lack of interest and turning away. "I have no need to convince you. Believe what you will, it is no concern of mine. Let us speak of it no longer."

"I know all about what happened," I said. Although I was guessing, I could not imagine it any other way. "What truly happened with you and Joan."

"Oh?" he said, warily, half turning and pausing where he stood.

"You discovered her, did you not? Knowing of the prophecy about a maiden from Lorraine who would save the kingdom of France, you found a girl who would act the part. You engineered the theatrics of her appearance. And then, when you were done with her, you cast her aside and she burned for it."

He turned slowly and gazed at me, his eyes narrowing twinkling dark in reflected lamplight. Then he snorted. "Yes, yes," he said. "That is it. How insightful you are."

His manner was profoundly irritating. Childish, almost. It was enough to make me want to throttle him. "Tell me the truth, then."

He wafted a hand in the air. "The truth? You would not believe it."

"Do you not understand that you will face the Inquisition, Gilles? Whatever you are doing with your attempts at delay, they have failed. The King is not coming to save you. We have had word from the King's agents. You are abandoned. There will be no reprieve. All that remains is to have you put to the Question and there we will get the truth of your crimes from you."

His face took on the aspect of true despair, then. It seemed he had been hoping that the King would come.

"So be it," he managed to say.

"I will ensure they ask you about Joan of Lorraine," I said. "Everything about the Maiden. Where you found her, how you educated and trained her. It will be entered into the court documents and all France will know she was a fraud."

He sagged further and collapsed down into a chair by the window, hanging his head. "That is not it at all."

"Well, we will see," I replied. "I for one will delight in hearing your manipulations. You say that her trial was theatre to convince the masses that she had always been false but there are many in France who still believe in her. In her divine mission. One might say it yet moves the hearts of the common soldiery so that they fight with her inspiration stirring their hearts. But the Inquisition will pull the truth from your flesh and you will tell how you turned a young girl into a blood drinking demon and manipulated her into doing your bidding. Into deceiving even the King. Do you think France will still be inspired by her after the masses hear your words? Do you think the King will remember you well? Yes, I shall enjoy the sight of your tortures very much indeed, sir."

He gaped at me as I spoke and when he did not respond, I turned and strode away from him to lift the latch and so leave him to his fate.

"Wait!" he cried. "Wait. I will confess."

I turned from the door. "Come again?"

396

His face was white. "Call the Inquisitor. Call him now. I will confess my crimes now, this very night. The illusion has gone on as long as it needs to. I will tell it all."

"All?" I asked. "You will tell them that you are over two hundred years old and a drinker of blood? You will tell them of William?"

"Oh?" he said, a sly look creeping onto his face. "The whole truth concerns you, does it, Richard? You will be undone if I do, is that it? Perhaps I *will* tell them everything, not only about my own crimes but about yours as well."

"Feel free to do so. It will serve only to condemn you to die as a madman as well as a murderer."

He sagged again. "Yes, yes. What you say is true. And so I mean only that I will confess my crimes with the poor children. Then they will hang me." His voice shook as he spoke. "They will hang me and then, praise God, it will be done."

"You will hang," I said. "And you will burn."

He nodded, though he hid his face with his hands as he did so.

"Stephen," I said through the door. "Can you hear this?"

From the other side of the oak timbers, he replied without delay. "I will bring the Inquisitor at once," Stephen said.

While we waited, I observed Gilles de Rais, slumped in his chair. He seemed defeated but whether it was an act, a play performed only for me, I could not say. I recalled then the grand play he had put on in Orléans, an event so lavish that it had almost ruined the richest man in the kingdom. He had been playing the parts of so many men for so many years that surely deceit came easily to him. It certainly came increasingly easily to me and I had suffered and continued to suffer the consequences of it. All I could hold on to was that I was, by birth and by heart, an English knight. With that core knowledge of who I was, I could weather the storms of self-doubt and look to sustain the moral framework that such knowledge provided.

But Gilles was nobody. The son of a carpenter, he had said, who had likely gone off to war and done well. Perhaps he was destined to be a man-at-arms, for a lord or as a mercenary or as a roadside robber. But then he had become immortal, required to drink blood, and had been given a quest by a powerful immortal to grow rich and powerful and he had done it. To get there, however, he had been one man after another. Whatever his birth name had been, he had become Charles de Coussey, a *routier* knight. Later, he had made himself into a noble, and become Jean de Craon, a famed brute but a lordly one. And finally, he had become Gilles de Rais, a famed soldier, companion of Joan the Maiden, become a Marshal of France. Who was he, really? Was he any of them? Which one of those men was sitting before me in that luxurious prison in Nantes? Did he even know himself?

"You need blood," I said, drawing his attention. "You need blood every day or two. Every three at the most, or else you will grow sick and lose your wits."

He eyed me warily. "Yes. But I am strong. From all the blood I have taken."

"Someone has been feeding you blood," I said.

He scoffed. "No."

"Who is helping you?" I asked, considering that his vast wealth would open many doors and perhaps even veins. "You have bought off servants, even here?" He clamped his mouth shut and turned away. "I suppose it hardly matters. Of course you have paid men to care for you. You have spent many lifetimes accumulating riches but you have never been shy about spending it to achieve your aims. You made and spent a fortune as if it were nothing to you. Are you being honest about your low birth? Or are you a nobleman after all?"

"I have no need to convince you of anything further," he said, and yet he continued. "I was born as low as can be. My father was not even competent as a carpenter. He could barely construct a coherent sentence, let alone build well or make wealth. If he had seen me as I was to become, he would have bowed and scraped low, like the miserable fool he was. I am to him as an angel might be to a mortal. The worlds I have seen would be so far beyond his comprehension that he would be forever blind to them and yet look what I became. It was difficult, at first, painful even. Learning to read and to write but there was some indefinable magic to it all that drove me on, some deep fascinating at the wisdom that might be contained in those black scribblings upon the page. In time, I found such a great love of literature in Latin and in Greek. By God, how I have loved the Lives of the Caesars by Suetonius. Do you know it, sir?"

It sounded familiar, but I could not bring myself to admit my ignorance to such a monster. "I cannot say that literature has touched me as deeply as it has you."

"Ah, such a magnificent work. Do you know, he describes the third emperor, who was Tiberius, as a man who enjoyed the secret practice of abominable lewdness? At his secluded palace, he entertained companies of young girls and catamites and assembled from all across his lands inventors of unnatural copulations, who defiled one another in his presence to inflame his ardour. He had several special chambers set round with pictures and statues in the most lascivious attitudes, contrived recesses in his groves for the gratification of lust, where young persons of both sexes prostituted themselves in caves and hollow rocks, in the disguise of little Pans and Nymphs before he himself—"

"Enough of your damned perversions!" I snapped. "Your professed love of literature is revealed as nothing more than your love of depravity. Not finding enough of it in Christian lands, you found it in the wicked texts of pagan kings and sought to fulfil it in life. It is all very clear, sir. Now, hold your damned tongue until the lords of the court come to hear your confession."

Gilles curled his lip in disgust and could not control himself enough to cease his crowing. "The subject may be depraved but the quality of the literature is itself inspiring. You would not understand. My lord said your soul was a small and shrivelled thing and I see that it is so."

"My soul is not perfect but yours has led you into a miserable existence, scurrying from murder to murder in the dark."

"Are you certain that you do not speak of yourself, sir?" His lip curled as he regarded me. "I made myself the most celebrated man in France. I wrote poetry and plays. I won the war for France, did I not?"

"And yet here you are. Soon to be hanged. A wasted life, is it not? You failed my brother."

His eyes flashed. "He failed me!"

"How so?"

Gilles almost wailed as he spoke. "He has abandoned us."

Us, he said.

"Who has William abandoned other than you? Certainly you do not speak of your vile servants in such terms."

Gilles covered his eyes with his hands and when he looked up and spoke, he seemed calm once more. "He has abandoned Christendom. A betrayal. Such a betrayal. And where does his betrayal leave me? What now am I?"

"A murderer of children?"

He grimaced. "Am I? Is that what I am? That is how the world will remember Gilles de Rais, no doubt. But that does not undo all that I have become."

"Some deeds are so evil that they define a life."

"I suppose that is true. I did try to stop it. I hope that I am allowed to beg you this much. That you believe I did try to stop it. But I was weak. I was powerless."

"There can be no excuses for this evil."

"I remain a good Christian. A perfect Christian, from my youth until this moment."

"You make a mockery of your words. You are a heretic."

"Never! Never that, never. I love Christ. He will forgive me. I will enter Heaven."

"If you make it to Heaven, I will slay you there, also."

He smiled. "What makes you believe you will go to Heaven? Do you attend Mass? Do you confess your sins? Do you believe in your heart that only Jesus Christ can bring you salvation?"

"I will not be questioned on my faith by you, demon."

"You and your traitorous brother are the cause of this evil, not me. I am a victim of it."

There was more truth in that than I cared to consider. "After you, William will die also. Have no fear of that."

"I pray that you each slay the other."

"What else has he done to you? Other than to abandon you after promising to return. You say he has turned against Christendom. How can you know this, if you have not heard from him?"

He opened his mouth, whether to answer or to deflect I do not know, as the door behind me was thrown open and the Chief Inquisitor strode in with the other chiefs of both courts trailing behind him in a swirling mass of robes and finery.

"What is this about a confession?"

"Praise God!" Gilles cried, and fell to his knees, clasping his hands together. "Please,

Inquisitor, I beg you. Hear my honest and true and freely given confession and after, have me executed so that my torment is finally ended!"

***

Present for the confession along with the Inquisitor was the Bishop of Saint-Brieuc representing the ecclesiastical court, and Master Pierre de L'Hopital from the civic court, Captain Jean Labbe on behalf of the Duke, and Stephen, the prosecutor. The Inquisition's scribes wrote down what was said and servants attended to their masters.

I was present, as a squire in service of the ecclesiastical court, and none of those great lords attempted to be rid of me, for they were rightly afraid of Gilles de Rais, a big and powerful soldier as well as likely heretic and murderer, and needed a brute like me to make them feel secure.

He was seated in a chair by the narrow window, facing us. We stood or sat or leaned in a great arc around him, from one side of the room to another. The Inquisitor sat at the centre, upright and leaned forward on a rather high stool.

"So, then," the Inquisitor said. "On the subject of the abduction and death of many children, and the libidinous, sodomitic, and unnatural vice, the cruel and horrible manner of the killings, and also the invocations of demons, oblations, immolations or sacrifices, the promises made or the obligations contracted with the demons by you, you wish to make a statement of confession?"

"Yes," the Marshal said without hesitation. "Yes, to all."

The Inquisitor sighed and looked down his nose. "You shall have to do better than that, my lord."

He nodded frantically. "I will say anything that I am required to say to swiftly end this ordeal. An ordeal I richly deserve, of course, my lords. And so I must say that I freely, voluntarily, and grievously confess to committing each and every crime for which I am charged by both courts. I have committed and maliciously perpetrated on numerous children the crimes, the sins, and offences of... of homicide and... sodomy. I confess also that I have committed the invocations of demons, what was it? Oblations and immolations. That I made promises and obligations, as stated, to demons. And done all the other things to which I am charged."

"Very good. We will require more. We must have details. We must have reasons."

"Reasons, my lord?"

"Your motivations, no matter how perverse, for committing these crimes."

"Yes, yes, of course. How would you like me to say it?"

"In your own words, tell me, when did you begin committing these crimes?"

"In the Champtoce Castle, during the time when my grandfather was alive. I do not know what year. I suppose it really started when my grandfather died and Gilles de Rais took over. When I inherited."

"Who persuaded you to commit these crimes?"

"Persuaded me? No one persuaded me. I committed them according to my imagination and my ideas, without anyone's counsel and following my own feelings, sir."

"But, for what purpose?"

For the purpose of blood, I thought. *For his need to drink.* But of course it was far more than that.

"Solely for my pleasure and my carnal delight. And not with any other intention or to any other end." As he said this, he glanced briefly at me and then looked quickly away.

"I struggle to understand," the Inquisitor said, shaking his head. "I find it very surprising that a man could commit crimes such as this for no reason. To what ends have you had the children killed and committed on them the sins we have heard about and had their cadavers burned?"

"I confess that I took pleasure in the hurting and the killing of them. Some I killed by removing their heads from their bodies, others by striking with clubs on their heads or necks. Others I throttled by hand or by ropes and cords, suspending them from hooks and pegs on my walls. It gave me joy to watch their anguish and confusion as they died. I delighted in destroying innocence, I suppose. It was satisfying to me to eradicate their innocence in every way that I could imagine. I am the opposite of innocence, you see. It is the antithesis to what I have become. It is something so far removed from what I have made myself that I sought to destroy it from the face of the earth. And my perversions knew no bounds. Even in death, I enjoyed defiling their corpses further. After so many killed, it slowly became tedious to me and I had to become ever more creative in my activities in order to maintain the joy. Even then, it grew ever more mundane until I found myself filled with misery but unable to stop." He broke off, his voice shaking.

"Please, continue to explain your crimes."

"Alas, my lord, you torment yourself and me along with you!"

The Inquisitor looked down his nose and replied calmly. "I do not torment myself in the least but I am very surprised at what you have told me and simply cannot be satisfied with it. I desire and would like to know the absolute truth from you for the reasons I have already told you."

Gilles glanced at me again. "Truly, there was no other cause, no other end nor intention, if not what I have told you. I have admitted to enough to kill ten thousand men. Let it be done but once to me."

"Well, my lord, we shall certainly see it done but it must be done in the proper, legal fashion. And so I will have you speak of your dealings with the invocation of demons and the oblation of the blood of the said small children and the places where you performed these acts."

"In order to solicit from the demon's evil, I had a note drafted in my own blood promising to give the devil, when he appeared, whatever he required excepting my life and my soul. My soul is still mine and God's and has always remained so. I must be sure that you understand that. I must be sure."

"I hear you and your assertion is so recorded. Continue."

Gilles took a slow breath and nodded. "Prelati summoned them many times and told me he saw them and spoke to them but I never did see them, not once, sadly. I gave him whatever he needed, whether it be blood or limbs or gold."

"Why did you wish to summon a demon or many demons? For what purpose?"

"To have powerful creatures to do my bidding. Prelati assured me that a demon would help in the transmutation."

"You wanted the demons to help to create gold?"

"Yes, indeed. I found myself in financial difficulties due to large expenses and I wished to recover it, and to make more. To make a fortune. To make myself richer than any king. Alas, alas, it did not work."

"We have heard from Prelati, who stated that you provided him the blood, the hands, eyes, and the hearts of children. You did this in the hopes of creating gold?"

"It is true, yes."

The Inquisitor sighed and rubbed his eyes. "We shall end this now. I suggest that you repeat what you have spoken here during the next session of the court and the Bishop will move to pass sentence."

"I will," Gilles de Rais said. "Praise God."

We filed out and before I left I looked back at him. He seemed relieved and that was understandable, assuming he was seeking the relief of death. But I thought I sensed something else. Just a hint of triumph, quickly suppressed. At the time, I convinced myself that I was imagining things. I would soon discover it was triumph indeed and everything was going according to his plan.

But the overwhelming thoughts on my mind after I left was how impassioned Gilles had been when he spoke of Joan.

Do not speak of her! he had said, raging at me. *Even you must know her trial was a nonsense. Everything about it, from start to finish. It was theatre, played to convince the masses that her brilliance was not only over but that it had always been false.*

It was plain to see that it had affected him profoundly. Perhaps her death was what had finally driven him into madness.

I wondered also whether he knew how close I had come to capturing her myself.

18

The Trial of Joan

March 1431

AFTER THE DAUPHIN was crowned and became the King, Joan had urged the new king to storm Paris, as she had foretold.

We fought off the assault and Joan was wounded in the leg by a crossbow bolt. King Charles ordered the retreat from Paris and sought to find a diplomatic solution with the Burgundians that would allow him to be rid of the English and at the same time he quietly excluded Joan. Her manic pleas for endless assaults and grand pronouncements ceased being helpful and began to be a hindrance. In the hope that she would take the hint and go away, he made her and her family into nobility. They were awarded an annual sum from the crown and were allowed all the other legal benefits of being above the station of commoners. Such a thing was not unheard of but usually was granted only to a fabulously wealthy and successful soldier or courtier after a lifetime of service and most people, lords especially, saw the ennobling as the farce that it was.

As the King withdrew active support, so too did other lords and knights until the number of men around her dwindled. Of the great men, only Gilles de Rais remained at her side. And he did so almost to the end.

But Joan did not take the hint and she would not give up her struggle. She would not be sidelined by anyone, not even the King of France, and so she continued to throw herself into any conflict that she could find in the hope that her strength of will would carry the day.

In May 1430, a year after her triumphs at Orléans, she led a force that attempted to attack the Burgundian camp at Margny north of Compiègne.

But I was hunting her.

Together with a handful of loyal archers we had tracked her from Saint-Pierre-le-Moûtier to La-Charité-sur-Loire to Compiègne but she was always too well protected. Once, we saw her at a distance and Rob had begged to be allowed to shoot her with an arrow but I had denied him.

"It must be over two hundred yards, Rob," I said. "It would serve only to alert them to our presence and we would be killed."

"I can hit her in the crown, I swear it."

"And you could hit her in the eye if only she was looking up," Walt said. "And shoot it up her arse if only she was bending over."

But with every failed attack that Joan led, her protectors dwindled in number and we got closer and closer to springing an ambush on her so that I could cut her damned throat.

When the French army withdrew into the fortifications of Compiègne after six thousand additional Burgundian soldiers arrived, Joan stayed with the rear guard of the army. We stayed close, moving parallel to Joan's position at the rear, keeping our distance. But when the Burgundians caught up with the French, they began skirmishing as they moved. Darting attacks by mounted men attacked stragglers and picked them off, which drew more French soldiers back to protect their comrades. And so the Burgundian vanguard crept up and slowly consumed the French rearguard, nibbling away at it until their flanks started to envelop them like a snake swallowing a rat. Joan's banner was visible as she attempted to rally her soldiers.

"This is our chance," I said, kicking my heels back and started out toward them. "We have to get through the lot of them and take her."

"They'll take us for Frenchmen," Walt pointed out, using his spurs to catch up with me.

"What's the Burgundian cry, now?" Rob asked, coming up behind with the archers.

"We will cry for Duke Philip," I said.

And that is what we did, crying his name as we pushed our horses boldly through the flanks of Burgundian forces and they cheered us on. Many even followed us in as we clashed with desperate Frenchmen and cut them down or drove them away.

The Maiden's white banner fluttered above the mass of men so closely that I could have thrown a stone and hit it but there were many fighting to protect her. I did not know whether I would have the courage to cut her down or if I would have to take her prisoner but I was saved from making the decision.

From the opposite flank came a massive charge by two hundred Burgundian men-at-arms, crying out for their lord and for their duke and the hooves thundered and trumpets blasted and the fear of it overwhelmed the French, who dropped their weapons and fled as the assault crashed into them. It was slaughter and they abandoned their beloved Maiden to her fate.

Many ran toward the rest of their army but even more ran directly opposite to the attack, which meant they were driven into us. We cut them down and pushed on through the press of desperate men and I shouted and cursed but it did no good.

Amongst so many men and horses, she appeared to be very small to my eyes. She wore a helm with no visor but I could not get a good look at her face. At a glance, it appeared snub-nosed and quite unattractive. Her armour was excellent, and her horse was one I would have killed to have under me but she did not use his size and strength in an attempt to break free of her encirclement. Perhaps it was my imagination but she seemed stunned by being abandoned and surely believed that it was all over. Still, she refused to lower the great banner and her squire, the only loyal man remaining, did not lower his sword. The Burgundians shouted at her to dismount and to give herself up but she sat and stared back at them.

"I could shoot her now, Richard?" Rob suggested from the saddle, his bow in hand with an arrow nocked. Even from horseback, I expected he could hit the target.

I sighed. "A thousand Burgundians would tear us to pieces for denying them their prize. Leave it, Rob. It is done."

The Maiden of Orléans was pulled from her horse by a Burgundian archer who rushed forward to do the deed and she fell hard. This brought others crowding in close about her so that when she regained her feet, covered in mud, she found herself surrounded by half a hundred soldiers with no ally but her squire at her side. Even then, she was too proud to give herself up until a nobleman from Luxembourg volunteered to be her captor. This she agreed to and she was seized. Her famous banner was grabbed and torn and trampled as men tried to take a piece for themselves.

It was done but I could not entirely rid my thoughts of her.

Joan was imprisoned by the Burgundians at Beaurevoir Castle, north beyond Paris and I made sure to follow closely what happened to her by employing Stephen and Eva's agents. The girl made several escape attempts, one of them being her leap from seventy feet up. When she recovered the use of her legs after a few days, she was moved further north to the Burgundian town of Arras.

Throughout her imprisonment, the lords of England negotiated with the Burgundians to transfer Joan into our custody. Eventually, we bought her for ten thousand livres, which was a vast sum.

Immediately, she was transported to Rouen, our soundest stronghold on the continent and I took my men there. Lucky that I did, for the French launched a number of small campaigns against us there in the hopes of rescuing her. One campaign occurred during the winter of 1430-1431, another in March 1431, and one in late May shortly before her execution. Of course, each time we beat them back. We were not so far gone as all that.

The French were outraged that we had their beloved Maiden of Orléans. King Charles VII threatened to exact vengeance upon Burgundian troops in his captivity and also he threatened a terrible fate for the English and women of England in retaliation for our treatment of her. Many believed that the French meant to invade England but I doubted such a thing was even possible for a kingdom still so divided and in turmoil as that of France. Still, they were angry to say the least.

The English celebrated the coronation of Henry VI as King of France at Notre-Dame cathedral in Paris on 16 December 1431, the boy king's tenth birthday. Charles VII however continued to act as if he was the legitimate king and it was difficult to argue. Indeed, his diplomacy was far greater than ours. Before we could rebuild our military leadership and replace our veteran archers, we lost our alliance with Burgundy when the Treaty of Arras was signed in 1435. The Duke of Bedford died the same year and Henry VI became the youngest king of England to rule without a regent.

But back in January 1431, in Rouen, Joan was put on trial. The tribunal was composed entirely of pro-English and Burgundian clerics and overseen by the Duke of Bedford and the Earl of Warwick. They meant to not only destroy her but also to humiliate her and through her, all France.

"It is we who shall be humiliated," Stephen grumbled after it started. We sat drinking in our rooms in Rouen one night after the trial had begun.

"You believe she will be acquitted?"

"Ha! No, indeed. Far from it. These bastards are going to convict her no matter what. The law be damned."

"What law?"

He waved his hand. "Ecclesiastical law, English law. Bishop Cauchon lacks jurisdiction over the case but he oversees it anyway purely because of his open support of us. And the English crown is paying for the entire thing, all expenses, so what does that mean for a fair outcome? The Inquisition has very clear rules regarding the standard of evidence allowed for the trial but this has been utterly disregarded and the evidence so far submitted is absurdly weak."

"Oh?"

"Look, the testimony gathered by the notary does not even technically allow the court to initiate the trial but they have gone and done it anyway." He took a great gulp of his wine and wiped his lips before ploughing on. "And then they violate the rules again by denying the girl the right to a legal adviser."

"That girl is an enemy of England, Stephen."

"The rule of law should be followed nevertheless. The law must be applied equally to all or else it becomes a worthless thing. If she truly is a heretic, she should burn. Of course she should. But every member of the tribunal is bought and paid for by the English, one way or another."

"The Inquisition are supporting it," I pointed out.

Stephen laughed. "The Vice-Inquisitor objected to the trial from the outset and yet his life was threatened."

"Rumours, that is all."

"It is true for him and for other clergy at the trial. I spoke personally to that Dominican Isambart de la Pierre, and he swore to God that Englishmen had threatened the lives of his family, Richard!"

"If true, that is rather heavy-handed, I admit." I pointed over my cup at him. "If true, that is."

"The standards for heresy trials are very clear. They must be judged by an impartial or balanced group of clerics. It is heresy, Richard. It hardly gets more serious than this and yet the rules are being discarded in order to achieve the desired outcome. The law is what protects the common man from the rampant predations of their lords. Disregarding it demeans us to ourselves and also to our enemies. Were we not better than this, once? Do you think the third Edward would have allowed this? Or the fifth Henry?"

"They would not have lost the damned war in the first place," I said, growling as I thought of it. "And yet you are right."

"I am."

"You know so much about the law, Stephen. Perhaps you should use your coming time away from London to train as a lawyer. You have mentioned wanting to do so in years gone by, I believe."

"Bah, I have so much else to do from afar. I would not like to leave it all to Eva in my absence, there is too much business to attend to on behalf of the Order."

"And yet you have such a passion for it. The Order's finances are strong enough, thanks to you, that we can do without you for a while. Why not take a decade or two? Perhaps if you had already made yourself into a powerful lawyer, you could have had an influence on this trial. Perhaps you could have persuaded them to follow the rules a little more."

He took a long while to answer but, in the end, waved it away. "They will have her destroyed no matter what. I could do nothing to change her fate."

I shrugged. "Especially as she is a heretic."

"So sure, are you?"

"She is either a heretic or God Himself is a Frenchman. And that is too terrible a notion to entertain."

Even Joan herself complained on her first day being questioned that the tribunal were all enemies and she requested that ecclesiastics of the French side be invited to provide the balance required in law. This request was simply denied.

The Maiden of Orléans continued to do very well for herself when questioned in the public court. I could not bring myself to attend for most of it and the couple of times I did, I stood at the rear of the hall. When she spoke, however, she did not sound like an illiterate commoner from Lorraine. That is, she had the rough accent of such a girl. But she spoke with such forceful confidence that it seemed she was filled with the righteousness of one of noble birth. And not so much a princess as she seemed a prince, arrogant and dismissive when questioned and openly contemptuous of the intelligence displayed by the members of the tribunal who launched questions at her unceasingly.

Somehow, without the presence of legal or ecclesiastical advice, this young girl was able to evade the theological pitfalls the tribunal had set up to entrap her.

One day when I was there, a bishop launched one of those traps.

"Tell me, do you know if you are in God's grace?"

Stephen, at my side, winced.

"What is it?" I whispered, while Joan hesitated in answering.

"If she says that she *is* then she is admitting that she knows God's will."

I shrugged. "And?"

Stephen sighed. "If she says *yes*, she is admitting to heresy, Richard!"

A single question with the power to convict her before all the lords of the Church. After so much of her grandstanding and insisting on her closeness to God's angels, it seemed impossible that she would avoid falling for it.

Finally, she spoke up in a clear voice that echoed like the ringing of a bell. "If I am not, may God put me there," she said. "And if I am, may God so keep me."

The lords of the church sitting behind their benches were struck dumb at her answer and the public muttered and sighed.

Stephen let out a surprised exclamation. "Well, I never."

"That was a fine thing to say," I said.

"It was brilliant, Richard," he replied, shaking his head in wonder. "Quite brilliant."

On and on the trial went, with repeated days where she was questioned for hours and in between was kept in awful conditions in prison under the guard of English soldiers. The Inquisition's rules dictated that she should have been kept in an ecclesiastical prison with nuns watching over her but again this was simply ignored. She appealed to the Pope but her appeals were not passed on. Over the weeks, she grew thinner and paler. Never an attractive girl, she became quite unpleasant to look upon. All this was of course another attempt at breaking her will. It grew hard for me to maintain my anger at her.

When she was stupefied by the physical and mental exertions, they cornered her and forced her to sign a document on pain of execution if she did not. The girl was illiterate and knew not what she had signed and even then the admission of guilt which she signed was substituted for another before it was submitted to the court.

But even conviction for heresy was not a capital offence. She was condemned to live her life in prison and all expected her to be transferred to a convent for the rest of her days. It seemed done and dusted and few English or Normans complained about the sentence. It seemed fair to me and to everyone I spoke to.

And yet the lords could not abide her getting away with her life and so she was set up in such a way as to condemn herself.

Ever since setting out from Lorraine on her God-given quest, Joan had dressed a page and also in armour, although this was allowed under Church doctrine where cross-dressing was permitted if it was to protect the wearer from rape.

Joan had agreed in her signed abjuration document to from that day on to forever wear feminine clothing. A few days after her abjuration she resumed male attire as a defence against molestation and because her dress had been taken by the guards and she was left with nothing else to wear.

The lords of the court were conveniently marched in at that very moment to catch her in the act of wearing a man's clothing. And thus she had gone back on her abjuration agreement and so she was now legally a lapsed heretic.

This verdict meant death.

I heard in the taverns and inns after it happened exactly how it had occurred. It made me miserable to hear it but the place was awash with the tale. Joan was brought out into the marketplace in Rouen. They had put her in a pretty, long white dress. She was far from her former, fierce self and came on with her head bowed and her body shaking. In the square was a great stake standing up, twice the height of a man, with bundle after bundle of branches and logs all around it, drenched in oil. It was to that stake that she was bound with chains and they came forward with a torch and set the mass of it ablaze. The oil went up quick, catching the dry sticks and burning white hot.

"An English soldier gave her two sticks tied together in the shape of a crucifix," one old man said to me, showing me the size of it with his hands. "Little one, about so high. She placed it against her bosom."

"Shut up, did she," another man said. "I never saw that."

"She bloody well did and I'll knock out the teeth of any man who says otherwise."

Most agreed that the girl said nothing the entire time. The girl who had said so much, who had spoken with such certainty that an entire nation had been moved to action, moved to victory, hung her head and said nothing when she was burned. Nothing, that is, until the flames took her and blackened her feet and legs and blistered her skin in boiling agony, when she cried out the holy name of Jesus Christ in a plaintive, terrible cry.

The fire was enormous and burned high and hot and turned the girl's body to ashes, even the bones. All swore, though none knew how they knew, that the only part to survive was her heart. But they swept up her ashes and threw them into the Seine, and then they tossed her heart in after.

And although I saw none of it, I could see it all in my mind's eye as if I had been witness to the terrible event.

"You feel guilty," Stephen pronounced.

"Nonsense," I replied. "It was nothing to do with me. Anyway, what happened? She had told them what they wanted to hear. She was bound for a convent, perhaps one day they would have freed her and sent her home. What occurred to cause her to destroy herself?"

"After she signed the paper of abjuration, she lay in her cell for two days, wearing ordinary women's dress. But someone meant to do her in, I must suppose. Someone wanted her to fall. To burn. So they took away her dress and in its place brought the clothing of a boy and laid it before her. It was the very same clothing that she had been forced to give up before. For a time, she refused to don that clothing, knowing what it would mean. But she was naked. Naked before her guards, the English guards, who leered at her and told her what they meant to do to her body. She was yet in chains and confined to that cell and had no one to turn to for protection. And so she put them on."

"That was enough to convict her?"

"It was theatre, of a sort. A pantomime. The next morning, after she dressed in the forbidden clothing, a procession of judges burst in on her while she lay in bed. They crowded around her and demanded to know why she had sinned once more. Why she had relapsed into heresy. She did her best to explain that she had worn the clothes only to protect her modesty, they railed at her and named her a witch and a prostitute and a heretic and they were overjoyed to condemn her. Joan would be burnt after all."

"She would have known that they would have killed her. Why did she choose to wear the clothes? Surely, better to be shamed and abused than burned on the pyre?"

"Is it? Would you allow your body to be so violated? Think of it. Think how she guarded her maidenhead. Her virginity was in part the source of her holy power. Perhaps she knew they meant to destroy her by any means necessary and so she decided to embrace it. Would you live life as a slave, Richard?"

"Not if there was no hope of escape."

"Why did you not attend the execution?"

"Why would I wish to witness such a thing?"

"She has been your enemy. She was the instrument of your losses in the war."

"Our losses, Stephen. England's losses. But was she the cause of it all? Or was she a victim? There must have been a man telling her what to say and how to act. More than one, perhaps. How could a mere girl do such things as she did? How old was she at the end? She had not yet twenty years. Perhaps it was this man who inveigled to have her so executed, in order to stay her tongue for eternity lest it might reveal his hand."

"What man?"

"What man indeed? The new King of France or one of his courtiers?"

"Do you not think she may have been one of William's? That business with her wounds, and the leap from the tower."

"Yes, it is of course possible, but it is not enough in itself. These things are perhaps within the limits of mortal endurance, just about, if that mortal is filled with passion."

"Or perhaps God truly did send angels to speak with her."

"I refuse to believe that God favours the French," I said but I did wonder whether it was true. "Anyhow, it matters not at all. Not any longer. The heretic has burned and that is the end of it."

"It is," Stephen said, his face grey and drawn as he looked up at me. "You know, Richard. I do believe I may take up your suggestion. To become a lawyer. It would be a good thing for the Order to have me educated in such matters and perhaps... perhaps one day I might even see some justice done thanks to my hand. Justice done for the common people against the exploitations of the powerful lords."

I thumped him on the shoulder. "A noble intention, sir. I wish you well in it."

Whether she had been an immortal, or the victim of a clever lord's manipulations, or inspired genius or even, heaven forfend, a genuine messenger from God, she had not deserved her suffering and her awful death. And I felt guilty for my part in all of it, as small as it was.

At least, that is what I thought and felt for many years, until shortly after the execution of Gilles de Rais when I would finally discover the terrible truth.

19

The Execution of Gilles de

Rais

October 1440

IN THE ECCLESIASTICAL court in Nantes on Saturday October 22nd 1440, I watched the prisoner Gilles de Rais admit before the assembled bishops, vicars of the Inquisition, and members of the public, that he was guilty of every crime that he was accused of.

He wept as he spoke, though he spoke at length and detailed his actions, drawing gasps and exclamations from his audience.

At one point, as Gilles described his processes of dismembering, the Bishop of Nantes stood and covered the golden crucifix behind him with a white cloth, lest it be tainted with the evil before it.

He also named his accomplices, pointing them out in their iron cage, and condemning them utterly, though not all would suffer the same fate. During his confession, he also reaffirmed with passion his assertion that he never promised his soul to the demon he wished to summon with Prelati.

Finally, it came to the long-awaited pronouncement of guilt and the sentencing from the ecclesiastical court.

"We decree and declare that you, the aforesaid Gilles de Rais, present before us in trial, are found guilty of perfidious apostasy as well as of the dreadful invocation of demons, which you maliciously perpetrated, and that for this you have incurred the sentence of excommunication and other lawful punishments, in order to punish and salutarily correct you and in order that you are punished and corrected as the law demands and canonical sanctions decree."

"My soul remains mine and my soul remains God's!" Gilles cried, shaking with passion, with tears streaming down his cheeks. "I am a sinner, I confess it, I am the worst sinner who ever was and I beg God for His forgiveness before I die. I humbly implore the mercy and pardon of My Creator and most blessed Redeemer, as well as that of the parents and friends of the children so cruelly massacred, as well as that of everyone whom I could have injured in regard to which I am guilty, whether they are here present or elsewhere. And I ask all of Christ's faithful and worshippers for the assistance of your devout prayers."

At this theatrical confession, the Bishop was almost weeping himself, for such great sin allowed for equally great forgiveness and so was delightful to a true Christian.

It was a convincing spectacle, though Stephen and I exchanged a look. I admit that even I was halfway convinced of his contrition.

"You will have opportunity to undo the sentence of excommunication," the Bishop said. "It is clear that, despite your crimes, you remain a true Christian in your heart and I confirm that you will be allowed to make your final, secret confession. And you will have the opportunity to be absolved of your sins, and you will have imposed on you for all your sins a salutary penance in proportion to your faults, as much for those you have judicially confessed as for those you will confess at the tribunal of your conscience."

"Oh, God bless you," Gilles cried, falling to his knees. "Praise God!"

Afterwards, the accused was brought to the civil court, where his previous confession was read aloud and he confirmed it was true and then he was condemned for the murders and rebellion that he had admitted to. And then he was sentenced.

"We declare that you are to be immediately taken from this place to be hanged and then burned," the President of the court said. "But, in conjunction with a request from the ecclesiastical court, you will be given time to make holy confession and then to beg God's mercy and prepare to die soundly with numerous regrets for having committed the said crimes. The clerical servants Prelati and Blanchet are sentenced to spend the remainder of their natural lives in prison, on account that neither are found guilty of committing murder by their own hands and were found to be orthodox in their faith. The servants Henriet Griart and Poitou are sentenced to be hanged and then to be burned."

"Thank you, my lord!" Gilles cried. "May I beg that my servants, Henriet and Poitou, be executed immediately after I am so killed? And might it be that I, who am the principal cause of the misdeeds of my servants, might be able to comfort them, speak to them of their salvation at the hour of execution, and exhort them by example to die fittingly. I fear, if it were otherwise, and my servants not see me die first, that they shall fall into despair, imagining that they were dying while I, who am the cause of their misdeeds, go unpunished. I hope, on the contrary, with the grace of Our Lord, that I who made them commit the misdeeds for which they are dying would be the cause of their salvation."

The President of the court was clearly deeply moved by Gilles' profound contrition and accorded him this favour.

"Praise God," Gilles said, crossing himself and gazing adoringly at the President.

"What do you make of it?" I asked Stephen, when the court was adjourned.

"Do you mean is he mad or is he truly seeking salvation?" Stephen asked.

"I mean, what the Hell is the sneaky bastard up to, Stephen?"

"Up to?" Stephen asked. "What can he be up to? He is about to be hanged and burned to ashes. What can he do?"

"I do not know," I admitted. "But I know that I do not like it. He has obviously been drinking blood in his captivity. And so have the servants, who are revenants and require it every day."

"So you say," Stephen said. "And yet you have been unable to discover who has been paid off."

"It could be the whole bloody episcopal staff, for all I know."

"You are allowing your apprehensions to get the best of you. He is in irons. He will make his last confession and then he will burn, along with the revenants. So what does it matter?"

"Yes, yes," I snapped, irritated by his damned reasoning. "Let us go and watch them burn."

"The crowds already gather," Stephen said. "But we can witness it from the balcony in the palace. Come. I am going to enjoy this greatly."

"As shall I."

By the time we reached the chamber on the fourth floor of the Bishop's palace, the square was packed with people standing shoulder to shoulder and nose to neck. None of them had ever seen anything like it in all their lives and every road approaching the square was likewise filled, as were the bridges across the river. The entire city had come to a standstill and the Bishop and the Duke's soldiers struggled to keep them back from the scaffold and the stakes with their mounds of logs and kindling already prepared. A noise welled up as the condemned were led out from a doorway into the hall on the far side, and the soldiers fought to push back at the surge of the crowd.

As Gilles stood before the dangling noose, he raised his hands and called for silence. We were very far distant and far above him but his voice was loud and it echoed from the four sides of the square.

"Pray to God for me, good people," he said. They fell quiet, perhaps astonished at his brazenness or his piety. "I confess once more, this time before you, to all the crimes to which I was charged and found guilty. Before you, I beg my two servants to in their hearts seek the salvation of their souls and I urge them to be strong and virtuous in the face of diabolical temptations, and to have profound regret and contrition of their misdeeds, as do I. And also to have confidence in the grace of God and to believe that there is no sin a man might commit so great that God in His goodness and kindness would not forgive, so long as the sinner felt profound regret and great contrition of heart and I ask Him for mercy. Dear God, have mercy."

Poitou and Henriet appeared distraught but hopeful and they thanked their master for his words.

Gilles then fell to his knees, folded his hands together and begged God's mercy again. "My friends, who have come here to see a sinner, you should know that as a Christian, I am your brother. Those amongst you whose children I have killed, for the love of Our Lord's suffering, please be willing to pray to God for me and to forgive me freely, in the same way that you yourselves intend God to forgive and have mercy on yourselves."

"What a disgusting display," I said.

"Nothing he says is inconsistent with orthodoxy," Stephen said.

"I know that I am uneducated in these things but surely you see that it is monstrous, Stephen. He compares himself with them."

Gilles raised his voice. "Let me be killed first," he cried. "And my men to follow. Please, good fellows of Nantes, build the fires and prepare the noose."

"Finally," I muttered.

The fires were started in the base of the three bundles and the flames grew. I wished that the living, conscious Gilles would be placed in the fire so that his agony would be prolonged and terrible but he would hang first.

"Now we will see," Rob said.

"Prepare your coin, sir," Walt replied.

"Coin?" I asked, turning to them. "What coin?"

"Ah," Rob said. "It is nothing, Richard."

Walt suddenly studied the clouds above, pretending not to hear me.

"What are you up to?"

Rob sighed. "Walt does not believe that the noose will kill him. But I say that it will throttle the life from an immortal and the revenants, just as it would a mortal man. How can it not?"

I stared at them both. "And you are betting coin on the outcome?"

Walt looked at me, then. "Do you wish to place a bet, Richard?"

"I wish that the noose does nothing and that the man dies in the fire in the full possession of his wits. I wish that his immortal strength prolongs his suffering in the flames. I would cook him slowly, if I was down there. I would feed him my own blood to keep him in agony for hours or days so that he begs me to end his life."

"So," Walt said, "how many ecus do you want to put in?"

"There he goes," Stephen said.

A heavy silence filled the air. Down in the square, Gilles stepped up to the noose and up onto a short stool. The noose was placed over his head and tightened around his neck. A shouted order was given and the stool pulled away.

Gilles dropped and his feet kicked and his body thrashed. It did not take long until he was motionless and he was lifted by the executioners, the noose removed and he was carried to the fire. His body was placed upon the burning logs at the base of the fire and his hair was singed and his clothes caught fire. His skin reddened and shone.

Then they pulled him out.

I grasped Stephen's arm. "What are they doing?"

The executioners patted the fire from his clothes and lifted him onto a handcart and pushed him through the lines of soldiers back toward the hall on the other side of the square to us.

"What in the name of God is going on?" I asked again.

Stephen turned to me, his eyes wide. "I do not know."

"Where is the Bishop?" I asked the men behind me. "Where is the bloody Bishop?" I grabbed a priest by his robes and glared at him.

"He is viewing it from his chambers, sir," one of the other priests said.

We raced through the corridor and threw open the Bishop's door with his guards trailing after us, shouting warnings even as Walt and Rob held them back.

"What is going on?" I shouted at the Bishop, who turned from his window with fear and outrage in his eyes. "Why was he not burned?"

"Who are you to speak to me in such a way?"

I grasped him by the neck and lifted him from his feet, pushing him against the wall. "Where are they bloody-well taking him, you God damned fat fool?"

The Bishop's eyes flicked over my shoulder, searching for rescue. I slapped his face and shook him.

"He... he... he begged to avoid being turned to ashes. He begged for his body to be allowed to be buried. His request was granted. What does it matter if he is dead all the same? He died in a state of—"

"You fools!" I said, and threw him down to my feet. "He is escaping. All he needs is human blood and he will be returned to full health. Where did they take him? Who took him?"

The Bishop shook his head. "He was to be taken by certain ladies of high rank and prepared for burial. I know not where."

I turned to Stephen. Behind him, Walt and Rob held five of the palace guards prisoner with their own weapons.

"We must cross the square to the hall," I said. "But we cannot go through that crowd."

"I know a route," Stephen said. "Through the palace, crossing by the cathedral and then on to the hall."

"Lead the way!"

We raced through the palace after Stephen, clattering down stairways and pushing priests and servants aside. We were faster than mortals and left the trailing guards behind but once we left the palace, the crowds were so great that we had to force our way through men and woman and children. As we crossed a street, I saw over the heads of the crowd into the square. Two great plumes of raging red fire and filthy smoke lit up the blackened corpses of Poitou and Henriet Griart.

By the time we made it to the hall, the body of Gilles de Rais had disappeared.

"He was taken for burial by high-born women," many told us.

"What does that mean?" I cried. "Where did they take him? Where?"

No one knew.

We raced from the city and watched the roads south and north and chased down every possible wagon and company that it might be but none were Gilles, nor these supposed high-born women.

"It is my fault," I said to Stephen as we looked down yet another empty road as night approached. "The entire time, he has been getting help from people in Nantes. Someone was bringing him blood, even to the servants, but I did not care about that. I thought it mattered not and yet he somehow retained servants, guards, these damned women. I thought we had him. I am a fool. Such a fool."

I had lost him.

He was gone.

2 0

A B l o o d y M e s s e n g e r

O c t o b e r 1 4 4 0

WE SLIPPED BACK into the city before nightfall, hoping to avoid the Bishop's palace and any guards who we knew would certainly still be looking to arrest us.

"Where would he go?" I asked Stephen in the darkness, riding toward the centre of Nantes. "Surely, not to Tiffauges. He knows that we would look for him there."

"He has a dozen castles to choose from and surely it must be at least one of them. Where else can he go?"

As a mounted group, we seemed too conspicuous and so we dismounted, pulled our hoods up or hats down, and moved on through the crowds hurrying home. Many who had attended the executions were steaming drunk and rowdy, while others stumbled away from the city or to their rooms as if they were yet stunned by what they had witnessed. The hum and hiss of voices echoed through the streets. I felt for them because in their ignorance they believed that their tormentor was dead and that justice had been done.

"It would take days to travel to each of his castles," I said to Stephen. "Weeks to search them. Months, perhaps. He escapes, Stephen. Now, as we speak, he escapes and if we do not catch him now, he will be in the wind. Who knows what evil he will do in the years to come?"

"Do not despair," Stephen said. "We will find him."

I turned on him. "How?"

He looked away, for he had no answer. We stopped and looked at the crowds filing by us. A woman wept, her husband's arm about her shoulders. A group of young men argued and jostled each other as they passed us, agitated and spoiling for a fight.

"What do you reckon they would do if we told them?" Rob asked.

"They would not believe it," Stephen said. "Even if they could be made to understand it."

"Shame them two servants got burned up, ain't it," Walt said. "Might be they knew where their master might have gone."

Stephen and I exchanged a look.

"The others yet live, do they not?" I said. "The priest and the sorcerer."

"They are yet held at the gaol in the castle. If we go there and are reported, we are likely to be seized by the Bishop's soldiers."

"Then we must move swiftly and if they do attempt to take us, we will cut our way free. Are we agreed?" Walt and Rob were quick to do so and Stephen hesitated only for a moment. "How much silver do you have on you, Stephen?"

We made our way to the prison as quickly and quietly as we could. With the help of fistfuls of coins, Stephen quickly talked the gaolers into granting us access to the guilty servants who had somehow avoided the sentence of death.

While my men watched the exits, the gaolers escorted Stephen and I through to the cell of Dominus Eustache Blanchet, who was horrified to see me step into his cell.

"Where is he?" I said, unable to keep the snarl from my face. "Where?"

"Who, my lord?"

I stepped over him and resisted the urge to thrash him senseless. "Gilles de Rais has fled. Following his execution, he has fled. And you know, by God, you know where he has gone, and you will tell me."

"Surely, sir, he cannot have survived the noose and fire," Blanchet cried. "Do you think he is coming for me, my lord? Because I turned on him and confessed and so condemned him?"

I slapped him and shoved him over and slapped him again. "Can you truly be so stupid? Is it a part that you play so well or are you a simpleton? You may have convinced the court but you do not fool me. You know what your master is. You know what the others were. And you must have known his plan to survive his execution. Tell me where he went!"

He sobbed and fouled himself and trembled, begging forgiveness for not knowing anything, tears running down his face. He swore that he would say whatever I wanted him to say, if only I would tell him what it was.

Stephen pulled me back. "I believe him, Richard. He is ignorant, of this at least."

"I am going to kill him," I said.

Blanchet whimpered and closed his eyes, his lips moving silently.

"He is not an immortal," Stephen said. "For the sake of your own soul, Richard, do not murder him."

"Damn you, Stephen," I said and pushed by him to where the gaoler stood waiting. "Where is Prelati?" I cried.

We were shown to his cell where, having heard my brutal interrogation through the walls, he already crouched in the corner.

"Sorcerer," I said from the doorway.

"I know nothing!" he shouted as I advanced on him and dragged him from the corner by the hair.

"Blanchet is a simpleton," I snarled in his face. "But nothing gets by you, does it, Francis." I wrapped my hand tight about his throat and squeezed. "You know what Gilles was. You know that he has avoided death for decades and you know that he has cheated it once again with this trickery. If you wish to avoid your own demise in the next few moments, you will tell me where he has gone."

He did his best to nod and I loosened my grip enough for him to speak. "I believed when he gave himself up that he had some way to escape. When the murders could no longer be denied, he sacrificed himself and us also, so that he could get away and carry on elsewhere, with the man Gilles de Rais considered to be dead. That was why he contrived to give himself up, it was obvious and he even admitted as much, in his way. But he would tell me nothing more and whenever I pushed him he would strike me and rage at me. I was certain he would kill me in one of his black moods even before we were finally arrested and so—"

I slapped his face to shut him up.

"There were men supplying him with blood," I said. "After his arrest, here in this castle. Who was helping him? What are their names?"

He gasped for breath. "I never knew any of that. He would never have told me. I was not one of *them* and he would not make me so. He used me and discarded me."

I let go of his throat but stood over him, ready to throttle the life from him at a moment's notice.

"And so get your revenge on him and tell me where he went."

"If I knew, I would tell it gladly."

I almost killed him from the frustration. It was maddening. But I pulled myself back from the brink and instead asked him a question.

"Where do you think your lord would go? Which one of his own castles? And if not one of his own, who were his allies? Surely, there were other lords or knights nearby who would shelter him in their home and you, who spent so much time at his side, you would know of them. So, who would put him up in his hour of need?"

He frowned, casting his red-rimmed eyes up and down me momentarily before answering. "Do you have any conception of his riches? Of how many men served him and serve him still? He owns a score of fortresses, a hundred villages, thousands of people. When we served him in his crimes and in his other deeds we used half a hundred peasant homes, spread across his lands. So many places, bought and paid for, or taken from men that we killed for him. It is conceivable he is at any one of them. But for how long? And I doubt he has gone to any place associated with the names Gilles de Rais, sir. Even in his arrogance, he would not be so witless as that. But in truth, my lord may end up hidden a dozen miles from here in some foul, dilapidated peasant house or in a grand palace in the East, feted by the Turks."

"You are a talker," I said, squeezed his throat once more. "A man with weasel words who thinks himself so very clever. Well, let me see you talk your way out of strangulation." His eyes grew wild and round and he thrashed and clawed at my throat and I revelled in his fear and suffering, which he had himself certainly inflicted on children before they were murdered.

"You can't do that!" the gaoler said, grabbing me to no effect before appealing to Stephen. "He can't do that, sir, or I'll get strung up myself for allowing it."

I did not care and would have committed another murder but Rob banged into the open door, breathing heavily. "Some bastard," he said, "tipped off the Bishop's men. They're on their way."

Growling, I pushed Prelati down and stalked out of his cell, hearing him gasping for breath as I did so. Following Rob, I hurried toward the way out of the gaol.

"When they come, we will subdue the Bishop's men and then question them," I said to Stephen. "One by one, to find who has helped him escape."

"You assaulted the Bishop of Nantes," Stephen said, lowering his voice. "Once we are cornered they will send more and more until you can kill no more. If we do not leave Nantes almost immediately, they will throw us in here with Prelati and Blanchet."

"He ain't wrong, sir," Rob said.

"We got to leg it now," Walt cried as we reached him.

"God save me from my temper," I muttered, recalling what I had said and done to the Bishop of Nantes in his own palace. "Come, then. Let us be gone from here. All we can do is go south and search those places that we can find. Someone will have seen something."

We made our escape from Nantes, with all of our horses, our belongings, and our valets. The enormous crowds were well on their way to drunkenness and the soldiers had their hands full keeping order so we slipped out without any trouble. Still, I looked behind me repeatedly as we rode to our inn at Mortagne which we reached as night fell.

***

"Can it be true?" the innkeeper Bouchard-Menard asked when we arrived. "Is the demon finally dead?" He stood in the middle of the communal room downstairs with a big, dumb smile on his face and two cups of wine in his hands.

"Yes," I said, lying. "Gilles de Rais is dead."

"Praise God," he said, weeping. "God bless you, good fellows, for all what you have done."

"We shall need food and wine for travelling. Five days' worth for seven men, if you have it and we are leaving well before sunrise," I said to him. "Now, what do we owe you?"

While the valets packed the remainder of our belongings, we sat inside by an open window facing the courtyard, eating in silence. I chafed to be gone, to be chasing after our quarry before he got too far, but also knew we had to wait until morning. It was obvious that the men needed sleep and I found my own eyes closing and my head nodding close to my stew. The poultry was soft and nourishing, and the broth was savoury indeed, laden with salt and fresh herbs and I knew it would likely be the last hot meal I would have for some time.

"Bleed the valets," I said to Rob. "You three all must have blood. We will ride hard in the morning and for every day after until we find him. Wherever he has gone."

"Going to be hard on the lads," Rob observed. "Keeping up with us."

"We will run them ragged and send them back to Normandy and London, if they cannot keep pace. There is plenty more mortal blood for the taking in France."

My men did not like it. Not treating loyal men so poorly, nor risking their regular blood supply. But what were such things compared to Gilles de Rais escaping justice?

"Horses, too," Walt said. "Already looking ropey. Noticed that mare favouring a leg on the way here and the grey's breathing ain't improving, none."

I nodded. "How are our finances?" I asked Stephen.

"Well enough to keep us in food and horses for a month or two," he replied. "After that, we shall have to travel to Rouen to collect additional coin."

The thought of chasing around blindly through the country for more than a month turned my stomach and I put down my spoon.

"Can't we just take what we need?" Walt asked. "We done it before."

"That was war," I said.

"What," Walt replied. "Ain't we at war still now? Ain't we Englishmen and ain't this France?"

"Keep your voice down," Stephen hissed, looking around to see if anyone had heard while Rob laughed.

Outside, the hooves of a single horse sounded on the cobbles of the courtyard. I thought nothing of it because so many came and went at such times but then a voice, filled with anguish, cried out.

"Richard! Where be Richard?"

Looking out of the window, I saw a man attempt to dismount a skittish horse before falling to the ground. His horse danced away from him and I saw in the lamplight that the man's belly and loins were shining with fresh blood.

"Dear God," I said, rushing to the doorway. "Is that Paillart? Stephen, that is Ameline Moussillon's servant."

With Bouchard-Menard clearing the way, we carried him into the ale room and laid him on a cleared table. Stephen opened his clothes while the innkeeper generously poured wine into Paillart's mouth and over the wounds on his belly.

The wounds stank of shit and bile, and I knew his guts had been hewn by a blade. Such a wound would certainly go bad and rot a man inside out, sooner or later.

"I am killed," Paillart said as he smelled it also, his voice rasping and his face pale. "She has killed me."

For a moment, I thought he meant Ameline had been the one who stabbed him but then I shook myself, for that could not possibly be true. "Who has killed you?"

"The damned girl. The girl."

"Tell me what has happened, quickly. Who is the girl who did this to you?"

"No true girl. A demon," he said, gasping. "A demon in human flesh. She broke through my master's door with her bare hands. My master attempted to seize her but she threw him. Across the room, into the wall. I stabbed her in the back, ran her through right and proper." He laughed in disbelief as he recalled it, eyes wild. "She withdrew my blade from her body and used it on me. As you may see, sirs. She held my master down and sucked blood from his throat until he struggled no more. Dear Ameline attempted to save her father but the girl dragged Ameline away. The demon girl looked at me, with her demon eyes. Tell Richard of Ashbury what has befallen his beloved, she said. Tell it to Richard. That's you sir, is it not? It must be. And then they was gone. She took Ameline, out the door to where others waited, men with horses, and they trussed her up and..." He gasped. "You must save her, sir. Save her from the demon."

"*Who* was the demon?" I asked. "A child?"

"La Meffraye's girl. Her familiar. Evil creature. Pure evil."

I staggered away, clutching my head at the implications.

"The girl," Stephen said, coming up behind me. "The young woman that we heard about who accompanied the Terror in her business taking the children. She was a revenant all along."

"Perhaps he made more revenants before his end," I said. "In order to carry out this task."

"Strong, eh?" Walt said, holding up Paillart's head so that Rob could pour some brandy wine into his mouth. "Could you break through a door with your bare hands, Rob?"

He had been in possession of an archer's strength in his mortal life and his immortality had increased it beyond measure. "The physician's house, in Tilleuls? Solid oak door with iron fixings, weren't it? Not bloody likely."

Stephen scoffed. "He exaggerates," he said, indicating Paillart, whose eyes were rolling. "There were others there who no doubt threw down the door prior to the girl's assault."

"Maybe," Walt allowed, and lowered Paillart's head back to the table where the man closed his eyes. He was not far from his death.

"Why would he make some young woman into one at all?" I asked, speaking half to myself. "But not Prelati or the priest or Roger de Briqueville or even La Meffraye herself?"

Walt scratched his nose. "Wouldn't want to stare at some dried-up old bird for a hundred years, would you? Get yourself a nice, round young woman instead, right? Lovely."

"But he does not like young women, does he," I said.

"Well," Rob said, a small smile on his face. "Only one."

I looked at him, not getting the joke.

"Joan of Lorraine," he said, sheepishly.

We looked at each other, arriving at the same enormous thought like a thunderclap.

"But it cannot be," Stephen said. "She burned."

I nodded. "People think that Gilles de Rais burned. We know differently."

"But Joan was burned to ashes." Walt said.

"*Someone* was burned," I replied. "Some poor girl. Who's to say that burned girl was the same Joan?"

"Well," Stephen said, "it should be easy enough to resolve. Did La Meffraye's granddaughter look like Joan?"

"I never saw her. She was not present when the old woman was arrested. Did you see the girl, Walt? Rob?" They all shook their heads. "Surely, though it cannot be that Joan not only avoided her execution, and that she truly was an immortal, as we expected, but that she has been under our noses for months."

"And abducting children," Walt said.

"And feeding on them, perhaps every day," Rob said. "And so growing strong enough to break down a solid oak door with her bare hands."

"Do you really think it can be true?" Stephen said.

I walked to the door and looked out at the night, recalling the fierceness of the young woman at her trial. Her impossible leap from that tower in an effort to escape captivity. A leap that only an immortal could hope to survive. My heart raced, filled with fear and guilt for Ameline, and the death of her poor father. I pushed the feelings away, for I needed my wits about me.

"He's gone," Walt said, his hand on Paillart's chest. "Poor old bastard's had it."

"Remember this man in your prayers," I said. "For with the last of his strength, he did his duty."

The innkeeper's servants carried his body into a storeroom and began scrubbing at the blood and so we filed into the courtyard to continue our discussion.

"The demon girl must be Joan, the Maiden of Orléans," I said. "But even if she is not, she told Paillart that she wants me to follow her. Which means that such a thing is possible. But to follow her, we need a destination. A place that we know. So, tell me, where has she gone?"

"Tiffauges?" Walt asked. "Machecoul?"

"Any truly likely suggestions?" I asked the others.

"Where was Joan from?" Rob said. "Lorraine, no? People go home when they get afraid."

Rob was a family man at heart and wanted nothing more than to go home, so that was where his mind would run.

424

My own mind returned to thoughts of Ameline. The poor girl had simply been at home with her father, living her life, and she was taken in such a manner only because of me. Because of my actions.

"If the girl ever was from Lorraine in the first place," I said. "If she was a revenant at the time, and surely she was, then why believe anything else about her? She was a myth, originally, that notion of a maiden from Lorraine who would be the saviour of France and so surely it was a prophecy that Gilles fulfilled when he created her. He moulded this girl into the shape of that myth and then set her off to charm the lords, and the people, and even the Dauphin. Her true home, where the human girl was born before she was made, could be anywhere in France."

Stephen massaged his temples. "Reason would dictate that *you* know where she went."

"Stephen, you ever assume that others are as reasonable and logical as you are. Most men are fools, monsters, or madmen, and women are even worse. The girl may have lost her mind long ago. In fact, if she is Joan the Maiden then surely we know she is madder than a box of frogs and nothing she says or does can be assumed to be due to reason."

"That is noted," Stephen said. "So, to where would a madwoman go?"

"Paris?" Rob said.

"She failed to take Paris, she would not return there," I said.

Stephen turned. "What makes you speak with such certainty?"

I could not say but something I had said to Ameline came back to me.

People stay away from pain, like an animal fleeing attack, or a child flinching from a hot candle. But we are also drawn to places where we once felt strength and love. And no doubt that is why he returns home.

"Where was Joan's greatest victory?" I said.

"Patay," Rob said, his face darkening. Of course that was where his mind would turn, the place where thousands of archers were cut down.

"That was Gilles de Rais' victory more than hers," I said. "Besides, what is there at Patay? A few houses? Fields, a woodland? It is nothing."

"Bloody Orléans, weren't it," Walt said. "They smashed us, over and over, when they had no right to and they did it because she riled them up into believing it."

"What is in Orléans?" Stephen asked. "Why would she go there?"

"She must be with the Marshal," Rob said. "Is that not what we think, sirs? Joan may have taken Mistress Moussillon but where she has gone, she has gone with Gilles de Rais at her side. The pair of them together won Orléans. And he was rich beyond mortal imagination. He could have bought anything, on the sly, through middlemen and agents. Like you do, Stephen."

"Dom Eustache Blanchet," I said. "He said something about Orléans during his confession, did he not, Stephen? What was it?"

Stephen frowned. "He went there with Prelati on the way back from Florence."

"By God, yes. Blanchet said he went to Gilles de Rais' *house* in Orléans. Prepare the horses. We will not wait for sunrise. We ride for Orléans."

2 1

Desperate Pursuit

Oct 1440

IT WAS A HUNDRED and eighty miles up the Loire to Orléans. Pushing the horses, it took us four days of riding ten hours a day, through bitter rain and the howling winds of the fall. Every mile of it, I swore vengeance and murder and pictured myself tearing my enemies to pieces when I caught up with them.

But also I recalled my conversations with Gilles and his servants. I remembered all over again the battles I had fought where Joan had been their talisman and Gilles had been their commander. Searching my memories for the times when I should have said or done this or that thing differently. If I had acted with great virtue and clarity of purpose. If I had just killed them both myself years ago instead of acting like a lawful commoner instead of a righteous lord of war.

"I have been going over my words with Gilles," I said on the first night when we stopped, exhausted, at nightfall, at a small inn beside the road. "He confessed when he realised he would have to speak about Joan during his torture. Like a fool, I believed he wished to protect her good name. But in truth, he wished to hide the fact that she was still alive."

"You could not have known," Stephen said.

"More like he was hiding his plan," Rob said. "Didn't want to admit he was going to get taken away."

"Yes," Stephen said, as if struck by inspiration. "Surely, Richard, it was his intent to confess all along. Think on it. It was only due to his confession and his vile apologies that he was able to strike his deal to avoid being burned to ashes."

"Why delay such a confession, then?" I asked.

"Can't admit you done wrong right off," Walt said. "People don't believe it if you do that."

Stephen nodded. "The Inquisition would have put him to the Question if he had confessed at the outset. As it was, he seemed contrite and so avoided giving up his plan."

"Might be they took time to plan it," Rob said. "Who was them women who took his body away? Do you reckon Joan was one of them?"

I slammed my fist down on the table. "I should have taken my revenge from the first day. Damn the peasants and their need for justice. Damn the law. Damn the Bishop and the Duke. Next time, I will wait for none of it and I shall kill the bastards wherever I find them."

My men would not meet my eye. We retired early and got up and on the road before dawn, pushing the horses through the freezing dark until we were warmed by our exertions and then exhausted by them.

It seemed I was not the only one wrapped in my thoughts during the long days in the saddle.

"I think I saw her," Walt said suddenly, at the close of the second day while we shoved bread and cheese down our throats in a busy inn. He stared at his wine cup, a deep frown on his head.

"What are you talking about?" I asked. "When? At the execution?"

"No, no," he said. "At the church in Tilleuls. When you got them peasants to promise to make statements. When I come in, there was this woman at the back. Young, short, little thing she was, with a hood over her head even though she was inside the church."

"What makes you think it was *her*?" Stephen said.

"She was alone, keeping in the shadow. I thought at first maybe she was that old lady, the Terror, but then I see she was right young. Something off about her. The peasants kept away from her. Seemed like a spy. I thought maybe she was one of the Duke's or the Bishop's or maybe even the Marshal's but then when I went back to nab her after I spoke to you, Richard, she was gone. Weren't outside, neither. Forgot about it until just now. Sorry, Richard."

"You could not have known," I said, though internally I cursed his witlessness. "Do not give it another thought."

"She was under our very noses," Stephen said. "I wonder where else she came so close to us?"

"He was nervous," Rob blurted out. "When we went to arrest him and you read out the charges, Stephen. Do you recall when he asked if the charges were for him alone?"

"My God," Stephen muttered. "How relieved he seemed when I named his servants also. I, too, thought it strange and now I realise it was that he dreaded the name of Joan of

Orléans in the warrant."

"If we had made more effort to seize La Meffraye," Rob said, "you know, lain in wait for her more, we could have nabbed her and the girl at the same time."

"Only, you'd have thought her a girl, hiding under her hood, and gone to grab her and the little monster would have cut your head off," Walt said. "Be glad we never tried it."

"That is why she was always hooded," Stephen muttered. "And none knew her for a young woman of small stature. It was because she is a revenant and had to cover her skin even more than we do."

"And she needed to hide in case anyone did recognise her," Rob said. "Might be many thousands what saw her in Orléans and elsewhere."

"That old woman kept up the lies," Stephen said. "She claimed even to your face that the girl was her granddaughter, did she not?"

I rubbed my eyes and pinched the bridge of my nose. "It might be that I let my expectations get the better of me. Now I recall it, she said that the life of her family would be in danger if I found the girl. Something of that nature. They had threatened her family, I assume, should the secret be revealed."

"I thought I misheard," Rob muttered, before looking up. "So many times, the villagers spoke of the Terror, La Meffraye, and it seemed that they were speaking of the girl, not the old woman. The little demon, they called her. The demon spawn. Words such as that. And I thought they misspoke, or I misheard. But the Terror was the girl all along. La Meffraye was Joan of Orléans."

"It is all in the past," I said, still so angry at myself that I could barely speak of it. "All that matters is that we find her, in Orléans. Find her and kill her and tear Gilles limb from limb."

When we arrived at the city, our horses were in bad shape and our valets were miles and perhaps even days behind us.

But we did not need them. Walt, Rob, and Stephen had drunk their blood and I commanded them to reach Orléans when they could. If they found us dead, they were free to share our wealth between them. They were good lads and they wished us well as they begged our pardon for their weakness.

Orléans was almost unrecognisable without the English forts and camps outside the walls and the thousands of soldiers inside and out. We came into the city through the western gate just before it closed for the night and though the rain had stopped it was still bitterly cold and we were all sore when we dismounted to stable our horses. The stable hands claimed to be ignorant of the location of the house we sought, though they crossed themselves as they did so.

"I will pay you for the location," I said but none would so much as look at the silver coins I held.

"Where's the market?" Rob asked them, and they told him readily enough.

We hid our weapons as best as we could, keeping them out of sight beneath our coats.

Rob used his bowstave as a walking staff and kept his arrow bag close behind his back and covered himself with his cloak. Praying that we would be unchallenged, we pushed deeper into the city through the stream of people heading home, their business done for the day.

"Pardon me, sir," I said to a man closing up his leatherwork shop. "Can you direct me to the home of Marshal Gilles de Rais?"

He looked me up and down from beside the table that displayed his wares. I was filthy from the road and moving as stiffly as an old man from the hard riding. His son or apprentice began to answer but the leatherworker clipped the boy about the ear, spat on the floor and turned his back on me to finish closing his workshop.

"Don't be wanting to go there," a woman said from the shop next door. "It's cursed."

I walked up the street to her shop, which displayed an array of ready-made shoes. Her husband the cordwainer sat within the workshop behind her. "Where is it, good woman?"

"What business you got there?"

"We are not friends of the Marshal," I said. "Far from it, in fact."

She screwed up her face. "On the river. Past the bridge." Crossing herself, she closed her eyes. "Got red painted doors on the front, don't it. Red as blood."

We hurried on through the streets, looking for the house as darkness fell.

"There," Rob said. "Is that door red?"

If the doors were red, it was the russet colour of old blood. The house was enormous, a high wall built all around the perimeter, with two and three storeys and a tower on the riverside reaching even higher and the gateway with the red doors was high and wide enough to allow a mounted man or a small cart into the courtyard beyond.

We ducked into the shelter of a dark doorway across the street and a few yards up. The fine porch had an awning and hid us remarkably well from casual glances, though if the residents came or went then we would be swiftly ejected.

"Can't see no lamps lit within, can you?" Rob said.

"Perhaps we have it wrong," I said. "I have brought us to the wrong town, or to the wrong house within it."

Walt nodded. "There's light behind them shutters," he said, nodding. "Faint enough but it's there, sir."

"I will take your word for it," I said. Their eyes were better than mine.

"Is that smoke coming from the tower yonder?" Stephen muttered. "Or from a neighbouring house?"

Smoke rose from chimneys all over the city, of course, and so it was difficult to make out for certain. But it seemed as though the Marshal's residence was in use by someone, at least.

"Break it in, you reckon?" Walt said, nodding at the door.

"I'll use my axe," Rob said, patting the weapon where it was hidden beneath his cloak.

I was afraid to go in because I knew, in my heart, that Ameline would not be inside. Not alive, at least. It had been a ruse to bring me to a place of strength so that they could kill me, but they had no need to keep her alive and so she would be dead. Drunk dry and discarded, like so many others. Still, I had a faint glimmer of hope that I expected to soon be snuffed out.

"They are expecting us to come," I said. "They wanted this, precisely this, and we have done as they designed and so they will be well prepared for us to rush in. They know we are three, at least. How can the Marshal and one girl, revenant or not, expect to stop the three of us? The three soldiers that is, Stephen."

"Perhaps they are not within after all," Rob suggested, his eyes flicking up and around us. "Might be it is only mortal servants within, but the immortal lords sit watching this place, awaiting our arrival. Might they not trap us within and burn us alive?"

I shuddered at the thought. I had been in raging fires before and knew that there was no more agonising way to die. "It would have to be a quick fire to be sure of killing us before we escaped."

Walt cleared his throat and mumbled. "Hold up, my dear fellows. They have men within. Soldiers. Bound to be revenants."

"Perhaps," I said, nodding. "Perhaps he does have more men and so when I go rushing in, they will take me by force of numbers."

"Begging your pardon, Richard," Walt said. "It was no suggestion I was making but an observation." He pointed up and across the street at the Marshal's grand residence. "A man walks upon that wall, do you see the top of his helm bobbing along? He has a spear or polearm, which you can see bobbing beside him. And in the alcove there by the window, another man, unmoving."

"I thought it was a statue."

"On the tower," Rob said, nodding. "A man turned from the top with a crossbow in his hand. Gone now to the river side of the tower."

"Damn me but your eyes are good, lads," I said. "How many more does he have within? A dozen? A score?"

"Plate armour and mail, a steel helm," said Rob, nodding at the unmoving man in the shadowed alcove. "They are his famed army, are they not? Some of them, at least."

"How can we kill so many veterans, clad in such fine harness?" Stephen whispered, his eyes wide. "Four against a score? What if it is more? What if he has fifty revenants in there with him?"

I placed a hand on his shoulder. "Stephen, it is three against however many are within. I do not expect you, a monk, a merchant, and a lawyer, to fight soldiers. Revenants nor mortals, neither a score nor one alone."

"I am immortal," he said, shrugging my hand off his shoulder. "I have strength, I have speed. I can fight."

"You will help us, that is certain," I said. "But not by killing. That is our trade. Look at our brother Walter, here. His is a face made to do violence and one that declares to the world that he can do nothing else but that. Look at Rob, feel the breadth of his shoulders and the steel of his eyes and know that his trade has ever been the piercing and hewing of the King's enemies. Yours trade is and has always been your wits."

Stephen sighed. "Should I ready the horses?"

"I'm afraid that you may have the most dangerous task of all," I said, surprising him. "For you must spring the trap."

2 2

The Master

Oct 1440

CLINGING TO THE WALL, I inched my way out along the outer edge of the city wall with the dark river flowing below me. I could barely see my hands in the gloom and found my way more by feel than anything else.

We would attack the building from multiple sides at once and so take the enemy by surprise, cutting through whatever guards there were and forcing our way in to meet in the interior, tapping Gilles de Rais and the Maiden of Orléans before they could escape.

Against my men's wishes, I had taken the riskiest point of entry upon myself. With every sidling step, I regretted my decision.

My task was to climb the outer wall of the house's tower that thrust up in the corner of one wing, which meant first finding access to the river bank fifty yards away at a landing stage before picking my way along the walls that guarded the city from incursion by the river. It had not looked such a long way before I had committed to it and I had confidently declared it to be in a poor state of repair, with ivy clinging in patches and great chunks still missing from the damage caused by English cannonballs.

And yet, I found it was taking me far longer than I expected and already I was tired. The stone under my fingers was freezing and damp and I had lost most of the feeling in my fingertips immediately. The hard riding and lack of rest were taking their toll and I fretted that I would fail even before the assault began. Though night had fallen, I was exposed to view from anyone watching from across the river or from the bridge downstream. I also had the furthest to climb, all the way up the wall and then up the tower built alongside it. One slip and I would fall into the river.

I wore no armour and carried no weapon but my dagger, having learned from experience what an impediment they are and yet it meant placing myself at a disadvantage if I did make it to the top.

Walt and Rob were on the other side of the house and their task was to scale the perimeter wall from the street side without being observed or stopped by the citizenry. It was at least a far shorter climb that would allow them to carry their swords. Rob wanted to bring his damned war bow with him, but I ordered him to stop being so foolish.

Our assault was to be coordinated, as far as we could, and I was supposed to be in position near the top of the tower when the signal was given.

I climbed, as quickly as I dared. Breathing heavily, I chanced a look up at the wall and tower above me. It seemed almost impossibly far.

If I survive this night, I swore to myself, *and even if I should live a thousand years, I shall never climb a wall again.*

From the other side of the building, Stephen banged on the front door and cried out for them, in the best imitation of my voice he could muster, to answer the damned door and to let him in.

That was the signal.

I was far from the top of the tower.

Stephen was supposed to flee from the door after he cried out, and Walt and Rob would then throw themselves over the wall from the street below and begin their attack.

Gritting my teeth, I climbed faster up the crumbling, aged stonework, aiming now to climb up not to the top of the tower but the top of the perimeter wall directly above me. The top was almost within reach.

A man coughed, so close that I looked up, imagining that he would be looking down at me over the side.

There was no face there and a foot scraped on the boards of the wall walk as he moved on away from me.

I let out the breath I had been holding and launched myself up the final stretch, throwing myself over the top. The soldier stood twenty feet away at the end of the section of wall, about to turn to return along the wall toward me.

I yanked my dagger out and sprinted toward him.

He flinched in surprise but recovered quickly and drew his sword, stepping forward to break off my timing. He thrust the blade smartly, which suggested that he knew his business, but I twisted around it and slipped my knife hand up inside his arm and pushed my dagger into his throat as I checked him with my shoulder and brought him to the ground. I ripped my blade back, tearing his throat out and bathing the wall walk with his blood before he could let out a cry.

Nevertheless, I found myself exposed.

Looking down into the shadows of the inner courtyard below, there was a soldier looking up at me. He stared, as if unsurprised and unafraid.

I turned and looked up as a voice cried a warning from the top of the tower, echoing between the wings of the house.

"He is here! The river wall!"

Snatching up the dead man's sword, I pulled open the door at the end of the wall walk to find two soldiers rushing toward me from within, both dressed in armour and helm. One had a mace and the other a short-hafted war hammer, both men began roaring like madmen as they came on.

Retreating outside, I stepped over the dead man lying in the shadows and the first armoured man, his vision limited by his helm, tripped over the body and fell flat on his face. The man behind did not hesitate but jumped over his comrade and swung his war hammer overhead, trying to crush my skull. I rushed in, grasped his hand and ducked low into his body. Lifting him up, I heaved him over the side of the wall and a moment later I heard him splash into the black Loire below.

The first man was getting to his feet when I pulled up his helm and sawed through his throat with the sword.

A cry behind me forced me to spin about and back away. Good thing, too, because a crossbow bolt cracked into the stone where I had been standing. The man on the tower had shot down and then his shouts, too, joined the others echoing in the courtyard. More soldiers rushed from the wings of the house into the courtyard, a couple carrying lanterns that they held high, illuminating the lot of them.

I realised then that the trap Gilles de Rais had set was greater than I had imagined.

He had filled his house in Orléans with his veteran soldiers. The few on the outside were but a hint of what lay within. I wondered how many of the armoured veterans he had made into powerful revenants by the power of his blood. And I had climbed into the trap without armour, armed only with a dagger and now with a dead man's sword.

How many more were within? A dozen? A hundred?

I considered bellowing a warning for Walt and Rob to fall back, thinking that perhaps we could retreat from the building to try a better approach another time.

Yet, how could I flee? Even the slim chance that Ameline was still alive within somewhere meant that I could never have left her to her fate. No doubt, Gilles de Rais had known that about me and used my sense of honour, faded and fragile though it may have been at times, as a weapon against me.

And anyway, there could be no safe retreat. More soldiers were coming up behind me to close off the way out and so I plunged deeper into the east wing, where three soldiers met me in the first chamber.

They each brandished polearms with deadly hammers, axes and spear points arranged on the ends, but the ceilings and close walls meant they could hardly swing the things. Each man thrust his weapon at me and I darted forward past the iron heads and thrust my weight against the wooden shafts, sending the men reeling against each other. Quickly, I slashed at them with my sword and cut each of them down.

Shouting echoed through the wing and footsteps pounded on the stairs. When they came rushing from the stairwell, I came at them from the side and bundled them to the ground, my two blades, the sword and the dagger, flashing and stabbing them to brutal, bloody deaths.

Jumping over them, I hurried down the stairs only to find a dozen men below waiting for me in a small hall. Without hesitation, I rushed into them trusting my speed and skill and aggression to carry me through.

Killing three immediately, the others cornered me and I found a wound in my shoulder streaming blood. I had not noted receiving it and the sudden anger and fear pushed me to rush them again. They were fearful of my speed. They could not have witnessed anything like it in their entire lives and after throwing down a pair of them, the rest fled. Or rather, they tried to. I caught up with each man and speared and slashed and hammered them to death with their own weapons.

A gash had appeared over my temple and I recalled the desperate swing that caused it, fast and strong enough to cleave my head into two pieces had I not slipped the blow.

As I pushed open the door that led out into the courtyard, eight more men rushed me and pushed me back into the hall with a fury that for a time I could not match. These men were certainly revenants, and their speed was greater by far than any I had fought so far that night. In desperation, I retreated further and found myself with gashes opening on my arms and hands and on my jaw.

Still, as they cut me, I cut them, and my strokes had precision and timing that theirs lacked and soon the eight attackers became six and then I was chasing down the three that fled toward the front door of the house.

The wounds all over my body were terrible but I had cleared the entire wing of the house and no more came for me. I rushed back to the hall and out into the central courtyard, where I found an armed man creeping along in the shadow. I swung my gore-spattered blade at his face but he spoke and I checked my blow.

"Richard!"

"Walt? What are you doing? Come in here, out of sight."

When we stepped back into the doorway to the hall, I saw that he was breathing heavily and had blood all over his face and mouth.

"Thank Christ it's you, sir. Me and Rob cleared the other wing, murdered the lot of the bastards." He looked at the bodies in the hall. "As you did, it seems."

"And where is Rob now?"

"Got separated," Walt shook his head. "Heard him fighting for a bit but then I couldn't find him and when I called, he didn't call back. Hiding maybe, or he's dead."

"Damn. What about Gilles? Joan?"

"Killed about a dozen of the bastards when I cleaned that wing." He jerked his thumb behind him. "No Gilles there. No demon maidens, neither."

"I also killed many soldiers and yet found no sign of our true enemies."

"Maybe they ain't here at all."

"The tower," I said, easing open the door to look up at it across the courtyard. "I was supposed to clear the tower but I never reached it. Come, through the courtyard, we shall finish this one way or another."

We crossed the dark courtyard quickly and Walt heaved open the door at the bottom which led into the base of the stairwell beyond.

"Thought it'd be locked," Walt said, a grin on his face as he half turned to me.

A crossbow clanged from the darkness within and I shouted a warning but the bolt hit Walt somewhere between his chest and his face with a wet thud. He fell back, his cry of pain cut off almost before he could utter it.

I charged through the doorway just as another bolt clanged from within, throwing myself down onto my face just in time so that the bolt missed me and shot over my hunched back.

Knowing I was close to death once more and at the mercy of anyone close by, I rolled over in order to get up.

A hand grasped my hair and a knife slashed over into my belly, cutting me deep once, twice, and almost a third time until I caught the attacker's wrist in both of mine. The wounds were agony and I was sickened greatly by the damage done. *By God, he is strong*, I thought, *as strong as I, at least, and perhaps stronger*. As I held his wrists and twisted, trying to pull him down off his feet while avoiding his blade, another man fell upon me, wrapping his arms about my legs.

I kicked out, not thrashing but with a swift blow from my heel. Through luck rather than judgement I caught him clean enough to crack his jaw or perhaps his nose.

The other man yanked his knife away from my grasp and swiftly drove that blade into my chest.

I had twisted before it plunged into my heart but still it pierced me between the ribs and I knew I would instead soon drown in blood if they did not slay me first.

Still kneeling behind my head, he drew his knife out and tried to cut my throat. Somehow, I got my hands up to my neck just in time and so instead of sawing through my neck he frantically worked the blade back and forth, cutting deep lacerations into my palms and fingers.

Grasping the sharp blade and twisting, I pulled it from him and rolled over. He lost his grip on his knife and I got my knees under me and drove myself into him so that he fell back against the lower steps of the stairwell, pulling the knife from his hands and stabbing it into his body once, then twice, and I was about to finish him off when the other man rushed me from behind.

I twisted and slashed out, catching him across the face. The blade cut across his eyes and through the bridge of his nose. Screaming, he fell to the side and I turned to finish off the wounded man under me at the base of the stairs.

"Please," the man said, almost wailing. "No, no."

There was no reason to hesitate and yet I recognised the voice and it stilled my hand.

"It is you," I said, in the dim lamplight seeing that it was in fact Gilles de Rais cringing beneath my knife. He was the man who had almost killed me. Blood welled out of the wounds on my chest and I knew that he had done me mortal damage. Without human blood I would myself swiftly die and so I wanted nothing more than to cut off his head. He deserved to die, for all the murders he had committed, least of all my own.

"Where is she?" I asked, coughing up blood along with my words.

His eyes flicked up the stairs above us.

"Thank you," I said and placed the knife against his neck, though blood streamed from my lacerated hands and I struggled to keep hold of it.

"Wait, wait," he said, lifting his chin and inching up the steps as he strained to pull away. "Your woman will be killed."

"Ameline?" I stopped. "She is above us?"

"With my lady," he said, gasping and wincing.

I gritted my teeth. "With your..? Joan the Maiden is up there?"

His mouth twitched at the corners. "And she will kill your woman before you can stop her."

The flicker of hope kindled in me but then faded as I realised he would say anything to prologue his life a moment longer.

"If the Maiden harms Ameline then I will kill her immediately. Nothing will stop me."

"I can save her," he replied, coughing up blood. "Save your woman. If you let me."

"A trick," I said, shaking my head as blood dripped from my mouth.

"I swear it."

"Meaningless words," I growled and pushed the knife against his neck.

"Kill me then," he said, closing his eyes and lifting his chin. "I beg you. End it, please. Please. End me now as I pray."

I rolled him over and pushed him. "Up, then. Up, up."

Staggering up the stairs with one hand over my chest and belly, I crept up behind him with my knife at the ready. The soldier I had blinded below continued to wail about his blindness, banging around at the base of the stair. I wondered if Walt was dead yet or if he was still lying in the dark courtyard, dying alone and in agony. He would have wanted me to try to save Ameline, for he was a knight at heart. It galled me to leave him behind but I was dying myself and I had only so long before I would bleed to death.

Shoving Gilles faster and faster, I crawled up, step after step. My head swam, and my vision clouded. One of my bloody shoes slipped on a step and I fell to a knee. Whipping my knife up, I saw Gilles peering down at me. He made no move to attack and instead turned and continued up.

We rounded the final bend and came immediately into the chamber at the top of the tower. A fire burned in a hearth on one side. A ladder led to a closed hatch in the ceiling.

Ameline stood upright in the centre of the room, her hands bound and her face a mask of terror and exhaustion. Behind her, a low iron cage. Inside that cage, three young children huddled together in the far corner.

And there stood Joan. La Pucelle. The Maiden of Orléans. I recognised her pug nose, small mouth, and her wild, shrewd eyes.

Joan held a knife to Ameline's throat. Though the Maiden was far smaller, she was possessed with an immortal's strength and so kept her prisoner from freeing herself with a hand wrapped like a vice around Ameline's upper arm.

"Halt there, Richard," Joan said, sneering at me and pushing her knife against Ameline's skin, threatening to break it. "Unless you want to see this girl's blood spilt."

"How is it that you live?" I asked her, inching forward.

"My Gilles saved me," she said, smiling at me and then at him. "You did something right, once."

I inched forward again. "Who was it that you burned?"

She scoffed. "It is a simple thing to find a girl that the world has discarded. They are so many, and they can be bought, threatened, and owned, really rather easily. If you take one more step I shall cut this bitch's throat."

I froze.

Gilles cried out, clutching the wounds I had given him. "Joan, please, no."

"I knew you would fail," Joan said to Gilles, bitterly. "You useless dog. Look what you have brought us to. He has killed you."

"He dies also," Gilles said, gesturing to me as he fell sideways against a table near to the fireplace. "And his men are dead."

Joan looked me up and down. "Yes, yes, I see it. So, Richard, my useless Gilles has killed you after all. Finally."

"Not yet," I said, coughing up blood and spitting it to the floor after I spoke.

Joan scoffed. "Drink one of the children," she said to Gilles, jerking her head at the cage behind her.

"No," he said, slumping against the wall. "No, I will not."

"Do it," she hissed. "Quickly, while you still can."

"No more," he said, weeping and leaning his head back against the wall. "No more killing. No more. Not the children."

"You are weak," Joan said. "You were always weak at heart. Die, then. You may as well die, for your will is long broken. When my lord returns, you will be no help like this."

"Your lord?" I said, a chill about my heart because I thought I knew who she meant. And I dreaded it.

"My lord," Joan said, her eyes shining in the lamplight. "My lord, the Archangel Gabriel."

"She means Milord William de Ferrers," Gilles said, glancing at me as he pulled himself to his feet once more. "Your brother, sir."

"Brother," Joan said, scoffing at him before turning to me. "You are Judas. My angel said that he would deal with you when he returns to these lands."

I laughed but the pain of it racked my body. "Yes he said that," I said, wincing. "Said it a long time ago."

She lifted her chin and glared triumphantly. "He sent word. He comes. Even now as we speak, he comes with a great army that will save France and all Christendom from the heretics."

"You are the heretic," I said, not believing a word. "And a lunatic."

She ground her teeth then snapped at Gilles. "Take a child before it is too late."

Gilles slid along the wall toward the fireplace where an ornate short sword leaned. I forced myself to straighten up, feeling my wounds open and more blood seep from me, and prepared to defend myself with my knife. Gilles grasped the sword, turned and brandished it.

Brandished it not at me, but at her.

"No more killing, Joan," he said, almost wailing. "I cannot bear it. I want only peace. All I did, for nothing. William comes not to save Christendom but to *destroy* it. Everything he said, everything he promised. It was all lies."

Joan snarled like an animal. "Unfaithful. Heretic!"

Beside her, Ameline attempted to pull away but Joan held her fast.

I was fading quickly, my sight darkening. My wounds were not healing swiftly enough and I lost more blood by the minute. I meant to save Ameline before I fell but could think of no way to achieve that. So I sought to draw things out further.

"Destroy Christendom?" I asked Gilles. "What does William mean to do?"

Gilles scoffed, disgusted. "He comes from the East with an army of Turks to overrun us. An army of a hundred thousand Turks who come to conquer Christendom forever, to conquer us and subjugate us under his rule for a thousand years. So his messenger said. I do not believe it, but the man swore it was true. He has betrayed Christ."

A *messenger*, I thought. *A man. A man who could lead me to my brother.* "I can believe it," I said. "He attempted it before, centuries ago, with Mongols instead of Turks. Where is this messenger?"

He shrugged. "Long gone. Two years past."

"Tell him nothing," Joan snapped. "Traitor."

"He dies," Gilles said. "What can he do?"

Joan looked me up and down, noting the blood pooling at my feet.

"So William made you both," I said. I wiped the blood from my mouth. I knew I would have to rush Joan and somehow reach her before her knife could mortally injure Ameline. "How many more of you are there?" I asked. "Who else have I missed all these years, other than you?"

440

"We are the last," Gilles said, his head dropping.

"We are the *faithful*," Joan said, raising her voice. "The only ones who had faith all these long years. We worked, we toiled. We were nothing, nothing at all, until he lifted us up and gave us eternal life and the true purpose. Oh, the glory. My angel, my sweet angel. How we toiled for thee."

"How did you so toil?" I asked, shifting forward.

She tossed her head back, smiling. "We began a rumour, a prophecy, that a maiden would come and save France. An armoured maiden from Lorraine. And then we worked to better ourselves. To learn the art of war and the war of art. Theology, poetry, philosophy. How we toiled. What riches we made. Always, we spread the word that the maiden would come. And then, when the time was right, I fulfilled the prophecy that I had written for myself two centuries prior." She laughed, a mad, peeling laugh and her knife pressed at Ameline's throat.

"Let her go or I shall kill you," I said, taking half a step forward.

"If you come closer, I will kill her," Joan said. "Then kill you all the same."

We both knew that if I did nothing, I would bleed to death on the floor and nothing would stop her killing Ameline and the children.

"No!" Gilles shouted.

His voice was filled with sudden and powerful anguish that I did not understand.

And then I did.

For I turned in time to see Rob come through the doorway with his bow in hand, an arrow nocked and pulled to his cheek. Blood streamed down from a gash on his head but his eyes were focused and his arrow point did not waver.

Joan was frozen in shock but Ameline was so close beside her.

I started to cry out to wait but Rob did not hesitate.

He loosed his arrow, the cord whipping through the air.

Rob's arrow hit Joan square in the chest and she fell back, dragging Ameline down with her.

As I lurched toward the two women, Gilles hefted his sword with a cry and ran forward, his wounds forgotten in his despair and his rage. I twisted, raising my knife and preparing to meet his attack once more.

But he was not coming for me.

His eyes shining with mad grief, he swung a wild cut overhead and brought it down, meaning to split Rob's skull in two. Surprised by the sudden flank attack, and the speed and ferocity of it, it was all Rob could do to raise his left forearm to protect his head and rush in to grasp his attacker.

The sword blade sliced through Rob's arm above the wrist and his hand tumbled to the floor as Gilles and Rob clashed together, both growling like beasts.

Ameline screamed as she struggled to get away from Joan who grasped her long hair in a hand.

I rushed in and fell on Joan, breaking her grasp and pulling Ameline away to safety before pushing her aside. Blood poured from my wounds as I looked down at Joan. The great arrow, a yard long and as thick as a thumb, had run her through the chest, wedging itself fast between her ribs or perhaps in her spine.

Turning, I watched Rob, one-handed now, stabbing Gilles in the guts with his own sword as he stood over him. It was done.

Beneath me, Joan gasped, her arms flailing. It seemed that she had lost the ability to speak and perhaps to stand.

"You killed all those children," I said. "It was you and him together."

She coughed up a mouthful of blood and spat it out. "My lord comes. My lord comes to begin a new age. And... to kill you."

I scoffed. "I have stopped him before. I shall do so again." I looked up at the children in the cage and at Ameline, who hunched against the wall. "Look away, children."

"Do not kill her," Gilles cried from the centre of the room, pleading. He crawled away from Rob, who tracked him slowly with his sword at the ready.

I pulled her up by the hair, cut into her neck and threw her across the room into the fireplace.

"Joan," Gilles wailed, slithering forward. Rob moved to finish him off.

"Leave him be," I commanded.

Rob stopped, confused.

Gilles fell to his knees deep in the fireplace and reached into the hearth to drag Joan out. Before he could do so, I grabbed the nearest lamp and threw it at them. It smashed and the oil burst over Gilles and Joan, immediately bursting into flame.

They screamed as they burned and as they died, clutching each other to the last, the flames burning hot until they screamed no more.

"Rob?"

"I'm alive," he said, clutching his arm while he stared at his severed hand where it lay on the floor. His face was white.

"Ameline," I said.

She stared at me, her eyes white in her dirty face. "Get away."

"I will not harm you."

"You are like them?" she asked, eyes flicking to the burning corpses. "A drinker of blood? Ageless. Monstrous."

I knew I was dying and could not bear that she would think so badly of me after I was gone. "Ageless, yes. But not like them. Never an innocent." Slumping against the wall, I eased myself to the floor and closed my eyes. "Be sure to free those children, won't you, Rob?"

He moved toward the cage. "Might need two hands, Richard."

"I will do it," Ameline said.

"God bless you," I muttered, feeling myself going.

"Blood heals you?" she asked.

I nodded, not daring to ask. She had suffered so much and suffered it because of me. I could not ask her. Better to die.

"Drink mine," she said, taking up my knife.

At heart, she was ever the healer.

Rushing down the tower, I cut off the head of the blind crossbowman who lurked still, hoping to catch us as we escaped.

We reached Walt, mere moments before he died, and I withdrew the bolt from his neck, spilling even more blood from his terrible wound. He clung on to the last vestiges of life for long enough to drink of Ameline's blood and was healed. Rob also drank, and soon his stump stopped bleeding and began to mend itself. Together with the children, we made our way out the building. The townsfolk of Orléans had heard the commotion and greeted us warily at first until we explained that we were agents for the Bishop of Nantes and had freed the children from the Marshal's soldiers. Then, they gave us wine and food and bandaged our wounds and found us rooms at an inn.

Two days later, we escorted the children and Ameline back home, to Brittany.

2 3

I n v a s i o n

O c t 1 4 4 0

POOR ROB. THE LOSS of his hand meant he could no longer draw his bow and that more than anything else broke his heart. We had all known men who had suffered such injuries in battle and so knew also that it takes a man time to come to terms with becoming an invalid. He had to learn new ways to dress and care for himself, and to eat and fight. But one thing that we had plenty of was time. And life is easier when one has servants to help fasten your clothing.

Walt had taken a bolt to the neck and had bled so profusely and come so close to death that even with days' worth of blood in him, the skin where the wound had been remained scarred and he spoke with a hoarseness that he had not had before.

"You might never shoot a bow again," Walt rasped at Rob on the road back to Nantes. Ameline and the children slept in the chamber upstairs at the inn while we toasted our survival below. "But what a final shot that must have been, eh? Wish I had seen that, by God. As far as final shots go, to kill the Maiden of Orléans and to save Richard, that gaggle of children, and a beautiful maiden all with a single arrow." He slapped his knee and laughed until he winced and held his neck.

"I suppose that is true," Rob said, attempting to smile.

"It was the finest shot in all the world," I said. "And I take back every jest and gibe I ever spoke against that bow, for you were right to carry it as you did. With that arrow, you ended the last of William's servants. The last in Christendom, at least."

"Yes," Rob agreed. "A hand is no price at all to pay for such a victory."

"A fine thing to say," Stephen said.

It was too soon for Rob to mean the words that he spoke, but he would, in time.

We were wanted men, in Nantes, for the assault I had committed on the Bishop, and for my assault of prisoners and bribery of the gaolers and all the other mischief we had caused. The lords of Brittany wished to put the entire matter quietly to bed and so we had to be careful. At the final stretch, we sent Ameline driving the wagon into Nantes with the children in the back. They were yet terrified beyond words and whether their spirits and their wits ever recovered from their abduction, I did not know. At least they had their lives.

"I am sorry," I said to Ameline. "They did this to you because of me."

She had healed me with her blood and did not believe I was evil, yet she could not stand to lay eyes on me.

"I know," she replied. "Because they believed you cared for me."

"They were right about that, at least. But still, I wish that I had not put you in such danger."

She nodded, absently. "I must see to burying my father. And Paillart."

"I am sorry."

Her eyes roamed the landscape before fixing on mine again. "I will never be able to speak of this. To anyone. Not without them thinking me mad."

"The truth is that it is over," I said.

"Is it?" she asked, her eyes looking through me.

The wagon rumbled on toward Nantes and I sat in the saddle with my men watching her and the children go.

***

Astonishing as it may seem, a number of the accomplices avoided justice. After my abduction of him from that tower, Roger de Briqueville had provided the evidence necessary to produce the arrest warrant for Gilles. He was certainly guilty of being present at a number of murders and as far as I am concerned that was enough for him to be hanged. But Roger was a knight from a good family and had a rich and noble father. Ultimately, the man was freed and entered the service of Pregent de Coetivy, an Admiral who proceeded to request a pardon for his new servant. The letters of pardon pass Roger off as an unwitting and unknowing participant in the crimes and who, upon discovering them, immediately left the company and service of his lord. Those letters paint the knight as a good and decent man but there is no doubt this Admiral Pregent de Coetivy wanted Roger to provide some vile, base service suited to his depraved mind. So, he got away with murder, and more than one, but he was not the first mortal to do so and was not the last.

Francisco Prelati, the vile cleric, alchemist, sorcerer, and mountebank, managed to avoid the noose but was condemned by the court to life in prison. Practised charlatan and rogue that he was, with his gift of the gab and sleight of hand, he somehow managed to escape from gaol. From there, he found his way into the service of another enormously wealthy nobleman, Rene de Anjou, who he convinced he could make richer by the alchemical creation of gold. The gullible Rene even made Prelati into the captain of La-Roche-sur-Yon, to where flocked other former servants of the Baron de Rais, including the pathetic priest Dominus Eustache Blanchet.

The damned prideful idiot that he was, Prelati could not contain his delusions of power and he had a minor lord named Geoffroy Le Ferron arrested as he passed through La-Roche. Le Ferron was the brother of the priest that Gilles de Rais had abducted years before and Prelati meant to exact some sort of revenge for all that had befallen him and his old master since that abduction. But Prelati had bitten off more than he could chew, and the affair brought to light his escape and his new crime resulted in Prelati being hanged. Finally, justice had been done.

Dominus Blanchet had been protected by the Church and received a sentence of banishment from Brittany, which was appallingly lenient. Especially as he left for a short time but then returned until Prelati was killed and his last allies were gone. For all I know, the weasel monk and priest lived a long life.

And then there was Perrine Martin, La Meffraye, the Terror of Tiffauges and Machecoul, who had personally taken away so many boys over the years with her tricks and honeyed words and heartlessness. She had claimed to be acting only as commanded by her lord. She said also that if she had not done as they asked, Joan the Maiden would have murdered all of Perrine's family. But still, there had to be some punishment for someone who could knowingly supply innocent boys for slaughter.

But they let her go.

If she had been a man, she would have been hung and burned also but convinced that an old woman could never have a will of her own in such crimes, they simply opened the door to her prison and set her free. Ever a cunning one, she immediately disappeared, along with her family.

There was an entire network of servants and associates who had been involved to a greater or lesser extent. Men like the porter at Tiffauges, Miton, and all the other porters who certainly had known about what was going on. Servants who scrubbed away the blood and washed clothes or burned mounds of linen. Others who heard the screams of the tortured and the dying.

If I had been able to remain in Brittany, I am not sure I would have been able to resist executing the worst of them. Prelati certainly deserved death, as did Briqueville.

But I had business in the East.

The war between England and France limped on a few more years, with treaty and truce bringing the conflict to an end. Altogether it had been a hundred and sixteen years and I had been there since the start and for almost all of it, on and off.

In the end, what had it all been for?

Henry VI was the weakest king England had ever known. He gave away all we had won for his kingdom in return for peace. It was the most pathetic capitulation imaginable but then he was a weak and useless man, so what else could one expect? If only his mighty father had not died so young. His weakness of character and the madness that came to take his mind led to his loss of the throne to Edward IV. From what I hear, he was a good man, an excellent knight, but another lacklustre king. He ruled until 1483 but the nobility of England warred over control of the crown for decades in a conflict that became known as the Wars of the Roses.

I did not take part in those wars, though I wish I had been able to knock some sense into the damned lot of them. In time, I would return to England when a new dynasty ruled. That of the Tudors.

After so long looking inward, England would emerge onto the world stage once more and I would be there with them as we reached out to counter the rampaging Spanish and began to settle in the New World. Most of the Tudors were a miserable bunch but Elizabeth was quite something else entirely.

As far as the world was concerned, La Pucelle died a heretic. But the French knew she had been wronged. A posthumous retrial for Joan was opened after the war ended. The Pope authorised the proceeding, known as the nullification trial, and its purpose was to investigate whether the original trial of condemnation and its verdict had been handled justly and according to canon law. Investigations started with an inquest by Guillaume Bouillé, a theologian and former rector of the Sorbonne. A good man, so Stephen said.

They found a huge number of strange and contradictory accounts with regards to her supposed upbringing, but they brushed all that aside lest it affect the outcome of the new trial. It was to be fair and legal in all ways, so they said, which meant that they intended to find her innocent and clear her name.

Before even reaching a new verdict, the Church declared that a religious play in her honour at Orléans would allow attendees to gain an indulgence by making a pilgrimage to the event. Which tells you all you need to know about the fairness of the process.

In 1456, they declared Joan innocent, of course, and also that she died a martyr. What is more, they formally accused the now-dead bishop who had conducted the first trial with heresy for having convicted an innocent woman in pursuit of secular, political outcomes at the behest of a foreign kingdom. Of course, they were not wrong about that, at least.

Over time, her legend grew until she became something like a talisman for the French people, and for the lords of the Church in that nation. At some point, they began calling her Joan of Arc, as they believed that was her father's name. In truth, he was likely just some poor fool who had been paid to say the girl was his and had become trapped in the lie.

During the Wars of the Reformation, Joan became a symbol of the Catholic League, who were an order dedicated to eradicating the Huguenots and Calvinists from France. In the 19th century, the bishop of Orléans led the efforts which culminated in Joan of Arc's beatification in 1909. This meant that Joan had not only officially entered Heaven but could now intercede on behalf of those who prayed in her name.

What she really did, along with Gilles, was rile up the French so much that they threw us out of France. The commoners had for a century been subjugated in misery while we rampaged through their land but then Joan had come and through her madness, on behalf of William, had bestirred the passions of those same people to such an extent that neither Gilles nor Joan could control them. No one knew the truth about her and so they made her into whatever they needed her to be, whether they wanted her to be a heroine or villainess. Who was the real Joan? Whatever she was in life, in death she became a symbol of something great. There was a real Joan and there is the myth of Joan. It is the myth that has the power and always did.

But there need be no wonder for anyone, for she always insisted, no matter how they threatened and mistreated her, that she was guided by the voice of an angel. It is only I who knew that the voice she imagined all those centuries was William's.

He had abandoned her, and Gilles, and all the other monsters he created, to their fates. And when he sent word of his return, it was too late. The centuries of death and murder had taken their toll on their souls and Joan and Gilles had been driven mad. Driven to consume ever greater numbers of children in order to increase their power, they had succumbed to the relentless damage it had done to their souls.

Gilles would be remembered down the centuries as the beloved captain and companion of Joan but mainly of course for his enormous crimes. He has taken all of the blame when it was equally Joan's, or perhaps much more so, and so he has entered history as one of the first and greatest serial killers. Some of the other men who share that appellation were the sons of Priskos. Those murderers also I tracked down and killed in the years to come, one near Cologne and the other in Bavaria. But none had the power and the wealth and authority that had allowed Gilles de Rais and his servants to commit the crimes they did, for as long as they did.

In all my long years, I swear I witnessed no crimes so depraved and so evil.

***

Watching her drive that wagon toward Nantes, I knew Ameline's heart was broken. The loss of her father was too great to be overcome quickly, if at all, and she was alone in the world. I wanted to stay and take care of her but I could not.

"Perhaps I could see her right," I muttered. "Keep an eye on her for a while. From afar."

"We must be gone," Stephen said. "There are too many questions. The Bishop's warrant for our arrest is still in effect. The Duke's soldiers are looking for us."

"Who will look after her if I do not?" I asked him.

"You cannot save everyone, Richard."

I turned on him. "I do not wish to save everyone. Only her."

It was my actions that caused her such loss, such pain but I could not undo it. Some deeds simply cannot be undone.

"You have saved her," he insisted. "We saved everyone in this land from Gilles. From Joan. There will be no more murders and missing children. The weight of the curse has been lifted and the fear will be thrown off. The people will heal, in time. The land can be lived on again, fully lived. Marriages will be celebrated joyfully, and their children will be able to play and grow to adulthood without threat."

"In time, yes," I said. "But she needs someone now."

"She has property," Stephen said. "Some wealth, an education. She is a beauty. There will be suitors nonstop, now, and one of them will make her a good husband."

He was right enough but I wished so very much for that husband to be me.

I knew I was not evil and prayed that I would never become so. Perhaps it was in me to turn to depravity, like Gilles and Joan had done, and if I gave in to it then I could become just as deranged and Satanic as they had. Whether it was the nature of William's blood rather than mine, or if there was something especially rotten in the both of them to begin with, they had over the decades and centuries, turned into demons themselves.

There was only one way that I knew to stop myself from taking the same path. Whether he is a commoner or a lord, a man must strive to live a virtuous life. When confronted with the choice of virtue or sin, one simply must choose virtue. One will not succeed, not always. But as long as one lives, the choice between virtue and sin remains in every act, in every day, and one must wrestle oneself onto the right course. It is simpler for a sinful man to chose sin than virtue but when one is virtuous in his heart, acting virtuously becomes easier every day.

"Come, then," I said, turning my horse. "Let us be gone."

"Too right," Walt said. "If I never see Brittany again, it'll be too bloody soon."

Of course I could not stay. For I knew that William had finally returned, just as he had promised he would. It had been almost two hundred years, as hard as it was for me to believe, but he was finally coming. Just as I had both dreaded and longed for all that time.

And he was returning to conquer Christendom at the head of an army of a hundred thousand Turks.

I did not know it then but the only man standing in his way was from a small, mountainous principality called Wallachia. A man who would become a hero of his country. A hero, in fact, for all Christendom, although he is not remembered that way.

He is remembered as Vlad the Impaler.

A man known to his own people as the Son of the Dragon.

They called him Dracula.

VAMPIRE

IMPALER

The Immortal Knight
Chronicles
Book 6

Richard of Ashbury
and Vlad Dracula
1444 - 1476

1

The Battle of Varna

1444

A HUNDRED THOUSAND Turks faced us across the plain. Banners snapped in the wind coming down from the hills and from the Black Sea close behind us.

It was to be the last battle of the last true crusade. The last time the kingdoms of Europe united to wage holy war on the enemies of Christ in a great battle.

"What do you reckon, Richard?" Walt asked me. "Biggest army you ever seen?"

We sat in the saddle in our armour, with the mercenary company I led around us. A hundred good fighting men, well equipped in steel and riding warhorses, plus their attendant squires, pages, grooms, and other servants which made me a minor though welcome addition to the crusade.

I looked out at the swarming mass of enemy horses and men filling the land from hills to hills and beyond, shining in their riot of armours and colours and raising noise enough to startle Heaven.

Across the plain in front of us, the azab infantry were robed and armed with spears. They were in effect a peasant militia, unmarried men who fought because they had no choice but were no less dangerous for all that. They might have been armed with just bows and spears, but there were many thousands of them that would have to be overcome.

It was not only low-quality men who were arrayed against us on foot, for the Anatolian infantry behind them wore mail with small plates, armed with spears and shields.

Beyond those infantry, in the centre of the entire army, thousands of elite Janissaries massed behind palisades, in their white or yellow robes, holding powerful recurved bows or the new hand-guns, and long, wicked polearms with spear heads, axe blades and hooks all on the same weapon. They also fought on foot but they were the most well-trained, well-equipped forces that the Sultan could deploy. At their sides were slung long, thin, curving swords that could split a man's flesh to the bone in a single, swift cut. Beneath their robes, they were protected by a light coat of mail, some bore bronze shields with shining bosses and on their heads they all wore tall, white felt hats that made them impossible to miss even from across the battlefield.

The *sipahi* horsemen from Anatolia and from Rumelia – that is the Turkish-held lands of Europe such as Bulgaria - were heavily armoured, wearing steel turbans on their heads that had mail hanging down to protect their necks and long white feathers trailing from the top. Some wore mail shirts, others wore lamellar armour of hundreds of small steel plates sewn together. Their horses were likewise well armoured in strong, light steel. Their steel shone in the dim light as the masses of cavalry rode this way and that on the two wings of a front two miles wide.

Our great army of Hungarians, a few Serbs, and German and French knights, was far smaller. Vlad II Dracul of Wallachia sent a force of seven thousand men, though he would not join us for the whole campaign and had left us in anger before the battle.

We were led by King Vladislaus of Hungary but the true commander was a knight and great lord named Janos Hunyadi. His countless military successes against the Turks in the Balkans over many years had so invigorated Christendom that the Pope had called the crusade and so it was Hunyadi, as the best soldier in Christendom, who chose our strategy and our tactics.

"Can we win?" Walt asked.

The eyes of my closest companions, Eva, Rob, and Stephen, also turned to me.

I said nothing.

"One Christian is worth a dozen Turks," Rob said, raising his voice. Some of the men of my company overheard and called out in affirmation.

"If we cannot win," Stephen asked, speaking softly as he sidled his horse closer me, "would it not be reasonable to withdraw? Our company, I mean. Richard?"

"I took the cross," I said. "I am sworn to fight. And so my men, who are sworn to me, are sworn to fight this battle also." I looked at him. "You included, Stephen."

"So, then, we fight," Stephen said, scowling. "Even if our deaths are almost certain?"

"Yes," I said.

"Nothing is certain," Eva said, almost speaking over me. "Even our reasons for being here."

I ignored her barbed comment. We were there because William was there, fighting for the Sultan. It was Eva and Stephen's agents who had discovered him but she was right that it was not certain. Even so, I felt it in my bones that he was across the field that day. Hidden from my view by the blur of distance and the swirling of the ranks of men and horse, perhaps, yet there all the same.

And the odds were against us in the battle but we had not meant for it to be so.

Hunyadi's plan for the crusade had been straightforward enough, in concept. We had followed the line of the Danube before crossing it in September 1444 and then westward into Bulgarian lands up to the Black Sea to the town of Varna. Instead of slowing our advance to take numerous, small enemy fortresses we had ignored them.

We knew of a great Turkish army coming to do battle with us but they refused to engage and so our advance to Varna was rapid.

From there, so we planned, we would push south into Turkish Rumelia and throw our enemy from Thrace and Bulgaria. The Turk had been in possession of those European lands for far too long already. And then we would go on, chasing them back across the Bosporus and back into Anatolia.

In all this we would be supported by fleets of Burgundian, Venetian, and Genoese ships who would close the Dardanelles and the Bosporus, denying the enemy the chance for reinforcements. Once we had the Turk on the run, we could pursue all the way to Jerusalem and win back the Holy City once and for all.

That was the plan.

But first, we had to defeat the great army of the Turks, led in person by Sultan Murad II.

We had reached Varna on a bitter day at the start of November and were shocked to discover the entire Turkish army camped just two miles away to the west beyond the hills. It was a failure on the part of our scouts and our leadership but once it was done, it could not be easily undone. Our army found itself trapped with the Black Sea to the east and the thickly forested hills in the north from where we had come. Between the northern hills on our right flank and the sea close behind us was an extensive marshland that meant we could not slip away quickly without being surrounded and destroyed.

"It is victory or destruction," I said, raising my hand to point at the Turkish centre. "Besides, William is there."

My companions looked at me once more.

"You do not know that," Eva said.

"I know it."

"You *wish* it," Eva said. "Because your desire for revenge is so strong that it has overcome your reason. You do not *know*."

"Your own agents have said he sits at the Sultan's ear, whispering that Christendom must be destroyed. And the Sultan is here, and so William is here." I looked at the vast host. "He would not be elsewhere."

"We are not certain that the man calling himself Zaganos Pasha is truly William," Stephen pointed out. "None of us have seen him with our own eyes."

"They say he is a tall and dark-haired Christian and none knows from where he has come. Some say he is Serbian, others Greek, and others that he is a Frank. It is typical of William to cause such confusion, sewing a dozen stories so that the truth is lost amongst the lies. This Zaganos Pasha has come from nowhere, at no time, and others whisper that he has always been there. He is feared and respected even by his enemies and the other pashas and viziers at the Sultan's court. Who else could Zaganos Pasha be but William?"

"Even so," Stephen began, "we are throwing our lot in with this doomed army without certain proof that—"

"You and Eva will retire to the *wagonberg*," I said to him.

Stephen broke off and turned to look to our rear. Behind us, the centre of our position was a vast ring of a hundred fortified war wagons, emplaced on a section of higher ground.

"I would rather fight at your side," Eva said.

"And I would rather that the work of the Order of the White Dagger continue," I replied. "Should I fall today."

She wished to argue but for the sake of appearances before my men, she simply nodded and pulled back to the *wagonberg*. Those one hundred war wagons were defended by hundreds of expert hand-gunners from Bohemia. The combination of war wagons and firearms were a remarkable military innovation by the Hussites that had been proven effective in their repeated victories against the great kingdoms of Christendom in the decade or two prior. An innovation embraced enthusiastically by our Transylvanian-born Hungarian leader Janos Hunyadi.

The wagons had high, solid walls on all sides from which the hand-gunners and crossbowmen shot at the enemy, along with men armed with polearms to protect their fellows should enemy cavalry ever reach the wooden walls of the wagon fortress. The solid wood sides dropped down to protect the wheels and the wagons were joined together by strong chains. I had seen wagons pulled into defensive formation before, indeed the Tartars had been well-known for the tactic, but first the Hussites and now the Hungarians had developed the concept into a sophisticated weapon of war that had proved all-but unassailable in previous battles in central and eastern Europe.

Indeed, the day before, when we had discovered the enemy horde were so close, a council of war was called. By that day at Varna, I had fought with Hunyadi for over a year and ever since I had impressed him in my first battle at his side he had invited me to join him at such councils.

It was the king's tent, and King Vladislaus sat in a large chair at the high end of it, but it was Hunyadi who commanded proceedings from where he stood, to the side and two paces in front of the King.

Hunyadi was about forty years old at Varna, in the prime of his life, and he had been a soldier for all of that life already. He was no more than middling height, was rather dark, and he had a heavy brow and a magnificently large nose, but he was not unattractively featured for all that. His eyes were shrewd, pits, twinkling with the intelligence of the man behind them.

456

In his youth, Hunyadi had served as page for a famous Florentine knight, then as a squire for a great Hungarian lord who loved battle, before serving the Despot of Serbia. Because of his brilliance even as a young man, he had been brought into the retinue of Sigismund, the old King of Hungary, who ordered Hunyadi to join the army of the Duke of Milan so that he might learn the modern ways of battle in Italy. Later, Sigismund brought Hunyadi into Bohemia where the young knight had learned to admire the tactics and technology of the Hussites that he would later replicate.

I had arrived in Hungary, still assembling my own mercenary company, just in time to join Hunyadi in his campaign against the Turks. We fought the Turks in a dozen battles and won almost all of them, though we had ultimately failed to break through the Turkish strongpoints in our efforts to invest the Turkish capital of Edirne, which had once been called Adrianople by the Eastern Romans. Still, we had thrashed the Turks three ways from Sunday and I had been mightily impressed by Hunyadi's tactics and his ability to lead men.

Still, many of his betters were jealous of his rise above them and they doubted his abilities to lead a crusade, even if it was in the name of King Vladislaus of Hungary.

"We are outnumbered and trapped," Cardinal Cesarini had said, his eyes wild. He was a tall man, as finely armoured as a prince, and in the prime of his life. "It is not possible that we should win. All we can do is fortify ourselves within a *wagonberg* and wait for our great fleet to arrive, which surely they must at any moment."

He was not just a representative of the Church of Rome but was a great lord in his own right, as were the other bishops and Church lords who had come as leaders. Each led their own contingents of powerful knights and other men-at-arms, meaning their words at a war council carried weight.

Many of the nobles in the tent called out their agreement.

Janos Hunyadi looked at each man who spoke and seemed to be fixing each of them in his mind as he did so. One by one, they fell silent. Some hung their heads, as if they were chastised boys.

"But even if it did arrive here, would the fleet be large enough to take all of our men from the coast?" Hunyadi asked. The lords spoke in French, occasionally in Latin, and sometimes in Hungarian. My Hungarian was improving every day but thankfully French was spoken by all lords, even those from the mountains of Thrace.

"God willing," Cardinal Cesarini said, to general muttering. "Surely, my lords, with the fleets of the Burgundians, the Venetians, and the Genoese, we shall be saved from this disaster."

"Indeed," a young princeling said, raising his voice. "Indeed, my lords, we must not engage with the enemy. I will not lead my men into a fight they will not survive. We must withdraw tonight under cover of darkness. By morning we could be away toward the Danube."

Voices were raised in agreement and many a man nodded to himself and to his neighbour.

Hunyadi caught my eye and nodded once to me.

I peered over the heads of the men in the command tent and looked down at the princeling that spoke to the great lords of Christendom with such surety. He was a stocky lad with a fluffy beard and moustache beneath a long, sharp nose.

"I beg your pardon but how old are you, little lord?" I called out. A round of stifled laughter flowed through the tent. Even Hunyadi's mouth twitched and he covered it by scratching his cheek.

"Who said that?" the young prince snapped, turning around from the lords at the front. "Some coward who speaks from behind the safety of—"

He stopped as I pushed forward through the men and looked down at him. "I meant no offence, my lord. Your suggestion is not such a bad one. I simply wondered how much experience you have in warfare."

The swarthy young fellow drew himself up as tall as he could and lifted his long nose. "I am Mircea of Wallachia, eldest son and heir of Vlad Dracul, Voivode of Wallachia. I bring seven thousand horsemen and am one of the leaders of this army. Who are you, you great Frankish oaf, to even address me?"

I smiled widely and bowed low. "Of course, now I recognise you. I met your father a few months ago, when he returned to his homeland. I believe your revered father said at that time that we had no chance of victory, did he not? In fact, I recall his very words. The Sultan's hunting party is larger than your entire army, Hunyadi." A few men behind me snorted and young Mircea of Wallachia's dark face darkened further and I quickly raised my voice. "And he was right."

The tent fell silent.

Mircea nodded and spoke warily. "So, you agree with me, sir? We must withdraw tonight, is that not so?"

I lifted my head and pursed my lips, tempted to ask whether he still demanded my name now that he thought I agreed with him but there was no purpose to humiliating the fellow further, especially when he wielded such power. "A withdrawal through the hills at night is possible," I said and turned to address all those present. "For some of us, perhaps. A thousand men might make it out, escaping detection. Two thousand, perhaps." I turned back to Mircea. "Seven thousand, even." His eyes widened. "But any man that attempts to leave this place shall be breaking his oath. What is more, he will be committing a great sin. The greatest sin, perhaps. Yes, any man who attempts to take his men away from the battlefield will not only be abandoning the King of Hungary and his fellow Christians, he shall be abandoning Christ."

Mircea of Wallachia stiffened. "What are you suggesting, sir?"

"Yes," Janos Hunyadi said. "Make your point, sir. There is much to discuss. Surely, you do not suggest dividing our army?"

"My lord," I said and bowed, then I paused while every man looked at me, including the King of Hungary from his throne. "I suggest that tomorrow, we attack the Turk and drive him from Bulgaria forever!" Men cried out and began arguing with me and then with each other. Many seemed to agree with me, especially the French and German lords. But others disagreed, calling into question my sanity and my ability so that I raised my voice above them so I would be heard.

"We do not have the numbers!" the Bishop of Talotis cried. "Even with God on our side, we cannot defeat so many."

"Do not let your eyes fool you, my lords," I said. "Their numbers are swelled by the many thousands of *azabs* they will throw at us. These men are peasants, with no armour and almost no will to fight. We shall run them down without slowing our horses."

"It is not the peasants but the *sipahis* that concern us," said a young Hungarian nobleman named Stephen Bathory who was the Palatine of Hungary, which I understood to be as high a rank as a man could achieve in that kingdom and he was well-favoured by his king. "The *sipahis* are equal to our mounted men and they have two or three times our number. They are our only concern."

"They are not our equal!" Michael Szilágyi said. He was another Hungarian noble and Hunyadi's brother-in-law. I liked him, although he did not feel the same about me and mistrusted outsiders. Which is right and proper, of course, and I did not hold it against him. "Our armour is stronger and our horses far larger."

"Precisely," said Bishop Dominek of Varadin. "Our beasts shall tire while theirs remain fleet and strong throughout the day."

Hunyadi, watching and listening, glanced at me.

I raised my voice over theirs and silenced them with sheer volume and the refusal to cease speaking. "What else can we do, my lords, but attack them and destroy them? If we take shelter inside the wooden walls of a *wagonberg*, with no army in the field, the cannons of the Turks will blast down our walls and destroy us. Our only way out is over the corpses of the Turks."

Cardinal Cesarini raised his hand and cried out. "We also have cannons, sir, thanks to God. And so with our cannons we shall destroy the Turks first, from a position of safety. Until the fleet arrives."

"There will be no fleet!" Bathory shouted. "If they were coming, they would be here by now, would they not?"

The discussion continued and Hunyadi nodded his thanks, so I stepped back into the crowd and held my tongue until they had talked themselves into action.

There really was no other choice but to attack and Hunyadi won them over with his plans. The king gave all appearances of backing Hunyadi's plan of action and once Vladislaus stated that we would indeed attack tomorrow, the others fell in line or fell silent.

It had always been the case that no matter what anyone said, or hoped, there was no way out but forward, through the Turks.

It was to be a battle.

"He may be just sixteen years old," Hunyadi said, nodding at the back of Mircea of

Wallachia as the lords filed out. "But he is not a fool. He has the cunning of his father. And, like his father, he will continue to play both sides in this crusade. He will pay tribute to the Turks with one hand and offer the other to Hungary."

I sighed. "He is a devious little shit if ever I met one. But one can hardly fault a lord for protecting his vassals."

Hunyadi scoffed. "His vassals? Vlad Dracul and his son care only for themselves." He sighed. "But I must give him some credit. The Turks hold his other two sons as hostages and he certainly risks their lives by sending his men to join us. So, Richard, no matter how we dislike them, we must try to not judge him or his father too harshly."

"And we need them."

"I wish it was not so but yes, we need them."

"His men must be guarded in case Mircea attempts to withdraw his men in the night," I said. "It is clear that he believes we cannot win the battle and so he will flee. He does not seem to be a man overly concerned with honour."

Hunyadi sighed again, rubbing his eyes. "Unfortunately, you are right. Yes, they shall be watched. The Wallachians are always watched. But if he takes his seven thousand horsemen away from me, what can I do? Send ten thousand to stop him? Begin the battle by fighting amongst ourselves? If he decides to abandon us, all I can do is let him go."

"We cannot afford to lose seven thousand."

"No."

"Whether or not we win this battle," I said, "we must not allow any Christian land to fall to the enemy, by force of arms or diplomacy. The Wallachians have the most defensible land in the region and they must be brought to heel."

He nodded. "It is easy for you, an outsider, to say such things. You are more right than you know but it is not so easy to do. We shall deal with such matters later. Tonight, we must prepare. Tomorrow, we must fight. God wills it."

"He does, my lord, He does." *And so do the Turks*, I thought. "With your permission, I will see to my men."

After an uncomfortable night camped on the plain, exposed to the wind off the sea behind us, we rose in the morning and were arrayed in a crescent, with Lake Varna on our left flank and the hills rising to our right. Our forces were spread across a mile or two. My place in the centre was not far from Hunyadi and his enormous bodyguard of superbly equipped men-at-arms.

The thousands of mounted Wallachians were behind us and were under orders to act as a mobile reserve to counter any breaks in the line or any flanking attack that came around by the lakeshore or from the hills. I prayed that young Mircea would do his job well, for if the swarms of *sipahis* could get in amongst us and behind us, we would be finished.

Behind the Wallachians was the *wagonberg*, our wooden fortress protected by the Bohemian mercenaries with their hand-guns and great polearms. If it came to it, we could fall back and rally at the *wagonberg* under cover of the guns. That was where I had sent

Stephen and Eva, along with those of our servants who would be of no help in the fighting, and the youngest of the pages and grooms.

"Turks in the hills, now," Walt said, nodding that way. "See the little bastards glinting in the woods on the ridge there?"

I could see little enough in the trees. Walt had good eyes and a good nose for danger, so I believed him.

The Sultan's empire was divided in two by the waters of the Sea of Marmara and the straits of the Bosporus and Dardanelles. With Anatolia on one side and Rumelia on the other, the lands of Europe that had once been ruled by Constantinople or Bulgaria or other Balkan kingdoms. And the Sultan had deployed his army in the same way, with the lords and soldiers of Anatolia on his left flank and those of Rumelia on his right.

"Their Anatolian cavalry will engage our right," I said, "and their infantry will push through the woods, beyond our flank, and get behind them. They will have bows with which to shoot our men and they will have spears to ward them off."

"What can we do about that?" Rob said, frowning as he squinted up at the hills.

"Nothing."

"God damn them," Rob said, turning to spit.

"It is a rather standard ploy, is it not?" I asked. "When one has the numbers on their enemy."

"I do not damn the Turks but our own lords," Rob replied. "Why in the name of God do we have almost no infantry? We need men on foot. Spearmen, peasant levies, even townsmen would do. Have they lost their wits?"

"They believe that infantry would slow them down too much," I said. "Others say they cannot afford to pay for the upkeep of such low-quality men when we already have so many veteran mercenaries, and that the supplies required to feed them would be more than could be procured. Others I have heard state simply that they have no need for such useless oafs blundering about against our Turkish foes, being that our enemy are mostly horsemen themselves."

"Madness," Rob said. "Peasant spearmen could cover the woods up there. They could screen our mounted men here at the front. They could fill gaps in our lines, hold positions out on the field for us to make charges from. Anyone would think our great lords have never been to war before."

"They haven't," Walt said.

I shrugged. "Some of them know. Others know that nothing can resist a heavy horse charge. Not all the Turks on earth. And they are trusting to that."

"Can't they bloody see how many spearmen the Turks have?" Walt said. "How many, do you reckon?"

Sighing, I pointed out vast formations all across their lines and made an estimate. "Twenty thousand? Thirty? Difficult to see through all the horsemen galloping here and there."

"They have more in infantry than our entire army, Richard," Rob said. "You are certain we must fight this battle?"

We have no choice, I wanted to say. But that is not what my men needed to hear.

"What happens if we do not smash them here? They may push on to the Danube and then along it all the way to Belgrade, and from there to Buda, then to Vienna. Where to then? Prague? Nuremberg? And then into France?"

Walt laughed, shaking his head. "You exaggerate, Richard. A dozen kingdoms would rout the Turk well before then."

"How many men can France put into the field, would you say? Twenty thousand?" I pointed at the Turks. "There stands a hundred thousand veterans, armoured in plate and mail, with more and better guns than us." I jerked my thumb over my shoulder. "How many more men could they bring up from Anatolia, if they needed to? As many as this again? Four times this many?" I pointed at the centre of the Turkish army again. "And William may be there, at the heart of them. Driving them on. It is our duty to be here. It is our duty to defeat the enemy. And so that is what we shall do."

A few men around me cheered but their apprehension was apparent.

We had around three thousand men in the centre, mainly King Vladislaus' Polish and Hungarian bodyguards, the Hungarian mounted mercenaries, and the Hungarian nobles and their men. The mercenaries were commanded by Stephen Bathory.

Our left flank was commanded by the very capable lord Michael Szilágyi. He had around five thousand Transylvanians and German mercenaries and a few Hungarian lords who were sworn to him. They were enormously outnumbered on that flank by twenty thousand *sipahi* cavalry, each man with mail or lamellar armour and quality helms, with long lances and shields for the charge. Their horses were fast and could run all day, if handled well.

Still, I hoped that Szilágyi could hold them.

It was clear from the deployment of Turkish light infantry moving through the forested hills that they would attempt to turn or crush our flank there. And it was clear that Hunyadi had seen the danger, as he weighted our strength most heavily on our right. Bishop Dominek of Varadin had six thousand men alone. Cardinal Cesarini commanded thousands of well-equipped German crusaders, and the Bishops of Erleau and Talotsi, the governor of Slavonia, commanded their own contingents.

I prayed it would be enough.

In the centre, the Sultan stood behind ten thousand Janissaries.

These were his best men. They were also men who should have been ours. They were ours by blood and by birth but they had been stolen. Taken, by the Turk's *devshirme*, the Blood Tax, imposed by the Turks on all Christians who they had subjugated. Every year, the Sultan's agents, often Janissaries themselves, would collect Christian boys from the Balkans and make his personal slaves. These boys would be aged eight or ten or even older boys close to becoming men. When they were taken, these poor innocents were indoctrinated into believing the alien religion of Mohammedanism. They were trained in military pursuits and administration until the age of around twenty and then placed into the Sultan's personal army or the civil service. And they were utterly loyal to the Sultan, and he used the existence of these elite troops to keep his great lords under control.

It was only the Christians under the Turks who were subject to the *devshirme*. Not the Jews, nor the wild Turkmen tribes in the east, or the Mongols of the Golden Horde. Only Christians—whether Anatolians whose ancestors were Romans and Greeks, or Bulgarians from Rumelia—a people strong in body, quick in wits, and loyal to a fault, were desired for the Blood Tax. Some of the highest ability might one day, after a life of service, become landowners and a very small handful might one day become governors or viziers. But no matter how high they rose, they would never be granted complete freedom.

And the Janissaries alone, the most highly trained soldiers in the world, numbered ten thousand. Not only did they hold the centre, on a small hill, they were well dug in behind barricades and were supported by an incredible number of levy troops.

And we would have to somehow overcome them all to achieve victory.

A sudden wind whipped up from the Black Sea behind us, wailing and powerful enough to stagger us and frighten the horses. Hundreds of banners were blown down and standard bearers pulled off their feet. Only that of King Vladislaus III stayed upright. It seemed to be a sign from God but what meaning the sign had, no one could agree.

"Here they come," Walt said, pointing to our right flank.

Up along the row of hills, thousands of Turkish horsemen advanced in a staggered series of lines.

"By God," Rob said, crossing himself. "They are so many."

"Our men are stronger," I said, sitting as high as I could and peering through the upright lances and banners between me and the right flank that curved forward. "All we need to do is keep our heads."

Even as I spoke, though, thousands of our horsemen on that flank advanced away from our lines to meet the massive Turkish attack.

"What are they doing?" Walt cried. "Why advance now? They must wait."

"They must," I agreed. "Yet they do not."

We watched in horror as the horsemen under the bishops of Erlau and Varadin plunged headlong into the massive Turkish advance. Rather than leave the others to their fate, the two thousand men under the Bishop of Talotsi, also advanced into the enormous melee. All together, our men were outnumbered three or four to one and soon there was little chance for them to withdraw, no matter how frantically Hunyadi's men signalled that they should do so.

With the right flank advancing so far forward, there was now a huge gap between them and our men in the centre.

"Richard?" Rob said. "Perhaps you might ride across to Hunyadi and suggest he close the gap?"

"Hunyadi knows his business," I said. "But tell our men to prepare themselves. We shall see action soon."

It was then that the Turks sent their other wing forward against our left, by the lake. Michael Szilágyi was a capable man and the Hungarians were disciplined enough to meet it in good order. The clash was incredible, with dozens of companies charging and wheeling repeatedly with neither side gaining any immediate advantage.

"There are gaps between us and both flanks," Rob said.

"And if the enemy push between one of them?" I said.

"I suppose we in the centre would counter and crush them from both sides," Rob admitted. "But the Sultan has enough men to attack both gaps and get around our flank on the right."

"He is holding, for now," I said, watching the Turkish centre. The tens of thousands of infantry and horse there were still dug in behind their barricades and in their trenches. "He fears Hunyadi's ability."

"You think the Sultan afraid?" Walt asked.

"He *respects* Hunyadi's ability," I said. "And so he should. Here is a signal, men."

Trumpets sounded and flags were waved from the centre where Hunyadi and his bodyguard advanced. I ordered my men forward and we moved away from King Vladislaus and his loyal troops who stayed back. I turned my horse to review the state of my men and noted behind them that the Wallachians were advancing to take the position that we were leaving. They would plug the gap and they would help to defend the King. Hunyadi really did know his business.

"Where is he leading us?" Walt called out over the wind and the growing din of battle. "Left, right, or centre?"

"We shall see," I said. The noise of the clashes on the flanks was like a distant sea, rising and falling but relentless and growing louder as more and more men were drawn in.

"Care to wager on it?" Walt asked, grinning.

"Do not be crass," I said as the men-at-arms of my company rode past us. "Thousands of men are about to die."

"Ten ecus says that we attack the left flank."

"You do not have ten ecus," I said, nodding and holding up my hand to this or that man of mine as he advanced.

Walt patted his breastplate. "Got more than that right here, Richard."

"Very well. Hunyadi must seek to save our right before it collapses," I said, confidently. "And that is where we will go."

"Richard wagers we go into the hills, very well, and I say it shall be the left." Walt grinned. "Rob?"

"*I* do not have ten ecus," he said. "But surely we will attack the centre?"

"Only a madman would assault ten thousand hand-gunners, Rob," I said. "Protected by ten thousand spearmen."

He scratched his nose. "I'll not wager what I do not have."

"Our lads look keen enough," Walt said as the last of our men-at-arms advanced past us, raising their hands or their lances in salute to me as they went. "Hard-hearted bastards, ain't they?"

We had French, Burgundians, Britons, English, Irish, Scots, Welsh, all desperate men seeking fortune and glory. But I had personally tested each one before allowing them to join my company and Rob and Walt kept a close eye on them. Since leaving England, we had recruited those we needed as we crossed Europe and we had expelled those who were found wanting, either in ability or in moral character. Some were brutal men, killers with little education and even less fear, but I would not allow disobedience or men not in possession of self-control. They were a good company and I was pleased with them.

"Will we get close to the Sultan?" Rob asked. "You believe William to be there, at his side. But if the centre is unassailable..."

"The more that I think on it, I believe if we drive off the flanks, we will have a stalemate. We cannot assail their central position and I doubt they will attempt our *wagonberg*. If his *sipahis* are crushed, the Sultan will likely withdraw. William will have to wait for another day."

"If he's even there at all," Walt said.

"The time for discussion is over," I snapped. "Come, let us catch Hunyadi and his men and do our duty."

With a final glance back at the great banner and bodyguard of King Vladislaus and the vast *wagonberg* behind him, I closed the visor on my helm. I could see ahead through the slits and down at my body through the breathing holes but due to the solid armour covering my neck, I had to turn my shoulders along with my head in order to see to either side. My nose was filled at once with the sourness of my breath.

We galloped forward and with surprise I saw Hunyadi's banner continuing straight toward the centre of the enemy. We were yet far enough away that their Janissaries' handheld firearms would not reach us but still I thought I had overestimated Janos Hunyadi. He was going to charge straight into a hail of deadly lead balls and the battle would be lost. All would be lost.

But I should have had faith for, with a waving of signal flags and blaring of trumpets, he finally ordered us to attack the enemy flank.

Not toward the hills where our right was crumbling, as I had wagered ten gold pieces in expectation of, but instead to our left, where Szilágyi's Hungarians were holding.

We had advanced so far that we crashed into their flank and slipped behind them, attacking the rear.

"Keep the men together!" I ordered. "Stay together!"

My company formed up together on either side of me and we charged into the *sipahis*. I thrust my lance into a Turk and shoved him out of his saddle before pushing on into the man behind him. The press of men was enormous and the sea of horses swelled and crashed under the weight of our charge. My men knew not to advance too far, too quickly, and we helped each other to disengage and pull back. Once we and our horses had paused for breath, we dressed our line and advanced again into a charge at their crumbling flank.

As their centre pulled back to meet our charges, Szilágyi pushed them further with his own men. Hundreds died in the charges and hundreds more in the press of the fighting but they were unnerved due to being surrounded and their will crumbled until the *sipahis* fighting us fled in something close to panic.

"Stay here!" I ordered, and Walt and Rob and my other key men ensured my company stayed together. There was little better in life than pursuing a fleeing enemy and many a soldier let it go to his head, whooping and cheering as he chased the *sipahis*. But the day was far from over and we would need every man on the field and so my company reined in and came back to the centre with me.

Other captains and lords were not so fortunate in their soldiers as was I. For the Turks fled so far that the chasing Hungarians disappeared along the lakeshore. Later I would hear that they in fact got fully behind the Turkish lines and began looting enemy camps that they found there. The damned fools filled their purses with loot and sport as they ran through panicking camp followers and servants while the rest of us fought on.

As Hunyadi attempted to rally us back to him in the centre, Walt rode up, shouting and pointing his bloody mace behind me.

Opening my visor, I turned to look up at the hills.

Our right flank was destroyed.

The men there were outnumbered in horse but they had also been surrounded by Turkish archers in the woods, shooting down at our knights as they fled the field. Some of the Germans were pulling back to the *wagonberg*, still in good order with banners raised, but the flank was still open.

"Are we finished?" Rob called. "Should we return for Eva?"

"The Wallachians must hold the line in front of the wagons," I cried. "The battle is yet in the balance, men. We have won a flank apiece but both centres hold. All is well. We shall yet win the day."

But I had underestimated Mircea, son of Vlad Dracul, and his Wallachian horsemen, for they did not hold, nor did they engage the enemy. Even as the rest of the Christians watched, they galloped their seven thousand men, perhaps a fifth of our army, along the banks of the lake through the gap the Hungarians had opened up by crushing that flank. Later, I would discover that young Mircea stopped only to join in the looting of the Turkish camp before continuing on all the way back to Wallachia.

"Those duplicitous bastards," I shouted as they cantered by in their thousands. "Treacherous little shit. I swear by Christ I shall have his head."

"Is that it?" Walt asked. "We can't win, now, can we?"

"No," Rob said. "Only a matter of time before some other lords decide to follow the Wallachians."

"We are not lost! But we must assault the horsemen on our right," I shouted to my men, pointing up at the hills. "The only enemy cavalry on the field is there, do you see? We can still kill them all. Do you hear me? We will kill the enemy cavalry and then the day is not lost." When wearing a helm, it was difficult to hear a lord's voice especially with the wind and the roar of battle, and so I shouted something clearer my men would understand. "We will kill them!"

Hunyadi and his Hungarians were forming up to do just that and I led my men forward with them. We rode slowly across the field and squires and pages handed out water and wine and some men stuffed bread or slices of sausage into their mouths. Exhausted horses were exchanged, and damaged weapons replaced. It appeared that some of the Hungarian nobles who had remained in the centre with the king were moving rightward to join us in the rising ground. I wondered whether the Turks would chance an assault against the King, but we were now between him and most of the enemy's remaining horse so it seemed likely he would be safe where he was.

The Turks were superb horsemen. Their horses were well-bred and trained for war, just as the men riding them were. Big fellows with bow legs and broad chests, just like the Mongols and other Tartars from whom they were descended. Hundreds of years of success on the battlefields of the steppe, and the hills of Anatolia, and the plains of Thrace and Bulgaria, had made them experts at war and had provided them with enormous riches plundered from the collapsing Roman Empire of the east.

Even so, there was nothing in all the world that could stand up to a charge by the knights of Europe. We were superb horsemen, too, raised in the saddle, practised in the proper use of the lance from boyhood. Our steel armour was the finest the world had ever seen, whether Italian or German made, and as long as we were led by a lord who knew the limitations of the charge, there was no hope for an enemy that attempted to resist it.

Hunyadi ensured that each of his companies were formed up before he ordered the attack on the Turks. His bodyguard were the centre, and Hungarian lords surrounded him. Near to the centre, Walt and Rob harangued my company into a line with voices louder than thunder. Contingents from Germany formed their own lines above us to the right. The Bishop of Talotis, God love him, somehow brought his defeated men back to join us in a renewed assault.

The order was sounded to advance and six or seven thousand of us moved toward the Turkish *sipahis*. They were busy chasing down the poor remnants of the right flank, desperately defending themselves from the wheeling Turks. When they saw us coming, the enemy galloped in all directions, attempting to form up against us. I thought that they would certainly do it but as we got closer and slowly increased our pace, they were still attempting to regain their order and were yet in several great, confused masses rather than ordered formations. At the last moment, our scores of companies charged in a staggered, broken line that must have been a mile wide.

I saw little of it, as I lowered my lance and raked my spurs against my horse, trusting that my men would be beside me. I thrust my lance into a Turk's helm with such force that he was certainly destroyed immediately. On, I charged, and my lance took the next man low on his flank as he turned to flee and his horse fell along with him. My lance broken, I used an axe to break through the Turks I came to. Beside me, my men attacked and we pushed on into the darkness of battle, with the cacophony of war filling my head so that all I could hear was a roar and the laboured breathing from my own lungs as I drove deeper into the enemy.

All of a sudden, there was daylight and sky, and no more enemies to kill.

They had broken and fled. Bodies lay everywhere underfoot and horses with no riders galloped in confusion this way and that.

Our men were celebrating our victory. We had killed the Beylerbey of Anatolia along with thousands of horsemen, and now the crusaders were the only horsemen left on the field.

"Now what?" Walt called, after we collected our surviving men and took stock of the damage done. Only six of my men had been killed. We were bruised and battered, some men nursing bad wounds, but my company had tasted a victory and only wanted more.

"No man loots the bodies," I shouted. "Unless it is to replace a weapon he has lost. We must reform on Hunyadi and either attack that damned fortress of a Turkish centre or withdraw."

"Richard?" Rob said, looking down the hill to our centre. "In the name of God, Richard, what is he doing?"

By *he*, Rob meant King Vladislaus III, who was riding at the heart of his enormous bodyguard. Thousands of heavily armoured horses and knights advanced along the flat of the plain straight at the Turkish centre.

"By God," I cried. "He means to attack himself."

"Stupid bastard," Walt said, pausing to spit a mouthful of blood to one side. "He wants some of the glory for himself, does he not?"

"He must be blind," Rob said. "Or mad."

"Glory," I said. "He seeks glory."

Walt scoffed. "He'll find a spear shoved up his arse instead, the silly bastard."

"Long has he been in Hunyadi's shadow. A lord should not be outshone by his vassal. And Vladislaus is a king."

"So he means to steal Hunyadi's victory and claim it for his own," Rob said, nodding.

"He's a fool," Walt said.

"What do we do?" Rob asked.

I looked for Hunyadi's banner. He was forming up his men but we were so much further away and the King, astonishingly, did not appear to be waiting for us. The trumpets sounded and we made our way across the slant of the hill toward the massive Turkish centre. By that point, we had been fighting for hours and our men and horses were exhausted. If we rushed toward the enemy, we would be on our knees by the time we reached them and so we were able to watch as the flower of Hungarian nobility charged the Turkish centre. It was the king's finest men against the Sultan's ranks of infantry, thousands of them, in prepared defensive position.

In front of the ranks of waiting Janissaries were lines of azabs, the peasant spearmen. These were swiftly overcome by the power of the Hungarian charge and the spearmen fell or were scattered as the nobles and their men rode them down and continued on, barely slowing or needing to reform. It was a magnificent display of bright colours and shining steel.

Behind were ranks of armoured infantry, armed with spears and axes, and wearing metal helms. But these men fled as the Hungarians rode down the thousands of peasant levies in front of them.

That left only the Janissaries between the King of Hungary and the Sultan of the Turks.

"He's going to do it!" Walt shouted. "Bloody hell, Richard, the king is going to kill the Sultan after all."

Many of my men and the others around us believed the same, for they raised their weapons and cheered, urging their king on. There were ten thousand Janissaries but their lines looked rather thin compared to that of the peasants the king had just run down. The Janissaries were barely armoured.

My heart fluttered at the thought that we might just do it after all. *If the Turks break, we shall have to pursue William through Bulgaria*, I thought.

As the king and his men approached the hill upon which the ten thousand Janissaries formed, the foremost ranks of the elite Turkish soldiers raised their long weapons to their chests, pointed them, and almost as one fired their hand-guns.

I had seen small hand-held cannons here and there for years. In Milan, decades earlier, I had watched a company of mercenaries displaying one such weapon which they propped up at the front with a long, forked stick and a man held at the rear with the pole attached to the iron barrel. When another of the fellows held a burning rope to the touch hole, the small cannon belched out a great stinking cloud of smoke with a sound so loud it caused my ears to ring for a day. The poor fool not only missed the target but fell over backwards after the shot, no doubt more from fear of mishap than from the force. How we laughed.

"Absurd of them to suggest such a device could replace a crossbow," I said to Walt, both of us grinning at the notion.

Fifty years later and we yet used crossbows but often they were used beside hand-gunners, whose firearms had developed into reliable weapons fired by couching the thing in one's arm at chest height while touching the firing pan with a lit rope. The Bohemians used them to great effectiveness from the safety of their wagons, as did the Hungarians who had taken up their arms and methods.

But the Janissaries had them also and trained to use them in the field and had done so with great success against Turkmen tribes in the east and against the poor people of the Balkans and so were well practised in technique and application. Far more than I had realised until that moment.

Thousands of Janissaries fired their guns in a great billowing of smoke that belched from their lines.

Moments later, the massive sound of it reached us and boomed and rolled from the hills.

Down on the plain, the royal and noble riders and horses fell in their scores but still they came on, their horses drumming their hooves on the earth. Before they reached the Janissaries, another volley of smoke and noise crashed and more knights fell tumbling back or rolling beneath their horses.

It was a slaughter. It reminded me of English archers shooting their longbows into French knights so many decades before. But instead of joy, I now felt horror.

Even though so many fell, the mad charge of the Hungarian nobles reached the Janissaries lines. We still rode closer and as we descended, it became more difficult to see but their charge crashed into the Janissaries at many places. They rode down the enemy palisades and then broke through the Janissaries' lines. Once through the first ranks of hand-gunners, they pushed deeper in.

I still had hope.

The king's banner wavered and slowed but it, and the king beneath it, pushed deeper into the Turk's camp to within a stone's throw of the Sultan's great tents.

But the enemy numbers were too many.

By the time we came down the hills and reached the flanks of the enemy lines, there was little we could do to reach the King, deep in the centre. We killed thousands of spearmen on our approach, we bowled over the armoured Anatolian infantry who had fled the king's charge, and we rode down Janissaries and cut at them. And yet they did not break. Far from it, in fact, and when they recovered from the shock enough to begin firing their hand-guns at us, we were forced back in our thousands and we retreated out of range for another charge.

"Come on!" I shouted. "We must break them. We will break them!"

No one wanted to charge against such an implacable enemy but I rode up and down the front rank of my company.

"We must not, Richard," Rob said. "It is madness."

"William is there," I roared. "He will be there, by the Sultan. This is our duty."

"Very well," Rob said, exchanging a look with Walter. They closed their visors and waved my men into line.

I led them forward and our charge was mighty indeed. We ran down the foremost ranks of the Janissaries and got in amongst those behind, cutting down scores of them.

"We are surrounded!" Walt shouted. "We must break free or be lost."

"Damn you, man," I swore. But he was not wrong and I ordered us to retreat once more.

It was a bloody and desperate battle. Even then, after so many of us had been lost, we might have won the day. Might have reached the Sultan and ended him and his son before all the devastation that they and their descendants would wreak upon Christendom.

But King Vladislaus III of Hungary was killed.

The cry went up along the line that the king had fallen and all remaining fight went out of the crusaders.

It was over. We knew we could not rally after such a loss.

I joined Hunyadi and we attempted to rescue the king or recover his body, at least, but scores of men fell all around us and it quickly became clear that we could do no more without bringing the remaining army to disaster. The Janissaries advanced on us and we had to retreat.

Our forces did not collapse and we disengaged carefully, though arrows fell and their hand-guns fired, we pulled away out of range. They were reeling from our assaults and their infantry could never have pursued our cavalry anyway.

We retired to the *wagonberg*, and together fled the field in some semblance of good order. The surviving Turkish cavalry limped after us but they never attempted a proper assault. In our various national groups, we formed up and fled beyond the Turks, either along the lakeshore or through the hills or marshes and we all attempted to get as far away as fast as possible. Indeed, we rode through a portion of the night before stopping to rest and tend our wounds.

I had just over fifty men left in my company and those that lived were battered and tired. Our remounts were needed but even those were exhausted and many of my servants rode two to a horse. We had left the company's wagons and much of our supplies back at the camp but there was nothing to be done about that. Eva was angry at the decisions that had been made but I think mostly she was annoyed that she had missed out on the fighting. Stephen fretted about what it all might mean for Christendom, muttering of dark things, but Walt told him to hold his damned tongue. We had no time to indulge in anything but flight.

The enemy did not have enough cavalry left to defeat our fleeing forces, for at least six thousand of our soldiers had survived. But we left ten thousand or so dead on the field and the Turks pursued us for days and weeks, as we rode back toward Hungary in a fog of defeat.

It was a hard ride. We could not stop for long without falling behind and those that fell behind were in danger of falling to the Turks chasing us.

But stop we did and word spread amongst us about what had happened at the end of the battle and I sought out witnesses.

Later, during the journey, I found a Polish knight who had survived the charge alongside the King. The knight was recovering from multiple wounds, and the ones on his head seemed at first to have robbed him of his wits. Or, perhaps it was the horror of the battle that had done so. We crouched, shivering, over a tiny campfire, and I urged him to speak of it.

"Did he reach the Sultan?"

The knight's eyes filled with orange tears that reflected the light of the fire. "Alas, no. It was not in some glorious combat with the Sultan or his son. First, he was shot by a slave armed with a cowardly, satanic weapon at a distance but that did not stop him. His horse was shot also, many times, but it did not slow. He charged on ahead of me, shouting for the Sultan to fight him. The king was almost at his tent when a man stepped forward with a long spear and thrust it up into him." The Polish knight stopped speaking and stared through the fire.

"A man?" I asked. "A Janissary?"

The Pole shook his head slowly. "He was bareheaded and unarmoured, in fine clothes. Not a Turk. He had the look of a Frank. Or an Englishman." He lifted his eyes to mine. "Like you."

A chill that was not from the night air ran through me. "His name is William. I believe they call him Zaganos Pasha, now."

"He was taken in the Blood Tax?" the knight asked.

I shook my head. "What happened after he was speared? You saw him die? Or was he merely wounded?"

The knight looked away again. "Your man, Zaganos Pasha, he pulled the king down from his horse as if he was no more than a child. Lifted him, in all his armour, and ripped off his helm with one hand and then he... he defiled him."

"Did he... forgive me, sir, did he *bite* the King?"

The man's eyes glowed. "Bite? He tore his face off with his teeth while the king screamed for God. And then with a long knife he cut his head from his body. The Janissaries cheered this."

"I am glad you survived to tell me what happened," I said.

He snapped his head up and glared at me. "I did all I could! My men pulled me away, forced me away, against my will, I would have died to defend him, would have died to defend his corpse from defilement."

I held up my frozen hands. "I meant no offence, sir, and apologise for having caused it. Others have told me of your bravery on the field and there is no man alive who doubts it, least of all me. Is there anything I can do for you?"

"Just leave me be," he said.

The Polish knight died of his wounds two days later. Like many men in that desperate retreat, he was swiftly buried in whatever suitable site could be found before the pursuing Turks caught up. We left a trail of crusader bodies many weeks long as we followed the course of the Danube, seeking support from the local people of Bulgaria and then Wallachia.

With the survivors of my company, I rode with Hunyadi's dwindling group of loyal men. Companies broke off at various points so that each group could slip through a number of valleys and passes on our journey back to Transylvania and Hungary without running into enemy forces.

Perhaps I should have abandoned Hunyadi but I wanted to help to defend him until he reached safety.

One morning we were surrounded at both ends of a steep vale by hundreds of Wallachian horsemen. Some of them I am sure were those who had treacherously abandoned us at Varna.

"We are here to escort you to my lord Vlad Dracul, the Voivode of Wallachia," said the fat nobleman leading them, addressing Hunyadi directly.

Hunyadi was furious but he controlled himself. "My thanks, sir, but we have no wish to do so. We are returning to Transylvania directly without your escort."

The Wallachian lord smiled through his beard, showing a mouthful of yellow teeth. "Forgive my unpractised Hungarian, my lord, but what I mean to say is that you are my prisoner. And soon you will be the prisoner of the Voivode of Wallachia, Vlad Dracul. Come with me now or we shall kill you here. Is that clear, my lord?"

Hunyadi's men stirred, some drawing their swords. I walked my own horse slowly forward closer to Hunyadi's. We were outnumbered three to one and we were exhausted. But I thought we could break through if we fought together and meant to say so.

Instead, Hunyadi gave himself, and all of us, up as prisoners.

"Damned bastard," Walt cursed him as we were escorted into Wallachia. "Bastard coward. We could have killed these useless dogs and been free."

"He is mortal," I said. "And mortals must preserve their lives where we would risk them. We cannot fault him for this."

Walt was incensed. "You seen this Vlad Dracul with your own eyes. You met his son. Insulted him, to his face. These treacherous Wallachians will cross us and give us up to their friends the Turks, mark my words, Richard. Mark my words."

Looking up at the forested hills of Wallachia, I thought that Black Walter might just be right.

2

Târgoviște

1444 - 1447

WE WERE ESCORTED northward through the Wallachian plains to the capital of Târgoviște. At the end of a long valley and at the foot of the hills that rose in the north to become a vast chain of mountains, the town had an attractive river running beside it that came tumbling and twisting down into a meandering course that irrigated the fields, then bare and cold. It would be a place I came to know and host to scenes that would haunt my nightmares for centuries, but the first time I laid eyes on it, it seemed a sturdy and well-appointed city in the German style.

Certainly, the defences of Târgoviște had been attended to, for it was protected by a high and thick stone wall with sturdy towers at intervals around the perimeter and over every gate.

Inside, the buildings were well made and of a good size, if far plainer when compared to the grand and intricate stonework of Buda or the ornate richness of Vienna. It had first been built by Saxon colonists and still retained that German character and, indeed, a large Saxon population who were responsible for most of the trade that went on in the city. But it was far more civilised than I had expected and as I entered through the gates I hoped that our captors would likewise prove to be more courteous than I had imagined.

"Vlad Dracul is in residence," Stephen mumbled, nudging me with his elbow and indicating a great dragon banner hung on the walls of the castle.

474

"Thought he was supposed to be off waging war on the Turk?" Walt said.

"So were we," Rob replied.

The ordinary soldiers, including my surviving men, were herded into tents in a huge field outside the walls and they would be damned uncomfortable but I reminded them to thank the Christ that the Wallachians had been so generous. They grumbled but they were hard fellows to a man, squires and servants included, and so they took to their quarters with stoicism.

"Do not attempt to run," I warned them before I went into the city. "We will play our parts and all will be well."

"Reckon they'll have work for us, sir?"

"We shall see."

As a leading mercenary captain and knight, I was allotted quarters for myself and my servants, those being Eva, Stephen, Walter and Rob and a handful of true servants. We were crammed into two dark rooms inside the castle within the city but it was warm and dry.

"This is the finest prison I have ever been in," I quipped as the door was slammed shut. "How lucky for us that warlords like Vlad Dracul rely on the services of mercenaries."

"We need blood," Eva said, her face ashen and eyes dark. "I will bleed the servants. You must free us from this place."

"Certainly, my dear."

I spoke to placate her, because she was suffering from the blood sickness. But I knew it would not be so simple to extricate ourselves. The Wallachians were a people that seemed filled with violence, many appeared to feel vitriolic hatred for the Hungarians and for the people of any other nation who followed the Pope of Rome rather than their own Orthodox Church. We had been captured with Hunyadi and that might have meant we were destined to share whatever fate he would suffer. On the other hand, they had treated us well by providing pleasant quarters.

We bled our servants and my immortals drank, sighing and calming themselves as the blood sickness symptoms retreated. Later, our captors brought bread, cheese, and cured pork, which we devoured, and even jugs of wine. Eva and I shared the main bed, Walt claimed one trundle bed and Stephen did the other. Our servants curled up where they could, and we passed the night in more warmth and comfort than we had experienced for many months. Still, Rob took the first watch and swapped with Walt, who swapped with Stephen. None came to harm us in the darkness. We may have been treated well but that did not mean I trusted our captors.

The next day, I was taken to the great hall where Vlad Dracul sat on his throne with his eldest son, Mircea, beside him on a throne of his own. Light from windows high above the thrones illuminated them, while the rest of the room was lit only with lamps around the walls. A hot fire burned in the huge fireplace behind the throne but it was still cold in the hall.

Vlad II Dracul was about fifty years old and he looked older but he was yet broad in the shoulder and straight backed. His face was fixed into a scowl, just as it had been when I had last seen him across a hall months before. I suspected from the depth of the lines on his face that the scowl was a permanent feature of it and had been s0 for decades. His dark eyes were narrowed beneath a low brow and his blade of a nose jutted from between them. His black moustache was as wide as his face and the oiled ends were curled up like two iron hooks.

Before the prince and his son, on one side of the hall, stood the *boyars*, the great lords of Wallachia. In Wallachia, the commoners were made up from the masses of free peasantry and then there were the lords, who were called *boyars*, above them and then there was the *voivode*, which was a title meaning the Prince of Wallachia. I did not yet understand just how much power those *boyars* wielded in Wallachian society, but I was about to.

On the other side of the hall stood the Hungarian and allied knights and nobles that had been captured along with Hunyadi, although Hunyadi himself was not present. There was an empty gulf between the two groups who stood glaring at each other and muttering amongst themselves. I slipped almost unnoticed into the rear of the hall and nodded to a couple of other knights who saw me. The *boyars* and Vlad Dracul's personal guards were armed and the Hungarians and other survivors looked about them, wondering what was about to occur.

It certainly seemed to me as though we were to be put on trial.

I did not fancy being subjected to judgements that Vlad II Dracul would make.

Almost as soon as I took my place, Janos Hunyadi was escorted into the great hall and every man turned to watch as he walked the length of the room. His servants were held back, and Hunyadi marched with his head held high to the base of the dais.

He and Vlad stared at each other in silence for a moment that stretched and stretched. Young Mircea glared at Hunyadi with a smirk but the mighty Hungarian warlord had eyes only for Vlad. The *boyars* began to shift and glance sidelong at each other.

"Janos Hunyadi, the White Knight of Transylvania," Vlad Dracul said at last, speaking Hungarian, "through your actions, you have brought the great crusade into ruin. And even now, when you have personally caused the death of ten thousand Christian men, and so ruined the crusade to throw the Turk back into the wilderness where he belongs, you stand before me filled with arrogance. I see it upon your features. You dare to cast your eyes at me and be filled with pride, in spite of your utter failure. What will happen now, Hunyadi?"

On the floor before the voivode, Hunyadi made to speak but Vlad spoke over him.

"I tell you what will happen! The Turk shall take his revenge. That old goat-fucker Murad will come to my land. He will cross the Danube and burn and destroy all of Wallachia before crossing into Transylvania and he will do the same there. Your own lands shall burn. After Transylvania, Hungary will fall to the endless hordes of the Turk and his demons. And it was you who did this." Vlad tore his mad eyes from Hunyadi and looked to his *boyars*. "I warned Hunyadi of what would happen. Did I not? Some men in this hall heard my words. You do not have enough men to face the Turk in open battle, I said. Your crusader army is smaller even than the Sultan's hunting party that he takes into the plains from Edirne. Take his fortresses, I said. Take his ports and his castles, one by one, and avoid a battle that you are incapable of winning." Vlad Dracul whipped his dark eyes back to Hunyadi and a mirthless grin stretched across his face. "Your arrogance is the cause of all this death. You believed in your own prowess more than you heed the advice of other, better men. You thought yourselves above all others and see where your hubris has brought us. Has brought all Christendom. You thought of yourself as greater than your king and now your king is dead, his body ripped apart and unburied. One wonders if this was perhaps not your intention all along? Will you make yourself king, Hunyadi? Is that what you have wrought with your convenient defeat?"

The *boyars* and watching Hungarians had been mumbling throughout the voivode's verbal assault, and increasingly so, but this final accusation brought a chorus of angry cries and outraged denials. The Wallachians shouted down the Hungarians and Poles, who roared their protestations in defiance of the threats against them. They loved and admired Hunyadi, who had led them to a hundred unlikely victories in the mountains of Transylvania and elsewhere over decades.

As subtly as I could, I sidled further away from the *boyars* and placed my hand near the handle of my knife.

Mircea, the son of Vlad Dracul, sat still smirking at the riotous lords. Once I reached the side of the hall, I stayed as still and quiet as I could, feeling utterly adrift in the turbulence of Balkan politics. Also, I could understand only one out of every ten shouted words that filled the hall to the rafters.

"Silence!" Roared Vlad Dracul, slamming his hands on the arms of his throne and standing. He was not a tall man, but he was broad and powerful, with a barrel chest and a herald's piercing voice. Gradually, the lords calmed themselves and Vlad pointed at Hunyadi before sitting down. "You will now speak, Hunyadi. What do you have to say for yourself?"

Hunyadi waited until silence had settled once more and when he spoke it was with his customary clear and strong voice. "All men here know what happened. All men know who stood on the field and fought with honour and for Christ." His head turned toward young Mircea, who blanched and glanced at his father. "And all men here know who did not."

The hall erupted once more, with the *boyars* on one side of the hall pushing and shoving the Hungarians and Poles and other crusaders on the other. Vlad's personal guards pulled lords apart from one another and it took even longer for the noise to settle while Vlad stood with his hands raised.

"For your crimes against Christ, the Church, and the King of Hungarians," Vlad said. "I sentence you to be executed."

Guards stepped up, ready to stop any violence, as the crusaders raged in shock and dismay at the sentence. I assumed the Wallachian *boyars* would come to blows with the outraged crusaders. And yet, to my great surprise, the *boyars* did not argue with the

Hungarians. Instead, the *boyars* sided with them against Vlad and they protested the sentence with almost as much vigour as did Hunyadi's allies. It seemed the *boyars* did not wish to anger the entire Kingdom of Hungary over such an extreme act.

I could not quite follow what was said but it was clear that Vlad Dracul and his son Mircea were also shocked by the resistance to the voivode's order.

And no matter how he raged and threatened, the *boyars* stood as one and defied their prince. Their stance could not be overcome and so, infuriated, Vlad cursed them and strode from the hall with his son on his heels.

The *boyars* muttered to each other when he had gone, not at all pleased by their victory. Instead, they seemed disturbed by the implications. And when Hunyadi and his men sought to thank them, the *boyars* were grim in their acceptance of that thanks. Hunyadi was cautioned to remember what the *boyars* had done for him and then we were ordered to be removed from the hall.

When I was escorted back to my quarters, my men stood and waited, pained looks on their faces as they tried to read my expression.

"What is it?" Rob asked.

"Are we to be put to death?" Stephen asked, aghast. "We are sentenced to death, aren't we. I knew it. What are we to do, Richard?"

"Had to happen sooner or later," Walt said, with a shrug. "Would have been nice to see old England one last time."

"Be silent," Eva snapped at them. "Speak, Richard."

"We are to be freed and sent on to Hungary," I said. "Along with Hunyadi and all his men."

***

A week later, we were sent from Târgoviște along with a large escort of *boyars* and their loyal men, heading north into the mountains of Transylvania. The passes were clear of snow but the mountains were heavy with it and the thick forest was dense with shadow.

"I do not understand how they could defy their lord," I said to Stephen as we trekked through a vale with jagged rocks jutting up into mountains on either side. "Why is the prince so weak in his own kingdom?"

"It is a mountain land and they are a mountain people," Stephen said, wiping his nose and looking miserable. "Precisely the same as mountain folk everywhere. Every valley has its lord and every lord is king of his valley. A hundred valleys, a hundred tribes and a hundred petty kings. Their feuds go back who knows how long and are so complicated that no outsider can ever hope to understand."

"Same as the Welsh," Walt observed.

"You would know," Rob said, quickly, a grin on his stubbly face.

Eva rolled her eyes and kept her own counsel.

The cold was astonishing and for the most part we kept to ourselves until we descended on the Transylvanian side of the mountains. Here, Hunyadi visibly relaxed and our Wallachian escort left us, to head back once they had rested and recuperated. For us, the journey continued, and I found myself invited to dine with Hunyadi in a large and fine town named Brasov at the foot of the hills.

"What will you do now?" Hunyadi asked me, once the wine was flowing. His look was at once penetrating and easy to return. There was no doubt he was a remarkably intelligent man and he had turned all his wits to mastering the art of war. But he had suffered a great defeat on the field and for some men who experience such a thing it defeats their spirit. Whether Hunyadi had been broken by it, I could not yet tell.

"I came here to wage a crusade against the Turk," I said. "I shall continue to do so."

His face did not change and yet I could tell that my answer pleased him.

"What of your men?"

"Most shall follow me for a while yet, as long as we have a master willing to pay for our services. Even then, there are some who I suspect would rather wage war elsewhere. Italy is far more civilised, as far as these things go."

He nodded. "And if I do continue to pay for your services, how will you wage this war, Richard, with such a reduced company?"

I drank the wine. It was rather good, if sweet for my taste. "That depends on what happens now, my lord. You were in command of the crusade. That has ended in practice but to my mind, you are the moral leader of the crusade still. If this crusade is considered to be ended, perhaps the Pope might consider calling another?"

Hunyadi took a deep breath and let it out slowly. "The king is dead. His own vanity cost him his life, and cost the crusade victory in the field, but he must be properly mourned. More to the point, however, is that Hungary needs a new king."

I watched him closely, for the men often muttered that Hunyadi should be made king, despite his relatively low birth into the knightly class rather than the upper nobility. It would certainly be unprecedented but they could not find a more able king to lead them in war, of that I was certain. He did have healthy sons, but the crown was not a hereditary one. Surely, if the lords had any sense they would see he would be the strong arm that Hungary needed if it was to resist the Turkish menace. For all his bluster, Vlad Dracul had been right enough about the danger.

"And who will be that king?" I asked.

He smiled. "Not I, if that is your meaning." He waved away my half-hearted protests. "I have the hearts of the minor nobles of Hungary but the truly powerful there shall never vote for me to be made king. No, they will make another wear the crown but it is my wish and my expectation that we shall continue the war. It is my wish also that another crusade be called, for this very year, if there is the will for it. But Hungary comes first. A king must be crowned and soon and then the war may continue."

"A sensible order of business, my lord. But what do you mean to do with Vlad Dracul?"

He raised an eyebrow. "Do? Whatever do you mean, sir?"

I glanced around and lowered my voice. "Surely, my lord, you have a great enemy in this man. His desire to have you executed will now have only grown and should he come into possession of your person once again, he will not hesitate to act, this time without consulting the lords who defied him." I shook my head to myself.

Hunyadi seemed to find this amusing. "The *boyars* revolt against the voivode disturbs you?"

"Surprises me, somewhat. That they have such authority against their own prince."

"You would have me believe that the King of England acts as a tyrant?" He smiled. "That he may go against the will of his lords without consequence?"

The thought of the useless, witless fool who was King Henry VI acting as a tyrant brought a smile from me, also. "Nevertheless, Dracul and his son have proved not only duplicitous but treacherous. How long before Vlad resumes his subjugation before the Turk? It is a vast land, the border of Christendom. We cannot afford to lose Wallachia."

"It pleases me to hear you say *we*. But if you had the power to act, what would you do?"

"Whatever has to be done."

"You would murder a prince?" he asked, his voice low and steady.

"What is one life compared to the lives of all of our people?"

"I wonder if I could ever truly trust a man who is so quick to jump to murder," he said, as if speaking to himself. "Do you know why Vlad is called Dracul?"

Of course I do, I almost said but stopped myself. "He is a member of the Order of the Dragon. It is a chivalric order, established by Sigismund, King of Hungary, in order to fight against the Turk. He was another great man who led a crusade against the Turk that ended in defeat, at Nicopolis."

"You were educated regarding it?" he asked.

I remember it, I wanted to say, *and heard from those who were there how victory was snatched away by arrogant knights charging before they should have*. Instead I merely nodded.

"I was raised and trained by men who survived it," he said. "A defeat that hung heavy over them, and so over me, all my life. I wonder if my defeat will echo through our sons." He shook himself from his melancholy. "And yes, my lord Sigismund founded it. The Brotherhood of the Dragon, or the Order of the Dragon, or any one of a number of other names. It is a society with no official name, you see, and yet the members must each bear the symbol of the society on his person at all times. This sign or effigy is in the form of the dragon curved into a circle, its tail winding around its neck. The dragon sign also includes a red cross, in the same way that those who fight under the banner of the glorious martyr St George are accustomed to bear a red cross on a white field."

"I have seen the emblem. And Vlad Dracul not only wears this sign on his person in the form of an amulet but he has made it his personal coat of arms. By doing so, he proclaims to the world his closeness to the Order and to the King of Hungary, whoever that shall be."

Hunyadi smiled. "Precisely. His membership of the Order is no small thing. He cannot simply be murdered."

"I never said he should be, merely that there should be no limits on actions that ultimately defend Christendom. But I suspect that he cannot be brought to heel. Not a man such as he. Can he be deposed? Would the *boyars* allow such a thing?"

"The position of Voivode of Wallachia has never been a stable one." He inclined his head. "If there was a suitable candidate, ready to step in, once the current voivode is removed, certainly he could be replaced. There are a couple of leading families that tradition would allow, especially those of the Danesti, who are the great enemies of the Draculesti."

"I assume you have a specific candidate in mind. How would you remove Vlad?"

"How would you?"

"I am a simple man. I would march an army to his gates and demand his surrender."

"If I were to do so, would you and your men join me?"

I hesitated. It was dangerous for a mercenary such as I was to tie himself too closely to one lord over others and some of my men had joined specifically to wage war on the infidel, not other Christians, even Eastern ones. Despite all that, I did not hesitate for long. "He and his son have proved themselves to be treacherous. They cost us the battle and so the crusade. I would see them removed."

"It will have to happen, in time." Hunyadi nodded slowly to himself. "But first, Hungary."

Our business concluded, I made to leave but Hunyadi leaned forward and placed a hand on my arm. "Richard. What is your interest in Zaganos Pasha?"

Slowly, I eased myself back into my seat. I considered denying it but it was obvious that men had told him of my enquiries. "I believe he was born a Christian but now he is a man who must be killed."

"Why?" he fired the question at me.

"He means for all Christendom to be destroyed."

"More than other Turks?"

"Yes."

"How do you know this?"

"I know."

"You know the man personally? How so?"

"He is an old enemy of mine."

Hunyadi smiled to himself, no doubt amused by my apparent youth. "He has wronged you personally?"

I had an urge to explain everything to Hunyadi but there was a good chance he would believe me to be a madman. "He has, my lord."

"At Varna, you took your men into an attack on the Sultan's position. It was foolhardy and you lost many of your men and you suffered extensive wounds. After hearing of your interest in this man, it seems to me that you were not attempting to slay the Sultan but this Zaganos Pasha." When I said nothing, he nodded once and continued. "I wonder if, should we come to battle with them again, you could be trusted to obey orders. Your passions may overcome you once more."

"My passions did not overcome me. I am not some fragile king who cannot let better men win glory. I know how to read a battlefield. My charge into the Sultan's position was only possible because Ladislaus acted like a mad fool. He threw away his life and that of his men but it almost worked, did it not? If only we had the Wallachians with us. Seven thousand horsemen would have overrun even the Janissaries and the Sultan and his son would be dead. And so would Zaganos Pasha."

Hunyadi kept very still. He was not distracted by my clumsy attempt to change his focus back to the Wallachians. "Men say that you bleed your servants every day. Why do you do this?"

I shrugged, attempting nonchalance. "All men should be bled every few days, especially servants. It keeps them servile."

"They say," Hunyadi muttered, "that Zaganos Pasha has a taste for human blood. Have you heard this rumour?"

I smiled. "I could very well believe it."

"There are tales in Transylvania, my homeland, of creatures who live by ingesting blood. Creatures who look like men. Who once were men but were turned into monsters by another. Have you heard of such tales, I wonder?"

Holding myself still, I attempted a smile. "There are many tales of monsters and the like amongst peasants. Even in England. There, they are called revenants."

"We have many names also. In Serbia, I heard these monsters called *vampir*. Here in Transylvania, they are called *strigoi*. It is not only peasants who believe they walk amongst us but lords and priests and learned men also."

"And you believe that I am a demon because I have my servants bled each week? Truly, my lord?"

Hunyadi said nothing but sipped from his wine. "My friends tell me that I should no longer associate with you. They tell me that you are unnatural. That many of your men are unnatural. One of your men is even a woman and yet she has the strength of ten knights."

"How absurd."

"But you do have a woman for a squire, Richard, do not deny that to my face when I have seen her with my own eyes. Who is she? Your wife? Your sister? Your whore?"

I flinched at the last word and fought down an urge to strike him. He was attempting to provoke me and knocking his teeth out would be satisfying for only a moment before his men attacked me. But what could I say about Eva? That I had known her for two hundred years? The truth was that we had been man and wife for decades while also fighting our way around Christendom and the East, as mercenaries and as crusaders and for our own purposes. Our love for each other had become friendship and our ardour had turned to tedium. After a mortal lifetime of companionship, she had needed to be apart from me and that was how we had lived for decades more. Many times since, we had found ourselves in each other's arms and beds. It was inevitable. And ever since leaving England for Hungary, three years before, we had slipped once more into comfortable companionship, sharing our bed when one was available and lying curled together under the stars or in a tent when one was not. How could I explain to Hunyadi that there was no word for the nature of my relationship with Eva? She was not my wife, not really. She was my squire, she fought by my side and saved my life more often than I saved hers. More than anyone else, she understood my stomach, my heart, and my wits, and offered better advice than I could find anywhere in the world. Simply, I suppose, she was my friend but at the same time Eva was such a part of me that I could not imagine life without her in it.

"She is no one," I said.

Hunyadi sighed, exasperated. "I must say that I feel inclined to agree with my friends about your nature. We have seen you and your men training. Seen how you fight in battle. I have seen you move as swiftly as an arrow and I have seen you throw a man, in full armour, clear over a horse. There is something utterly unnatural about you, Richard, and I do not like it."

I nodded to myself, trying to understand what it was he wanted. Reassurance that he was wrong? Or confirmation that he was right. I tried for a middle path. "And yet in spite of my unnaturalness you wish to use me and my men to help you achieve freedom from the Turk?" I said.

He tilted his head. "You do not deny it?"

"Deny what? That I am stronger and faster than any living man? That I have turned the tide of battle more times than I can count? Janos, you have been content to let me fight for you all this time, what has changed?"

"We return to Buda and the court there is far more dangerous, for both of us, than the Sultan and his Turks. I must be above reproach and while you are an asset on the battlefield, you are a liability at court."

I almost laughed, for I had heard that very thing many times before.

"You and I have the same enemy, my lord. Whatever else I may be, I seek to always be a good Christian and a good knight. Mistrust me if you will, I quite understand. I will find another way to defeat the Turks."

He almost smiled again. "All of them?"

"If they stand between me and my enemy."

His smile dropped and for the first time, he seemed uncertain. "I can protect you from rumours at court but you must keep yourself and your men on a tight leash."

"I understand."

"And so you will restrain yourself until I am ready to act?"

If he thought I was a *vampir* or a *strigoi*, then perhaps he was asking me to stop drinking blood. Or he may have been merely warning a foreign mercenary captain to know his place.

"My lord," I said, "I am a courteous man, in full control of myself and my actions. If it does not take too long, I shall wait like a peaceful Christian for you to once more aim your lance at the Turk."

"Oh, I shall take aim, sir." Hunyadi pointed a finger at me. "And you shall be the point of the spear."

***

A new king was raised to the throne of Hungary. A young boy of five years, named Ladislaus V, and Janos Hunyadi was named as the Regent. This young fellow was in the physical possession of the Habsburgs in the Holy Roman Empire and they would not let him return to Hungary, so while Hunyadi ruled the boy king remained in the care of his guardian, the Holy Roman Emperor Frederick III.

The politics of the crowns of Europe were complicated beyond my clear understanding, no matter how much Stephen and Eva explained the web of alliances and debts and feuds between hundreds of major and minor noble houses. All I knew was that Hunyadi had been made king in all but name and I chafed to be freed from the luxuries of Buda into the wilds of the southeast once more. The Turks were rampaging through Serbia and it seemed to me that we did almost nothing about it.

I kept my men sharp by leading them into Serbia multiple times each season, where we raided and harassed Turkish soldiers. I pushed my men hard and they won themselves enough wealth from fallen enemies that they were reasonably happy. Two years of such warfare was enough for some and they returned home. Others wanted more. More wealth and more glory.

Hunyadi did not go to war but, as Regent of the enormous Kingdom of Hungary, he was never still. He spoke often of the traitorous Vlad II Dracul who had betrayed the crusade and so had turned against Christendom and God Himself.

And the voivode of Wallachia turned once more to the Turks and negotiated the subjugation of his people in return for not being destroyed.

To give the man his due, the Turks held his two youngest sons as hostages, and no doubt that played some part in it. Those two sons were named Vlad and Radu and they had been hostages for many years. The boys were being raised as future Princes of Wallachia, who would be friendly to the Turks when it came time for them to be placed on the throne. The Turks were cunning and forward thinking, in ways that we simply were not. I do not doubt for a moment that my brother was responsible for imparting this deviousness into the barbarous mind of the Sultans.

Whatever the circumstances, Vlad II Dracul once more agreed terms with the Turks in 1447, agreeing to pay the usual enormous tribute in silver as well as the *devshirme*, the Blood Tax that would take the best sons of Wallachia and turn them into the Janissaries who would overrun their brothers and then all Christendom. Vlad Dracul also agreed to give up the fortress of Giurgiu, on the Wallachian side of the Danube, and a key to unlocking the destruction of the country.

"Enough is enough, my lord," I said, when I had finally been granted an audience with Hunyadi. "Vlad is bargaining away Wallachia. The Turks will have free reign to push right up to Transylvania once more. Christendom's border is now a hundred miles closer to Hungary."

Hunyadi seemed to have aged a decade in the two years since he had assumed the regency. Soldiering will keep a man young and vigorous but politics will take his soul.

"Ah, another man who likes to explain to me what I already know. And what would you have me do?"

"What you said you would do. You must act."

"And I shall. And you and your men shall come with me."

Taking a small but powerful force, we travelled to Transylvania and met with a young *boyar* lord named Vladislaus, who Hunyadi favoured for replacing Vlad Dracul. The fellow certainly seemed agreeable enough, and no doubt for he was being offered a princely crown, but I wondered if he would be strong enough to resist the power of the *boyars*.

We crossed the mountains between the two kingdoms at the end of the year, just before the snows filled the passes, and we descended into the valley like a horde of barbarians and there invested Târgoviște. We had a handful of cannons and these were wrestled into place while soldiers dug trenches and threw up palisades around our camp.

Word was sent demanding that Vlad surrender, though we knew he would not give up his throne without a fight. The city was a strong one and it seemed that we would need to reduce a section of the curtain wall to rubble before we could assault it. Our army was not huge but Hunyadi believed it would be enough to take the walls, if it came to that. There were not enough men to seal the city entirely but it was reckoned we could stop supplies from getting in.

"Why could he not have done this in summer?" Stephen asked, looking up at the snow drifting down on our camp. "It will be Christmas soon."

"Hunyadi has a vast kingdom to rule and a dozen allies who might become enemies. He could not have come in summer."

"The bastards in the city will be warm and dry and we will freeze."

"And come spring, they will have eaten themselves into starvation and they will be ready to talk."

"War is a miserable and tedious pursuit," Stephen grumbled.

"You could have stayed in Buda," I pointed out. "Warm and cosy in bed beside that fat Polish girl."

"Do not remind me," he said, miserably.

And yet we did not have to settle in for a winter siege. Only three days after our arrival, before our trenches and camps were even half established, a great cacophony came from within the walls.

Hurriedly, we assembled in whatever armour we could quickly don, ready to fight off a sally that was surely coming.

When the gates were thrown open, instead of the voivode and his knights charging at our camp, it was unarmoured citizens who emerged bearing a flag of truce on a tall pole.

"What is it that they are saying?" I asked Eva, suspiciously, taking off my helm.

"They say they have overthrown Vlad Dracul," she replied. "And they welcome Hunyadi as their overlord."

"Is it a trick?" Rob asked.

Walt scoffed. "Course it bloody is."

Just then, Hunyadi sent for me and I rode up to him. "Richard, would you be so kind as to enter the city and see if what these men claim is true?"

I laughed aloud, drawing sharp looks from his lords and bodyguards. "You want me to risk my life and the lives of my men because you suspect this to be a ploy by the treacherous Vlad?" He turned to look at me for the first time and I laughed again. "Better a mercenary than your friends, My Lord Regent, I quite agree. And of course I shall go, happily, and if it is a trap, I shall slaughter every man in the city."

Some of his men crossed themselves and I brought my men forward to the gates where the *boyars* bowed and urged us to come within.

"You cannot mean to take us in there," Stephen said, his face white.

"He ain't wrong, Richard," Walter said. "Can't be nought but a trap."

"Walt, you will take twenty men and hold the gate while the rest of us go within. If they attack, we shall keep moving and we shall fight our way out."

"God save us," Stephen muttered, crossing himself.

"Grow a spine, man," Eva said. "And ready your sword."

Passing into the shadow of the gatehouse, I saw scores of grim-faced men in the streets beyond. Many were brandishing drawn weapons, and some of the blades and clubs they bore were bloodied. Those men watched us as we rode slowly through the streets, deeper into the city, our horses' hooves clacking on the stones in the frozen road surface.

"Here, my lord, here, you shall see, here he is," one of the men leading us said as we came into the market square. He was dressed in his finery and his hat had an enormous feather in it that bounced and fluttered each time he bowed and backed up, further and further. He was fair haired and I took him for a Saxon. Trailing him came a group of other men, almost all of them were old and fat. Rich townsfolk and merchants, nervous and yet proud.

"What has happened?" I asked them, not bothering to hide my contempt and distrust as I looked down at their worried faces.

"Come, come," they said, beckoning me on.

A large, silent crowd stood at the edges of the square and they turned to face us as we drew to a stop at the corner.

In the centre was a single post, prepared with faggots of wood. A stocky young man was tied to it, his bloody and bruised face a mask of anguish.

"It is Mircea, son of Vlad Dracul," the Saxon man leading me said, nodding and seeking acknowledgement. "Do you see, my lord?"

"By God, it is him," I said. "What is wrong with his eyes?"

"Ah, they were burned out, my lord."

"Merciful Christ," I said. "You burned out his eyes?"

"Burned out, as punishment for his crimes."

"What bloody crimes?"

The Saxon townsman blanched and turned to the *boyars*. "Why, his misrule, my lord. His misrule and that of his father. We... we thought you would be pleased."

"He is a treacherous little shit but his blood is royal."

"No longer, for his father has been deposed. And so he will now receive his final punishment."

The lord grinned, raised a hand and called out. A group of men rushed forward and ignited the pyre beneath young Mircea, who screamed and wailed as the fire took him. The crowd stood in grim silence, watching their young prince until his desperate prayers became screams that faded into silence. Soon, the smell of cooking flesh filled the square.

"What of the voivode?" I asked. "What did you do to Vlad Dracul?"

The Saxons, merchants and *boyars*' faces dropped. "We did everything in our power, my lord, but he is a very great knight and his men were too powerful. Even with the help of the Saxons, we are simple townsfolk, and—"

"Where is he?" I shouted.

A *boyar* raised a hand and pointed to the eastern side of the city. "He fled, my lord. But he cannot have gone far. It is a mere half a day since he—"

I turned to Stephen. "Ride to Hunyadi and tell him Vlad has escaped. Send Walt and the rest of the men to me, now." Stephen nodded and his horse clattered through the streets. "Leave anything heavy with your squires and pages, take only food and water. We ride hard and fast." My men prepared themselves. "You will provide me with guides, on good horses. Men who know the country and who can ride like a centaur. Hunters, soldiers, anyone dependable, strong, you understand?"

The *boyars* shakily agreed and began shouting orders. Almost at once, an old man in rough country clothes came forward.

"This man is a hunter and a fine rider," a lord said, presenting him. "He says he will lead you."

"You can find Vlad Dracul?" I asked him.

He looked me in the eyes and nodded once.

"Give him a bloody horse, someone," I said to my men.

"The company is ready," Rob said as we rode through the city to the south gate. "But why don't we let the prince go free? Seems to me we're well shot of the bastard."

Eva answered him. "Because he will raise an army and fight to regain his throne, weakening Wallachia and only making Turkish conquest all the more likely."

"Right," Rob replied, nodding to himself.

"And because he is a treacherous dog who would sell his soul to the Turk if we but let him," I said. "Come on, you men," I shouted as we came out of the city. "Who wants to kill a king?"

My men roared their approval, despite Vlad Dracul not technically being a king at all, and we rode south in pursuit.

***

He had half a day on us and he knew the country better than anyone. But it seemed clear that he was making for the fastest, straightest route possible toward the Danube, straight down the valley toward the plain and the great river beyond. Whether he was aiming for one of his many fortresses on the river or was contemplating riding beyond into Bulgaria and into the hands of the Turks, I did not know. But clearly, we had to catch him before he reached safety and so I pushed my men hard.

Our horses suffered from the ride and from the intense cold and we were forced to leave more and more men behind every time we paused for rest. The guides provided to us failed in their strength or their will and on the first night one young lad curled up weeping and so we told him to return to Târgoviște at first light. Another man feigned an injury and could not be persuaded to continue, even when Walt lifted him from his feet and spat insults into his face.

Soon, only the grizzled old peasant who had volunteered in the city remained. He rode hard before us, his weathered face set into a wrinkled frown and his narrow eyes pointing ahead.

"Reckon he's got a score to settle," Walt said while we watered our horses halfway through the second day.

"What gives you that idea?"

Walt laughed. "Tough little fellow, ain't he. How old do you think he is? A hundred and one?"

"Younger than you, whatever he is."

He turned from his crouched position and looked at us. "My name is Serban," he said, in French.

Walt and I exchanged a glance. We had been speaking English but he had detected that we were talking about him. I switched to French to ask him a question. "Few men here speak French, especially commoners. How did you come to learn it?"

"In my youth, I travel. I fight. I return to my land. But I remember."

"You were a mercenary?"

He raised his chin. "A soldier."

"You own land?" I asked.

His face darkened. "Once. My family land is lost to me, now." He pulled his horse toward the stream and let it drink just a little before he mounted and rode south again, hooves flinging back sods of frozen soil.

"Best get after him," Walt said, "or he'll kill the lot of them before we catch up."

The winter day was short but we found Vlad as darkness was falling. He had attempted to hide his men in a wooded marsh, on the flat plains by a meandering river, but Serban had found his tracks and he knew where the prince was hiding.

"There is a small place there," Serban said, speaking softly. His voice was like a growl. "Through the trees, high and dry land. Some people live there."

"A village?"

He shrugged. "Some houses. It is called Bucureşti's place. Wet earth beyond, very soft, all the way to the river."

I turned to my men. "Sounds like the prince and his men are camped on something like an island of dry land, protected by that beech wood, there."

Rob scratched his stump. "Easily defended. Especially in the dark."

"We should wait until morning," Eva said. "Hunyadi's men will have caught up with us, then. We can surround the wood, and the marsh, and either he gives up without a fight or he does not. Either way, we have him."

Serban's head snapped around at the mention of Hunyadi's name. "Not wait for Hunyadi. Vlad Dracul is there, now. We go. We kill him."

"I am inclined to agree with you, Serban," I said.

"Hunyadi wishes to use him to keep the new prince in line," Eva said. "He will be grateful if we provide him this prisoner."

"And yet it will not be us who provides him, if the entire bloody army comes down here in the morning to roust him out," I said. "Hunyadi will take Vlad prisoner, lock him in Buda and use him in his political games. These people are too keen by far on their politics. Vlad is better off dead. And it is better by far if I am the man to do it. Our influence at court wanes every day. This act shall purchase for us some influence. We go in, now. Tell the men. We take no prisoners."

Eva grabbed my arm and pulled me to the side. Lowering her voice, she leaned in. "How do we know to trust this Serban? He volunteered to help you rather quickly, did he not? Perhaps the prince left him behind in order to lead you into a trap. Vlad may be there, waiting for you. Or he may be miles away in another direction."

Straightening, I turned and raised my voice. "Serban, are you leading me into a trap?"

"No, lord."

"If you are, then you shall be the first one I kill."

"Yes, lord."

"There you are," I said to Eva, who pinched her nose and said nothing.

We followed Serban through the darkness beneath the trees. Admittedly, it was not as eerie a place as the dark green woods of the mountains in the north and beech forests were as familiar to me as the back of my hand. Even so, there was a wildness to Wallachia, even on the lowland plains. Much of it was unpopulated and untamed, and deer and wolves roamed the woods and I half expected us to scare up a boar big enough to disembowel my horse. My men were disciplined and there was not a word spoken as we advanced but still the noise we made crashing through the brittle undergrowth was loud enough to wake the dead, let alone alert Vlad's sentries.

"Faster," I said to Serban just ahead of me. "Faster, man." I turned to Rob beside me. "We shall rush them."

A noise clacked in the trees ahead and a bolt whipped unseen through the darkness.

Rob drew his mace and spurred his horse forward. "Sir Richard!" he cried, not as a warning but as a war cry. "Sir Richard!"

I raced after him and my men came behind, all them taking up the cry.

"Sir Richard!"

The enemy were ready for us, dismounted with their spears in hand, the blades flashing in the twilight, their roars of defiance filling the darkness. "Dracul! Dracul! Wallachia!"

My men dismounted and rushed in close, overwhelming the defenders with our numbers and our ferocity. Crossbowmen on the flanks shot at us and horses in the rear of the enemy position drummed their hooves as their riders galloped away from us.

"Vlad flees," I shouted to Walt, before forcing my horse around the remaining men. Something banged against my helm, a bolt or a spearhead, but then I was through and chasing the fleeing riders through the trees. They thinned and the ground grew soft and my horse began lifting his hooves high and tossing his head. Ruthlessly, I raked my spurs and forced his head up. "On, you bastard, on!"

I was chasing three riders through the dwindling light. The moon, low over the horizon ahead, shone through wisps of cloud even as the last of the day's light faded behind me. My horse splashed through shallow water and then onto dry ground again before running into wet ground once more, softer and slower. Ahead, my quarry had also slowed, though they struggled on toward the silver glint of the river in the distance.

Opening my visor, I raised my voice. "Coward!"

They ran on for a few more strides but their horses slowed and turned. Almost as one, the three of them slid from their horses and came back toward me, standing three abreast with their weapons drawn.

The man in the centre was broad and short.

"Vlad!" I shouted. "There is nowhere to run, now."

I slid from my horse and strode forward through the freezing water, which was almost up to my knees, and the ground beneath sucked at my feet. The three of them had stopped on the edge of a dry patch of land and so they were above me as I came forward, right at them, lifting my feet high as I advanced.

At the last moment, I rushed to the right, spraying icy water everywhere and stabbed up into the groin of the man there, sliding my sword point deep into his thigh as he swung his axe at my head. I continued on, caught his hand and took the haft of his weapon as I slid my blade out.

Vlad Dracul roared like a bull and thrust his sword at my neck. I batted it aside and pushed him as hard as I could, throwing him away from me. The last man caught me on the shoulder with his mace but I swatted him down and finished him on the ground.

The voivode got to his knees and launched himself at me, attempting to grapple and pull me down. I swung the axe at his arm, crushing the bone and half-severing his right hand. He cursed me and drew a dagger with his left, still trying to kill me.

I twisted it from his grasp and held him on his knees before me, pulling his helm from his head to ensure I had the right man.

"You," he snarled, speaking French. "Hunyadi's English dog."

"My Lord Prince. You fought with spirit. I will tell Christendom that you died well."

"Ah," he said, suddenly, looking up at the sky. There were tears in his eyes. "My sons. Forgive me."

"You should know that the men of Târgoviște burned Mircea alive after you abandoned him."

He snarled and tried to stand but I held him. "All I have done, I did for my sons. That monster has them, my youngest two. Vlad and Radu. He has corrupted them, by now, I fear but I had to try."

I paused. "What monster? Murad?"

Vlad scoffed, looking at the emerging stars once more.

"You mean Zaganos Pasha?"

He snapped his eyes back to mine. "You know of this monster." It was not a question.

"I shall kill him," I said. "Know that, as you die, the man who has your sons will one day die by my hand."

"But then we share an enemy," Vlad said, quickly. "I did as I was bid by the Turk in order to save my sons. Free my sons and I shall be free to fight the Turk once more."

"You have been a slave to the Turks too often to ever be trusted," I said, shaking my head. "You will not live."

His face clouded again. "Then protect my sons from the monster, sir. With my last breath, I ask it humbly, from one Christian to another." I hesitated and he continued. "With my death, Murad will seek to place Vlad on my throne. Or Radu, if Vlad is too obstinate. Help them to fight the Turks."

"If the Turks free them, they will be Turkish slaves already in their hearts and they will die, also."

Vlad smiled. "Not my sons. Not the sons of Dracul."

"Any man who fights the Turks will be my ally. That is all I promise."

"Grant me a single favour, then, from one knight to another. Give my sword to my son. My oldest living son, Vlad. And this." Reaching up to his neck with his one remaining hand, he pulled up a circular metal insignia on a thin silver chain. He held it out to me. "My sword and this. Vlad is to wear it always."

"If I can," I said, taking it from him.

He sighed. "God strike you down if you break your word. I am ready. Make the blow clean."

"You are strong, my lord, and you have killed many men in war. Your blood is strong and I shall take your strength into myself. Know, as you die, that I shall use your strength to kill the Turks and drive them from your lands."

He frowned in confusion as I lifted him up, slit his throat and drank the hot blood gushing from his neck. He fought me, with all the will left in him, but his will soon leeched from his body and I drank until my belly was full and his heart slowed into nothing. I dropped him at my feet.

Filled with the power of his blood, I arched my back and let out a roar at the moon.

I turned to find the old Wallachian named Serban a few paces behind me, shaking in what I took to be shock, fear or simple awe. I thought I was going to have to chase him down and kill him before he spoke to his fellows about what he had seen.

Instead, he dropped to his knees in the freezing water. The moon shone down on his wrinkled face.

"My lord, I see that you are *vampir*," he said, shaking. "I would serve you."

I walked forward, filled with a blood rage, and considered taking him also. But I had had my fill.

"You may serve me. Your first act will be to remove the head of Vlad Dracul. I shall bring it to Janos Hunyadi. And then we shall go to war."

3

The Battle of Kosovo

1448

HUNYADI WAS SO flushed with the quick success against Vlad Dracul, that he let it go to his head, somewhat. He announced that he was now the ruler of Wallachia.

It did not go down well with the Wallachian *boyars* who had risen up to depose one lord only to find a far more powerful one was now above them. And Hunyadi's own lords and friends urged him to reconsider, on account of him having more than enough to occupy his attention as Regent of Hungary.

"Can't help it, can they," Walt observed one night in Târgoviște, when the arguments were still raging. "Never enough for these great lords. Give them a regency and they want a crown. Give them a kingdom and they want another, and then one more."

"Perhaps he *should* take them all," Stephen said. "Is that not what our great problem is, sirs?" We looked at him, waiting for him to go on. He always did. "The Sultans, for a hundred years, have sought only conquest. They take us, piece by piece, year after year. No matter if they lose a battle, they keep coming. The sons and grandsons of Turks who were thrown back now live on those lands."

"Does he think he's telling us what we do not know?" Walt asked Rob in a stage-whisper.

"But why?" Stephen said, turning on Walt and Rob. "Why do they come on and on while we fight amongst ourselves?"

"William is there, whispering in their ears," I said. "He was probably there beside the first Mehmed, and perhaps even with Beyazid or earlier, with the first Murad. Seventy or eighty years, perhaps."

"You do not know that," Eva said.

Stephen replied. "But it makes sense, does it not? All that time, they have been pushing into Christendom, taking over or else forcing the Wallachians and Serbians and Moldavians into vassalage. Consistency, across generations."

Eva pursed her lips. "Yes, perhaps. What is your point?"

"It was only possible with a strong leader, who could dictate policy at will. Or close to it. The Sultans have accumulated personal power through all that time until Murad and his son Mehmed can expect to rule almost as tyrants. How can our scattered Christian kingdoms possibly stand in opposition to that?"

I nodded slowly. "So, you would have Hunyadi seek to hold the crown of Wallachia."

Stephen crossed his arms. "And Hungary, and Transylvania."

"And then Serbia," Eva said. "And Moldavia."

"You are in this together, I see."

"We are of one mind about this, yes," Eva said, holding up her hand with her fingers spread, before closing her hand tightly. "Only a strong king can hope to unite these kingdoms into one fist." She punched her other hand.

"And who better than Hunyadi?" Stephen said. "He has healthy sons who could rule after him."

"And when better than now?" Eva asked.

I snorted. "Have you two prepared your words before time?"

"Are we wrong?" Eva asked.

"Of course not. But what can *we* do about it?"

"He trusts you," Stephen said. "You gave him Vlad Dracul's head."

I scoffed. "He does not trust me, Stephen, I assure you."

Eva leaned forward. "He *likes* you, Richard. That is plain."

"He respects what I can do on the battlefield but he fears me. He knows we are different. And his men absolutely do not like me, nor do they trust me. Vlad Dracul's head or not. Whatever position I take, if I take one, they will argue against it purely for that reason." They sighed and I continued. "Listen, both of you. You have bent your attention to the southeast for so long that you have forgotten what lies north and west. The kingdoms of Poland, the Holy Roman Emperor, the bloody Pope, and who knows who else. If Hunyadi attempts to make himself king of so many kingdoms, he will have war on Hungary's northern border as the Habsburgs and all the rest strive to bring him down. And how will that help us resist the Turk?"

Walt snorted. "Without Hungary, all is lost. And that's the truth, no mistake."

Stephen wheeled away and kicked a bedpost. "Why are our people so bloody-minded? Why can no lord follow another?"

Rob answered. "Every free Christian man is the king of his own household, Stephen.

494

Every wife is a queen and their children are princes and princesses." He shrugged. "From Scotland to Italy, and Castile to bloody Wallachia, it's the nature of our people. It just is. I ain't learned much in all my years but I learned that. We do not good slaves make."

"He's right," Walt said, his arms crossed and nodding decisively. "It makes us strong."

Stephen pinched his nose. "No, it makes us divided. And divided, we are weak."

"Our greatest strength and our greatest weakness, then," Eva said. "Be that as it may, Richard, I would have us be *patient*. Clearly, William has laid his plans for decades, perhaps a century or more. These mountains are not easily conquered, nor are these mountain kingdoms easily overthrown, especially by armies of horsemen. You must be patient. If not Hunyadi, then perhaps someone else. Perhaps his son, or the son of another. Or a man not yet born. But we have time."

"You speak as though I am one to rush in without thinking the matter over." After I spoke, Walt burst out laughing and Rob covered his mouth and turned away. "What amuses you, men?" I said, which only caused them to laugh harder. "I shall be patient," I said, "if you damned fools cease your bloody mirth-making."

"We must discuss also the new man you have taken into your service," Eva said.

"What is there to discuss?"

"He saw you drinking blood. And then offered himself to you."

"Yes."

"Does that not disturb you?"

I looked around at each of them. "Should it?"

Walt shrugged. "The old boy must have been shitting himself. He thought he would be next. And he swore to save his own life."

"So what if he did?" I asked.

"If he swore only in the moment to save his neck," Rob said, "then how can he be trusted to hold his tongue about what he saw?"

"He knew what I was. He called me *vampir*. It was a word that Hunyadi used before to describe stories of blood drinking demons. It is a Serbian word. In his own country, the word is *strigoi*. And now this man Serban saw me and calls me *vampir*. Am I wrong in thinking William has his own immortals in these lands?"

"It seems likely," Stephen said. "And if they are here, then we must be careful. We must watch our backs. Any of Hunyadi's men could be one of William's."

"Or Hunyadi himself," Walt said.

"Do not be absurd," I said.

"Right, yeah," Walt said, covering his eyes with a hand. "Probably not."

"We must watch for enemies in our midst," I said. "But why wait for them? We must seek them out and destroy them first, if we can."

"How do we do that?" Rob asked.

"I will speak to Serban and find out what he knows. He has rooms in the city, I believe."

"Why not summon him here?" Stephen said. "It will be safer."

"He's above that tavern off the square," Walt said. "The one with the good German beer."

"We will go to him," I said. "I will take only Walt, so that we do not overwhelm him."

Walt rubbed his hands together and grinned. "Lovely. I'm right parched, I am."

Serban came down from his quarters above the tavern's ale room and the innkeeper directed us to a table and bench in a quiet alcove, bringing beer, wine, bread, cheese, herb sausages, and pork in jelly.

"I would have come to you, my lord," Serban said as he sat opposite us, staring at the food.

"Eat, please. You must eat and drink. We cannot finish all of this by ourselves." Walt glared at me but I ignored him as Serban grabbed a piece of bread. I poured him a mug of beer and handed it over before doing the same for myself. "Serban, you swore to be my man."

"I did," he said, not meeting my eye.

"Tell me about yourself."

He looked up. "My lord?"

"You were a soldier in your youth. You said you once had land but no longer. I like to know all of my men and I would have you tell me about the things you have done so that I will know how to best use you."

Serban bobbed his head slowly. "Yes, my lord. I was born in the west, near to the Iron Gates."

"The great gorge that the Danube flows through," I explained to Walt. "Near Serbia."

"That is just so," Serban said. "My father had good land. We grew almonds and figs. But there was not enough land for me. I was the youngest. So I go and fight."

"Where did you campaign?"

"Many, many lands. Bulgaria, Albania. And across the sea to Italy."

"Is that so? We fought there, also. On occasion. Where did you fight?"

"Oh, for this lord against that. A duke against another duke. Milan against Venice. Venice against Genoa. When I return home, a new lord ruled over my father's land and had given my family land to another. My parents had died. My brothers and sisters fled, or died. I was lost. But there is always work in Wallachia for a man who fights. I come here. That is all."

Walt and I exchanged a look and Walt shrugged.

"When you offered me your service," I said, lowering my voice. "You called me something. You knew what I was."

Serban held my gaze. "Yes."

"How did you know?"

He stuffed a large slice of sausage into his mouth and took his time chewing it, looking around the room, in every corner, rather than look directly at us. Walt's eyes twinkled with amusement but I was impatient.

496

"You have heard tales of these things?" I prompted.

Slowly, he nodded, pointing to his ear. "I hear things."

"Have you ever met one before?"

He scratched at the stubble on his chin before answering. "All people know these stories."

"All people of Wallachia?"

"And other places. These hills have long hosted *vampir* and *strigoi*."

"So they are two different things?"

He shrugged, as if he did not care to answer. The man seemed nervous but was trying not to show it. "Different, yes. One is more powerful. The *vampir*. But both..." he lowered his voice. "Drink the blood of man."

"Tell me more."

"More?"

"Where are they found? Where do they live, Serban?"

"Why do you want me to speak of such things?" he said. "Do you not know these things yourself? You are one of them. You must know. No?"

"Humour me," I said.

He frowned.

Walt cuffed his lips and spoke with his mouth full. "He means tell him what you know anyway."

Serban nodded. "I know very little. Stories all mothers tell their sons and daughters. Do not go out at night, or the *strigoi* will catch you. They will drink your blood. If you are lucky."

"What if you are unlucky?" Walt asked.

With a small smile on his lips, Serban continued. "The *strigoi* take the little children back to their master, the *vampir*. And there you will be eaten. Or some other evil thing. It was not clear."

"So it is just tales to frighten children?" I said. "What do you know of real men who are *strigoi*?"

"Forgive me, my lord, but are you afraid of them?"

"Of course not," I said. "I simply wish to make their acquaintance. Perhaps we might become friends."

"I do not know of any," he said. "But there are old folk in the villages. They may know more."

"Older than you?" Walt said, grinning.

Serban stared back. "Perhaps I can find one who knows more. They would need paying."

I nodded to Walt who stared at me for a moment in contempt at my gullibility but he pulled a few silver coins from his purse and, scowling, pushed them across the table to Serban.

"And not a word of this to anyone," I said before he took them. "One word from you to another lord and I will cut off your head and drink you myself, do you understand?"

"Yes, lord."

***

He may not have been able to make himself into an emperor, even if he wished to do so, but Hunyadi's dominance of the political and martial landscape was far from finished.

After pushing for support from the Pope, he organised a new crusade to be launched against the Turks, this time to save Serbia.

Serbia had capitulated to the Turks just a few years earlier, under their leader George Branković. The Turks had occupied his lands and, caught between two great powers, ultimately, Branković had simply been more afraid of the barbarous Turks than the Hungarians and so he had promised the usual great sums and the *devshirme*, the Blood Tax. What is more, Branković held a number of territories within the borders of southern Hungary and these he passed over to Sultan Murad II as part of his capitulation. Of course, this was never completed in practice, because physical possession is a fact that legal documents cannot themselves overcome and so Hunyadi had simply seized these lands for Hungary, considering them forfeited by the Serbian capitulation.

And Branković had even refused passage of the crusader armies through Serbia before the battle at Varna. Now, in 1448, Hunyadi demanded that Serbia join the new crusade. Not only did Branković refuse but he denied passage of the Hungarian army through Serbia.

Hunyadi swore that once he defeated the Turks, his very next act would be to destroy Branković and place a worthy prince on the Serbian throne.

"Branković is finished," Stephen declared, as we rode south with the new crusader army. "He cannot be allowed to defy us like this. Hunyadi will set all Serbia aflame for this continued defiance."

"One task at a time, Stephen," I said, looking ahead at the thousands of men spread out over the march south.

"It is worse than defiance," Eva said, turning in her saddle to speak to Stephan. "After refusing to join us, refusing passage, what do you think Branković did? There is no doubt he sent word to his master, Murad II, and so there is no doubt that the Turk will be fully prepared to meet us. There is no doubt, also, that Serbians are watching our advance and taking stock of our composition and dispositions. The enemy will be able to intercept us at will and offer battle."

"You do not seem confident in our grand crusade," I said. "What would you suggest we do?"

She was silent for a time before she replied, looking out at the hills in the distance. "Hunyadi seeks to retake Southern Serbia and Macedonia, to drive on to the coast and so split Turkish Rumelia into two parts, with Bulgaria on one side and Greece on the other."

"A fine plan, is it not?"

Eva turned to me. "If it works, certainly it is. If it fails, then all is lost."

498

Stephen laughed. "One can say the same with all plans!"

"What I mean, Stephen," she said, glaring at him, "is that it is both unspecific and dangerous."

"Describe to us a better plan," Stephen said, "If you would be so kind to impart your wisdom."

She ignored his goading and spoke to me. "If the Serbians had joined us, it would be different. But not only has Branković refused to take up the crusade, he is opposing us. He sends word of our movements to Edirne, or to the Sultan's army, if it is already in the field. Worse still, Branković has forbidden the lords of Serbia to join us. This means our army is smaller than planned for and we have fewer men who well know these lands."

"Some Serbians have joined us," Stephen pointed out.

"A fraction of what we expected. What we need. And how does Hunyadi react? We are pillaging and burning through Serbia, treating it as an enemy land but without conquering it."

"What would you have him do?" Stephen asked. "We have been defied."

"Either make the Serbians our allies, or destroy them in battle, and make them a vassal." Eva glared at me. "Hunyadi instead takes a middle path so that we march through and leave an enemy behind us."

Rob came cantering back along the line to where we rode and fell in beside us, his squire and servants trailing behind. He was sweating, though the air was cold.

"Thank Christ you have returned," I said. "It has been days. What news?"

Before he even opened his mouth, I knew it was not good.

"Skanderbeg and his Albanians cannot reach us," Rob said, wiping his dry lips and calling for water. "The damned Serbians under Branković himself are blocking the passes and fords between Albania and Southern Serbia."

"God damn that man," I said. "Still, surely there is time. Perhaps we can meet further south, in Macedonia. No?"

He cleared his throat, took a long drink of water and frowned at the sky. "There is a hope that we can meet Skanderbeg's forces on the plain of Kosovo, yes. And that is where we are now headed."

"And the Sultan has not returned?"

"Hunyadi's agents say again that the Sultan is campaigning in Anatolia," Rob said. "I asked about local forces but every one of the bastards told me either to not concern myself with such matters or to flat out mind my own business. And then I was asked to return to my master."

"What did you do?" I asked.

"Nothing," Rob said. "Nothing at all. I simply seized the man who had told me to mind my own business and I pushed my bare stump into his face and explained to him that killing was my business. Other than that, I was entirely courteous."

"To the Kosovo plain, then," I said. "Is there anything we can do to speed Skanderbeg along his way?"

"No," Eva replied, before Rob could reply. "Skanderbeg may be the most competent commander for a thousand miles." She looked at me. "Present company included. He does not need our help. If there is a way to get to us, he will find it."

"I think our Eva is enamoured with the new ruler of Albania, Richard," Stephen quipped.

I ignored him. "What makes you so confident in him?"

"Look at what he has achieved already. He was raised by the Turks, trained by them. He will certainly have come across William in that time. We must speak with him. If Hunyadi falls, Skanderbeg is one who may be able to take up the mantle, who may be able to lead all these kingdoms to victory together."

"He has won a few skirmishes," Stephen argued. "No more. Perhaps he has potential but let us see it in the coming crusade before jumping to conclusions."

I agreed. "That seems like a good notion."

Walt scoffed. "No one from a civilised kingdom is going to follow an Albanian, Eva."

"Let me tell you about Skanderbeg," Eva said to me. The wind whipped at a strand of hair streaming from beneath her cap. She tucked it back inside. "His name is George Kastrioti, and according to all reports, he served the Ottomans loyally until he deserted them at Nis, the year before Varna. The Turks called him Iskander Bey, and so we called him Skanderbeg even now, though he has since proved himself to be a loyal son of Albania and a good Christian. Which is remarkable in itself, as Albania, do not forget, was long a vassal of the Turks. He was sent to Edirne as a noble hostage, and it was the Turks who trained him in battle. He even became a Mohammedan, completely embracing the religion of the infidels. Or seeming to, at least. He was rewarded with a *timar*, near to the territories ruled by his father. His loyalty to the Turks was tested, time and again, and always he proved himself to them. There was a rebellion in his homeland and his relatives invited him to join them but he resisted and the Turks rewarded him with further advancements. They made him a cavalry commander, a *sipahi*, and after the revolt was put down the Turks installed him as a governor, for a time. But he was better suited to war and they gave him a cavalry unit of five thousand men."

I whistled. "He cannot have been deceiving them, surely he was a committed Mohammedan and loyal to Murad."

"Perhaps. Who can know what is in a man's mind? But he was rewarded again and made Sancakbey of Dibra. It was now that he must have been in contact with the people of his homeland. Had he already decided, long ago, to rebel against the Turks? Or did someone change his mind?"

"Seeing his homeland," Walt said, suddenly. I had not known he was still paying attention. "A man is tied to his homeland, to his ancestors, by the blood of his people and the soil of his homeland, is he not? Bloody foolish of the Turks to send him home and expect him to resist what cannot be resisted. It's inevitable."

"But a man who has turned against his own people, then turned against his masters," I said, "can he be trusted not to turn once more?"

"He can never go back," Eva replied. "It was a year before Varna, at the Battle of Nis, when he was fighting for the Turks, that he took himself and three hundred Albanians from the Turkish ranks and fled the field. From there, he went to Kruje, in the heart of Albania." Eva smiled. "He handed the governor a forged letter, supposedly from Sultan Murad, and gained control of the city. He overthrew those loyal to the Turks and proclaimed himself lord of the city. Then he conquered a dozen fortresses in the area and raised his battle standard, which is a double-headed black eagle on a red field and proclaimed himself a Christian. What is more, any Mohammedans in his lands, by birth or by conversion, he commanded to embrace Christ or face death. Somehow, he united the disparate Albanian princes under his leadership."

"I remember when the Sultan sent armies to stop him," I said. "But he defeated them."

"I heard it from a Serbian mercenary who was there. Ali Pasha had thirty thousand men and Skanderbeg just half as many. Skanderbeg, knowing how Turkish armies fight and deploy, pulled the enemy into battle at a place of his choosing. Prior to the arrival of the Turks, however, he had already placed three thousand of his strongest cavalry unseen in a forest to the Turkish rear. The Turks were surrounded and crushed. The Albanians killed ten thousand Turks that day. He smashed two more armies. At Otonete, he surprised them in their camps and slaughtered at least five thousand, taking only three hundred prisoners. Then it was just this summer when he beat Mustafa Pasha in the field at Diber."

"He has had a good run," I said, "no one would deny that. But is he a Hunyadi in waiting? We shall see in the coming battles what this Skanderbeg can do. And yes, I shall request an audience with him and ask him about William. Let us all pray that he can throw off the Serbians and join us at Kosovo."

We advanced southward where we were met, finally, by the Wallachians under their new voivode, Vladislaus II, who was loyal to Hunyadi. A handful of Skanderbeg's men made it to us but they only confirmed what we dreaded; that the main army was caught up manoeuvring against the damned Serbians. At a vast plain named Kosovo Polje, our army rested and waited for our allies to arrive before we continued on to begin assaulting Turkish-held cities in the south.

On the morning of 17th October 1448, an uproar spread through the camp until it reached us.

"What is it?" I cried, throwing back the flaps of my tent.

Walt approached, his face grim. "It's the Turks, Richard. Sultan Murad is not campaigning in Anatolia after all. He is here."

***

"My lords, we have two choices," Hunyadi said to the assembled leaders of his army within the vast command tent. "The Turks have got behind us to the north, cutting off any chance of direct retreat back toward Hungary, and so if we are to retreat, it must be southward, towards Macedonia."

The men were grim and quiet but they grumbled their dislike of this proposal.

"That would be madness," one of Hunyadi's companions said. "We would move closer to their routes of supply and reinforcement and further from ours. Manoeuvring will be possible but only for a time and we will be dependent on what can be foraged or taken by force as we move deeper into winter."

"We must cross the mountains into Albania and join with Skanderbeg," another lord said.

Hunyadi sighed. "Using those passes, with an army of this size, makes it likely we are drawn into skirmishes and perhaps a battle with our backs to the mountains. And that says nothing about the Serbian army of Branković out there. If we attempt Albania, we will be trapped between Branković and Murad. What is more, much of Albania remains Turkish. We cannot go that way."

"So, my lord," I said, in my rough Hungarian, "our choices are between retreating south or something else? Perhaps you would provide us with the alternative."

A few of the greater lords scowled at my speaking out of turn, which I had a reputation for, but other men smiled because every one of us knew what the alternative was.

Hunyadi lifted his head. "We may retreat. Or we may fight."

The lords wanted to fight but they were rightly cautious. Once more, we found ourselves outnumbered. Perhaps more important was that we were not prepared in our minds for a great battle.

"How might it be done?"

"We have three thousand German hand-gunners, war wagons, and scores of artillery pieces," Hunyadi said. "The Turk cannot assail our position and overcome us."

"Then why would he attack at all?" I said. "They have only to prevent us returning to Hungary or trail us into Macedonia and need not risk an assault against our wooden walls." Some lords shouted me down and told me to mind my tone. I ignored them and looked only to Hunyadi. "And if we wait, the Turks can bring reinforcements from a number of directions."

"No," Hunyadi said. "Their most likely reinforcements will come from the passes to Albania." He turned to one of his men. "Alex, take a thousand of the Transylvanian light cavalry and take the passes. They must take them and hold them. We cannot be surprised at our rear or all is lost."

"How might we assail their position?" A German mercenary leader asked. "They are yet taking their places on the field but it seems the Sultan is deploying with the River Lab at his rear, so we cannot get behind him easily. There are hills on his left flank, and the River Sitnica will no doubt guard his right. He has nested himself in tight."

"Do we know how many they are?" I ask. "Their true numbers, I mean, not panicked

502

guesses."

"It appears they are sixty thousand," Hunyadi said, to nods from his men. "*Sipahis* from Rumelia and Anatolia both and of course his Janissaries are in the centre protecting his camp. We shall see what their final dispositions are but it seems the Anatolian peasant levies are being sent out to his right which we assume means the Rumelians will be put on the left, out by the hills."

"No cavalry at all in the centre," a Polish knight said. "My men confirmed it. Just lines of infantry, mostly *azab* levies with spears. And then artillery and behind are the Janissaries. A tough centre to break with cavalry but it can be done. A massed charge of heavy horse to overwhelm them and send them flying into their own guns and on to the Janissaries. We almost broke through at Varna, we can do it properly here."

"Begging your pardon, my lord," I said. "My own men have ridden so close to the enemy today that some were wounded by hand-gunners. They report that between the front line of *azab* levies and the Turkish guns, the enemy are digging deep and wide lines of trenches. We cannot ride over with ease."

They grumbled and some doubted me enough to send their own men forward to see for themselves. But Hunyadi did not question my assertion.

"We form the *wagonberg* on the hill here," he said. "The German and Bohemian hand-gunners will man the war wagons. The artillery will position between the wagons and from there fire across the field into the Turks. Within the *wagonberg* we will have the crossbowmen and the archers. We shall keep a unit of Wallachian horsemen safe within, also, who will follow up when the Turks break under our fire and shot. All our cavalry will be on the wings. The Albanians and Wallachians, the horse archers, and the men-at-arms also. Before the *wagonberg* in the centre, we shall have light horse in the first line and heavy horse in the second. I shall command the second line in the centre, with the royal troops, my mercenaries and the Transylvanians. I want the Wallachian lords under their own banners with me." He then pointed out which great Hungarian lords he wanted on which wing and what they were to do and we were dismissed.

"Sir Richard," Hunyadi called and I crossed to him. "You will be with me and I would have you and your men kept out of the fighting for as long as possible, until the time comes. It may not come until late. Do you think your men can restrain themselves?"

"They can. Each knows if we slay the Sultan then he will be famed and showered with wealth."

He grasped my arm. "When you strike at his heart, it must be with everything. Those damned Janissaries will be hard to break."

"I shall not need them to break if I kill them all instead."

He shook his head at my arrogance and said I could go.

"How's the boss?" Walt asked as I joined him outside.

"Worried."

"Ain't we all."

It was a tense night on watch, half expecting a horde of Turks to come screaming out of the night. I went from man to man in my company and explained that we would need to avoid fighting until late in the battle, even if it started before dawn. But the sun rose in the morning and we assembled in our thousands and stood watching each other across the plain.

"The Turk ain't ever going to attack," Rob said. "Why do we not push forward?"

"Hunyadi knows his business," I said.

"God save us," said Stephen, crossing himself. "This shall be another Varna."

"Look out there, Stephen," I said, pointing. "Do you see those massing lines of levies? Behind them, the field guns? Behind them the Janissaries, beneath the Sultan's banners? There stands William de Ferrers. Our enemy. We have a chance to end it once more, today. You should be filled with joy."

Stephen nodded. "You are no doubt correct, yet I am filled with the sense that our illustrious leader is going to repeat the mistakes he made at Varna and so I am retiring once more to the *wagonberg*. Eva, are you coming?"

She stared across the field. "I am not."

"Very well, I wish you well and look forward to joining you for the victory feast."

"Bloody coward," Walt muttered. "Always slipping away, ain't he. Back there, sipping on wine while we do the work."

"We all have our strengths and weaknesses, Walter," I said. "You would best him in feats of arms and yet in a battle of wits, you would be defeated even by a drunken Stephen."

Rob snorted. "Walt would be defeated in a battle of wits by a drunken chicken."

"Our men are wheeling ever closer on the right," Eva said. "They are goading the enemy."

"That'll do it," Walt said. "The Turk can't control himself."

We watched as best we could. Our light horse advanced, shooting arrows into the Rumelians. When they countered, our heavy horse came up to fend them off while the horse archers retreated behind them. It was a highly effective manoeuvre and the Turks were growing frustrated, pulling ever more forces into attempts at counter attack. So much so that our flank was reinforced also.

"This is it," I said. "It cannot be resisted now."

Sure enough, Hunyadi was forced to send knights and light cavalry from his centre lines onto the right. It was then that Murad ordered his Anatolians against our left, where the light Wallachians met the enemy advance.

It was difficult to make out what was happening but suddenly the Wallachians, essentially our entire front line on the left, suddenly broke and fled straight back away from the Turks.

"Damn them," I said, with a sinking feeling in my guts. "The Wallachians are the most useless bloody men in Christendom!"

Hunyadi led us out from the centre, two thousand heavy horse, to stem the collapse of the left. I kept my men back from the press of the fighting, as ordered, though it galled me to do so.

Now that we had weakened our centre, Murad sent forward masses of the *azab* infantry to attack us there. I watched from the flank with my fresh and unused company as thousands of Turkish infantry marched right behind us and straight toward the *wagonberg*. Our last line of heavy cavalry in the centre charged the *azabs* and I was certain they would run down the weak, useless levy infantry. Instead, it was our heavy horse that broke and fled to the flanks.

"Good God Almighty," Rob said. "What is happening here? God is against us."

Walt sneered at the cavalry fleeing from the peasants. "Useless bastards."

"All is well," I said. "They shall not break the *wagonberg*."

The German mercenaries inside unleashed the power of their hand-guns and blasted away the *azabs* in a hail of shot and smoke. Our cannons fired into the masses of Turkish levies and drove them back. Hundreds were killed, and then thousands, and they edged back from the storm of fire and massed together like frightened sheep. Finally, our damned cavalry returned and charged into the panicked *azabs*, cutting them down gleefully as the Turks fled back to their own lines and the safety of their cannons.

It was growing late and we had stopped the Turks on both flanks and in the centre. With the spare men in the centre, Hunyadi reinforced the right further and broke that flank, sending the Rumelian cavalry fleeing into the dark hills or back to the Turkish camp.

Darkness fell and we drew back into our camp.

***

Our cannons continued their firing as night fell, and the Turks did the same. I had never seen such a thing before, the flashing of the cannons in the darkness and the endless repetitive crashing of the guns. It unnerved everyone, the horses especially, but Hunyadi insisted that they continue.

"We must force them from the field," he said in his tent. We all ate and drank standing up in our armour, even those lords who had taken light wounds.

"Perhaps an attack in the night, my lord," a Hungarian noble suggested.

Many scoffed. "Such a thing would be chaos. No man could see what he was aiming for."

I cleared my throat. "What if a small company was to make an assault on the enemy guns, my lord? They are flashing and banging for all to see. We could come at them from the flanks and so avoid their danger. Kill the crews manning each cannon. That would give us a fine advantage tomorrow, would it not?"

For once, no one shouted me down. They were tired, having fought a battle and were dreading fighting another the next day. Anything that might make their task easier was worth considering.

"Who would lead this attack?" Hunyadi asked all those present. The lords suddenly found the contents of their cups incredibly interesting. It was not that they were cowards, far from it. It was simply that only a madman would take his men in a night attack.

"I will do it, gladly, my lord," I said. "It is just that I have a mere fifty men to lead. Even with the advantage of surprise and the confusion of the enemy, we could only do so much with so few men."

"I want your men fresh, Richard," Hunyadi said.

"Then I will leave my men in their tents and lead others. If any are willing."

Hunyadi looked around the scores of lords crammed beneath the canvas walls. "Who here will place his men under Sir Richard's command for this attack?"

Again, men shuffled their feet and cleared their throats but said nothing.

"I would happily lend some of my men," a lord said. "Alas, they cannot see in the dark." Others murmured their assent.

"This discussion is all for nought," another Hungarian snapped. "Who here has ever heard of a Turkish army staying on the field for more than a single day?" There was muttered agreement. "Even now, their army will be retreating behind the guns and in the morning we shall find that they have withdrawn, only to offer battle elsewhere on another day. Or perhaps to move on altogether. We certainly hammered them today. Hammered them hard, my lords, did we not?"

There was much agreement to this and my suggestion for a night attack was dismissed as unnecessary. Certainly, these men, their fathers and grandfathers had been fighting the Turks for decades and I was willing to believe their expertise.

Despite the endless cannon fire, I lay down in my tent and slept for what seemed like a few moments before Eva shook me awake and bade me come outside.

The sun was lightening the sky in the east and already we could see the glints of metal and fluttering colours of the banners in the blackness across the field.

"They did not move," I said, shaking my head. "Damn them."

"What are they playing at?" Walt said. "Who wants to bet they come straight at us today? Stephen, how much gold do you have?"

"If we had some prisoners," Eva said, "we would not have to bet." I turned to look at her and saw that old glint in her eye. "We would know."

"Rouse the men," I said to Rob. "Prepare the horses. We are going to snatch up some Turkish sentries before the sun rises."

At the command tent, as a haggard-looking Hunyadi made his finishing remarks, I strode in, covered in dust and sweat, breathing hard. They turned to look at me, scowling.

"By God, you did not make a night attack alone after all, did you man?" some knight quipped.

"My lord," I said, "just before dawn, I took a small company out to the left flank and we brought back five sentries to the camp where we questioned them, separately. Two were Greeks. Well, Thessalians. They said almost the entire Thessalian cavalry was sent far around our left flank in the night. A small number of them were left with banners, so that we would not notice they had left the field. They will attack our left flank from the rear once battle is joined."

Everyone began speaking at once until Hunyadi's men shouted them down and commanded silence. Eyes fell on Hunyadi.

"Where are these men?"

"Outside. I brought them, in case you wished to question them yourself."

Hunyadi nodded to one of his men who ducked outside the tent to do just that. "If what you say is true, Richard, then we must strengthen the left at all costs. The only way to do that is to take men from the centre. And also from the reserve. And so that is what we shall do." He turned to the German mercenary lords. "And also ensure your hand-gunners are ready for a cavalry assault on the *wagonberg* from the rear. If there is nothing else? Then, God be with us all."

Hunyadi crossed the tent as they went back to their units and he grasped my arm in two of his in a powerful grip, nodding. His eyes were watery from exhaustion and the lines of his face were deeper than ever.

"They will come at us hard, today," he said, letting me go. "Harder than yesterday."

"You still want my company to assault the Sultan, my lord?"

"You still wish to do so?"

"More than anything."

"And if it is a choice between your enemy, Zaganos Pasha, and the Sultan?" He peered at me. "What will you do?"

"I would slay the Sultan, of course," I said, which was a lie.

"Then God be with you," Hunyadi said.

Stephen elected to join us on the field, clad in the most expensive Italian armour that could be bought, though he was careful to ensure he hid its brilliance behind poorly-applied paint and unremarkable cloth. He had no desire to be mistaken for somebody of importance.

"The Germans seem to think they will be attacking today," he said to me. "And I do not relish being guarded by the camp followers and the wounded."

I slapped him hard on the back. "That's the spirit, Stephen. And remember, if a cannon shoots in your direction, ensure that you duck."

"Very amusing," he said, closing his visor.

The battle began much as it had before but both armies were full of tired men and perhaps it was my imagination but everyone was tense and fearful. The entire plain was soon filled with the drumming rumble of thousands of horses and the blaring of trumpets and banging of drums.

The Anatolians came hard against our left but we had so many men there now that it held. On the other side of the plain, the Rumelian light horse almost turned our flank but the reserve drove them off.

With our flanks holding, Hunyadi committed his entire centre and all our infantry into an attack on the Turkish centre. The *azab* infantry were pushed back by our hand-gunners who advanced and fired, advanced and fired. Our cannons were pulled forward and deployed again behind our advance.

When we came into range of the Janissaries, our hand-gunners and the Sultan's elite soldiers stood in ranks and shot into each other. The Janissaries had the advantage of their prepared positions, their trenches and palisades, which protected them from our infantry's fire. Even when our cannons opened up on them, blasting holes in sections of their palisades, it made little difference. Battalions of infantry in lines, shooting their firearms into each other would in coming centuries become a familiar sight for me. But at the time, it was truly astonishing. Billowing clouds of smoke and the endless crash of the guns filled the air while we watched from a distance.

Our Germans began edging back from the withering fire of the Janissaries.

"Prepare to attack!" the cry went up and down our line and the men-at-arms in their armour prepared to charge the Janissaries lines.

"Lances!" I cried and my men called for the same from their squires. "Lances!"

"By God, no," Stephen said. "It shall be Varna all over again, Richard. You must stop them."

"No man can stop this now, Stephen. The battle has become a beast with its own mind. All we can do is ride it and try to hold on. Come, we shall join the charge."

We were many thousands of heavy cavalry and our front must have been half a mile wide. Ahead of my company, I watched the steel clad men and horses weaving through the trenches on their way to the Janissaries and I led my own men through safe routes.

The Janissary line broke against our charge, fleeing in sections until the entire line turned and fled. Our cries of victory went up all along the line of our attack and we pushed deeper in toward their camp, cutting down fleeing Janissaries left and right. Our horses were tired and the men's arms grew heavy but the elation that we had won gave strength to us all.

Ahead, the flags atop the Sultan's great tents fluttered in the breeze.

"Pull the company together!" I roared at Walt and Rob. "We make a final charge there, do you see?"

Eva threw her horse against mine and nudged me with her bloody mace. "What is that? Richard? What is that, there? There!"

I followed her pointing and saw the advance of a reserve unit of Janissaries coming forward in good order, shoulder to shoulder, about five hundred of them. The front ranks with their guns levelled and pointed. They were equipped as Janissaries, with the long robes and headdress, with polearms, hand-guns, bows, and side swords at their waists.

But their robes and long felt hats were dyed a vivid, blood-red.

"There!" Eva cried, jabbing her mace.

I tore my eyes to their right flank, on the far side of the formation from me.

William.

Riding an enormous iron-clad warhorse, he wore heavy mail, and had a Turkish helm on his head, with his face exposed. I would know it anywhere, as I knew his bearing and manner. A chill shot through me.

William's unit of blood-red Janissaries stopped as one and couched their gunpowder weapons.

"Halt! Pull back!" I ordered and led my men away from the front of the firing line. Just in time, as the Janissaries fired and scores of Hungarians fell to the volley.

I expected more gunners to step forward and take another shot but instead, the Janissaries dropped their guns and advanced quickly, drawing their wicked swords. Others in rear ranks raised their polearms, long spears with axe blades on one side.

Another order was called and they broke into a run, advancing like lightning on the Hungarian horsemen.

"Good God," I muttered.

They moved with unnatural speed.

Inhuman speed.

In moments, they crashed against the advancing men-at-arms and killed them. Their spears flashed and their swords whirled into men and horses. The red-robed Janissaries swarmed up onto mounted knights in the saddle and killed the riders. They grasped horses with their hands and dragged them to the ground, crushing the men's helms with maces or cutting off their heads with their swords.

"William!" I roared.

Eva had hold of my horse's bridle and would not let go. She commanded Walt and Rob to hold me back.

"He has five hundred immortal soldiers, Richard!" Eva shouted. "We cannot defeat them. Richard, we cannot! We must live so that we may kill him."

I allowed them to pull me away and I ordered my men to retreat away from the advancing immortal Janissaries. The red-robed monsters cut a swathe into the rest of our army before the retreat was sounded and we fell back, riding across the plain all the way to our reserves before the *wagonberg*.

Instead of pursuing us, William held his Janissaries back and the mortal Turks came forward to occupy their positions amongst the trenches and surviving defensive works. Our men were shocked and confused by the sudden reversal in the battle but they saw we were safe for now and they trusted Hunyadi to see them through and order was restored.

"What now?" Stephen asked, flipping open his visor. "Can even our entire army defeat so many immortals?"

"God damn his soul," I said. "God damn that bastard."

"Can we get around to his rear?" Walt suggested, gesturing with his weapon. "Slip through between their flank and centre, and circle in to the Sultan's camp and close on William's position?"

"He's right," Rob said. "We go around those red-robed bastards and avoid them altogether."

"We shall do it," I said. "Ready the men."

"Richard," Eva said, her tone level, pointing at our centre, where the surviving knights were preparing for another mass charge at the Sultan. "Hunyadi must be warned not to attack again."

It would undoubtedly be suicidal to assault hundreds of immortal soldiers, that was true, but there was a problem. "What can I say to him? What reason can I give that he would believe or even understand?"

None of them had an answer.

It was at that moment that the Turk's Thessalian cavalry finally arrived on our left flank in their thousands and assaulted the rear of the men still engaged there. We watched from our position in the centre near to the rear as our men were surrounded by the flanking manoeuvre.

"All is well," I said to my concerned men. "Hunyadi heeded our warnings and placed the Wallachian reserves there, you see? They are advancing and the Thessalians will themselves be pinned by the Wallachians. The flank will be ours again and their horsemen will be destroyed."

But it dawned on me that something was very wrong.

The Wallachians were not fighting.

"By God, those treacherous dogs are at it again!" Walt cried. "Do you see? Do you see it?"

"What is it?" Stephen asked us, turning from me to Walt, to Rob. "What is happening?"

"The Wallachians," I said, knowing then that the battle was lost. "The Wallachians, thousands of fresh horsemen, our reserve. They are surrendering to the Thessalians without offering battle."

"What?"

"We are betrayed. The Wallachians are surrendering! The battle is lost."

4

Dracula

1 4 4 8 - 1 4 5 2

HUNYADI MIGHT HAVE been defeated but he and his Hungarians again showed their ability and experience during the retreat, saving much of the remaining army.

The Wallachian's treacherous surrender allowed the Anatolian *sipahis* to overwhelm our left flank and so Hunyadi ordered the retreat. Their professionalism allowed the left and centre to disengage, with units taking turns to hold the Turks at bay while we did so.

However, the entire right wing was isolated and destroyed. We were still pulling back into the dark of the night. He left behind a screen of infantry to man the camp and sent cavalry to feint attacks while the majority of us slipped away. It must have taken the Turks all the next day to overwhelm the *wagonberg*, even poorly defended as it was, because they did not pursue our army. The men we left behind were slaughtered, of course. God bless their souls.

And despite the sudden change in the course of the battle, we still lost only about six thousand men while the Turks certainly lost forty thousand.

Their enormous losses were the main reason we were not pursued far and we broke into smaller groups to travel back to Hungary, for we would have to skirt far around the Turks on our way back north.

"It is like Varna," Stephen said during our flight. "Like Varna all over again."

"Yes, yes, you were right, Stephen," I said. "Be quiet."

Throughout the journey, riding hard through cold passes and sleeping on thin, hard, freezing soil, I could think only of William and his red-robed immortal army. In the hills many nights later, we crowded into the shelter of a roofless hovel and outbuildings but I was too angry to rest easy.

"If not for William and his immortal Janissaries, we would have killed the Sultan," I said, leaning against the ruined wall and watching the growing fire my men had lit in the centre of the room. "And his son. We would be throwing the Turks out of Europe. If not for William. How could he do such a thing? How could he make so many? How does he find enough blood for them?"

"The Turks have learned to be efficient," Eva said, looking up through the ruined beams at the clear sky above.

"How can we hope to defeat so many?" I asked. "We five against five hundred."

"There is always a way to achieve a goal," Eva said. "Now, sleep. Have patience. Trust that we will yet cut off his head and burn his foul body into ashes. Dream well."

Disaster followed disaster, however, and when we reached Hungary, we discovered that Hunyadi had once again been caught in his defeat by an enemy. George Branković, the ruler of Serbia, had chased down and captured Hunyadi as he and his men cut across his territory, threatening to hand him over to his Turkish masters.

Hunyadi immediately promised a vast ransom if he could be released, to which Branković agreed. The Serbian despot was like a whipped Turkish dog but he saw gold showering down from a desperate Hungary and so he let Hunyadi go. Still, the delay in returning, and doing so in such an ignominious fashion, took more of Hunyadi's remaining lustre and Christians began to wonder if the great Janos Hunyadi could be so great after all, if he only ever lost the battles that truly mattered.

In his defence, it was undeniable that on the field he had done everything correctly, even brilliantly, and yet still he had lost. It was not his fault that he faced an immortal regiment of Janissaries. Even then, he might have saved his army if not for the betrayal of the perfidious Wallachians.

The Turks were on the rise again and Hunyadi had been brought low in the minds of many. The Turks focused now on taking Albania and they invaded in 1449, and in 1450. Each time, the brilliant Skanderbeg threw them back. It seemed for a time that he might truly be the brilliant leader who could unite eastern Christendom, but then he promised peace and entered into negotiations, promising to pay six thousand ducats and swore he would accept Turkish suzerainty. I was saddened by the news but it was all just another clever ploy on his part as he never paid the promised sum and then renounced his subjugation when it came time to pay. Immediately, he began raiding Turkish forts and the invading army, he attacked supply caravans and carried off enormous quantities of booty, eventually forcing the Turks from the field without ever fighting a grand battle.

"Perhaps that is the way to do it," I said, on reading the reports and after listening to men who had been there or claimed to have been. "Force them to withdraw."

512

"That'll work for mountain lands," Walt pointed out. "What you going to do on the plains, when they can see you coming and chase you down when you flee?"

We were comfortable once more in our house in the city of Buda but it seemed so far from the action.

"Is it time to travel to Albania?" I asked Eva and Stephen, seeking their advice.

"How many men can they put in the field?" Eva asked. "Ten thousand? Lightly armed, at that. Enough to protect their hills and valleys but would Hungarians follow an Albanian, no matter how successful he is in raids and small battles?"

"Damn these people, all of them. The Wallachians most of all."

"Patience, Richard. We have time. Years, decades. We know where William is, now. He has shown inhuman patience and so must we."

"You need not repeat yourself," I said.

"I think I do. You wish to fight. Always. I know. But to defeat William you must first defeat that need to always fight and kill."

"I know, I say. I know, woman, now leave me in peace."

The Turks assaulted the city of Kruje, led in person by the Sultan, but the garrison defeated every attack. The Turks attempted to cut the water supply, and undermine the walls, and they offered vast bribes, literal fortunes to any man who would open the gates. Every attempt failed and Skanderbeg's brave Albanians resisted. The Turkish siege was struck by camp sickness and eventually the Turks, clutching their painful, watery bellies, limped back to Edirne in defeat.

And there, in early 1451, Sultan Murad II died.

He had ruled the Turks for thirty years and had been fighting and winning for most of that time. Christendom rejoiced at his passing and there was a sense that things may just improve, now. The Sultan's son came to the throne as Sultan Mehmed II. He was very young and already in his life he had been the Sultan, when Murad had attempted to retire in his old age and hand the reins of power to his very young son. But the boy Mehmed was not capable of ruling a vast empire, nor could he lead vast armies. Indeed, the young Mehmed had supposedly been Sultan when the crusade of Varna had been launched.

We had heard that young Mehmed II asked his father to reclaim the throne but Murad II refused. Our agents had reported that Mehmed wrote to his father thusly. "If you are the Sultan, come and lead your armies. If I am the Sultan I hereby order you to come and lead my armies."

It sounded to me like the sort of thing William would say but whatever the cause of it, Murad had returned for Varna and for every battle since.

"We shall pray that the boy Sultan remains incompetent," Stephen said.

"Was it incompetent to command his father to return?" Eva said. "Or was it in fact the only thing that saved their damned empire from destruction?"

"It was William," I said, "Whispering in the boy's ear. I have no doubts. But the old man is dead and now we have this young fellow. What is he now, nineteen years old? In command of a vast empire. No, William will have this lad wrapped around his finger, mark my words. We may wish for incompetence but we must plan for further conquest."

"Have you thought any more about making us our own immortal army, Richard?" Rob asked. "To counter the Janissaries in red?"

"I think of little else," I said. "But the questions remain, Rob. Who can we trust enough? Can I make a hundred Hungarian immortals and trust them to keep the secret? If I make a hundred, let alone five hundred, how will we find blood enough for them? Already, there are endless rumours about us here and the drinking of blood. William had Murad to shelter him and now he has Mehmed. Who do we have? You think Hunyadi would comprehend it? He is already walking a knife edge and if we brought him into it, his lords would overthrow him and then we would have chaos. And if there is chaos, William will walk right up to the gates of Buda."

A knock at our door proved to be one of Hunyadi's messengers. "My lord wishes to speak with you, sir. At your earliest convenience."

That meant immediately. My servants prepared my finest clothes and I made my way through the city to the royal palace, whereupon I was brought at once into Hunyadi's private audience chamber.

"Vladislaus II has not proved himself to be the ruler that I hoped he would be," Hunyadi said, inviting me to sit with him by a window overlooking the Danube below.

"You mean he is not obeying your commands," I said. "And you were the one who placed him on the throne of Wallachia."

"I do not issue him commands," he snapped. "But I have just had word that Vladislaus has sent a delegation of *boyars* to congratulate the new Sultan."

I shrugged. "Wallachians are duplicitous. None can be trusted."

Hunyadi eyed me, weighing up his next words. "And yet some can be trusted more than others. And it seems that Vladislaus can be trusted to throw in with the Turks, just as Vlad Dracul had done. We need a loyal man on the throne, or at least one who hates the Turks more than he fears them."

"You need a man who hates the Turks more than he does Hungary," I said, which did not please the Regent. "Are there any such men in Wallachia?"

"Perhaps there are not," he admitted. "Not amongst the *boyars* in Wallachia at this moment. But perhaps there is one who feels this way who is not in Wallachia?"

"Very well," I said. "Who is this man?"

Hunyadi looked out of the window before speaking. "We have had word that the Turks recently released a Wallachian who was their hostage for many years. He is the eldest of the two surviving sons of the former voivode, Vlad Dracul. The son's name is also Vlad. He is coming here."

I nodded. "The son of the man I killed is coming to Buda?" As I spoke, Hunyadi smiled. "And you wish me gone before he comes, is that it?"

"It would not be for long. You see, I have a task for you. We must begin to move against

514

Vladislaus by taking at least two of the fortresses on the border of Transylvania and Wallachia so that we control the passes and not him. And while you are away, taking possession of these places for Hungary, I will speak to this young Vlad and I will see how he feels about things. And, yes, it might be best if the man who cut off his father's head was not present when he arrives. It may have an undesired effect on the young fellow."

"I am pleased to hear that he is coming," I said. "When I do meet him, I will be able to fulfil a duty that I swore to uphold."

"A duty? Swore to whom?"

"Before he died, Vlad Dracul asked that I look after his sons. He gave his sword, and a dragon amulet, into my care, and requested that I pass them to his eldest, this Vlad. I wondered if I would ever get the opportunity."

"Truly? Well, that is well. Perhaps the bridges can be mended, in time. Nevertheless, the Transylvanian fortresses must still be taken. There will be no fighting, but the garrisons must be replaced, you see."

***

The fortresses in the duchies of Fogaras and Amlas were willing to give up without a fight but honour demanded they go through the motions of demanding the legal proofs and the commanders stated they had to receive confirmation from the lords before vacating the defences.

Although I took my company and four hundred other mercenaries in Hunyadi's pay and Hungarian soldiers, there was a lot of talking and even more waiting. I did my best to be courteous to all and remembered that it was *supposed* to take a long time. I was supposed to be keeping out of the way while Vlad, son of Vlad, made himself at home in Buda.

"Perhaps we can raid into Wallachia a little," I suggested to Eva. "Keep the men busy."

"Because you are bored," she replied.

"It would make Vladislaus look weak," I said. "And his people would demand his removal. Which is what Hunyadi wants."

"He does not want lawlessness on his borders, and he does not want the Wallachians subject to raids by Hungarian soldiers. Or soldiers loyal to Hungary."

"We would disguise ourselves," I said, warming to the idea. "Perhaps we could find some Turkish armour?"

"You should train against Walt and Rob. Take out some of your excessive vigour."

I scoffed. "They are no challenge. They have only three hands between them."

"We will not raid Wallachia, Richard. You would not be so rash. Once, perhaps, but not now."

"Have I changed so much?"

She smiled. "There will be war enough even for you, soon. Have patience."

After a few weeks on the Transylvania-Wallachia border, my business was concluded.

The towns and fortresses had written letters to the voivode, begging for forgiveness for accepting the protection of the Hungarian crown. My Hungarian soldiers and most of the mercenaries I left as garrisons in the towns. They would not be enough to resist the Wallachians should the voivode decide to take them back by force and instead the garrison soldiers were there to keep an eye on the towns. And no one believed Voivode Vladislaus would go so far as taking the towns back by force.

When I returned to Buda, the young Vlad had been welcomed into Hunyadi's service and had sworn allegiance to Ladislaus V, the King of Hungary. Even so, I felt it best to keep my distance, literally. Until I was once again summoned by Hunyadi to the palace.

I knew what to expect. At least, I thought I did.

The summons was to his private quarters and I expected that the conversation would again be a quiet one with just him and his chamberlain and other servants.

Instead, when I was escorted in, there were dozens of men and lords present, surrounding Hunyadi. He was somewhat hidden behind those lords, engaged in serious conversation while wine was served and men drank in small groups, and I waited until his business was completed.

Some men nodded in greeting but I was not well liked by most lords, great and small, and most ignored me. I was an outsider and also I made no effort to play the game of politics by building friendships and alliances, which was unusual and so made the men who would be my peers mistrust me even more. Some looked down on me as a mere mercenary knight and others wondered if I had some secret motivation to have remained at the Hungarian court for so long.

Of course, they were right to be suspicious. I was indeed there for secret, ulterior motives, and I did not care what they thought of me. I was not a part of their society, or any society, existing outside of it. And Eva said I had a stillness that disturbed people, and I moved with a fluidity reminiscent of a wolf. Some lords were so powerful that no lesser man, even an unnatural one, was a threat to their position and so I was welcomed by kings and princes.

It was fine by me. Their opinions on warfare were idiotic, and I often listened to impassioned arguments for one tactic over another where both men were woefully wrong. Even those infuriating discussions were preferable to the fools discussing the minutiae of this piece of armour over that, or a new weapon they had obtained. Worse still was the ravings over items of clothing that they were having made, or even the absurd shoes they were wearing. Other than that, it was complaints about their sons, fathers, wives, daughters, their servants, or their vassals. It was incredibly tiresome.

"Who is that man there?" an outraged voice cried out in Hungarian.

The room fell silent and I looked up. Across the chamber, Hunyadi was on his feet and beside him a short, young lord stood glaring at me with his hand outstretched and his finger pointing at me.

Nobles on either side of me cleared their throats and stepped backwards, creating a space around me.

Hunyadi looked anxious but restrained, watching me carefully.

The top of the young man's head came up to Hunyadi's nose but he was otherwise powerfully built and had a strong face, with a long, sharp nose and the beginnings of a fine moustache beneath it. His clothes were of rich cloth, in red, with sable edges.

"I am the mercenary captain known as Richard of England," I said and bowed. "And who are you, my lord?"

I knew who he was.

"I am Vlad Dracula, son of Vlad Dracul, the former Voivode of Wallachia." He stalked forward, approaching slowly with a face fixed in an unreadable expression. "I have heard of you," he said, his voice deep and steady. "You are the man who did slay my father in the marshes."

Lords and knights shuffled further away from me.

"I am," I said, looking him in the eye. "And I did."

He stopped just an arm's span from me, looking up through heavily lidded eyes and thick black eyebrows. "In that case," he said, speaking slowly. "I must thank you, sir. My beloved father was for too long a friend to the Turk. And so it is right and proper that he was removed from power and a loyal Christian put in his place."

Around me, I heard many a breath being released.

Still, it seemed rather convenient to be swiftly and publicly forgiven.

I bowed my head a little. "I am glad you feel that way, my lord."

"However, Sir Richard the mercenary captain, we do have a problem, do we not?"

"We do, my lord?"

"Why yes. Certainly, we do. For there is now one on the throne of Wallachia who has also forgotten his duty to God. He also must be replaced by a man who knows where his true loyalties lie."

I glanced at Hunyadi, who stood motionless across the room. He met my eye but I could not read his expression. "I hope that such a replacement of the Voivode of Wallachia can be swiftly brought about, my lord."

"Will you help me?" Vlad asked, suddenly. He cleared his throat and spoke more slowly. "That is, if you would agree, I would much value your assistance in claiming the throne that is mine by right."

Over his shoulder, Hunyadi made the smallest nod of his head. "My only desire is to kill Turks," I said, watching closely for his reaction. "My only goal is to drive them from Europe, once and for all."

"Your *only* desire?" Vlad raised his eyebrows and smirked. "Truly?"

In fact, my only desire is to kill William and the Turks are in my way, I thought.

"Yes, my lord," I said.

He smiled beneath his moustache. "I am pleased to hear it. And since that is my only desire, also, then you should help me."

"I should?" I said.

The young Vlad frowned, his eyebrows lancing down over his dark eyes. "You would be paid, of course. You and your men. You are a mercenary company after all, are you not? And you are currently unemployed."

"It seems to me, my lord, that you have much work to do before you begin slaughtering Turks. Not least of which is taking the throne that you say is yours by right. When you have armies to throw against our enemies, I will gladly fight beside you. Assuming, of course, that my lord Janos Hunyadi, who currently pays to retain my company for his service, grants us leave to take up employment by the new voivode."

Vlad scowled and turned to look at Hunyadi, who appeared annoyed.

"The Turks have a new Sultan, Richard," Hunyadi snapped. "And they will be on the march once more. Our new ally, Vlad Dracula, has accepted responsibility for guarding the Transylvanian border against Turkish incursion. If Vladislaus has indeed thrown his lot in with the Turks, they will march straight through the Wallachian plains and seek to cross the passes. Vlad Dracula, therefore, shall indeed soon be engaged in your favourite pastime. And because, as you say, I pay you well in order to retain your service, I will ask that you join him in his new responsibility."

Vlad Dracula turned back to me, his dark eyes full of expectation.

It seemed quite possible that he intended to get me alone, away from the court, and out in the wilds so that he could take revenge for his father's murder. There was no chance at all that he meant what he said about being glad I had killed the older Vlad. No matter how one feels about one's father, no man alive could break bread with his killer, much less serve beside him in battle.

On the other hand, he seemed willing to throw himself into the fight. Perhaps his long years amongst the Turks had created in him a desire to destroy them, or at least resist them, as it had done for Skanderbeg in Albania.

There was still a good chance that the young man was in fact a Turkish agent, biding his time until he betrayed Christendom and opened the gates to the swarming hordes beyond. He would not be the first Christian hostage to convert to his captors' religion and throw his lot in with them. If that was his plan, to kill me, and to betray his Christian brothers, then the best place to stop him would be at his side.

No doubt Hunyadi was playing his own games. Indeed, although he paid to retain my service, I was not sworn to him and could refuse a task. Breaking our contract would not go down well with my men, who would feel their reputation was at risk of being tainted and who always made more money on campaign than sitting idly.

By arranging for me to be confronted by Vlad publicly, Hunyadi was hoping to pressure me into accepting the task, even if I had doubts about my safety and the young lord's chances of success.

But I thought I could protect myself against an inexperienced young knight. And if he failed, then I would not have lost much. More important was keeping Hunyadi on my side.

I bowed. "I will guard the border with you, my lord."

And I will guard my back from you, I thought.

"Do you consider yourself an equal to me?" Vlad asked, watching me like a hawk.

Just in time, I stopped myself from bursting out into laughter.

Instead, I bowed. "You are a great lord, who will one day soon be Prince of Wallachia. I am a mere knight, albeit one of great renown and personal ability, with a small but loyal company of veteran soldiers."

A Hungarian lord growled from across the room. "He is a mercenary dog who will do as he is commanded, if the whip hand is firm enough."

I smiled. "And you are a fat old man who cannot hold his wine. Would you care to do combat with me, fat old man? You may choose the weapons, as I am your superior in them all."

His face turned purple and he threw his goblet down with a crash upon the floor. "How dare you! I demand an apology!"

"You may try to take it, if you dare," I said, holding out my hands.

"Enough!" Hunyadi roared. "Radol, I forbid you to fight my mercenary."

"Listen to your lord, Radol," I said. "Or you won't live to regret it."

Hunyadi turned on me. "Richard, you will go with Vlad Dracula or you will leave Hungary forever!"

Sighing, I imagined Eva mocking my inability to hold my temper.

I bowed to him and then to Vlad. "To Transylvania it is, then."

Vlad Dracula watched me with a strange look in his eye. I could not be certain but it seemed as though it was a look of delight.

***

On the journey to the mountainous southern border of Transylvania, I was sure to keep myself and my company far from Dracula's. His new personal forces, some gifted by Hunyadi, others by loyal Wallachian *boyars*, and a number of Moldavians, outnumbered mine many times over.

Before we left Buda, I had explained to the men of my company that we were heading into danger and that the threat might come from our host, Vlad Dracula.

"But the main threat is to you," a grizzled Frenchman named Claudin said. The leading men in my company had assembled in my tent and it was crowded and unpleasant inside and I wished for it to be done as swiftly as possible.

"Well, thank you for your concern, Claudin," I said. "My heart is touched by your compassion."

Some of the men laughed but he continued. "Without you, my lord, we would have a company no more. But I merely ask whether Vlad Dracula means to kill you and you alone."

"I do not know if he means me harm at all, Claudin, but it is a distinct possibility, would you not say?"

He shrugged and pursed his lips, for he was both deficient in wit and a Frenchman.

"Might he not kill us all?" Garcia asked. He was a young man, forced to leave his homeland in his extreme youth due to some indiscretion or other, but he was a sharp one. "If Vlad Dracula, son of Vlad Dracul, wishes you dead and kills you, might he not wish for there to be no witnesses to his crime? After all, Hunyadi would not wish to see you murdered. It would be a crime to blacken his name. Cause him trouble, no? But if the entire Company of Saint George is killed to a man, he might well swear that it was the Turks that did the deed."

The men muttered and looked around at each other in the tent.

"Indeed, Garcia," I said, "that is the case. So you must each of you be on your guard at all times. We shall ride and camp as if we are in enemy territory. Any Wallachian or Transylvanian that comes near us, day or night, must be stopped and questioned and if he is on proper business then he must be watched and well guarded in every moment."

"What about Serban?" someone called and others chuckled.

"All Wallachians other than Serban," I said. "He is sworn to me. None of you will treat him as the enemy. Do you all understand what we are riding into? And do you all agree to follow me in such circumstances?"

Thanks to God, and the men's love of money, they all came with me into Transylvania.

We rode away from our supposed allies in the day and camped with an established perimeter that we closely guarded. Each night, my close companions and I took turns to sleep, lest Vlad Dracula or his men attempted an outright attack or an assassination.

And each night passed without incident.

"Biding his time," Walt said confidently one morning, after we had been in Transylvania for two weeks.

Rob agreed, as his squire strapped his vambrace on his handless arm. "Luring you in by being patient and waiting until you let your guard down."

"Ah, well," I said, tapping my nose. "Little does he know that I never let my guard down."

Eva scoffed. "Every night, the whole of Transylvania can hear you snoring."

My companions found this highly amusing. "I snore so that you, my friends, will each be wide awake enough to guard me in my slumber."

One by one, Vlad Dracula toured the fortresses of the border that fell under his command, and each commander swore loyalty and agreed plans of action should the Turks attack. A few men he removed and replaced but the tour was largely without incident. Eventually, we took quarters outside a fortress in the east called Crăciune.

I had kept my distance from Vlad for weeks and what had started out as sensible precaution had begun to look like rudeness and, ultimately, outright fear. I did not like to skulk about and to always be where our leader was not. It made me appear unimportant and disinterested, as well as fearful.

"Perhaps I should join our young commander in the fortress," I said to Eva, who lay beside me in our low, narrow bed inside my tent. "He seems committed to taking his throne and waging war against the Turks after all. If that is true then it is likely he would be a friend to me."

"That would be taking an unnecessary risk."

"If he was going to do us harm, he would have done it already. It stands to reason."

"A man may use reason to convince himself of anything," she said. "Many pathways of reason appear sound all the way to the conclusion and then men choose the one they like the best."

"I am not prone to such failures in reasoning," I said.

"All men do this," she said. "And all women, too. You cannot out-think a problem to a certain conclusion. It is not possible."

"But one may weigh up decisions. Come to a reasoned decision based on this outcome or that having more or less likelihood of success."

"Precisely. For instance, you cannot reason whether Vlad Dracula will be a friend or an enemy to the Turks. Or to you. Perhaps he will be an enemy to the Turks and an enemy to you also. What you wish to be true is that he seeks to destroy his former captives with every ounce of will he possess, and so you look for reasons that this is true. You speak to me of the hatred that must have grown in his heart at being held prisoner by hostile and strange people. And you look for evidence of this in his actions since being freed, or in the words he uses, or the tone he takes, or expression his moustache makes when he speaks of the Turk. But it is all wasted effort, do you not see? Either of your suppositions could be true, or neither."

"Out of all of the women I have ever known, you have the most elaborate way of telling me to shut up and go to sleep."

She tutted. "I am telling you to be patient. Be prepared for any eventuality. Even better, be prepared for every eventuality and you can never be surprised."

I pinched her suddenly on the flank and pushed her gently onto her back, shifting myself over her. "You did not expect that, did you?"

She rolled her eyes and smiled. "With you, Richard, I never expect anything else."

"You expect me to always take your advice," I said.

"Because it is always good advice," she said.

"Perhaps. But how would I ever know if I did not on occasion disregard it?"

She frowned as I slid off of her and climbed from my bed, calling for my valet.

"What are you doing?" she asked, sitting up.

"I will not live like a whipped dog, cringing at the sound of his master's boots. I am going to speak to Vlad."

"At this hour? He will be abed."

"Or drunk."

"Aye, or drunk, which would be far worse."

I grinned at her as my valet entered and pretended not to be staring at Eva's breasts.

"I am going to call on the future Prince of Wallachia so prepare my fine clothes," I commanded and he bowed and crossed the tent to do just that.

"Richard," Eva said, climbing from the bed. "Why would he grant you an audience at this time of night? Why not wait until morning?"

"I have something in my possession that he will want," I said. "He will see me."

Eva scowled and snapped at my valet. "Leave the clothes be, I will see to them. Go and rouse Sir Robert and Black Walter. They are to attend Sir Richard at once. Go, now."

"Thank you, Eva," I said.

"Wear the green jacket with the loose sleeves so you may hide a blade inside each arm," she said, crouching naked by my clothes chest and searching through it.

I bowed. "Whatever you say, my dear."

We crossed the field into the fortress by the light of lamps alone. The sky was low and rain threatened, with a cold wind bringing damp air down from the east.

"You sure about this, Richard?" Walt asked, scratching his chin.

"It does seem contrary to your previous advice," Rob said, carrying the long wooden case that I had entrusted to him.

"All will be well," I said. "Just, for God's sake, be on your guard."

It was a small fortress and the hall was likewise diminutive. When I was escorted in and instructed to wait, the remains of the meal eaten earlier were being cleared away and the trestle tables taken apart. We stood in front of the high end of the hall where the permanent chairs of the lord sat empty. A couple of soldiers sat slumped in the corners, heads lolling onto their chests.

Behind me, Walt scoffed. "Wallachia's finest sons, there."

"Useless bastards," Rob said, before yawning. "Though I wish I was in a drunken stupor."

Walt snorted. "Remember that time in Prague when that little Bavarian lad challenged you to—"

"Will you two old maids cease your prattling?" I snapped. "Someone comes."

Footsteps approached from the rooms beyond the hall and Vlad Dracula entered, followed by a dozen of his companions. All were armed.

He did not acknowledge me until he had taken his seat in the largest chair upon the dais. It was not raised high but still it was a demonstration that we were not equals. Far from it.

"Sir Richard," Vlad said. "What is the danger?"

"My lord?"

"I asked you what is the danger, sir." He gestured with his palm up. "I assume there is some danger imminent and that is why you had to see me immediately. I was just about to get into bed, such as it is."

"There is no danger, my lord."

"Oh? Then what is the meaning of this urgency? After all, you have kept yourself and your company so far from me and from any service that I had concluded that you were workshy. It seems that your reputation as a fierce soldier was no more than lies. You have taken your pay and done nothing of note other than to camp in this field or that with your men. What has changed, sir, that you felt so compelled to insist I see you in this very moment?"

"We are a fighting company, my lord, that much is true. Thanks to Christ, though, that there has been no fighting these past weeks, for us or for you. Clearly, your powers of diplomacy are significant and worthy of praise and you have done so much to secure the lands of Christendom against the Turk. Indeed, I was so impressed by your ability to secure the length of the borderland that I suddenly recalled a duty I swore to perform. This duty is why I have come to you."

I left it there so that he would be forced to ask.

"A duty?" Vlad said. "What duty must you perform tonight?"

"I swore that I would support you, as long as you were an enemy of the Turk."

Vlad sighed, gesturing at me to hurry up. "Yes, yes, you swore to Hunyadi, I was there."

"I stated my terms in Buda and Hunyadi agreed. I swore nothing to him that is not in my contract."

He was confused and growing frustrated. "Well, who did you swear this oath to?"

"To your father."

He and his men bristled and I noted a few hands drifting toward their swords. Most would have spent the last hours of the day drinking wine and would be quick to anger and slow to see subtleties.

"You swore to my father to support me," Vlad said, "before you killed him?"

"I pursued him and his men into the marshes. We fought and he was injured in the arm and neck. Before he died, he asked that I help his sons, Vlad and Radu, to fight the Turks."

Vlad was very still, though I thought I saw him flinch at the name of his brother. "My father would not have said that."

"I beg your pardon for disagreeing, my lord, but he did. He begged me to deliver these to you and to urge you to remember your duty, just as he had failed in his."

I turned to Rob who handed over the long wooden case that he had carried for me from my tent, and I held it out to Vlad.

The case was covered in intricate patterns of moulded boiled leather in a deep red, with gold leaf in recesses throughout. The corners were protected by polished brass. The pattern on the top of the case in the centre was that of a dragon with its tail in its mouth and a cross on its back.

One of his men took it from me, his eyes widening as he saw the beauty of the designs and brought it reverently to his lord.

"My father gave you this?" Vlad asked, rightly suspicious.

"The case I had made in Buda," I replied. "Though it was a Wallachian who did the work. He claimed to have trained in Florence and I did not believe him until I saw his work. It is the contents of the case that were given to me by your father that I might give them in turn to you."

Vlad did not take his eyes from the case as he undid the clasps and opened it. His men clustered close about him and peered over his shoulders.

The interior of the case was moulded to the shape of its contents and covered in red silk.

Vlad reached in and lifted out the sword, staring at it with such fervour that I feared his eyes would pop from his head. With his other hand, he took the dragon amulet on its chain and looked from one to the other as his men took the case away.

Finally, Vlad lifted his eyes to me and I saw that they were damp with threatened tears.

"Did he say anything else?"

"He asked that I protect you."

"Protect me?" Vlad repeated, bewildered. "And you agreed?"

"I said that any man who was an enemy to the Turk would be a friend as far as I was concerned."

Vlad thought for a moment and stood, stepped down from the dais as he approached, still with the sword in one hand and the dragon amulet in the other, its silver chain dangling down.

Walt and Rob slid forward but I waved them back.

"Thank you, Sir Richard," Vlad said, standing before me and looking up. "You have done your duty in this matter. And you have done it well."

"It pleases me to hear it, my lord. As I said to your father. I am here to fight the Turks. The Sultan and his closest men in particular."

Vlad glanced up at me. "I hate the Turk more than any man alive. Once I have my kingdom secured, I shall do everything in my power to destroy them. Every one. The Sultan and his closest men in particular."

For a moment, I thought he was about to embrace me but instead he dismissed me. As I left the hall, I saw him showing off his father's sword to his companions.

"How did it go?" Eva asked.

"I think perhaps we should throw in our lot with this Vlad Dracula. We might help him to win the throne and if we do, he may well become a great ally. Or even more."

Alas, it was not to be. The Turks were not sitting still and allowing us to make our plans and live our lives. They were bent on conquest.

In the morning, a frantic messenger came from Hungary, with letters for Vlad Dracula but others for Stephen from his agents in Buda.

"What is it?" I asked Stephen when his face turned grey. He continued reading. "Stephen!"

He dragged his eyes from the words. "The new Sultan, Mehmed, is not coming for Transylvania after all."

"Damn," I said. "Where is he headed? Albania? Not Moldavia, surely, they are nothing."

Stephen swallowed. "There is no doubt that he has chosen to concentrate the efforts of his entire empire on the final reduction of Constantinople."

"Constantinople?" Serban said, crossing himself.

"Bastards," Walt said.

"Can it be true?" I asked Eva.

Stephen answered, flicking the letter in his hands. "It is Constantinople herself that calls for aid. Letters have been sent to every Christian kingdom, begging for help before the Turks arrive."

"Then that is what we shall do," I said. "Prepare the men. We leave for Constantinople."

5

Constantinople

1453

THE TURKS HAD LONG sought Constantinople and yet it was impossible to not see William's hand in this new assault. It was the sort of grandiose monstrosity that he brought forth into the world. Yet it was certainly in the interests of the new young Sultan, for if he achieved his aim it would secure his position within his empire, as well as make him famous everywhere in Dar al-Islam, even in Arabia and Egypt where they looked down on the Turks as barbarian upstarts. Indeed, such fame would help to secure his empire's porous eastern borders, for who would dare attack the man who had destroyed the great Constantinople?

The Byzantines had long been forced into vassalage under the Turks. Under the terms of their vassalage they had not even been permitted to strengthen the great walls of their city and had been sending troops to fight for the Turks for decades already. Even sixty years earlier, the subjugated Byzantines had sent troops to help destroy the city of Philadelphia, the last Byzantine possession in Anatolia. All that was left of the once great and vast Roman Empire of the East was the city of Constantinople and a handful of outlying ports, fortresses and villages. Such a disgrace and humiliation to suffer and yet the city itself, with its vast walls, had resisted every previous attempt at taking it.

There remained many elements in the city's favour. Provided that Venice and Genoa and other fleets came to Constantinople's aid, the Turks would have enormous trouble crossing the Bosporus without coming to disaster. The Turks were good soldiers but their fleets had always been weak compared to Christian navies. And if they attacked the great chain gate that protected the Golden Gate harbour, they would be risking a counter assault by the Christian ships safe in the Golden Horn.

"Do not think the Turk is unaware of this," the Byzantine officer said as he escorted us along the top of the inner wall of the city's main defensive fortification. The officer's name was Michael and he was a grim fellow though he had welcomed me and my company with open arms when we arrived. "One of the first acts that alerted us to the Turk's intentions was his construction of the fortress six miles north of here, on the European side of the straits. It is at the narrowest point of the Bosporus, do you see? It was when the towers of the fortress grew as tall as our own walls that Emperor Constantine sent his letters requesting aid. That fortress is armed with vast cannons, powerful enough to threaten any ship passing through."

Michael came to a stop beside a tower at the northern end of the inner wall and we looked out through one of the enormous crenels to the empty land beyond. The fields were untended and there were hardly any people on the roads, all the way to the horizon. On our right was the inner portion of the Golden Horn, the protected harbour so precious to the city. Within the harbour, hundreds of ships, large and small, bobbed on the blue waters.

On the other side of the harbour mouth was the walled town of Galata, which was largely populated and controlled by Genoese colonists. Unseen beyond Galata, further along the strait, was the new fortress that Michael had spoken of. It was technically, legally, on Byzantine land but the Turks had not cared about that. They meant to take everything for themselves anyway, so why quibble over such things? The local peasants had protested but there was nothing they could do.

"So they now control the northern half of the straits, at the least," I said. "But still, the Turk cannot truly sail."

Michael scoffed. "No, he takes to the water like a stone," he said and spat. "And may they all drown like rocks, also. But no, they have been building ships everywhere in Anatolia. And they have promised fortunes for Christian crews and captains for a thousand miles and they have answered, the treacherous, mercenary, bastards. With hundreds of new ships and Christian crews, the Turk may be a challenge for the Venetians and Genoese."

"Surely not, sir," I said, thinking him far too fearful.

Eva and Stephen exchanged a look and Stephen began scratching down notes. Walt leaned on the merlon and looked out at the landscape beyond, pointing down at the lower, outer walls and muttering something to Rob and Serban.

"Four hundred Turkish ships in the straits, so they are saying. Eighteen great warships, another twenty galleons and a score or more built only for transporting horses across the straits. They have made a fleet and made it for the sole purpose of contesting the Bosporus and for moving an army across the waters."

Stephen stopped writing for a moment to stare, Serban crossed himself and Rob muttered a short prayer or an oath.

"Even so," Stephen said, "the Venetians alone could defeat the Turks, could they not?"

"That is assuming more Venetians come than have already," Michael said. "They are not a people to be trusted, as I am sure you know. They care only for gold, for making wealth. They are a people without honour."

"They are Christians, sir," I said. "They will come. All of Christendom will come."

He scoffed openly. "An easy thing to say. Yet, where are they?"

Stephen answered. "Constantine has promised to heal the schism between the Roman and the Orthodox Church, has it not? And the agreement allows the Pope in Rome to be the lord of all Christians in the East."

The soldier sucked air in through pursed lips. "Old Constantine has promised it, yes, and the leaders of the Church have agreed. But ordinary people will not have it. Mark me, sir, the people will not be subject to Rome."

"They would rather be destroyed by the Mohammedans?" I said, irritated by his obstinacy, and that of his people.

"They would rather be free to worship as they believe in their hearts."

"But if it is a choice of surviving or being destroyed, surely they can see they would be better off changing the form of their worship somewhat rather than seeing their sons murdered and their wives and daughters raped and sold into slavery."

He shrugged. "They see it as subjugation also. But they believe the walls will save us. And God will save us. This is God's city. He will not let it fall."

I shook my head in disbelief, and Eva placed a hand on my arm.

"Who has come so far, sir?" Eva asked him, smiling pleasantly. "We have seen Venetian ships in the harbour and men of many nations in the city."

His face flushed as he answered, annoyed at being addressed by a woman. Normally, she held her tongue amongst strangers but we were not in normal times. "Catalan mercenaries have been hired but silver was stripped from the churches to pay for them and the people are not happy. Not happy at all, madam. Some of the silver went on repairing the walls, at least, and few men complain about that. The Venetians, though, already lost ships to the great guns of the Rumelia Hisar fortress and so they are keeping clear of it until the battle is won. To that end they have sent us the ships you see, along with two transport ships now departed which was filled with Venetian soldiers."

"So they have come," I said. "In numbers."

"A few hundred soldiers, perhaps. But will they stand or will they set sail when battle is joined?"

I had no answer for him. "Who else has come?"

"Cardinal Isidore arrived yesterday and his men are now disembarking. I believe he has brought hand-gunners and archers but a mere two hundred soldiers. In the streets, the people are rejoicing and saying that this is the vanguard of a vast army which comes even now to save us. After all, why not think this? The Pope could send tens of thousands but he demands Constantine publicly heal the schism first. Outrageous. I tell them that the Pope's army is not coming but few have listened. Even my own family tell me to have faith. Ha!" He turned and spat over the wall, the wind catching it and sending it flying away horizontally. I guessed he had spent a lot of time up on that wall.

"And what of the Genoese? Is there word?"

"They say that they will come. But will they? They are almost as bad as the Venetians and perhaps they are even worse, for they occupy the Galata quarter, across from the Golden Horn, and many are saying that they must remain neutral if there is a battle. Neutral! Can you imagine it? Almost as bad as the Hungarians." He eyed me, watching my reaction, for he knew that we had come from that very place and that my company had been in their employ.

I spoke lightly. "You have reason to hold the Hungarians in contempt, sir?"

He lifted his chin. "I do. We have had word back from this jumped up poor knight made Regent of Hungary, named Hunyadi. He lost the battle at Varna, the bloody fool. And now he sends word in reply to a request for aid from the *Basileus* himself. Do you know what he says to my lord?"

"I was the one who bore the letter," I said.

Michael scowled. "So, you know. You know that your master Hunyadi says that he will only send soldiers here if we promise him land in Greece in return. Land that is not even in our possession now that the Turk has taken it! It is as if he has intended an insult. Is that what he intended, an insult to the Emperor?"

"I do not know."

After leaving Vlad Dracula in the province of Transylvania, I had returned to Buda and asked Hunyadi how many men he was sending to protect Constantinople. He told me it had yet to be decided and that I was to wait. It soon became clear that the Hungarians were interested only in making the most of it as an opportunity to extract concessions from the Emperor. In truth, there was little he could give, for he had no territory, no men, and no money. He did have historical claims to certain territories and other rights and these were what Hunyadi asked for.

"So, you will not go?" I had asked Hunyadi. "Truly?"

"We may go, by land or by sea, but there must be the will of the council and the lords see Constantinople as a lost cause. We may bring them around yet, Richard. Have patience, sir."

But I did not have patience and could not sit around waiting while the last bastion of Christianity in the East was at risk. And so I had begged that he allow my company to go, at least. When Hunyadi agreed, I had the distinct feeling that he did not expect to see me ever again. At least he had paid me and my men and had helped arrange our ship from Venice.

On the high, inner wall, I turned and looked in toward the city. Below me, protected by the ancient wall, was a huge plain dotted with fields and houses. In the distance, where the peninsular narrowed, I saw the massive dome of the Sancta Sophia and the other grand buildings with the sea around on all three sides. I had been there before, many times, and each time the venerable city had declined. It had become a collection of small villages, communes, dotted about, with the densest areas along the northern and southern walls and in the heart of the old city where the government administrators and merchants lived.

"What will Emperor Constantine do?" Stephen asked Michael.

"He has promised Hunyadi the land in Greece he has asked for. What else can he do? He has embraced humility and is willing to give all in order to save what is left. But these Christian kings think only of themselves. Do you know that Alfonso of Naples demands the island of Lemnos in return for sending his ships? As if it is not his *duty* to do so all the same."

"I agree, it is madness," I said. "But more men will come. I am sure of it. But how many men do you have in total?"

His face coloured and he looked out at the waters. "So far? Not eight thousand proper soldiers. More will come, yes. Yes. They have to."

We exchanged looks. Eight thousand men to defend the greatest city in the world? It was ludicrous. It could not be done.

"What of the militia?"

He nodded. "Yes, we have thirty-five thousand militia under arms inside the walls. And they have been trained. But they are not soldiers, they are men with weapons."

"Men defending their homes," I pointed out. "Their families."

"Yes," he said, looking wistful.

"You have family still here?"

"Of course," he said, looking both offended and confused.

I thought it best to change the subject. "What of the walls? You are repairing and rebuilding certain sections, I see?"

The walls of the city were famous throughout the world. For a thousand years, they had helped keep the city safe. But they were old. Built for a time that was long gone.

Extending across the peninsula from the Sea of Marmara in the south to the Golden Horn in the north, they were four miles long and dotted with almost one hundred towers. The main, inner wall was forty feet high and the smaller outer one beyond it was thirty feet. Beyond that was an enormous moat sixty-five feet wide and thirty feet deep.

Where they reached the water in the north and south, the walls turned sharply and ran all the way around the peninsula so that the city was entirely encased in stone and brick, with battlements on top.

Repairs and additions had been made over the centuries, of course but there were few emplacements for cannon or firearms. Michael and his men escorted us along the top of the inner wall and showed us the sections they had repaired and other terraces where they had installed small cannons.

"What do you think?" I asked my men.

They were silent, looking in various directions.

"I think it is still a wonder of the world," Stephen said. "Even after so many years of degeneration."

"There are no defences like this anywhere else on earth," Rob said. "The scale is... inhuman."

"I think we were fools to come," Walt said. "This place is doomed."

"There is hope yet," Rob said. "Think of the floating chain, with the massive buoys. It yet closes the Golden Horn, from the Acropolis Point to the sea wall of Galata. It is in place. It is functional. No assault can be made there.

"Stephen?" I prompted. "You saw it two hundred years ago, just as I did. It is much changed, is it not? The walls are still here, yes, but the people are so few. It is like the countryside in here, not a city."

"And yet we must remember that this city has been besieged so many times, Richard, and almost always it has resisted. Look here, behind the walls. Yes, the people are fewer than they were. But we see vast fields under cultivation. Orchards. Livestock of all kinds being reared, sheep, pigs, even cows. Pasture for horses. They bring in great baskets onto the docks every morning, filled to bursting with fish caught just off the many harbours. There are cisterns all over the city storing more water than can be used. No siege can starve us out, that much is certain."

Walt held his hand over his eyes. "But they ain't going to settle in, are they, Stephen? You heard how many men the Turks are planning to bring here? That are already gathering beyond all four horizons." He slapped a hand on the towering merlon beside him. "They mean to break *through*. Perhaps not these walls, perhaps instead by the sea ones there or there. But they mean to break us open. We should not have come here. Eight thousand proper soldiers, Richard. Look at this wall. Look beyond it. Imagine the plain filled to the horizon. How many will William and his pet Sultan bring here? A hundred thousand? Surely, knowing what we know, we must leave while we still can."

I sighed and leaned on the top of the crenel, trying to imagine the army that Walt described.

"These walls have stood every assault," I said. "Well, other than the madness of the crusade in my youth when the Christians of the West took the place by the power of deceit and confusion. But look how high they are. How broad. Of the hundred thousand they might bring, how many will be horsemen? What will horses do against this mighty fortress?"

For fortress it was, more than a mere wall. With its multiple layers, stairs, gates, tunnels, and towers, the word wall did not do it justice. It was a fortress complex, only one that was stretched across four miles.

"All they need do," Walt said. "Is fill the moat with the bodies of their horses and climb over the walls. A hundred thousand against eight thousand? You ain't thinking straight, Richard."

"With the walls under our feet, we will even the odds."

Eva sighed. "There is word that the Hungarian cannon maker named Urban has been casting guns for the Turks for months. Probably years."

"Why is the bastard not making cannons for Hungary?" I asked, irritated.

"He was, and then he came here to do so. But the Emperor would not pay for the great cannons he wished to build, and they could not procure the metals and would not provide him men with the expertise. And somehow the Turks persuaded him to go to them."

"So because of the weakness of our leaders, the enemy shall have the cannons that we should have," I shook my head. "But surely there is not a cannon that has been made that could bring down these mighty walls."

"Perhaps it has not been built yet," Eva said. "But perhaps it shall be."

I sighed. "William is bringing his Sultan here to destroy this city. It is our duty to stop him. We must stay. But our mortal company are not duty bound to do the same. I will speak to them and give them the opportunity to leave before it is too late."

***

In December 1452, Constantine XI accepted that the only way he was going to get more men from Christendom was to go through with his promised union of the churches. And so a service was dedicated to the official union in the Santa Sophia, with all the heads of the Orthodox Church agreeing to end the schism with Rome.

The old soldier, Michael, had been right about the mood of the people, however, and that of the lower clergy. Immediately following the service of union, the city erupted into rioting as the furious people felt betrayed.

We stayed well out of it, of course, but it did not bode well. Instead of preparing for the fight of their lives, they were fighting each other. It was madness. It was as though they could not see what was coming.

Or perhaps they could.

Unseen beyond the walls, the Turks were busy. They reinforced Byzantine bridges and cut down Byzantine forests for timber.

All the men in my company had stayed with me and had not deserted. I called a meeting in order to give them a chance to leave with their honour intact and I did not lie to them about our chances.

"It does not look hopeful," I said, looking over the sea of their faces.

We were crammed into the main chamber of a tavern near our quarters and every man had a cup of wine in his hand.

"What do you mean, my lord?" Claudin called out. "We not getting paid?"

I rubbed my eyes and sighed. "We will not get paid, Claudin, because we will all be dead." That jolted them and they muttered unhappily.

"Is it truly so bad?" Jan the Czech asked. "There is no hope?"

The muttering died down as they waited for my answer.

"We are certain to be vastly outnumbered. The Turks are crossing the straits and massing to the west. We were expecting more soldiers to come. Many more."

"Perhaps they will yet come here," Garcia said. "Perhaps there are tens of thousands of soldiers on their way in this moment."

"It may be so. Yet, it seems unlikely they will be here before the Turks close the trap."

"So there is hope?" Claudin said, gesturing so vigorously with his cup of wine that he splashed it on himself. "Hope that help may come?"

"I am giving you all a chance to leave," I said. "The Emperor has forbidden it but I have spoken to a merchant captain who is willing to take any and all of us in his ships, for a price I have agreed per head."

They fell silent.

"What will you do, my lord?" Jan asked.

"I am staying. Black Walter, Robert, Stephen, and Eva are all staying, as are our servants. But I will not hold you to your contracts. You came here to save this city in the name of God, not to die here in a battle we could never win. I will pay each of you your due before you depart."

Again, they fell silent. Some looked at each other, while others looked at the floor or the ceiling above. Outside, a seabird screeched overhead.

"God knows, I do not favour their Church," Jan said. "But I came here to fight for Christ against the heathens. If I run now, I could not be at peace with myself for the rest of my days."

Heads around the room nodded.

"I had a feeling I would die here," Garcia said. "So be it."

Claudin raised a hand. "Could we get our coin paid out now anyway, Richard? If I am to die, I think I will spend my last days drunk as a lord in the brothel house by the Gate of the Neorion."

Not one of them chose to leave. I was touched beyond words but also filled with sadness. It seemed likely they would all die.

Soon after, the first Turkish troops arrived on the horizon and began clearing trees, bushes, and vineyards so that their cannons would have a clear shot at the walls, and so that their horsemen could roam quickly across the peninsula.

Turks set up camps and began digging trenches, banks, and other groundworks. It was early spring 1453 when they brought their massive guns up and systematically took the last remaining fortresses outside the walls.

At the start of April, the great chain was drawn across the Golden Horn, closing it off to ships.

Before the chain was drawn, however, a Genoese captain named Giovanni Giustiniani Longo sailed into the Golden Horn with two enormous war galleys and seven hundred excellent troops. The soldiers were young and enthusiastic and it raised the spirits of all inside the walls to see them. I half hoped that it presaged a sudden deluge of Christian soldiers but in fact, Longo and his men were the last to arrive.

Longo was well known as an expert in siege warfare and his fame was such that he was swiftly given the rank of *protostrator*, made overall commander of all forces in Constantinople, and gifted the island of Lemnos for payment. It was a token, of course, for he would have to save the city in order to take possession of it and perhaps it spoke of Emperor Constantine's desperation more than anything. But Longo seemed a sharp and capable man who knew his business. He treated me with respect and gratitude and gave me clear instructions about what he expected from my company. I liked him.

I do not know when or where it started but there soon spread an excited report that Hunyadi had personally led a great seaborne campaign to outflank the Turks. It soon turned out to be no more than a rumour. I was bitterly disappointed in Hunyadi and irritated at the hope I had felt when I believed it to be true.

Gradually, it dawned on each and every one of us that Christendom was not coming. The mighty kingdoms of Europe, from the Atlantic coast, to Spain and Italy, to the Holy Roman Emperor, Poland, and to the Balkan kingdoms who were already engaged in a war of destruction against the Turks, decided for their own reasons, to abandon Constantinople to her fate. Perhaps some believed that she would not fall, that her walls would prove too strong. Others no doubt expected that the rest of Christendom would act and so they would not need to. Others, I am certain, felt that the city was a lost cause. All were, of course, engaged in their own local struggles against some other kingdom or against over-mighty lords or other rebellions within their own lands. But whatever their reasons, by their actions, a withered, shadow form of Constantinople would stand alone against the mightiest empire in the world.

Turkish troops filled the peninsula beyond the walls day after day until they covered the plain from the waters of the Golden Horn in the north, to the coast of the Sea of Marmara in the south, all the way to the horizon.

Their ships surrounded the city in their hundreds while those allied to us were safe within the Golden Horn. While thousands of us watched from the walls, the Turkish fleet attacked the great chain but they failed to make headway against our superior ships. They tried again three days later but were also thrown back. We rejoiced but we did not yet appreciate their cunning, nor their determination, or the resources that they could bring to bear. For they were building a wooden slipway behind the Genoese town of Galata that nestled in the promontory, unseen behind the hills. This would create an overland link between the waters of the Bosporus to the waters of the Golden Horn at a point *behind* the great chain, bypassing it entirely.

We did not know but we would discover it soon enough.

A few days after their attack on the chain, they made a sudden night attack on the walls.

We had expected their great guns to spend weeks or even months reducing the walls before they attempted an assault and so we were almost caught off-guard.

Almost.

Our Genoese *protostrator* Giovanni Giustiniani Longo was no fool. He had ensured the walls were manned at all hours and when the Turks attacked, signals were lit and trumpets blared. Walter shook me awake and I sat up to see Eva in her undershirt clambering up the ladder to the roof over our house.

"Assemble the men," I ordered Walt.

He nodded, grim faced. "Rob's already at it."

I climbed the ladder and joined Eva on the roof. She was looking west to the Great Wall, where signal fires were flaring. "False alarm, perhaps?" I said to her. "The militia are a jumpy lot."

"Their families are here," she said, not looking at me. The moonlight softened her features and I watched her face rather than the distant walls. "It is no wonder they are fearful."

"By the time we get there, order will have been restored and we will return to our bed. Perhaps we will have an hour or two of night which we may spend together."

She looked at me and rolled her eyes. "If it is a real attack, it may work."

I scoffed, placing a hand on her shoulder. "The moat alone would stop them. Then the walls. They have no hope."

She shrugged my hand from her. "Imagine fifty thousand soldiers advancing on the walls. How might it be done?" she said to herself. "Five thousand in ten divisions, each assaulting a different section. Might they not bring up boats, or rafts, with which to cross the moat? Ladders to scale the first wall and the second? If they are unopposed, might it not be done in half a night?"

"God damn them."

"Such a combination of daring and disregard for the lives of his men would be reminiscent of someone we know, would it not?"

I looked out at the distant wall and listened to the shouts and footsteps of the men running through the streets toward it. "The Catalans are quartered just behind the wall. They will hold them."

"Come on," Eva said, returning to the hatch. "We must hurry."

It was more than a mile from our quarters on the northern side of the city to the closest point of the Great Wall and once I was in my armour and had gathered my men, most of the fighting was over. When we reached the walls along with thousands of other soldiers, we found the Turks fleeing in the night.

It had not been a massed attack in force, as Eva had feared, but a probing attack intended to take us by surprise and perhaps take a gate and hold it open for others to come through. But our soldiers manning the walls had moved into action, both the city's professional soldiers and the militia, as well as the Catalans who had snapped into action rapidly. The arrows, gunfire and cannons had been enough to send the Turks fleeing without much of a fight.

"Your tactic would probably have been successful," I said to Eva on the wall as the sun rose behind us.

"What tactic?" Stephen asked, his helm tucked under his arm.

"Never mind," I said. "We should find quarters closer to the wall. Can you see to it? And we must find more horses."

Stephen shook his head. "New quarters are not a problem. But each horse in the city is worth a fortune."

"Then we must pay it."

He lowered his voice. "I would rather us retain enough gold and silver to pay our way out of here, should things turn bad."

I sighed. "Damn you, Stephen, but you are right enough about that. Well, do what you can. Even a donkey or two would help."

It was that very morning when their mangonels began their work on the walls. Later in the day, the first Turkish cannon fired. It was a sound we all had dreaded hearing and there it was, splitting the air with its blast. Soon it was joined by a dozen and then scores of others. Before long, the cannonballs were making their mark, blasting holes in the outer surfaces of the walls and towers and working their way inward.

Out of the dozens of guns, a handful were enormous. But there was one beast mightier than them all. The work of that traitorous gunsmith Urban, it was truly enormous. We knew from prisoners taken that it was called *Basilisk* and the Sultan and Zaganos Pasha were very proud of it. Every time it fired, the very air shook, the walls cracked, and the people grew more afraid.

It was less than a week after the night assault on the walls that the Turkish ships suddenly appeared within the Golden Horn, brought there by the slipway. People were confused for hours and then, when they understood that their indestructible chain had simply been bypassed, they grew to wailing and despair. It was almost as if they could not comprehend it. The commanders at least worked quickly to transfer soldiers from the walls and other places to defend the sea wall facing Galata.

But we were surrounded now on all sides.

Because so many Turkish ships had been taken from the Bosporus, it meant there were fewer guarding the actual straits themselves. It was an opportunity to strike back at the Turks and so one night at the end of April, fire ships were deployed. Two big transports were packed with cotton and wool and oil and were sent with the tide and the wind toward the Turkish fleet at anchor out in the straits.

Although the Turkish fleet scattered in terror, our fire ships were sunk before they could inflict any damage. Still, it had been a good idea and one I made sure to remember for the future.

The first breach of the walls was made at the gate of Saint Romanus on 30th April. The militia repaired the breach as well as they could with stones and timber prepared for such an eventuality.

Another new type of gun was brought up. This invention was a long-range mortar that fired up and over the walls, to fall within the city, wreaking great destruction. The first to fall prey to this monster was a Genoese merchant ship which sank like a stone in the harbour.

"Our lads are getting nervous," Rob said as we watched the fires burning.

I smiled. "I'm getting bloody nervous."

Rob laughed. "Couple of them came to me yesterday."

"Oh?"

Rob scratched his stump. "They said they know what we are."

"They what?"

He sighed. "They know we take strength from the blood of our servants. Everyone in the company knows."

"Do they, by God? For how long?"

Rob shrugged. "You know what rumours are like."

"What did you say?"

"I said I didn't know what they were on about."

"What did they want?"

"They wanted to become like us. Wanted our strength."

"Who was it?"

"I promised not to say."

I looked at him. "Rob."

"It was Claudin, Garcia, and Jan."

"Truly? Those three are friends?"

Rob pursed his lips. "I reckon they came representing their friends. Jan spoke for the Czechs and Germans, Garcia the Castilians and that lot, Claudin for the French and for the idiots."

I sighed. "What do you think?"

"I think we need all the help we can get," he said. "And if they decided to betray our trust, they would not be able to flee from us. And I think that most of them will die anyway. So why not gain a few immortals? What if it is enough to swing the balance in our favour?"

"It will take more than a few immortal soldiers to save this God-forsaken place. But let us discuss it with the others."

"We must do it," Stephen said at once. We had assembled in my new bedchamber which was close enough to the walls to hear the booming of the cannonballs striking them all day long. I considered moving away again lest a giant cannonball fall through my ceiling at night but sometimes one must simply live with danger. And besides, it was a remarkable old building, with many chambers on two storeys above and a long hall below where we could all assemble to eat as a company. "With an entire company of immortals, we stand a better chance of surviving whatever comes."

"Eva?"

"They would have to take our oath and join the Order. They will have to understand it would be a lifetime commitment to serve you and that if they survive this place, they will have to follow you for centuries. What if they then decline? We will have dozens of mortals aware of our existence and our purpose. It could be a greater danger than leaving them as they are."

"That is true. I do not know that I trust all of these men. Where is their loyalty? They are from a dozen or more kingdoms. Some have already betrayed pervious masters. One or two are certainly criminals."

Walt, leaning by the window, turned and straightened up. "Ain't they already proved themselves loyal, Richard? Some of these lads have been with us for almost ten years, now. You forget how long that is for a mortal. We've seen some of these fellows join us as little more than boys and grow into men under our command. Whatever some of them once may have been, they see themselves as serving you. They're proud of it, have you not noticed? You gave them a chance to flee before coming here and the ones that didn't fancy it, they left. Then you gave these lads the truth about our chances and offered to pay for their passage and send them off with their purses full. They stayed. Every bloody one of the stupid bastards. I reckon they've proved themselves loyal, don't you?"

Eva pursed her lips and shrugged. Rob nodded to himself.

"I had not seen it that way," I admitted. "It is as you say. Ten years passes almost without me noticing sometimes and I often cannot easily recall how this year or that has been spent."

"They'll be giving up their chance to be fathers," Rob said. "Though some of them have bastards, none have proper wives. They need to understand that, at least."

"And some may well die if your blood does not take," Eva pointed out.

"We'll have to bleed more of the servants, and all," Walt said. "Soon as our lads are made immortal, we'll be committed to feeding them regular."

"We will assemble the men only," I said. "No squires or servants. And we will lay everything out as clearly as we can."

"And those that decline?" Eva asked. "Perhaps we should wait before taking action."

"Perhaps."

"We are out of time!" Stephen said, advancing on me. "We need them. Have you forgotten William's army of red-robed immortals? They are out there, right now. And they will be coming here. How can we hope to stop them if not with an army of our own? If we had any sense we would use your blood to turn the entire garrison. Imagine if we had five thousand immortals, Richard, we could stream out and defeat the Turks in a single blow. We could take their entire empire!"

I stared at him. We all did.

"Would I get a say in this grand plan of yours, Stephen?" I asked.

He sighed and sank down to sit on the top of a closed chest. "Turn our company, at least. What Walt says is true. They are loyal to you now. They will be loyal in this."

"Assemble the men," I said to Rob.

After they filed out, Eva came to me and took my hands in hers. "I know that you do not wish to do this. It is not too late to change your mind. Who knows how they might turn on us or who they might tell? But Stephen is right that we need to consider William's army."

I leaned down to rest my forehead on hers. "If they betray me, I may have to kill them."

"You will have to," she said, softly.

I straightened up. "Do you think it was Stephen who started the rumours amongst the men? Suggested they come to Rob?"

"It is his nature to do these things."

"Damn him."

"It may be what saves us. It may be what helps you to fulfil your oath."

"Do not defend him," I said.

"He serves you faithfully. In his own way."

"I suppose so," I admitted. "Come. If we are going to do this, we must get started. I can only bleed enough to change so many every night."

When the men were in the hall below, I came down and stood before them, with Walt and Rob at my side and Eva and Stephen behind us. I noted that Serban stood at the side of the hall, watching me closely, his eyes questioning. My men fell silent and stared at me, full of apprehension. I was full of worry myself but I forced it down and drove on regardless.

"The rumours are true. I am not like other men. Nor, indeed, are your captains." I watched them closely as I spoke, watching for signs of fear or revulsion. "We have lived longer than the span of mortal men and are gifted with strength and speed beyond any man here or on any battlefield in the world. Wounds that would kill any of you in hours or days will be healed on our bodies. But these gifts do not come without a price."

"You must drink blood," Garcia said. "We know."

"Oh?" I said. "You know, do you?"

He was wary but he nodded, as did a few others. "We have seen you. Now and then. You bleed your servants, you drink their blood. I saw you after that battle in the woods, with Hunyadi, when that Serb cut your face. Before Varna. I saw you, though you did not see me, and I saw you drink from his throat and the cut across your face turned to nothing."

"By God," I said. "You have known all this time?"

He and others nodded.

"Why did you not say?" I asked.

He shrugged and Jan answered for him. "We were afraid. Some men left, giving false reasons out of fear. Some of them call it the work of Satan. Only one who has a pact with the Devil could have such power. It is witchcraft, so they said. And they left."

"And yet all of you stayed," I replied. "Why?"

"We are not all so ignorant," Garcia said. "You acted always with honour. You treated your men well. We were content to follow one with such power."

"And you always paid up," Claudin said. "Always was fair."

I glanced at Serban and wondered if he had been whispering to the others about us. He stared back, his face rigid.

"Sir Walter was seen," Jan said. "And Sir Robert. We knew it was blood magic. Some of us have long hoped to have this power for ourselves."

"And we saw the Janissaries in red at Kosovo," Garcia said. "They moved like you do. They moved like you, Richard, and Walter and Robert, and Stephen and the Lady Eva. We saw them."

Many of my men nodded their heads, their eyes staring through the floor into the memory of those red devils tearing our army apart.

"And we knew it was the same magic," Jan said. "Somehow."

"We tried drinking the servants' blood ourselves," Claudin said. "Couple of us did, anyway. Didn't work."

"It was hoped you would reveal to us your secrets," Garcia said. "But you did not. And so we did speak to Sir Robert."

"We have seen your power in battle," Jan said. "We want it, also, my lord."

"And you have not aged a day," Claudin said. "Don't think we haven't noticed. None of you. Not one day has marked your flesh. Not one line more, nor one scar. I was as young as you when I joined the Company of Saint George and now look at me. It's the blood what does it. And we want it, and the magic that goes with it, my lord."

"You think that the price for this power is that you must drink blood?" I said. "That is not much of a price. No wonder you are willing to pay it. Slurping up some warm blood fresh from a fellow's arm. It is nothing at all." They regarded me silently, suddenly more tense than before. "But that is not the cause of the power, as you discovered. If you have this power, you will drink blood to increase your strength and heal you, yes. But you must drink every day or two. If you go three days without drinking, you will begin to feel sick. Your stomach will turn in knots and your mind will ache. Go without for longer and your skin will turn grey and then green. Your flesh will blister and your hair will fall out, your eyes will become red and you will begin to lose your mind. You will think of nothing else but drinking the blood of a man or a woman and nothing will stop you from getting it. Is that a price you are willing to pay?"

They stared but some already nodded in agreement.

"There is more," I said, holding up a finger. "Once you are granted this power, there is no going back. You will never be a mortal man again. You will be as ageless as we five before you." Many grinned at that, glancing at each other. "And you will never father a child." Their smiles fell from their face. "You may try for all you are worth but no matter how many women you lay with, no matter how often you do so, your seed will never grow."

They were rightly appalled and I gave them time to consider it.

"It is a steep price," Garcia said. "I had hoped to return home one day."

"And you may do so," I replied. "If you decline what I offer. And if you survive the assault on this city."

"Is there more?" Jan asked.

I nodded. "You will never again feel the warmth of the sun on your skin without it burning you. Wherever sunlight falls on your flesh, it will swiftly redden, and blister, and then burn. You must cover your skin and always cover your head."

"And pray for clouds?" Claudin quipped.

"Even overcast days will burn you, I am afraid. But night will be your friend. You will be able to see into the dark better than any mortal."

"But I have seen you," Jan said, frowning. "I have seen you many times with the sun on your face, Richard. You take pleasure in it, just as any man does."

"Ah," I said. "But you see, Jan, I am different. I am not as you will be. I can make immortals but you cannot."

I did not admit that my immortals could use the same process to make mad, savage revenants. I would hide such knowledge for all I was worth.

"So, where did you get your power?" Garcia asked.

"Let me tell you a story," I said, "about a man named William de Ferrers and the Order of the White Dagger."

After speaking for so long that my throat grew hoarse, I answered their many questions until they fell silent. Serban stared at me in surprise and wonder and I nodded to him before turning back to my men.

"Each of you must decide for himself whether to join the Order. I will welcome you all but you must know that some of you will not survive being turned. I do not know why but some men cannot take it. It is not strength, nor age, nor any other common factor as far as I can see but it is unavoidable for some. With that in mind, I ask that you make your decisions. Certainly, you have been thinking on it for some time."

"I will do it," Claudin said, getting to his feet.

"As will I," Jan said. "I will risk death and pay the price for the power it will give."

Others agreed, one by one, until only Garcia and Serban had yet to speak.

"Serban?" I asked. "You have not been with us for as long as the others but you have been welcomed by all. You knew what I was within days of meeting me, having witnessed me drinking the blood of a fallen enemy. And you have heard stories about people like us in your homeland. What do you say? Will you become one of us?"

He stood upright, looking me in the face, and crossed himself. Then he fell to one knee and bowed his head. "Please forgive me, my lord, but I cannot. I do not think you evil, nor have I ever divulged your secrets, but I cannot do it."

I shrugged. "Very well. You will continue to serve me faithfully as a mortal."

Serban looked up, relief on his old face. "I will, my lord."

"Garcia?" I said. "You have spoken of your desire to return home and make a family. It is a good wish. You do not need to give it up."

"No, sir," he replied, standing. "I will join you, gladly. It is a worthy cause for a knight. To fight evil. I see now why you named our company after Saint George. I believed that the saint was a warrior of Christ and the serpent was the Turks. But now I see that the saint is us and the serpent is evil. It is your brother William."

"Very well," I said. "You will all take the oath. And I will make you into immortal men."

***

Before I was halfway through turning the men of my company, the Turks attacked again in the night.

They came in force against many parts of the wall, attacking the partial breaches and crumbling towers. Where the walls were damaged, the rubble fell down and out to fill the gap between the two walls and to partially fill the moats. The piles of rubble created unstable slopes for the attackers to climb up to the top of the breaches and down the other side or up onto the wall walks either side of the breach.

But the militia worked tirelessly every day and through many a night to repair the breaches, to clear the rubble, and to throw up new walls and barricades of timber. These repairs would be blown to pieces by the cannons and the garrison would repair them. Every day and every night, the pattern repeated but the Turks and their cannons were irresistible. We could not repair and rebuild as swiftly as they could destroy.

And so they came in the darkness on the 7th May, crossing the moats on rafts and throwing in vast quantities of earth and rock to create causeways. All the while our men shot arrows, fired cannon and guns at them, killing hundreds. Still, they crossed the moat in many sections and climbed onto the lower, outer walls through the breaches.

I held my men back. I would not lead them down into that hell amongst the fires and the cannonballs unless there was no hope.

And the militia and the proper soldiers of the city did well. The Catalan mercenaries also threw themselves into the thick of the fighting and the Turks were turned back from the outer walls.

We cheered as hard as anyone when the sun rose that day but we knew it had merely been the start. Repairs continued and the cannons fired, bringing down the battlements on four towers in just one day.

As quickly as I could, I turned the rest of the men in my company, each and every one of them, apart from Serban, who still declined. I lost five good men in the process. They were drained of their blood and they drank mine but they did not wake up. We buried them and I felt enormous guilt for their deaths, even though they had accepted the risk. And though I lost five, I gained thirty-nine immortal soldiers who swore to follow me until the end of their days in my pursuit of William and his monsters. Eva said it was a good trade.

"If we meet the immortal Janissaries in battle," I said, "they will still be outnumbered ten to one."

"Far better odds than we had last week," Eva said. It was hard to argue.

It was five days later when another attack came, again at night.

The Turks focused their forces on the north-western section of the walls by the Golden Horn in the Blachernae district. In their attacks there they were supported by their fleet in the Golden Horn and it seemed for a while that they would break through. By the time my company arrived, the fighting on the walls was confused and it was hard to know where best to place my men. I held them back in reserve, ready to counter any breach into the city that occurred.

At sunrise, fighting slowed as the Turks stopped receiving reinforcements and it became clear they would not get through. Still, it had been a close run thing and, no doubt because of their success that night, the Turks concentrated their efforts on that district even more.

Serbian miners had been sent to Mehmed by the Despot of Serbia George Branković, along with two thousand Serbian cavalry. It was the miners, working tirelessly to undermine and breach the walls, that became the greatest danger and many of the tunnels were aimed at the Blachernae district. Our militia dug their own tunnels to counter those of the Serbs before they could undermine the walls or even come up inside the city.

Some of the Serbian tunnels were flooded and others were set on fire and the miners smoked out.

For others, though, where there was danger of them breaking into the city, we had to get down there and kill them.

"It is good work for us," I said to my company. "We can clear out the enemies in the tunnels with our strength."

My men were unconvinced that it was a task for knights and mercenaries.

"Any wounds we receive we can heal by drinking the blood of our enemies and we can do so without being seen by our allies," I said, which they were intrigued by. "Besides, I have already volunteered our services to Longo."

It was horrible fighting. As bad as war can get, and that is saying something. Dark, sometimes black, smoky, often cold but sometimes roasting hot. No room to flee because of the men behind you. It was dirty, awful work and two of my men were killed before I could get blood into them and another was crushed when a tunnel collapsed. But because of my company, we defeated all of the Serb's best efforts.

Our successes in the tunnels and the militia's tireless work in sealing breaches meant that the Turks would only find success through storming the walls. Incredibly, in just a few days, the Turks constructed a bridge across the Golden Horn, allowing them to bring up their troops much faster. Sorties were carried out in an attempt to burn the bridge but it remained intact.

On 24th May we stood on the walls and silently watched a lunar eclipse.

What it meant, whether it was a good omen or bad, none could agree.

Word spread that a vast crusader army was approaching to relieve the city. Many rejoiced at the news but others were cautious. Previous rumours of the sort had proved false and we had received no official word of such a thing and so cooler heads questioned where the rumour had started. For many, this in itself was somehow proof of the army's existence, reasoning that the crusaders would not have sent word that could have fallen into Turkish hands.

During the night of the 27th May, fires appeared all over the Turkish camp. There was further rejoicing, for it was concluded that the Turks had seen the approaching crusaders and were burning their supplies before their flight back to Anatolia. Indeed, many a Greek began drinking to their victory and drank themselves into unconsciousness.

"Sieges can drive people mad," I said to my company. "The fear causes them to lose their wits."

"What if it's true?" Claudin said, grinning. "See the fires burning out there. They must be burning their supplies, what else could it be?"

But in the morning, the enemy was still there. In fact, there seemed to be more than ever before, and the enemy soldiers began coming forward to fill the foremost defensive ditches closest to the walls.

"It was a feast," Stephen said, looking out at the distant scenes. "A celebration of some sort."

"What was?" I asked.

"The fires. The great fires in the night was not them leaving, it was a celebration of the victory to come. A great feast where they ate until they were bursting and they burned their fuel, as they will not be needing it when they take the city."

"By God," I said. "You think that is it?"

He pursed his lips. "Perhaps the Sultan had his supplies burned so that his men would have to achieve victory or starve?"

I sighed. "So you do not, in fact, know anything at all."

"Looks like rain," he replied. "I know that much."

Stephen was not wrong. A great rainstorm started and did not end, drenching everything. The gunners stayed within the towers and fought to keep their gunpowder dry and the fields turned to mud. On the walls, I met the commander of the Catalans, Pere Julia, who cursed the rain and the Turks with equal vigour.

"They will come soon," he said. "Mark my words, Richard, they will come. Look at them, the dogs. You see the stacks of ladders there? They do not care that we can see. They want us to see. They want to break our hearts."

"How are your men?"

"My men are angry. They want the Turks to come. They want to kill them."

"I am happy to hear it," I said.

"Oh, you think mercenaries do not have passion, sir? Is that how it is in England?"

"I am a mercenary, sir," I replied. "And I want to kill them, also."

He nodded, barely placated. "My men love God, Richard. Above all, they love God. They will do their duty for God, mark my words."

"I believe it," I said.

"Look at the dogs," he muttered. "I hope they drown."

The rain continued to fall.

Just a couple of hours before dawn on the 29th May, the Turkish cannons sounded. All of them fired at once and then over and over again, as quickly as each one would allow. As the dawn lightened the sky behind us, thousands of *azab* infantry emerged from the darkness. They were massed at the gate of Saint Romanus where the great cannon, the Basilisk, had created a wide breach in the outer and inner walls.

We brought up three thousand soldiers from the reserve behind the line and filled the walls either side of the gate. Longo himself came, as did Emperor Constantine, though he kept well back.

The *azabs* advanced through the rain in their thousands toward the breach and our cannons fired, blasting them apart. Our gunners fired from the crumbling towers and from the battlements of the inner wall. Crossbowmen shot down at the advancing battalions, killing and wounding hundreds. Before they even crossed the moat, the *azabs* suffered massive casualties.

Along the sea wall in the north, Turkish ships came swarming through the Golden Horn to the base of the walls and threw up ladders for the troops in the ships to scale so that they might breach them and get into the Blanchernae district. Reports came through to Longo that the fighting there was terrible and he sent a few of his reserve forces to the north to ensure that the assault by the river was thrown back.

In front of us, the azab assault ground to a halt under our terrific fire. The sound of the guns was endless and trumpets blared and banners hung limp in the relentless rain. I made my way to Longo's position so that I might through him gauge what was happening throughout the battlefield. He sat upon his fine horse with a confident expression on his face, receiving messages and sending riders in all directions. In the distance, the Emperor's guard held position.

"What do we do now?" Stephen asked behind me.

"We wait."

The great guns sounded again, in another timed and almighty barrage that shook the walls over miles at once. As the echoes died away, thousands of Anatolian soldiers came charging out of the rain, attacking the breaches by our position at the Saint Romanus Gate.

All the breaches made by their guns were too high and too narrow for them to walk through but still they tried. The Anatolians were armoured in mail and lamellar and good, steel helms. They crossed the moat and attacked the lower, outer wall and attacked our soldiers there. Longo ordered militia units forward to reinforce those positions.

"Should we help?" Rob asked.

"We keep our men back for as long as possible," I said, and pointed at the breach in the inner wall and the fan-shaped hill of rubble that lead up to the broken top of the breach. "When the Turks come charging down that slope, we will stop them. Not before. Tell the men."

When the Anatolians retreated, our men cheered for a long time but there was sense of dread settling on the defenders. We were already exhausted by the struggle and yet the Turks had used only a fraction of their strength. Still, we had killed thousands of them and lost few ourselves.

After the Anatolians retreated, we received yet another bombardment and a hit by the Basilisk brought down a massive section of wall at the breach, throwing up an enormous cloud of white dust and sending chunks of masonry and brick flying in all directions. When the dust settled, we realised that the walls were now beginning to crumble with almost every shot and I am sure the dread spread further.

Beyond the walls, the enemy's war drums started again and their horns sounded.

"Here they come again," Walt said, before raising his voice and turning to my company. "Here they come again. Prepare yourselves."

The Anatolians came back to assault the breaches in their thousands, swarming the outer walls. Our gunners shot down from the inner walls above us and the elite crossbow units shot and reloaded and shot again, with incredible speed. In every moment, I expected to see the helms of the enemy appearing at the top of the breach.

And yet we threw them back again. Banners were waved and the men cheered their victory. The wounded and the dead were carried back from the walls and filed past us, heading east toward the rear.

"Jesus Christ, there's a lot of them," Walt muttered, crossing himself.

Riders came galloping in from the north, drenched and covered in mud kicked up by their horses, calling for Longo and other commanders.

I caught Pere Julia, the commander of the Catalans, and asked him what the panic was.

"They assault the Blanchernae Walls also, in force, and threaten to break through. Just Minotto and the Venetians there to stop them."

"Is that where your men are going?" I asked him.

"No," Pere Julia said. "I am ordered to defend the imperial family and the great and the good in the southeast."

"You what?" I said. "Why?"

"The Turks are making an attack also on the Contoscalion Harbour. If they break through the walls there, we must stop them."

"Then God be with you. All of you."

"And with you," he said. I watched him ride away with his men following through the rain. It was a long way and when they got there, they would be on their own and at the opposite side of the city from the ships that might take survivors away.

"Shall I take some of our men north to the Blanchernae, Richard?" Rob asked. "Sounds like it's in danger."

"Everywhere is in danger. And we must stay together. It is for others to guard that way. All we can do is protect this breach. This is where the hammer blows are falling. Here is where the Basilisk has done its work. The Sultan's flag is flying behind it. Here is where we must be."

Later, we had word that the assault in the north was thrown back by the Venetians. Indeed, it had been a long day but we could sense it coming to an end. And we were still standing. There was fight left in the men, whether militia or professional soldiers, and despite the breaches, we had slaughtered thousands of the enemies who had attacked us. We had a sense now that it could be done after all. The Turks had thrown their worst at us and we had done what was necessary, and more. I saw Longo congratulating his men and drinking wine with them.

But the Sultan had not thrown everything he had at us. There was one part of his army that had yet to engage.

"Janissaries!" came the cry from atop the wall. Trumpets sounded and men jumped to their positions, racing back up to the tops of the walls. Our cannons fired again and again.

"Wait here," I said to my men and went forward toward the wall, pushing my way through the crowds. I was one of the few men dressed entirely in plate armour so they tended to let me through and so I stood at the top, looking out through the crenellations at the scene beyond.

Thousands of Janissaries advanced from their defensive ditches. They came marching in tighter formations than I had seen from any infantry in my life until that point. Our hand-gunners fired from the walls and brought down the advancing Janissaries in their dozens but sill they came on without hesitation and without breaking formation. Arrows rained down on them, killing more and their lines became wavered. Still, they reached the filled in sections of moat and the half-burned pontoons and rafts and crossed without hesitation to the lower outer wall, where they threw up ladders.

Our soldiers on the wall below stood ready to meet them either side of the great breach that led through the outer wall to the inner one.

"Those bastards," Walt said.

"I told you to wait below," I said, turning to see not only Walt but Rob and Eva, also. "All of you."

The Janissaries reached the breach, as we had known they would, and cut into the militia, spreading out even as they were shot and killed by the men in the towers and on the inner wall. On they came, relentlessly, as if they cared nothing for their own lives.

"Our lads are getting nervous," Walt said, nodding to the Greeks along the wall. I saw at once how right Walt was. The men were inching back, afraid of the assault. In no time, they would find false reasons to escape from the wall in ones and twos and then they would be in full flight.

"We will hold them," I shouted. "They are no better than us. They are weaker than us. We have the walls!" I turned to my men. "Take up the cry, lads. Spread the word." I raised my voice again and called in Greek as loudly as I could. "We have God on our side. We have the walls. We have Constantinople! Constantine! Constantine! For the Emperor!"

They took up the cry in time, and it spread along the wall until they were cheering themselves. The crossbowmen were a steady lot who took immense pride in their skill and they worked tirelessly. The soldiers with their halberds came forward and climbed down in their hundreds and fought the Janissaries hand to hand in the breach. Bodies tumbled down into the gulf between the walls. The white mounds of rubble turned pink with blood even with the rain turning it to rivers and washing it down. It was brutal, bloody work. Bodies piled up. Guns were fired from both sides and the air stank of filthy smoke and blood and entrails.

We threw them back. The Janissaries cowered below the outer wall, afraid of attempting the breach again and they began falling back in pairs and then in dozens, trudging back toward their trenches beyond the moat.

The day was almost over and the enemy were in retreat. Some of the men indulged once more in congratulatory cheering.

"They did it," Walt said, chuckling. "God love them, the mad bastards, they did it."

"They will have to do it all over in a few days," I said. "And again a few days after that. Assuming the Turks did not break through today along the Marmara wall in the south."

Walt laughed and slapped me on the shoulder, splashing droplets of rain. "You know your problem, Richard, is you're never—"

"Wait," Rob said, grasping Walt with one hand and jabbing his stump out at the field, "there!"

From the smoke and the rain advanced a new formation of Janissaries.

These were clothed in red.

"William's immortals," I said.

"By God," Eva said. "How can we stop them?"

I cried for all guns to be turned on the advancing Janissaries, and all cannons too. Bring back the crossbowmen, I shouted. Return to the walls.

But this next wave of attackers had caught us by surprise. Only two cannons fired, and one missed. The other ball cut a small swathe through the corner of the formation, felling no more than half a dozen, and the rest missed not a step. Crossbowman shot their bolts but they were running low and replacements had not reached us. A few hand-gunners fired but again their ammunition or gunpowder was wet or had been expended and more was not yet in place.

"They are coming on fast," Rob said and he was right. William's red Janissaries crossed the moat and swarmed up the outer wall and spread out along it like a drop of blood falling into a bowl of water.

"We will have to hold them at the inner breach," I said to my men. "We cannot let them inside. You know who they are and what they can do. We cannot let them inside. Come, back to the company. Come, now."

Before I followed my men down the stairs, I turned for one last look at the immortal Janissaries. They breached the outer barricades and rushed forward in a surge, swarming up and over them. Our soldiers came on to meet them and raised their spears and swords and axes but were cut down in moments by the Janissaries' inhuman speed and strength. Our defenders were exhausted and their enemies were faster than they could imagine and they stood no hope.

Even so, they did not break. They knew that if the enemy broke into the city, all was lost. And so they stayed and they died in their hundreds.

"Richard!" Rob shouted from below. "Come on!"

"What is this?" a captain on the wall shouted to his men. "What are they?"

"Whatever they are," I said, "they will not break. Will not flee. They must be killed."

"How?"

"One by one," I said. "A score of ours for one of theirs. It is the only way." I rushed down the steps as quickly as I could and ran across the open space by the breach. I saw Longo approaching the wall with his men around him and hoped that they would stand and fight with us. "This is it, men! Now, we do our duty. For Constantine! For the city! For Christ! Deus vult!"

My men lifted their weapons and roared in response.

"Deus vult!"

The red robed immortals appeared at the top of the breach and began to descend the rubble pile into the city. Above on the wall, the Greeks shot down into the advancing men, no doubt stunned by the speed of this new enemy, and their resistance to arrow and lead. I led my company forward up the loose rubble to meet the enemy, pushing through the ranks of Greek soldiers who held back, no doubt in shock at the ferocity of the approaching red tide.

Suddenly, they were there. With their long red, felt hats and red robes, they were big and powerful men with polearms and swords whipping up and down and thrusting forward. I caught the first one unawares as he descended, spearing my sword point into his face. Still, he fought even as he died and the axe blade of his polearm banged against my breastplate. More came behind him, cutting down the mortal Greeks with ease and stepping forward.

But my men had arrived and spread out along the rubble to stem the rising tide. A part of me wondered if they were surprised to find enemies who fought as well as they did. Better, in fact, for my closest companions had fought more than a hundred battles and lived more than a hundred years and our armour was the best that could be bought and the Janissaries' weapons glanced off when they struck. The rest of my company were as good as could be found anywhere, with decades of experience between them and now they fought with the strength and speed of immortals.

In mere moments, a dozen immortal Janissaries soon lay dead before us, and then a score more. My company cut into them like a scythe, cutting down a field of red wheat.

But we were outnumbered ten to one and my company was swarmed on all sides. They got around our flank and there was nothing we could do to stop them.

"Stay together!" I shouted and cut down the Janissaries in front of me. "Stay together!"

Suddenly, the immortal Janissaries simply pulled back from us. They retreated and avoided our position, like water moving around a rock in a stream, and they pressed on around us into the city.

"With me!" I shouted, and pushed on up the rubble slope to where more came up over the top of the breach. If we could stem the gap, we could cut them off and stop any more mortal Turks from coming in behind them. As I pushed deeper into their ranks they could not so easily get away from me and I cut down all those who stood before me, slicing through their necks and chopping through their faces.

Walt grabbed my shoulder, leaned in and banged his helm against mine and held it there while he shouted. "They have gained the wall!"

I followed the line of his axe and saw dozens of red Janissaries swarming up the breach to the shattered tops of the wall on either side of it where they cut down the men at the top.

"We must throw them down," I shouted.

But now we were close to the top of the breach, we were surrounded by immortals trying to kill us and for a time all I could do was defend from the men all around. Men in my company fell, overwhelmed by the numbers. Still, we held them close to the top until the pressure was relieved. Once again, the Janissaries pulled back and left us alone, refusing to engage with us.

"William must have taught them this," I said, cursing his cunning. "We make for the wall!" I called to my men, turning to see who was still alive.

With shock, I saw that most of my company were gone. Many had been cut down behind me and lay dead on the rubble and others had been carried off down to the base of the rubble hill by the waves of immortals pushing forward. The ones who yet lived, half my company, perhaps, fought the enemy on both sides and behind us. I swore and cursed but nothing could be done. If the Janissaries took the wall then they would take the gate and if they opened it and held it, then all the Turks in Europe would pour through and end the city forever.

"On!" I shouted to my remaining men. "On, on! To the walls!"

I pressed through into the immortals that still came on, cutting down one man and then another. Hands grasped me and I cut off a hand and then sliced through a throat, spilling hot blood. I longed to drink mortal blood, longed for the strength it would bring. We slowed, as the press of men grew dense at the breach itself. Mortal Janissaries had joined the fray and they poured over the breach in their hundreds, mingling with their red brothers who yet fought. The mighty wall was right above me. How I would climb it with so many enemies around, I had no idea. I knew only that it must be done.

A great cry went up and I glanced up, seeing through my helm a quick glance in the smoky, wet gloom. It was Longo's personal banner, up on the top of the wall above the gate, advancing toward the Janissaries there.

Praise God, I thought. *Well done, Longo.*

He had seen the danger and thrown himself into it, to inspire his men by his personal leadership.

It was a view gone in a moment, as the enemy crashed into me again with such force that I was lifted from my feet and thrown down onto my back, tumbling down the pile of masonry. Blades whipped down even as I fell, seeking to end me. I slashed at them and rolled to get up, grabbing at a Janissary and pulling him down. Together we slipped in the loose, wet scree. My sword was pulled from my grasp and I raised my armoured arms over my head as I got to one knee, feeling my armour bend and break from the blows that crashed down on me. Standing, I grabbed a spear and ripped it from my attacker's hands and used it to fend them off, whirling it around until I broke the shaft across a Janissary's face.

There was a great commotion all around but I did not know what was causing it, whether it was to do with me and my men or with the battle elsewhere.

And then suddenly the enemies rushed beyond me. I saw that I was close to the ground once more, having fallen down forty feet of the slope. My men rushed toward me, sliding and falling down.

I wheeled about, peering through the dented eye slits of my skewed helm to see what was happening.

A mighty hand clapped me on the back, in a familiar way, and then Walt was before me, his helm gone and blood streaming down both sides of his head. Eva, Stephen, and Rob were there also and a mere dozen of my company. All around us were bodies, Greek soldiers and Janissaries in red and in white, many writhing and crying out.

Beyond them, our army fled from the wall.

Thousands of soldiers and militia walked or ran or rode away from the wall toward the distant city.

"What in the name of God has happened?" I shouted.

Walt spat a mouthful of blood before he answered. "Longo fell. His damned fool men lowered his banner and carried him off."

I looked at the wall and the Turk's banners were held aloft by Janissaries atop the gate towers. The enormous gates themselves were being prised open.

"Pull back to the city?" Rob said. "Fight them in the streets?"

"We must flee from here!" Eva shouted at me. "Now!"

Beyond the breach and through the rain and by the last of the daylight, I saw thousands of infantry and horsemen approaching.

"The city is lost," I said, turning to the survivors of my company. "We must escape."

6

Escape

1453

THE *PROTOSTRATOR* GIOVANNI GIUSTINIANI Longo had not been killed outright, merely wounded by a gunner's shot. If his men had only withdrawn him a little way and held the line, perhaps we would have thrown them back. Perhaps we would have held the wall, and so held the gate, and so held the city. Perhaps Constantinople would be Byzantine to this day, if only the handful of men around him had chosen differently. If only they had loved their captain a little less.

Such is the way of battle and of the world. The smallest decisions can have enormous and irreversible consequences.

In the chaos of the break through, Emperor Constantine disappeared also and every man, woman, and child in the city knew by the spreading panic that it was lost. Darkness enveloped the city, illuminated by distant fires and flashes of cannons and guns, and lamps and torches held aloft by soldiers and citizens fleeing one way or another.

We made for the ships yet moored in the Golden Horn, knowing that even if it was unlikely to be successful, it was our only chance of escape.

And so did thousands of others.

We walked and ran in turn toward the docks, many of our company limping and breathing heavily. Some of my men removed and dropped dented pieces of their armour. Others begged a servant for a cup of blood

"The servants slow us down," Stephen said. "Perhaps we might consider going on ahead and meeting them at the dock?"

"You mean abandon them?" I said.

"No, no," he said. "We shall hold a boat for them."

He knew that in such chaos, once separated, we would never meet up again.

"At least have the courage to make your true argument," I said.

He sighed and shook his head. "Do I really have to make it? If we move at their pace, all of us may be killed. What of the Order, then? What of William?"

I grabbed his shoulder, stopping him. "It is their duty to follow their masters and it is ours to not abandon them. And what will you and the others do for blood if we leave them?"

"There are always mortals around," he muttered but would not meet my eye.

I shoved him so that he would continue on. I went back to help and to hurry them on. Despite what I had said to Stephen, he was not wrong about the danger their weakness meant for us.

Turkish horsemen were through the gate and into the farmlands behind us.

"Might have to fight soon, Richard," Walt said, loping along with his axe in hand.

"Should we not head north?" Rob called. "Or south? Protection there? The Catalans guard the palace, no?"

Along the southern and northern edges of the peninsula, the confined streets between dense housing and churches and public buildings seemed to offer a way to fend off the cavalry.

"We cannot stop. The Catalans are finished, Rob. They will soon be surrounded with no way to escape. And if we do not reach a ship tonight, we shall never escape. We push on. Come on lads, you can do it, we'll find a ship home, shall we? Come on. On, on!"

We hobbled further toward the city proper while shouts and cries sounded behind us.

Eventually, we made it to a street lined with houses and from there I led my men north, towards the gates that led out to the harbours of the Golden Horn.

"Richard," Eva said, jogging up beside me, "you hope to find a ship to take us from the city, yes?"

"That is where the fleets are," I said.

"But the great chain has closed the way," she pointed out. "And already the Turks have their ships behind, in the Horn."

"The chain must be drawn in," I said. "Or broken."

She stared at me in disbelief. "How? Are we to do this ourselves?" She indicated our shattered, limping company.

"If we have to."

Eva coughed and wiped blood from her eye. "Even if that were possible, the other half of the Turkish fleet is *beyond* the chain. Any ships attempting to flee will be boarded or sunk before they can get beyond the Acropolis Point and then we—"

I turned to her, stopping her with a hand on her shoulder. "Listen, Eva. I do not know what will happen. I do not have all the answers to your questions. All I know is that we must take a ship, tonight, to be free of this place. And I know that we shall not be the only ones who know this. We go to the docks. We find a ship. We do what we must to escape. Agreed?"

She took a deep breath, nodding at me as she let it out.

"Good," I said. "Let us do it."

The docks were chaos. Thousands of people swarmed there, looking for a way out. Some were Greek residents, some merchants and workers, others were foreign soldiers or their servants.

Of all the thousands of soldiers left alive, most of the militia had returned to protect their homes and their families. It would do them no good. They would be overwhelmed and killed, their homes looted, their wives and daughters raped, and the survivors taken as slaves. But the foreign soldiers had to either fight to the death, surrender, or flee. And they had nowhere to go but home and they were the ones fighting each other for access to the ships in the harbour. The many gates had been forced open and crowds pushed and shoved through, shouting and wailing at each other. Others called for calm but the panic could not be contained.

"There is an entire army here," Rob said. "If these fools had stood, the city would not have fallen."

"Why don't you explain that to them," Walt said. "I'm certain they would welcome your observations, sir."

"Come on, let us stay together," I said. "Tight together, everyone. Hold on to each other, protect our mortals. Rob, take up the rear, will you? See we do not lose any of our fellows in the crush."

Using our strength, we pushed through protesting soldiers and batted down any outraged hands who attempted to hinder us. We were armoured in steel and had immense strength and so we were irresistible. Salvation lay beyond in the water and I would not stop for anyone, even if he was a desperate Christian soldier looking to make his way home. The noise of the crowd filled my ears.

Pushing through the Neorion Gate, we came out to the docks ringing the harbour where a dozen ships were moored. The Golden Horn glittered in the light of dusk and the lights on the hundreds of ships on the water. Far to my left was the Turkish fleet, many of which assaulted the walls. In front, across the Horn, lay the Genoese town of Galata. Ships and small boats headed straight across the Horn toward it, while others came from there to the harbours to collect refugees and take them to relative safety.

Most of the moored ships around the harbour before me were taking on scores of desperate people and those would be no good for us. But one galley further up the arm of the harbour was defended by sailors with pikes who fended off those attempting to swarm the pontoon and board the ship.

"Venetian," I said to my men. "Do you see it? We shall make our way there."

"How?" Stephen asked. He was keeping very close to me at all times, which was sensible but irritating. I ignored him.

"With me, men, with me! Stay fast together, come on!"

I pushed forward through the crowd, drawing irate curses. When they saw that we were foreign mercenaries, some flinched away in fear and space opened around us so that we advanced swiftly. Some of those same people cursed us for abandoning our posts and betraying the city. That they were doing the very same thing perhaps had not occurred to them. In no time, I approached the galley I was aiming for. In front of me, an Italian man shouted at the sailors to let them on, shaking his fist at them. He had lost his helm but was otherwise very well armoured.

"What are they waiting for?" I asked the armoured man.

"We are Venetians," he replied. "They must take us, they must."

I grabbed him. "Why do they not?"

He sneered. "They wait for the Catalans. Bastard sailors care only about money." He raised his voice again. "We are your countrymen. We serve Cardinal Isidore! We are your brothers, you dirty bastards!"

"Come on," I said to my men and pushed through the angry men.

"Keep back," a Venetian sailor shouted at me in Italian. "Keep back, I say."

"We come from the Catalans," I said. "We come with a message."

"Lies!" the man next to me shouted. "He lies!"

I elbowed him in the face and he dropped down in a clatter of steel, out cold.

"I will give you their message, sir," I shouted. "I will give you the message from my friend, the Catalan commander Pere Julia, and then I shall go."

"Just you," their commander said, pointing to me.

I pushed forward with my hands up and palms open, slipping through the points of the spears they brandished.

"I was with the Catalans," I said to the man. "They were cut off at the Great Palace when the Turks broke through. The Catalans are certainly cut off and surrounded. None shall escape. None shall come here."

He scowled. "You lie."

"I do not. Besides, the Turks are through the walls at the Saint Romanus Gate which they held. They are likely within the city already." I jerked my thumb over my shoulder and the Venetian's eyes looked at the walls behind me. "At any moment, you shall see the enemy attacking the rear of this mob and then your ship will be swarmed and you will not leave at all."

He nodded and glanced at me, sneering. "So you are telling me to flee. Without my payment. Without my protection, should the ship be boarded."

I looked him in the eyes. "I will pay. I will bring my men. A score of knights, just as many squires, and as many servants again. But we must be gone before it is too late to do so."

He scoffed. "You will pay? What will you pay for your sixty men? I am awaiting the payment of five hundred Catalan mercenaries."

I turned and called to Stephen. "Let my man there in the Italian armour come forward and offer you our gold."

The commander nodded to his men and Stephen stepped up and pulled a heavy purse from his belt. With an unhappy look, he passed it over.

"All ecus," I said. "All gold."

He hefted it and was impressed, though he attempted to hide it. "Hardly what I am due."

"You will not get what you are due. The Catalans are dead or captured, I swear it to Christ. If not by now then certainly by morning. If you do not wish to take us, please return my gold and I shall seek another vessel. I see dozens ferrying men across to Galata. The Genoese know a good deal when they see one."

He snorted at my jibe as he hefted the bag. "Your men only. A score of knights you say?"

"Twenty-three soldiers and their squires, all experienced fighters, and those that serve us must come also."

With a last look at the crowds and the gate beyond, the Venetian nodded and took my hand. "My name is Alvise Diedo."

"Richard Ashbury."

"Get your companions onboard, Englishman."

We boarded quickly as the men on the dockside cursed and damned us all. Once we were through and onto the ship, they began to push off while men rowed us out onto the black waters of the harbour toward the fleet in the Golden Horn. The desperate soldiers on the dock surged forward and grabbed for the sides of the galley as it departed. Some were fended off by the sailors, falling into the lapping water.

"You said you had five hundred Catalans," I said to the master as we watched the scene in silence. "This boat would not hold even one hundred packed to the gills."

"That is my ship also," he said, pointing to a great three-masted cog out on the water, with a high sterncastle and forecastle. "And two more, beyond."

Silently, I thanked God.

"Was it true?" the master asked. "What you said about the Catalans?"

"I wish it were not," I said. "Pere Julia is a good man."

"They are all good men." He sighed, looking me up and down. "You were at the walls?"

"I was."

"They say the Emperor is dead. Did you see it?"

"I heard it also but I did not see. I believe he fled southward along the wall. Later, word spread as we ran that he had fallen. Whether it is true, I cannot say."

The master grunted. "Small fleet of Genoese ships by the Golden Gate at the south, leading into the Sea of Marmara. Going for them, I would wager. Should have stood and died for his city. What of Longo?"

"Wounded. His men drew him back and it caused the rout. He was alive long enough to order a full retreat, I heard the trumpets sound. Or perhaps one of his men gave the order. His men were taking him to a ship but we went on separate roads and I do not know where they went."

The master shook his head as he gazed back at the dark city. "She has fallen, then. She has truly fallen."

His eyes glittered with tears.

"How shall you break through the Turkish fleet?" I asked him. "And before that, the great chain?"

"Word was that the Genoese in Galata would pull in the chain but it has not happened yet. I doubt the useless bastards shall do it, fearful as they are of breaking their oaths of neutrality. But if they do it, we shall be ready for the Turks. Their ships are weak, they cannot sail."

"I heard they hired Christian crews."

He smiled a little. "But we are Venetian."

We were transferred to the great cog, with its slab sides and square sails on the masts. Many of the Greek lords had sailed or were sailing across to Galata but everyone knew they could not stay there. The Genoese might have sworn to remain neutral but they had sent men to the defence of the walls and they were assisting in the evacuation of the city and so they would soon surrender to the Turks or have their gates broken and their people slaughtered. Through the swarming ships of all sizes in the Horn, word was passed that Longo had indeed survived and he was on one of the ships. Though he had failed in his duty, he was still loved by the Genoese, the Venetians, and the Greeks, and they were pleased to find he yet lived.

"I know you are all tired," I said to my men as we bobbed at anchor. They lay in heaps, half tangled with each other, on the deck of the cog, relieved to be away but afraid of what might come. "And we will take what rest and sustenance we can. But we must be prepared to fight once more. When the ship sails, we shall keep well away from the crew and we will not obstruct them in their work. But if a Turkish ship attempts to board us, we must be ready to repel them. Do you understand?"

They did and I left them to rest.

"I'd rather have died on my feet," Walt muttered beside me as we looked out at the burning city. "Than get sunk out here and drown beneath the waves."

Drowning was a great fear of my own but a leader must show confidence at such times. "We must have faith in our Venetian friends. They are the masters of these waves."

"If you say so."

The night drew on and the fleet signalled to each other by lamps and by whistles, bells, and trumpets and by shouting across the waters. Small boats were rowed between ships and gradually, some sort of plan was agreed upon. The darkness made it hard to see what was happening but soon our ship was underway. To the east, the great chain was broken by Genoese ships and in several groups the fleet of Christian survivors sailed out toward the

Turks beyond the Horn.

There were hundreds of us, and the Venetian master had not been lying when he said their skill outweighed that of the enemy. Some of our ships fell to enemy assault. Arrows flew and guns fired, flashing and banging in the night. Men were killed and ships boarded, even sunk in collisions. My men were called to arm themselves and to stand ready many times through the night but the enemy ships were always avoided before they could close with us.

We made it through the strait and south into the Sea of Marmara, and from there we forced our way through the Dardanelles into the Aegean. Once there, we had days out away from the coast and our small fleet aimed for Greece and the few free Venetian port cities that the Turks had allowed them to keep when they took Greece.

We spoke little during the journey. Even of what would happen next. The fighting had been hard enough but the defeat was far harder to bear.

The city was sacked for three days. Some quarters resisted the Turks for a time before surrendering but the Catalan mercenaries fought to the last man. The Turks looted homes but focused of course on the churches and monasteries, desecrating them with their heathenry and stealing their wealth. Constantinople was looted on a massive scale. The richest lords of the city and their families sought sanctuary in the Santa Sofia, hoping that the sanctity of that greatest of churches would save them. Instead, the vile Turks broke down the doors, raped the women on the floor of the holy church, and dragged the survivors off to be ransomed or sold into slavery or defiled until death.

Later, Mehmed rode into the city and into the Santa Sophia where he had the building converted into a mosque and held afternoon prayers that very day.

That was the Turkish way. They had stolen everything from the Byzantines by force. Stolen her cities and her towns, her fields and orchards. Stolen her sons for their Janissaries. And now they had stolen the most beautiful, the most magnificent building on earth and defiled it by worshipping their false god within.

Genoese Galata surrendered. The terms were negotiated by William himself, no doubt because he spoke the language so well. The thought of William's red Janissary regiment forcing their way through the walls and into the city turned my stomach every time I recalled it. The fact that William had not fought alongside them enraged me further, but I did not know why.

In return for winning him the city, Sultan Mehmed made William his official Grand Vizier, the second most powerful man in the Turkish Empire.

"What now?" Eva finally asked me, days later as we approached Negroponte, on Euboea.

"What will William do?" Stephen said, when I did not answer. "Where will he strike next?"

"Where else is left now for him to conquer but to the north?" I replied, finally. "Whether he strikes at Serbia, Wallachia, Moldavia, Hungary, the line must be held."

"But how can we stop William?" Stephen said. "How can we stop his Janissaries?"

"You urged me for so long to build a great company of immortals but I resisted. For good reasons, I thought. And then we made our Company of Saint George into members of the Order of the White Dagger. I had hoped it would be enough."

"We know now that we need more," Stephen said. "More than two score. We need as many as William has. Five hundred at the least."

"And yet the problem remains. How can we find and support and supply so many? Already, I worry about the men we have."

He nodded, warily. "We would have to trust the men completely. We would need enormous amounts of mortal blood. And it would need to be done in secret, lest we are challenged, declared enemies, outlaws, expelled from Christendom."

"All great challenges that must be overcome," I said. "I see it now, with my eyes clear and open. Because the only way we will ever stop William from conquering all of Christendom is with our own army of immortals."

7

Wallachia

1456

OF COURSE, CREATING an army of immortals was more easily said than done. It was a clear goal but how we could accomplish such a thing was far from resolved.

It took months to make our way back to Hungary in safety, first by sea and then by land.

In Buda, the court was subdued and focused on internal issues. When we told our friends and contacts, whether merchants or knights, that we had been in Constantinople for the siege, few seemed interested in discussing it further. It was a matter that people already seemed to believe best forgotten, even though the implications were enormous. It was as though they could deny it had ever happened, if only it was never spoken of.

The Turks continued to reinforce the frontier. And all the Christian lands under Turkish authority continued to be subjected to the *devshirme*, the Blood Tax. Hunyadi had a report compiled by a group of monks who believed that fifteen or twenty-thousand Christian boys were being incorporated into the Janissaries every single year. Twenty thousand of our strongest boys, every year, taken as slaves and used against us. That says nothing of slaves taken from the Rus and other people of the north by the Golden Horde.

Our Albanian warlord Skanderbeg made a swift and secret visit to his allies in Naples to discuss the strategic implications of the loss of Constantinople and discussions were begun regarding a new crusade to retake the city. We long held out hope, for all of the years 1454, and 1455, but it came to nothing. In the meantime, I trained the survivors of our company and we sought new armour and weapons and supplies. Hunyadi was glad enough at my return to fund us once more so that we would be on hand, though he did not have much use for us. Still, we took the opportunity to regain our strength and improve our skill. The new immortals delighted in their new abilities and they gave me little trouble.

Eva and Stephen re-established contact with their agents and brought many to our company's house to provide regular reports of enemy activity.

By 1456, the Sultan had about ninety thousand soldiers in Edirne and a fleet of sixty ships at the mouth of the Danube. Agents provided word that the Turks were producing cannons in new foundries in Serbia, which would save them the time and effort needed to bring them up from Greece or Anatolia.

It became ever clearer the Turks meant to take Belgrade.

Swiftly, Vladislaus II the Voivode of Wallachia turned even further toward the Turks and was said to be making ever more promises to the Sultan. If Wallachia could not be brought to heel then it would soon fall, perhaps without a fight. More immediate a problem though was that Vladislaus had begun raiding across southern Transylvania with Turkish soldiers. This raiding tied down thousands of Hunyadi's best men who were guarding against this new Wallachian assault.

"But I need those men," Hunyadi said, after summoning me to his private chambers. I knew that it meant he had finally found a use for me and my company. "I need them for the defence of Belgrade. It is there that the Sultan's hammer blow will fall next."

"Why not remove Vladislaus now?" I asked. "You have known it needed to be done for a long time. But it cannot wait any further."

"You are more right than you know. Vladislaus has stirred up the people of Fogaras, encouraged them into a full rebellion against me. Against Hungary. They sent word that they are no longer my vassals but the vassals of Sultan Mehmed. This means they will throw themselves into the arms of the Turks when they arrive and so already we have a Transylvanian town lost to us and gained by the enemy. We cannot allow them to do this."

"So send an army, take back Fogaras and march over the mountains into Wallachia and be rid of Vladislaus."

"An army, Richard?" he shook his head. "I cannot take even more men from Serbia and send them into Wallachia. You have seen the country. Seen those mountains. You have fought in them. If Vladislaus refuses battle, which he will do if he has any sense, we could have ten thousand men tied up there for years. We do not have *time*."

I could not disagree with that. "But you have something in mind, or you would not have asked to speak to me."

Hunyadi sighed and gestured to a servant to bring us more wine. "You seemed to do well with young Vlad Dracula last time you were with him, in Transylvania. Are you on good terms?"

"I kept my men clear of him, truth be told. But I made my peace with him before I left for Constantinople and we parted on good terms, certainly."

561

"What did you think of his abilities?"

"We did not do any fighting and neither did he. But throughout the negotiations and during the journey from place to place, he seemed a perfectly steady young prince."

"Steady?" Hunyadi drank his wine and frowned. "Do you damn him with faint praise, sir?"

"Not at all. Young Dracula knew what he wanted, he told his men clearly what he expected, and they obeyed him. He knows how to lead."

"Good, yes. But you were not impressed?"

"It is not that I was unimpressed. He is young and untested. But most of all, I still wonder where his true loyalties lie. You wish to put him on the throne and so make a true ally of Wallachia again. But this is what we did ten years ago, and your man has turned to the Turks even more thoroughly than the old Vlad Dracul ever did."

He sighed and scratched his cheek. "And you fear I will make the same mistake again. It is certainly a possibility. But there seems to be a deep well of contempt in the young man's heart, reserved above all for the Turk."

"Perhaps he is deceiving you. Perhaps he has been their man ever since they released him. After all, why would they do so? I believe the Turks yet hold his younger brother, Radu. Is that still the case?"

Hunyadi made an unhappy growling sound in his throat. "It is. It appears that he is serving the Sultan in a military capacity."

"Perhaps they threaten to end Radu's life if Vlad does not do as they command."

"Do you have a brother, Richard?"

I swallowed. "Why do you ask?"

"I merely wondered what you might do for the life of a younger brother. How far you would go. What would it take for you to trade your honour as a prince and a knight, and a life as an independent ruler for that of a slave subordinate to the Turks? Would you do it to save the life of your brother?"

"You are speaking to a lowly and landless knight with no family, my lord. I have never had to consider such a question. But I take it you do not believe the threat to his brother's life would be enough to bind him in servitude to the Turks? Perhaps not. We cannot know what is in his heart. But you have asked me here and you speak to me of Wallachia and Vlad Dracula instead of the coming battle at Belgrade. And so I take it that you have decided to make your move with young Vlad? To place him on the throne?"

"No." Hunyadi drank off his wine and snapped his fingers for another. "I cannot *place* him there. He must take it for himself. But I will provide him with a small number of soldiers, as many as I can spare from the defence of Belgrade. Perhaps Dracula can make his way into Wallachia and overthrow the voivode, with the help my men and of loyal *boyars* who have been exiled by Vladislaus."

"How many men do you mean, my lord?"

"*Boyars?* Almost thirty, with their retinues. And I have secured the services of six hundred Hungarian mercenaries and five hundred more from Transylvania and Wallachia."

I laughed aloud. "You are sending, what, fifteen hundred men against the armies of Wallachia and the Turks he controls? They will be outnumbered ten to one. It is madness."

"Madness, yes," Hunyadi said, smiling. "And that is precisely why I thought of you."

***

"We're doing what?" Walt said, after I explained it to them. He sat at my right hand at the top table and I looked down at him from where I stood before looking around at the rest of the men seated below me.

Our hall in Buda was large enough for the company to assemble. I had not recruited anyone to make up our numbers as I was concerned about a company of immortals and mortals mixing together. Certainly, the servants could not be trusted to hold their tongues about the nature of their masters and any new mercenaries would have to become members of the Order. Indeed, the Company of Saint George had become essentially synonymous with the Order of the White Dagger. The outside world saw us as a small but elite mercenary company retained by the Regent of Hungary and yet we knew ourselves to be the Order, committed to destroying William de Ferrers and all his evil, immortal followers.

Some of the men took time to understand what a fine line it was to thread between these two realities. Indeed, I struggled to do so myself every day.

"It might be done," I said. "Though it will be a challenge, I do not doubt it."

They all looked at one another and said nothing.

"What is in it for us?" Stephen said. "How does agreeing to win Vlad Dracula his kingdom help us make the immortal army we need to defeat William?"

I nodded and clasped my hands before me.

"If it works," I said, "and if we show ourselves to be indispensable, then we might find ourselves with a ruler in Dracula who can give us the sanctuary we need."

Rob rapped his knuckles on the table and pointed across the hall to Serban, sitting far away below the salt. "What do you say, Serban? What do you make of Vlad's chances?"

Old Serban dragged himself to his feet and glanced around the hall, all eyes turned to him. "It can certainly be done, my lord. It has been done before. The throne of Wallachia changes hands more often than a halfpenny strumpet."

Walt burst out laughing and banged the table and most of the men laughed with him.

"I take it you taught him that?" I asked Walt as he wiped his eyes. "Thank you, Serban, for sharing with us your expert local knowledge. That will be all from you."

Stephen cleared his throat. "Do you truly believe Vlad could be the ruler we need? He may be working for the Turks. He may be a weakling. He still may turn on you and have you killed because of his father."

"Yes," I agreed, clapping my hands together. "All that you say is true. But where else might we find our friendly ruler? So, before we conclude, are there any other objections to be made?"

"So," Stephen said, getting to his feet. "No matter what we say today, you have decided that we will ultimately agree to this mad scheme?"

"I have agreed already. Make your preparations. We return to Transylvania."

It was June 1456 when we slipped over the mountains from Transylvania and into Wallachia with our small, makeshift army. Those mountain peaks were black and jagged, with grey streaks and were inhumanly large and intimidating and entirely unscalable. On their flanks clung dense forests of pine trees so dark when in shadow that they seemed black as charcoal. The passes and valleys were prone to sudden changes in elevation, but they were often lush and green, whether with meadows grazed by hardy sheep and mad goats, or in broadleaf woods thick with herds of pigs. Below, the lands were crossed with rivers running from the mountains to the distant plains and on to feed the mighty Danube, sometimes becoming long, narrow, and spectacular lakes. In between was a wild land of forests of beech, oak, and elm in the lowlands, or pines and spruce and fur above.

Our leader, the young Vlad Dracula was in fine form. Whether with the exiled *boyars* or the mercenary captains, he was always at ease. His own men, young lords or sons of lords or other Wallachian adventurers who had thrown their lot in with him, clearly adored him and hung on his every word. Though he was often the shortest man in any group, he seemed to dominate it with his loud voice and sure gestures. The young prince was born to rule and had been raised in that very expectation. Despite his prolonged period of confinement in the lands of his enemies, he certainly appeared to believe in himself deeply.

The only man he was wary of was me.

Despite my presentation of his father's sword and dragon amulet, young Vlad kept his distance. At councils of war, though he was courteous enough and listened to my suggestions just as he did for others, with me he was always reserved.

"He does not favour me," I muttered to Walt as we left his tent a week after crossing the border.

"You cut off his dad's head," Walt said.

"There is that."

"Reckon he means to take yours?" Walt asked.

"I think it is a distinct possibility."

"Don't worry, Richard, I'll watch your back."

Vlad's plan relied on bringing as many of the *boyars* to his side as he could before open fighting began. Without wooing former allies of his father and enemies of Vladislaus, the attempt on the throne would be doomed to failure. With that in mind, we made for the fortress of Copăceni at the head of a severe valley in the north. Once our army filed into the valley and approached the fortress, Vlad took some of us up the final steep approach and there demanded to see the lord, a *boyar* named Bogdan.

At the gate, our horses were breathing heavily from the climb. I was at the rear of the party, with a few of my men to accompany me. The gatekeeper looked down on us and raised his voice, which echoed from the rocks and thick stone walls. "Who are you and why do you come here?"

I looked up at the dragon banner held aloft over our party and shook my head at the gatekeeper's absurd attempts at haughtiness.

"You know who we are," Dracula said, his voice projecting over the entire fortress. "Tell your lord I will speak with him."

"State your name," the gatekeeper said.

Vlad paused for half a moment before answering, the silence filled with his contempt for the stupidity of the question.

"I will not be kept waiting," Dracula replied.

The man hesitated, looked at the soldiers flanking him, and disappeared into the tower. We stood in silence on our horses.

It was not long before the gatekeeper reappeared. "You, my lord, and ten men. No more. And no weapons."

"Ten men it is," Dracula agreed. "But we shall keep our weapons. Open the gate."

The gatekeeper pursed his lips and his gloved fingers drummed on the parapet before he muttered to the man beside him, who hurried off. A few moments later the gate below creaked into life as it swung slowly inward.

"That was easy," Walt said, grinning. "We'll be camped in the valley tonight, then. Wonder if the lads might shoot a deer. Do you reckon there's boar in these woods?"

"Undoubtedly," Rob said, his tone miserable, staring at his stump.

Before he dismounted, Dracula called out the names of his men, commanding them to accompany him inside the fortress of Copăceni.

The tenth name he called was mine.

Caught off guard, I hesitated but swung down from my saddle.

"Do not do it," Rob muttered. "It may be a trap."

"Might be," I said, adjusting my clothes and slipping an extra knife up inside my doublet.

"This may *all* be theatre," Stephen said, hurrying forward and whispering. "This entire event."

"What do you mean?"

"It was rather easy to gain access to this supposed enemy stronghold, was it not? What if it was prearranged? What if the purpose was to separate you from your men?"

I turned to Serban. "What do you think?"

"I think at such times a man must flee," he said, shrugging. "Or go forward to meet his fate."

"Do you know something about this trap, Serban?" Stephen said, reaching for him. "Are you in on it? Are you a part of it? If you are, you will speak now, or I shall flay you myself."

Serban stared back, his wrinkled face filled with contempt and bitter amusement.

"Enough, Stephen," I said, smiling and patting him on the back. "Our Wallachian friends are looking."

"Be careful," Eva said. "And hurry up. They are waiting for you."

I winked at her and followed Dracula and his nine companions into the fortress. It was a small place but sturdy enough. Like so many such structures in those highlands, it was a stronghold where a lord could feel safe from raids and assassinations and other mischief started by his neighbouring lords, while ruling over the villages in his valley below.

There seemed to be no more than forty soldiers and as many servants. A hundred men and women in the entire place, mostly men.

We were escorted into the small, dark hall. A table and benches had been set in the centre of it while a fire burned in a surprisingly modern fireplace on the side.

At the head of the hall sat Lord Bogdan of Copăceni, a big man even seated in his chair, with wild eyes and a thick, greying moustache.

"So," Bogdan said, his voice gruff. "You have come. Sit at my table and take refreshment. Then I will hear your requests."

While we stood in a line at the rear, Dracula said nothing and strode the length of the hall toward the seated old *boyar*. He stopped an arm's span from him, looking down.

"You, Bogdan, have sworn to follow the false prince Vladislaus," Dracula said.

The *boyar* shifted in his seat, discomforted. "But of course. He is the Voivode of Wallachia."

"Not for long," Dracula said.

The *boyar* peered around Dracula, looking at his men for help, even at us. I glanced at Dracula's men, his bodyguards and exiled *boyars*. None moved to help Bogdan. Some were smiling.

"Come, let us drink," Bogdan said, attempting to take control of the situation. "Let us eat. Then we can discuss things."

"There is nothing to discuss," Dracula said.

The *boyar* coughed and shifted in his seat again. "Then why are you here?"

"To accept your apology," Dracula said.

"Apology?" The *boyar* snapped. "For what? I have done nothing to you."

"I have come to hear you beg forgiveness."

Bogdan's mouth gaped. "For what? I supported your father until they killed him. What else could I do then but support Vladislaus?"

Dracula half turned to the men behind him at the back of the hall. "These men went into exile rather than follow a false prince. And yet you did not. Why?"

Bogdan attempted a consolatory tone. "Let us eat."

"Why?"

He slapped his hands on the arms of his chair. "Why do you think, you upstart? I am a lord. This is my castle. This is my land. I rule it. They are my people. Give that up, for what? For the memory of my dead lord? His sons were in the claws of the Turks, I did not know if they would ever return. If you would return. What was I supposed to do?"

Vlad stared at him, unmoved. "I will accept your apology, once it is given."

"And what will you do if it is not?"

Dracula said nothing and I could not see his face. But the *boyar* could and his eyes opened wide and his skin turned white. He coughed again, before looking around at his men. Many shuffled with unease.

"Very well," the *boyar* said with his chin up. "Very well, then. I do here before witnesses say to you that—"

"On your knees," Dracula said.

Surely, it was too far.

The *boyar* stood. He was taller than Dracula but it somehow seemed as if he was still looking up at him.

"If you would step back, my lord," the *boyar* said. But Dracula did not move. The man smiled in discomfort and edged around the younger lord before dropping slowly to one knee. Now, Dracula was the one with his back to the lord's seat and the man before him appeared to be a supplicant in his own hall.

"I beg my lord to forgive me for following the false Voivode Vladislaus instead of taking myself into exile. I should have honoured my word. In the name of God, allow me to make amends."

Dracula held out his hand with his silver dragon ring and shining rubies. "You may swear fealty to me and follow me as I retake the throne of my ancestors."

The *boyar* took Dracula's hand in both of his and kissed the ring, swearing that he would do so.

"Very good," Dracula said, smiling and clapping his hands. "Now we may eat."

***

In the sweltering heat of the valley, as June turned to July, we rode hard in pursuit of Vladislaus II and the last of his loyal men.

It had taken Vlad Dracula a mere four weeks, going from lord to lord, stronghold to stronghold, to gain the support of the majority of the Wallachian *boyars*. With his support fading away and even his Turkish troops drifting south back across the Danube into Rumelia, Vladislaus had seen what lay in store for him.

And so he ran from Târgoviște.

To me, it was a familiar feeling. Ten years before I had pursued Vlad II Dracul from the very same city, only this time my quarry had a greater start and he was not fleeing down into the plains and toward the Danube and to his friends the Turks but instead east across the valleys toward the last of the *boyars* who remained loyal to him.

We sweated and our horses gasped but we had to catch him before he could raise a spirited rebellion. If Wallachia descended into a civil war, even if Dracula won it would be weakened and open to invasion. A swift victory on the other hand would mean Wallachian troops and the mercenaries we had with us could all be directed to the vital defence of Belgrade.

And it was my company who had finally scared Vladislaus into full flight. If I could catch him and hand him over to Dracula, perhaps it would bring me such favour that I could approach him about our immortal army. Perhaps, at the least, it would start us down the road that would lead us to that place.

Just as I had years ago, I followed Serban once more, who proved to be an excellent rider. The rest of my company followed behind along the road. Miles behind, I expected Dracula himself and the core of his followers to be advancing as swiftly as they could.

It was late afternoon when we found them, stopped on the side of the road by a pond where they watered their horses and fed themselves with cold meats. We were surprised to come across them so suddenly but they were astonished at our unexpected arrival around a bend in the road. They rushed for their horses and half of them stood to fight while others took flight. Some that attempted to stop us were on horseback and others were on foot. Frightened horses without riders ran in panic. Without waiting for my men to come up beside me, I charged in amongst the enemy, killing one and knocking another from his saddle and charging through their line and on for Vladislaus. I recognised him by the crest upon his clothing and the excellence of his German armour and helm. With a glance over my shoulder I saw that some of my men were with me but not many, most having become entangled with the prince's men.

When I turned back to the road, my horse tossed his head and attempted to turn away, for Vladislaus and his men had turned and were starting to come back for their friends.

Gritting my teeth, I pulled my horse back onto the track and raked my spurs on him. My bloody sword raised high, I shouted a wordless cry and crashed through them, taking a blow on my shoulder from a warhammer that almost knocked me sideways. I cut at them, wheeling my horse around and around, fending off blows from all sides.

My company was outnumbered but Vladislaus and his men were outmatched. They were unable to conceive how much stronger we were than they and their misplaced confidence proved to be their undoing. We killed a great many of them and caught the rest. Out of sight of the survivors, a handful of the dying were drained of their blood and we finally stopped to take stock of our victory.

Rob and Walt grinned, for between them they held Prince Vladislaus. He was shaken and furious and behind his anger was a deep fear.

"Well done, men!" I cried. "You have unseated a prince, this day!"

We began escorting Vladislaus down the mountain and had reached a flatter section of the track where the river curved away to reveal a wide meadow on one side and the woods on the other.

Approaching us was a great mass of galloping horses.

"Line up!" Walt roared. "Defensive line here! Prisoners to the rear!"

"It is Dracula," I said.

"He got our message, then," Rob observed as Vlad Dracula's enormous column of horsemen came to a stop between the woods and the swift flowing river, spreading out into the meadows on either side with their long grass and array of red, purple, and white flowers.

"Bring up the prisoners," I called.

Vlad rode closer before throwing himself off and stepping away from his men into the open space between my company and his bodyguard.

When Vladislaus was brought forward to me, I took him by the arm and walked toward Dracula. We had removed his helm when we captured him, along with most of his expensive armour, and all could see who it was that I had beside me. Vladislaus glared at me once but then he had eyes only for Vlad.

The young would-be prince stepped forward. Dracula said nothing, his face cold and hard and his eyes glaring as they came together. He looked up at Vladislaus who sneered down.

"They told me you were a skilled knight," Vladislaus said. "But now I see that you are nothing but a little boy."

Dracula's face did not change, he simply stared into Vladislaus' eyes.

"What?" Vladislaus said, scoffing. "You think you can frighten me? I know I am to be executed. What can you frighten me with?"

I spoke up. "Your men burned his older brother to death, did they not? I wonder if that's how you will go? Or if they will remove your skin first?"

He glanced at me, angry. I laughed.

"No," Dracula said, the first word he had spoken. "No, you shall not be burned. Nor flayed."

Vladislaus looked down his long nose. "What is it to be, then?"

Dracula seemed not to have blinked at all. "You shall not be executed, Vladislaus."

The voivode scoffed but I saw hope kindle in his eyes. "Ransom, is it? A wise choice. You will earn for yourself a fortune, have no doubts about that."

Dracula did not smile but I saw that he was amused. "And who would pay this fortune for you? The *boyars* will raise a fortune for a man who cannot protect them and their people? Or do you mean that the Turks will pay for a king who cannot hold a kingdom?"

Vladislaus sneered. "There are many yet loyal to me."

Dracula shook his head. "There will be no ransom."

"What then?" Vladislaus snapped, unable to stand it a moment longer. "Not execution, not ransom. Then what?"

"It is to be combat, my lord," Dracula said, calmly. "You against me. To the death. Now."

Vladislaus looked at the men behind Dracula and then back to the young man. "Even if I win, I will lose."

Dracula raised his voice but still did not turn away from his enemy. "If Vladislaus defeats me in this fair trial of combat, you shall let him and his men go free. This is my command as your lord. Do you agree to honour it?"

They called out their assent. If it came to pass, I doubted they would honour their word. Still, it was enough to give Vladislaus hope and I understood later that it was as much a matter of Vlad's cruelty as it was his sense of honour.

Vladislaus was ordered to prepare himself and his surviving men were allowed to approach and dress him for combat, with his own armour and weapons. I was mildly annoyed because I had already claimed those fine items for myself and I was not about to have my men strip the dead man in front of his former subjects.

"You disapprove, Richard?" Vlad asked me as his squires strapped his armour on.

"I approve very much," I said. "It is always a pleasure to see young people embracing the old ways."

He smiled. "And you know about the old ways, do you?"

"A little."

"And yet you do not seem happy. Is it because I have not thanked you for catching him for me?"

"I have no need for words of thanks. It is the favour of the Voivode of Wallachia that I seek."

He stepped forward, scattering his surprised squires, and held out an armoured hand. I took it as he looked into my eyes.

"You have it, sir. We must talk, you and I. There is much to discuss."

"Then we shall do so," I replied, letting him go and pointing over my shoulder. "After you kill that bastard."

His eyes were mirthless as he nodded to the squire holding his helm. "It will not take long."

Eva came close to my side. "Walt and Rob are taking bets."

"I would not bet against our young lord, here."

"No? Do you not often say that in battle experience more often bests youth?"

I glanced at her. "I say no such thing."

She scoffed.

Fully armoured, the great lords stalked toward each other as the sun touched the rim of the ridge to the west, casting deep yellow light into the valley.

Dracula feinted an attack and Vladislaus covered himself, but it was clear he had not been deceived. Their blades clashed and they withdrew, feeling each other out for a few more moments until Vladislaus launched into a furious attack. Vladislaus was taller and his blade longer and he used his reach advantage to thrust at Dracula's face. The shorter man parried as he stepped back and back. But he was not in a blind panic and he did not retreat in a straight line, stepping and moving at oblique angles as he defended. Both men had been raised since early childhood to be great knights and had received superb instruction by experienced masters, and they had made it their business to practice throughout their lives since. Even when he had been a hostage of the Turks, he had received martial instruction.

But Vladislaus was taller and older and it became clear that he had the advantage, as slight as it was. Dracula's attacks came up short and it seemed to all watching that the combat was certain to end only one way. Certainly, Vladislaus had sensed it and he redoubled his efforts to break through Dracula's defence before exhaustion overcame him. After their sharp start, their movements had taken on the rhythmic state that one reaches when weariness begins to take hold. And there are few activities in life more wearying than prolonged armoured combat.

Vladislaus gave a sudden burst of speed and caught Dracula on his helm with a powerful blow, powerful enough to knock any mortal man from his senses. The watching crowd cried out.

But Dracula did not fall. Nor was he dazed, even for a moment. Instead, a change came over him. He stopped defending and instead attacked and all trace of weariness was quite suddenly gone. Indeed, he used his sword with one hand instead of two, almost casually, as he advanced on his tired opponent.

I realised then that the fight up to then had been all deceit on Dracula's part, feigning lesser skill than he had. It stunned Vladislaus, who began retreating in panic.

Dracula surged forward so quickly that he was almost a blur, and his sword whipped through the air, left and right, knocking away his enemy's sword and driving him to his knees with a flurry of blows. Eva grabbed my hand and squeezed it.

Advancing on his kneeling opponent, Dracula twisted the helm from Vladislaus' head and tossed it aside. The Voivode of Wallachia's eyes were wide, and his face and hair were soaked with sweat.

"Look at me," Dracula said, grasping Vladislaus' slick hair in his gauntleted fist and pulling the man's head back.

Just as Vladislaus opened his mouth to speak, Dracula lifted his sword hand high and drove the pommel down into the fallen man's face, breaking the bones of his cheeks and eyes. It was powerful enough to knock Vladislaus unconscious, as his raised hands fell limp. But Dracula held his head in position and brought the pommel down again and again, until the man's face was caved in and the insides pulped. When there was nothing left but a sucking hole, he pushed the dead man down and walked slowly back toward his horse.

The hundreds of watching men stood in silence for a long moment before one of his men cheered and then suddenly, they all were.

"Richard," Eva said, speaking rapidly. "Did you see? See the way he moved? The speed. Do you think—"

"Yes, I saw it," I said. "There is no doubt. Dracula is an immortal."

8

The Battle of Belgrade
1456

"I WOULD HAVE you stay," Dracula said as I prepared to mount my horse. All around us, the field swarmed with men and horses, assembled for the ride to the west. "You and your entire company."

"It would please me to stay," I said to Dracula, "and there is much to discuss. But there is not a moment to be lost. Belgrade must not fall."

"There is no doubt about that," he replied, shading his eyes with a hand and wincing. He wore a broad-brimmed black hat and gloves. I recalled that he had always been well covered when outside, especially in the bright summer sun. "I wish that I could fight also. There is little I would prefer in all the world than to fight a great battle against Mehmed. Alas, it shall have to wait. I cannot leave the land I have not yet completely won."

"I understand, my lord, and when we have smashed the Turk at Belgrade, I shall return."

"Do you think you shall?" Dracula replied.

"Return?"

"Smash the Turk. Hunyadi has not managed to do so yet. Not when it truly mattered."

"We must," I said. "If Belgrade falls, they will be across and into Hungary and from there, where can they not go?"

He nodded, his face unreadable. It was as though he did not care either way.

I hesitated. So many questions were on my mind but I could not ask them. Not yet.

"What will you do now, my lord, if I may ask?"

"There are many men I must speak with. Wallachia must be put into good order. The traitors must be discovered and punished, and good men put in their place. I hope that you will return soon, with as many of my soldiers as possible. I need them. Wallachia needs them."

"You need them to return?" I asked. "Or do you need them to kill the Turks?"

Dracula's mouth twitched. "They have been poorly led in past years. My predecessors gave orders that they stay intact, no matter what. I have ordered these men to do their duty and kill twice their number in Turks, and to show Christendom that Wallachia is resolved to destroying the enemies of Christ. I will not have my people shamed once again."

"I am very glad to hear it, my lord."

"Come back, Richard."

He held out his hand and I took it.

"I will, my lord."

Dracula had already turned away to speak to his lords as I mounted and rode to my men, who sat watching me.

"Getting on rather well with the little bastard," Walt said, "aren't you, Richard?"

"I think he likes me," I said.

"He is luring you in with false courtesies," Stephen said. "So that he can catch you and kill you."

I tilted my head. "Thank you for your unique insight, Stephen, it had not occurred to me that one of William's immortals may mean me harm."

He blustered. "I simply meant that he will kill you the moment he has the chance and—"

"But he *has* had the chance," Eva said, cutting him off. "Many times. Something has stayed his hand. Perhaps he is not certain about Richard, or perhaps there is some other reason. Perhaps there is something he wishes to know before he acts. Or it may be that he wants you as an ally after all. Perhaps William has sent him with orders to win you over."

"Fat chance of that," Rob said. "Right, Richard?"

"We do not know what he wants," I said. "I do not know how much it matters. There may be an advantage in capturing him and questioning him about William before we kill him. And before we capture him and kill him, we must come up with a plan that does not lead to us all being slaughtered by an army of his men. But first, before all that, we *must* go to Belgrade. For all we know, the Turks have already reached it."

"We ride with Wallachian horsemen," Walt observed. "Many of them are the very same Wallachian horsemen that abandoned us at Varna."

"Yes," I said.

"And they deserted again at Kosovo."

"Many are the same men, certainly."

Walt nodded. "And these same lads are our allies now?"

"We are riding with them, that is all. When we reach Belgrade, Hunyadi will know not to trust these men." I thought of Dracula's earlier words. "Besides, they may not act as they have before."

My men were not convinced.

"What if they do not flee," Walt said, "but instead attack. Dracula is one of William's and he will have ordered these men to fall upon the Hungarians at just the right moment. Did that occur to you?"

"I will warn Hunyadi, do not fear. Until then, we must treat our companions with respect and courtesy. Understand?"

"Can I not just keep apart from them instead?" Walt grumbled.

"Once our business in Belgrade is finished, we must return here and capture and kill their new prince. We cannot make enemies amongst the soldiery before then, and so you will be courteous," I said, wagging a finger at him. "Like the knight you are. Come on."

***

We marched first with the Hungarian and Transylvanian mercenaries from Wallachia across the plains to the Danube, crossing by boat, and then up into the mountains toward northern Serbia. The mercenaries knew they would be paid when they reached the Hungarian army at Belgrade but they also looked forward to the prospect of enormous quantities of loot, assuming of course that the Turks could be defeated.

We pushed hard and I drove my company faster than many of the others, gaining distance every day. The land was teeming with soldiers from all over, heading for Belgrade. There is no doubt that there were Turkish spies everywhere also, whether they were Anatolian, Bulgarian, Serbian, or Wallachian.

My company gained half a day and then a full day and soon we were one company out a day ahead of the mercenaries and the Wallachians a day behind them. It was no simple thing to cross from the plains of Wallachia into Serbia and the hills and valleys between the two seemed endless. It was a sparsely populated land but our guides knew their business and every day we rose early and stopped late. It was gruelling travel, especially for my mortal servants, but I dared not miss the battle. There was no doubt in my mind that William would be there and God alone knew what atrocities he could commit with his red-robed immortals. We could not face him directly, not yet, but we could not abandon our allies to face them alone, either.

Once we dropped down from the hills into the long, north-south valleys of Serbia, the going was far easier. We headed north, toward the Danube again, before crossing three wide, fertile plains as we headed west once more.

I grew up in hill country but where Derbyshire was rounded and filled with bright, verdant greens, and the rocks were warm, soft limestone and sandstone, Serbia was a land of all dark greens and the stone was jagged, hard and harsh, in deep greys and red-browns, and the soil thin and black. It seemed nowhere in the entire land was flat, other than their three valleys in the northeast, even as we followed the Danube for the final leg of the journey to the massive city that was our destination and our great hope for stopping the relentless advance of the Turks.

Belgrade was a Hungarian possession, but it remained to all intents a Serbian city. And the Serbs had, for once, decided to defy their Turkish overlords and were intent on defending the city. Indeed, they must have known that once Belgrade fell, there would be no Serbia left to resist the Turks at all.

The local Serbian population around the city had added to the number of defenders within it and the land all around had been well prepared by them for the siege. Defences had been dug, erected, and extended and fields of fire cleared for the cannons and gunners on the walls and towers. Indeed, Hunyadi had been lavishing vast sums on enhancing the defences at least since I had arrived in the region more than ten years earlier. But recently there had been a final surge in effort and the locals had been building the walls higher and stronger for months. Anything edible had been removed from the enemy's line of march, all the water sources poisoned, and bridges destroyed. It would not stop the Turks but it would not help them, either.

"Come on," I said every morning to my tired and aching men, "just a little further." Our guides were eager to get us into Serbia and they ranged ahead every day to ensure the way was clear. When we reached the city, they came back and urged me to bring just a small party ahead to see for ourselves what awaited us.

Belgrade sat nestled between the River Sava where it ran into the Danube and as we approached the peak of the highest point a few miles from the city, we were awed by the scale of the fortress on the horizon.

And yet the triple-walled fortress city was not what stilled our tongues. We had been avoiding Turkish patrols in the hills for days before we arrived and dreaded what we would find as we crept through the long grass to the top of a ridge.

"We are too late," Stephen muttered, looking out at the city close to the horizon where it sat at the confluence of two great rivers.

"Damn the bastards," Walt hissed.

The army of the Turks was arrayed before Belgrade, encamped in an arc completely cutting them off. Tens of thousands of soldiers, horses, and great artillery pieces, already intent on reducing the outer limit of the fortifications. On the wide Danube, an enormous Turkish fleet swarmed the waters. The tributary Sava River looked clear of Turkish vessels but still the city was close to being cut off. More wagons and groups of riders trailed from the south up to the camp, bringing supplies and more men.

Though camp fires burned in the Turkish camps and lines and lines of trenches and earthworks were thrown up between the army and the city, the walls were intact and there was no fighting going on.

"The city is untouched," I said. "We cannot have missed much."

Walt scowled. "How are we going to get in past that lot?"

Stephen laughed. "Well, I think it is clear that we shall not do so, Walt."

"What, then?" Walt said. "We going back to Wallachia?"

"William is down there," I said. "And the Sultan, too, do you see his banner there in the centre camp? His vast tents below them. We will not flee."

"Shall we camp in the hills, then?" Rob asked. "Sit and watch from afar, shall we? Move in when the fighting starts?"

"Patrols will find us before then," Walt said. "It'll take the Turks months to get in there. Look at the walls, by God. We should go north, cross the Danube, go into Hungary and back to Buda. I bet our good Regent is yet building his army, don't you? Reckon we should join it."

I scanned the river beyond, where it curled away into the horizon. There were no allied ships to be seen and no army on the banks. "Listen, Hunyadi knows just as well as anyone that a city, even one as well-fortified as this one, cannot resist these new cannons for long. Weeks or a month, perhaps. But they will blast away at the walls, like at Constantinople, and they will break through. Not in months but weeks and perhaps even days. Look how many cannons there are. A hundred? Three hundred?" They looked at me, waiting for the good news. "And that is why he was building an army which can bring the Turk to battle before that occurs."

Walt held his hand out to the scene before us. "And where is this army?"

"He will come now, right away. He will be here any day. Tomorrow. Soon. He knows he cannot leave Belgrade to its fate and so he will come. He has to."

"Remember that old Cardinal?" Rob said. "The one preaching for a crusade in Hungary before we left, commanding Christians to take up arms and come to the defence of the city."

"John of Capistrano," Eva said.

"That's the fellow. Perhaps they are coming also?"

I shook my head. "The only men who listened were peasants. They started assembling in southern Hungary but they had nought but slings and clubs, for God's sake. What do you think they will do against the Janissaries?"

Rob shrugged. "Better than nothing."

"Hunyadi is coming with the soldiers of Hungary but he is coming from the other side of the city. The other side of the siege, beyond the Sava. We must do two things. First, send word back to the mercenaries behind us and Wallachians behind them that if they come this way they will be seen due to their great numbers, and then they will be chased down by thousands of sipahis and defeated in a pointless battle. Secondly, once our message is sent, we must cross the Sava and join with Hunyadi's approaching army."

"Why not join the mercenaries behind us?" Stephen said. "There are thousands of them and we would be safer in numbers if we force a crossing of the tributary."

"A small company like us can evade notice. Even if we are seen, no one will be overly concerned. If we are a force of a thousand or more, we will find ourselves run down by entire divisions of Turks. Their only hope of joining the battle is going around for miles or waiting in the east. It is up to them."

"They'll run," Walt predicted. "They'll just run."

"Perhaps we should, too," Stephen said. "This is too much. Too much."

"It would do us no harm to take a few days to ride around," Eva said.

"Longer we wait, the more dug in they'll be," Rob said. "Less chance of getting in at all."

"And I will say it again," Stephen snapped. "We need not fight every battle, especially when we are so likely to lose. William and the damned immortal Janissaries are there, I understand that. But approaching the city in these circumstances seems foolhardy at best."

Walt shrugged. "Might be all right."

"It is suicide!" Stephen said. "If we had any sense at all, we would flee and find another place to defend."

"After Belgrade," I said, "it will be Buda. After pacifying Hungary, it will be Vienna. And then where? Prague? Venice? If Venice, then Rome? We will not run. We will do our duty." I pointed due west across the rear of the great Turkish camps with their hundred thousand soldiers and tens of thousands of horses and servants spread across the plain. "We make our way there, to the banks of the Sava."

***

We reached the Sava a few miles upstream from the city in the night, at a place where the tributary curved into a great bow shape. Our guides had made contact with Serbian spies, and they assured us there would be Hungarian forces ready to ferry us across. I did not know what to expect but we moved across the Turk's line of retreat to the water's edge as dusk fell. Enemy horsemen roamed the countryside all around and we were certainly spotted more than once but we moved quickly and were not challenged directly. No doubt, they assumed we were allies or too small an enemy force to be concerned with.

"We're in danger," Walt muttered as we huddled in the orchard on the outskirts of an abandoned village for our guides to return. "Sat here like a bag of plums, ain't we."

The residents had likely fled into the city days or weeks before the first Turks arrived and they or the enemy had later burned half of it to the ground for good measure. The obvious thing would have been to take shelter in the ruins but I did not like my men to be so confined, should enemy cavalry find us. The banks of the river were a stone's throw away and our position was sheltered by a rise on the landward side and I had positioned a few men up there to keep watch, and at our rear. Others kept an eye on the waters for the approach of the ships that would collect us. Our horses were nipping at the grass on the ground beneath the apple trees.

"The men are ready to repel an attack," I said. "And we shall be across the river before dawn."

"Balls, we will," Walt muttered. "We'll be sat here with our arses wet when the sun rises and an army of Turks is coming over that ridge down onto us."

"Then we will fight our way clear. Or we will die. What has got your gizzard, Walter?"

"Don't mind him, Richard," Rob said. "He wagered Serban we would make it inside the city before the Turks arrived."

"I would have thought you would welcome a quick death then, Walt, rather than part with your silver."

"We've been abandoned," Walt said. "Our damned guides have led us here and fled. Probably found a tub and rowed across to save themselves. Lying bastards, I'll skin them alive when I find them."

"They have not let us down so far." I raised my voice just a little. "Serban?"

"My lord?" he said, shuffling over.

"Do you trust our guides?"

He scratched his weathered face. "They are Serbians. They can be trusted only so far."

Walt scoffed. "There, you hear that? We have to run, now. Head south and see what's what."

"We shall wait."

As the night drew on, I could not contain my own fears. In frustration, I went out on foot toward the river to see what was happening. The moon's light was shaded by wisps of cloud and the wind whistled in my ears. The river was far wider than it had seemed at a distance, when I could compare it to the mighty Danube. Half of me had expected to be able to swim in, with our horses, should the boats not come, but looking at it close up I knew we would never make it across. Not even those of us who knew how to swim. Somewhere downstream along the bank, a grebe chattered its frantic, warbling trill and then a loon gave its long, mournful, two-tone wail. Further away, the loon's mate gave it's answering call which echoed across the water. It was eerie and unusual to hear them in the dead of night. I wondered if someone had disturbed them.

"You are afraid," Eva said, from just behind my shoulder, startling me.

"Good God, Eva," I snapped. "I am when you are creeping about like a bloody wraith, woman."

"You are deciding whether to wait longer or to take the men away."

"Walt is right," I said. "Being here at sunrise is too great a risk. It is a wide river but perhaps there is a ford upstream."

"The Sultan is five miles downstream."

"Closer than that, even."

"And William is very likely with him."

"With tens of thousands of soldiers and five hundred immortals guarding him, so do not suggest we attempt to steal through their ranks to slit William's throat. Believe me, Eva, if I thought it was possible, we would be attempting it."

"I was not going to suggest it. All I suggest is that perhaps your mind is focused upon your brother instead of the battle ahead."

"What do you mean?"

"The city is encircled by land and almost closed off by river. And you said it yourself, the Sultan has hundreds of cannon. Hundreds. Have you ever seen so many before? There are more here than at Constantinople, are there not? The city is doomed. And where is Hunyadi? Where are the Hungarians? Not even the crusader army of peasants has come."

"Hunyadi will be here."

"You like him as a man," Eva said. "You like him as a fellow old soldier."

"Speak plainly. You believe my judgement is clouded where Hunyadi is concerned? He has faced the Turks a hundred times and defeated them more times than he has lost. Who else can say such a thing?"

"He has done well. But he is old, now. His sons are taking their own commands. Hunyadi's losses have taken the shine off the man and the lords of Hungary, who have always been jealous, are asking what comes next."

I turned from the river and looked at her. "You think he will not come."

"Already at Easter, the Hungarian lords were refusing to answer his summons. You said it yourself, all the crusade could recruit was useless peasants. You must consider the fact that Hunyadi may not have an army to bring."

"He will come," I said. "Alone if he has to."

She did not reply. The loons had fallen silent and splashed out onto the dark river. Only the grebe still chattered, as if it was as nervous as I was.

"What would you have us do?" I asked.

"As you said. Go upstream, find a ford and head north until we can cross the Danube into Hungary."

"Abandon Belgrade?"

"Only so we may fight another day."

"You and Stephen are both pragmatic to a fault. Our Christian duty is to defend Christian lands from the infidel."

"Our duty is to defeat William. Our oath is to accomplish what no one else can."

"Perhaps—" I broke off at the sound of a large splash, staring out at the water and straining to hear it again. Whether it was a large fish jumping or a bird landing or something else, I could not say.

Eva said nothing, listening also.

Rob approached quickly, wading through the rustling tall grass behind me. "Riders approach," he hissed. "Heading into the village."

"Turks? How many?"

"Anatolian light horse," Rob whispered. "Two score, perhaps."

"We could kill them," Eva said. "And flee south."

"Not before some escaped and then we would be in a fighting retreat, looking for a ford and—"

I heard it again, only this time I was certain that it was not an animal.

"What is it?" Walt asked.

"Water slapping on wood," I said. "Oars. A boat. Something. What can you see?"

They both peered out at the river, their eyes far better than mine at seeing into the darkness.

"It is boats," Eva whispered. "Galleys, heading for the bank. For the landing stage by the village."

"Ours? Or Turks?"

"I do not know."

Leading them back quickly to the rest of the men, I called Walt, Stephen, and Serban to join us.

"Turks in the village," I whispered. "Galleys coming to pick us up from there."

Eva and Rob shot me looks but I ignored them. We would have to assume the ships were meant for us rather than for the Turks. And if they were not, perhaps we would have to kill the crew and row ourselves across. Sometimes one simply has to act decisively and push through.

"Walt, take your half of the men around to the north. Rob, take your half to the edge here. Our cry shall be Belgrade. Let our boats know who we are, yes? Do not pursue any riders that flee. All that matters is that we board the galleys and get across the river. Questions?"

We mounted in the orchard and got our horses lined up ready to attack. The Anatolian's campfires in the ruined village suggested they were simply looking for a place to wait out their night patrol and I hoped that meant they were unprepared to defend themselves. I was determined to wait until Walt got his men in position on the far side of the village but it was impossible for so many men and horses to move in silence and the Turks were alerted to our approach.

A voice cried out a query.

"Hold the men until Walt attacks," I ordered Rob and kicked my horse forward. "Be ready."

"Good evening," I called out in a friendly tone in my best Arabic. "Peace be upon you!"

The closest man on watch shouted back in Turkish. Another man further away called a query and the guard rattled off something in reply.

"Do you speak Arabic?" I called, riding slowly forward into the space between two burned houses. Their roofs had burned away but the walls were solid. I was sure they could not see me very well out in the darkness.

The guard shouted something back and I caught both the surprised tone and the word *Arabiyah*.

"Yes, friends, I am a peaceful and humble merchant from Damascus. Could I share some of your food?" I asked, politely, riding my horse at a slow walk forward.

He came forward, drawing his sword and two more men hurried behind him both bearing their lances.

"You should tell your men that they should not be seated around staring into the fire in that manner," I said, keeping up my friendly tone. "They will not be able to see a thing when we attack."

They shouted at me to stop and I whipped out my sword and roared at them. "Belgrade!"

Raking my spurs to startle my tired horse into action, I charged into the first man, knocking him down. One of the two men froze in shock but the other rushed at me with his lance up and thrust it at my chest. I twisted and leaned in the saddle, the point missing me by an inch, and I cut the other man across the face, spilling his blood and drawing from him a terrific wail. I rode on into the centre of the village, shouting and slashing at anyone I came near, then I rode on through toward the river to draw some after me.

A great cry of *Belgrade!* went up as Walt's twenty-odd men attacked from the north and Rob's company came up behind me, shouting the name of the city.

We made short work of them, and Walt had found their horses before he attacked and so none got away. Still, we had raised an awful cry into the pre-dawn night and all suspected the enemy would be coming to investigate before long.

I hurried to the landing stage where the first galley waited. One of our Serbian guides jumped out and came forward, waving and grinning, very pleased with himself.

"Give him some silver, Stephen," I said, as the man beside him began speaking rapidly in Hungarian. "Give him a lot of silver."

"Come, you must come now, now!" he said. "Now, my lord. Before it is too late."

"We shall do just that," I said. "Where is the army? Where is Hunyadi."

"Coming, coming," the boatman said. "Yes, he is coming."

"When?"

"Soon, soon. Come, you must come. You are fifty men, yes?"

"With servants we are over a hundred," I replied.

He almost swooned, crossing himself repeatedly. "No, no, it cannot be done."

"It will be done. Do it well, and there is silver in it for you."

He eyed me, looking me up and down in the darkness. "You must hurry, we will have to use four boats."

"How many horses can you bring across?"

The man was horrified. "No, no, no. It cannot be. Men, yes. Horses, no."

"Get the men across first and then we will bring as many horses as we can."

"No!" he snapped. "Horses take too long. The Turks will shoot us from the banks. We must away."

"Just six horses then," I said. "I will pay much more."

He crossed his arms and stared at me. "No horses. Not one. You come now, come, come. Just men. Come."

We crossed in five boats, a score of men to each one with our gear piled in amongst us as the sun came up. I waited until the last so I could be certain that all would escape and said farewell to my fine horse.

"Hurry," Stephen said. "Leave the beast be."

"What a fine fellow you are," I said softly, holding his chestnut head in my hands and looking into one of his big, dark eyes. "You crossed mountains without complaint and you always fought well. You never hesitated and did everything I asked of you. I hope that your next master treats you well."

"Perhaps we should kill them?" Stephen said, behind me. "So that the Turks cannot make use them against us."

I turned and stared at him. "Get in the boat, Stephen."

By the time the sun came up, we were out on the river being rowed rapidly downstream toward the city. The galleys were part of a small fleet that yet plied the River Sava, though the Turks had two hundred warships on the Danube. Their fleet nestled behind an island in the mouth of the tributary where it flowed into the massive Danube. Commanding them was a lord I knew named Osvát and he had me brought across to his ship to speak to him. The walls of the castle and city were across the channel to the east and the smoke from the cannons and the campfires filled the air, along with the smell of a summer siege. The cannons sounded continually since dawn, unseen on the opposite side of the city.

"I doubted it was true," he said, taking my hand. "And yet here you are. How did you get by the Turks, Richard?"

"A handful of Serbians have guided us since we crossed the mountains and they helped us reach the river."

"My men believed they were lying and even I thought they must have been mistaken. Is it true you brought thousands of Wallachians with you? Where are they?"

"I expect they went back to Wallachia. There is no way through for a sizeable force and if they had stayed, they would have been destroyed. It is just us."

His face was grim. "Every man will make a difference. We are so low on soldiers. Did you make out their number from the east?"

"Perhaps ninety thousand. Rumelians on the Danube, Anatolians against the Sava there, and Janissaries and the Sultan's camp in the centre. Light horse on the flanks and rear but it seemed as though he has brought mostly infantry this time, in addition to the Janissaries, of which there were perhaps ten thousand."

He sighed. "That is what we have heard. Did you see the cannon?"

"If I had not seen them, I would not have believed it. We counted as many as three hundred, if you can believe it. And a great smoking workshop at the rear churning out smoke and casting even more cannon."

His face was ashen. "I have been praying that the Serbians were exaggerating the number. Three hundred cannon. Even those mighty walls will not stand such an assault for long."

"What of the Sultan's fleet?" I asked. "There were hundreds of ships but they were upstream, beyond the mouth of the Sava in the Danube."

"They are there to block reinforcements and supplies coming from Hungary to the city." He shook his head. "Turks with two hundred war galleys. Can you believe it?"

"And Hunyadi?" I asked. "He is coming?"

Osvát hesitated before answering, turning to look northwest as if he might see that very thing. When he spoke, his voice was sharp. "He is coming. We have had word. Hunyadi is coming."

"And yet you sound embittered, my lord."

He leaned on the side rail and spoke without turning. "They have abandoned him. Our great lords have not come. Our kingdom is on the eve of a terrible disaster, for neither with our own resources nor with the aid of the mercenaries we have engaged can we bring enough forces to cope with the Turk. Our only hope is that God will listen to our prayers and move the hearts of our treacherous princes to bring their fleets and men. And yet so pressing is our peril that the delay of a day or even an hour may bring about such a defeat as shall make all Christendom weep for evermore."

"What of the crusaders?" I asked. "Led by Cardinal John of Capistrano?"

"They came down the Danube to meet Hunyadi. Ten thousand at least, camped miles up there with the Regent."

"Well, that is something to thank Christ for."

"Common men with sticks? There are thousands of them but what can they do? Even if they get into the city, all they can do is fetch water and rebuild walls and so on but as for fighting the Turks..." he trailed off.

We watched the horizon. "How is it that you are still here? You must have over twenty boats here."

"Forty," he said, smiling. "I have forty boats, most small but some as you see. The others are hidden in bays around the island, or pulled up on shore and some are patrolling, keeping watch. Yes, forty boats, thanks to Christ."

"But how has the Turkish fleet not assaulted you?"

"They do not wish to come under the guns on the walls. And I do not believe they know how many we are. We are hidden here behind the island. If they knew what a threat we were to their fleet, they would perhaps chance it."

"Well, then, I thank you for sending the galleys to pick us up. It was a risk to you. But can you now transport us to the opposite bank? I would like to take my men along the south bank of the Danube, find Hunyadi's army and join it for their assault on the enemy."

He turned, surprised. "The Turkish fleet holds the river and they have men on the banks, also. You will not make it through by land or by river. Hunyadi cannot bring his army by river, due to the Turkish blockade upstream."

"So he will march along the banks, to the Sava?" I said.

"And then I am to ferry them across. As many as I can before we are destroyed by the enemy fleet. I will get Hunyadi across at the least, if it is the last thing I do. With his leadership to inspire the men inside the walls, perhaps we will have a chance."

"You can get him inside the city?"

Osvát pointed to a landing stage at the base of the wall, right at the river. Large enough for three galleys to moor against at once, there was a short stair up to a small postern gate. "I can take your men across now, if you like."

There was no point in trapping my men further inside a doomed city. "No," I said. "With your permission, my men will serve on your fleet until Hunyadi arrives."

And if he does not, we shall have to flee.

"Glad to have you," Osvát said. "But if the city falls first, I am to evacuate as many as I can to the far bank. I shall have to disembark your men there first. Perhaps you can help escort them to Hungary?" He crossed himself. "But God will not allow that. Hunyadi will come. By one way or by another, Hunyadi will come." Osvát crossed himself again.

I hung my head. Through my own recklessness, I had brought my company, all of the Order of the White Dagger, into a trap from which there might be no escape.

***

For two days, my company was distributed amongst the fleet where we manned the boats and we all waited anxiously for word of Hunyadi's army. As subtly as we could, my immortals consumed the blood of their servants without any of Osvát's men noticing. If they did, they said nothing about it. Perhaps they had bigger concerns. The cannons never ceased their firing and it seemed certain that Belgrade would be assaulted on the far side of the city at any moment. Smoke from fires and cannons and guns drifted over the walls and across the waters and birds wheeled overhead. What they made of it all, I could only wonder.

"I have been thinking," I muttered to Eva at the rail, leaning close to her. Like all of us, she stayed in her armour all day and she stank just as much as I did.

"Then times are desperate indeed," she quipped, looking across the Sava to the northwest, where we hoped every hour to see sign of Hunyadi's army.

"I have been thinking about your suggestion to sneak into William's tent at night and there assassinate him."

"Richard, I suggested no such thing. That was your notion, not mine."

"Well, whoever suggested it, I think the time has come to—"

"Wait," she said, grabbing my vambrace. "Christian riders."

From the opposite bank of the Sava, those riders pushed through the long grass and reeds to the water's edge and signalled to our fleet. Boats were sent to bring the men across to the island and finally to Osvát's boat. I made certain I was present when the message was delivered.

"My lord comes with every boat and every man that he can find," the messenger said, a fair Hungarian youth with ruddy cheeks and fluff on his cheeks. "When he attacks the Turkish fleet, he asks that you bring your fleet to attack their rear."

"Your lord?" I said. "Hunyadi?"

The messenger bowed. "Indeed, sir."

I looked at Osvát, who seemed astonished. "Hunyadi is going to attack the Turkish war galleys? By Almighty Christ. How many boats does he have?"

"Almost two hundred, my lord."

Excited, I could not hold my tongue. "That is as many as the Turks have, is it not?"

Osvát nodded but he turned to the messenger. "What manner of boats are these? They cannot all be warships?"

The young man's cheeks coloured, as if he were personally embarrassed. "Crafts of many kinds, my lord. Transports, galleys..." he trailed off. "Fishing vessels. Many kinds."

"Dear Christ," Osvát said, crossing himself.

"And the army is on the ships and we will fight our way through but there is also the army of the crusaders," the messenger said. "Lead by Cardinal John of Capistrano. They come in a great body of many thousands, keeping pace with the fleet as best they can."

"Many thousands of peasants with sharp sticks?" I said. "Just what we need."

The young man was offended by my cynicism. "They have taken the cross to fight for Christ, sir, and they are filled with His strength."

I bowed to the fellow. "I am sure they are."

Osvát nodded to himself, looking out at the waters. "Are you and your men to return?"

He shook his fair locks. "We barely made it through the Turkish patrols on our way here. Besides, there is no time. He comes now, my lord. We are to join you for the battle, sirs, if you will honour us so."

"No time? When will he assault the Turkish fleet?"

"Today, my lord."

Osvát, to his credit, smiled and took the young fellow's hand for a moment before turning to issue a stream of commands. Boats skirted off in all directions, taking messengers to the city and to other vessels in the fleet.

"I will drop you on the far shore, if you wish it," Osvát said. "So that you can go out to meet the force by land. Or I could send you into the city, perhaps, if there is time. But I would rather have your men fighting in my ships."

More than anything, I hated boats. I hated the sea most of all, with its impossibly high waves and the motion of the boats in it. But the Danube was a river like few others. As wide as a lake and endlessly long. Fighting on boats was as brutal and bloody a battle as one might find. Then again, I had done it before.

"Certainly, we shall join you."

Osvát stepped closer and lowered his voice. "We shall fight with all we are worth but it is likely that we shall fail to destroy their fleet and we will have to withdraw. But I mean to make a hole big enough, for long enough, for as much of Hunyadi's army as is possible to reach the city. If we can draw the Turks close to the city, perhaps they will break off and flee. Do you see?"

Damn. I wished I had thought about offering my services before knowing the plan.

"Very well. We shall do what we need to. I would fight with my closest men beside me, if you will send me to their galley."

"We will bring them here, no more than a dozen, and you will fight with me." Osvát grinned. "I have seen you and your men in battle."

It was not midday when the fighting started. Hunyadi's makeshift fleet came down the Danube flying flags and banging drums.

The Turkish fleet manoeuvred to face them and we edged out through the channel into the Danube behind them, trapping the enemy's war galleys between Hunyadi's larger, makeshift fleet and our smaller, well-equipped one of forty ships crewed with Hungarians and Serbians.

"You look unhappy, Serban," I said to him as we approached the enemy.

"I do not swim," he said.

"Then do not fall in," I said, and clapped him hard on the back. "Have you fought on ships before?"

"No," he admitted, shielding his eyes from the sun and pulling his hat down.

"The most important thing above all else is to keep your feet. Stay away from the sides as much as you can," I advised. "Remember that boats move, sometimes drastically, even when they seem stable. And the decks are slippery, especially when the blood starts to be spilled. If you fall, roll away and keep moving as best you can. We will stay together, all of us, and fight as one."

Rob elbowed him. "Stick with me, Serban. I'll keep an eye out for you."

Serban glanced at Rob's stump and attempted to smile in thanks.

Our rowers heaved for all they were worth and the ships with sails made the most of the diagonal crosswinds. Still, it took us a long time to join the battle that had by that time already been raging for hours. As we approached the sound of guns firing grew and the shouting of the crews and soldiers filled the air. Arrows streamed in all directions and small cannons on the boats fired at each other.

It was like heading into hell.

Hunyadi's fleet may have been thrown together but there were some magnificent vessels that were a part of it. His flagship was the biggest of all the ships on the river by far and it poured fire from hand-gunners into the enemies on all sides. His ships were filled to the rails with archers, hand-gunners, and soldiers armed with pikes and halberds and axes but it was not his entire force.

On the southern bank were ten thousand men or more in a great swirling mass. I recognised banners from Transylvania that I knew belonged to horsemen. But most of the men were the peasant crusaders I had heard about, armed with slings, hunting bows, threshers and probably sharpened hoes and pointed sticks. They massed on the banks and shot arrows and slung stones and shot at the Turkish ships that came close to shore.

"The Turks are outmatched!" Osvát shouted in my ear as we approached, grasping my arm and shaking me. He turned to his crew. "Signal the fleet to spread out. We can trap them all. Kill them all. Let none escape! Christ be praised, the Turks are outmatched."

Their ships were pushed aside by ours and many were forced hard against the banks. There, the crusaders swarmed them and slaughtered them. One was swiftly set on fire and it went up like a demonic candle, burning hot and bright.

Osvát steered our ship into another galley that attempted to flee and crashed into it hard enough to throw us onto our knees. The Turkish galley was stuck with arrows and the side was covered in charred timber and soot where a fire had been put out. Wounded men lay in the bottom of it already but when our hulls ground against each other, they seemed keen enough for a fight.

"With me!" I shouted and led my companions across and down into their galley. My men made short work of the enemy and soon we got back on board our own vessel and looked for more prey.

Osvát cheered us and even Serban had a smile on his face.

We captured or destroyed at least a hundred and fifty of their fleet. By the end, they were burning their own immobilised ships before abandoning them so they would not fall into our hands. The remaining handful fled downstream, being peppered with shots from the walls and towers of Belgrade as they went.

The battle lasted many hours and the men were exhausted but were buoyed by the elation that victory brings. The way was clear now for Hunyadi's army to be ferried into the city by the docks on the Sava side, protected from the Sultan's army by the walls and mass of the city itself.

It was a relief of sorts to see my company through the postern gate and finally into Belgrade, where we had hoped to be for so many days.

And yet even while the river battle raged, the enemy cannon had not ceased their bombardment and we knew we would soon have another fight on our hands.

This time it would be a fight to save the city itself.

***

A week after the river battle and the outer walls of Belgrade were crumbling.

Our cannons would fire out at the Turks as often as they could, hoping to destroy an enemy cannon but often as not hitting Turkish earthworks or ploughing a useless furrow into the mud. There had been a giddy moment of joy days earlier when a cannon on the city's easternmost tower shot and killed the Beylerbey of Rumelia, striking him down, killing him, his horse and at least two of his servants. The damned fool had been inspecting the front lines of the siege within range of our guns, in broad daylight, flying his banners and gesticulating toward us as he no doubt propounded to his men on how the city would fall. It was a lucky shot, to be sure, but many in the city took it to be a sign from God and who was I to argue with that?

We certainly needed the victory, no matter how small it was. The city was as well prepared for a siege as it was possible to be. Indeed, it had been preparing for over a decade, for it was no secret that it would be so assaulted, and there were supplies enough to last months, even with twenty thousand extra mouths to feed with the arrival of Hunyadi's army and the crusaders. And with the river cleared, it meant more supplies could be brought in at will along with reinforcements. We knew we could therefore survive a siege indefinitely.

And the Sultan would know it, too.

The only way he could take Belgrade now was by direct assault and so we waited, day after day, night after night. Waited for the sudden assault by tens of thousands of veteran infantry on the outer walls of the city. The repairs on both the outer and inner curtain walls went on ceaselessly. Every breach was filled with rubble and shorn up by enormous timbers. When these were blown apart, they were built back up again, stronger than before.

"I made a mistake," I admitted to Eva as we stood on the steps of a church and watched the repairs from a distance, the air filled with smoke and dust and the shouts of the men rebuilding and the ringing of mallets and hammers. "I should never have brought us here. Especially after Constantinople. I have trapped us once more."

"Your reasoning was not faulty," she said. "But I sometimes do wonder..."

"What do you wonder?"

"You often make it so that you will have an impossible victory or death. When instead you would do better to wait and pick another battle. What is it to the likes of us if Hungary falls? Might we not in our long lives see a dozen kingdoms fall and another dozen rise in their place?"

"You sound like Priskos. As if mortal matters mean nothing."

"Not nothing. And yet we are so much more than they." She jerked her chin at the men toiling at the walls. The streets near the landward walls of the city were where the crusaders had been quartered, packed in with a dozen in each room and others sleeping huddled on the streets. Some were active in helping with the repairs while others seemed to do little but pray, while others lay slumped in alleys, drunk or sick. Our holy army.

"It is easy to feel contempt for the smallness of their lives," I said. "At the same time, I feel less than they are. They are natural, living, dying. Raising sons and daughters. While we... endure."

She lowered her voice and glanced around. "It is not too late to flee. We could go through the castle, down to the river. Take a boat."

"We cannot."

"No," she admitted. "No, we cannot."

The next day, in the full light of day, the enemy broke through,

The Turks assembled in their tens of thousands and charged the walls in waves. Our brave garrison poured down fire from cannon and the hand-gunners and crossbowmen shot as quickly as they could, and arrows flew into the advancing men but still they came on and assaulted the high breaches and the gates with ladders and ropes while others behind them shot back at our men on the battlements.

"We must stay out of it for as long as possible," I said to my company in our quarters near to the castle. "The mortals must do their work at the walls. We must save ourselves, where we can, for our true enemy."

Claudin raised his hand. "We will look like cowards, no?"

"No. We will stay close to Hunyadi and the other commanders. We must have patience. There will be fighting enough for all of us before all is said and done here. Now, bleed your servants and drink while you can."

Late in the day, the Turks breached the outer walls. The garrison and the mass of crusaders fell back in panic while the professional soldiers attempted to stem the tide in every street and courtyard. But the blind retreat was unstoppable. They swarmed by our position in their hundreds and ran across the drawbridge into the inner fortress where they hoped to be safe. And yet that drawbridge could not be closed before the pursuing Turks reached it. The Janissaries swarmed over the drawbridge into the fortress courtyard and they began slaughtering the crusaders, militia, and soldiers inside.

By the time we rushed to the fortress, the streets were so packed with panicked peasants that we could not get close to the enemies that had broken through.

"We are close to disaster!" Stephen shouted at me. "What do we do, Richard?"

"Guard this position," I commanded my men. "Walt, with me."

I pushed forward through the bodyguards and lords crowding Hunyadi, meaning to discover what his plan was. If something drastic was not done, the city would be taken before sunrise the next day.

"We must secure the city walls," one of the lords shouted at Hunyadi.

"Yes," another cried. "We must assault the walls, my lord!"

"No," he shouted. "The Janissaries are enclosed within the inner fortress. We attack their rear, trap them within our fortress, and kill them to a man. They are the Sultan's best troops and we shall slaughter them all, then retake our outer walls. All of you, with me. Bring every man you can. God be with us."

I pushed back to my company and told them that we do as Hunyadi commanded.

"Are they the red bastards?" Garcia asked. "These Janissaries?"

"If they are, we will kill them."

We rushed through the panicked streets to the inner fortress, where there were so many Turkish infantry and white-robed Janissaries that they could not all fit inside the fortress and instead massed on the drawbridge, as if waiting their turn to kill our men. Our assault on their rear took them by surprise and they had no room to manoeuvre. Hunyadi's men killed them, cutting them down and stepping forward and killing the next man and the next but the approach to the fortress was so dense with enemies and they could not fly through them with ease. The flagstones underfoot ran slick with blood and the air was filled with the smell of it, along with the screams and shouts of the dying Turks.

Holding my company back behind the Hungarians, we finished off any survivors that writhed on the floor.

"No immortals!" Claudin shouted.

"Quiet, you fool," Walt snapped at him.

Soon, Hunyadi's men reached the edge of the drawbridge, slaughtering the men who stood shoulder to shoulder now. Beyond the drawbridge, still thousands more Janissaries attacked our men.

"Damn the bastards for this," I muttered, feeling a desire to throw myself at them.

"A fire!" someone shouted. "They set a fire!"

Smoke billowed up beneath the men on the bridge and then the yellow flames flickered behind and amongst the Janissaries.

"What is happening?" Rob asked.

"The Turks have fired the drawbridge," I said, raising my voice so my men and allies could hear.

"But they have cut off their means of escape," Jan said.

"And they kill their own men who stand on the bridge," Rob said.

The fires grew and many of the Janissaries on the bridge jumped thirty feet down into the dry moat below, breaking their legs and trapping themselves.

"They are burning the bridge so that we cannot save our people within. They trust their reinforcements outside the walls to come in and take the city."

"There is no other way into the fortress, now," Stephen said.

"Aye," Walt said. "Best go to the outer walls instead, Richard?"

"Wait," I said. "The entrance from the river into the city comes up through the fortress."

"From the boats?" Stephen said. "That is all very well but how do we get out of the city and reach the river in order to come in through the back door?"

"We shall fight our way clear of the city walls and get down to the river," I replied. "The defenders within the fortress will hold out long enough for us to do so and—"

"Richard!" Eva said, grabbing me by the armour and yanking me around to face her. Her eyes were wide and angry. "You do not have to do everything yourself. You said the mortals must do their work and we must save ourselves for our true enemy. So tell Hunyadi. He has thousands of men."

"Yes, yes," I said. "But can anyone do the job but us?"

She pulled my arm and shook it. "And when William's red Janissaries come marching through the streets, who here can do the job of stopping them?"

"Damn you, woman," I said. "Where is Hunyadi?"

It was a fight just to get close to the man but when I suggested he send a message to the fleet to assault the fortress from the Sava, he cut me off and began issuing orders for that very thing. Six lords or knights were given the task, along with their retinues and companies, to reach the river by different directions so that one at least would get through.

As they made off, Hunyadi glanced at me. "Something else, Richard?"

His helm was off and his cap beneath was soaked with sweat. Hunyadi looked old, the light of torches, lanterns, and the fire of the burning bridge picking out the deep lines in his grey face.

"Have the red Janissaries been sighted, my lord?" I asked. "Or the banner of Zaganos Pasha?"

He shook his head. "Ask Michael," he said, jerking his head and turning to command his men for the defence of the city.

Pushing through the soldiers, I made my way toward the banner of Michael Szilágyi, the commander of the fortress of Belgrade, a great lord, and the brother of Hunyadi's wife.

"My lord," I said, raising my voice and interrupting the knights speaking to him. "My lord, have the red Janissaries been seen within the walls?"

"Richard?" he looked me up and down. "Last I heard, the red-robed bastards are yet beyond both walls, outside the breaches, guarding the Sultan. I doubt we shall see them anywhere that the Sultan is not. Where is your company?"

"With me."

"The Turks are within the city walls but they have not broken through everywhere. We are holding them in every quarter. If we act *now*, we can get behind them and trap them inside before we slaughter them. I will take my men along the Danube wall before attacking their flank. Will you join us?"

If William's immortals were beyond the breaches, we would do well to keep them there lest they slaughter their way to victory. And Szilágyi's flanking attack would take me close to the red Janissaries' position.

"It would be an honour, my lord."

Szilágyi was a good leader and a competent commander. His lords liked him and the men trusted him and so when he marched off for the walls, he drew hundreds along behind him. A more cautious man would have waited until more precise orders were given and until more men had assembled, but there are times for caution and there are times to throw oneself into danger.

Our numbers overwhelmed the Rumelian infantry on the northern flank and we pushed on through the streets, spreading out where we could. The fighting at each juncture was hard but brief, and the Turks fled, in one company after another. It soon seemed that the battle had swung in our favour, for our men were filled with vigour and high spirits and the Rumelians and Anatolians were crumbling, their morale shattered. No soldier likes to find his enemy has gotten behind him but the Turks were taking to their heels before we could even reach them.

"Is it a ruse?" Stephen asked beside me after catching his breath. We watched two hundred well-armoured Rumelian soldiers pushing each other aside in an effort to get back to the breach in the outer wall. "Will our men be trapped and counter-attacked?"

"Perhaps," I said. "But it is difficult for ordinary soldiers to feign fear so effectively. They expected no resistance. They believed that breaking into the city would be like Constantinople all over again, and all the fighting they would need to do would be over wine jugs and women. Our resistance broke their spirit."

"The Red Janissaries have not yet engaged?"

"That seems to be the case."

"Why would he not throw them in now and push on to victory?"

"Even immortals can be killed, especially in narrow streets. Anyway, tonight's battle for the walls may be over but the enemy is not defeated. They will come again, tomorrow perhaps, and again until one of us is truly broken."

By sunrise, the fighting was essentially over. The Hungarians and Serbians had forced their way into the fortress and had slaughtered the Janissaries trapped within. After the killing had been going on for some time, Hunyadi and Szilágyi's men threw down a makeshift bridge over the remnants of the still-smouldering drawbridge, crossed the chasm and sent hundreds of heavily armoured men across. Caught between the two Christian forces, the Janissaries died in their thousands. The fortress ran with blood and the dawn air was filled with screams.

Watching from across the bridge, it turned my stomach to see it. The Janissaries were our enemies, it was true. They worshipped the God of the Mohammedans. But they were our own people by blood, our sons and brothers, and they should have been fighting beside us instead of dying beneath our blades.

But the job was done and done well.

It had been a close thing, perhaps, but the Serbian militia, the Hungarian peasant crusaders, the foreign mercenaries like me and my men, and the Hungarian lords and their retinues, had all held fast and so done their duty.

But the task was not yet done.

***

"I had hoped that they would pack up and leave," Walt said from the top of the city's inner wall walk when I joined him and the others in the morning. He yawned and rubbed his eyes, squinting at the light. "What did our great lords have to say?"

"As much as always," I replied as Eva passed me a jug of wine. I drank two great gulps and wished it was blood I was supping. Our squires stood ready with our helms but we were clad in the rest of our armour.

Beyond was the lower outer wall with its crumbling breaches. Outside of that was the enemy siege works and the huge camps themselves. Tens of thousands of men, ready and willing to come back and kill us. The crews for the hundreds of cannons were busy preparing their weapons for the day's bombardment.

Rob sat in shadow with his knees up and his back to the parapet wall, head back and eyes closed, snoring away like he was in a feather bed.

Walt followed my eyes and smiled. "You made him a knight, Richard, but he'll always be an archer at heart."

"What have they decided?" Eva asked.

I shrugged. "Repair the breaches, restock the powder and shot, and pray the Sultan does not come back again tonight."

Walt sighed and his head drooped. "These people lack boldness."

"It is true," Serban muttered. "They fear losing more than they long for victory."

"What did you say to them?" Eva asked.

"I politely suggested we might assemble every able man right now and drive the Turks from Christendom."

"Politely?" Eva repeated.

Walt snorted.

"I *was* polite," I snapped. "I even suggested a compromise. A limited sortie on the enemy lines to destroy their cannons." I pointed at them in the distance. "Perhaps they would then withdraw. No Janissaries, no cannons. It would be enough to force Sultan Mehmed to withdraw, surely."

"And our lords declined, I take it?" Stephen said, pulling the brim of his hat down. His eyes were yet wild. He had seen more of war than most mortal soldiers ever would and yet he never grew used to it.

"We would be outnumbered on the field. We risked more than we might gain. The battle would more likely be lost than won. The usual."

Walt slapped a hand on the parapet. "Bloody fools. They would rather sit here and die slowly than die like a man?"

Stephen smiled. "One suspects they would rather not die at all, Walt."

"It's no easy thing," Rob said from where he sat, his eyes yet closed and his head back. "Leaving the safety of these mighty stone walls. No easy thing to be bold. A man would have to be halfway mad to leave his castle to attack an army of barbarians beyond the gates. And you're right enough, Stephen. Most soldiers, lords especially, would rather victory be won by someone else so that they might live to fight another day."

"Truly spoken, brother." Walt grinned. "Shame we ain't got an army of madmen here instead of great lords, ain't it."

"But we do," I said, turning to look down into the city. "Come on."

We made our way through the city to the quarters of the Roman delegation, led by John of Capistrano.

He was a Franciscan friar and a powerful Catholic priest and cardinal, a friend of the Pope, no less, and he had at least a score of priests and monks trailing him wherever he went, along with dozens of servants and suppliants and desperate souls wishing to hand him some pathetic gift or to beg for his prayers. As such, he was never a difficult man to find but he was always difficult to get close to.

John of Capistrano was holding court in a large house in the north-eastern quarter, not far from where the cannons once more took up their bombardment of the walls. The streets were filthy with grime and it stank of wet shit everywhere.

A mass of crusaders pressed in close to the cardinal's house, hoping for sight or sound of their illustrious and beloved leader. Luckily, I have never minded pushing a gaggle of peasants and priests aside when it is called for.

"And who are you, my lord?" a fat monk asked, pushing his belly between me and the interior of the house. "And what might be your business?"

I leaned in close to his face and lowered my voice. "I am a soldier of Christ and my business is cutting the heads off Turks."

He furrowed his bushy brows. "If you have business with Brother John, I will take to him your message, my lord."

Pushing him aside, I stepped into the room where John of Capistrano was speaking, surrounded by monks and priests hanging on his every word. An old man with a bald head and masses of grey hair over his ears, he wore nothing grander than a plain monk's robe. But even had I not seen him before, I would have known which of the men in the room he was, for he had a commanding presence and a magnificent, booming voice.

"What is it?" he said, his Italian accent very strong, breaking off from his discussion. "What has happened?"

"Nothing, my lord," I said in French. "I merely came to speak with you."

He frowned and replied in kind. "I recognise you. Richard the Englishman, is it not? Do you mean me harm?"

"Harm? Why would I wish you harm, my lord?"

"I have heard the stories about you. The bloodthirsty slayer of Vlad Dracul. You have never been seen in a church. They say you drink your servant's blood."

Spreading my hands, I smiled. "It is all true. But I am a Christian, my lord, and more than anything I love Christ and pray daily for my salvation."

He snorted. "You have the smell of heresy about you, boy."

"Never, my lord."

"They say you are sympathetic to the Hussites," he said, his voice ringing from the walls of the small chamber. "And you enjoy the company of the Jew."

The meeting was not going as I had intended. "Perhaps someone heard me express admiration for the Hussites' ways in battle, which our own regent has emulated with great success. But I do not hold with their views. Indeed, I do not know what they are, precisely, only enough to know that I will not stand for such heresy."

In truth, much of what I had heard, especially with respect to indulgences, sounded rather appealing to me but I knew never to say such things in company. Whenever there were discussions on the matter, I held my tongue. But that is the way with heresies. Either one joins in wholeheartedly in condemnation or one is considered a sympathiser, which means one is a heretic also.

John of Capistrano lifted his chin. "So you do not deny enjoying the company of Jews?"

I sighed. "Of course, my lord, I hold the Jews in contempt, just as much as anyone. It is merely that myself and my companions often seek information about our enemies, the Turks. And as you know, the Jews are welcomed in those lands, travelling to do business whether mercantile or diplomatic. And many of these Jews will happily speak of the things they see, if your coin is good."

The great priest shook his head in disapproval, lifting a finger and taking a deep breath. "A good Christian would never commune with Jews, as you do, sir. A man of godly character could not stoop so low as that. And he who trusts the word of a Jew makes himself a fool before God and the world. No, no, I will not abase myself by conversing with a friend to Jews."

"We are hardly friendly with them," I snapped.

"Do you break bread with them? Do you share wine?"

I floundered, irritated at having to discuss such a pointless thing. "It is a transaction, no more. A trade. We purchase their words with coin and while we discuss—"

"You purchase *lies*," he said. "And I will not listen a moment longer to one who breaks bread with the murderers of Christ. Mind your tongue and begone from my sight, sir."

In the silence, the room resounded with his loud voice. Monks and priests stared at me while the greatest amongst them pointedly turned his back on me and began conversing with the man beside him.

I turned and pushed my way outside and through the crowd to my men.

"What happened?" Eva asked, aghast at my expression.

"I am not certain," I said.

"Is he willing to lead his men against the Turks?" Stephen asked.

"We did not reach a point in the discussion that allowed the question to be raised."

"What do you mean?" Stephen asked. "How could you not ask him?"

Ignoring him, I addressed Rob and Walt. "What do you think of the crusaders?"

"Keen as mustard," Walt said.

"They are stark raving mad," Rob said. "Which is what we want, of course."

"Serban?" I asked. "Do these men want to attack?"

Beneath his steel hat, his face was grim. "More than anything, they wish to strike a blow against the enemies of Christ."

Walt nodded. "Some of them keep trying to sneak out and have a go at the Turk all by themselves. You know, groups of young lads, that sort of thing."

"What about the rest of them?"

Rob gestured with his stump. "Speak to them yourself, Richard. They came here to drive the Turks from Christendom. After last night, with their mallets and clubs still bloody, they know for certain that God is with them. God wills this. There is no fear or doubt amongst them. Come on."

When it came to knowing the hearts of common folk, whether soldier or peasant, Rob was never wrong. And so it proved.

Men asked if I had seen their actions the night before or if it was time to make an attack on the enemy. Others stopped us to ask for advice on how to use this weapon or that, or what was the best way to kill a man in armour. Some wished to show me their knife or the spear they had taken from an enemy. A few men strutted about in pieces of armour they had stripped from corpses. Their mood was high indeed. And dangerously high, for we witnessed more than one angry argument and two fellows almost came to blows before their friends drew them apart.

"Won't take much," Walt said softly, raising his eyebrows.

"We would be sending them to their deaths," I replied. "All these fine people."

Rob held his nose. "These fine people have turned the streets into rivers of shit. It is no wonder they would rather be outside."

"It is what they want," Walt said. "We'd be sending them to glory."

"Not much glory dying in a ditch, Walt," I said, looking at the filthy people, some laughing and others clutching their bellies.

"There's glory in saving Christendom, though."

"Rob?"

He scratched his stump as he regarded the men, nodding to one or two who caught his eye. "We must all make sacrifices for our world. The order of things does maintain itself. Walls are nothing without the blood spilled to protect them."

I sighed. "It must be all of them, or it would be better for it to be none."

"Start the stone rolling and the mountainside will fall," Stephen said. "Where one peasant goes, the rest shall follow."

"How will they even know where to go?" Eva asked. "They will get bogged down out there, trapped, and destroyed. We will have gained nought but lost a great deal."

"It is as I said before," I replied, sighing. "They must be led."

"But John of Capistrano will not even speak to you."

"We shall lead them. Each of us."

Eva shook her head. "Richard, this is not—"

I placed my hands on her armoured shoulders. "You were quite right last night. There is no need to carry out such a task when there is another who will do it. I agree. But now there is only us."

She looked up at the sky. "Your heart's desire is to fight and so that is where your reason leads you."

"I would never argue with you, Eva," I said, drawing scorn from her and quiet laughter from the others. "But we can have victory today or defeat tomorrow. And I know what I chose."

She gave a small nod. "We should none of us get ourselves cut off from retreat back to the city, agreed?"

We all gave our assent.

"Rob, Walt, you find a group of angry young fellows and rile them up. Tell them to spread the word."

"What word?" Walt asked, frowning.

"What should we say, Richard?" Rob said.

"Men rarely wish to be the first but they will fight the devil to avoid being last. Tell them that we are attacking. No, tell them that the attack has begun. We must hurry or we shall miss the attack. And lead them out. The fighting will be desperate, disorganised. They will have to cross from ditch to ditch, killing the Turks hiding in their trenches and their holes. But we must push on and on. Serban? You take some men and find drums, trumpets, and go to the walls and make some noise. It need not be proper signals, just make it loud. Raise your voices and sing if you must. Stephen? Eva? You must go to Hunyadi and Szilágyi and tell them that the crusaders are not only attacking but they are *winning*. The crusaders are driving the Turks away. They are going to destroy the enemy cannons. But they must have support from the soldiers."

"But that may not be so," Stephen argued. "Even by the time we reach the lords."

"If you do not say it, Stephen, then it shall never be so. By speaking it, you will make it come true, do you understand?"

Walt grinned. "We done some foolish acts in our time, Richard, but this is—"

"None of that, Walter. Hurry now, let us gather our men, and then we shall stir these shit-stinking warriors into action."

The Hungarian crusaders were filled with their recent victory and they jumped into action. Few doubted the words we spoke, even the first of them who pushed their way up and across the breaches and down toward the enemy siege works while the cannons blasted the walls overhead. The stream of men turned into a torrent and soon there were hundreds and finally thousands of common folk wading their way over the churned mud toward the enemy lines.

Surprise was on our side. I doubt the Turks could believe what they were seeing at first. To them we would have looked like a mass of desperate civilians fleeing the city but if they had any doubts initially, we soon showed them our true intent. Forward positions with small cannons and hand-gunners were overrun with barely a shot being fired. Our crusaders ran gleefully through the trenches, battering any enemy who stood to fight. We swarmed each palisade or position and overwhelmed it before doing the same to the ones beside and behind it. Every time I looked back toward the city, our numbers had swelled further and there was a line of men all the way back to the walls.

Whether we lived or died depended on Hunyadi and Szilágyi. Would they abandon the fools who had attacked without orders or would they seize the opportunity?

A huge cheer spread through our men and at first I assumed the Sultan had fled or, more likely, Hunyadi had come. Instead, we discovered that the ancient priest John of Capistrano had come to join the attack. A while later I saw him, still wearing his monk's robe, swinging a bloody mace over his head into the skull of a cowering Turk while roaring some prayer.

Turkish cavalry finally came to attack, as I had dreaded, charging our flanks in a thundering of hooves and flashing blades.

We lost a lot of men but the crisscrossing earthworks now worked in our favour as the cavalry could not charge through them to kill our peasant soldiers. Still, they pushed slowly in between the lines of interconnecting trenches and palisades and did their bloody work more slowly. Our crusaders did not break, though. Far from it. They swarmed the slow or stationary cavalry and killed the riders.

Finally, Szilágyi and Hunyadi led out their men against the entire Turkish line.

With their help, we pushed the Turks away from their cannon and because we now had professional gunners with us, we trained the enemy cannon on the enemy. Although the massive guns could only be turned with teams of men and horses, the smaller cannons were turned about or brought up and aimed toward the Turkish centre.

Where the Sultan was.

He yet had thousands of men defending his central position, not to mention William's immortal Janissaries but slowly we crushed or drove off both wings and the cannons opened up on the Sultan's men.

"We need to get to Hunyadi," I said to the men of my company. "Tell him not to engage the red Janissaries again. Let the cannons do the work."

"He knows by now," Walt said. "Surely to God, he knows."

"He may know," Rob said, jabbing his arm across the battlefield. "But someone should have told his men."

The Hungarians and Serbs made a series of assaults on the dwindling Turkish centre. But they broke themselves repeatedly on William's Janissaries who could not be pushed aside or broken, no matter how many charges crashed against them.

We went from gun to gun, begging those in charge of it to aim their fire at the small target of the Janissary formation. Kill those five hundred men, I would say, and we win the battle and save Christendom.

Some men agreed but most of the rest told me to mind my own business or said they were determined to kill the Sultan himself. Considering the unreliable accuracy of those guns, other than a lucky shot, there was little hope of that. But still, every artilleryman I ever met, from the earliest days down through the centuries, claimed he could shoot the cock off a gnat if only I would stop talking to him.

"Should we attack?" Rob asked, shouting over the noise of the cannons. "William and his men are there, deep in that formation."

"I cannot lead us into that death trap, Rob," I said. "Our new cannons may do the work for us."

"If not?" he said.

"We shall have to be content with a victory," I replied. "We must be patient."

Night fell and it was a dark one. The battle turned to skirmishes and those to withdrawals.

The Sultan took his remaining men away with him in the darkness, and William was gone with him.

Belgrade had been saved.

And yet there would be more casualties to come.

***

The Turks left behind a staggering amount of treasure and provisions in their abandoned camp.

Once the bodies were collected and burned and buried, the priests calculated that we had killed about twenty-five thousand Turks within or outside the walls of Belgrade. It was an incredible and unlikely victory.

Later, we found out that the Sultan had retreated to Sofia and then had several of his generals executed. Sadly, William was not one of them. He had done his job.

We would also hear that Pope Eugenius IV called the salvation of Belgrade the happiest event of his life.

And the battle was hardly over when the plague struck.

It was a camp sickness, brought about by fouled water and hundreds of thousands of people eating, drinking and shitting in proximity for weeks on end. We knew even in those days that bad water and rotten food caused sickness and we knew that stricken people spread their afflictions to others. But what could we do in such situations as sieges, when it was bad food or no food? Whenever armies camped in one place for long, many more people than usual would fall ill. But sometimes, as during that hot, wet summer in Belgrade, a terrible plague might appear. In this case, it was probably brought by the invading army and contracted by us when we killed them and looted their camp. Or perhaps the peasants brought it and spread it due to their filthy conditions in the city.

Whatever the cause, the crusaders died in their thousands, the Serbian residents died, mercenaries from all over died.

Janos Hunyadi died.

He was over sixty years old and had been leading vast campaigns for his entire adult life. After the pressures at Belgrade, he was weakened in spirit and in body. And the illness took hold of him mercilessly.

Before he succumbed, he sent for me. I was surprised, to say the least, and it was clear from the grave and displeased faces of his men that they felt the same.

"Do not tax him," Szilágyi said, grasping my arm. "Do not go within, Richard."

I stared at him for a moment and looked at his hand. He withdrew it and stepped back.

"You are afraid that he might die," I said, understanding his anger. "But he summoned me."

"Why?"

"I have no idea. You know, my lord, if you wish it you could bar me from entering and he will likely not live to voice his displeasure."

Szilágyi, shamed, nodded his head toward the door and I ducked inside. The room was hot and humid, with fabric over the shuttered windows and curtains around the bed and a crowd of people crammed within. His servants and physicians busied themselves and priests prayed.

"Sir Richard," his chamberlain said. "My lord is awake, come closer."

Hunyadi's face was pale and he stank of foul shit. A servant wiped his lips with a wet cloth and Hunyadi raised a hand to mine. I did not want to take it but I did. It was ice cold and sweaty.

"Richard," he said, his voice a whisper. "Protect Dracula."

"Dracula? My lord, he is dangerous." I lowered my voice. "More than you know."

Hunyadi shook his head. "He will save his people."

"Perhaps he will, or perhaps he will not."

"Do not abandon him. Help him. Secure the borders. Hold the enemy at Wallachia."

Dracula is an immortal and I will use him however I can before I cut off his head.

"I know, my lord. I know. All will be well."

Hunyadi's will was iron, and he survived for days after I last saw him. They moved him to Zenum and many hoped he would recover but his body and mind had been through too much and so passed the White Knight, Regent of Hungary and Christ's Champion, Janos Hunyadi.

Cardinal John of Capistrano died also, leaving the crusaders without a leader. The survivors made their way back home.

The Despot of Serbia George Branković, for so long a thorn in Hungary's side and latterly an unwilling ally, died also and Serbia fell into the chaos of a succession crisis. Even Mehmed II submitted a claim to the Serbian throne, his rights based on his Serbian stepmother but he had enough problems to deal with following his defeat and did not press seriously.

Skanderbeg, seizing the opportunity our victory provided, brought his men out of the mountains of Albania to raid the Turkish garrisons stationed in the lowlands.

Hungary turned into itself as they looked to a future without their great leader. Hunyadi's son Laszlo took command of Belgrade.

And I took my company back to Wallachia, and to the immortal voivode Vlad Dracula.

9

The Boyars

1456 - 1458

DRACULA WAS FORMALLY elected by the high *boyar* council in August that year and confirmed by the metropolitan in the cathedral of Târgoviște with the title Prince Vlad, son of Vlad the Great, sovereign and ruler of Ungro-Wallachia and of the duchies of Fogaras and Amlas.

I half expected to be seized in the borderlands and every night our company slept in or near a new *boyar* stronghold on our way to Târgoviște I expected to be set upon in the darkness. And then when we reached that fine city, we set up our company camp in the great meadows to the west, alongside a few other mercenary companies and with the retinues of visiting dignitaries.

I wondered whether Vlad would send an army out to greet me. When his messenger came with word that the prince begged my presence, my men urged me not go.

The walls of the city were somewhat intimidating, I will admit. I had seen the citizens burn young Mircea alive years earlier, after burning his eyes out, and I had no friends within who would speak for me were I taken.

"Send us in, Richard," Walt said. "We will explore the city and decide on places we may flee to, or fight our way from, and points where we might escape the city. Then we will spread ourselves at various places, ready to act if things go against us. And then you can go in and speak to Dracula."

"Black Walter, when did you become so very sensible?" I quipped.

He shrugged. "Must have been sometime this last century."

"Well, it is good advice. Let us not rush straight at danger for once. Take as many men as you need, see what you can see, and return before dark."

The messenger was sent away with my apologies, explaining that I was fatigued from the long journey and would be well enough to call on the prince in a day or two, God willing.

While my men roamed the city, I had my servants clean and repair my armour and clothing. A few of them went into the city to purchase cloth and thread and clothes brushes and it was these men who came hurrying back across the field with word that Vlad Dracula himself was riding from the city with a hundred lords behind him.

"He has come for you," Eva suggested, before ordering her squire to fetch her armour.

"I do not think mail and plate will save us," I said to her as she ducked inside our tent.

"You should prepare yourself," she called in return.

"He could be going anywhere," I said but I saw the great party of riders now on the road and they turned from it onto the track through our great field. "Although it seems he is coming here."

His bodyguards and lords stayed far behind him and the prince rode up in his finery on a magnificent charger. I went forward from my tents to greet him.

"I see you are feeling better, Richard," Dracula called, smiling beneath his broad-brimmed hat. "That makes me so very glad."

"My lord," I said, smiling. "I did not expect such an informal and intimate greeting as this, considering that you are now the Prince of Wallachia in the eyes of God and of all men."

His expressed turned serious. "I do not think such close friends as we need be beholden to formality, Richard."

I bowed. "What an honour to be named friend by one such as you, my lord."

He seemed amused again, though he did not smile. "Indeed? Well, then, as a friend who feels honoured, I ask that you join me on our hunt today."

"Thank you, my lord, but I am much weakened by the weeks of riding and the hard-fought battle."

"Nonsense. I can see with my own eyes that you are as strong as a bull. Have them bring your horse. I shall insist if I have to, and I would really rather not do so."

I glanced at his waiting men. From the corner of my eye I saw Eva inside our tent with her sword drawn.

"It would be a pleasure, my lord," I said and bowed again for good measure.

While the grooms prepared my courser, I dressed as swiftly as I could.

"These clothes are suitable for riding," I said to my valet, "though they are not fine enough for noble and royal company."

"It's all you got, Richard," he said. "You want better, you got to buy better."

"Watch your tone," Eva warned him. "And Richard, I think your attire is the least of your worries, don't you?"

"Oh?" I said. "You think our prince means to have me murdered in the trees?"

"It would not be the first convenient hunting accident to befall a prince's enemy."

"I wish Walt and Rob were here," I said. "Or Garcia, Jan, or even Claudin."

"Take Serban," she said. "He did not go into the city with the others."

"That is something, I suppose, though an immortal would be better."

"You could take me?" she said. "And damn their judgments."

"That would be unnecessarily provocative. I will be well. All will be well."

"Do not placate me as though I am a child," she scowled. "I know full well this may be the last time I see you."

I crossed to her and looked into her worried eyes. "I mustn't keep our prince waiting." I bent to her and kissed her lips. There was nothing more to be said.

On the hunt, we rode down through the valley while the hunting masters and dogs ranged ahead into the broadleaf woodlands. It was a good day for a pleasant ride.

"Not a bad day to die on, right, Serban?" I called to my Wallachian servant.

He scowled under his hat, hunched over in the saddle. "Too hot."

"You would rather die in winter? Come on, man, if they do turn on us I will ensure I give myself a glorious death. I will kill a score at least, what about you?"

Serban shook his head and muttered something about Englishmen I could not quite catch. "Death is not to be mocked."

"I do not truly believe the Prince will murder us today," I said. "He could have me executed in a dozen simpler ways. So, enjoy the ride. Perhaps we will scare up a deer or two."

"Not much deer in these parts no more."

I shook my head. "Serban, assuming we survive the day, you must do as agreed and find word of immortals in these lands. Any stories, any legends. Anything at all."

He did not meet my eye. "I will, my lord. I will."

Dracula sent word for me and I was escorted through the masses of horsemen until I rode beside the prince. A hundred men before us and a hundred behind but we were alone, side by side. The woodland was ancient but large sections had been cleared for timber, revealing distant mountain peaks over the tree tops. Crows cawed and hopped between the branches overhead as we crossed a wide clearing.

Dracula glanced at me from beneath his hat. "This sun does not bother you, Richard?"

"I love the feel of the sun on my skin," I said, grinning. "Do you not, my lord?"

He smiled back at me, his long moustache curling up with his lips. "In my youth, I delighted in Wallachian summers, whether in the mountains or on the plains. However, I was sent to Anatolia when I was a prisoner of the Turk. The sun is different there. Relentless and punishing. I learned to despise it."

And since you were turned, it burns your skin most frightfully, marking you as something not quite human.

"A terrible shame, my lord, for the summers of your land are delightful."

"Is it different in England? I hear the land of your birth is dark, and wet, and cold, all the year around."

"Indeed, no, my lord. The weather of England is perfection itself. The summers are warm and long, though rain falls at night so that the crops grow tall and strong every season. Spring comes early, with an abundance of rain to enrich the soil for planting, and the harvests are the most bountiful on earth. Our winters are cold but not deadly. If there is an Eden on earth, my lord, it is England."

He grunted in disbelief. "I have it on good authority that England is a deeply unpleasant land for civilised men."

"Oh? And from where did you hear such a thing?" I asked, suspecting that William had filled his ears with it.

He waved a hand dismissively in my direction. "I received an excellent education, as befitting a future prince. I learned many things about England, even though it is a distant and unimportant kingdom. Perhaps I shall journey there and see for myself if what I have learned is true."

I will kill you before you go causing mischief in my homeland.

"That would be a great honour for me and my people, though I fear you have much to occupy you here, at the moment."

He smiled again at that. "You are quite correct. Hunyadi is dead, and Hungary looks inward. Branković is dead and Serbia is without a leader. What do you believe Sultan Mehmed will do now?"

"Why would I know better than you, my lord?"

He smiled. "I would very much appreciate your advice, sir."

A wiser man than I could turn such situations in his favour. If I had the wits to do it, I could have given Dracula false advice in order to manipulate his actions or plant seeds which I could later harvest. I even had a distant, fantastical notion that I could turn him from loyalty to William to joining our cause in bringing his destruction.

But I was not a wise man and so I decided to speak the truth, as I saw it, and to advise him as if he were a mortal ruler.

"The Sultan will invade Serbia again, though he will not attack Belgrade. He has patience. Mehmed will slip into the rest of Serbia almost unopposed and his garrisons will embed themselves."

Dracula tilted his head. "What do you believe I should do about this?"

"Your western border with Serbia will become a possible line of attack from the Turks and so you are right to be concerned. But there is little you can do to stop it. If you move alone to push the Turks from Serbia, you will be invaded on your southern border. If I were you, my lord, I would ask the Hungarians what they intend to do about the Turkish threat."

He nodded noncommittally and said nothing for a while before casually asking another question. "What else needs to be done with regards to the Hungarians?"

"The west is not the only border you need be concerned about. You must understand what is planned for Transylvania, whether the lands will be properly protected by Hungarian armies or if the towns there will have to stand alone. And if they must defend themselves, how will they do so? Which of them, if any, are considering bowing down to the Turks to protect themselves?"

"How might I discover these things, Richard?"

I looked up at the distant mountains. "You would write to the mayors of each of the important towns of Transylvania and ask them explicitly. But you cannot be certain that what they say is honest and so your messengers will have to attempt to discover the truth by whatever means they can before they return with the message."

He pursed his full lips, seemingly amused by something. "What of my eastern border, Richard?"

To the east of Wallachia was Moldavia, which had traditionally been in vassalage to Poland, to the north. Its position, northeast of Wallachia and the Danube, had spared it from conquest by the Turks until about 1420 when the old Sultan Mehmed I had raided. And then Moldavia had turned inward to wage a series of civil wars in the 1430s and 1440s which Sultan Murad had taken advantage of by promoting one side over another. And by 1455, Peter III Aron had accepted Turkish suzerainty and agreed to pay tribute.

"Moldavia? I have little knowledge of it, my lord, other than to suspect that Peter III Aron should be removed by some means or other and your cousin Stephen should take his place on the throne. And Stephen is in favour with the Hungarians so it would draw Moldavia away from Poland and into the fight alongside Hungary and Wallachia against the Turks. Assuming you believe Stephen capable of resisting the Turks, of course."

He snapped his eyes to me. "What do you know of my cousin Stephen?"

"Nothing at all," I said. "I believe he is in Wallachia, however."

Dracula snorted a laugh. "He is with us on this very hunt, sir. At the front, with a bow and a spear and keen to bring down both stag and boar. He loves hunting and he loves war."

"I am sure that he does. And how many wars has he fought, my lord?"

Dracula whipped his bulging eyes to me. "Do you mock me, sir? Do you mock my cousin?"

"I would never presume to mock royalty, my lord. I merely wonder how a man can love something he has so little experience of."

Dracula held himself stiff in the saddle. "And yet a man may love women before he has ever had one for himself."

I laughed. "Very true, my lord."

We rode into shadow beneath ancient trees once more. "What would you recommend I do with regards to my *boyars*, Richard?"

I turned, surprised at his question. Asking me about foreign matters made some sense, as I had spent over a decade at the Hungarian court and travelling through Transylvania and latterly Serbia but Wallachian politics was almost entirely opaque to outsiders.

"I am afraid I know nothing of your *boyars*, my lord and so my advice can only be general.

All princes should reward his most loyal and most capable men and all disloyalty and incompetence must be punished."

"Ah," he said. "What punishment would you recommend?"

"That would depend on the crime, my lord."

"And a severe crime would require a severe punishment, would you say?"

I wondered if I was being set up in some way. Dracula held himself with a stiffness that suggested suppression of some high emotion and I feared it may well be murderous rage. Was he leading me to condemn the guilty to a terribly punishment only for him to then accuse me of some such crime in turn?

"The punishment of crimes is surely established by the law?" I ventured. "And by custom."

He scowled. "The prince is the law."

That was very far from being the truth, as I had seen for myself when Dracula's father had attempted to have Hunyadi summarily executed only to be refused by his council of *boyars*. But I had no wish to argue the point so I held my tongue and we continued in silence.

"Much of what you say is true," Dracula said eventually. "I must discover what my enemies and allies intend. But it is imperative that my cousin Stephen takes Moldavia, for that shall be a new kingdom to join us in our struggle."

Yes but for Hungary or for the Turks?

"So you will lead your armies into Moldavia?"

"I would dearly like to do so but I have work here. Instead, I shall send six thousand horsemen with my cousin. With these men, he can take his throne, as I have taken mine."

"Forgive me, my lord, but will that not weaken your defence of Wallachia against Turkish incursion?"

"It will not. For I shall welcome the Sultan's emissaries and I shall agree to their demands."

"You will do what? My lord, you took the throne from a man who was too acquiescent with our enemies and yet you will now do the same?"

He lowered his head and glared at me. "I shall acquiesce only for as long as is necessary to strengthen my position and my kingdom."

It sounded like the justification a man makes to himself when he knows what he is doing is wrong. It is only this once, he says, lying to himself. It is for a good reason that I do this thing I know is wrong. All men do this, and women also, though for a peasant it may mean nothing more than encroaching on his neighbours' land, or for a merchant it may mean undercutting a partner, or for a woman it may be betraying the trust of a friend or her child. But for a prince, it might mean beggaring away his kingdom.

Whether it was that or whether Dracula was William's man, working for the Turks all along, I could not yet say.

"How will your lords react?"

"Those loyal to me shall react by demonstrating their loyalty."

606

"That is quite a test. You are asking your *boyars* to trust that you will not..."

"Not go the same way as my father? The father that you killed with your own hand?"

"Yes."

"You disapprove of paying tribute to purchase myself time?"

"What could possibly be worth the cost, my lord?"

"There are a great many *boyars* in Wallachia who care nothing for their people. They care nothing for their prince, nor for Christendom, nor for God above. They care only for themselves and so these men must be dealt with. I must have time to clear Wallachia of its rats. A prideful man would not stoop so low as giving in to the Turks but I consider my pride as nothing when compared to the continued existence of my people. I shall sacrifice my pride and my morality for them. And when my people are free and safe then I shall feel pride in myself once more. Do you understand?"

It sounded ominous to me. "I do not know."

"You will, in time. And I hope that you will help me."

"What would you have me do?"

Dracula hesitated, as if he was about to say more but stopped himself. "I would ask that you have patience and trust me for a while longer."

"Have patience? That has rarely been a virtue of mine."

"I find that hard to believe," he said, smiling and watching me.

"My lord, I am nothing more than the captain of a mercenary company. If you will pay us, we will remain on hand."

Dracula smiled. "I am delighted to hear it. You will be right where I want you."

***

"You are a fool," Eva said.

Stephen nodded emphatically. "It is clear now that he is both an immortal of William and an agent of the Sultan. We must dispose of him immediately before he turns on us."

"Keep your damned voice down, Stephen," I said. We were meeting in our house in Târgovişte, in my bedchamber, without servants in attendance. It was as private as we could manage in that city but one never could know who might be listening. "It is hardly a surprise. We knew this would happen."

Earlier that day, Vlad Dracula had done as he had said, receiving the Sultan's emissaries at Târgovişte with extreme courtesy. I had expected Dracula to pay the annual tribute, and it was agreed at two thousand gold ducats, but then the Turks had demanded the resumption of the rights of access that Vladislaus II had given. That was the right of free passage through Wallachia for Turkish soldiers so that they could raid the rich towns of Transylvania. In exchange, the Sultan would recognise Dracula as the rightful ruler of Wallachia. This meant the Sultan would not seek to remove him or undermine him nor would he invade or raid his lands.

Dracula readily assented.

He did at least decline their offer to travel to Constantinople to make his obeisance to the Sultan in person but how much meaning that had we could not agree.

"And there is Moldavia to the east likewise rolling over without a fight," Eva said.

Stephen of Moldavia had taken the throne there with Wallachian support and so there was now a unified front of sorts but it seemed as though both kingdoms would simply continue to pathetically submit to the Turks.

"Can you really blame them?" Stephen had said. "By submitting, they hold on to their lives and their position. Why challenge the established order when it is that very order which keeps you where you are?"

"I do blame them," I said. "Not just the princes but the *boyars* of both kingdoms who allow it. It is weakness. It is treachery. They throw their people to the wolves so that they may sit in their palaces and pretend to be lords and kings."

"What now?" Eva asked.

Walt scoffed. "Obvious, ain't it? What we always said. Get close to our dear Prince Vlad and..." Walt drew his thumb across his neck. "And then we make off to some other likely kingdom and there attempt to make this immortal army."

"There is no likely kingdom left," I said. "And even if there were, we must first do as you suggest with the prince. It can be done, of course, but how shall we then escape this damned country? We will have ten thousand Wallachians after us."

Rob had a suggestion. "We wait until he journeys to the lowlands, close to the Danube. We do him there, in the south, then we can reach the river by nightfall."

"And then what? Sail to the Black Sea? And then?"

Rob shrugged.

"Anyway," I said, "he never leaves the safety of the north. This is where his power is located and he stays clear of his enemies within the country."

"We need allies," Eva said. "Or at least one powerful *boyar* who will protect us after the deed is done and help us escape, perhaps into Transylvania."

"Dracula has his own possessions in Transylvania," Stephen said.

"Yes, who could we possibly trust enough there who could shelter us?" I asked.

Eva pursed her lips. "We shall have to make further enquiries while avoiding suspicion."

"Everyone here is suspicious of everyone else," Rob said. "It is a nest of snakes. I would not wish to trust any of them."

"What of the Germans?" Stephen said. "The Saxons have their towns all over and they almost all hate and fear Vlad. Perhaps they might be trusted? They are more civilised than these Wallachians after all."

"The Saxons here are merchants and craftsmen," I said, "how much can they be trusted?"

"We do not have very many choices."

"Very well, Stephen, perhaps you should develop your contacts with the Saxons. Eva, see what you can discover about any *boyars* who might be willing to see our prince meet his end. But be subtle, for the love of God."

"We know what we are doing."

"I hope you do. A wrong move here may mean we have to fight our way through hundreds of miles of forests and hills. Get to work."

We stayed with Dracula's court wherever it went, and it rarely strayed far from the northern mountains. His family was from those parts and the bonds of decades and centuries of familial ties meant the people of the region were the most loyal of all his subjects. And the mountains would offer safety from assaults from any direction. He never strayed far from his Transylvanian possessions either.

Poenari Castle was his key fortress, located in the mountains on the Wallachian side of the border and the most defensible of all his fortresses. It was also a little way north of Curtea de Arges, the ecclesiastical capital of Wallachia which also held extensive political power and influence over the people. Dracula worked hard to make it so that the security and prosperity of the Wallachian church was increasingly tied to him personally.

The fortress at Poenari was at least a hundred years old, probably much older, but it had fallen to ruin when Dracula declared that he would bring it back into use. It was perched high on a steep rock precipice and its position alone made it almost impregnable. Dracula ordered it rebuilt grander and more modern than it had ever been.

In fact, he brought in highly skilled and very expensive engineers to do it. They started to construct five towers which were positioned so that when completed they would be able to provide crossfire on any section that might be assailed. The grand central tower was being built with stone reinforced by brick which was supposed to ensure it would withstand shots even from massive cannons. It was a long, slender fortress and when completed it would only need a hundred soldiers to defend it, as well as all the necessary servants. It was clear that Dracula meant to have a place that no one, whether king or sultan, *boyars* or Hungarians, and perhaps whether William or me, would be able to roust him out of.

By starting to rebuild this fortress, Dracula was in breach of his agreements with both the Hungarians and the Turks who prohibited him to construct any defensive works, lest he be seen as planning mischief.

"Does this building of fortresses and fortified monasteries mean you will be going to war again soon, my lord?" I asked him at a feast in the hall at Târgoviște. Many of the Wallachians muttered their disapproval at my impertinence. "But, my lords, I am a crusader and I wish only to know where best to fulfil my oaths."

Some cursed me openly.

"You are a mercenary and will go where there is payment to be had," one fat lord said, to much approval.

"Quite right," I said. "And will there be war here?"

"There will always be war here," another said.

Dracula would not answer me and he would not comment at all.

In fact, he avoided me and over the winter declined to offer me a formal post at his court or give me a task to complete. It was possible he believed I intended to assassinate him and yet he did not banish me and my company and he did not have me arrested. Instead, he sent word that he would have work for me and my men in spring and that I was to have patience. It would be work that we would be richly rewarded for, so he said. And I told my company that we would bide our time and receive a grand payday when the weather turned.

It was not just Poenari Castle that he began building. Down on the plains near the Danube, he began construction of new fortresses that he could garrison with his own men. It would mean extending his power into the lowlands and they would also provide much-needed revenues. One of the first that he founded was a fortress called Bucharest, at a place which was almost exactly where I had killed his father.

He also fortified a monastery called Snagov and built a line of minor forts right along the plain and the river.

And then in early spring he invited me to dine with him in his new hall in the almost-completed Poenari. There were over a thousand steps to climb on the path up to the first gate, and the men gleefully told me there were a thousand more up to the top of the central tower.

It was a small gathering of his closest men, the strongest and most capable soldiers loyal to him.

Even though the summons had said to encamp my company in the valley below, I had been allowed only a single valet to attend me into the fortress itself. Of course I chose Walt but even together we would have a hard fight if Dracula meant me harm.

"Do not go," Eva had urged. "Do not take the risk."

"There is no way forward without risk," I had replied. "I have been patient for months waiting to see what he would do next. Well, let us see."

"You seem on edge, Richard," Dracula said during the meal. These were his first words to me since I had arrived, the first to my face in months, and they drew laughter from his men.

"I am filled with longing, my lord."

He furrowed his brow. "Longing?"

"Longing to know why you asked me to join you, my lord. I can only assume that you have some task for me and my men and I am overjoyed at the prospect of action after so long a winter, doing little but training with the sword and in wrestling and other martial pursuits."

Vlad's long moustache twitched under his long nose. "Come up from down there, sir. Come here and sit at my side."

I moved to do just that and Walt came with me until Dracula waved him away. Walt's face clouded in warning but what could we do? He trudged back to his place below the salt and sat watching us from the corner of his eye, tense and ready to leap into action.

610

Dracula peered at me as I took the stool at his right hand, cold amusement on his face. "Do you know, Richard, that Wallachia has had twelve princes on the throne in the last forty years? That makes one prince for every three or four years. How long do you think I will last? Tell me, I wish you to answer."

"I shall pray that you last a lifetime, my lord."

He laughed, briefly. "You are a cleverer man than you seem, Richard. There is more to you than meets the eye, is there not? Tell me now, who do you think might become voivode if I am killed?"

I shrugged, as if I had not given the matter much thought. "I suppose there is your younger brother, Radu, who has elected to stay with the Turks."

Dracula's eyes looked through me. "My beloved brother, yes. Such a delightful boy, so obedient and lovely to look upon. The Turks love him dearly, though I do not think he will find much favour with our *boyars*. They are a rough people, do you not think? Of course you do. Have you heard any talk of my father's other sons?"

I had, of course, but I pretended ignorance. "Others, my lord? I had no idea."

He smiled. "My father left a string of bastards behind him wherever he went. Some of them are still alive but they know enough to keep quiet, for now. If I am killed, they shall be brought out of their holes and one promoted over another by this *boyar* or that one. Such endless intrigue. We are a people at war with ourselves when our enemy is united behind the Sultan. How can we hope to win the war for Christendom when we cannot win this war over ourselves?"

It was an old point, made many times before but I sensed this time he had something specific in mind that he was alluding to. "My lord?"

He waved away my confusion.

"Certainly, you know that my greatest rival is the *boyar* Albu? Have you heard that his men call him Albu the Great? He pretends his name comes from his grand achievements but in truth it is because of his gross corpulence? Admittedly, he is powerful, but what has he achieved in his life that men would think him great, other than attempt to unseat me during my first few months on the throne? I shall tell you, he has maintained his private army and has ceaselessly agitated for my removal. What do you think I should do about this largest of my subjects, Richard?"

"Take your men to his fortress, besiege it, capture it, capture him, and cut off his head."

Dracula wagged a finger at me. "Good advice, Richard. You always have such good advice. But what if you could take him on the road, when he is travelling between one fortress and another, in order to build his conspiracy against me, what then?"

"You know he is moving?"

"My men captured one of his messengers. He did not give up his secrets easily but give them up he did. So, Richard, do you advise that I move against Albu the Great?"

Another test for me. Did he wish to test my cunning or did he believe that I was engaged in this conspiracy against him? I wanted Dracula to leave his castles so that I could potentially kill him myself and flee, so I knew I should certainly advise him to pursue this Lord Albu in person.

But if I said as much explicitly, it would reveal me for a fool or as a possible assassin.

"I have known lords to give their men false messages," I said, "in the hopes that they will be captured. Perhaps Albu the Fat has done this very thing as means to draw you out of your fortresses and into the open. Your ambush on him might become an ambush on you, my lord."

He grinned. "I am relieved that you are so wise, Richard. Yes indeed, we suspected a ruse but then we captured a messenger, quite by chance, from the *boyar* who Albu is meeting. This messenger did not even know why he had been told to repeat the name of a place near to Pârscov. But he was confirming the meeting place. And so we know where, and we know when, and it is good that you and your men are here because we must leave at first light if we are to spring the ambush in time." He leaned in closer. "You will help me to secure my throne, will you not, Richard?"

Dracula was leaving the safety of his fortress with a small number of men and travelling into hostile territory.

I knew I might never have a better opportunity to kill him.

"I will join you gladly, my lord."

***

We rode out, fewer than three hundred fighting men and our servants. Each servant, from groom to valet, and squire to page, was able to ride hard and keep discipline. The Prince of Wallachia disguised himself beneath clothing provided by his men and no man was to kneel or bow to him at any time, on pain of death, lest we give him away to someone observing from afar.

Killing Dracula was on my mind. I might have been able to kill him while he slept but just as likely was being caught in the act, either before or after. Perhaps my company could manage to kill all of Dracula's men, especially if we took them by surprise.

But still I wished to question him. How did he become an immortal, what was his task in Wallachia, and most importantly of all, what were William's plans?

There was time enough yet for a better opportunity to emerge and so I continued to wait and to play the part of an obedient mercenary.

We came in time to the place of ambush and disported ourselves amongst the trees and rocks in preparation for the party to come by. We waited one afternoon all the way until dark, and then an entire day where the only excitement was a partly-sprung ambush on a shepherd and his sons. They were detained, lest they give our position away. I expected Dracula would have them killed but instead he treated them as honoured guests, poured them wine from his own skin and asked them about their lives. It took the shepherd some time to answer fully, and he looked terrified for much of it but by the end him and his sons were smiling with their prince.

"Friends of yours, my lord?" I asked, partly in jest when he passed by my position near sundown. I sat leaning back against an oak. "The shepherds?"

"They are now," he said, seating himself on the fallen tree trunk across from me and leaning forward with his elbows on his knees.

"You mean to befriend every man in the kingdom one by one?" I said, making it clear that I was speaking lightly and meant no criticism.

He almost smiled. "You think it a ploy? To pretend to enjoy the company of the peasant so that he will speak well of me to his fellows? I can see why a man as cunning as you would think that but no, that is not it. I do truly love my people. Not the *boyars*, though many are my good and dear friends, but the people who make this land. It is all but barbarous, this land of my blood, and would be so if not for the toil of the peasant who sculpts beauty and function from the wilderness by his labour. When I see my people going about their daily business, I am filled with joy and good cheer, for it is they who work the soil and they who make the land what it is. It is they who I mean to save from destruction."

"An interesting notion, my lord. Was this how your father felt, also?"

Dracula tilted his head, remembering. "In part, perhaps. It was never stated so clearly, not in my hearing, but he had a love for his people that caused him to make the choices he made, as poor as they were. But no, he did not instil this feeling in me. It was only after being kept away from my people for so long that I learned what it meant to be Wallachian. Every year, every month, every day, and every hour I was held by the Turks, I missed my homeland more. And all the while I was there, I believed it was freedom that I longed for. My homeland meant freedom and freedom is what every imprisoned man desires above all. But when I was free, I realised it was not freedom from bondage that I longed for, it was home itself. It was this, what we have before us now." He took the glove from one hand and dug his bare fingers down into the mulch between his feet, pulling out a handful of black, damp earth. "This, Richard. All of this. The sunlight blocked by dark green trees, filtering through to the pine needles underfoot, and this dark soil and the fast rivers cutting through the hills above and the wide, winding waters of the lowlands. And above all, my people. It is the people who make the land, the people who give it voice and soul and its heart. Not the *boyars*, even the loyal amongst them, and not the soldiers, though I love them also. No, it is the shepherds and the woodsmen and hunters and the peasants who make Wallachia and it is them who must be saved. They must be saved from the Turks, from the Hungarians, from the Catholics, and from the *boyars* who would see them fall to one or all of the aforementioned enemies." He wiped his hands on his woollen hose and put his glove back on. "Do you understand now, Richard?"

"I think I am beginning to," I said.

Was it true, I wondered, what he said about his land and his people, or was it meant to deceive me? And if it was true, did it not sound a little like the mad ramblings that William had spouted so many years ago, in Sherwood or was it my imagination?

613

And what did it say about me that I found his paternalistic affection for his people to be endearing, even a touch inspiring?

I could not risk asking my companions these questions, not when there were so many of Dracula's men around us. But I did not have to spend long alone with my thoughts.

It was the next morning when the ambush was sprung.

Albu the Great and his men rode hard and fast through the narrow defile, certainly aware of the danger such a path presented. But we were well prepared for their rapid passage. They were cut off at the front by a barricade and we moved to block the rear. A mere handful of Albu's followers escaped capture. Dracula's men, positioned amongst the trees and rocks of the slopes both sides of the track shot their arrows and guns down into the horsemen until those that survived surrendered.

"There you are, sir!" Dracula called out as he rode down to where Albu stood, bleeding from a wound to his head. "Albu the Gluttonous. How in the world did the bolts and shot miss your great girth, my lord? You must be blessed by God, dear Albu. Truly, you are blessed."

Amongst the fifty survivors was Albu and his entire family. Afraid to leave them unprotected, he had risked moving them to a better fortress only for his entire clan to be captured by us.

They were escorted to a close-cropped meadow near to a fortress called Bucov. Our prisoners were sullen and frightened, and it distressed me that Albu's children and nieces and nephews were as mistreated as their parents. And I was not the only one who felt that way.

"He ain't going to kill the little ones, is he?" Rob asked me during the journey.

"Of course not," I said, confidently. "Dracula was raised as a knight."

Outside of Bucov, Dracula assembled his men about the huge clearing which had dense trees on every side. Most of the servants and many of the soldiers were set to work felling tall pine saplings from those trees all around and trimming off the spindly branches. Other men dug a series of narrow, deep pits in rows.

Naive as I was, I believed they were working to prepare the materials for a palisade to keep the prisoners safe in overnight rather than keep them in Bucov itself.

Almost three hundred years old, having seen and done evil that would break the heart of any sane man, and still there was the remnants of innocence in me. But there was some evil, even then, that I had not yet seen.

Sheep shit was everywhere underfoot though the sheep and their shepherds were nowhere to be seen and I wondered idly if Dracula had not discovered the field through his discussion with the passing locals.

However he had found the secluded spot, once all was prepared, he assembled his men in an arc around the prisoners and declared that "Albu the Rotund" was a traitor and a friend to Turks.

"Lies!" Albu shouted over Dracula's speech. "You are the Turk, Vlad Dracula. You and your father before you. And your Turk brothers. It is you who are traitor! God knows it. All honest men know it."

Dracula stared at Albu with an unreadable expression on his face. It might have been anger but there was such coldness in the young man that it was difficult to be certain.

"For your crimes, Albu the Bloated, I sentence you and your family to suffer death by means of impalement."

The women in the party began wailing and Albu and his brothers cried out, begging that their children be spared. If not the sons, then the daughters at least.

"I am merciful," Dracula said, holding up his hands. "All daughters present who have less than twelve years shall be spared."

There were but two who met this criteria and they were carried off from their wailing mothers by rough-handed soldiers. There were four young boys and three older girls who were not so lucky as that. Albu's entire family were trussed up and some or all of their clothing removed.

"We have to stop this," Rob said, appalled.

Stephen crossed himself and mumbled endless prayers. Eva took my hand and turned her back on the scene.

"Ain't right," Walt muttered. "God knows, this ain't bloody right."

I nodded but I knew there was nothing that could be done.

The prisoners were impaled through their backsides. Each person writhing and screaming in agony as the sharpened stakes penetrated deeper and deeper into their bodies. One by one, they were heaved upright and the bases dropped into pits so that the impaled body was held aloft. Many were already dead or unconscious by that point but others remained alive, if it could be called living. They writhed in mindless agonies, causing their bodies to slide down the poles and the points to work their way deeper inside them until the tips travelled through the guts and into the chest causing the victim to suffocate or burst their heart.

The Wallachian soldiers did their work grimly but without hesitation, even with the children. And grim though they were, they took great pride and pleasure in the occasions when a stake could be forced through a body to emerge through the mouth so that they resembled a pig being roasted vertically.

Dracula appeared, throughout the entire event, to be almost uninterested in what he was witnessing.

Albu was saved until last, so that he witnessed the appalling death of his entire family, his entire clan, and would know that he had brought his line to an end by his folly. He cursed and growled at Dracula, his tears all shed and his throat ragged from wailing.

"Make sure his stake is sturdy enough," Dracula quipped to his men. Most were too appalled by their own actions to even pretend to find it amusing but there were plenty still who grinned and jeered at the broken man. For they had prepared a longer, and wider stake for Albu than for any of the others. Holding him down, they smeared blood from his wife onto the sharpened point of the stake to make it penetrate him more easily, and they prepared the way by first stabbing his arse with a spear to split him open wider. His screams of agony and rage were the only sound while Dracula's men worked the timber deeper into him, three grim soldiers twisting and heaving the stake in unison until Albu, mercifully, fell silent.

When they heaved him upright, he was the tallest of all the bodies. The weight of his body caused it to slide further down. Not fast enough for the soldiers, who pulled on his ankles until the point emerged from Albu's mouth, ripping off his jaw. They were proud of their precision and shook hands.

Even to the end, Vlad seemed entirely unaffected by the horrors he had witnessed.

Once Albu was dead, Dracula ordered the bodies cut down and burned, and the remains buried.

"Why?" I managed to ask the prince before we set off for Târgovişte. "Why perform such an appalling spectacle at all if it is to remain a secret?"

"It was to ensure that Albu suffered as much as a man can suffer for his betrayal. It was also necessary to spread fear amongst my enemies, for the tale shall certainly be told to all in time. You think my men, yours, and our servants will hold their tongues about this? And finally, simply, my men needed the practice."

"What practice? You mean impalement practice? What are you planning, my lord?"

He smiled, though there was no mirth, nor even pleasure, in it. "Come, Richard, we must hurry home. It is almost time for Easter, and we cannot miss the festivities."

***

The Easter celebrations were lavish and rather joyful. Vlad had invited more than two hundred of the *boyars* to the palace, along with their families, and a great and delightful time was had by all. I was honoured with a high place, though there were so many nobles in attendance. Not just *boyars* from across the country but leading citizens from Târgovişte were invited also.

"I am sorry that you were witness to the recent unpleasantness in the woods, Richard," Vlad said after I was invited to sit by him at the end of the meal. "Do you understand why it was necessary?"

Unpleasantness, I thought, recalling the screams. "In part, my lord," I said. "Though there is some of it that I wish I had not seen."

"Come, Richard, you must have seen worse things than that in your time." He peered at me, his look loaded with significance.

"You mean in my time as a mercenary?"

"But of course, Richard. What else could I mean?" He drank from his wine, looking over his goblet at me with his dark, bulging eyes. "You do understand that ruthlessness is a most desirable trait in a prince, do you not?"

"I understand that a king must be the dispenser of justice in his kingdom."

"Ah, so you disapprove? How interesting." He frowned, not in displeasure but in what seemed to be genuine curiosity. "How is it that you have retained such squeamishness over your long life when your older brother has embraced all aspects of personal and political tyranny?"

I froze, preparing to grab one of the knives at my belt or within in my sleeve.

Dracula glanced at me just for a moment, as if we were good friends having a pleasant conversation.

"So it is true," I said. "William gave you the Gift of his blood. And in return you will give him Wallachia."

Dracula bent his head and looked at me through his thick, raised eyebrows. "You have misjudged me, sir. Sorely misjudged me." He sat upright and clapped his hands before rubbing them together. "We must, of course, discuss this further, Richard, but would you be so kind as to excuse me for a few moments? I must speak briefly to my honoured guests."

He got to his feet, and I made ready to fight off any assault. But none came. Instead, Vlad nodded at his seneschal who raised his voice and roared for silence.

It took mere moments for the conversation in the hall to die away into nothing while all eyes turned to Vlad III Dracula, who smiled and raised his hands, palms up, in a gesture of welcome.

"My comrades, my brothers, my friends. Once more, I thank you for honouring me with your presence on this most holy day of celebration. This feast of feasts, celebration of celebrations, is a joyous occasion on which we praise Christ for all eternity. Christ is risen from the dead, trampling down death by death, and upon those in the tombs, bestowing life. And so it is that Wallachia rises once more into greatness. My friends, it has been a trying time for our people. You have known such disruption, from the times of our fathers and our grandfathers."

Vlad picked out an old man and pointed at him with a smile. "Michael, my lord of Giurgiu, you are as venerable as many here." Vlad glanced at me before smiling broadly at Michael of Giurgiu once more. "Barring perhaps one or two exceptions. Tell me, my lord, how many Princes of Wallachia have you known in your life?"

The old man shifted in his seat. "Difficult to say, my lord. Seems at times like it may be thirty of them." He finished with a grin and many in the hall laughed lightly.

I glanced at Vlad, but he laughed also. "You would have to be two hundred years old for it to be thirty, my lord, but you are not wrong in spirit." Still smiling, Dracula picked out another older man on the other side of the hall. "Alexander? What say you? How many princes have you served?"

This old man did not smile and he his eyes were dangerous. "In my lifetime, perhaps ten or so. My lord."

Dracula clapped his hands, grinning. "You are close to the truth, Alexander, very close, but it is in fact more than ten. Even the youngest of the lords here have likely known seven princes. Tell me, my lords, how do you explain the fact that you have had so many princes in your land?"

Vlad looked around the silent hall, while the smile on his face died away. The smiles on the faces of the *boyars* died away, also.

"As I see that you are all too afraid to speak, I shall tell you," Dracula said, his voice hardening. "The cause is entirely due to your shameful intrigues."

The lords protested, while their sons and their wives looked from man to man, worried about the sudden turn of events.

"No longer!" Vlad roared, his voice filling the hall like thunder, silencing hundreds of people. Dracula looked around the room, fixing man after man with his bulging eyes. "For the sake of my kingdom and of the people of Wallachia, I sentence every person here to death."

The soldiers must have been waiting at every entrance around the hall for they filed in at that moment from all directions and surrounded the *boyars* and townsfolk. A number of the *boyars*, unarmed though they were, attempted to fight the soldiers but these great lords were immediately murdered by spears and axes, bringing screams of terror and outrage from their women. Soon enough, the lords held their wives and children close while the soldiers escorted them from the hall.

"Come," Vlad said to me, still as a cat before it pounces and yet raging with cold fire behind his wild eyes. "You must bear witness to this, also, Richard."

There were close to a thousand prisoners in all, including the wives and children who had not attended the feast but who had been dragged from their lodgings throughout Târgoviște. All were rounded up and marched through the city and out of the gate to the assembly fields before the walls and beyond the suburbs.

When I reached the top of the wall and looked out over the battlements, it was just as I had dreaded. A thousand great stakes, twenty feet long or more, had been prepared and without fanfare or ceremony, Dracula's soldiers began impaling the great lords, their wives, and their children.

Just as I had witnessed in the clearing near Bucov, they were partially or entirely stripped and held down. Many were split first by sword, spear, or knife, and then the sharpened stakes were pushed within while the victim was held in place by up to four men, one on each limb. I noted that the points of the stakes were being smeared with white lard or oil to facilitate the ease of passage. The sheer mundane practicality of it filled me with revulsion and I wanted to turn away but I could not.

The wailing and screaming that filled the air was unbearable. Others around me walked away, and others stood watching but with their hands over their ears. One of Dracula's veteran bodyguards, sturdily built and old enough to be a grandfather, loomed nearby with tears streaming into his moustache.

Worst of all was the silent terror and confusion on the faces of the children and their

618

mothers' futile attempts to shield their eyes and ears from the fate that awaited them.

Beside me on the wall, Vlad watched the scene wordlessly, and with a complete lack of expression on his face.

"You spared the youngest children before," I managed to say to Dracula. "You must do so again."

It seemed to amuse him. "You are truly unlike your brother. That is good, Richard. He said that you were yet limited by archaic and idealistic notions of morality instilled in you by hypocritical mortals centuries ago but I assumed that was down to William's rhetorical tendencies toward hyperbole. And so, I will admit to being surprised to see it in action. But it pleases me to see I was wrong. Yes, you are different indeed."

"The children, Vlad."

He sighed. "Very well." Dracula turned to his seneschal. The man's face was ashen and he had vomit on his embroidered silk doublet. "Have the children under ten years of age separated. Chain them, one to the other, in view of their parents. Tell them that their youngest sons and daughters will be used as labourers on my new castle. They shall be slaves until they die from the work. Ensure each man knows that despite this act of mercy, his line is ended. Do this now."

The seneschal bowed and hurried away.

Below, there were dozens and then hundreds of dying bodies hoisted aloft and fixed in place. The sounds of men begging for the lives of their sons and the screams of women and the stench of blood and shit aroused in me the most profound horror I have ever felt.

"You think me a monster," Vlad said quietly from beside me.

"This *is* monstrous," I said, slapping the top of the crenel in frustration. "The *boyars* and their eldest sons, I can understand, but their wives and daughters? They should not be made to suffer this."

"You are at liberty to feel outrage at my actions because you are a knight," Vlad said.

"So are you!" I snapped.

"I was raised to be a prince," he said, speaking so softly it was difficult to hear his words over the screams. "And now I am the ruler of Wallachia. I cannot afford the sensibilities of knights, nor commoners, or *boyars*."

"Kings are not above God," I said. "And God says what is just."

"Oh? I thought you said that law and custom are paramount?"

"And what does your law and custom say about this?" I said, jabbing my finger at the carnage.

He turned and looked at me with those bulging, dark eyes. He seemed utterly calm and entirely unaffected by the unfolding scene of inhuman horror beyond his walls. "When the laws of the land are leading your people to destruction, it is time that those laws be changed, is it not?"

I had no answer for him. But I did have questions.

"How then does this act help to save your people?"

"I shall kill every Turk in the world and every man who stands in my way." He nodded at the dead and dying.

"Every man, and his family?"

"Precisely this."

The sheer barbarity of it, the totality of it, was stunning to me. His unwavering certainty, his seeming lack of guilt or shame for the acts of slaughter he had instigated, was breathtaking. He reminded me of my brother.

Vlad stayed to watch until most of his victims were dead and then he turned to the men around us. "You may all return to the hall where we shall complete our feasting. The cooks have prepared an array of fried pastries, marzipan cakes, and sweet custard. I shall undertake a brief perambulation about the walls and join you shortly, my friends."

Dracula walked away along the walls with his bodyguards, as if the air was pleasant to take in, and his remaining companions left for the castle.

I stayed on the wall and watched until every person had taken their last breath and still I watched as the flocks of crows came swarming onto the bodies from the darkening sky. Watched as they feasted on the eyes and entrails of the people who had earlier been feasting themselves.

"That's that, then, Richard," Walt muttered at my shoulder. "We'll have to kill him now and be done with it."

"Not yet," I said, watching a crow stabbing its mighty black beak into the wound around a neck where the stake had emerged on its passage through the victim's body. A long piece of skin stretched impossibly before it snapped and the crow gulped it down.

"He returns," Walt mumbled, covering his mouth. "We can do it now and flee."

I placed two fingers on Walt's sword arm and watched as Dracula returned from his tour around the walls of Târgovişte. "Richard, you are still here. If I had not been told so much about you, I would have thought you were revelling in this scene. But that is not it at all, is it?"

"Is it not?" I said, aware that Walt was like a coiled snake beside me.

Dracula took up position beside me, leaning on the crenel and looking out through the battlements to the scene of death that he had wrought. His flank was exposed to me and I knew I could run my dagger into his kidneys, force him down onto his chest across the parapet and strike his head from his shoulders before his bodyguards could reach me.

"William told me that you were prone to melancholia, brought about by a surfeit of personal responsibility and a desire to do penance for the sins of yourself and all of mankind, combined with the guilt of never carrying out said penance on account on your choleric nature."

"Utter nonsense," I snapped. "What is he now, a physician or a priest?

"He is a demon, Richard," Dracula said, speaking softly. "A demon that walks the earth in the form of a man. You think me evil for my actions here today? I did this evil only because I must overcome the greater evil of another."

"Overcome?"

"I need your help, sir," he said. "I cannot do it alone."

"Do what, Vlad?"

Dracula stood and looked up at me, his face in shadow. "I will kill him, Richard. If it is the last thing I do, I shall kill my maker, William de Ferrers."

10

Vlad and William

1458

IT WAS AFTER DRACULA massacred the *boyars* at Târgoviște that people began calling him Vlad *Țepeș* which meant Impaler in the Wallachian tongue.

The children of the *boyars* were indeed spared impalement. Instead, they were manacled and chained together in a horrific procession and were marched, hard, for two days up the River to the construction site of Poenari Castle. Those children were made to carry bricks up the dangerous slopes and steps to build the towers and the walls, and one by one they were worked to their eventual deaths through exhaustion and accidents.

With the massacre of their parents, the core of the ancient *boyar* class of Wallachia was smashed. Even many of those of the old families who had been spared an invitation to the feast decided to flee to Transylvania. Some even fled to the Turks, which certainly lent weight to Dracula's argument that the *boyars* were infested with traitors.

All the deaths and voluntary exiles meant that enormous tracts of land were now in need of new lords and Dracula offered those confiscated domains to new men, many of whom were of astonishingly low birth. It was quite clever of him to do so because those commoners now owed everything to their prince and their fortune was tied entirely to his fate.

He also set about rearranging his state and created a new body to be set above the grand council of the *boyars*, called the *arma*. In theory, the *arma* was designed to administer and carry out the policies decided by the grand council of *boyars* but everyone understood that it in fact would simply do the bidding of the prince.

The *arma* was set above the *boyars*, who had never had anyone above them before other than the prince himself. The *arma* was made up from many of the new, loyal *boyars* but Dracula installed other men also, such as peasants elevated to officers in his new army and even a handful of foreign mercenaries.

In fact, he named me as a member of the *arma*. My duties would be to attend these meetings and offer my opinion on matters and to then carry out the tasks assigned to me.

It was not only the civil administration of the state that Dracula set about reforming. He needed to pay swift and drastic attention to the organisation of the army, such as it was, and so he created an officer class called the *viteji*. The *viteji* were drawn from the free peasants who had proved themselves extremely capable in battle and they were intended to form a leadership role over the peasantry who the prince intended to call to war.

"You have been busy, my lord," I said to Dracula as we rode away from his latest batch of *viteji* who were undergoing military training in the valley beneath Poenari Castle.

"Not busy enough. We have much work to do and I cannot wait any longer."

Our horses walked at a steady pace along the track. It was a warm day and Vlad had spent it all sweating in his fine clothes, giving a steady stream of observations and orders to the men organising the training of his new officers. He knew precisely what he wanted. Efficiency, consistency, and obedience.

"You wish to rush to make war on the Turks?"

"We are not yet ready for that. No, there are more enemies within my borders who require bringing to heel before we can turn our attention to our common foe."

"Who?" I asked.

He frowned at my tone. "You will hear when I am ready to speak of it."

Vlad cultivated an air of supreme confidence and calmness, especially in physical confrontations and when arguing with another. But I had seen his mask slip when he was defied. I sensed also that he was more unsure of himself around me than he wanted to let on. I decided to push him by allowing more of my true self to come out. I was his superior in arms, in years, in ability, in strength. We had continued to play our parts in the days since his admission that he wanted to kill William but I could not wait patiently for ever to know more. I wanted to hear it now.

"You must tell me about William, Vlad," I said. "It is time. You have avoided the question long enough."

He scowled. "You cannot speak to me in that manner. Do you forget that I am a prince?"

I shrugged and spoke lightly. "Do you forget who I am, my lord?"

Vlad scoffed. "And who are you, Richard?"

"I am pretending to be a mercenary who is pretending to be a crusader. But you know who I am. You know what I am. And I want to know what my brother told you about me."

Dracula almost smiled. "Everywhere I go there are ears listening. We shall make our way to a paddock in the next village."

"A paddock?"

"I would very much like to test my skill against yours, Richard. And I shall not ask your permission, for I am the prince and you are one of my loyal men, are you not?"

I did not answer him, and he seemed content to let his jibe rest.

The village ahead was disbursed over half the width of the valley, on either side of the river. Each house had a large kitchen garden and pens for pigs, which were numerous, and tethered goats that stared at us as we rode by.

The villagers came in across the fields where they worked and out of their small houses as our party approached, calling out praise and blessings to Vlad Dracula. He smiled and blessed them in turn, flicking small coins to this man or that who caught them out of the air or stooped, laughing, to pick them out of the dust. The chief man of the village escorted us to his house, bowing repeatedly and babbling constantly until his wife shushed him and drove him into the house.

"He fought with me years ago when I was with my cousin Stephen in Moldavia. A good soldier, though getting a little long in the tooth to serve in the *viteji*."

"Oh? I would have thought experienced older men were a good counter to the young ones. If you breed two hot-blooded horses you may find yourself on an uncontrollable beast. Sometimes it is better to temper the hot blood with the cool and so steady the animal."

"Perhaps you are right. And if he cannot keep up with our pace, I can always have him dismissed. I shall speak with him once we are done."

The man's servants led the sturdy ponies out of their paddock and away toward the village.

Vlad declined the offered wine and food but did so with politeness. The man and his wife went away smiling at each other while I opened the paddock gate. Their children peered out of the open door, their eyes wide and round.

The bodyguards and servants distributed themselves around the village, accepting offered food and drink, while Vlad's squires provided wooden practice swords to each of us before retiring to beyond the wooden perimeter of the paddock and closing the gate.

"It has been some time since I used one of these," Vlad said, hefting his wooden weapon.

"Oh? I ensure my men utilise them regularly. There is nothing quite like being thumped by a length of timber to let you know you made a mistake."

"Not as true to life as using blunted swords," Vlad replied. "And I often use sharpened blades when I spar with my men. It adds true danger to one's practice that cannot be achieved through these sticks."

I shrugged. "When training in full armour, I might agree but otherwise a man will always pull his cuts a little short for fear of hurting his opponent."

Vlad smirked. "Not my men."

"Yes, your men," I said. "Especially your men. Your men most of all. If they killed you in practice it would mean their death and so they are careful to fight below their true abilities. You do yourself a disservice by using sharp weapons. Perhaps you are not as skilled as you believe yourself to be."

He narrowed his eyes. "I do not think so."

I shrugged again, as I had no care either way. "We shall see."

"Keep away!" Vlad snapped at two of his men who had drifted to the edge of the paddock to watch us. "I do not perform for your entertainment, you dogs. Turn your backs and move away."

They did as they were ordered, slumping off chastened.

He was irritated by my tone, I am sure, as no one had spoken to him with anything but deference for years. Perhaps it reminded him of his past, when he had been no more than a hostage. Perhaps my tone reminded him of my brother. I decided to push him further and the next time I spoke, I used French. He spoke it perfectly, but it was another passively aggressive way to anger him.

"Your bodyguards are afraid you will be hurt but they are too afraid of your wrath to tell you so. That is a mistake. A lord needs men courageous enough to draw their master back from acts that are a danger to him."

"Enough talk," Vlad said and lunged at me.

He was quick but after my gentle goading I had fully expected him to make a sudden attack.

Instead of feeling out my ability by a series of noncommittal exchanges, he instead continued to advance and attack with a flurry of cuts, feints, thrusts from all angles, changing directions and speed as he did so.

Our wooden blades clacked at a furious rhythm and our shoes stomped on the dry, short-clipped grass underfoot.

There were many styles of swordplay and it varied from place to place, with one kingdom adopting a certain style while a neighbour would develop another. Different masters had their own methods and practices which they would teach and this one or that would find favour with a monarch or with a series of powerful lords and their influence would spread across regions and down generations. And the practice had changed over the centuries as weapons and armour developed. Some men still liked to use shields or bucklers in practice or on the field but most that fought in plate armour had little use for them and so two-handed swords and polearms had become standard. As experience developed down through the years, certain tricks and their counters were developed and became established and new ones were introduced until duelling and sword practice had taken on a sophistication it had not had in my youth.

But I had kept up with it all. It was my business and my life depended on it. Indeed, it could not be avoided. My lifespan meant I was more experienced than any mortal man and most of the immortal ones also and my strength and speed meant I was essentially unbeatable in a one-on-one duel.

And yet there were gifted fighters. Men who were born with natural abilities beyond their fellows, who excelled at their chosen martial art, whether it be jousting, or sword and buckler, or spear fighting. Amongst many thousands of professional soldiers, I would find one every now and then who was a true master.

To my surprise, Vlad III Dracula was one such man.

I had seen his exceptional horsemanship on display before, and indeed he was known for it, and I had seen him thrash Vladislaus in a duel to the death. But I had not known what skill he possessed in the sword.

He came at me with such expertise that I had to leap out of my sense of complacency to avoid being thrashed by him. And when I stepped up my defence, he likewise adjusted and improved his attacks. Again and again, I moved to shut him down and he ramped up his skill and speed.

It was clear that he meant to beat me. With everything that he had. And yet his expression remained impassive, even when he began taking heaving breaths and the sweat streamed down his face, sticking his sodden black hair to his forehead.

His wooden sword snapped above the handle, sending the blade part spinning through the air so far that it landed beyond the paddock, causing the bodyguards there to duck as it bounced between them.

We stood, breathing heavily, with scores of Dracula's men staring at us from two sides of the paddock.

Vlad straightened up and lifted his hat. After wiping the sweat from his face he clamped it down on his head again and looked at me through his thick eyebrows.

"You are almost as fast as your brother."

Almost.

"You fought William?"

"Could you have beaten me?"

"Yes."

"Easily?"

"You are as gifted a swordsman as I ever met. But yes." He stared at me, still breathing hard. "You should not feel too disheartened, Vlad. How old are you?"

"I have almost thirty years."

"And I have almost three hundred."

He jabbed the broken stump of his sword toward me. "Perhaps in three hundred years, I shall have you."

I smiled. The courtly thing to do would have been to accept his attempt at saving face. "In three hundred years, Vlad, I shall be six hundred years old and you still will not beat me."

He scoffed. "Perhaps you will be dead. And then I will be the greatest swordsman."

"Perhaps I will be. But then we would never know who was the best, would we?"

Vlad tossed his broken sword to the side and turned back to his watching men. "Attend to your duties. I will not repeat my order again."

I could see why they had drifted over, in spite of themselves. The sounds of the fight must have drawn glances and the speed of our movements must have moved their feet close out of astonishment.

"Have you told your men what you are?" I asked.

"Do you take me for a fool?"

"You are their prince. They have sworn themselves to you. They have committed mass impalements for you."

"Not enough. They must do more and so I cannot afford doubt from them. Look at yourself, Richard. Ever since you came to Hungary, years ago, there have been rumours about blood drinking where you and your closest companions are concerned."

I shrugged. "We used to make extraordinary efforts to conceal it. Once, when I was in the east many years ago, I used only mute slaves who could not tell others about our bloodletting. They were rather difficult to procure. One slaver was particularly adept at procuring these mutes and after a while it became clear he was cutting out their tongues before selling them to us in order to raise the price. Later, we brought in servants from foreign lands who did not speak the local languages but you can imagine the difficulties that brought as far as their duties were concerned. Soon, we would change any servant we suspected of spreading the tales. But servants talk. They always talk. And word always gets out."

"And you have them killed?"

"Why? When one or two in the next batch would talk, also. Word always gets out, Vlad. No matter what we tried, there would always be the rumours of our bloodletting and what we did with the blood we took. Blood magic, dark magic, communing with the Devil."

"And blood drinking."

"Of course. What secret does any man hold alone who has servants in his house? In London, our house was often swamped in rumour. Some merchants would stop doing business with us or one or more of us might be expelled from a guild."

"I would have such men killed. Quietly, of course."

"That is one way. But pay a man a few coins and it is often enough to buy his silence. Or there are other secrets he might hold himself that he does not wish to be made public. We grew rather adept at bringing powerful men into our net and using them to discover even more secrets."

"You have been doing the same here," Vlad said. "Your man named Stephen and the woman who shares your bed. They are drinkers of your blood also? They have been made by you into one such as I am."

I considered holding back, suspecting that he was seeking to extract information that he intended to use against us. But sometimes one must throw away caution and embrace uncertainty.

"What did my brother tell you?"

"That you have a small and pathetic company of useless commoners that you drag behind you through the centuries."

How does William know that? He has not seen me for two hundred years.

I smiled. "Ah, you truly have spoken to him. Please, Vlad. Will you tell me about it?"

He stared through me and then up at the wooded hills, the rocky peaks and the blue sky beyond, shielding his eyes. Vlad nodded slowly, almost absentmindedly, and ambled to the far edge of the paddock which looked out at a field of green wheat and the river beyond. I followed and watched him from the corner of my eye as he locked the fingers of both hands together, rested his forearms on the top of the paddock fence and leaned on it. Were it not for his ornate clothing and muscular build, he would have looked for all the world like a peasant surveying his land.

"We were young when he first came to us. My brother Radu and I were almost alone there. The servants sent over with us had been stripped away, one by one, for spurious reasons. We were instructed in Turkish and Arabic. Taught to ride their horses, in their saddles. We ate their food and listened to sermons about their Prophet and their God. And then he came to us, big and loud and filled with movement and passions, speaking French and Latin and Greek, to talk about Christ and knights and jousting and bedding beautiful women. He brought us gifts of familiar horses and the saddles in which we had first learned to ride. This food makes me sick, he would say, come and dine with me and we will eat stews with sausages of pork. But do not tell the Turks about this, for such things go against their law and their God, it is a special thing just for us good Christians who are alone together in this strange land."

"He has always been a snake."

"It is so clear now that it shames me. How easy it was for him to make us love him. As easy as breathing. Mere child's play. But we *were* children and we were so desperate for home and for our father and so, yes, we loved him. Rejoicing at his visits. When he was absent it was as though we simply counted the days until the sudden brightness and joy of his presence."

"You are not the first he has charmed."

"Charm, yes. We were enchanted by him. And yet I knew something was wrong with him. The servants, the guards, our instructors and tutors, the behaviour of every other man changed when in his presence and it took some time before I recognised it for what it was. Fear. I rationalised that they were fearful of his power as a pasha of the Sultan but in fact it was something deeper than that, something deep inside them. It was terror. A terror one might feel when trapped in a cage with a hungry lion. Or the terror of finding yourself before God with a heart full of unrepentant sin. And I noticed that Zaganos Pasha enjoyed their terror. Revelled in it. He was amused by it and would draw it out further by engaging them in conversation."

"It frightened you."

"No. By God, no. I wanted that for myself. I wanted men to shiver as I passed them in the hall. I wanted soldiers to shake so hard when I addressed them that they dropped their spears and fumbled to pick them up again. But Radu is not like me. His enchantment turned to fear when William revealed his true nature."

"He told you of his immortality?"

"Later, yes. Before then, he turned his attention on Radu by humiliating him in public whenever he committed the slightest error. William would instruct him in the sword in good humour until Radu made an error, at which point William would strip him and whip his bare legs bloody, all the while proclaiming him to be entirely without merit. And at night, in private, William would come to him and whisper sweet words and embrace him and cover his hair with kisses."

"By God. He forced himself upon him?"

"Forced, perhaps or manipulated my brother into allowing it or even desiring it. I do not know for certain. Radu, in his shame, would not speak of it nor hear it spoken of. Whatever perverse delights he felt, it became clear later that William was in fact preparing Radu for Mehmed."

"I do not understand."

"Sultan Mehmed lies with many women. It is his duty to get sons on them. But his passion has always been for young men and the older sorts of boys. You see, my brother was always fine featured. It was often said that his face was more beautiful than that of a ripe young woman, with skin as smooth as silk, his limbs elegantly proportioned and supple as an almond sapling. Grown women and girls fell in love with Radu on sight but he was not allowed to go to them. Instead, William first made Radu his own, body and soul, and then sent him into the tent of Mehmed to win his heart."

"To spy on Mehmed?"

"To fill Mehmed's head with whatever William wanted, I suspect. Men are uniquely vulnerable when sated in the dark of the night, do you not think? It helped to secure William's place by Mehmed's side when old Murad died."

"William had been advising a succession of Sultans already before Murad."

"Yes and each time the transition between one lord and another was the most dangerous time for him, threatening to undo everything that he had done before."

"He told you this?"

Dracula took a deep breath and turned away from the scene before us to look back at the village where his men lounged and laughed in the sun. "I attempted to help Radu. I urged him to resist, to fight every time, every night, to fight even if it meant his death. That is what I did to survive. When William attempted to discipline me in public, I would harangue him in turn and call him a traitor to his people and a pathetic servant who should bow down to me, who was of royal birth." Vlad smiled to himself at the memory. "Sometimes he would make a joke of it. Other times he would strike me or beat me badly. But next time I just fought all the harder, even when William crushed the bones of my sword hand in his fist. Even when he broke my ribs one day and my jaw the next, still I fought. Radu would not. Or could not. He was younger, of course, and weaker in his heart.

Always. And so I gave him up. He would not save himself and so I would not save him. How can one respect a man who does not respect himself? His weakness was contemptible."

"Not all men will choose death over subjugation."

Vlad replied without hesitation. "All true men would certainly choose death over dishonour. Only the slave chooses slavery over death. All slaves have chosen their slavery."

"Is it not better at times to live so that one may take revenge?"

"If one chooses that path, he must know that he will never be whole again. He will never be a true lord."

"Forgive me but how is that you then continued to live amongst your enemies?"

"I was a prisoner, not a slave. I was never subservient and all recognised me as a king."

"They intended for you to become their king. A client king, subject to the Sultan."

"They did. But always I knew I would fight them to the death rather than kneel and call them lord. And I wanted William's power in order to free my people."

"His power to fill men with terror?"

"That, and the terrible power of his limbs. When I witnessed him tear a man's throat out with his bare hands and bathe his face in the blood, I knew that he possessed a great magic. It was unnatural. Perhaps evil. And I wanted it."

"And you got it. How?"

Vlad looked pained and glanced at the sky. "It grows late. We shall return to Poenari and feast."

I wanted desperately to know it all but I knew it would be a difficult thing for him to speak of. No doubt, Vlad wanted time to compose himself and to fortify his heart with wine. And as impatient as I was, I wanted that too.

"I will see you there, my lord," I said.

When I walked back toward my horse, Rob strode over with a stiffness to his hunched shoulders that told me had important news to impart. What it might be, I could not imagine.

"Richard," he said, keeping his voice low. "There's a woman in this village. A very interesting woman. You should speak with her."

"Oh?" I said. "Pretty, is she?"

He sighed. "Please, follow me."

***

The house was tiny, out away at the edge of the village and with a small patch of woodland behind it. With a steep thatched roof and a stone wall around the lower course and plastered wattle and daube walls above, the neat garden was surrounded by a hazel fence.

Walt and Eva lounged beside the open door on a low, stone bench. Both sipped on a cup of something.

"What is this?" I asked them as I approached.

"Rob made a friend," Walt said. "But we can't understand a word she's saying."

"Why do we need to understand what she is saying? Who is she?"

Stephen stomped from the door with a scowl on his face. "She is a hardnosed old crone and we are wasting our time, Rob. She knows nothing at all."

From inside the house came the sounds of someone banging around.

"She knows," Rob said. "If only we could understand what she was saying."

"Did you find Serban?" Eva asked.

"You know what he's like," Walt said. "Workshy old bastard sleeping it off somewhere."

"Richard speaks the Roman tongue like a native," Rob said. "He can question her."

"Will one of you fools tell me what is happening here?"

An old woman appeared in the doorway. Her hair was tucked under a scarf, and she wore a vividly white shirt beneath a sort of embroidered waistcoat and a long, plain skirt down to her shoes. She scowled up at me and threw up her hands.

"So, you have come? What is wrong with you that you send these fools to me to ask their foolish questions when they will not listen to the answers? Well, I suppose you had better come inside, if you must." She held up a bony finger. "I warn you. If you try to take my blood, or turn me into a *strigoi*, I shall cut off your head, do you understand?"

I dragged my eyes from her outstretched finger and looked into her dark eyes. "I understand, good woman."

She scoffed and disappeared into the darkness.

"You could understand her fully?" Rob said.

"Of course," I said. "You speak the same tongue as she does well enough. And Wallachian is almost the same language as Italian, which you speak like a native. It is not so far away from Latin. What is wrong with you lot?"

"But her accent is so strong to be indecipherable," Eva said. "And there are the peculiar words these mountain folk use."

"She refuses to speak slower," Walt said. "Just won't bloody do it."

"You are all hopeless," I said, ducking to pass through the doorway into the dark house.

I took off my hat as I entered, only to find myself whipped across the face by a great bunch of dried herbs.

"What are you doing?" I said, fending off the next blow from the old woman.

She clucked her tongue and thrashed me on the hand and arm, then on my body, sending pieces of dried plant matter into the air and onto my clothes. She muttered some sort of spell or prayer under her breath as she did so. Apparently satisfied for a moment, she threw down her bunch of herbs onto the table and grabbed a head of garlic which she crushed together in both of her hands and held up to my face, muttering the spell once more. The pungent smell filled my nose and I moved away, wafting at the stink.

"Aha!" she said, "you are *strigoi*. I knew it. The herbs do not lie."

"Are you finished?" I said, looking around the room. Her house was a single room, with a table, a fire place, a sideboard, a bed, and not much else. It was spartan to say the least, but it was impeccably clean.

"No!" she said, fishing something out from beneath her waistcoat. "Not finished."

She whipped out a small crucifix on a leather thong and dangled it before me. "Take this iron into your hand and close your fist about it."

I sighed and did as she commanded, holding the simple little thing in my closed hand. "Is something supposed to happen?" I asked.

Eyeing me warily, she sidled over to her table and took a seat on one of the benches. "You will hold the iron cross in your hand until you leave, do you understand?"

"Fine, fine," I said. "May I sit?"

She nodded and indicated the bench across from her. On the table was a jug and two cups. Crudely made but with a blue bird upon the jug and a pattern in the Greek style on the cups.

"My friends asked me to come here to speak with you," I said, looking at the herbs on the table and still smelling the crushed garlic. Amongst the bunch of dried herbs I recognised the yellow flowers of wolf's bane and the leaves of belladonna. "And I can well imagine what it is that they wish for us to speak about." She watched me closely and said nothing. "My name is Richard."

"I will not tell you my name."

"Another method of protection against evil?" I asked but she only glared. "Thank you for welcoming me into your home. That was quite a welcome. Do you do the same for all of your guests?"

She grunted. "Only the ones that are dead."

"Dead? My dear woman, I am not dead."

"Perhaps," she said.

"Do you receive a lot of dead visitors?"

"Not as often as I would wish," she said, speaking quietly.

I sighed, hearing my friends muttering outside in muted conversation. A bee flew in through the window, flew around the room in one quick circuit and then flew out again. It seemed increasingly plausible that the old woman was not in the full possession of her wits but Rob had summoned me for a reason and he was not a man prone to flights of fancy.

"Do you know stories of immortal people? Those that live forever, and who are very strong, and who drink blood?" I watched her for a response as I spoke but her scowl did not waver. Her brown eyes were so dark they were almost black and her eyebrows knitted almost together above her axe-blade of a nose. But it was not an unpleasant face for all that. "You seem to know spells and herb craft to ward yourself against them. Can it be that you think me and my men are immortals? Surely, if you truly thought that was the case, you would not have let us in. So, what can you tell me?"

She lifted her small, pointed chin to look down that nose at me. "I know that you are one of great power. I see it in your eyes." She jabbed a crooked finger at the doorway. "And I know that your friends are the lesser creatures. Yes, yes, I know this. Do not deny it."

"What do you know of it?"

"Why do you ask what you already know?"

I tapped my fingers on the table, smiling at her scowl. "Well, how about this, then? Would you tell me how you know about these people? What tales you have heard."

"Oh," she said, waving her hand in the air. "Everyone knows. Everyone. The tales are told to all children."

"What are these tales?"

She reached forward and poured a cup of water for me and filled her own before drinking from it. "I was born in the west. By the Iron Gates. There were stories about the *strigoi* and I knew they were true because my mother and father never lied to me. But I never expected to see one." She took a drink of her water and I noted her hand was shaking. "My husband was from here. He came with his father across the hills many times with their wool and it was a good match. My husband was a good man. A good man. We lived well. We had a daughter and I was going to have a son but he died. One summer, a man came through, claiming to be an apothecary but he had little enough to sell and we thought him nothing but a vagrant. He had a monk with him, though, so we thought he must be right enough. The vagrant asked if he could collect leeches from the pond and we saw no harm in it and both men were put up by the blacksmith and his wife." She stopped to cross herself and then she stared past me to the open door and the colourful, sunlit world beyond.

"They were blood drinkers?" I prompted. "The leech-collector and the monk?"

She glanced at me, seeming surprised I was there for a moment before nodding and continuing. "In the morning, Rab and Maria were found dead. Their children found them, both their throats torn and bloody. Both drained of the blood."

"And the vagrant and the monk?"

The woman nodded. "Gone." She sighed. "So we thought."

"They came back?"

"They never left. I do not know where they went in the day but at night, they came and they killed us. We barred our doors and we listened to them outside, knocking on the door and the shutters and laughing. Some nights would pass and everyone would be safe in the morning. But every two or three days, another would be found dead. I picked and hung herbs. We made crucifixes and placed them around. At night, we prayed together over our child. My husband wanted to fight them. He said he knew how to kill them." She peered at me sidelong.

"How does one kill them?"

"Iron."

I lifted my fist up. "Held in the hand?"

She scoffed. "That merely traps them. To kill them, you must drive a rod of iron through their heart. Or elsewise cut off their heads."

"Yes, I find cutting off the heads to be the best method."

"You mock me," she said, planting her hands on the table and getting to her feet.

"I do not," I said, with sincerity. "The iron rod, I had not heard of before. Please, do go on."

Warily, she sat down. "My husband said that was why they had killed Rab first. He was the blacksmith. And my husband went there to find iron with which to kill the *strigoi*. But it was all gone. They had taken it all. Hidden it. Buried it. There was nothing else for it, he said. He would not wait around until we were killed. He would take the ploughman's riding horse and ride down to Arges. If he left at dawn, he could be back with soldiers by nightfall."

"Then what happened?"

"He did not return. They came for me that night. They hammered on my door and my window, they attacked the thatch. My girl, she cried and wailed. But my husband had strengthened the house everywhere. New timber across there, and there, do you see?" She pointed up at the roof above. Instead of the underside of thatch showing, the inside was lined with sturdy planks. The shutters and the inside of the door were likewise crossed with old oak an inch thick. "They cursed me. They said they had my husband and they were going to kill him slowly and then they would come back for me."

"And then?"

"They did not return. I never saw them again. I raised my daughter alone. She lives in Domnesti now, with her family. She visits me, sometimes, but her leg is bad."

"You never saw them again? Why did they leave?"

She looked at me. "Who can say?"

I had the sense she knew something more but was hesitant. "Is there anyone else in the village who might know?"

She smiled with genuine amusement and just for a moment I had a glimpse of her as she might have been in her youth, before grief and loneliness had taken her. "All who survived the *strigoi* are now dead. Their grandchildren or new people live here now. They all think me mad. Even my daughter. It was the Turks that raided the village, mother, she would say. The Turks or the Serbs. My baby, who I covered with my body and prayed over while those blood drinkers shook my house, my dear girl grew up to be a fool. But that is what happens when a girl grows up without a father. I beat her as best I could but it takes a man to do it properly." She waved her hand in the air, as if she could chop away the words she had spoken.

"Why did you tell me this?" I said. "Why did you speak to my friend Robert about it?"

"Would you pour me some more water, sir?"

"There is none in the jug, my dear woman," I said.

"The pail," she said, gesturing at the sideboard behind her, a high bench along the wall where she prepared her meals below shelves with her pottery and utensils. A bucket sat on one end. "Fill it for me."

Putting down the iron crucifix on the bench, I dipped the jug into the water in the bucket and poured the woman a glass of water. She nodded her thanks and sipped at it while I took my seat opposite her.

634

"You are a great lord," she said. "A soldier for the new prince."

"I am."

"You command those blood drinkers outside?"

"What makes you call them that?"

"I know it. I can see it in you. In all of you."

"That is not possible."

She smiled and pointed through her doorway. "I saw him. Your man, the one handed soldier, he had his servant bleed into a bowl, behind my cow shed."

I looked out at the ruined shack beyond the woman's garden. "Our servants are bled regularly for their own health. The most sanguine of them require it or else they forget their duties. That is all."

Lifting her gnarled hand, she pointed at me again. "You, sir, are a liar. And I do not converse with liars."

"Very well. You have it right enough. My men must drink blood to stay alive and in good health. But we do not kill innocents. The blood of the living, freely given, sustains us."

She nodded but was not completely placated. "You deny that you are *strigoi* also?"

"I do not require blood. But I am ageless, yes. What is this word that you use? *Strigoi?* What is its meaning?"

"Meaning? It is what you are. You and your men. And it is what those men that came were. And it is what my husband became."

"Your husband? He was not taken on the road as you said?"

She closed her eyes as she spoke, her voice little more than a whisper. "He was taken, yes. Taken, and bled. Taken away. But not killed. He was turned. He became *strigoi.*"

My heart began to race. "How do you know this?"

"I thought he was dead. For so long, he was dead. More than ten years, he was dead. But one morning, as the sun rose behind the mountain, I saw him in the trees behind the house. I ran after him but I could not find him. My daughter said it was madness taking me. My friend Anca said it was his ghost and that I had to pour a line of salt across my door and window so he could not enter at night. I told her that I wanted his ghost to enter at night and then she called me mad also, the fat old cow. She is dead now. But my husband returned. I saw him and this time he did not run. I expected him to turn to smoke when I embraced him but he did not. He was real! Solid as this." She slapped the table top with her palm and closed her eyes as she breathed in a great, happy breath. "Ah, my husband. To feel him again. I wept like a girl."

She sat, lost in the memory, a smile on her thin lips.

"Where had he been?"

The woman was irritated that I had intruded on her thoughts. "Some things he told me, others he did not."

"Where is he now?"

"Gone. Never to return. Why would he return to an old woman like me? In the years since, I have prayed and I have asked travellers for stories of the *strigoi*. I hear things. I hear that you are looking for these things, also."

"You heard I was looking for *strigoi*?"

"A man who serves a foreign soldier lord has been seen here and there, asking for stories of *strigoi*. He has never come here but when I saw your man, I knew it was you. And so I sent for you. Your men are fools. And you have a woman who dresses like a man? You are *strigoi* but I see now, you are not evil. You are like my dear Petru. Cursed for eternity but not evil. And so I tell you this story, which you have sought, and in return, you will send Petru to watch over his daughter and grandchildren in Domnesti."

"But I do not know your husband. If I find him... I will tell him what you have said. But I fear yours is the first story of the *strigoi* that I have heard and I have been searching for years. I had begun to doubt if there were any stories to hear."

"There are many stories. Many thousands. But none that you shall hear. None but mine."

"Why should I not hear them?"

"You are an outsider. We cannot speak of such things to foreigners."

"You did."

"But I want something."

"Everybody wants something."

"Not us. Not Wallachians. All we want is for you to go. You, the Turks, the Hungarians, the Serbs. All we want for us to be happy is your absence. Alas, you all want our land and you want us dead or enslaved. No, none shall tell you these stories. None but the monks."

That caught me off guard. "The monks? What monks?"

"In the south, there is a lake called Snagov. And there is a village there, called Snagov. And there on the lake there is a monastery named Snagov. The monks, they know. They collect the stories, also."

"Stories of *strigoi*?"

"They will tell you the stories and then you will find Petru and tell him to watch over our family. No matter what else he has sworn, he must do his duty to his family. You tell him. Now, you must go." She held out her hand. "Return to me my cross."

"I left it beside your pail when I filled your water."

She scowled and snatched up her bunch of dried herbs and thrashed against my back as I left, before slamming her door behind me.

My men stopped halfway through their conversation to stare.

"Always ends the same way, don't it, Richard," Walt said. "You and women."

"Actually, it went rather—"

The window shutters slammed closed.

"What did she say?" Eva asked as we walked back toward the village.

"It turns out that Serban has not been so useless after all. His questions somehow reached her and then today she saw Rob bleeding a servant in secret."

"Robert," Eva scolded, "for the love of Christ, you have to be more careful."

"How was I supposed to know anyone was looking?" Rob said.

"It matters not. Anyway, she claimed that she somehow knew us for immortals on sight." Walt scoffed. "How?"

"She did not say. But she wants me to find her husband, who was turned into an immortal decades ago, in this very village."

"We been looking for years," Rob said. "Did she say where to look?"

"Yes. A place where they have collected the stories of immortals. A monastery named Snagov, in the south."

Rob whistled. "Fancy that."

"Well, then," Walt said. "What are we waiting for?"

"Patience," I said, looking up the valley at the mountain peaks. "The monastery will wait. First, I must finish my business with Vlad Dracula."

***

"Your forces are growing in strength," I said to Vlad later as the wine flowed in the cramped hall at Poenari.

The towers were still being built but the central keep had been largely completed and that was where we had dined. It was barely large enough to feast two score men but that was about all who could garrison the entire fortress, as small and incomplete as it was. In time, a separate hall would be constructed in the narrow space between the walls but for now, only his closest companions could join him at the top of the mountain, while the rest of his men, and mine, stayed in the camp below where the workmen and soldiers slept and ate, and fought when they were drunk.

I could well understand Vlad's preoccupation with Poenari. His life had been in a state of constant change. As a child, he had been sent to Târgovişte to begin his training as a knight, only for it to be interrupted when he was sent first to the Turk's capital Edirne and then on to a succession of palaces and country estates in Anatolia, surrounded by enemies and assaulted by my brother. When freed by the Turks he had been unable to return to Wallachia which was controlled by his enemies, and so he had fled to Moldavia with his cousin Stephen only for them both to be forced into Hungary by intrigues in Moldavia. The boy and the man had never had a home to call his own, had never known true security or stability.

Târgovişte was not safe, not even the castle within the city. The Saxon and Wallachian merchant burghers of the city had turned on Vlad's father, executed his brother, and forced the elder Vlad to flee. The young Vlad Dracula could never have forgotten that.

And so he had built himself a modern fortress on the highest, most inaccessible mountain ridge in his kingdom, far from the border with the Turks. And although the Transylvanian border was close, that border was with the Duchy of Fogaras, which was in fact a vassal land under Vlad's personal possession.

If his enemies, internal and external, ever pushed him then it would be to Poenari that Vlad would turn.

Watching him feasting with his men that night, I saw him converse more than I had at any other place. He even laughed aloud once or twice. If I had not been paying close attention, then I might have assumed that he was drinking more wine than he customarily did but in fact he hardly seemed to drink much at all. He seemed simply to be a lord at home with his men.

I took a chance and moved from my place to sit beside him.

"Earlier, my lord, we were about to speak of William."

It was not a company of men that enjoyed carousing and conversations had quieted as the hour grew late. Vlad glanced around to see if anyone was listening. If they were, they gave no indication of it.

"I imagined, Richard, that you would wish to speak of such things where others cannot hear it."

"These are your men. Your chosen men, who will gladly die for you. I wonder how many of them know about the blood."

A couple of them glanced at me and then at Vlad.

"Not all know," Vlad said, slowly. "And not all who know fully understand."

"If you are going to defeat William then perhaps it is time that they be made to understand."

His eyes narrowed as he regarded me. "Perhaps."

"You said that you sought William's power. Clearly, he gave it to you. Why?"

Some of them were paying attention now, and Vlad thought for a while before answering.

"The day I witnessed him tear a soldier's throat out and drink the blood, I was surprised by it. It was a brutal act and a demonstration of inhuman strength, the way he held the man, in heavy mail armour, aloft with one hand as if it were nothing. But the others around us responded not at all. Some wore the hint of a smile. And yet it was as if nothing was out of the ordinary."

"They were immortals also."

"Some, certainly. Others were hoping to become so. Under Murad, William had become a lord with great wealth with many estates but every other noble Turk viewed him with suspicion or loathing and they sent assassins with some regularity. William dared not make himself too powerful without the total and complete backing of the Sultan or else he might find himself surrounded by a dozen armies. Even if he escaped such an assault, he would be outlawed and all his work undone. And so he kept the number of his true followers quite small at this time. How many they were, I never discovered."

"He told you all this?"

"When I told him I wanted his power, he laughed and said I would never be worthy. I knew it was a challenge. That he wanted me to prove myself. And so I did whatever I needed to in order to gain his favour."

"Such as?"

"He told me he could never give the sacred Gift to one who had never killed a man. And so I snatched the knife from William's belt and cut the throat of the slave serving our *sherbet*. His blood soaked into the ice while he died, glaring at me and trying to keep the blood in with his hands."

"I wager William was pleased."

"He sneered and said a child murdering a servant was contemptible. He needed soldiers not cowards. And so I waited until I was training in the sword with a soldier I believed I could beat. William was not there but I said to the instructor that I intended to kill him in the next exchange and that he should attempt to do the same to me. He did not believe me until I wounded him across the face and then he did indeed fight for his life. He very nearly took mine. When I came to myself, many days later, William was there. It was then that he began to instruct me in his ways."

"Ways of fighting?"

"In part. But it was more to do with his ways of moving through the world. His cunning methods for manipulating societies that he had learned in the East amongst the people of Cathay. Particularly, he said, he had grown too powerful and had fought to keep his position. He spoke of successions of weak kings that proved incapable of defending themselves and securing their kingdom. And so he had been determined to make the Turks into a powerful empire while keeping himself in the shadows, coming into the light when he needed to and fading away if that was in the best interests of the great plan."

"Which is?"

"Do you not know, Richard?"

"To rule," I said. "To conquer a land and to rule it as a king."

Vlad nodded. "But not just any land. He expects that all Christendom will serve him. And he will rule as a king like no other. He will be worshipped as though he is an angel descended to Earth, as though he is a pagan god in human form, immortal and all-powerful."

"He told you this?"

"After he gave me the sacred Gift of his immortal blood. He believes that it ties a man's soul to his. Why would he not tell me this?"

"He believes those that ingest his blood become tied to him? Through magical means?"

Vlad took a sip of wine. "Is that not how your followers are tied to you?"

Walt had not even been turned by my blood but by the blood of a son of Priskos. And he had been always the most loyal man to ever serve me.

"No. I do not believe so."

"Then why are they loyal?"

"My closest companions are my friends. My brothers. Why do your friends follow you, my lord? I do my duty. They do theirs. That is all."

"In many ways, you remind me of William. And in others, you seem to be his opposite. An anti-William."

"Well," I said. "Quite. And were you ever his man? Magically or otherwise?"

"His words have a strange power. His eyes seem to posess a kind of magic. I will not say that I felt no temptation to join his cause, in spite of myself. God knows, I felt the pull of that magic for years. But always in my heart, buried deep, I held on to my hatred of him."

"And he never suspected?"

"He suspected everyone. Always. Unrelenting, he was suspicious. We had been friends and companions for years and I had sworn to obey him and had done many crimes, committed many sins, all for him, when one day I held his gaze a moment too long and allowed a spark of hatred out of my soul and into my eyes. Up until that moment, it had been hidden and I had not known it was coming and no mortal man would have seen it. But he seized me and beat me and had his men carry me away and strap me to a rack. He pulled the levers himself, all the while saying I should admit to my treachery and he would end my life. He cut me and bled me and fed me blood to keep me alive so he could inflict more pain. It was some weeks before he was satisfied."

From the corner of my eye, I saw some of his men cross themselves.

"And after that William trusted you again?"

Dracula affected William's tone and accent and wagged a finger as he spoke. "You are lucky that you are so useful, my dear Vlad, or else you would have found yourself returning to Wallachia without a head. I have killed better men than you for less. But you will give me a kingdom and so you will live in gratitude for the life I have allowed you."

"One way to inspire loyalty is to kill all those around you who do not demonstrate obedience," I said. "Personally, I would prefer to inspire fidelity."

Vlad snorted. "He had much to say about you."

"He did?"

"Especially after you killed my father."

I glanced at the men around us, all listening intently to every word. They looked back at me, their faces impassive and unreadable in the lamplight of the hall.

"He wished to loose you against me," I said. "Use you as a weapon to destroy me."

"I think he was delighted to be able to relay it to me. We both share an enemy now, my dear Vlad. My brother Richard stands in our way. We shall kill him together. Draw him close, pretend to be his friend and isolate him. He is nothing without his companions. Richard is witless, quick to anger, impatient as a child, and filled with mad passions. Never fight him. Be his friend and then betray him."

My heart racing, I looked again at the men around the hall. They were all armed in one way or another.

"Good advice," I said, shrugging.

"It was," Vlad said. "The only allies you have in my fortress are two mortal servants to attend to you. And even they are not here."

"But I have you," I said. "My friend and ally, Vlad Dracula."

"Yes," he said, smiling at last. "You do. William is truly my enemy and you have proved yourself to be a friend. More importantly, you are a good Christian who has fought for years to keep the Turk at bay and so you are a friend to all Wallachians."

I let out a sigh and drank off my wine. "So you played along, no matter the cost, for years. And when the Turks released you, they believed you to be theirs. Do they believe it still?"

"I think that they do, yes."

"But you mean to fight. And you mean to defeat William?"

"I do."

"How?"

"He is more powerful than ever. His Blood Janissaries might be impossible to stop. But if I can draw William in, draw him close and away from his men, I mean to surround him and kill him."

"And how will you do that?"

"Sometimes I imagine filling him with arrows, other times having a hundred hand-gunners shoot him at once, or to blast him in half with a cannon. Whatever is left, I shall cut into pieces and burn."

"A very pleasant fantasy, I am sure. But how will you isolate him from his... *Blood Janissaries*, as you called them?"

Vlad glanced at his men. "I wondered if you might consider using yourself as a lure? If he knows where you are, I believe his hatred for you is so strong that he would come for you in person."

"And how do you propose to do that?"

"Send men with messages through Turkish territory and have them captured and—"

"That trick may work on a *boyar* but William would not fall for it."

"Well, then, there are many ways in which—"

"I have a far better idea," I said. "William has his immortal Janissaries. The red robed Blood Janissaries. As you say, they will prove almost impossible for mortal men to overcome and I am certain William will never leave their protection. That is why he created them, I assume."

"He made a personal army that is loyal to him. My intention is to avoid them and to kill William directly. To cut off the head of the snake. After that, they will be unable to replace their numbers and so I can grind them away into dust."

"We cannot isolate William from those men. We will have to go through them to get to him."

"But if, as you said yourself, they cannot be overcome then—"

"Not by mortal men. What about by immortal ones?"

"Your men? How many is your company? Twenty-five soldiers? You are outnumbered, sir."

"My immortal men, yes. And me and you, also." I glanced around the hall. "And your men."

"What do you mean, my men? I have no immortal men."

"Ah, yes. But I could make you some, Vlad. If you wished. I could make you five hundred of them. I could make us an immortal army of our own."

1 1

The Saxons

1 4 6 1

"REPEAT AFTER ME. I swear to serve Richard Ashbury from this day until the day of my death. I swear to obey him in all things and to obey the orders of his captains without question. With the strength of my arm, I will fight the enemies of Wallachia without flinching or fleeing and with the strength of my heart I will protect the people of Wallachia with unwavering fidelity. Together with my brothers, we serve the Voivode of Wallachia Vlad III Dracula against his enemies, wherever they are found. I swear also to take no wife, to have no sons and no daughters, and to have no father but my lord and to have no brother but my brothers of the *sluji*. All this I swear in the name of Christ."

I released the young man's hands and took one step to the side while Vlad Dracula took my place, holding the dragon amulet in one hand and his father's dragon sword in the other. The young man leaned forward to kiss the amulet and the hilt of the sword. Walt and Rob helped him to his feet and led him to the Blood Altar, a stone table at the top of the hall. Wearing no more than his undershirt, he shook in the cold air. No doubt, he was also terrified. Many of them were when it came time to be initiated into the blood brotherhood of the *sluji*. Over three hundred of the men who would soon be his brothers stood in the hall, silently watching.

Dracula had chosen to name our new immortal army the *sluji* which was a word that meant "to serve" and was meant to emphasise that our blood brothers were sacrificing their mortal lives for their prince and their people. The true nature of the *sluji* was hidden from outsiders, even most of the men close to Vlad. To everyone else, we were a special bodyguard, loyal to Vlad with foreign mercenary officers, namely me, my close companions, and the immortals of the Company of Saint George.

The young initiate lay on the altar. Walt sliced an incision on both of the initiate's wrists and his blood flowed into bowls. The bowls were taken when almost filled and passed amongst the watching blood brothers, who each took a drink and passed it on to the man beside him. There were many bowls of blood in a man's body.

Those chosen for the *sluji* knew that they were giving up their families and their chance of ever fathering a child again. Most of the volunteers we chose were peasants but all had proven themselves in one way or another to be competent or courageous in battle, or at least in training.

It had taken a lot of arguing to reach agreement about the immortal army. Vlad had argued that they should be loyal to him. I had refused to make any man an immortal who was not personally loyal to me, which Vlad could not agree to. Eventually, we came to a compromise of sorts. The *sluji* swore loyalty to me but they would only fight the enemies of Wallachia. I could never order them to England and expect them to follow me. And I could never order them to fight against Vlad or his allies. All the initiates understood that.

The newest man was so drained of blood that his eyes were clouding and his eyelids fluttering. Taking a knife, I cut my own wrist and held it to his mouth. He knew to drink quickly and so he did, grasping my arm in both hands and sucking the blood from my wound. When he had a bellyful, he fell back, unconscious.

My companions had argued that I could make no concessions as far as loyalty was concerned. They feared that Vlad would work to subvert my authority and take command using his rights and power as their royal lord. And the immortal knights and men-at-arms in the Company of Saint George had argued against adding so many men of one nation to our number, lest they turn against us. They were also contemptuous of the new men's abilities. I assured my men that this was a new venture, separate from the company that they had earlier joined. They were placated by being granted positions of authority in the *sluji*, with responsibility for first training and then leading the men in battle. Along with an accompanying increase in pay. They found the terms acceptable.

The young man was carried away to the quarters behind the hall, where he would either die in his sleep or rise an immortal brother of the *sluji*. I drank a bowl of his blood to replenish that which I had lost and came forward to meet the next initiate, who came forward and knelt.

"Repeat after me."

While we made more immortals and trained them to fight as an army, Vlad was also busy.

He drew as much personal power to himself as was possible. He became a most generous patron of the Orthodox Church, granting tax immunities and other privileges to monasteries and built new church buildings and extended old ones. In return, he expected and received both submission to his will and passionate support from the pulpit. Vlad needed the peasantry to believe in him, in his vision for Wallachia and he knew it was going to be a hard fight. Peasants must be told something in the simplest terms and for them to retain it they must be told repeatedly and so the priests of the Church explained to their flock that the changes Vlad was making was in their interests and to trust in their prince as they trusted in the Lord.

In fact, the sermons that were preached were perfectly truthful. As the *boyar* class was weakened, the peasants and the Church gained power.

Vlad especially favoured a monastery at Comana which he founded himself and filled with loyal monks. The Catholic Church had long been exerting its own influence in Wallachia, especially since the recent crusades, and Vlad had many of these Catholics thrown out of his lands before replacing them with Orthodox appointees. I heard that several obstinate Catholic priests and abbots were impaled.

"It is evil," Stephen said to me, when this news reached us in the north. "He does great evil."

"He is making these lands his own, Stephen. All will be loyal to the Voivode of Wallachia. No divisions anywhere that can be exploited. This is just as you wanted."

"Under the Hungarians," he replied, as if I were a simpleton. "Under Catholic Hungarians, not barbarian eastern heresy."

"What else could we do?" I asked. "Beggars cannot choose their benefactors, Stephen."

"Please, Richard, do not let *axioma* dictate our actions."

"Come, come, Stephen. You know as well as I do that no man ought to look a gift horse in the mouth."

He tutted and huffed but we were certainly not about to challenge Vlad on his opposition to Catholic priests when it was Christendom itself at stake should we fail in our military duty.

"There will be no schism to heal," I said, at least a dozen times, "if we all live under the Turkish yoke."

All the while, Hungary continued its internal strife. Back in 1456, the young King Ladislaus V of Hungary had come to post-siege Belgrade which was under the command of Ladislaus Hunyadi, Janos' eldest son. The Habsburg-allied lords who controlled the King of Hungary were the enemies of the Hunyadi and no doubt meant to remove the commander of Belgrade from his position. And so Ladislaus Hunyadi seized the king and killed his ally Count Celje in the ensuing row. Capturing his own king was a bold move by young Hunyadi and he only released him after receiving assurances that the king would take no action in retaliation.

The king lied.

He arrested and then executed the eldest son of Janos Hunyadi and took prisoner the younger son, Mattias Corvinus. Michael Szilágyi, the elder Hunyadi's brother in law and the boys' uncle, rebelled against the King.

Szilágyi was an able commander and many were ready to follow him. God alone knows what a civil war would have done to Hungary but then King Ladislaus V died. He left no heir and the crown was once again up for grabs.

Wasting no time, Michael Szilágyi brought fifteen thousand soldiers to Buda and with such a force present, convinced a council of nobles to elect Mattias Corvinus Hunyadi, son of Janos Hunyadi, as King of Hungary.

Having a Hunyadi on the throne of Hungary was a good thing for us. Now, we did not know Mattias, but both Vlad and I had been supporters of his father and so we hoped and expected that we would be favoured in Wallachia's looming conflict with the Sultan.

But we did not realise just how difficult it was for Mattias to do anything but fight tooth and nail for his crown and for the true authority to wield his power. The first years of his reign were spent attempting to throw off the control of his uncle Michael Szilágyi.

And later, Mattias seemed almost uninterested in the wars on his south-eastern borders, preferring to focus on the struggles for dominance in central Europe. In fact, he did nothing to prevent the extinction of Serbia as a separate entity from Turkish Rumelia and clearly viewed Belgrade and the Danube-Sava junction as the natural defence line he would hold against the Turks.

In Wallachia, we were beyond that line.

Young Mattias Corvinus Hunyadi looked to the German elements within his lands for support and this included the enormously wealthy Saxon merchant colony towns of Transylvania and along the Wallachian border. Whereas his guardian Szilágyi looked for support from vassal lords.

Dracula was long a friend to Szilágyi. In fact, he admired the man greatly. When Dracula had been under Hunyadi, Szilágyi had shown him great friendship, helping him with words in ears and even with gifts of gold and men and such favour was not soon forgotten.

So when Szilágyi asked Dracula to help him with a rebellious Saxon town, Vlad readily agreed. He assembled a small but powerful force and we rode into north-eastern Transylvania to the town of Bistri.

"Bring the *sluji*," Vlad commanded me. "We will see what they can do."

"They are not at full strength," I replied, "and we have so much training to do before they will be battle ready."

"Bah!" Vlad said. "There will be no battle. We will raid. We will threaten. They will capitulate. This will be no more than another form of training."

Still, there was much to prepare, even for a short campaign close to home. We had to procure the horses, the servants, wagons, tents, and other equipment needed to maintain a force of almost five hundred fighting men. And immortal ones at that. The experience of my mercenary captains was invaluable, however, and we were ready to march in time and joined Dracula's other forces as we made for Transylvania.

"We have long tolerated the Saxons in our lands," Vlad said as we rode through the

646

mountains. "This rebellious town of Bistri is one such colony. Their forefathers were invited to settle in our mountains and ever since we have allowed them to prosper. It cannot be denied that they generate a significant amount of revenue through their trading and the making and selling of goods. Some of these towns were swift to support me against Vladislaus, although it is clear that they make decisions based on mercantile reasons rather than for honour and duty. For they honour only themselves and are not tied to our land the way our own people are. There is one town, you know Brasov, yes? Of course you do. The townsmen of Brasov were especially generous in their support of me and so I had to respond in kind. When I wrote to them that they were honest men, brothers, friends, and sincere neighbours, they knew my true meaning."

"It was more than empty flattery?"

"How can mercantile men ever be honest? How can they ever be brothers to those so different to them as we Wallachians are from Saxons? How can they be sincere neighbours when both they and us know they do not truly belong in our lands?"

"How did they take your jibe?"

"They will have taken it for what it was. A warning."

Not only was Vlad keen to put the Saxons in their place for Szilágyi, and to see the *sluji* in action, it was an opportunity to exercise his own men and to test the skills they had been training. His army was small and new and he had to find out what already functioned well and what did not.

Bistri was well-fortified and that was no doubt one reason they felt they could defy Szilágyi and refuse to send him the requested revenue.

"The *sluji* can assault it immediately," I said to Vlad. "We can cross the outer works at a run, throw up ladders, storm the walls and open the gates for the rest of the men."

Vlad smiled. "That would be a sight to see, Richard. But our Saxon friends and our own men would certainly see the somewhat more than human nature of your soldiers. And we should do our best to avoid that, for as long as we can. Besides, there is no need. My boys can do the job almost as well. Bistri is nothing."

He was not wrong. The Wallachian cannons blasted holes in the town gate and the hand-gunners and crossbowmen kept the town militia ducking down behind the battlements while infantry rushed forward to assault the walls and the gatehouse. It took no more than that. Our soldiers soon penetrated the defences and looted and burned the town.

All the while, I stood and watched from a safe distance. Before the sack was completed, the ringleaders of the rebellion fled to the larger Saxon towns of Brasov and Sibiu and Vlad was content to let them go.

"We do not need to exterminate them," he said. "Our point is made."

"What is your point?" I asked Vlad.

He laughed. "It is that the Germans are guests in Transylvania and Wallachia, no matter how many generations they have been here. Do not rebel against our good will or you see what will occur."

In Buda, Michael Szilágyi was delighted with Vlad's swift work of retribution and rewarded him with a castle dominating the Borgo Pass. Having made his point, Vlad led us all back home and we called it an informative exercise. Adjustments were made to the organisation of the soldiers and the supply train and I continued to recruit and train the *sluji*.

But Vlad Dracula had stirred up a great mass of ill-feeling amongst the Saxon colonies in Transylvania. The German cities came together in rebellion and the royal captain general of Transylvania, Count Oswold Rozgony, threw his support behind the league.

The burghers of Brasov moved to materially support Vlad's great *boyar* enemies the Danesti. They were a dynasty long in opposition to Vlad's ancestors and they saw themselves as rightful rulers of Wallachia.

They began a campaign of subversion within Wallachia against Vlad III Dracula. They spread whispers that Dracula was in fact sworn in vassalage to Sultan Mehmed II and always had been. They sent men out to spread tales that Dracula was lying about his opposition to the Turks.

"Damn the bastards of Brasov," Vlad said when he came through and stopped to inspect the *sluji*. "Always those Saxon dogs have been ungrateful, disloyal, and treacherous. Have you heard what lies they are spreading? Have you?"

"I have," I said.

The most effective slander has the ring of truth to it and for years Wallachia had been in vassalage to the Turks. It was undeniable as the effects of that vassalage had been felt by every family in the kingdom. After all, the payments required under the terms of vassalage were calculated by Janissary tax collectors who went from place to place in the country, assessing the plenty or scarcity so that the rulers could not deceive their overlord the Sultan with regards to what was available. The taxes were paid in coinage and silver but also in livestock and in grain, supplied by the hardworking peasants to their lords and thence to the Turks. The Wallachian lowlands were so productive that the Turks viewed their northern vassal in large part as a vast granary which could be relied on to provide enormous quantities of grain that would feed its armies on campaign.

There was of course the *devshirme*, the Blood Tax, in which thousands of healthy boys were dragged from their homes and turned into Turkish slaves. Wallachians were a hearty and wily people who made the Sultan reliable soldiers and able administrators.

No matter what the rumours said about Vlad's subservience, the truth was that in 1459 Dracula refused to pay the tribute to Sultan Mehmed II. That act would bring the wrath of the Turks down upon us from the south and it was at that moment that the Saxons began stirring up open rebellion in the north.

Up until that Saxon rebellion, I had never seen him express much in the way of anger. But when he was told of the accusations spreading amongst his people, Dracula threw an ancient oak table across his hall with force enough to shatter it, sending jagged boards flying back to where his men stood. While they ducked and cringed, Vlad stood unflinching with the crushed letter in his gloved fist.

"What else?" Vlad asked his messenger, a new *boyar* raised up from the peasantry and granted lands on the Transylvanian border.

The young man who had conveyed the message got back to his feet and stopped shielding his head with his arms. "Dan III, brother of Vladislaus II the former prince, has established himself in Brasov," the man said, clearing his throat. "He has claimed the throne of Wallachia for himself and was elected as such by a group of Danesti *boyars* and other lords who fled from you or who you banished when you took your throne, my lord."

"He calls himself voivode? And these landless, illegitimate *boyars* claim to have elected him?" Vlad spoke with his voice level. "Do you have word of Sibiu, Alexander?"

Another lord stepped forward and bowed. "I have word, my prince, of a man who claims to be the son of your father, and half-brother to you. All lies, I am sure. He calls himself Vlad the Monk."

"He is my half-brother, of that I have no doubt. My father was not shy about spreading his seed. He is called Vlad the Monk because he was squirrelled away in a monastery so that he would be out of sight until he came of age. He has been stirring up trouble ever since. What does he have to do with the town of Sibiu?"

"The Monk has based himself at Sibiu, my lord, and they have granted him great sums of money with which to raise forces. He likewise has exiled *boyars* at his side."

Vlad's lip curled beneath his thick moustache. "A bold move for the burghers of Sibiu. I would have expected them to follow their brothers in Brasov, not go against them."

"I believe Vlad the Monk has promised to extend the trade rights of Sibiu and the towns allied with it."

"Those money grabbing fools. I already extended their rights when I took the throne and now they want more? And are willing to rebel in order to get it? Do they not fear my displeasure, Alexander?"

His face pale, the man bowed. "I cannot say, my lord."

Vlad pursed his full lips and glanced around at me. "It seems that we must put down two rival factions and two rival rebellions. Is there anything else?"

A new man stepped forward and fell to one knee before his prince. "My lord, I have had word only this morning from one of my sons that a third candidate for your throne has declared himself. I do not know much but it is another one of the Danesti clan. A son of Dan II, named Basarab Laiot."

Vlad raised his eyebrows and scoffed. "And who is backing this Basarab Laiot, who is the son of my father's great enemy?"

"I do not know, my lord. All I know is that he made a series of promises to *boyars* in Wallachia and Transylvania and he has promised great things for certain Saxon towns."

Dracula thanked the man and looked around at his lords, one after the other. "Is that all? Or are there any other of my father's enemies or offspring in open rebellion?" His men shuffled their feet and glanced sidelong at each other. "Just three, is it? Well, three is enough, do you not think? It is clear that our enemies mean to overwhelm us with problems. While I attack one, the other will come in behind me and assault my lands or attempt to pin me between them. But we shall do nothing so foolish as that."

Vlad broke off, looking up at the arches of the vaulted ceiling above.

"Shall we assemble the army, my lord?" one of his men said, as if prompting his overwhelmed prince.

"In time, certainly," Vlad said, looking down again and searching the faces of every one of us present. "But this is a war on many fronts. Their claims that I am a Turkish lackey must be countered by the truth. And we shall move first of all to strike them in their most precious, most sensitive, most beloved parts." He smiled, cupping a hand down low before him. "Their purses."

If I had been a prince, I would have gone to war. My armies would have smashed my enemies one after the other. But Vlad had been raised to consider statecraft and had studied cunning under no less a tutor than William de Ferrers.

He countered his enemies with writ and with sanction, with declarations and proclamations. Vlad withdrew all previously awarded protections for trade for the Saxon towns and encouraged Wallachian merchants with highly favourable tariffs. He imposed exceedingly disadvantageous terms on all Saxon merchants in his lands. There were many declarations issued, one of which required them to entirely unpack their wagons for inspection by Wallachian officers and merchants at Târgoviște. Every time I passed by, there were Saxons complaining and arguing with the officials while their produce was spread across the square being poked and ruined by grinning Wallachian customs officers. The Saxons were forced to sell to Wallachian merchants at far lower prices than they could have received further along the trade routes.

All his economic warfare frustrated the Saxons and reduced their revenues enormously, while boosting Vlad's. It also meant that the entire Wallachian merchant and artisan class became besotted with their new prince and he had swiftly won the loyalty of another caste in his nation.

The Saxon merchants of course did everything that they possibly could to avoid Vlad's newly empowered customs officials and so Vlad had a perfectly legal cause to bring them and their cities to heel.

"Now it is time, Richard," Vlad said to me one morning as I entered his hall. "We shall put the *sluji* to good use at last."

"Against the Saxons?" I said. "I would much rather take them south to raid across the Danube to kill Turks. That is why we made them."

Vlad scowled. "In fact, Richard, we created them to kill William's Blood Janissaries. Not ordinary Turks."

I sighed. "They are not yet battle hardened. They need honing further before facing William's men on the field."

"Well then," Vlad said, spreading his arms. "What difference does it make if they kill

Saxons or Turks? Both are the enemies of Wallachia. Both are the enemies of Vlad Dracula. Anyway, Richard, by this rebellion the Saxons know they weaken a Christian kingdom in the face of the Turk. By rebelling against me they are working in concert with the Turk, if not in full collusion with him. It is a good and proper thing for a commander to test his men before throwing them into battle, yes. The *sluji* have trained together and now we will see how well they fight together? We must know. And these are the only battles they will see before Mehmed and William come. And come they will."

I knew that Eva and the others would disagree with our immortals being used to attack Christians but nothing Vlad said was incorrect. It was one thing to see them march and camp and deploy but we had to see the *sluji* in action to be confident in them. And anyway, the Germans could be bloody well damned for their treachery, as far as I was concerned.

"Very well."

And so we put the *sluji* to the test.

***

Both the towns of Sibiu and Brasov deserved to be punished. They were the most Saxon of districts in Transylvania and they were also within the duchies of Fogaras and Amlas, which were possessions of the Prince of Wallachia. And so Vlad was in his rights to order Sibiu to give up its support for Vlad the Monk and Brasov was formally instructed that they were harbouring a traitor to the crown in Dan III.

Neither city so much as sent a letter of response to Vlad's demands.

While a light rain fell beneath a low grey sky, I approached the assembly field outside of Târgoviște leading my five hundred mounted *sluji* as well as the servants who would provide their blood and all other logistical support. There were hundreds of horsemen present but there was not the army I had expected to see.

Vlad had brought his bodyguard and a small number of *boyars* and their own retinues.

"Where are the cannons?" I asked Vlad, riding to him. "Where are the infantry?"

"Cannons, Richard?" Vlad asked, innocently, while his men laughed. "Infantry?"

I came close enough to him to drop my voice. "You want to take these towns, do you not? How do you expect to do it quickly without destroying the walls or storming them? If you expect my men to storm the walls of these wealthy places, one after the other, I will lose scores at least and possibly hundreds. You will throw away all I have built with the *sluji* if you mean to do such a thing."

"You fear I mean to overrule your command of your men, Richard?" he asked. "Do you worry that I will command them and they will obey?"

I was confused and caught off-guard because that had not even occurred to me. The fact that he jumped right to that raised my hackles and I was about to tell him he was welcome to try when he smiled.

"I jest, Richard, I jest. No, you are quite right, of course. I do not have time to make a siege of these places, one after the other. While I am in one place, the other will run riot. No, no. We will simply destroy their *lands* instead. Each town has a dominion filled with productive villages. Well, we will burn every village and drive off all their people. All the merchants we find shall be killed, of course. Soon enough, the towns will capitulate. And if they do not, well, my dear friend Michael Szilágyi has given his word that he will bring his army down upon them with all the cannons and infantry that we might possibly need. Either way, the Saxons will give up before they are conquered. All they care about is money. Shall we depart?"

Our cavalry force moved swiftly across the mountains in spring 1458, passing by the Turno Ro, the Red Tower, which the Wallachians swore was stained red due to the blood of all the Turks who had bled upon its walls in their futile attempts to take it. Absurd, of course, but they seemed to believe it. Our destination was the valley of the River Hirtibaciu. These were the lands of Saxons who continued to support Vlad the Monk and so the people there were rebels. Their punishment would be death.

"We must not do this," Eva said when we were about to order the men into the valley. "We did not make this brotherhood of blood to make war on the innocent."

"They are not innocent. They are rebels."

"Do not be so pig-headed," she muttered. "You know this is wrong."

"Very well, this is wrong," I snapped, speaking quietly so that no one would know I was arguing with my woman. "But this is the path we are on. This path leads to William's head on a spike and so it is our path."

"Unleashing our men on women and children?"

"I will order them to leave the women and children unharmed," I said.

She scoffed and walked away, because of course such a thing was absurd. Even so, I ordered the men to spare the lives of the women and to let the children flee.

"This will spread panic," I said, projecting my voice over them all. "And send hungry mouths to Sibiu, which will cause them to surrender."

The *sluji* broke off into companies, each commanded by a captain. Walt and Rob took the strongest, the steadiest of them in their companies. Claudin, Garcia, and Jan, took the rest. They knew their business and the *sluji* brought fire and death to the villages of the valley. The men they found were killed. Some of my men delighted in making spectacles of it, forcing their kin to watch as their menfolk were executed, sometimes in artful ways.

Rob made sure to protect the children at least, as best as he could, but even he struggled to keep the women from being violated. One might as well attempt to stop a white-topped wave from reaching a rocky shore. Such is the way of war. Everything a man does must be to make his own people strong so that war does not descend on his lands.

Thus, the valley of Hirtibaciu was turned to a smouldering ruin. Without resting, we moved on to the lands around the town of Brasov.

First, we destroyed the village of Bod. The houses were burned, as were the fields and the trees, and the waters were poisoned with corpses. Everyone was killed, other than a handful who were taken prison so that they could be publicly executed back at Târgoviște.

The village of Talme we also burned to the ground and every person slaughtered.

Any Saxon merchants who were captured attempting to flee the area were tortured before they were killed. At Birsei, a community of six hundred merchants were captured trying to force their way clear of our encirclement. They had banded together in hopes of overcoming us. But they were merchants and we were soldiers.

"Do you know," Vlad said, his voice ringing out over them. They were tied up, on their knees, in a great mass. Many were bruised and bleeding and most had ropes around their necks tying them one to the other lest they attempt to flee again. "Do you know that I have promised to impale every Saxon merchant I find in these lands?"

The wind was the only answer. Somewhere, a man groaned in agony, physical or spiritual, and many of Vlad's men laughed.

"Why is it then that you would stay?" Vlad asked them. "Can it be that you do not fear impalement?"

Again, they hung their heads.

Stephen cursed under his breath beside me. Even Serban looked sickened.

"Where is Eva?" I asked him.

Serban did not look at me. "I think the mistress would not wish to see more men put on sticks," he said.

"She ain't the only one," Walt muttered.

"Impalement does not seem to frighten the Saxons overly much," Vlad called to his men, as if he was astonished. "I think we must try other methods. Have them boiled."

When it was clear that the prince was not joking, great cauldrons were brought from the kitchens of grand houses, fires were lit, and one or two bound men at a time were dumped into the boiling water. The fires had to be built high and hot and hundreds of men brought wood for the fires for hours on end. Every so often the executions would have to be stopped while masses of boiled skin were scraped from where it accumulated on the sides of the cauldrons. The screams of the dying were nothing when compared to the sobbing and begging of the Saxons who lay shivering on the ground watching their friends boiling to death before them. It was hard work for the Wallachians, but their prince had set them the task and they were committed to seeing it done. At the end, a couple of dozen merchants were released before their time was up.

"In my great mercy, I have decided to grant your freedom," Vlad pronounced. "You fortunate fellows will return to your homelands. If any of my men lay eyes on you again, you shall suffer a fate worse than the one you have just avoided."

It was not mercy of course. Vlad wanted the tale to spread to the other towns. And spread it did, not just to the Saxons of Transylvania but to all German-speaking peoples and beyond. The tales of Vlad's bloodthirsty depravity had begun.

As promised, Michael Szilágyi brought his forces down from Hungary and besieged

Sibiu in October 1458 and though he did not take it, the Saxons towns as one agreed to come to the negotiating table.

Just as Dracula had predicted.

The murder and terror we had inflicted had shaken their resolve and the Saxon rebels gave in. In November, the burghers of Brasov agreed to surrender the would-be prince Dan III and his supporters to Vlad Dracula. They even agreed to pay Szilágyi ten thousand florins in restitution for the revenues they had withdrawn from Hungary. In return, they would have their previous commercial rights and privileges restored.

And all was well. Vlad congratulated all of us on a campaign of terror well waged. The *sluji* had done their part superbly, following the orders of their captains. They had drunk the blood of their enemies only when no mortals could bear witness and they now felt themselves blooded as a company. When we returned to the valley of Poenari, I told them I was proud of them and that with peace on our northern border, we would soon face their true enemies the Turks in battle.

Sadly, that was not to be. Not yet.

King Mattias Corvinus Hunyadi was not his father. He was far more ruthless and far less honourable. The king was displeased at the way the rebellion had been handled. Indeed, he was furious at the amount of blood that had been spilled and he felt that the terror we caused had blackened his name by association. In order to distance himself from the massacres, he had Szilágyi captured and imprisoned and it was clear to all parties that everything Szilágyi had agreed in the negotiations no longer had value.

Even more astonishing for us, for Vlad Dracula, was the King Mattias Corvinus declared his support for the rebel Dan III.

"It is all falling apart already," Stephen said when we heard. "Corvinus hates Dracula."

We were in our camp, seated around a table in my tent. The company busied itself outside while we discussed what it might mean for us.

"He fears him," I said, nodding. "Fears his resolve."

"We should all fear his resolve," Stephen replied. "What happens to us, to the *sluji*, if Vlad is overthrown? With the King of Hungary for an enemy, with a replacement prince in his pocket, surely it is all but certain."

"Keep your voices down," Eva snapped.

"The treaty with the Saxons is finished," Stephen said, leaning forward. "And so we are at war with Brasov again when it is the Turks we are here to fight. We have our immortal army, but they are being squandered on these ridiculous dynastic squabbles. We wanted a king who was strong. And now we have Vlad who is still unable to suppress his nobles or his other vassals despite the evil he wreaks and what is more we find that the King of Hungary is favouring a new prince for Wallachia."

"These people are mad," Walt said. "No offence, Serban."

Serban looked up from his position guarding the entrance to the tent and looked away again.

"Do you doubt that Vlad will emerge victorious?" I asked them. "Even without our help, I would not doubt him."

"He is a perfectly capable soldier," Stephen said. "But with so many enemies how can he ever—"

"He is more than capable, Stephen," I said, surprised at the fervour with which I found myself speaking. "He is decisive and he leads his men well, whether peasant or lord. He knows how men think. His own and his enemy's. We are committed, now. We cannot abandon the *sluji* here and I fear that they would not follow me away from Wallachia. Not without Vlad's permission at least. Not yet. We must make it so that Vlad emerges victorious. That is our path to throwing the *sluji* against the Blood Janissaries."

"Everything you say is true," Rob said. "But this way of waging war does not bring glory. Only blood."

"Well then that is lucky for us," I said. "For blood is what we need."

They were not amused, and I could not blame them. It did not get any better and indeed, it grew to be far worse.

Early in the year, we raided the valley of the River Prahova, destroying the villages there which belonged to Brasov. We burned crops and killed everyone in our path. We reached Brasov swiftly, and they were not expecting us for many days yet. Much of the town lay outside its walls, having grown through its success so that many homes, large and small, lined the roads toward the town.

Unprotected by a wall, we smashed our way right into those suburbs and captured hundreds of residents.

Outside the walls of Brasov, Vlad ordered the prisoners be impaled.

They were raised aloft in their hundreds, writhing and screaming in full sight of the residents lining the walls. Those residents were the friends, business partners, and family, of the prisoners dying upon the stakes outside. On the walls, they screamed and begged and hurled insults, wailing as they watched their kin dying in the most horrific way imaginable.

Even the veterans of my Company of Saint George quailed at the sight and the sound of it and most of them walked away. But I could not. The sheer horror of it was breathtaking. In all my years, all I could recall that was the like of it was the massacres of the Mongols. They had dreamed up satanic punishments for their conquered foes but they were a savage, barbarian people. To see Christians killing Christians in such a fashion was a fresh horror that stunned me.

"Astonishing," Stephen muttered, for he alone had stayed to watch. "Truly astonishing."

"You sound almost as though you admire him for this," I said.

"Do you not?" Stephen replied, not looking at me.

"Admire him? It is monstrous."

"Precisely," Stephen said. "Who could bring himself to do this? I could not. I could never. Never. Could you, Richard?"

"No."

"Do you think William could? Of course, I am sure that he could. It is the sheer will of it, do you not think? The sheer will that is to be admired."

"Keep your damned voice down, Stephen."

In response to the wailing and the begging from the residents of Brasov, Vlad had a large trestle set up in amongst the dying people around and above him. There, he was served a hearty breakfast and he tucked into sausage and cheese and bread with gusto. While the citizens of Brasov watched from the walls, he had a man's throat cut and the blood caught in a bowl. This was brought to him and he delighted in dipping his bread into it with every mouthful.

"By God, it is true," Eva said, coming up beside me. "Serban said Vlad was drinking blood in full view of everyone. I did not believe him."

I looked around and Serban was there beside Eva his face a mask of anguish. "No one will know what it means," I said. "He is merely dipping his bread in the blood. It is a display of barbarity. Meant to break the will of Brasov."

"He's a madman," Eva said.

Eventually, a quaking messenger was sent out under a flag of truce, while he covered his mouth to stop himself from vomiting or perhaps to block to reek of blood and ripped bowels.

"You bring word of your unconditional surrender?" Vlad asked, still eating.

The man's eyes were rimmed red and his gaze kept wandering up to the dead men and women all around him. "Prince Dan is not in Brasov."

One of Vlad's lords stiffened. "Address your lord properly, or you shall join these men in the sky, you fat Saxon pig."

He bowed and spoke again, shaking like a leaf. "Forgive me, My Lord Prince. It is just that..." he swallowed and tried again. "My lords the elders of Brasov send word that the rebel who names himself Dan III, left our city ten days ago. Neither he, nor his men, nor his soldiers, are within our walls or within our lands."

"If you are lying, then your entire city shall suffer this same fate." Vlad gestured above him.

"It is no lie. My Lord."

"Then tell me. Where is he?"

The messenger fell to his knees and vomited onto the ground. "Please, my lord, have mercy."

Vlad put down his piece of cheese and got to his feet. He strode across to the man sobbing over his own vomit, pulled his sword from the scabbard and used it to lift the man's quivering chin up. "Where is the traitor?"

"He... he... he has invaded Wallachia!"

It was true. Unbeknownst to any of us, or Vlad's agents, Dan III had moved decisively to invade Wallachia while we were moving on Brasov. It seemed that there were traitors yet in Vlad's army, or at least that Dan had been incredibly lucky in his timing. Either way, he had got into Wallachia behind us and he had begun his campaign of insurrection. He intended to do just what every would-be Prince of Wallachia had to do in order to gain the throne. He had to get assurances from *boyars* one by one.

I expected Vlad to be furious. I thought that he would rage and order his men to find what traitor had sold him out.

Instead of fire, though, he was ice. After Brasov was subdued, Vlad turned our army around and led us straight into Wallachia. If Dan had been counting on us besieging Brasov for weeks and months, allowing him free reign behind our backs, he was sorely mistaken. Due to Vlad's atrocity outside the walls, Brasov had fallen immediately and so Dan was shocked at our sudden appearance at his rear.

We caught up with him in April 1460 and defeated his small army before he could do too much mischief. It was not much of a battle. He was outnumbered and outclassed and I led the *sluji* on a wide manoeuvre around his rear, falling upon him when he was already engaged with Vlad's forces.

His men surrendered at once, throwing down their weapons.

Before the assembled *sluji* and the rest of Vlad's bodyguard and leading *boyars*, Dan III was brought forward. Dracula had ordered a proper grave to be dug and Dan was made to stand before it.

"What is this farce?" Dan said, shaking with rage. "You inhuman monster. Do you expect me to grovel in fear? Just kill me and be done with it."

"You misunderstand, sir," Vlad said, speaking loudly so that all could hear. "You see, you are already dead. Yes, you see, you died when you thought you could rise against me. This is simply your funeral."

Vlad nodded to a black-robed priest who stepped forward and proceeded to recite the funeral for Dan III while he stood bound before his own grave.

When the ceremony was completed, the priest hurried back and Vlad Dracula stepped up to Dan III, drew his sword and cut off the man's head in a single, effortless stroke.

It was masterfully done. Dan's body and head both tumbled into the grave.

"Now," said Vlad, turning to us. "Let us find my brother Vlad the Monk, shall we?"

We continued to plunder the Saxon lands and refused to make lasting peace with any of them until Vlad the Monk was captured. We hoped that the Saxons would collectively find the Monk and give him up but they seemed set against us. One could hardly blame them. We raided their lands all of the summer of 1460, taking their wealth and their people. Prisoners divulged that Vlad the Monk was in hiding in the Duchy of Amlas and so we burned the town of Amlas and impaled the citizens, after forcing a priest to lead them all in a repulsive procession to the site of their execution. My *sluji* burned and killed through half of the duchy and eventually everyone in the city and many in the villages were killed by one means or another.

How many it was that died, I do not know. Thousands, certainly. And the town of

Amlas was so reduced that it never recovered.

It was disheartening.

"We waste our efforts against these people," I said to Vlad in the smoking ruins. "Anyone can slaughter peasants and merchants. The *sluji* was meant for greater things."

He turned his bulging eyes to me. "My enemies must be destroyed."

I gestured around us. "I think they have been."

"Not enough," he snapped. "They resist, in their hearts if not in their actions."

"Would you expect any less? You say they do not truly belong in your lands and that is true, of course. But then you still expect them to come to heel. They are not Wallachian. They know it as well as you do. You are a foreign ruler to them and always will be. You can never trust the Saxons but while they yet live and their cities still stand, will you not let them make peace? And then we can turn our efforts against the true enemy."

"I will have their obedience."

"Let them offer it. Let them offer some terms, at least. Everyone in Christendom knows they have been beaten."

Mattias Corvinus acted as peacemaker, ironically, as it was his endorsement of Dan III that had encouraged the Saxons into open rebellion. But with his mediation, accommodation was reached. Commercial privileges were returned, which is all the mercantile people really care about. And for their part, the Saxons agreed to pay an annual fee large enough to maintain an army of four thousand mercenaries who would be employed against the Turks.

Thus strengthened, we could turn our soldiers south again.

1 2

Ottoman Invasion

1 4 6 2

"DID YOU HEAR what he's gone and done now?" Walt whispered.

We stood in Vlad Dracula's great hall in Târgoviște along with hundreds of *boyars*, burghers, monks, priests, and soldiers milling around waiting for the prince to arrive. Their muttering filled the air to the rafters.

"I do not know," I replied. "What has he done?"

"You heard about him going around and capturing all the beggars in Wallachia? All the beggars and the vagabonds. And he's had them executed."

"I heard. My heart does not bleed for the wastrels."

Walt nodded and smiled in greeting at a soldier who had called out in salutation. "And did you hear that he had all the beggars rounded up and brought to a vast tent where they were served a mighty feast? And while they were eating, your man Vlad ordered that they be burned alive. See, he had the stools and benches soaked in oil, and the cloths upon the tables also, and when the order was given the whole lot of them, hundreds of the blighters, all went up like a bonfire."

I scoffed. "If that had happened, Walt, I would have heard about it."

"You don't want to hear, that's your problem, Richard. You have closed your ears to the truth of your friend."

"Nonsense."

"Did you hear what he done to that gypsy leader not a week last Tuesday?"

"No."

Walt shifted closer. "Well, what he done was, he had the leader of this clan of gypsies boiled alive while his whole clan watched. See, his flesh was boiled all nice and so Vlad had the leader carved up into little pieces while his people, what was in irons, watched and despaired. And then, this is the worst part of the tale, so listen well, then he had pieces of the flesh forced into the mouths of every one of the gypsy clan. Force fed them their own lord and father, imagine that."

I looked at him. "Where did you hear this?"

"One of Vlad's lads, you know Michael One-Eye? He split that Saxon in two with his poleaxe outside Amlas."

"I believe I do recall the fellow. He was there?"

"He swears it upon his mothers grave and all that is holy that his cousin Pepu was there."

I chuckled. "Well, there you have it then. It did not happen."

"Michael told me Vlad done a speech to the peasants who was watching. He said to them, he said, these men live off the sweat of others, so they are useless to humanity. Their lives are but a form of thievery. In fact, says Vlad, in fact the masked robber in the forest demands your purse but if you are quicker with your hand and more vigorous than he you can escape from him. But these vagabonds take your belongings gradually by their begging but still they take more. They are worse than robbers. I will see to it, Vlad says, that such men are eradicated from my land. And then he had the lot of them killed."

I grunted. "That does sound like something he would say."

Walt smiled, pleased with himself. "Told you so."

"Silence now. The envoys are here."

We knew that Sultan Mehmed and William's policy of conquest was now to conquer across the Danube and secure at least the lowlands of Wallachia and the lower Danube all the way to the delta where it ran into the Black Sea. That part of the river was controlled by Vlad's cousin Stephen in Moldavia.

Indeed, it was clear to all Christendom where the hammer blow would next fall.

The Turks would next attempt the conquest of Wallachia or Moldavia. Or both.

Pope Pius II called a congress of all Christian princes at Mantua for the necessary crusade. He even tried to create a new military order of knights, bearing the name of Our Lady of Bethlehem, who would be dedicated to waging war on the Turks while based on the island of Lemnos. But the Pope's congress and his new order were born lame. Nothing came of the new order and it was quietly dropped, no doubt embarrassing the Pope. Worse, almost no kingdoms answered the call to take the cross.

It was no longer surprising to me that Christendom could not be relied upon. In England, the great lords loyal to Lancaster or York were fighting over the Crown. The French were pouting about a decision the Pope had made to favour Aragon's suggestion for the throne of Naples rather than the pretender put forward by the House of Anjou. The Holy Roman Emperor Frederick III decided to taunt the Pope by sending Gregory of Heimburg as his representative, a man who had been excommunicated. The Holy Roman Empire was moving ever closer toward open defiance of Rome and Gregory was apparently openly hostile to the Pope in person during the congress. Ultimately, he promised to send thirty thousand infantry and ten thousand cavalry to the Danube in support of the crusade, which would have been a magnificent force to have on the frontier. In fact, though, Gregory never even attempted to raise them and the whole thing was no doubt simply an overt snub for Pope Pius II.

Poland, too, was engaged in its protracted conflict against the Teutonic Knights and even commanded Moldavia, her traditional vassal, to avoid conflict. The Albanians, isolated and threatened as they were, had secured a three-year truce with Mehmed II and they refused to break it, preferring to stay on the sidelines. It was short-sighted, for they would soon fall utterly before the Turks but mortal men act almost always in their immediate interest rather than doing what is best for their nation.

In an act of complete desperation, Pope Pius II sent a monk named Fra Ludovico da Bologna halfway across the world to the east of the Turks territories. There, he urged the Mohammedan states in the far east of Anatolia to attack the Turks and so open up two fronts at once, drawing away their strength from both.

I imagine that Fra Ludovico da Bologna was met with the same response wherever he went. Something along the lines of *what do you think we have been trying to do for a hundred years, infidel?*

Pope Pius was certainly being industrious, although some would say he was being desperate. He travelled to Ancona on Italy's east coast and declared he would lead the crusade in person but no one flocked to join him. It was certainly desperation that caused him to write to Sultan Mehmed II in an attempt to convert him to Catholicism.

I imagine William laughing down to his belly when he read that letter.

It was all rather pathetic. All it did was signal to our enemies that we were weak and disunited and desperate. They could scent our blood more than ever.

But Vlad Dracula responded to the Pope's call.

He was committed to destroying the Turks and all Mohammedans. As his father before him, Vlad was a member of the Order of the Dragon.

So few were with us.

Michael Szilágyi was one of the few good and honourable men left in the Balkans and he swore he would wage war against the enemy. But Szilágyi made a fundamental error. He was carrying out forward reconnaissance in Bulgaria in preparation for the invasion we knew was coming. But he failed to take the proper precautions despite being in enemy territory and he was captured.

This great man had not long previously been in effect Regent of Hungary and had by his actions secured the crown for his nephew. But the Turks captured him and took him to

Constantinople and was passed over to Zaganos Pasha; my dearest brother. There, William tortured him mercilessly for information about Hungary's military preparations and the state of specific defences.

How much Michael Szilágyi gave up, I do not know.

But what I do know is that William had my friend and Vlad's mentor sawn in half.

Soon after, a large party of Turkish envoys arrived from Constantinople. Vlad made them wait for days for an audience which was a deliberate and obvious snub. Many townsfolk in Târgovişte were made nervous by the presence of the increasingly agitated envoys, knowing as they did that any provocation made it more likely that war would begin. The soldiers and leaders amongst them, though, knew that war was inevitable. The only question was when it would begin.

Finally, Vlad had them brought to the castle and he awaited them in his hall in all his finery. The Turks were irritated by the sneering soldiers who escorted them so closely that they at times dragged the envoys by the arms. When they protested, the soldiers laughed and mocked them.

But on they came in their colourful robes and great headdresses of wound cloth with jewels set over the forehead.

When they bowed before Vlad III Dracula, then, their blood was up. The audience of *boyars* and burghers was clearly hostile and the envoys frowned and huffed to be so disrespected. Even the priests scowled at them.

"Not a happy bunch of lads, are they," Walt whispered.

"He means to send them back to Mehmed fully insulted."

Walt shrugged. "Good for a laugh, I suppose."

"It is an act of defiance. To shake his enemy and to show his men that he does not fear the Sultan. Hush, now."

The Turks made their introductions and bowed. "I thank you, my lord Vlad, Prince of Wallachia, for welcoming us to—"

"What is the meaning of this?" Vlad said, his voice overwhelming them and silencing every murmur in the hall.

The envoy broke off and traded glances with his fellows. "My lord? I am afraid I do not understand—"

"How is it that you come to me so attired?"

The envoy looked down at his robes. "My lord, this is the clothing commonly worn by my—"

"Look around you, Turk." Vlad commanded. "Look at the men in my hall. What do you see?"

All of the envoys looked at the hundreds of lords and soldiers and priests all around them, glaring in hatred. "I see the great and noble lords of Wallachia and no doubt of other Christian lands who serve—"

"What do you see upon their heads?"

He looked startled for a moment before recovering. "My lord," he said and bowed. "At your court and at the courts of Christian monarchs, it is the custom for your people to bare their heads when addressing their king, their prince, as a sign of respect. And yet it is the custom of the Turks to wear such turbans as you see us wearing before you as our own form of respect. For us to remove our turbans would be signifying that we disrespected you and this of course we could never dream of doing, my lord."

Vlad stared at him and allowed a heavy silence to descend once more. "Where are you, envoy of the Sultan?"

"My lord? We are in your fine hall, my lord. In the magnificent city of Târgoviște."

Vlad nodded slowly and wagged a finger once at the envoy. "Indeed, sir. Indeed, you are. And so would you not wish to follow our customs when in our lands?"

The envoy swallowed and bowed again. "I wish that I could, my lord, but as you know I am merely the servant of my master and he has bidden me to wear the attire you see before you. I cannot remove a piece of it without his command."

Vlad frowned, tilting his head as if confused. "So, you refuse to remove this hat?"

"It is not a hat, my lord, it is... that is to say, it breaks my heart but it cannot be removed without offending my master, the Sultan Mehmed II."

"In that case, my friends, I cannot allow you to offend your master. I cannot allow you to remove your hats. Not ever, for the rest of your lives. Would that be acceptable?"

The envoy hesitated, sensing a trap. "I... yes, my lord. I am most thankful for your courteous understanding in this matter."

Vlad clapped his hands once. "Wonderful." He gestured to the captain of his guards who came forward with his fist clasped around some sort of bundle in one hand and hefting an iron hammer in the other. "And to help you to keep your hats on your heads, we shall hammer them into place with these iron nails."

The envoys were confused and then they attempted to flee and then to fight. But they were seized by the soldiers and forced onto their knees. One by one, great iron nails ten inches in length were driven through the turbans and into the men's skulls. Some of them died or at least collapsed immediately but others continued screaming and begging, despite the iron in their brains. However, those men were also not long for the world.

"Take the bodies to their servants and send them back to Constantinople," Vlad commanded. "Along with my warm regards."

"Did you see that?" Walt said in my ear, chuckling. "He must have had those nails and hammer ready the whole time. Whatever anyone says about him, you can't say he doesn't have a knack for a good jest."

Most of the hall emptied temporarily and wine was served to the guests out in the courtyard below while the hall was decked with tables and benches ready for a feast. But Dracula stayed by his throne and called me to him as the work went on around us.

"Was that for Szilágyi?" I asked.

"Hardly. When I have Mehmed and William as my prisoner, and both are tortured for weeks before being sawn in half while they scream for their mothers, then we shall say that it was for dear Michael. This was…" Vlad shrugged. "A playful taunt. No more."

"You hope to move him to attack sooner than he wishes?"

"Not through insults, he is too hard of heart to be moved by such petty things. If we can draw him close by military means, then perhaps we can get him to move this year, before his full force is readied."

"And you have a notion of how to do that?"

Vlad brushed a finger along his moustache. "You know about the raids across the Danube?"

I nodded. "The *razzia* parties grow bold. They are taking plunder, which we cannot afford, and killing the men and ravishing the women to death but they are taking children now, also."

"Taking them for the slave markets in Constantinople. I have lost too many people along the river and I will not lose any more. The *boyars* are doing their best but they cannot guard against all incursions. Every time they arrive, it is too late."

"I am sure we could do something to help," I said.

"It is not only the raids but they are certainly testing the defences. They want to take every fort on the river before they launch their invasion."

"You want us to hold the fortresses? I am not certain the *sluji* will make good garrison troops."

"I do not want to hold them. Not all of them. I am of a mind to allow some to fall but to fight for others."

"So that Mehmed comes across where we want him to."

"And you know where, Richard. Can you be ready by tomorrow?"

"I will go now."

Vlad smiled. "There are not many men who would rather ride to war than feast with his friends."

I bowed. "My Lord Prince, I will feast on the blood of Turks."

***

Throughout 1461, we threw back many raids and in our turn raided enemy camps. The *sluji* were swiftly learning to fight together, and together we drank the blood of many Turks. The villages and fortresses by the Danube saw us as saviours, despite it becoming common knowledge that we killed our prisoners and sucked the blood of the dying from their very wounds. All the people knew we were fighting for them and so it did not matter what we were said to be doing to their enemies.

Despite our best efforts, we were only so many and we could only be a certain number of places at once. I requested that Dracula send more soldiers to help us but he wanted them, the peasant army that they were, to undergo further training together before the true invasion began.

The most important and greatest of all Wallachian fortresses on the Danube was Giurgiu. It was situated amid mud-flats and marshes on the left bank of the Danube where it swerves north for a stretch. There were many islands in the river there which made it easier to cross, and the land to the north produced enormous quantities of grain so it was a vital point in the defences. The fortress being surrounded by marsh made it difficult to assault from the land but the Turks swarmed the walls from the riverside and took it.

They held it for close to a year and Vlad said he was content for them to hold it, for he was not going to waste men on a frontal assault. As important as it was, I was likewise not going to waste any of my *sluji* when it was likely to continue to be fought over anyway.

And so, as much as it rankled, I let it be.

During that year, I captured and questioned hundreds of men before I killed them and they gave up as much as they knew. Often I would start the same way.

"What can you tell me that might save your life?"

It is remarkable the things that men say at such times. Almost always what they said was useless but I asked all the same.

One man, in the very depths of a freezing winter, gave me far more than most.

"An ambush!" he screamed. He was a captain of some importance, as evidenced by his clothes and his fluent Greek.

"What ambush? Our ambush of your men? Is that all you have? Very well." I placed the edge of my knife on his throat. He had a bulging Adam's apple and I poked at it.

"Vlad Dracula!"

I moved my blade away a fraction. "Say that again?"

He gulped, shifting so that his knees crunched the ice on the frozen ground. "An ambush on Vlad Dracula, my lord."

I put the blade under his chin and lifted his face up. "A likely story." I leaned down. "Where? When?"

"At Giurgiu!"

"He's not in Giurgiu, you damned fool. The Turks have Giurgiu."

He held up his hands. "That's true, yes, but Dracula is *coming* to Giurgiu. And before he gets there, in the woods in the north by the marshes, he is to be ambushed and killed."

"Why would he go to Giurgiu? In the depths of winter at that. Why would he risk his life in such a fashion? It is absurd."

"I do not know. All I know is, he is coming there. There will be a Wallachian bodyguard of a hundred men and so we needed to be at least twice that number."

Behind the man, Rob shrugged.

"You have less than a hundred here," I said.

"Yes, it was to be my men, many Turks from Anatolia, a company of Bulgarians and some other Greeks who serve Hamza Pasha."

"When?"

"Soon. Dracula has already left Târgoviște, so they say."

Rob waved Walt over to listen.

I leaned down. "If you are lying to me then I promise that your death will be long and dreadful. Admit that this was all a lie now and I will end you swiftly."

He swallowed. "It is the truth, I swear it."

"We shall see. Bind him and bring him. Drink the rest."

"Bring him where?"

"The road to Târgoviște."

We intercepted Vlad Dracula's company about twenty miles north of Giurgiu where Vlad was building a monastery at a place called Comana. Being so close to the Danube, it needed to be heavily fortified against raids and it looked more like a castle than a house of prayer. The building work was far further along than the previous time I had seen it and the great walls were almost completed. I had most of the *sluji* keep back out of sight and went up with just a handful of my men at first light. Dracula's bodyguards were alert to any danger and I was escorted inside.

"Where is the prince?" I asked them when I was through the monastery gates.

"Preparing to depart, my lord," the senior soldier said, blowing warmth into his hands. "He is eating in the refectory with Catavolinos."

"With who? And what in the world are you doing bringing the prince so far south?"

Vlad's bodyguard scowled, though it was not me. "Thomas Catavolinos, a Greek in the service of Hamza Pasha. There is to be a negotiation to avoid the coming war. Or delay it, at least, while we grow stronger. Hamza Pasha was due to come to Târgoviște but he sent this Catavolinos instead and the meeting place was changed to Giurgiu."

"But why would you let him risk himself by coming to the Danube?"

"He is our prince. We do as he commands."

"You men are supposed to protect him. Even from himself. Remember that. Take me to him."

Vlad's soldiers outnumbered the monks at least ten to one, crowding every corner of the monastery. But the refectory was empty other than Vlad's bodyguards, a handful of servants, and the prince and his guest. It was mercifully warm inside.

The Greek named Thomas Catavolinos was a sophisticated and charming gentleman who smiled ingratiatingly and made it clear how truly delighted he was to be able to make my acquaintance. I told him the pleasure was entirely mine and begged he allow me to speak to my lord for just a few brief moments. Catavolinos bowed and said he would be delighted to take a stroll around the remarkable walls.

The moment he was gone, I turned on Dracula. "What in the name of God are you doing?"

"Good morning, Richard," Vlad said, chewing on a piece of bread. "This is a pleasant surprise."

"Why are you here, Vlad?"

He frowned as he leaned back. "I believe I should be asking you that question. Why are you not on the Danube?"

"It is a day's ride away. The real question is why are you so close to it? Why are you riding into a fortress on the river that is held by the Turks? Have you lost your mind?"

Vlad's moustache twitched. "There is no danger that I cannot overcome."

"Did you not expect a trap?"

He shrugged. "Of course. But I have a hundred of my best men."

"Do you not know that they would send a thousand? In order to kill you they would send ten thousand and you feel safe with a hundred? You would blunder inside Giurgiu and never come out."

Vlad lifted his chin and looked along his long nose at me. "Do not think me a fool. I would not enter the walls. It was my condition that Hamza Pasha meet me outside the fortress and so I shall be free to flee if there is danger."

"You will not reach Giurgiu."

He stopped eating. "What do you know?"

"I have a man. A Greek captain who was to be one of the men leading the ambush. Just north of Giurgiu before the ground becomes a marsh, there is a woodland."

"I know it. The garrison cut wood for fuel there. It is dark and dense, even in winter, as it is a pine woodland but they could not hide ten thousand men there, Richard."

"At least two hundred will attack from all sides. There could be as many as five hundred, if they lay in the marshes also."

He nodded and began picking at his food again. "Where are the *sluji*?"

"With me. Here. Unseen to the south."

"Can you get close to the Giurgiu woodland? Unseen?"

"Not in daylight. After sunset, certainly."

"Then I will delay here. The food has produced in me a sickness and I will only be able to travel at first light tomorrow. I shall ask Thomas Catavolinos to send my apologies ahead later and then I shall see you on the road to Giurgiu tomorrow."

"You mean to spring the trap yourself? That is not necessary."

"I am the Prince of Wallachia. It is necessary."

It was a test of our men that they maintain discipline throughout the approach to the woodland. It was a cold and wet night and they were sodden and freezing as they crept with me through the marsh, walking where we could on top of the thick ice that had formed on top but just as often crashing through it. We hid ourselves behind tussocks of frozen grass and stands of bare bushes and waited in silence for sunrise. In truth, I doubted we would make it until the prince's party arrived. I was certain one of the Turks would wander close to relieve himself and discover us but even if that happened I thought we could fight our way through them. Even if they were five hundred. I left half our men beyond the marsh with our horses, in case we needed to flee or pursue an enemy and hoped that my remaining two hundred and fifty immortals were strong enough.

But Vlad came along the road early, their horses surrounded by a cloud of steam illuminated by the morning sun. Even after his earlier bravado, he was sensible enough to wait beyond the wood and send most of his bodyguard in ahead while keeping the Greek Catavolinos back with him.

As the Wallachian riders disappeared into the darkness of the pine trees, I heard Walt and Rob whistling like birds, prompting me to order our men to attack. But I wanted to ensure no enemy escaped.

I whistled back.

Not yet.

When the sound of fighting started, I called out the order and rushed through the icy bog. As I stood, I realised that ice had formed around my legs and flanks and it shattered as I strode forward. All around me, the *sluji* emerged from behind tussocks and long grass and bushes and we swarmed over the ice toward the woodland. The cold and wet Greek, Turkish and Bulgarian infantry were trying to break the fresh, mounted Wallachians but they were biding their time as more of their men got into position.

My men came up quickly and cut the enemy to pieces. We cried the name of Vlad Dracula and the Bulgarians were so surprised they tried to surrender but we killed most of them without hesitation. The Greeks instead tried to flee but they were intercepted by my men and cut down by the Wallachian bodyguard.

When Vlad came up, he had Catavolinos bound to a horse.

"It was done well, men!" Vlad shouted beneath the trees. "I am proud of you all. Now, we shall go on to Giurgiu."

I strode toward him, still damp and shivering despite my exertion. "What do you mean to do?"

Vlad ignored me for a moment and called to his men. "Find the biggest Turk you can and strip his armour." Vlad turned back to me. "How is your Turkish coming along?"

"Still not as good as my Arabic. Why?"

Vlad grinned.

It was not long before I sat on a horse beside Vlad before the vast gatehouse of the fortress of Giurgiu. It was a massive, squat castle covering the only section of dry land for a mile in any direction, barring the road. Beyond the fortress, the great Danube was a sheet of white ice and beyond that was Turkish Rumelia which had once been Bulgaria.

Behind us, almost fifty of our men sat with their shoulders hunched and heads down in ill-fitting Turkish armour. In our midst, we had a cluster of Wallachian prisoners, including one wearing Vlad Dracula's fine clothes.

Vlad called out to the men on the battlements in perfect Turkish. "Open the gates, you fools!"

"Who are you?" the guards shouted.

Even Vlad's audible scoff had a Turkish ring to it. "Who do you think we are, you damned idiots. Tell Hamza Pasha we have Vlad Dracula."

"Where?"

"See for yourselves? He is here, the treacherous dog!" Vlad said, gesturing at the soldier dressed up in his clothing. "And hurry, would you. We have a hundred Wallachian bastards chasing us."

"Praise God!" The guard said, and they were all smiles behind their beards. "You must wait there for us to—"

Vlad's friendly tone shifted at once. "I shall not wait! I have ended the war! The Sultan will thank me himself, *inshallah*, and you will be praised also, my friend, for doing your duty. But if you do not open this gate at once you shall be executed, this I swear. What is your name? Tell me your name, immediately."

There was a sudden commotion above and their hands pointed behind us. I turned and although I could not see what the guards on the walls were pointing at, I knew what it was. A hundred Wallachian horsemen galloping from the distant woodland towards Giurgiu along the road.

"Quickly!" the guards in the gatehouse called to us. "The enemy approaches. Inside, quickly."

The gates swung open.

Before we rode in, Vlad turned to me and winked, a crooked smile beneath his long moustache. I had to lower my head to hide my own smile from the men on the walls above.

Our first task was to capture the gatehouse and hold open the outer gate and the inner gate. While we held open the gates, the poor Turks on guard were silenced forever and it did not take long for our Wallachian companions to come charging up to the fortress. We allowed them to charge right on in and then we closed the gates and followed the sound of the screams.

Once inside, we set about killing and capturing every damned Turk in the fortress. They did not understand what was happening and panic spread through the garrison. There was hardly any resistance at all and none of it was organised. Our men swarmed into every pocket of the fortress and dragged out those that attempted to hide in storerooms and under floors.

Giurgiu was a Wallachian fortress and the soldiers saw the Turkish presence as an infestation and as a personal affront. The Turks could not surrender fast enough and though we killed many, we still took a thousand of them prisoner. Most importantly of all, the treacherous Hamza Pasha was captured, and we ensured that he and Catavolinos were kept safe from the rampaging Wallachians.

Walt laughed to see it. We sat on our horses in the courtyard as the Wallachians took their revenge. "You remember capturing a castle with such ease before?"

"Never," said Rob.

"I am sure I must have done," I said.

"What a bunch of gooseberries, Richard," Walt said. "Never was a fortress so swiftly taken as this, not never. Got to hand it to your boy, Dracula don't muck about."

"There he is now," I said. "Come on."

I rode toward Vlad as he was issuing orders to his captains. The valuable prisoners were bound and bloody on the floor.

"You shall march these men to Târgovişte," Vlad said, pointing his bloody sword down at them, "and there impale them outside the walls. The longest of stakes shall be reserved for you, Hamza, and you, Catavolinos. I will see your rotting corpses there when I return."

"You are not going with them?" I asked.

Vlad turned and laughed, ejecting a great plume of steam. "The Danube is frozen, Richard! We can cross it at will. I shall send for thousands of horsemen and together we shall raid Bulgaria until the spring thaw."

"What shall we accomplish?" I asked. "William is coming with an army large enough to conquer your kingdom. We should rest the men through the winter."

"The Turk has ravaged our border and so we will ravage his. We shall weaken him and only grow in strength. Let Mehmed come. Let Zaganos Pasha bring his Janissaries. We shall reduce every point of strength on the border. Every point. God is with us and so we shall begin."

I turned to my men, who shrugged.

"Who wants to be warm, anyway?" Walt muttered.

It was as Vlad said. We crossed and re-crossed the great river at a hundred points along its length. We surprised the Turks at every point, from Serbia all the way to the delta on the border of Moldavia. We broke into smaller companies for certain raids so that we could strike at a dozen places at once. When we needed to attack a larger enemy position we assembled more of our number so that we always had the upper hand. We lived off the land, taking what we needed from the villages and fortresses that we attacked and burned. The damage we wrought in a single winter was remarkable.

In order to keep a tally of those killed, Vlad ordered that heads or at least noses and ears be cut off and counted. Our soldiers competed to outdo each other in how many noses and ears they could collect.

In February, we came together back at Giurgiu and took stock of the destruction.

"It is time that we informed our overlord Mattias Corvinus of these matters," Vlad said in the great hall after hearing twenty reports. "Are you ready to take a letter? It is to say the following. I, Vlad III Dracula, have killed men and women, both young and old, who lived at Oblucitza and Novoselo where the Danube flows into the sea, up to Rahova which is near Chilia, from the lower Danube up to such places as Samovit and Ghighen. It is a fact that I have killed... how many was it?"

A clerk referred to the tally he had earlier recorded and cleared his throat before answering. "Twenty-three thousand, eight hundred and eighty-four, my lord."

"I have killed that number of Turks and Bulgars, but this is not counting those that we burned inside their homes and those whose heads were not struck off by my men. Thus, Your Highness should know that I have broken peace with Mehmed II. That is all, add no more, do not include any of your niceties. Have it taken at once to Buda."

We hoped that we had done enough damage to delay the invasion or at least hinder it. Most of all, Vlad had scored a moral victory over our enemies by striking the first blow and it was a victory that had to be answered. We knew by then that Mehmed and William were in Greece, engaged in reducing Corinth but he sent another *wazir*, Mahmud, to conduct a raid in force across the river.

They had almost twenty thousand men and they struck first the port of Brila on our side of the Danube. We brought the army down and trailed them, looking for a good place to intercept. All the while the Turks marched and looted through the lowlands, repaying our winter raids.

"We must stop them," I said, watching smoke rise above the trees in the distance. "What was all of this for if not to stop precisely this?"

"Have patience, Richard," Vlad said. "I knew my people would bleed. We shall destroy them utterly but it must be at the right moment."

"But we could drive them off now," I said. "We have enough men for that."

"I do not wish to drive them off. The entire army must be destroyed."

Whispering to Eva in the dark, I said that Dracula would not listen to reason. "He wants nothing less than a stunning victory."

"He is vain," Eva muttered. "He says he will abase himself, suffer any ignominy, for the sake of his people. But he is a man like William at heart, who seeks greatness at the expense of decency and virtue. Greatness no matter the cost."

"What if he seeks greatness through the preservation of his people?"

Eva sighed. "When those come into conflict, which will he seek more?"

"You think he will choose himself over his people?"

"I think you should go to sleep."

Vlad waited and waited. And then, when it was almost too late, he ordered us into battle. In fact, it was only as the Turkish army of Wazir Mahmud headed back to cross the Danube at Brila that we finally launched the crushing assault Vlad had been planning for.

The Turks were loaded with Wallachian prisoners that they would make into slaves, along with tons of stolen food, wine, gold, weapons and everything they could carry on wagon and horse. Drunk on their riches, they camped by the river and prepared to ferry their piles of booty across.

It was there that Dracula got his stunning victory. We killed ten thousand Turks in that battle, shattering their army utterly.

And then in May 1462 we heard that Zaganos Pasha and Sultan Mehmed were coming.

***

The Turks needed their vast fleet on the Danube in order to supply and support their army and enable the crossing of the men and horses from Bulgaria and so to hinder them we had destroyed the ports along the river and deployed our men in certain strong garrisons. All our efforts then were turned toward discovering where the crossing would be made. We baited our traps by leaving certain regions lightly defended but William was cunning when it came to such things. We did not even know if they would cross in one place or divide to cross at multiple points and either join up or launch a series of smaller armies. Each one still might be larger than the entire Wallachian army all together.

Keeping up with the enemy troop movements on the other side certainly stressed our captains on the river but it had to be done. We needed to be able to respond quickly to the invasion in order to have a hope of stopping it before it reached Târgovişte.

We soon had word from our agents and spies that the Turks were bringing close to a hundred thousand men. This was as large an army as they could ever realistically supply in the field and so it showed Mehmed was determined to conquer Wallachia once and for all. It was as large as the army he had brought to Varna, to Kosovo, and to Belgrade and in all those places it had taken all the might of Hungary and her allies to fight the Turks to a standstill.

This time, Wallachia would stand alone.

The Turks had sixty thousand core soldiers with at least thirty thousand auxiliary forces including Bulgarians, Serbians and Anatolian *akinje* marauders. Of great concern was the hundred and twenty cannons that they would bring to the field.

Dracula did his utmost to bring allies to fight with us. For a time, we hoped the Venetians would send forces but nothing came of it in the end. No matter how many messengers we dispatched, Mattias Corvinus would send no one to aid us. Instead, he was facing off against Frederick III in the north and so it seemed he was happy enough for Christendom to lose another kingdom.

All we had was what Wallachia could provide.

The mass levy of Wallachian peasantry produced a rather motley army. Many were just boys, though they called themselves young men, and the elder of them were often bent-backed from their years spent tilling their fields. But the men knew their country and, in the woodlands and marshes and mountains of Wallachia, they were at home. And what is more, Dracula's *viteji*, his new officer class, had been recruited from these very same men and they knew their people, just as the people knew the land.

It was not just the country peasants but the townsmen also who were called up to fight. These fellows were the ones trained in the mass use of the hand-guns, as well as in the use of the precious few war wagons and cannons that we had available.

When the recruiters had gone out to find every able-bodied man and boy, many had come back with women also. These were not turned away and indeed many of them demonstrated their ability to shoot crossbows and even hand-guns and drive wagons. Most in fact acted as ammunition carriers and loaders for their husbands or sons but I saw plenty of women fighting in a murderous rage amongst their menfolk in the battles to come. Sadly, I saw some dead and injured, also. Women are sometimes driven to defend their homelands and they are brave to do so in spite of being weak in body. But it is always a tragedy when a people are forced into such positions and there is not a Christian man who has lived that enjoyed seeing a woman fight. They are the most precious thing in all the world and when they feel the need to take up arms then one knows her men folk have already failed in their duty.

Including women and children, our army numbered a mere thirty thousand.

Of those, we had about ten thousand cavalry, who were mostly experienced soldiers that knew their business. These men were well armed and wore lamellar and mail and their lords and their retinue were clad in plate armour.

And of course we had the *sluji*. Everyone in the army knew that if things were falling apart they were to rally around their prince, his bodyguard and the *sluji*.

As well as all this we had our very light cavalry, who were excellent riders with their wits about them riding fast horses. These men conducted lightning raids when opportunity presented itself but mainly served as our reconnaissance and messenger force.

With any army, it is necessary to be supported by thousands of servants to clean and mend and cook and support the soldiers in every way and in this we were blessed to have the entire nation of Wallachia behind us.

The old *boyar* families on the other hand completely abandoned Dracula and their own people and fled into the mountains. There is no doubt that they believed we would be destroyed and when we were they planned to come down from Transylvania and pledge allegiance to the Sultan and take up whatever positions they could under their new masters. Such men are so far beyond contempt that it is impossible to find a suitable punishment. I prayed that in time they would at least find themselves duly impaled.

But only if we beat an army three times our size made up of veteran soldiers.

They came at us in two parts.

First they were sighted at Vidin. Mehmed came up the river by ship in the hopes of traversing the River Olt so they could strike deep into Wallachia and directly at Târgovişte.

And another detachment came to force a crossing from Philipopolis in Bulgaria which would cover the first army's flank.

We were waiting for them.

The Turkish advance force tried to send men to the northern bank but we came out quickly from the woodland, took up firing positions and blasted them with our hand-gunners and crossbowman.

When the Turks fell back, we also retreated into the trees.

I expected that they would come again the next day but they were willing to be patient and instead moved their forces to Turnu. We had burned it the year before but our scouts had watched the Turks carefully rebuilding it and so knew it was a likely crossing point.

It was the dark of the night when they came in force.

We fought with everything we had but trying to organise peasants into effective night fighting units was harder than I could have imagined. Even so, it was the cannons that did it. Dozens of them fired through the night, their flashes lighting up the darkness and the cannonballs crashing into our positions across the river. Men and horses were killed and the living were panicked. We could not hold where we were and so we fell back, enabling even more of their boats across.

They even brought light cannons across with them and they dug in on our side of the riverbank. Our cavalry did their best to break them and drive them back into the river, charging repeatedly down on them, but the Turks had so many troops that no matter how many we killed, the men behind them continued digging defensive ditches until finally our horsemen could not approach the cannons.

Our war wagons had a commanding position above the landing area and our hand-gunners fired from the backs of them over and over, killing hundreds of Turks and wounding more.

More and more barges came across and we simply could not hold them. When morning came we counted seventy barges ferrying Janissaries across. Still, we attempted to hold them on the thin strip of land along the bank there. For hours, it was a close-run thing. We managed to kill hundreds of Janissaries, at least, and they were precious men the Sultan could ill afford to lose.

Vlad was everywhere, shouting encouragement as he rode from position to position. "We are holding them!" He rode close to the enemy and, taking a crossbow, shot at them before riding back to his cheering men. "Throw them back!"

While we focused on our side of the river, we did not pay attention to what was occurring across the water. The Sultan was there, and William and his Red Janissaries too, but we could not get to them and so we ignored them for now. But they had ordered up every one of their great cannons and positioned them in an arc. When the order was given, all one hundred and twenty cannon fired at once.

Our war wagons were hit, smashing them and sending shards of oak and limbs of hand-gunners spinning across our positions. Wallachian cavalry were blasted apart.

The shock of it alone almost broke our poor army. Even I had never heard a cacophony like it. A hundred and twenty massive cannons firing at once seemed enough to shatter the very world, splitting first the air and then the ground beneath our feet. It did not shatter the Wallachians but we knew we could not stand against such a bombardment and so Vlad ordered a retreat.

Without those Turkish cannon on the far shore, I do not doubt we could have sent the massive army back over the river by the end of the day.

As it was, we were defeated. And the Sultan's army was in Wallachia.

***

"There he is," Rob whispered. "Do you see him?"

"Yes, yes," Serban said at my side. "He is there. No, there, my lord."

Peering through the trees from a high ridge, I saw the banner and the man riding at the centre of the party. "By God, he looks just like him."

"Rather more handsome than Vlad," Eva said, squinting beside me.

"You cannot possibly tell at this distance," I said, glancing at her.

"Certainly I can," Eva replied. "He is a most striking young prince."

Vlad Dracula's younger brother, Radu, had joined the Sultan's army. Indeed, it was common knowledge that the Sultan intended to place Radu on the throne as Voivode of Wallachia once Vlad had been defeated. What is more, he had four thousand of his own horsemen with him. Radu was completely and totally under the spell of Mehmed and William.

"Do you reckon he's an immortal?" Walt whispered.

"Why don't you go ask him?" Rob said.

"What did Vlad say about it?" Eva asked. "Was his handsome brother turned?"

"Quiet, all of you. He is here, that is all that matters. With him here, it is worth the risk."

The Turks had moved slowly north from the river. We knew they were coming for Târgovişte. They were so focused on destroying Vlad's capital that they ignored the fortress at Bucharest and the fortified monastery of Snagov. Mehmed did not want to waste time and men on taking places that ultimately mattered little in his conquest. If Vlad could be removed and Radu put in his place, all the smaller places should either give up or could be conquered without consequence.

We knew we had little hope of winning a set-piece battle on the open field.

Instead, we started a type of war that I had fought before, in France and other places. Along the line of advance and for miles around, all grain stores were burned, as were the crops in the field. Every source of water was poisoned, and the livestock and peasantry were driven into the north where they would be safe.

As the Turks advanced up the valleys and through the dense forests, we harried them everywhere they went. Every scouting party, every group sent out for forage, we pounced on them and killed them.

Our purpose was to kill as many as possible, of course, but even more it was to break their spirit. To make it so that every man was afraid in his heart to face us.

We also damned small rivers and diverted their waters to create swathes of waterlogged marshland to slow down the progress of the army, especially of their supply wagons and most of all the dreaded but enormously heavy cannons.

Our peasants may not have been professional soldiers but they excelled at digging the earth. And so we had them dig man traps everywhere. Steep, deep pits with wickedly spiked stakes at the bottom which the peasants delighted in smearing with bog water and human and animal shit. These traps were covered with thin sticks and leaves to disguise them.

It was a scorching summer. By denying the Turks access to water, they suffered deeply from thirst and heat exhaustion as they advanced. The sheer size of their army worked against them and they spent thousands of men relaying water for miles and even then it was never enough. Without enough fresh water to drink, they certainly did not have enough to wash with, and they grew filthy and, rather quickly, disease spread. The camp sickness began killing almost as many as we did.

So their days were spent in misery as they crept forward in agonising thirst, afraid of each step and fearful of leaving the core of their army lest they be murdered most horribly.

And we made sure they suffered every night.

When they came to a stop for their nightly camp, they were exhausted and thirsty and short of food and then they had to dig their trenches and throw up their earthworks around their tents. And we made certain that they had to do it, for any man not within the safety of those defences we took and murdered and left for their comrades to find in the morning, often headless or skinless or somehow mutilated.

My *sluji* could see in the dark better than any mortal and they delighted in creeping up on sentries and drinking their blood while their screams echoed through the hills and forests. When the Turks took up their march again, they would pass scores of their friends, skinned, or headless, and impaled upon tall stakes. At first, the Turkish soldiers, outraged, immediately cut down every man we left for them but we knew we were breaking their spirit when they began leaving them until the slaves at the rear were ordered to do it. Thousands of men saw what conquering Wallachia would cost them.

The Turks we captured had begun referring to Vlad Dracula as *Kaziglu Bey*, which meant the Lord Impaler. It was a name we embraced. The Lord Impaler is coming to drive a stake through every man in your army, we would say to captured men, and then we would send them back to their men with the message on their lips but with their hands cut off or their eyes put out.

And yet we could not stop their advance. They were too many. Slow and shaken as they were, their sheer numbers combined with the relentlessness of the will driving them, they were inexorable.

"We must break their spirit," Vlad had urged us, on many occasions. "They must be made to see that even if they achieve victory it will be at the cost of their entire army. We are not their only enemies. The tribesmen in the east threaten them, and they have no friends among the Arabs. The Mamluks of Egypt would gladly see the Turks destroyed. We must break their spirit and they will retreat."

The bravest of his friends on occasion risked asking for reassurance. "What makes you so certain, my lord?"

"I know these men. I know Mehmed. I know Zaganos Pasha. They are men who carefully calculate the cost of their actions."

It was true, of William at least, I could attest to that. He was a man well versed in cutting his losses in order to save his skin.

But it was not working. Not entirely. Not enough.

The Turks pushed us back into the mountains not far from Târgoviște. If they turned from us to besiege the city then we could fall upon their rear and work away at them. But with their cannons and their sheer numbers they could break into Târgoviște and take it before our methods of warfare could drive them off.

More desperate measures would be required.

Peering down on Radu from that high ridge, I knew it was time.

"Are you certain we can do it?" Rob asked, scratching at his stump.

"Too risky," Serban muttered. "To risk all when we need not do it, it is too much."

"Târgoviște will fall if we do not," Stephen said.

"So what?" Serban said. "It is a city."

"A city full of people," Rob said. "Families."

"It is the heart of the kingdom," Stephen said. "When it falls, the kingdom falls. Where will we stop William then?"

Serban shrugged. "We would live. You would live, my lords. To survive is all."

"Enough talk," I said. "Now that Radu is here, that makes every leader together in one place. It is worth the risk."

"I doubt that Prince Vlad will see it that way," Stephen replied.

"Then I must convince him. Come, we must retreat before we are seen."

We crept backwards through the trees until we were behind the ridge and we rode north for the heart of the camp. Our army was spread over three valleys and each had at least one pass leading north into Transylvania. If the Turks attacked any or even all of the valleys we could retreat all the way out of Wallachia if we needed to. However, we also had prepared defensive positions all the way up those valleys so we could mount an effective fighting retreat with every step. If the Turks did attack us they would pay dearly for it.

Few of us believed Mehmed would be so foolish. All he had to do now was hold Vlad's army at bay, take Târgoviște and install Radu as the new voivode. Gradually, loyal *boyars* could be found to support him publicly and they would then be granted the lands held by the *boyars* in Vlad's army. The Turks would garrison every town so strongly that we could not take them and then we would be starved of supplies until our army withered into nothing.

"We should attack," I said to Vlad, pushing into the cool shade of his tent.

Vlad was sipping on a cup of blood while his armourer measured and fitted a new or repaired gauntlet on his other hand. I could smell the blood, though it was mixed with wine, and I am certain the armourer would have smelled it, also. There were rumours of Dracula's regular blood drinking circulating amongst the army and the populous but it disturbed me to see him doing so openly.

"Attack? They still outnumber us three to one," Vlad replied, waving his cup in the Turk's direction. "Each one of his soldiers is more capable than most of mine. We could not kill enough to win. Instead, we must drag them further into the hills."

"We do not need to kill many men to win. Only three."

Vlad grunted. He looked tired. "You mean Mehmed and William and..."

"And Radu. Your brother is here. I have seen him this morning, with the four thousand horsemen Mehmed has gifted him."

Vlad ground his teeth. "I thought they would keep him safe in the lowlands. If he is here then we need not kill all three. Killing Radu alone would put an end to Mehmed's great plans for Wallachia."

"It would not. Mehmed would find any one of a hundred other puppets to place on the throne. He could pluck one of the Danesti at will and they would gladly accept. If Radu alone is killed, it does not save Wallachia."

Vlad fixed his dark eyes on mine. "You would say anything if it meant getting what you wanted. And all you want is to kill William. You do not even care about killing Mehmed."

I kept my voice level. "That is not true. I have fought him and his father before him, fought the Turks, fought for Christendom as a crusader, for almost twenty years."

"You have. But only because William was by their side. If William dies, you will leave here and abandon us to our fate." He glared at me. I could see white all the way around his irises.

I shrugged, as if it was a matter of small importance. "If William dies then I have other business to attend to. Once that is completed, I would fight the Turks once more."

"I do not believe you. You are just like all the other Catholics. Only interested in each other. You will only care when the Turks are at the gates of Rome. Even then, no doubt, you would prefer to fight each other than to do your duty to God."

He glared at me and my anger flared up in response to his words. I had done more than any man and to be questioned and doubted by one so young was deeply offensive. I could have happily struck him a blow.

But I forced my blood to cool.

"Perhaps you are right," I said, surprising myself almost as much as him. "But the fact remains that you are about to lose your kingdom, Vlad. Nothing can stop Mehmed from taking Târgovişte."

He sneered, curling his lip. "If they reach the gates of my city, I will make sure what they find will shatter their hearts in their chests."

"You will. But supposing they can bring forward their cannons and knock down the walls. Will that not give them cheer enough to carry them through?"

He waved away his armourer who retreated as quickly as he could. "You would have me gamble the existence of my people on a single throw of the dice."

"If you do not throw the dice then your kingdom is lost. Your people will be slaves forever."

Vlad walked to the open front of his tent and looked out at his army. "It might cost half of them their lives."

"It might."

"Even if I kill Mehmed then William will see another Sultan put into his place. Another puppet. And William will come again."

"That is why we must kill William above all."

"Above Radu? Above Mehmed?"

"Do you doubt that he is the most dangerous of them all? With William dead, with his Blood Janissaries wiped out, then our enemies are only mortal."

"Very well, then." Vlad turned to me. "How could it be done?"

1 3

Night Attack at Târgoviște

1 4 6 2

WE TORTURED TURKISH SOLDIERS and officers that we had taken in previous raids and questioned them about the precise location and disposition of the enemy soldiers within their camps. We had so many that it took some time but we combined the reports until we had a consistent picture of where Mehmed's tents were, and those of Zaganos Pasha and also Radu Dracula.

For all their heart and for all the deaths and mayhem that they had caused, we knew that the peasant infantry would not be capable of attacking in the manner we needed. Their officers were for the most part excellent but the peasants did not have the discipline needed. Not only that, they did not have the armour and weaponry required.

Instead, we took every single remaining mounted soldier we could gather together. They had to be mounted. We needed to penetrate deep within the camp at multiple points, kill our targets and retreat before the remaining soldiers surrounded us and killed us.

For a time, it seemed we would have only seven thousand men. Even after all their losses, to us and to plague and thirst, the enemy still had seventy or eighty thousand soldiers in the field. Some of the captured officers swore that they had received reinforcements bringing their numbers back to a hundred thousand but I was careful to silence those men and discount their testimony.

"What's the difference?" Walt asked, shrugging, as I cut a Turk's throat for claiming such a figure. "Seventy thousand is already impossible. Might as well be seventy millions."

"Quiet, Walter, or your throat will be the next one cut."

"When a man threatens violence it means he has lost the argument."

"Shut up, Walt."

At the last moment, our numbers were boosted to almost ten thousand cavalry when two more great companies returned from their ranging. They were tired and their horses would be in a bad way but they would be coming with us that very night. We needed every man we could get.

Such an assault could only have a chance of success if it was carried out in the dark of the night. By day, we would be seen and the enemy would be prepared. By night, we had a chance. Slim, yes, but a chance.

Our attack took place on the night of 17th June 1462.

"This could be it," I said to my companions as darkness descended. The air was still warm from the day and the pines released their sickly-sweet smell into the sky. "This could be the night that we kill William and fulfil our mission. Or... this could be the end of our Order. Let us not pretend that this is anything other than a huge risk. We are outnumbered and we are riding deep into the heart of the enemy. While I pray for victory, I also fear that not all of us will escape with our lives. But we have toiled here for years for the chance to get this close to William. He is as well defended as any man on earth and so surprise is our only chance for ending him."

"We understand, sir," Walt said. "Death or glory, ain't it. Same as usual."

"Well, let us pray for glory and for victory," I said. "You know what to do. Keep a tight rein on your companies and keep in sight or sound of the next captain, if not me. Any questions?"

They went to speak to their detachments and to take a last draught of blood before the fighting.

"Serban," I called. "Where are you, you little bastard?"

"Here, sir," he replied, hurrying over.

"Listen, Serban. We are going into hell. Even the *strigoi* will struggle to make it out alive. I want you to wait here."

He frowned, wrinkles creasing like canyons. "I have not slowed you down yet. Not once, my lord. And I never will."

"That is true enough," I admitted. "Still, I want you to stay at the camp until we come back."

He bowed. "I will prepare the servants for your return. And if you die in the battle, I must say it has been an honour to serve you."

"I could still make you a *strigoi* before I go? There should be time enough."

"Very kind, my lord, but I would rather stay as I am."

"Fine, well, you get going now. It is soon to get dangerous around here."

Our army would attack in two flanks. My *sluji* would accompany Vlad in the main attack while a boyar named Lord Gale was tasked with assaulting the Turks from the opposite direction. Our horses and their riders swirled in the darkness, a great mass of flesh and steel moving out of the trees, our lance points raised to the stars. I had seen countless battles and ridden in more raids than I could remember and yet my heart hammered in my chest as we swept down from the hills. William was out there in the dark. So close, I could almost smell him over the reek of the sap.

Ahead of my men, each forward detachment took a handful of Turkish officers with them to allow us to get close to their outer sentries before killing them. The prisoners were then killed, despite our promises to free them for cooperating.

"Close now," I muttered. "Be ready to charge."

Word spread through our lines.

Be ready.

Once we reached the trench lines around the camp, our foremost men roared and their trumpeters sounded.

Our cavalry charged in. Cries went up into the night sky and the hooves pounded on the hard, dry earth. We streamed into the camp, rushing by the outermost Turks and leaving them for the men who would follow us.

Some men bore flaming torches which they whirled and tossed out into tents and stores. Other shot their crossbows in volleys to create confusion and terror before dropping them and charging in with sword and spear in hand.

We charged in with the *sluji* keeping tight in formation, their lances lowered only when we needed to force our way through, deeper into the camp. I was determined to keep our immortals out of the fighting for as long as possible so that they could focus on the Blood Janissaries, when we found them, but of course there were so many enemies in the way that we had to join in with cutting our way through.

The Turks were in a blind panic. Somehow, they had not expected we would attack in force. At least, they were certainly not prepared for it. The only men who were armed initially were those sentries we had quickly dispatched and overcome and the men further within all seemed to be sleeping in their tents or even out in the open air. Most men rushed from us in full retreat rather than standing to fight and those who did were in various states of undress, let alone in armour. Our blades cut them to ribbons and the air filled with the smell of hot blood and the screaming of the terrified Turks.

It seemed to be going even better than I had hoped but I knew the sands of time were swiftly running out. In the distance, a gun fired and then another. It would not be long before they organised themselves. We had to find William before then or it would be too late.

Smashing our way through a line of Turks, we came across a vast and colourful tent surrounded by properly equipped guards.

"Mehmed's tent!" Rob cried nearby. "Or William's?"

"To me!" I cried. "*Sluji*, to me!"

A handful of them rallied to me and without waiting for more to come I ordered a charge and raced toward the tents myself. Our numbers and strength overwhelmed the guards. I had a sinking feeling that it could not be William's tent. He would surely be surrounded by his blood-red slave soldiers. The tent was hacked into and my men pulled down the ropes and poles holding it erect and they rushed inside even as it collapsed. A dozen *sluji* came out dragging a pair of finely attired Turks.

"Who are you?" I asked them in Turkish, dismounting and coming at them on foot. On their knees with my men holding them fast, they cringed away from me. "Who are you?" I asked, slapping their turbans from their heads. "Who are you?"

"We are wazirs. I am the Wazir of—"

I slapped his face. "Where is Zaganos Pasha?"

"In... in his tents."

"Where are his tents? Point them out. Where, man?"

Their shaking fingers both pointed the same way, deeper into the camp. I sawed through both of their throats and threw them down.

"Find the other captains," I commanded Rob. "I want all the companies with me now."

There was hardly room in the avenues between the tents for so many men to ride abreast but to my right and left my men tore into anything that stood in their way. We killed more men as we advanced, setting fires as we went. The flames lit up the night and also filled it with billowing black smoke. Sparks flowed up like a demonic rainstorm. In the distance, a mass of gunpowder exploded in an almighty blast that I felt through the very earth. We killed men and we killed horses and we killed camels.

The Turks came at us in confused charges, mounted or on foot, but these we beat back, though each time we lost a man or two. Some of the *sluji* were killed outright and others must have become separated in the confusion. Our numbers dwindled and always there were more Turks beyond the ones we cut down. Gradually, they became more organised and we came up against masses of heavily armoured men and their cavalry began cycling charges that slowed us down. At my flanks, my men were being killed and I could do nothing to protect them.

"Too slow!" Walt cried, riding toward me with his axe raised and dripping blood. "Too slow, Richard! We're getting stuck!"

"On!" I roared. "Kill them! Kill the Sultan! Kill the Pasha!"

We killed them and their screams filled the night.

"Great God Almighty," Rob cried, pointing ahead before pulling his visor closed. "Here they come."

Out of the swirling smoke and darkness, lit by the flames of the burning camp, the Blood Janissaries advanced with their hand-gunners at the forefront. Some knelt and others leaned into their weapons, bracing them against their chests or couching them under their arms.

"Beware gunners in front!" I shouted to my men but before the words were out of my mouth their weapons fired and my men and their horses were lashed by a hundred deadly shots. My men fell in their dozens, their lances thrown down as they fell. Some that were hit were wounded rather than dead but even those would bleed to death and expire without blood to heal them. And we lost many horses. Some horses could survive multiple wounds and continue to function but still they were mortal, and they collapsed under the onslaught.

The next two rows of Janissaries advanced beyond their front lines and they brought up their guns and lifted their sticks with the smouldering tapers to the firing holes.

"What do we do?" one of my men was shouting. "What do we do?"

Hesitation and uncertainty are the worst possible things at such times and so I made a snap decision. It was my default decision with regards to problems and which has caused me more trouble in my life than just about anything else.

"Charge!" I shouted. "Come on, charge them now!"

Perhaps I should have waited. Two hundred years later I might have ordered my men to dismount and to lie flat while the enemy fired but I did not yet have extensive experience with firearms. I imagined that if they saw three hundred charging cavalry they would be panicked enough to miss their shots or even to break altogether, seeing that they were without polearms in the front lines.

But they were far too disciplined for that. And all I succeeded in doing was ordering a partial charge from men who were not prepared that brought them closer to the guns that were shooting them.

Dozens of us were hit again.

As was I.

The flashes of the fire and the crashing of the weapons filled my eyes and ears. An impact hit me in the chest with such force it was like being kicked by a destrier. I found myself tumbling along with my horse who collapsed under me having himself been shot in the head and chest.

I smacked into the ground, the sound of my armour crunching filled my ears, and rolled until I was lying on my back, struggling for breath. Above, all I saw was darkness and the sparks from a hundred huge fires spraying up into it like the souls departing the dying.

Hooves drummed on the ground and men shouted and I rolled to my feet. My sword still in my hand, I looked about to get my bearings. It was hard to breathe and I instinctively touched my chest only to feel the metal of my breastplate. Whatever the damage was, it would have to wait. Bellowing horsemen rode past me at a gallop and crashed into the Blood Janissaries with an almighty crash of bodies and steel.

I hurried forward on foot to join them, feeling a mass of wounds all over me. I needed a horse but I could not see one spare and so I ran on toward the *sluji*. Our charge had ground to a halt by the density of the Janissary formation. We were better armoured and on sturdy horses but the hand-gunners were dead or had retreated and now they fought back with their long polearms. We could not break through.

Through the press of men, at their rear, I caught a glimpse of a large man on a large horse, directing his men.

It was William.

I looked around for my captains or any senior man and took a deep breath to shout for my companions to push on and kill my brother.

But the breath I took caught halfway through and instead of a shout I coughed out a mouthful of blood. I felt my breastplate again and found two holes had been shot through it, both in the upper chest near to my heart. A chill went through me. Would it be fatal? Would I be strong enough to escape from the enemy camp?

Pushing those unworthy thoughts aside, I looked for assistance.

Where are my bastard bodyguards? I snarled to myself before I remembered. *I made them charge to their deaths.*

A riderless horse nearby struggled to free itself from the press of men and I reached it just as another one of my *sluji* did.

"My lord!" he said. "Are you wounded? Where are your men?"

I tried to answer him and instead, blood welled from my mouth.

"Christ save us," he said and he helped me to mount and offered up his lance which I took with some difficulty. It hurt just to hold it but I had to try something, anything, to reach William. He was so close.

Walt's angry shouting reached me. "There you are, you daft bastard!"

He rode to my side along with Rob, both covered in blood and on exhausted or wounded horses. I pointed my lance, the point shaking with the exertion of doing so, at William where he sat behind his Janissaries. Both of my men shouted their understanding and their approval and they called in the others around us.

I waved a hand at Walt who hesitated just for a moment, no doubt concerned about my condition, before he ordered the charge. It was so clear to me in that moment. We would push through ten lines of immortal Janissaries and strike down my brother.

He saw me, I am certain. Through the darkness and the boiling smoke and the flickering radiance of the burning camp all around, he saw me.

I will kill you, I thought as I looked at him. *I will kill you.*

It was a mad risk but still I might have ended it right there. All those later centuries of death and horror inflicted by William could have been avoided. I myself might have been killed but at least William would have fallen also.

Instead, a thousand Janissaries dressed in white advanced out of the shadows on our flank.

"Watch out!" my men cried. "Look to the flank!"

They were in a wide formation, their white robes and long hats seeming to glow orange in the firelight. Already, they were prepared to fire. There was no time to react, no time to move.

The Janissaries took aim and fired.

We were cut down. The *sluji* were blasted, raked, from one side and all our men there

685

were riddled. Their armour providing no protection and only their immortality preserving the lives of some. Had I been on that flank rather than the centre, already wounded as I was, I would certainly have been killed. As it was, only the presence of Walt and Rob beside me served to shield me from the attack. Even so, my horse was killed and Rob and Walt were shot. As we climbed, dazed and in pain, to our feet, we found the Blood Janissaries advancing in front and their mortal compatriots rushing on the flank.

Unable to speak, I signalled as best as I could that we should retreat. I need not have tried. Not a man among the *sluji* was fool enough to think we could stand against such an onslaught.

There was no way forward, only back.

We fell into a desperate retreat, fighting any who came too close and fleeing as fast as our legs would carry us.

A group of our brave *sluji* rode up, threw themselves off their horses and helped me and Walt and Rob into their saddles while they stood and covered our retreat. Those Wallachian soldiers saved our lives that night at the cost of their own. I do not remember their names.

We soon rode amongst thousands of mortal Wallachian horsemen who had also turned to flee. Our raid was finished and I could not speak to ask what had happened. All I could do was try to stay conscious as I coughed up masses of blood and spat it off into the darkness. We fell back and enemy cavalry pursued us into the hills even after sunrise.

All I wanted to ask was whether Dracula had killed Mehmed. And whether Dracula himself was still alive. But all that came from my throat was more blood.

It was hours before we were clear of the enemy and by then the day had turned hot. My blood caked inside my ruined armour and I was stiff as a board, sweat and blood mixed and ran into my eyes. All I could think was that I had failed. William was still alive.

We returned on exhausted horses with thousands of tired and wounded men to the camps we had prepared.

Eva stood waiting, her face twisted in aguish as she ran to my horse. Stephen was everywhere shouting commands to the servants. My men had to help me dismount and I could not speak a single word of command though they knew what I needed. They took me to my tents where some of my servants removed my armour and others bled themselves into cups that I might drink. This I did, greedily, and at once began to feel as if I might just avoid death, though I could still barely take a breath. After undoing the straps and removing my plate, they cut the blood-soaked clothes from my body and washed my skin.

I had been shot three times in the chest. One of the balls had passed right through me and I had a corresponding wound in my back that they claimed was big enough to fit a fist inside, with shattered bones poking out. The other two shots had entered my rib cage but had not come out.

One shoulder had been torn up by another ball and I had a long gash on my thigh that could have been caused by anything but I assumed was the result of being shot also, as my armour had been penetrated but remained in place.

"You did not find William," Eva said. "I can tell it from your face."

I gestured for more blood and guzzled down as much as they could give me. The pain was excruciating and I faded between wakefulness and unconsciousness as they tended to me. I felt an intense itching in my chest and looked down to see first one and then another piece of flattened lead, shining with blood, emerge from the wounds in my body and drop onto my lap and from there to the ground. A servant picked them up and stared, mouth open, at them.

"Blood," I said. "More blood."

A short time later I was cleaned and dressed and had a belly full of servant's blood and fresh wine. Still bruised and exhausted, I knew I would live.

"What happened?" Eva asked, stroking my hair.

"We came close," I muttered. "Not close enough."

"You lived. You can try again."

"What happened with the rest of the attack?" I asked.

"You will have to ask someone who was there. I know we lost many men. Perhaps too many lost to win the war. You shall have to speak to Dracula."

"He lives?"

"Ask Walt."

I got up to do just that but Eva placed a hand on my chest, looking me in the eye and then all over. She slipped her arms around me and held me tight for a moment before letting me go.

Walt was already up and walking around the camp, taking stock, checking on his company. My surviving men were being treated and were drinking every drop of blood and wine that they could get. They watched me with the grim faces of defeated men.

"Walt," I said. "Where is Rob?"

"In there," he said, nodding at a tent. "Shot to bits. He'll live, probably."

"Is this all there is?"

Walt sighed, placing his hands on his hips and looking around. "Ain't finished counting but looks like we have a hundred and thirty men here. Worst of all is that Jan died, poor sod. Garcia lives. And Claudin is still with us, sadly. But most of the rest of the Company of Saint George didn't make it back. Reckon a few more will come in today. But not many."

"A hundred and thirty? Out of four hundred and eighteen?" I felt sick to my stomach. "We lost two hundred and ninety immortals? And we did not kill William."

Walt shrugged. "Near enough wiped out his red bastards, though."

"We did?"

"Did you not see? Easily half of them, probably more. If it hadn't been for those mortal Janissaries coming up then." He shook his head. "We nearly had the bastard, didn't we. Still, come out about even, I would say. Our lads are a wee bit disheartened, though. Reckon some of them are realising that being immortal doesn't mean you ain't ever going to die. Don't worry, I'll have a word. Me and Rob will sort them out."

"What of Mehmed? What of Dracula?"

Walt looked up the hill toward the rest of the camp. "Dracula lives. I reckon Mehmed does, too, or else them lads wouldn't be looking so heartsick."

"I am sorry, Walt."

He nodded, looking the men over. "I been thinking, Richard. I been thinking that it might be we should get ourselves some of those hand-guns after all. Pretty useful, it turns out."

I ordered my servants to fill Rob with blood and to take care of him as if it were me and I moved to speak to my men. There was hardly a man who was not wounded in some way. And all of them had seen their friends die or had been forced to leave them behind in the enemy camp as they died. I said whatever I could and perhaps my words helped to lift their spirits a fraction, even though they no doubt felt angry at me for having led them to such a crushing defeat. The Company of Saint George was almost entirely wiped out and the *sluji*, after so much promise, had been reduced by seven tenths.

Making my way slowly up the hill to Dracula's tent, I felt every one of my three hundred years.

"I did not kill him," Dracula said when I was admitted into the inner part of his large tent. He, too, had been wounded and was drinking wine mixed with fresh blood. "I did not kill him."

"You were shot?" I asked.

Dracula sneered. "It is nothing. My men were killed. My *friends*. And Mehmed lives."

"As does William."

Dracula nodded. "And Radu. That bastard Gale did not break through on the other side of the camp. We were two thousand men fewer than we should have been and it is Gale's fault. I shall have him impaled the moment he shows his face."

"You will do as you must. But perhaps he has his reasons."

"Gale is no friend to you. Why do you defend him?"

I shrugged. "If he is at fault through incompetence or cowardice, then I would gladly see him punished. But it was a difficult task. Impossible, or near enough. Even so, we came close to victory."

Dracula turned his face up, squeezing his eyes closed. "I *saw* Mehmed. My men wounded him before the Janissaries attacked. We were a hair's breadth from killing him."

"He was wounded?" I said. "How badly?"

"Not badly enough. What of William?"

"We killed at least half of the Blood Janissaries. But I lost almost three hundred of the *sluji*. Perhaps more will yet return but it was a bloody exchange. I suppose our immortal armies came out with somewhat even losses."

Dracula scoffed. "You failed. And Gale failed." He stared at me, as if daring me to speak. The words hung in the air between us before Vlad sighed and spoke them aloud. "And I failed. I most of all."

"How many men did we lose?"

"Perhaps as many as five thousand, including men surrounded and taken prisoner as we retreated. We are in no better a position than we were. In fact, we have only lost by this raid."

"How many of the enemy did we kill?"

"I do not know. A great many. Twenty thousand? Thirty? Not enough. Not nearly enough. There will be no way to stop them from reaching Târgoviṣte. All we can do now is prepare the way for them."

The Turks advanced on Târgoviṣte. Vlad Dracula had spent his years as voivode building the defences of the city, at great expense and using vast numbers of slaves to carry out the hardest of the labour. And so the walls and the gates and gatehouses had been strengthened mightily in preparation for the assault that he knew would come.

Their advance cavalry came first toward the city while we stayed back in the hills to watch. We could not stop them by force of arms, we knew that, it was just a question of whether the force of Dracula's spirit would be enough.

For the final two miles along the road to Târgoviṣte, Vlad Dracula had impaled twenty thousand Turks.

There were dozens of rotting, impaled Turkish for every single pace the advancing army had to take and the closer they got to the centre the more there were. It was a crescent of impaled soldiers, growing to be half a mile wide at the centre, so that they walked through a forest of their dead comrades.

Highest of them all were still the rotten corpses of the treacherous Hamza Pasha and his Greek Thomas Catavolinos.

The advancing Turkish cavalry, thousands of them, faltered during their passage through the twenty-thousand impaled men and their hearts and stomachs were not strong enough to get them to the gates of the city.

They turned tail and fled back to the rest of the army.

South of the forest of the dead, they made their camp for the final time.

And in the morning, they retreated south.

What force of arms could not achieve was done through breaking the will of the enemy. On the Danube, the Turkish fleet ferried their broken army back across to Bulgaria. Their rearguard spread out to protect the army while it did so and this we attacked and defeated near Buzău.

While we won that final small victory, the main army burned Brila and departed Wallachia, heading back to Edirne.

However, not all the army fled so far.

A detachment was left close to the border. This force of exiled Wallachian *boyars* and Turkish cavalry was commanded by Radu Dracula.

And he at once began agitating to take Vlad's throne.

14

The Throne

1467

"MY KINGDOM is broken," Vlad said. "And I am the one who has broken it."

The great hall in Târgoviște was empty but for the two of us and Vlad's guards and servants. Dracula drank off his goblet of wine and commanded that it be refilled. He gulped down half of that and leaned back in his throne.

"It was the Turks that broke it. You defended your people."

"I did. And at what cost? My people struggled and won and they are exhausted. So many crops and stores were burnt. Countless wells poisoned and all the while we fought the land has been untilled. There will be famine. Half of my best soldiers are dead or will fight no more. The bravest and strongest of the peasants who fought for me have been killed. Everywhere I go in my lands there are sons without fathers and wives without husbands. And worst of all, I have no allies."

"Your cousin Stephen of Moldavia will—"

Vlad chopped a hand down. "Stephen will do what is best for Moldavia. As he should. It is right and proper that he should. The Turks will turn on him soon enough."

"Perhaps if we go to Mattias Corvinus and—"

"Ha!" Vlad smiled but his eyes were filled with bitterness. "He considers me an enemy and always will. As do the Saxons. And half of the ancient families in my kingdom."

"They had to be driven out and frightened into submission. You could not have done otherwise."

"I was foolish to think I could unmake the ancient feuds of those lords. It would have only worked if I could have killed every one of them and their entire families. And that would be killing Wallachia herself. My methods enabled me to take and hold my crown. But now my people are shattered and my enemies gather."

"You shall weather the storm. You will endure."

"Yes. But why?"

"To defend your people."

He looked at me with something in his eyes. "You are not a subtle man, Richard. That is where you differ from your brother. You have cunning on the battlefield and in any feat of arms. But in politics, you have no subtlety at all."

"Of this, I am aware."

"And I am no different from you. I have never sought compromise or conciliation. It is not in my nature, as it is not in yours. My brother, however, is a peacemaker. Radu is a diplomat at heart and always sought to ease tensions and calm conflict throughout our youth, whether in childish games or in training or when William and I fell to arguing."

"You argued with William often?"

Vlad sighed, looking up at the dark beams of the vaulted ceiling. "As a son might argue with his father, perhaps. A father and son of differing temperaments. And Radu would stand between us and profess his love for us both and beg that we calm ourselves."

"Radu said he loved William? Is that true? Was this before William... violated him?"

Drinking down his wine, he called for more. "No. I think William loved Radu almost as much as Radu adored William. I speak as if it were all in the past for of course it is so for me but I do not doubt that their love endures even now. Radu begged William to give him the Gift of his blood but William said always that Radu was too young and he had to wait until he had grown into his prime years. And even then, William was reluctant to grant my brother what he wanted."

"Why would he not do so? He uses his blood to bind followers to him. It is what he attempted to do with you."

"Indeed and my own immortality was a source of great despair for Radu. He could not understand why William would give me the Gift, when William and I disliked each other so strongly, and at the same time deny it to Radu. But it was because of his love for him that William did withhold it, of that I am certain. He did not want my brother to become like one of us. Drinkers of blood, tied to the consumption of it, and denied the hope of a natural life. He tried to explain it to Radu but my brother heard only rejection. You are so pure, so beautiful. It would be an act of desecration to destroy you. Words such as that. But Radu wished only to be with William forever and William eventually promised that he would give him the Gift, in time. If he did not change his mind."

"You said they had love for each other. But from the way you speak, it sounds almost as though they were tender with each other. I can scarcely believe it."

Vlad took a sip and stared down into his drink. "They were, at times, I am sure. Radu is the fairest man in the world and his nature was always sweet and gentle but he is not a weakling. He has a sharp enough mind. I think William set out to make him his by seducing him body and soul but somehow William in turn became bewitched by Radu. They were at times like lovers, yes, but also like brothers, or a father and a son, or friends of the deepest kind, in the Greek tradition. Like Achilles and Patroclus or Alexander and Hephaestion."

"And you did not try to save Radu from this wicked, perverse relationship?"

His head snapped up and he glared at me. I held his gaze and then he slumped, shrugging. "At first, I did try, but Radu would never speak of ending it. And soon my contempt for him overcame my pity. I resolved to abandon him to the fate he had chosen for himself in his weakness. As I say, I have never been a subtle man. Now I am older, I see that I should have tried harder. He is my brother and the bonds of family should be stronger than anything else. I should have sought compromise so that he was not entirely lost to me. But I did not and now I find that he is working hard to replace me in my own kingdom. And so now what should I do, Richard? Harden my heart once more and fight him to the death, throwing my surviving Wallachians against him and his Wallachians until only one of us is left alive?"

"Yes."

Dracula scoffed, shaking his head.

"What else can you do, Vlad? If you give yourself up, he will have no choice but to have you killed."

He pursed his lips. "I could flee. Take myself into exile."

"You are the Voivode of Wallachia."

It was as though he could not hear me. "I thought I could change the pattern. That I would be the prince for years, for decades, bringing stability and peace and safety to my people. Instead, I find I am just one more name in the litany of Wallachian princes. If I had been a shrewd prince, as Radu will be, then I might have turned the *boyars*, made them my allies, instead of enemies." He threw back his head and downed the contents of his goblet before waving his servant over for more. "But a man cannot change his nature."

I could scarcely believe what I was hearing. For years, I had thrown my lot in with this man and had helped him to defend his kingdom against the mightiest army on earth and just when we had won, he was throwing it all away.

"All you did here was for your people."

He nodded slowly. "That is true. I swore I would do whatever was needed to save them. I would take any action required, no matter if it was a great sin or if it caused me personal danger or even humiliation. And so I find that I must follow this oath again by giving myself up in the interests of my people. By staying, even if I win the battle for the throne, it will be they that will suffer most."

"But what about William? He must be killed."

He pointed a finger at me. "That is your sacred quest, not mine."

"But Radu will be a puppet of Mehmed and William. Our enemies are still the same. And you are simply walking away? Giving up everything we have fought for?"

He smiled. "I will not be dead, Richard. Merely biding my time for more favourable circumstances."

"Such as what?"

He opened his arms, as if gesturing at his hall, at Târgovişte, at his kingdom beyond. "The *boyars* will grow tired of Radu, in time. His heart is too soft to rule. There will be rumours of his blood drinking and he will make many errors by trusting this *boyar* or that one. And in time, my people will want change. They always do. And I will be ready. My lands will have healed by then and the people will have grown fat once more."

I could not think of anything that would change his mind. "But it will be as though Wallachia has fallen to the enemy. Radu will have Turks at his court. And he will do what William commands him to do."

"And if William is foolish enough to come to Târgovişte, we shall come back and kill him, you and I."

I scoffed. "You expect me to come with you? Into exile?"

He could not meet my eye. "If I asked it, would do you do so?"

"I cannot simply wait in the distance for years for things to change. I must stop my brother." I took a deep breath. "And to do that, I need the *sluji*. William still has his immortals and so I need mine. I must stop him, Vlad."

Dracula shrugged, as if it was no matter. "You must. And you should take the *sluji*. They are yours. Loyal to you. It is your blood in their veins, not mine."

"I will take them, then," I said. "But take them where?"

"You may go where you wish," he said, sipping from his goblet. "I would have you go to my cousin Stephen and aid him. The hammer blow will almost certainly fall upon Moldavia next."

"And where will you go?"

Vlad looked up again, leaning his head on the back of his throne. "I think I shall lose myself in Transylvania. Perhaps there will be some friends who will give me sanctuary. I will have to disguise myself in some way, perhaps as a merchant. Can you imagine such a thing? It might even be amusing."

"Radu will pursue you."

"He is not the soldier that I am."

"I will go with you. I will bring the *sluji* out of Wallachia along with you and we will fight off any attempt to take you. When you are safe and if Stephen will give us sanctuary, I will take the *sluji* to Moldavia and continue the fight."

Dracula leaned forward and held out a hand to me, which I grasped. "You have been a good friend to me, Richard. That is just what we shall do. We must make our preparations in secret and then move without delay. All those men loyal to me who will face retribution if they stay must be urged to join us or to make their own preparations. I will leave you to speak to the *sluji*."

When I returned to my quarters and summoned my companions, they were distraught to say the least. I had to have the same arguments I had just gone through with Dracula, and with myself, all over again.

"Are we going to, you know," Walt said, dragging a thumb across his neck. "After all, if he's not helping us no more then he's just one of William's immortals. And we all know what we swore to do with respect to William's immortals."

"I hate to say it but Walt is correct," Stephen said. "We did our best as far as this land is concerned but it could not be saved. It is time to take our losses and put an end to it."

"No," I said. "There is still more that he could do for us."

"I understand that you do not want to harm him," Eva said. "Because you like him."

"He is a good man."

Stephen scoffed. "How can you say those words without them sticking in your throat? He is a monster. Surely, you can see that, Richard? Or perhaps you cannot."

"Because I am a monster myself, Stephen, is that your meaning? Do not beat about the bush, if so. You may quake in your boots at the monstrous things he has done but they were enough to break the spirit of the Turks, were they not?"

"Our night attack on their camp broke their will. Wounded their Sultan."

"What is that you say, Stephen? *Our* night attack? That is very interesting as I do not recall seeing you there."

"You ordered me to stay away!"

"Because of your utter incompetence as a soldier, yes, which you display here again. It was a remarkable feat, beating that army with a band of peasants. Have you ever heard the like of it done before? Where has it been done? Is there word of it in your books of history? Tell me."

He stood before me, almost shaking, but he kept his voice level. "It was done by the *sluji* and by your skill as a captain in leading them, not our dear prince or his useless *boyars*. This is not a proper kingdom, Richard. It is a loose collection of mountain clans who can never be ruled. We should never have spent so much time and effort here. Now we must leave and nothing has been accomplished at all. Everything is precisely as we left it only tens of thousands now lie dead and this country is ravaged."

Eva spoke quickly so that I would not argue against Stephen's words. "What is done is done," she said. "It is in the past. We have fought William and his pet Sultan to a standstill where if not for our presence he would have conquered. We all agree that is true." She looked at Stephen and he avoided her gaze but nodded his assent. "And we also agree that Vlad broke the will of our enemy but he also broke the strength of his people. More than that, from what Richard tells us, it seems Vlad has broken his will also. This is a land, a people, and a prince who are shattered. All we must decide is what to do now. What now brings us closer to William's death?"

"Whatever we do next, we cannot do it from here," I said. "Vlad Dracula is fleeing his kingdom. We shall go with him. And then I shall decide where we go next. But know this. Our quest remains the same as it ever was. We will find a way to kill William."

Rob cleared his throat and spoke quietly from the corner. "We might never come back to this place. To this kingdom. Ever. It might be destroyed, overrun. It might become a new part of Rumelia."

We all stared at him.

"Yes, Rob," I said, knowing he would not speak unless he had something important to say. "That is so."

"Well, we never did go to that monastery, did we. Remember, that old dear up near Poenari with the story about her immortal husband. We always said we would go there when we had a spare few days. But we were so busy with the *sluji* and everything that we just put it off. Because it seemed there was always time in the future to do so."

I nodded. "But if we do not go now, we may never go at all."

"Leave it," Walt said. "Who cares about that batty old bird and her nonsense? We ain't riding down south with Radu and his cavalry charging about the lowlands."

"She said they knew about immortals at Snagov. If that is true, it is not an opportunity we should pass up."

"That may be," Stephen said, "but we do not have time to ride there before our prince and the rest of the men flee the city. We must not be left behind in the country. What if our route of escape is cut off? What then?"

"We can be there and back in three days. There is time enough."

Walt raised his hand. "Does any of us reckon there is anything to find? All we've heard is stories from old Serban and a mad old peasant woman. If once there was immortals in this country, they are probably gone. If they weren't, we'd have run into them by now, wouldn't we? And, I might add, if there are any sneaking around, so what? Why do we even care about them?"

"They would come from the children of Priskos," Eva said. "They might know something useful."

"That is true," Stephen said.

"Wasting our time," Walt sighed.

"It is three days, Walter," I said. "We will be back here in no time and thence to exile."

"Just us?" Eva asked. "The Order."

I nodded. "Just us, and Serban, if you can find him."

***

The monastery at Snagov was on a small island in the middle of a long, narrow lake and we crossed to it by an ancient boat moored on the shore for just that purpose. The people in the village said it was used to ferry supplies to the monks, who they spoke of in hushed tones.

Other than the stone buildings of the rather small monastery, the island was green with fruit trees and the kitchen gardens where monks or lay servants hoed the earth. It was actually quite lovely and I felt peaceful just looking at it and decided that no matter what the monks had to say on the matter, I was glad that I had come.

Vlad had not really understood my desire to visit, when I had gone to him before we left Târgoviște.

"If you are abandoning me, Richard, at least have the courage to say so."

I frowned. "You think that I would skulk away like a coward? Is that truly what you think?"

He sighed. "No. But why ask them about immortals? They have never mentioned anything to me about it and I have been there many times."

"You have?"

He puffed out his chest. "I gifted them a new bell tower, a chapel, and a new roof. I even offered to build them a bridge to the mainland. They declined."

"Very generous of you, I am sure. I heard a rumour that they have some knowledge of immortals. All I will do is ask them to share it and return here."

"Why would they have such knowledge?"

I shrugged. "Perhaps an old text in their possession?"

Vlad snapped his fingers. "That will be it. They have a magnificent library there. The monk in charge of it, decrepit old fellow, blind as a mole but sharp up here. Very well, then, I shall see you when you return. If they give you any trouble, remind them of the bags of florins their prince bestowed upon their house."

"I will do so," I had replied.

There was a monk in his black cassock waiting for us on the island landing as we moored the boat. He was a young man but he had a rather magnificent beard.

"You are welcome, my lord," he said, smiling but hesitant.

"No doubt you are wondering why I have come," I replied. "I have questions regarding certain legends and I am told that you men here know the answers."

He frowned and opened his mouth to answer, then closed it again. The monk looked over his shoulder at the monastery buildings and then past me out over the lake, still frowning. "Perhaps you should speak to the *hegumen*, my lord," he said, finally. *Hegumen* was their word for the abbot.

"Perhaps I should," I said, smiling. "Well, lead the way, brother."

As we set off toward the buildings, Stephen hurried up behind me and whispered in my ear. "Actually, the common form of address for a monk here is father, not brother."

I turned around to tell him to shut up and saw Serban was on the dockside still. "Serban, what are you doing? Come on, I need you."

He slumped sullenly up the bank. "Someone should guard the boat, sir."

"Guard it against these dangerous monks, Serban?" I asked. "Come on." Still, he hesitated so I grasped him by the shoulder and shoved him into motion in front of me.

The handsome buildings were of a pale golden sandstone and the trees, and fruit bushes were neatly pruned and the pathways smartly swept. Evening sunlight glowed from the walls of the new bell tower. Before we entered the monastery, three monks emerged from a dark archway and came to meet us. The foremost of them was a man of middle age, his beard tinged with white.

"Ah, here is the abbot now," the monk from the dock said.

"Welcome, my lord," the abbot said, as we drew to a stop in the long shadows. "I am Abbot Ioánnis."

"I am Richard Ashbury, a soldier in service of Prince Vlad."

"Ah," he said, his eyes widening. "I have heard so much about you."

"You have?"

"You have come far and arrived late. It is almost vespers and I am sure you and your men will require refreshments. Do you intend to stay for the night?"

"If you would allow it, father, and if you have space. The villagers will put us up if not."

"We have a rather fine new hospital building with space enough for all of you with some to spare. It was enlarged due to the beneficence of our generous prince. Come, I shall escort you there myself."

He led us around the perimeter to the hospital which had beds and even a dining table where guests could take meals separate from the monks' refectory.

"Abbot Ioánnis," I said as my men spread out in the dormitory. "May I state my business here?"

"If you wish to do so," he said.

"It is somewhat of a strange question to ask but I have been looking for certain stories." I trailed off.

"Stories?" he prompted, a smile on his face.

"Stories of a rather strange nature. You see, I am looking for tales of men who drink blood."

His smiled faltered and his eyes darted around. "Oh? What could you want with stories like that, my lord?"

I sighed, sensing that I had perhaps wasted my time on the ramblings of a mad old woman after all. "I was told that you collected such tales here. It may be nonsense and if so, I apologise. Have you ever heard of the word *strigoi*?"

He peered at me, his mouth slightly open. "Well—" he began before breaking off, staring behind me. "Is that you, Serban?"

All of us stopped what we were doing and turned around to see Serban slouching in the doorway, his head down.

"Serban?" I said. "Come here."

He came forward, almost dragging his feet with every step.

"It is you, is it not?" Abbot Ioánnis said. "Praise Christ, you have returned. Gracious, it must be, what, thirty years?"

"Returned?" I said. "What is the meaning of this?"

Serban bobbed his head. "Father Ioánnis. Long time. You are abbot now, I see. That is well."

"Oh," the abbot said, chuckling, as if that was unimportant. "So, it is you who has brought my lord Richard Ashbury to our house. How wonderful."

"No, no," Serban said. "It was not me. I did not bring him."

"Ah," the abbot said, his face falling.

"Serban, you serve me and I command you to tell me it all, now."

He shrugged. "Not much to tell. I was here. Then I wasn't."

The abbot scoffed. "Oh, Serban, you feel guilty, I am certain. Please, do not. My lord Richard, allow me to speak of it. There is really not much to tell. One day, a soldier arrived on our shore, terribly wounded. He managed to tell us that he was looking for a place to die. Well, we are not unskilled in the arts of healing and in time, the soldier was made whole again. He stayed after and we spoke of God and His son Jesus Christ. You see, the soldier's body had been healed but his soul was yet wounded from the battles and horrors he had seen. For a time, the soldier embraced life here. He became a novice, wore the cassock and carried his prayer rope and recited in prayer with us. He confessed his sins and, my lord, there were a great many sins to confess, as is the way with soldiers, and I had high hopes that we would welcome him as a full brother." Abbot Ioánnis smiled. "But one morning as we rose for orthros, we found that the soldier was gone. And we never saw him again. Until this joyous moment."

I stared at Serban, who was looking at his shoes. "You sneaky little sod!"

The abbot chuckled. "Many novitiates end their time at a monastery in such a fashion."

"I know that," I said. "But why did you not tell me this at any point, Serban? Is your shame really so great that you could not speak of it?"

He looked up at me. "I knew that you had to come here. I did not know how to speak of it properly. In the right way. But Ioánnis has done it well."

I shook my head. "If only your battlefield bravery was matched by your moral courage, Serban."

"Please, my lord," the abbot said, "do not be overly firm with Serban. I can understand his hesitancy. But he need not fear us. We mean him well, always. Now, you are looking for stories of *strigoi*? Then you must speak to Theodore. Your men should remain here and I will escort you to the library."

Vlad had not been lying about the library at Snagov. The walls were lined with shelves packed with scrolls and there were more codices than I had ever seen in one place. Some of the books were richly ornamented and some even encased in gold and jewels. One wall was lined with windows that opened on to a view of the long lake beyond and there were two monks bent over copying manuscripts. In the corner, sitting by an open window with his face half turned to the view, sat an ancient monk with an enormous white beard.

Abbot Ioánnis dismissed the two scribes and called out to the elderly fellow. "Father

Theodore. I have brought with me one of Prince Vlad's soldiers named Richard Ashbury, the Englishman. He comes wishing to ask you if you have any stories of the *strigoi* that you may relay to him. Why he wishes to know this, I cannot say, because he has not told me and I have not asked him. Would it be well for him to speak with you about this?"

Theodore turned from the window and stared, glassy eyed, in my direction. The man was quite blind.

He dragged himself to his feet and I was surprised to find he was rather tall and, though his back was bent and his frame was frail, it was clear that his shoulders and chest had once been broad. Theodore surprised me then by offering his hand by way of greeting and when I took it I found his hand was even larger than mine and his grip was like iron.

"Richard Ashbury," he said, his voice thick with a strange accent. "I am Theodore. Welcome."

Beside me, the abbot spoke up. "Father Theodore, you will never believe who Richard has brought with him. It is none other than our old—"

"Leave us, Ioánnis," Theodore said, turning his cloudy eyes on the abbot, who immediately left without another word. "Come and sit by my window, Richard."

He strode back to his seat and eased himself down into his chair with a sigh, indicating that I take the chair opposite it, also by the window. The evening breeze ruffled the edges of the ancient monk's snow-white beard.

"Thank you for meeting with me, father," I began but he just spoke over me.

"What can you see, Richard?"

"Out of the window? Well, I see a small courtyard outside, well paved, with a low wall surrounding it. Beyond that is the graveyard, going down to the water's edge. A few trees there, looks like alder and a magnificent dark green pine, the top of which is lit by the sun. The trees are not enough to obscure the view of the long lake beyond, however. The water is clear and flat and hardly rippled by the wind. I see the sun setting off over the right bank where there is woodland and fields. I see sheep on the far bank and three shepherds, all boys, throwing stones into the water. Smoke from the village drifts across and catches some of the sunlight high above. It is peaceful. No danger. Everything is as it should be."

He smiled as I spoke and when I finished, he sighed. "Yes, that is what I see, also. You have good eyes, brother. A soldier's eyes. I would wager you watch always for danger on distant horizons, am I correct? Of course I am. And that is why you wish to know of *strigoi*, is that it? You fear these creatures?"

"Fear them? No. I would like to find them. If they cause others harm, I would kill them."

He seemed amused. "You would kill them, would you? You know that they have strength beyond that of mortal men, do you? So how would you do that?"

"I find cutting their heads off usually works."

Theodore scowled. "You have killed *strigoi*? Where? When?"

"I do not know if they were *strigoi*. What I do know is that I found them everywhere from England to Palestine."

The ancient monk's voice rose, incredulous. "And you *killed* them?"

"Most of them. So far."

He held himself still. "Well, Richard, if you are an expert killer of *strigoi* all over the earth, why would you seek stories from a simple old monk?"

Sighing, I sat back and looked at the lake. "All the ones I killed so far were created by one man. But I have heard there are more in these parts who, I assume, were not created by him. I would like to speak to those men and if you have word of them in your manuscripts then that might help me to do that."

Theodore eased himself back further into his chair. "You call them men. And yet you also say that you kill them. Is that not murder?"

"They are men, certainly. The ones I killed have all been murderers, also. Murderers who toiled at sedition and treachery and attempted to gain control of kingdoms so that they might rule as immortals for a thousand years. These I killed. If that is murder, then so be it. But you called them creatures. Perhaps we speak of different things."

Theodore sighed. "They have many names. All people have their own words for what these men are. The Wallachians call them *strigoi*. The Croats call them *mora* and the Czechs name them *pijavica*. In my homeland, they were called *vrykolakas*. And so on. But they all describe people who are turned from human into one who must drink blood to live. And they come only at night because the sunlight hurts their flesh and their eyes. Sometimes they are terrifying monsters, other times they are tragically cursed people. But they most certainly all describe the same thing."

"You seem to be an expert," I said. "I had assumed you would need to refer to some ancient codex. How is it that you know so much about them?"

He smiled. "I know so much about a great many things. All my life, I loved learning. Even when I was a soldier."

I had to suppress a laugh. "You were a soldier?"

Theodore frowned. "I was a fine soldier. I will wager I killed more men than you ever have, Richard the Englishman." He sighed. "But I was even better at fighting for lost souls. Alas, my time is almost up. I spent so many years in scriptoria and libraries like this one that I have wasted away into this frail creature before you. Yes, my time is almost up. If you learn nothing else from me, learn this. Never become a scholar."

I smiled. "Hardly much danger of that. But tell me, what do you know of the *strigoi* of Wallachia? How many are there here now, today? How might I track them and find them?"

"You do not fear them?"

"If anything, they should fear me."

"Because you wish to kill them all."

"No, not at all. If they live peacefully, I would have no quarrel with them. I merely wish to know how they came to be."

"What do you mean, son?"

"All *strigoi* were made into what they were by another. Do you know about this?"

Theodore sighed. "The *strigoi* drink the blood of the *vampir*."

"The what?"

"The *vampir* is the immortal lord who creates the *strigoi*."

"He is one man? Where is he?"

"No, no. He is not one man. There have been more than one *vampir*. No one knows where they come from but only they can make a man into a *strigoi*."

"Well then, yes, that is precisely who I seek. How can I find them?"

He hesitated for so long, staring out at the dusk, that I thought his attention had wandered. "I doubt even the *strigoi* out there know where the *vampir* are."

"You know something," I said, leaning forward. "There is something you are not telling me. Do you know where I can find one of these *strigoi*?"

Theodore turned his blind eyes to me and smiled. "It has been a joy to speak with you, Richard. Please do return another day."

"Thank you for seeing me," I said, annoyed that he was hiding the full truth. "I will come again if I can but it may not be for a long time."

"If God wills it, I will still be alive. And if not, I wish you peace."

"I am a soldier," I said, standing. "Peace is the last thing I want."

When I returned to the hospital, my men were eating. I sat at the table and gulped down two cups of wine.

"How did it go?" Eva asked.

"I am a *vampir*," I said.

"You did what?" Walt called out.

"The monk in the library knows all there is to know about nothing useful at all. I am sorry, my friends, this was a waste of time. In the morning, we will ride for Târgovişte and then into exile."

***

It was not long before Radu III Dracula was recognised as Voivode of Wallachia by most of the *boyars*. He was cunning in a way that Vlad never was. Word was spread by his agents in advance of his arrival that under the rule of Radu III, Wallachia would remain completely free of occupation Turkish soldiers. What was more was his promise that the *devshirme* would never be paid. There would be no Blood Tax under Radu's rule, no sons of Wallachia would be taken by the Janissaries.

William's devious hand was behind it, there could be no doubt. Only a friend of the Turks could get such concessions from them in order to secure his throne but the peasantry of any nation are a simple sort and they did not question the whys of this boon. All they heard was the promise of freedom from occupation and the freedom to raise their sons in peace.

And what man or woman in all the world would fight against that?

The only other option for the country was to retain their hero Vlad Dracula who many still loved but who could promise nothing more than a reign of relentless repeated invasions and further destruction of the land.

Before we had even fled far we heard that the people were calling their new leader Radu the Handsome. We did not get close enough to see his beauty but we were not far off. He and his soldiers pursued us right through the mountains and it was a close-run thing. First we raced up the valley of the River Arges and sought shelter in Vlad's castle at Arges. Radu's men were so close behind that we barely made it before they were encamped below the castle. By the end of that day they were bringing up small cannon with which to blast through the walls.

But Vlad was never a man to get himself into a situation he could not get out from and there was another exit from his castle that took us across the slopes to the north, with our horses and all.

We headed of all places to Brasov who Vlad—and I—had once terrorised. But after the peace had been secured with them it was neutral ground, of sorts and there we awaited the arrival of the King of Hungary Mattias Corvinus.

Vlad and he met in the town hall at Brasov and came to an agreement.

Radu had already sent word that he would favour and even extend the all-important commercial agreements of the Saxon colony towns and so they were inclined to back him over their old enemy Vlad. And Mattias Corvinus, cautious to a fault, was not one to pick an unnecessary fight. In fact, the king had signed a truce with Mehmed and had officially ended the crusade against the Turks. It was in his interest to do so in order that he could further concentrate his efforts on Frederick III the Holy Roman Emperor who still had eyes on Corvinus' crown.

Vlad agreed to give himself over to Mattias Corvinus as a prisoner.

It seemed like madness for him to do so but it was likely the safest course of action that he could take. Hiding out in one of his small Transylvanian castles would mean being besieged and taken by an enemy, eventually. And there were already plenty of Saxon enemies in addition to the Wallachian ones.

In spite of everything, it was to be a rather pleasant imprisonment for Vlad. He resided in the king's summer palace at Visegard overlooking the Danube and the Hungarians treated him well. He was valuable as a rival claimant to the Wallachian crown and that alone would serve to keep Radu the Handsome in check. The implicit and ever-present threat was that the Hungarians could remove Radu if he proved too troublesome and they had a ready alternative always at hand.

What is more, Vlad III Dracula was a name that stirred fear in the hearts of all Turks. He was Kaziglu Bey, the Lord Impaler, and Mattias Corvinus made sure that Dracula was at his side whenever he undertook diplomatic business with the emissaries of the Turks. I am certain that there was not a one of them who did not look upon the Lord Impaler without feeling a terrible itch beneath his turban.

Dracula was also offered a place in the Hungarian royal family on condition that he embraced Roman Catholicism in place of his Orthodox faith. They gave him an important position in the Hungarian Army where he served as a respected and feared senior captain.

As far as captivity goes, it was as comfortable and honourable as it was possible to get.

The Turks continued their work of encircling Hungarian territory, however, and as much as Radu the Handsome called himself a vassal of Hungary, I knew the truth. He was allowed to reign only by the grace of William de Ferrers, Zaganos Pasha.

Of all the kingdoms that might seek to resist him, the small and isolated kingdom of Moldavia, between Wallachia and the Black Sea, was perhaps the least likely to be successful.

But it was all we had.

1 5

Moldavia

1 4 6 7 – 1 4 7 3

"MY COUSIN WRITES that you are his finest soldier," Stephen of Moldavia said as I stood before his throne in the great hall of his palace in the city of Suceava. "Do you agree with that statement?"

"I am not a prideful man, my lord," I replied. "But it is the truth."

King Stephen looked rather a lot like Vlad Dracula, with his long nose and wide moustache but he did not have Vlad's piercing gaze and bulging eyes. Still, it was immediately clear that his men both loved and respected their king and I was sure to show proper deference.

"You are a mercenary," the king said. "And your men, the *sluji*, have fought the Turks and beaten them. And so I will have you, gladly. But I will not have you running around my kingdom causing trouble, do you hear me? I can use you but I do not need you. I can expel you at any moment and you must understand this?"

I bowed. "As you say, my lord. All my men want is the chance to kill Turks."

"All you want is to avoid the retribution of my cousin Radu the Usurper, you mean? Well, whatever you mean, you will have your chance. And perhaps you will have the chance to do both, for what is Radu if he is not the slave of the Sultan and Zaganos Pasha?"

"Indeed, my lord."

King Stephen smiled down at me. "I know all about Zaganos Pasha. My cousin and I spent years together before he claimed his kingdom and he helped me to claim mine and many a night we sat drinking wine and speaking about the evils of Zaganos Pasha." He lowered his voice. "Or should I call him William?"

"Call him what you will, my lord, all I ask is that, in your service, my men and I be used to counter the Janissaries of the pasha. It is why the *sluji* were created."

The king nodded. "You were right to come to me, Richard. Only Moldavia stands against the enemy. Albania, Bosnia, Montenegro, and Serbia have fallen. Wallachia is Turkish in all but name. And both the Turks and the Wallachians are massing on my borders."

"The Wallachians too, my lord?"

"Will it prove to be a problem for your men if they help me to defeat Radu, should he invade my lands? Your men are all Wallachians, are they not?"

"Most of them, my lord. But they are loyal to me, now. And anyway, Wallachia is not one people but many. There are more clans than I can name and they harbour hatred for each other and they seem to enjoy fighting each other whenever there is no enemy without. You can trust my men."

"That is good. But it may be your men will not have to fight Wallachians at all, as the Turks have sent Radu thousands of soldiers for his army."

I could scarcely believe he would be so open about it, after all his promises. "Radu has claimed to his people that he is holding the Turks at bay through clever diplomacy. But if this is true then his people will know him for a puppet after all."

"He believes himself strong," King Stephen said, a smile on his face. "He thinks he will conquer Moldavia and be only strengthened." He laughed and turned to his lords in the hall. "What do you think, my friends? Shall we sit back and allow Wallachia to conquer Moldavia?"

Their roar of defiance shook the very stones of the walls.

The king smiled. "I shall not wait for Radu to launch his invasion of my kingdom. I will not have war on my land, on my people, when I might wage it on my enemy's soil and spill the blood of his people instead of mine."

I was surprised. "My lord, you mean to invade Wallachia?"

"His Turks are still arriving. Would you prefer to wait for him to gain his full strength? But I thought you were a great strategist, Richard the Englishman?" His men laughed.

"I would never claim that, my lord. But Radu will flee to the mountains and avoid battle."

The king threw up his hands. "Wonderful! Then we shall raid his kingdom and rob it blind. In the end, his own men will overthrow him."

I had fought to protect Wallachia for years and now I would be fighting to destroy that very land, those very same people. The thought twisted my stomach but it was not so unusual a turn of events for a mercenary. At least there could be some good to come of it.

"If Radu is removed," I said, "you will be able to reinstate Vlad Dracula."

King Stephen frowned. "Why would I want to do that?"

I hesitated, surprised. "He is your cousin, my lord. He is your friend."

The king pointed at me. "Your friend, you mean. With Radu gone and my armies in his lands, yes, I could perhaps restore dear Vlad. But is that best for Moldavia? Is that best for me?"

"Is it not?"

The king stroked the end of his moustache. "He can be depended on to fight the Turk, that is certain. And yet we cannot always have war, eventually we must have some form of peace with the Turk. And the Turk hates Vlad Dracula."

"They fear him."

"Yes and they will come again sooner and with greater strength if Vlad is on the throne."

I sensed that this was not the first time King Stephen had considered these points. "You have another lord in mind for the throne? Perhaps yourself?"

His men bristled and cursed my impudence but Stephen waved them down. "I would not step into that snake pit. There is another I would make Voivode of Wallachia. A man I have here at court."

I remembered that there was an exile in the city. "You have one of the Danesti clan."

"Yes. Basarab Laiot will be what Wallachia needs in order to pull together the warring factions within the kingdom."

"Can he be trusted?"

King Stephen scoffed. "He can be trusted to act in his own interest. As can all men. Do you not agree?"

"All men, indeed. To one extent or another."

"And so, knowing what I will do, who I must wage war on, and who I must put on what was my cousin's throne, can I trust you to join us? And to follow my orders?"

What else could I do? I had to work to bring about another battle against the Turks for the chance to kill William.

I bowed. "War is my business, my lord.

King Stephen dismissed me and I was escorted back to my companions in our quarters in the palace. The city of Suceava was in the north of Moldavia, just on the eastern side of the mountains that separated the country from Transylvania. Even though Suceava was on the edge of Europe, with nothing to the east but the Tartars and the Golden Horde, it was finely built, with buildings almost as magnificent as those of Buda, though on a far smaller scale. I had expected Moldavia to be halfway to barbarous but it was no more so than Wallachia, at least in the large towns. The country, too, was fertile and crossed by countless rivers that drained from the north down into the Black Sea. The small country's southern border was the Danube and where it met the Black Sea it was wide and the area around it was marshy indeed. It was no wonder the enemy intended to invade from Wallachia.

My men were enjoying the delights of a Moldavian tavern when I found them, sinking tankards of beer and gnawing on chunks of bread.

"I like it here," Rob said as I sat down. "Serban likes it too much."

The old soldier had his head on the table, snoring audibly even over the din of the ale room.

"What happened?" Stephen asked, pushing me a plate of half-eaten boiled pork in jelly. "Did he accept us?"

I related everything that the king had said in between mouthfuls of pork and beer.

"Basarab Laiot instead of Dracula?" Walt said when I was finished. "He will be worse than useless. Have you met him?"

"Have you?"

"I drank with him a few days ago. We played dice. I was not impressed by his wits nor his character."

"Why?" I asked. "How did you come to play dice with a pretender to the Wallachian throne?"

Walt grinned. "An attempt to woo me, wasn't it."

We stared at each other. "Woo you?"

Walt was enjoying himself. "Promised me great wealth. Swore he would grant me an estate near Buzau. Said I would be a great captain in his armies. All he wanted was for me to tell him what the secret was. What the power of the blood magic was that gave you your strength and the strength of the *sluji*."

Stephen gasped. "He wanted it for himself."

Eva leaned over and punched Walt on his shoulder. "You did not think to mention this, you witless oaf?"

Walt rubbed his shoulder, still grinning. "Hardly seemed worth it. Wasn't going to accept, was I?"

"Our agents brought word of him years ago," Eva said as Stephen nodded. "We dismissed him as neither a possible asset nor a risk. He is a nobody."

"Basarab is a duplicitous *boyar* who attempts to be cunning but is not competent at it," Stephen said. "And this is who we would be fighting for?"

"No. We would be fighting to kill Radu and so remove one of William's immortals."

"Assuming Radu is an immortal," Eva said. "We have no proof."

I scoffed. "Come on, he must be by now. William would never have given him this much authority were he not bound to him by the Gift."

"Very likely," Eva allowed.

"And even if he is not then we should destroy him anyway, for Radu is an important ally in William's plan of conquest."

Rob snorted a laugh. "More than an ally. More of a sweetheart, no?"

Walt grinned. "We're going to break his heart."

I fished a piece of gristle from the back of my teeth. "William feels nothing for any of his spawn, no matter what the fools believe."

"That is a point to consider," Stephen said, sitting up straighter. "Whether William feels any true closeness to Radu, will he not come to fight for him if his rule is at risk?"

"Zaganos Pasha is in the East with Mehmed," Eva said. "Waging war against the tribes threatening to overwhelm the Turks there. He will not come here until his business in the east is concluded. You see, William understands the value of patience. His plans for conquering this entire land are almost complete. All he needs is Moldavia and he will have subjugated the lands from the Black Sea to the Adriatic. He will not be rushing back here in a panic, even if we threaten his beloved."

I gestured with my tankard as I spoke. "If he does not return, we shall kill Radu with all the more ease. And if William does return to save his spawn, we shall kill him also. It seems to me that it is in our interest to join this war against Wallachia and to win it."

"What about our lads?" Rob said. "The *sluji* are Wallachian. They will not want to fight their former lord's brother and they especially will not wish to do it for the Danesti clan to benefit."

Rob's concerns worried me because if he felt them they were likely worth considering.

"The *sluji* have sworn oaths of obedience," I said. "They will obey or they will suffer the consequences."

"You might first attempt to explain to them that they will be fighting the Turks, as they have sworn to do, when they are fighting Radu."

"If you insist, Rob," I said. "Now, enough of this disgusting beer. Have them bring me wine."

***

Stephen sent requests for aid to Mattias Corvinus, who was instead concerned with central Europe. Likewise, Moldavia's traditional overlords the Poles also declined to be drawn into the fight. Their concern was for the east and the north of Europe, not the Balkans to their south. They did not believe that the Turks could threaten them.

My men joined with companies of Moldavian cavalry and we raided the lowlands with hardly any opposition. Radu was careful to stay in his castles in the high places of Wallachia and no matter how many villages we burned and no matter how many crops we destroyed, Radu would not be drawn from his places of safety.

He sent companies of Turks against us, some of them Anatolian but mostly Rumelians from Bulgaria. When they were too many, we ran. When we had the advantage, we attacked them with everything we had and we destroyed them. And even then, Radu would not come to face us.

Eva and Stephen used their agents to spread word of Radu's treacheries and to seek *boyars* who would come over to Moldavia's side and many of the Danesti clan replied that they would be willing to turn on their prince, for the right incentives.

Still, Radu the Handsome stayed in the mountains.

Along with Moldavian captains that I rode with, I eventually persuaded King Stephen that only an all-out invasion would be enough to force Radu to lead his armies in person. In autumn 1473 we brought Radu to battle near Bucharest at a field near the River Vodnu. It was a rather sad and brief affair, with little glory to be had for anyone.

For all his charisma and personal command, Radu was not a bold general by nature. Far from it. But the presence of so many Turkish soldiers had emboldened him and we baited him into an attack in which we enveloped and crushed his army.

As his army crumbled, Radu abandoned his men and fled his camp. He fled in so much haste in fact that he abandoned his treasury and all of his wardrobe. The man had more clothes than a king of France. He left his battle standards and his new wife. He had lost all legitimacy in the eyes of his people and soon they would be willing to declare Basarab as the new Voivode of Wallachia.

But I would find out all of that later. First, I had to catch him and kill him. A company of Rumelian sipahis fled with Radu and I led the *sluji* after them. It seemed that they were making for the fortress of Giurgiu which Radu loyalists yet held and so we had to stop them before he reached it. No doubt King Stephen could besiege it and no doubt Basarb could command them to surrender but by then Radu would have been long gone across the Danube. And I wanted him.

"The woodland!" I said to my captains. "If we can reach the woodland before them, we shall have him."

I made half of my men dismount and told them to meet me at Giurgiu. We took their horses as remounts, stripped off as much armour and equipment as we dared and then set off across country. We stopped only in the darkest of night and I had them up again well before dawn, trusting their immortal eyesight to keep us on track. We cut across the marshland and finally reached the wood, exhausted and tired but ready.

We were hardly in position when Radu and his sipahis came cantering from the north toward the fortress. Radu, still the proud peacock that he was, rode at the head of them in shining armour and a great headdress upon his helm, with a glittering golden band around it studded with rubies.

"Do you reckon that's him?" Walt muttered before we sprung our ambush.

My *sluji* swarmed on the sipahis from both sides, pulling them from their horses and drinking their blood while they screamed.

I made straight for Radu and caught him in indecision. He began riding back to save his men before seeing the speed and strength of the *sluji* and he wheeled his horse about to make for the fortress. Instead, my lance point caught him in the flank and threw him from the saddle. He landed on his helm, his neck bending under him. I jumped down and was on him, pulling his helm from his head.

He looked so much like Vlad that for a moment I thought it was him but then I saw how the man's features were far more refined. His jaw was squarer and his brow higher and his nose less of a spear point. He roared at me and drew his sword half out of his scabbard before I wrestled it from him and threw it aside.

Still, he got to his knees and pulled a long dagger from his belt. I grappled with him as he rushed me and I knew at once that he was an immortal. Radu was strong and a well-trained fighter. He tried to trip me and twisted to get inside my guard. But I butted his face with my helm, crushing his nose and he released his grip. Tripping him, I forced him down and slipped his own knife under his throat.

Blood streamed down his face.

"Not so handsome now, are you, boy?" I said. "I am going to send William your head."

I was about to slit his throat when Eva stayed my hand.

"Richard!" She held my arm. "Let us not be so hasty."

"He is an immortal, Eva. He must die."

"And so he will," she said, trying to get me to look at her. "But why not speak to him first? He may know William's plans."

Radu's eyes glanced back and forth between us. "I will tell you nothing!" he said, in French.

"Quiet!" I said and cracked his broken nose with the butt of my dagger, causing him to flinch and wail, though I held him fast. "The world knows William's plans. Conquer Christendom."

"He may have some secret. Something. We should question him."

"Perhaps. But the Moldavians will not wish him taken prisoner. The Wallachians opposed to him would see him dead also, lest his continued existence give heart to his faction and to the Turks and so prolong the war. And what is my status that would allow me to take a royal prisoner? I cannot take him and expect to keep him unchallenged. He must die."

Eva looked around at the *sluji*, who were feasting on the sipahis or rummaging through their equipment. "What if we take him in secret? Tell the world he is dead and only we shall know he lives."

I hesitated, looking down at Radu. "They will expect to see his body. Let us provide one. We could use one of his men, although I doubt any of those filthy Bulgars could pass for Radu the Handsome."

Eva nodded to herself as she thought it through. "We must mutilate the corpse's face. We shall dress him in Radu's shining armour and fine underclothes and carry away the real one."

"But carry him to where? Where can I keep him for questioning that he will not be seen?"

Stephen stepped forward. "Richard? We are not so far from the monastery at Lake Snagov."

"Yes?"

"Perhaps that abbot would hide him there."

"Why would he do that?"

"All the money that Dracula showered on that place must count for something. The abbot loved Dracula, you could tell by the way he spoke about him. He's loyal to Vlad Dracula and I bet he would hold Radu as his prisoner without giving him up. The monks are, of course, utterly loyal to the abbot and none would speak of it."

Eva looked down her nose at him. "Radu is an immortal."

I sighed. "Oh yes."

"What's the problem?" Rob asked. "Ah, he needs blood. Well, you said the old boy in the library knew all about us. About *strigoi*."

I shook my head. "I imagine if we tell the monks we brought a cursed blood drinker into his house, he would throw us into Lake Snagov. He would have to bleed his brothers to keep Radu alive."

Eva sighed. "I suppose it is worth the attempt."

Rob nodded down at Radu. "Exactly. And if it all goes pear shaped, we'll just kill the bastard."

I ordered Radu's clothing swapped with a soldier of similar height and frame and stood admiring the finery he was now dressed in, Walt smashed his face in with his mace. As the false Radu's body was delivered by my men to Stephen, I took the real Radu north to Lake Snagov.

***

The abbot came down to the dockside and watched us row across the lake to his island. Behind him came first half a dozen and then a score of black robed monks, spread out across the bank.

"Richard Ashbury," he said, his face grim. "It has been some time since we saw you last. Do you mean us harm?"

"Harm?" I asked, confused, and then looked at my men as the abbot would. We were all, to one extent or another, wearing armour. Our men waiting with the horses behind us at the village were likewise arrayed for war. "My apologies for coming to you in this manner. Of course I mean you no harm, father. Why would we?"

He looked us over again, still not trusting my word.

"We come straight from the battlefield," I explained. "Hence our appearance."

"There has been a battle?"

"Not much of one. We have defeated Radu Dracula and have taken him prisoner."

"I see. I am sure that his brother is pleased. But what does this have to do with us?"

I hesitated for a moment and then gestured for the prisoner to be brought forward. Walt and Rob picked him up from the bottom of the boat and carried him up to me. Dressed in a commoner's undershirt and hose, he was bound with rope around the wrists and had a leather bag over his head. I nodded and Walt pulled the bag off to reveal Radu Dracula's face, swollen and covered with dried blood from his broken nose.

"Abbot Ioánnis, I am pleased to introduce Radu Dracula."

The abbot recoiled and the monks behind cursed and muttered until the abbot silenced them with a glare.

"Why bring him here?"

"The new Voivode of Wallachia will be a man named Basarab. He is a Danesti and he will have Radu killed. Basarab was placed on the throne by King Stephen of Moldavia, who will also have Radu killed. We preferred that he live. And so we left a defaced body in Radu's armour on the battlefield and brought him here in the hopes that you would keep him safe."

The abbot stared at me. "Why in the name of God would we do that? We survive here in peace precisely because we stay out of the dynastic wars of the Wallachians. If we are discovered harbouring a former prince, we shall not survive here much longer."

"No one will know. It is a secret known only to my men and yours."

The abbot was amused. "Secrets always come out, Richard."

A disturbance behind him made us turn and I saw the old librarian, Theodore, coming down to the dockside with a hand outstretched on the shoulder of a young monk walking before him. He walked with the aid of a long stick, his unseeing eyes staring into nothingness.

"Did I hear Richard Ashbury?" the old man said, his voice raspy from his aged throat but still deep from his barrel chest.

"You did, Father Theodore," I called. "How delighted I am to see that you are still alive."

The abbot bristled but Theodore chuckled as he came to a stop beside him and his guide sidled away. "And did I hear you say you have Radu Dracula as your prisoner, here?"

"You have good ears, father," I said. "He is here beside me. Angry beyond words."

"Free me," Radu said, his voice thick from his wounded face. "Free me, brothers, and it will rain gold on your house, I swear by—"

I punched him in the stomach, knocking the words from his mouth. Walt and Rob held him aloft, else he would have collapsed.

"He can offer you nothing because he has nothing to offer. He has lost his kingdom. But I would very much like to speak with him and I hoped you could find space in your house and in your hearts for a poor wounded soldier."

The abbot scowled. "It would not be an act of charity to put my brothers here in mortal danger."

I sensed it was not going well so I decided on a final throw of the dice. "Would it change your mind overly much if I told you that Radu here was a *strigoi*?"

The abbot and all the monks stirred and looked to each other, disturbed indeed.

"Even if that is true," the abbot said, his voice almost a growl. "Why should that concern us?"

Theodore placed a massive hand on the abbot's shoulder. "We would be glad to welcome Prince Radu into our house. I think we have a spare cell, do we not, Ioánnis?"

The abbot dismissed his brothers and led us through the monastery down into a

713

corridor with a row of four cells, one of which he led us into. There was a bed, a low table with a lamp on it, and a high, narrow window at the top of the far wall. I pushed Radu into it, forcing him down to his knees, and was followed in by the abbot and Theodore. My men and a handful of monks crowded outside.

"Periods of solitary contemplation are required for all of us," the abbot said. "Especially for novices. You will be comfortable here, Radu."

"There is something I must make clear," I said. "Being that Radu is a *strigoi*, he will require regular cups of human blood for consumption."

Radu snarled at me from his knees. "Your men are all *strigoi* also, Englishman. And you are worse. You are the father to them all! But you will be defeated. My master will come for you, traitor, he will come and he will—"

I kicked him in the guts and he fell forward and curled into a ball.

"We will have no violence here," the abbot said and moved to help Radu onto the bed.

Theodore had a smile on his face.

Neither of them asked me about Radu's accusations nor questioned the need for him to drink blood.

"I must return to my men. King Stephen will be looking for me. Before I go, I must question my prisoner."

"If he is in my care," the abbot said, "he is not your prisoner but my ward. And I refuse to allow you to harm this man, whatever he may or may not be."

"I must question him," I said, staring at the abbot. "And I will question him."

"You will leave, sir," he replied.

Theodore cleared his throat. "I must say that I am most curious to hear what the *strigoi* has to say. You can question our new brother here but only if I am present to hear what is said."

I shrugged. "Fine with me, father. I will try to avoid spilling too much of his blood."

The ancient monk smiled. "That will not bother me."

Abbot Ioánnis straightened up. "Yes, do what you will and then go. But I will have no part in it."

"Do not mind him," Theodore said. "He is young and is burdened by responsibility for the safety of his brothers."

"He is a good man," I said.

"Indeed he is. I wonder, Richard, are you?"

"I try to be. Although, I cannot deny that I have also done much evil."

"Haven't we all," Theodore said as he closed the door and latched it. He stood before it like a sentinel. "You may begin."

I nodded and turned to Radu who was now sitting on the bed, his bound hands before him. "Hold out your hands," I commanded him and proceeded to saw through and unpick his bindings until his hands were free.

"William always said you were foolhardy. And I see it is true," Radu said, rubbing his wrists. "For I am now free to kill you."

I smiled. "You are free to try."

"Perhaps I will bash the old man's head in before you can stop me. Do you think the monks would let me stay after that?"

I looked at Theodore. "I expect that old man knows a trick or two. Besides, you are not a killer, Radu."

He scoffed, outraged. "I have killed a hundred men."

"Perhaps you have but the fact remains, you are not a killer. I know a vicious, murdering bastard when I see one and you are not it. Your brother, now. Vlad Dracula is a killer through and through, down to his marrow. He can kill women and children without flinching. Even I could never compare with such a monster."

"Even you," he said, sneering. "Even you, with your three centuries and thousands of deaths at your hands? I doubt there is any who can compare to your evil."

I shrugged. "Perhaps there is only one who has surpassed me. Your master."

Radu spat on the floor at me feet. "Your brother."

"Where is he?" I asked. "Why did he not come to help you keep your throne?"

Radu said nothing but looked up at the narrow window high on the wall.

"I shall tell you," I continued. "William is in the east with his brother in arms, Sultan Mehmed. His truest friend in all the world. I hear that they lie together like man and wife. Tenderly, so it is said, and with great passion."

"They hate each other!" Radu snapped. "They are at war with each other. It is not love. It was never love."

I shrugged. "Not what my agents tell me."

"Your agents are wrong. William holds Mehmed in contempt and Mehmed has grown tired of William."

"But William has won him all Thrace up to Hungary, or near enough."

Radu scoffed. "Mehmed is sick of Europe. His armies are ground into dust here."

I smiled. "Because of me. I am the one who has ground his armies into dust. I smashed his armies at Varna, at Kosovo. I killed thousands even at Constantinople. I defeated him at Belgrade, smashing his army into nothing. I killed fifty thousand of his soldiers when he invaded Wallachia. All because of me. And now he despairs." I laughed.

"William could have defeated you a dozen times!" Radu said. "But Mehmed would never let him lead. He was ever jealous and held William back. But no longer." Radu smiled. "Soon, you will feel his wrath unleashed."

"Mehmed will unleash William?" I said. "How?"

Radu shrugged and looked away, a smug smile on his bloody lips.

"Listen, Radu," I said, crouching down across the room from him so that I was level with him. "Look at me, Radu." He turned his eyes to mine, smirking. "You mean to say that Mehmed is going to give William an army of his own? But I thought they now mistrusted one another, so why would he give William an army? You are lying."

Radu shook his head. "It is a chance to prove himself. To finish the conquest once and for all."

"And if he should fail, what then?"

He laughed. "He will not fail."

"Where will he lead it?" I watched Radu closely. "To Moldavia?"

Radu's mouth twitched. "He knows where you have been hiding. You and your pathetic little immortal company. He knows and he is coming for you and for Moldavia. You will not stop him. If you had any sense, you would run. But William knows you too well. He knows that you will stand and fight and that will be your downfall."

"Yes, William is the one who runs. I have defeated him before and each time he has fled like the coward he is."

"He could have killed you," he said. "A dozen times, William could have killed you but he did not because you are his brother and he loves you and he wants you to live."

I smiled, genuinely amused. "He has lied to you about that just as he has lied about everything else. He lies. It is what he does. He lies to all the poor fools who he subjugates and forces to do his bidding."

"Not me," Radu said. "He will come for me. He will find me and he will come for me here and he will kill all these monks and then he will kill you."

I glanced at Theodore who stared into nothingness.

"He will never know you are here. No one does. William will hear that you died in a grubby little ambush in the woods and he will believe it because he will know that you make for a pitiful soldier. And he will not mourn you. He will not give you a moment's thought."

His face was twisted in anguish. "Kill me, then! Why keep me?"

"I am sorry, Radu. You may prove useful one day. And I think that your brother would rather you live."

Radu sneered. "That bastard will have me killed the moment you tell him where I am. He cares nothing for me, nothing at all."

"You would be surprised. He feels guilty for abandoning you when you went over to William. Perhaps he would like to make amends."

"Nonsense," Radu said but quietly.

"I may be gone for a good while," I said, standing and looking down at him. "I suggest you make the most of your time in solitary contemplation."

His head snapped up. "I will kill you one day, Richard Ashbury."

"I told you, Radu. You are not a killer."

He sat slumped on the bed and I called my men in. We trussed him up again, this time tying him to the bed post by a length of rope. He gave us no resistance and did not look up when I said farewell.

Outside, Theodore turned to me with a smile on his face. "A most illuminating conversation."

"I must hurry to King Stephen and from there prepare Moldavia for an invasion." I pointed at Radu's cell door. "He will require a cup of blood every two or three days to stop him falling into illness and madness."

"I think we can manage that."

I peered at him. "You do not appear surprised or disturbed by any of this. You or the abbot. Are you not afraid of him? I said he was not a killer but I fear he may harm you, all of you, in an attempt to flee this place."

"We may be monks but we all answered this calling from a question we heard out there in the world. I am not the only former soldier amongst us and between you and me, Richard, we have a couple of ruffians here who would make even this William knock his knees in terror."

I smiled. "I doubt that. Remember, he has the strength of ten men."

Theodore leaned in. "But we, Richard, we have the power of God."

16

The Battle of Vaslui

1475

THE SULTAN HAD LONG been on campaign in the east and north of Anatolia against the forces of the powerful warlord Uzan Hasan. By all accounts the eastern nomadic horsemen were numerous and ferocious but they were not enough to overcome the discipline and sheer firepower of Mehmed's army.

There was now nothing to stop the Turks in the east and they ranged around the Black Sea to threaten the flanks of the lands of the Golden Horde and the Genoese outposts around the coast.

But the core of Mehmed's forces came back to Europe and William began his move to crush Moldavia. The Sultan even ended his siege against the Albanian city of Shkoder in the north in order to free up more soldiers for William's great horde. Those soldiers were not in a fit state, so our agents said, and we knew that it would take at least a month to march them to Moldavia. But Mehmed expected his soldiers to do extraordinary things and they usually managed what he demanded.

"I did not wish to tell you until I was certain," Eva said. "But now one of Stephen's men, that Genoese merchant with the nose, has confirmed it."

"Confirmed what?" I asked them.

We had a very large, very old house in the Moldavian city of Suceava that served as our residence and headquarters for the *sluji*. Our hall was almost large enough for every soldier to squeeze inside for meetings and ceremonies but that morning it echoed to the voices of the Order of the White Dagger only.

"Confirmed that the Turkish army assembled at Sofia and now marching here is being led by Zaganos Pasha."

I nodded. "So Radu was not wrong. William commands the army personally? And where is Sultan Mehmed?"

Stephen shrugged. "Possibly Constantinople. Possibly Edirne. But not at the head of this army, certainly. And it means that William walks into our arms once more. If he joins his men in battle, which he no doubt will, he is in danger. This benefits us."

"It means more than that," Eva said. "This perhaps confirms Radu's claims that William and Mehmed are indeed now in conflict about the direction of the empire. If Mehmed has given William one final chance to complete the conquest and if we defeat it, then William may have to find a new master."

Walt grunted. "Or kill his current one and take over."

"The Turks would not follow him," Stephen said. "They hate him enough as an advisor. If he attempted to rule directly, the empire would collapse."

Walt opened his arms. "Even better."

"Let us not get ahead of ourselves," I said. "We have to defeat this army first. Do we know how big it is?"

Stephen glanced at Eva. "The precise number is not yet known," he said, "as more are coming in to support the campaign but from the amount of grain they have requested, it cannot be less than a hundred thousand fighting men."

"Likely more," Eva said. "A hundred and twenty thousand, probably."

I whistled. "He has winkled out the biggest army the Turks have ever fielded, has he not? What soldiers does he have?"

Stephen unrolled a long piece of parchment and peered at it. "By meticulously calculating the cartloads of straw my Bulgarian merchant has been commanded to transport through Rumelia, it is like that—"

Eva spoke over him. "Thirty thousand *sipahis* for the core cavalry. But also Bulgarian, Serbian, and Tatar cavalry in support."

"Infantry?" I asked. "The Janissaries are the Sultan's personal troops so presumably we do not have to contend with them."

Eva and Stephen shook their heads in unison. "Janissaries for the core," Stephen said. "Thousands but we do not know how many. They are supported by an enormous number of *azabs*."

"Guns?"

"Many in number," Eva said. "Every size of field gun that can be transported has been assembled. More than Moldavia has in the entire kingdom, certainly."

"This is a conquering army," I said. "With William in command, it is one to be feared. How long before they reach our southern border?"

719

"They have dragged in thousands of Bulgarian peasants who are at work clearing forests and shovelling snow. They are building bridges across the marshlands in the south."

"Bridges across the marshes? Remember when they attacked Wallachia, their cannons were bogged down and they could not move. So, William has learned his lesson. They will move swiftly, for all the great number of the host. Do we really believe he will attack in winter and not spring?"

"He's coming now," Stephen said. "Perhaps he means to catch us unprepared. Perhaps crossing the marshes is easier when they are frozen. Perhaps the Sultan has given William a deadline that he must meet. But they are coming now. No chance he maintains a force that size for months of winter while they sit and do nothing."

"We will have to share all of this with King Stephen," I told them. "He will not like it."

They looked at each other, throwing meaningful looks. I knew they were each urging the other to speak.

"For the love of God," I snapped. "Spit it out."

"King Stephen will like this even less," Eva said. "It seems also that Basarab III Laiot has welcomed a large detachment of Turks across the Danube and has himself committed seventeen thousand Wallachian soldiers to the army."

I laughed and covered my eyes. "So, Basarab is another traitor to his people and to Christendom. I will never understand Wallachia. What is wrong with those people? Why do they continue to do this?"

"At least he has shown his true intentions," Stephen said, shrugging. "He is an enemy of all those who oppose the Turks and so in time he can be removed."

Walt scoffed. "Easier said than done. We just have to defeat this great army first. How many does old King Stephen have, anyway?"

I sighed. "He had word this morning from Hungary that the Pope's call to crusade has been answered by Corvinus who sends a paltry two thousand men from Hungary."

Walt shrugged. "Better than a kick in the bollocks. Is that it?"

"Poland has likewise sent two thousand. King Stephen has recruited five thousand mercenaries, though many of them look to me like nothing more than desperate fortune hunters and outlaws."

"Takes one to know one," Rob quipped, to much amusement about the room.

I ignored him and continued. "The Moldavians can field fifteen thousand of their own soldiers and Stephen's heavy cavalry can beat anything the Turks might field. There are just not enough of them. And the peasant recruitment of all able men aged fourteen years or older has resulted in thirty thousand sullen and incompetent sons of Moldavia assembling."

"Vlad defeated the Turks with less."

"King Stephen has heart and he is a bright fellow but let us not be fooled into thinking he is the equal of Vlad Dracula on the battlefield."

"Well," Walt said. "We'll just have to see, won't we."

"Are the *sluji* prepared?" I asked them. "In that case, we must assemble them. The weather grows ever colder and William will not hesitate to strike hard and soon."

***

The battle would be fought near Vaslui, deep inside Moldavia. But first, we had to draw the Turks to it.

We were by now experts at this type of warfare. When William's great army of Turks crossed into Moldavia, they found nought but burning fields and poisoned wells. Every resident had been removed north and there was not even a single animal larger than a cat in the entire country. Those people who could not fight were sent into the mountains in the northwest where it was hoped that they would be safe.

Every step that William's army took, we made them pay for by endless sudden raids. Every point that we held in force, they gathered a detachment with which to attack and when they did we fought briefly for a time before retreating. Every company that did so retreated toward Vaslui over prepared ground, stopping only to delay the massive army pursuing them. We used the *sluji* in some light skirmishing that helped to prepare them and also supplied us with enemy blood to drink. But I wanted them fresh and ready for the main battle to come.

The town of Vaslui had been well fortified by King Stephen. In addition, he had ensured that of all the lands for miles around across the march of the enemy, the fields and villages around Vaslui alone would remain whole. Livestock remained on the outskirts and stocks of grain filled storehouses, like a trail of breadcrumbs.

It was all a trap and the Turks, starving and cold and desperate, surged toward the city in their thousands, drawn by the promise of grain, meat, and fodder. Whether William knew it was a trap or not, he must have known he needed to capture the supplies we were sitting atop in order to complete his conquest and so save his plans for total domination.

What was more, our army blocked the route to Suceava, the capital, which William no doubt expected to use to quarter his army over the bitter winter.

They had to cross the River Barlad to reach Vaslui and our constant harassment of the massive army had served to funnel them into a narrow crossing over the river. The High Bridge was the only way across into the valley beyond and the fact that we had allowed it to stand was certainly a giveaway of our nefarious intentions. No doubt, William and the other commanders expected that whatever we planned by way of mischief could be overcome by their numbers and their hundreds of artillery pieces.

In comparison, we had twenty-one cannons.

The Turks needed to strengthen the bridge before they risked bringing their massive army and heavy pieces across it. And while they did that, our army waited anxiously unseen over the hills beyond. It was cold and damp and deeply unpleasant weather to be waiting around in but we could do nothing else until William took the bite and crossed into our trap.

"He will not take the bait," I said for the hundredth time.

"Stop saying that," Rob muttered, shivering.

"He ain't got no choice but to take it," Walt replied.

We peered at the vast army on the other side of the river from our vantage point on a ridge, hidden by the trunks of an unruly stand of scruffy pines. On our side of the river was a boggy valley almost entirely empty of soldiers. Across from us, though, William's army filled the plain as far as the eye could see. Low cloud and drizzling rain hid the full extent of the forces but even so it was enough to make my heart race.

"By God there's a lot of the bastards," Rob muttered, echoing my thoughts. "Have you ever seen so many men in one place in your life? Got to be a hundred and fifty thousand, all told. More than Stephen reckoned with his bloody idiot calculations."

"If only we could knock down the bridge while all their biggest cannons were on it," Walt said.

"Or when the Blood Janissaries cross," Rob said.

I snorted. "And William, also, but no doubt they would survive the fall and the dunking and come up merely smelling sweeter than when they went in. Come on, their woodworkers are almost done with the bridge and they will be across today or tomorrow. We must prepare for battle."

"Thank the Lord," Walt said. "It's bloody freezing."

We had discussed the battlefield for weeks and months. It was one the Moldavians had used in years past to defeat the Poles and it was as good a place for the purpose as I have ever seen in my life. The valley was surrounded on three sides by steep, densely wooded hills and the ground throughout the valley floor was soft and in many places marshy indeed. Horsemen would find their pace slowed to a difficult walk and even infantry would have difficulty fighting or even coming to order. I had walked it myself, lifting my knees high to make headway and found myself quickly exhausted. Yes, it was a fine trap but even so the odds were severely against us.

We waited overnight in our camps for them to come on but as the night ended and sunrise approached we were greeted by a thick blanket of freezing fog.

It was hard to see from one tent to the next, let alone across the battlefield.

"We must continue as if they will," King Stephen said as we stood sipping warm wine in his tent and stamping our feet. Outside, the Moldavian and allied forces prepared themselves and within the king's tent their lords and masters were subdued and apprehensive. "You will at all times listen for the trumpets and send riders with messengers. We must stay in contact. You each must send a rider to me at intervals to tell me where you are and what is happening. Do you all understand? You must select sensible men and give them good horses. Each must know where my position is before the day begins."

It was good advice and I was impressed by his command of the situation and of his commanders.

"Are the cannons in place?" the king asked.

"They are, Your Grace," said the Hungarian artillery commander. "Every one of them aimed at the bridge. We will knock a few of their heads off as they come over, will we not, my lords?"

They muttered their assent and some smiled. Still, they were subdued. No man feels victory is near when they are so outnumbered. I resisted attempting to give them good cheer. They did not like me and it was not my place.

"Cuza, you will keep the cavalry back here until it is needed," the king said. "We will send all the mercenaries out, infantry and cavalry, to screen the cannon. Send the mercenary captains in and we shall explain it to them."

Everything was in place and yet so was the fog. The reports coming back all morning confirmed that the Turks were probably waiting for the air to clear, afraid to march into what they could not see.

King Stephen called me to him. "If Zaganos Pasha is truly your brother, perhaps you know a way to encourage him to cross the bridge today."

I sighed. "He knows we are waiting in the hills to descend on him and yet he means to cross anyway, convinced that his strength will overcome ours. But he would be mad to march into it while he cannot see us coming. It costs him nothing to wait for the fog to clear. Once he can see, it might give him confidence to march across but he is by nature a cautious soul and he would rather delay than risk disaster."

The king scowled and sipped his steaming cup of wine. "I know all that. I asked you if there was a way to encourage him across today."

"Have you tried praying for the fog to lift, my lord?"

His men bristled but the king ignored my tone. "I have," he said. "And my priests are praying for that very thing as we speak. Very well, that will be all."

I did not obey him as I was beginning to warm to the idea of tricking William further. "If we could make him believe we have left the field, he might advance." One of the king's men scoffed openly but he ignored them, staring at me as if urging me to continue. I did so, thinking out loud. "How could we make him believe that? Why would we ever abandon such a perfect spot? Any army placing itself down there will be enormously disadvantaged. After all, that is why you did not—" I broke off.

The king stared, waiting. "Yes?"

"If we brought our army down into the valley, he would attack."

The king's men groaned and told me to get out.

"Of course he would attack," King Stephen said. "We would be suffering that very disadvantage which you have mentioned."

"But we have the fog," I said, still thinking as it came to me. "And the Turks could not see us assembling even if we did so." I clicked my fingers and grinned. "Your Grace, can you please summon all of your musicians. And all of those of the peasantry with loud voices for singing. And serjeants and captains who might be spared."

King Stephen peered at me. "I do not know how it is done in England but in Moldavia it is our tradition to hold the festival celebrating victory after the battle has been won and not before."

I could not help but laugh, briefly. "Please, my lord. Other than praying for the fog to lift, this may cause the Turks to act."

Taking the mounted *sluji* with me, simply as I did not wish to be separated from my men, I marched the hastily assembled drummers and trumpeters down into the boggy valley and advanced toward the bridge. There were hundreds of us and more came running after us down from the wooded hills.

"Spread out and play," I shouted at them. "Play for all your worth. Make enough noise to startle God in Heaven!"

I had the peasants sing together whatever working songs they knew and to raise their voices louder and louder. Other men amongst us were various captains and serjeants with mighty battlefield voices who I commanded to roar out imaginary orders to their imaginary companies.

In very little time, we had made a sustained and mighty cacophony that echoed through the valley and across the river.

"God help us but that's a nasty noise," Walt cried, his hands over his ears.

"Tell them to sing louder," I shouted to my Moldavian detachments. "Command the trumpeters to sound an advance and the signal to form a line. Send the serjeants forward to sing their orders. Hurry!"

Whether it was truly my scheme that motivated them, I cannot say, but all of a sudden from out of the fog came our riders who shouted that the Turks were now crossing the bridge.

Rob burst out laughing. "You mad bastard, Richard. You mad old bastard, you've only gone and done it."

"Back!" I shouted to the drummers and trumpeters and peasants, sending my men along our makeshift line to repeat the orders and get them out of the way. "Get back, now! Flee for the hills. Back to your companies!"

I grabbed a handful of messengers. "Ride to the cannon masters and tell them the enemy crosses. They must fire now, do you understand? Go!"

By the time we had pulled back, the twenty-one Moldavian cannons opened up from the flank, firing through the fog at the bridge itself and the bank on our side where the enemy would enter the valley and assemble. Our forward positions of archers marched into range and began to shoot, raining down volleys into the massed ranks of Turks who crossed and sought to assemble on our side. It was difficult to get a sense of what was happening down there but I was certain the enemy would be falling in their hundreds under such a barrage.

"I bet you he'll pull back from this," Walt said to Rob, shaking his head. "How much money have you got on you?"

But a handful of cannons and archers could not slow thousands of soldiers for long and so they advanced slowly, company by company, from the bridge and into our valley. Into our trap. Whether we would be enough to stop them, I still had no idea.

Through the swirling fog, I caught glimpses of the azabs advancing. The king brought up our hand-gunners and these men fired their guns from the front and from the flanks at the advancing companies, their filthy, stinking weapons massed together and scything down the *azabs* that marched like lambs to the slaughter into them.

Wherever the *azabs* managed to close with our infantry, our men turned and fled, retreating as far as necessary before turning to shoot or to hold position once more. It appeared through gaps in the fog that the *azab* infantry were running hither and thither like a leaderless mob and everywhere they went, they were killed by crossbows or by guns.

Behind them though came hundreds of *akinji* light cavalry. They too attempted to break through the infantry and cannon arrayed before them but again they found themselves surrounded on three sides and were no doubt confused about where our fire was coming from.

Our cannons kept firing at the bridge itself, blasting away continuously so that any who crossed were in danger of being blown to pieces before reaching the field beyond. Even when they crossed the bridge they would find more cannonballs crashing amongst them if they tarried there in order to assemble their companies.

"Fog's lifting," Walt said, his mouth full of slices of dried sausage.

"Reckon it's the cannons and guns blowing it away?" Rob asked.

"Do not be absurd," I said but perhaps he was right for in the coming centuries I would see that very thing happen for certain. Whether it was the gunpowder or the wind, the fog was rapidly thinning.

Perhaps it was this which gave William the confidence to send his Janissaries and *sipahi* cavalry across. They were superbly equipped veterans, professional horse soldiers who had fought everywhere in the empire and had won countless victories for their sultans. And William had thirty thousand of them.

They thundered across the reinforced bridge in a seemingly endless mass, their mail and lamellar armour a dull grey and their lances held high above them.

"Time to get to work," I said to my men and we called for our helms.

A great cry went up everywhere at once and my own men beside me cried out.

"By Jesus the Christ and all His saints!" Walt shouted. "Would you look at that!"

Through the swirling banks of fog, the High Bridge was collapsing before our eyes. It was jammed with *sipahis*, packed flank to flank and nose to tail along its entire length. Whether it was the weight of horses alone or if a few lucky cannonballs had helped, the bridge supports snapped and came apart and the entire bridge tilted and slipped, spilling men and horses from the side as it went before the entire thing collapsed and sent them crashing into the river below.

Every man around me crossed himself and sent his thanks to God, for half the enemy army was yet on the far bank and they now had no easy way to cross. William was there and would be unable to send orders to his soldiers on the other side.

But even though it was not the whole army, we were still outnumbered by those who had crossed already. The *sipahis* on our side rapidly organised themselves in, I must admit, a rather impressive fashion. A testament to the professionalism of the officers and obedience of the men. It was impressive and worrying in equal measure. The mass of surviving *azabs* were arranged into some semblance of order and they advanced on our flanks, pushing away the hand-gunners and archers by their sheer numbers and their mad bravery. This allowed the *sipahis* to advance out into the valley toward our mercenary infantry and cavalry. Behind them the Janissaries formed up and followed, ready to exploit any opening the horsemen created.

I ordered the *sluji* to fall back and we kept our distance, watching as the *azabs* finally engaged our infantry. It was hard fought but the Turks were driven back once more, suffering incredible casualties. *Azab* bodies littered the field already.

"What are we doing?" Rob asked, prompting me for orders.

"Keep the men back," I said. "Keep our distance. This is not yet our fight."

William was on the far bank with his immortals and I now doubted we would get the chance to kill him that day. Still, the enemy threatened to overwhelm the Moldavians and so we might well have to fight a retreat all the way back to Suceava, which might present more opportunities to come at him, so I thought I should keep the *sluji* fresh and unharmed. On the other hand, if we won the battle, we might destroy William's partnership with the Sultan. All I could do for the moment was hold my men ready at the flank.

Though the ground was soft, the *sipahis* advanced quicker than our infantry in the centre could retreat and so our mercenaries were ordered to hold their ground and fight off the cavalry. The *sipahis* began to charge and retreat in companies and larger formations. Cannons blasted continuously, sending their projectiles flying overhead and the hand-gunners fired at the enemy in front of them.

Behind the sipahis, the Janissaries began to manoeuvre out to both flanks. It appeared as if they meant to encircle our infantry while the *sipahis* kept them engaged. Our infantry were already being pushed back by the Turks and even if they were not surrounded by the Janissaries, their line might well have been broken and the order of the battle would disintegrate and in that chaos the numbers of the Turks, especially of mounted men, would mean the end for us.

It was the high moment in the battle, where most soldiers of both sides were engaged and only the reinforcements would decide the outcome. In the wooded hills all around us, King Stephen and his heavy cavalry waited for the moment when their charges would turn the tide in our favour.

But the enemy had tens of thousands of men close at hand, just across the river. If they could somehow be brought across before the day's end, while the king's cavalry was engaged, then everything might change.

"Rob?" I called. "Take ten men and ride around back to the river. See if you can see what William is doing. Do not engage anyone, even if it means returning without reaching the river."

He called out the men he wanted and they thundered off toward terrible danger. I wondered if I would see him again.

"He will cut his losses," Stephen said, riding forward to give me his opinion. "He will retreat. It is his nature."

"He needs a victory," Eva said in response, "or all his work with the Turks will have been for nothing."

"What is a century to William?" Stephen countered. "Even if Mehmed orders him from—"

"Enough," I snapped. "We shall see."

Trumpets sounded from the trees, echoing through the hills. From the fog-filled woodland ringing the valley, the sounds of horses and men built until I could make out the colours and banners emerging from the shadows between the pines. King Stephen's Moldavians in the centre, with the detachments of Hungarians and Poles on the flanks. As they advanced, I saw masses of the peasant army marching behind with their spears and flails and mattocks in hand.

Walt called to me. "Rob's returned, Richard."

A company of *sipahis* chased him but they broke off when they saw how many we were and retreated, allowing Rob and all ten of his men to approach.

"Turks trying to ford the river," Rob said, breathing heavily from his gallop. His horse shook beneath him, its chest heaving, and Rob patted and rubbed its neck with his stump. "Thousands of them trying to use pieces of broken bridge and other timber and rocks and anything to make a dam or a ford at least."

"Will they succeed?"

"Men being swept away. Water must be colder than ice. But there's thousands of them. They'll do it eventually."

"Damn him!" I growled. "He will win the battle."

"Should we stop them?" Eva said. "Take the *sluji* and stop them coming across?"

"They have cannons and guns. And he will send his Blood Janissaries to sweep us away while he remains unassailable on the far bank. No, we shall assist in the destruction of this army as swiftly as possible. Ready the men. We will assault the enemy after the nobles and the *boyars* complete their charge."

"Who do you fancy?" Walt asked. "Get us some *sipahi* officers, you reckon? Lots of nice stuff on them, jewels and gold and the like. Nice for a drink, and all."

I considered charging the *sluji* at the enemy cavalry but discounted it. "We will flank these Janissaries and wipe out as many as we can. They are the Turk's best soldiers. The more we kill, the better it is for Christendom. And tell the men to steal their hand-guns, the ammunition and the gunpowder. If we survive this day, we should arm ourselves properly."

The Turks had advanced so far into the valley that a good number of the Hungarian and Polish cavalry and Moldavian peasant forces emerged fully behind the main body of their army. There was no escape for them.

I brought the *slujis* close and arrayed them in two lines while the Polish horsemen rode by us, two thousand of them in whites and blues and reds, with pennants fluttering above them. The wealthiest lords were clad in shining plate and even the lowest of the riders were superbly armoured, as were their horses.

Like storm waves crashing against a promontory, the heavy cavalry crashed into the Janissaries, the *azabs* and the *sipahis* in the centre. The enemy were overwhelmed and crushed by the weight of the charge. Our men-at-arms were fewer in number than the enemy but were still unstoppable.

Their great charge flattened hundreds of Janissaries, many fell dead from lance strikes or were bowled down and crushed by the horses themselves. Those that avoided the first charge were met by a second line which brought down even more. The Poles slowed and turned about or moved through the Janissaries, thrusting with their lances or using their swords or axes or maces. Others formed up beyond them and prepared to charge the thousands upon thousands of *sipahis* in the centre.

My *slujis'* war cry had often been the name of Vlad Dracula or that of their country. But considering there were Wallachians fighting in William's army, we needed something else that would proclaim which side we fought for. There was one that all men knew, that was even older than I was.

"Christus!" I shouted, lifting my lance high over my head. "Deus vult!"

My men took up the cry behind me and we advanced on the Janissaries. I knew I would not need to tell my men to end the fight by taking a number of our enemies prisoner so that we might later drink their blood. We had fought together for years and they knew their business.

Despite being mortals, exhausted by their slog through the sodden ground and the shock of the heavy cavalry, the Janissaries put up a strong and sustained resistance. They were strong and well-trained individuals and even broken by our attacks they formed groups and fought back to back. None wished to surrender. For the thousandth time I cursed the Turks from ripping these fine men from their Christian families as boys and turning them into Mohammedan slaves, their minds broken and infested by the infidel religion. But my anger at the Turk and the sympathy for the boys that were and the men they might have been did not stay my hand when it came to cutting them down.

In time, all the living Turks in the valley broke and tried to flee. All were chased down and killed or captured.

And despite his attempted crossing of the gorge and freezing river, William did what he always did.

He took the remnants of his army, and he fled.

They all rushed south, back toward Bulgaria where they would be safe. All but Basarab and his Wallachian horsemen who abandoned William and rode west for Wallachia.

With William on the run, we knew we had a chance to catch him and kill him but he had a half a day head start and he somehow managed to keep his army in good order throughout the retreat. Though they were no doubt distraught by the loss of so many of their comrades, and the fact that they rushed through a winter landscape devoid of food or water, they maintained their cohesion. We attacked the rear guard repeatedly and each time we killed hundreds of them but our horses were no less exhausted than theirs were. The Poles and Moldavian light cavalry that rode with us were excellent soldiers but they were exhausted also by the battle they had fought. It was bitterly cold.

Four long days and nights, we whittled away their rear guard. We lost hundreds of men through enemy hand-gunners and ambushes and through accidents and exhaustion. We could not have pushed our people or our horses any harder. And still the Turks, and William, got away.

When the reports came in to King Stephen of the enemy losses, he had them checked again by his own priests and monks. And yet it was true. Our small army had killed forty-five thousand Turks in the valley and during the retreat. We had killed four pashas in the valley and a hundred enemy battle standards were taken.

In addition to the dead, we took thousands of prisoners of both low and high rank. The lords, King Stephen kept, while the commoners he had impaled.

It seemed he had learned a thing or two about frightening Turks from his cousin.

Unlike Vlad, though, he soon after ordered them cut down and burned rather than leave them rotting.

By any measure, it was a great victory, and King Stephen could do as he pleased without hearing a word of criticism from anyone. Indeed, the Pope proclaimed him an *Athletae Christi*, just as old Janos Hunyadi had been years before.

In Hungary, Mattias Corvinus did everything in his power to claim the victory as his own. In truth, not only had he not been there but he had sent the barest minimum of his men to fight the battle and yet he wrote a series of letters to the Pope, to the Holy Roman Emperor, and to all manner of other kings and princes of Europe telling them that *he*, Mattias Corvinus, had defeated a large Turkish army with his own forces. It was truly an incredible bit of dishonesty and whatever lingering flicker of respect I had for the man was gone the moment I found out.

King Stephen on the other hand not only refused to celebrate his victory but instead he fasted for forty days in order to show his devotion to God.

"It is to God that this victory should be attributed," he said when I saw him a week after it was fought. "It was God that brought down the High Bridge."

"It was your well-placed cannons that brought it down," I replied, frowning. "And Zaganos Pasha sending too many *sipahis* over it at once in his eagerness to crush us."

The king would not hear it. "God smote the bridge with his own hand."

"Perhaps he did but it was the drummers and trumpeters that brought the enemy across."

King Stephen smiled. He looked tired. "Yes, and I am certain that you would like to claim this victory as your own, Richard. But who placed that thought in your mind?"

"I did."

His smile dropped. "God put it there, Richard, so that Moldavia would be saved."

"Well then, My Lord King, I shall praise God for his deviousness and his martial cunning."

Stephen frowned. "For his wisdom, yes. Now, you asked to see me and I believe I know what you wish to discuss." He leaned back in his chair. "Wallachia."

"Basarab turned traitor. He must be removed."

The king sighed. "And your friend must be returned to the throne, is that it?"

"My friend and your cousin, yes, My Lord King."

He leaned forward. "What will Zaganos Pasha do now?"

"Our agents suggested that this was the last chance he had to conquer Christendom. Now he has failed, Sultan Mehmed will take his armies east and south."

King Stephen closed his eyes. "Then we shall have peace. Praise God."

"If those things come to pass, perhaps. But if the Sultan takes his army a thousand miles away and leaves only garrisons, would this not be the best time to launch a reconquest?"

The king interlocked his fingers and peered at me. "We would struggle to fight off another invasion at this point. Launching one of our own is out of the question. Do you comprehend the size of Bulgaria? What would you have me do, besiege and conquer Sofia?"

"To begin with, yes. But not alone. With an ally on the Wallachian throne and support from Hungary and the Poles, it would be possible to—"

"No," he said. "It would not. We have been ravaged by these wars. We need time to heal. Years, you understand, not months. By the time we are recovered, Sultan Mehmed may have defeated his enemies and then returned to assault us once more."

"Precisely why we must attack now."

King Stephen smiled and then laughed but it was with a certain affection. "I have long admired your military vigour, sir, and your relentless enthusiasm for war and conquest. But you have never understood us and our kingdoms here. We have been beset by the Tatars of the Golden Horde to our north for generations. The Turks have been at our gates in the south for almost as long. This is our life. Our burden. God is good to us. He has given Moldavia the wealth of the plains and the safety of the mountains. He has given us wheat and sheep and timber. He made our men courageous and our women strong. Moldavia will endure these barbarians from this day until the end of days and we shall prevail."

"I pray that you will."

"You want Vlad Dracula on the throne of Wallachia and I would not object. But he is bound to Corvinus, now. It is not my words of support you require but the assent of the King of Hungary."

"Perhaps you might consider sending—"

"Yes, yes," King Stephen said, waving his hand. "I shall have letters written."

"There is of course the small matter of Basarab occupying the—"

"If I can spare the men when the time comes, I shall spare them. You have my word. Is that all or would you like to cut my purse while you are here?"

I bowed deeply. "Your wisdom and generosity is matched only by your prowess commanding armies, My Lord King. I will take the *sluji* west and do what I can to restore Vlad to his throne."

The king nodded as if he did not much care either way. "And what will you do with regards to your brother? Our dear defeated Zaganos Pasha?"

"I pray only that he flees far from here along with the Turks."

King Stephen pursed his lips, nodding slowly and regarding me closely for a few moments. He then abruptly dismissed me without any courteous words and I was escorted from the hall with Walt at my heels.

"Not true, is it?" Walt asked me, following me out. "We're not praying William has fled with Mehmed?"

"Of course not, you bloody fool."

"What will we do then?" Walt asked, lowering his voice. "How are we going to kill William now?"

"I have a notion," I said. "But we will need to see Dracula return in order to achieve it."

17

Dracula Returns

1476

AFTER THE SNOW THAWED, I took my men into Transylvania to meet Dracula, where he had been residing. When we arrived, however, Dracula was not there. Instead, he had travelled to Bosnia with Mattias Corvinus and an army of five thousand soldiers.

We set off immediately for Bosnia but arrived too late.

The Hungarian forces had captured the city of Sabac and Corvinus declared his campaign a success and left Dracula in command with the task of taking the city of Srebrenica from the Turks. The area around the city was teeming with silver mines so it was no wonder Corvinus wanted it.

Any doubts that Dracula had lost his edge during his long relegation from the front lines was dispelled when we heard what had happened next.

He disguised his soldiers as Turks and sent them into Srebrenica during the monthly market day. Those men quickly captured the gates and then Dracula himself came charging in at the head of thousands of soldiers. While the gates were held open, Dracula and his Hungarians rode inside and caused chaos until the Turkish garrison surrendered the city.

Dracula had every Turk impaled. The city was burned to the ground and everything of value taken.

It was a brutal sacking that deprived the Turks of a key regional source of income and extended the strategic reach of the Kingdom of Hungary. What was more, it declared to the world that Vlad III Dracula was back.

When we returned with him to Transylvania, we set about building an army to retake Wallachia. With support from Hungary and Moldavia, plus soldiers from Serbia and loyal Wallachians, Dracula assembled a force of twenty-five thousand men.

King Stephen, good as his word, brought his army of fifteen thousand into Wallachia from the east while we swept in from the west in order to crush Basarab between us. In addition to his native forces, Basarb had eighteen thousand Turks.

Our armies met near a small town named Rucr in the Prahova Valley. Half of the battle was fought in a woodland and there it ended amongst the trees. It was hard fought and bloody but the *sluji* helped to win it, as they had done so many times before. This time, fifty of them were armed with hand-guns which added a considerable tactical advantage.

Each army lost close to ten thousand men. Basarab fled south and ultimately escaped to the Turks but his rule was over after that battle.

It was devastating for Vlad to witness so many of his people dying. In the aftermath, I found him sitting on a fallen tree, watching the wounded and the dead being carried away by their friends. He was alone but for his bodyguard standing at a respectful distance.

I sat next to him in silence for a while before he spoke.

"Wallachians slaughtering each other." Vlad shook his head. "Those men there should have been brothers and yet they died with each other's blades buried in their guts. I have come back to take my throne but, Richard, I wonder. I do wonder. The longer I go on, the more I think this war is nought but madness."

"They are fighting for survival," I said.

His gauntleted hands made two fists before him. "Why will they not unite against the most dangerous foe? Why can they not see it?"

I grunted. "I have been asking these same questions for thirty years."

He turned to look at me then. "Is that how long you have been in Wallachia?"

"In Hungary, Transylvania, Moldavia, Serbia, Albania, Bulgaria, Constantinople, and yes, most of all, in Wallachia. All of these kingdoms I have found peopled with strong, proud men and beautiful, terrifying women." When I said this, Vlad smiled. I continued. "On the one hand, these lands are wild and virginal and on the other it is as though the feuds within and between the peoples are as old as time. I know these lands, have fought in them, have fought for them, for longer than some men live. And I will always be a thorough outsider. I must admit that I do not understand your people and I never will. My own people, the English people, I know them in my heart. Although it is three hundred years or more since I was born and raised there, the people are the same as they ever were and I understand their concerns and their interests. I can predict, without conscious thought, how my people will respond to any given difficulty or boon. Whether commoner or lord, I know their sense of humour for it is also my own. They frustrate me and even enrage me at times with their manner but it is in the same way that a family feels about itself. For they are my family. Each time I return, the faces are new but the people are the same and I know that I am precisely where I am supposed to be. Your people are, I am sure, just as fine as mine. But I will never know them nor will I understand them."

Dracula ponderously raised a steel-clad finger to point at me. "You, sir, miss your homeland."

"I do. I think perhaps I am heartsick for it."

"And even though I am home, and victorious, and newly made Prince of Wallachia, I too am heartsick for my homeland. For a people who can live in peace. For a time, I thought I could give them peace and good fortune. But now I know I cannot. I shall never be able to do so."

"You may have peace if you crush your enemies."

Vlad shook his head. "I did that, many years ago. I killed two hundred lords and their families. It did not bring peace. I see now that I never could. How long will I go on, bringing nothing but war to my people?"

"Your people will have war whether you lead them or not."

"Yes, yes, that is true. But when my presence as their prince is the *cause* for war, how can I say I love my people? It is nought but pride, is it not?"

"What else can you do?"

"That is what I have been asking myself for years, Richard. What lies in my immortal future? To seek to be prince for a hundred years? How would I accomplish it? By killing hundreds and thousands of my own people? I have been thinking of William. And of you. How you keep to the shadows and let other men, mortal men, take the glory and the fame that should be yours. The Pope names this king or that lord as *Athletae Christi* when it is you who are the true champion of Christ. And yet you are humble enough to let it pass."

"I do not know that any man has ever named me humble."

"And yet you are. If I could but control my pride then why could I not do the same? Watch over my people from afar, protecting them, keeping them from harm where I can. Learning true patience and humility while I do so. Is that not a good life to lead?"

I looked at him, the mixture of hope and despair in his eyes, and wondered if I would have to kill him myself one day soon. He was spawned by William and so I was sworn to end his days. I still needed him in order to battle William but after victory was achieved, I would like as not have to cleanse the earth of him and his ilk. But was I bound to that fate? It was an oath I had sworn but what was to stop me from ignoring it in this case?

"It may be a good life, Vlad. But you will only get to live it if William is first killed."

Vlad nodded. "You think he would come for me?"

"I do not know what he will do now. What do you think?"

"Me? You are his brother."

"And you were his friend. His protege. You spent more time with him than I ever have."

Vlad raised his thick eyebrows. "Is that so? Well, for a long time after I abandoned him, I expected that William would come for me. Or that he would send his men to kill me. But he did not. I do not know why. Perhaps he feared me."

"Perhaps."

Vlad peered sidelong at me. "You do not think so."

"If he wanted to kill you, nothing would stop him trying. He may wish you dead but he would weigh the possible dangers of making it so and if it did not benefit him in some way, he would not take action. William has never let pride stand in the way of his continued long life. And I am sure that you are not as important to him as you might imagine. I have met many that he turned. He promised them the world and they loved him and were convinced he would return, even after a hundred years or more."

"And these people you killed."

"Yes. Like you, he swore that they would be the ones to help him bring about his new kingdom. He swore to so many that they would be the one sitting at his right hand to rule over millions of worshipful subjects for a thousand years. Some of the women he seems to have promised undying love for and they remained convinced they would be the immortal queen to his king."

Vlad nodded. "He knew enough to never promise such a thing to me. His honeyed words spoke only of power. The power to rule over my people and keep them safe. He knew me, I suppose, even before I did." He looked up at the sky. "Radu, on the other hand, wanted William's companionship. Craved it. And William was quite convincing in his own professing of friendship. I certainly believed their admiration and respect was mutual, though of course they were far from equals."

"Radu is also convinced of the sincerity of William's friendship."

Vlad turned slowly and scowled. "When did you speak to Radu? Before you executed him?"

"I have deceived you for a long time, Vlad."

He got to his feet and looked down at me. "In what way have you deceived me?"

"I did not kill Radu."

"Where," Vlad said through gritted teeth, "is he?"

I glanced around at Vlad's bodyguards. "He is somewhere safe."

Vlad breathed hard as he stared at me. "Why?"

I tried to make light of it. "I believed he might prove useful. But I am glad to tell you now that he is alive."

"You feed him blood?" Vlad hissed. "Whose blood?"

"His gaolers keep him well."

"Take me to him. Now." He clenched his fists as he spoke but I did not move or respond. "I *command* it."

I looked at him, careful to keep my expression neutral. "You are the Prince of Wallachia. But I do not answer to you. Despite appearances, I never did."

Vlad curled his lip. "So. Not so different from your brother after all."

"I will take you to Radu. I am sure he will be glad to see you."

Vlad nodded slowly, his lips curling with rage. "And then I will impale him myself. I wonder how long it will take an immortal to die upon the stake. Well, we shall see."

I stood, moving slowly lest I anger him further. "You must do as you see fit, of course. But, you see, my friend, I had hoped that we might use him first."

"Use him?" He scowled. "Use him for what?"

"To kill William."

18

Ambush

1476

TOGETHER, WE JOURNEYED to the monastery at Snagov. Our men waited in the small village and Vlad and I crossed with just a couple of men apiece, who rowed us smartly across the lake. The abbot and his monks had seen our huge party galloping up and they stood ready to greet us as we moored up.

"My Lord Prince," the abbot said, bowing to Dracula. "It is a great honour to see you again. We have all prayed for your return to your rightful place upon the throne."

Vlad nodded. "How fares my brother?"

The abbot glanced at me but his smile never wavered. "He does remarkably well, my lord. We pray together often."

"He *prays* with you?"

"Oh, yes, indeed. We converse every day and I or one of my brothers prays with Radu. If only we could allow him from his confinement, I believe he would enjoy our communal services."

Vlad scowled, horrified. "You have made him into a monk? He is a prince of Wallachia, not some black-clothed kneeler."

"Is that what he is, my lord? You are certain? Radu the Handsome, Voivode of Wallachia is dead. Slain by some brute of a Catholic mercenary years ago." The abbot smiled at me as he spoke. "We have here a man seeking to find peace and forgiveness."

"Have you considered that he is deceiving you with his good behaviour," I said, "and intends only to get you to drop your guard so that he might make his escape?"

The abbot smiled. "But of course I consider it daily. And that is why he always remains chained inside his cell."

"Chained?" I said, surprised but pleased. "That is well."

"Not much of a life," Vlad muttered.

"On the contrary," the abbot replied. "It forces a man to look inward. He must commune with his soul. And as I say, he is confined but not isolated. What is more, he has devoured every text in our library and is keen for more."

Vlad raised a finger and jabbed it in the abbot's face. "You have made my brother, a knight and a prince, into a scholarly monk. It is shameful."

To his credit, Abbot Ioánnis did not so much as flinch. "Do you believe, My Lord Prince, that taking holy orders is shameful?"

"For one who was a prince, yes indeed."

The abbot lifted his chin and stared back at Vlad. "The prince is dead. Only the man remains. The man and his soul. I can think of no greater pursuit than to attempt the mastery of the self. Especially for one who may find himself walking the earth, ageless and powerful, for all of time. Men such as yourself, my lord."

Dracula scowled at me.

I held my hands up. "I never said a word about you, Vlad."

The abbot stroked his thick beard. "Your brother speaks of you often. Almost as much as he speaks of your brother, Richard."

I sighed. "My brother wraps himself around these poor people's hearts so that they can never untangle their soul from him."

Abbot Ioánnis nodded. "He does have an unusual power, that is true. But we pray for the disentanglement. You will find Radu much changed, Richard, from when you saw him last. As will you, my prince."

"Take us to him," Vlad said. "Now."

We followed him to the monastery and down into the corridor with its row of cells. When the abbot opened the door, we found Radu in black monks' robes on his knees, facing away from us.

"Radu," the abbot prompted. "You have guests."

It was only when Radu climbed to his feet that I heard his chain dragging across the stone floor. He turned as Vlad stepped forward and they faced each other.

Radu had become thin, his handsome face now gaunt and his cheeks were deep hollows beneath sharp bones. Yet, for all that, he looked well. He had a composure and stillness to him that he had entirely lacked before.

"Look what has become of you," Vlad said, his voice breaking. "If our father could see you."

Radu's eyes flicked to me. "Your companion murdered our father. Otherwise, perhaps our father could see me."

Vlad half turned. "I thought he had killed you, also. I am glad that he did not."

"You are glad that I am kept chained like a dog? Whether you are here to kill me or to free me, please be about it. I have waited long enough."

I heard the abbot laugh lightly at my shoulder.

"We will do neither," I said. "We will use Radu in order to bring William to us."

"What do you mean?" Abbot Ioánnis said.

"My comrades have let it be known that Radu is alive and that he is held here."

"You have done what?" the abbot said, turning on me, furious. "You will bring an army down upon us, you great fool."

Radu likewise growled at me. "What is the meaning of this, Richard? You saved me and kept me here and now you wish me dead at William's hand?"

I waited until they had stopped. "You are nothing but bait, Radu. And William and his men will not reach Snagov because we will ambush him before he ever reaches this place."

Radu was incredulous. "And what if William evades your ambush and does find me here? He will slaughter these good monks to reach me, of that I am certain. But what then? I am no longer his man. I no longer share his vision. He will slay me also."

"Truly?" Vlad asked his brother. "You mean you will follow me?"

"No. I follow God, and myself. Under the guidance of the Abbot Ioánnis here and also Father Theodore who has wisdom greater even than William's, and that which he has is far more Godly and true. William will come for me, if he knows I am alive, but my love for him is at an end. Truly."

"Listen again," I said. "If William does reach Snagov, then you are in no danger. For you shall not be here. Not you, Radu, and not you, Abbot, nor any of your monks."

The abbot raised a single bushy eyebrow. "And where, pray tell, shall we be?"

"At the fortress of Bucharest. It is not twenty miles from here. We will leave at sunrise."

The abbot was calm but firm. "My brothers will not leave this place. It is their home. We have the laity to consider also."

"All will come. If necessary, they will be trussed up and carried off in sacks but they will come. I shall not have your deaths on my conscience should William avoid our ambush and fall upon this place."

An aged voice in the doorway made us all turn.

"How can you be certain William will come?" Theodore stood there, his hand on a young monk's arm.

"Theodore," I said. "You look just as well as ever."

He ignored my greeting. "How do you know, Richard?"

"My companions Eva and Stephen have sent messages alluding to Radu's presence here. Messages intended to be intercepted and they were. What is more, Vlad's coming here will also have been noted by Turkish spies. There is no doubt that they are everywhere in this country."

"That seems to me to be a lot of hope and no surety, my son," Theodore said.

"Well, there is also the fact that William has abandoned the Sultan with all of the Blood Janissaries. Our agents confirmed it. Whether he has left Edirne without orders or is acting still for Mehmed, we do not know. But there is a force of Turks newly stationed on the southern bank of the Danube. It is likely William will take command of them and rush here, to Snagov, to rescue Radu and kill you, Vlad, at the same time."

"So," Vlad said. "You have used me as bait. You have deceived me. Manipulated me. And now you expect me to *allow* it? You are so much more like William than I imagined."

"Perhaps I am. But just as you have acted immorally to achieve a greater moral good in the protection of your people, so I have betrayed your trust in order to put an end to his existence. It is not right but I will pray for God's forgiveness."

"It is not God's forgiveness you need but mine. In order for your ambush to be successful, you require my men and they are of Wallachia."

"I do, yes. But if you do not help me then I will use the remaining *sluji* alone. They will follow me and together we will overcome the Blood Janissaries and kill William. But I very much doubt he will come into Wallachia without those mortal forces in support. And so I would really rather also have the support of your small force out there. Together we will spring the trap. And together we will kill William, who is my enemy, and yours, Vlad, and yours, Radu, whether you accept it or not."

Vlad strode away from me and his brother, crossing the small cell in just a few strides. He went to the high, small window and looked up through it.

He grunted. "You cannot see anything from this useless window, Radu."

Radu smiled. "I can see the sky above my homeland. I see clouds and birds and the sun. I see rain and snow falling. A taste of God's creation is enough to remind me of it all. And that slice of blue sky, no larger than my outstretched hand, is all the kingdom I have needed since I have been here. Never in all my life have I felt contented before being brought here. I may have this chain upon my body but my soul is free."

I glanced at the abbot and Theodore who stood smiling proudly at their ward.

Vlad said nothing for a while before turning to Radu. "Brother, if your words are sincere then it brings me great joy to hear that. Perhaps, if you prove that you are loyal then when the time is right your existence can be declared to our people and you may be welcomed at my court. Or, if you prefer, I will found a monastery and you can be abbot there and live in peace."

Radu bowed his head. "Nothing would give me greater joy."

"Richard." Vlad turned his terrible gaze on me. "We will kill William together. But your manipulation of me I shall never forgive."

"I understand. Now, let us prepare to leave this place. Tomorrow, we ride to Bucharest."

***

The monks were incredibly efficient and had their valuables and victual packed and ready well before dawn. Being monks they were used to rising for midnight and matins services but still they worked through the darkness as if they were half-bat and half-soldier.

Still, with so many men, monks, soldiers, and servants, it was a somewhat chaotic departure from the side of the lake that morning.

"Where is the ancient one named Theodore?" I shouted at my men, not seeing the blind monk in the crowd.

Stephen called out from over the sea of heads. "The abbot said the old man is too frail and blind to travel."

"Too stubborn, more like. Well, may God damn him, then," I muttered. I knew if William managed to get by us and reach the monastery, then he would not take pity on the blind man's frailties. But we would intercept William before he reached Snagov and anyway I had too much on my mind to think of one surly old monk a moment longer. "We must hurry," I cried out, repeatedly. "If it is not essential, leave it behind."

Rob nodded at a group of servants carrying squawking baskets. "Would you say chickens are essential, Richard?"

"In the name of Christ, sort the daft bastards out, will you?"

Waving his stump at them and babbling in his appalling Wallachian, Rob scared them into dropping their baskets.

"Where the bloody hell is Serban?" I asked Walt as I pulled myself into his saddle.

He shrugged. "If you haven't noticed, the old bastard's always off somewhere when there's hard work to be done."

"Will you take some men and take position at the rear of the column, Walt? If there are any stragglers, whip them along. If they won't keep up then you have to truss them up and bring them forward."

Walt rubbed sleep from his eyes. "Can't we just leave them to it? They'll come up eventually."

"Absolutely not. Not a single one can be left behind. What if one of William's men scoops him up and questions him about Snagov? Better to kill them than let one risk the entire plan. Our only hope is through springing an ambush and trapping him. Do you understand?"

"None will fall behind. You can trust me."

I did trust him. Him and Rob, as well as Eva and Stephen. They had been with me for so long because they were trustworthy, reliable and competent. My captains in the *sluji* and all the surviving men had given every indication of similar reliability but I still could not trust them as I could one of my own countrymen.

We rode out in a long column, with the vanguard far ahead out of sight consisting of Vlad's cavalry and behind them a core of lightly armoured veteran infantry, mostly survivors of Vlad's peasant armies and led by his peasant officers. Then Vlad and his bodyguard rode at the head of the rear guard which was formed mostly of his bodyguard and fine troops they were.

I rode behind with the *sluji* and at the rear traipsed the monks and the lay brothers and other servants, some pushing hand carts and others leading ponies.

Radu I kept hooded and chained at the rear of my company, guarded by two trustworthy *sluji* under orders to keep him safe but above all to stop him riding off. Despite his seeming sincerity and newfound piety, I could never trust a man who had been for so long under William's thrall.

If all went well then we would sleep within the safety of Bucharest that night and in the morning could send out scouting parties to watch for the approach of William's Turks and begin planning our ambushes.

By the middle of the morning, Vlad rode back along the column and fell in beside me. We rode along a track with trees close by each side, the shadows beneath cold and still.

"I understand why you did as you have done," he said without preamble. "Until this morning I had not understood just how well you played your part."

"My part?"

"Your performance as a mortal man. As a crusader and a mercenary captain. Even though I knew what you were, how long you had lived and what you had done, I still believed in your subservience." He smiled, his moustache lifting, and a brief laugh escaped from beneath. "And yet it was all pretence. You see yourself as a man above kings. You obey what orders you wish and ignore the ones that do not meet your aims. And you manipulate your superiors into doing what you wish. Even the lords and princes that do not really care for you, still they see you as a straight speaking and morally upright man. But all the while you hold our hierarchy in contempt while you stand above it."

I rode in silence for a while to collect my thoughts while Vlad rode smiling beside me. We left the close confines of the wood and came out onto a long section of road where the woodland had been cleared. On both sides were wide and long meadows but they were covered in nothing but clumps of low weeds. The rear guard ahead of us filed through the woods where they closed tight by the road again beyond the meadow.

"I will not disagree with all you say," I said, finally. "There is truth to much of it. But I do not see myself as above a king. It is impossible for me and my close companions to fit within a mortal nation. We have many times attempted to do so but as you say it is more a dramatic performance than it is truth. We live in a city or pose as a lord but we have no father and mother that we can admit to and so we seem to come from nowhere. We have no brothers and cousins with which to make a family. And we can make no children of our own to raise and any that we might adopt will age while we will not. Not in a natural sense. When we fight as mortal soldiers, we must hide our need for blood from our comrades and so we can never be at peace amongst them. As for kings and princes, I have known so many, both good and bad, that the inherent power of their authority has somewhat lost its ability to cower me. We are not above anyone, as such, but we are outside of them. We are the eternal mercenary, doomed to wander and to never fit within a nation, even our own."

742

"What of my future as a prince?" Vlad asked. "If we as immortals are doomed to live outside of our nation, do you believe it impossible for an immortal to sit on a throne?"

"Impossible?" I sighed, thinking of Priskos and his claims that Alexander the Great was his grandchild, just as I was. Alexander and Caesar and other kings. All met their brutal ends. "How many kings have—"

I was cut off by the mighty blasts of coordinated firearms on both sides of our column. Hundreds of hand-gunners discharged their weapons and the men and horses around me, in front and behind were hit. Steel pinged and men cried out in pain and panic.

Horses fell and men fell with them. Ahead, I watched the cavalry of the rear guard riding one way and another in panic.

"We must charge the enemy!" Vlad shouted, drawing his sword and pointing across the meadow to the edge of the trees where clouds of smoke drifted from the shadows.

It would ordinarily be good advice but I knew it had to be William commanding this force. My mind rushed with realisations. William had somehow discovered my own plans and ambushed me instead from a prepared position. There could be stake pits, trenches or other defences that would cut charging Wallachian cavalry down before it reached the Janissaries beyond.

"Ride back for the *sluji*!" I shouted at Vlad and took my own advice, wheeling my horse and urging him back towards my immortal company.

Another blast ripped through the air and then another., far mightier than hand-guns.

They were cannons, firing from the head of the column behind me. Whether it truly was William or Basarab or Turks, they had planned their ambush well.

"Where is Radu?" I shouted at Eva.

"Who cares?" Stephen cried out. "We must flee!"

"William will be after him, you fool. Perhaps coming for him in person. Where is Radu now?"

"Rear," Eva said, pointing. "Put your amour on, first, Richard, please."

"There is no time," I replied.

"A helm at least," Eva said, fighting to control her horse.

"I will go get Radu," Rob said. "Bring him here."

"Very well. While you are there, tell the damned monks to flee into the woods if they have not already."

He nodded and wheeled his horse around. I called to my captains.

"Put on what armour you can, quickly. We must act decisively but not foolishly. And listen, we must use the *sluji* to kill William. Zaganos Pasha is here and here is where he will die. Your enemies the Blood Janissaries have come to kill Prince Vlad Dracula but we will kill them. Arm yourselves, now. We will ride around this flank. Bring up the hand-gunners, we will advance behind them."

Two of the *sluji* came galloping up from the rear. "My lord," one cried. "Master Robert sends word. Please forgive us, my lord, we did not know."

"Know what?" I shouted. "What is the message?"

"He said you had sent him for the chained monk and we released him to him. But then Rob came and asked for the same thing. He has chased after him and the monk. Heading due east, into the woods."

"Can you understand what these fools are saying?" I asked Eva. "Who did you release the chained monk to? Who is Rob chasing?"

"It was Serban, my lord. Please, forgive me."

My mind raced. Serban had freed Radu and led him away? What it meant, I did not know, other than one thing.

"We are betrayed," I said to Eva. "Serban has betrayed us."

"Let him go," Eva said. "Rob will catch him."

"One handed? No, I will go and I will bring Radu back here."

"He is not important!" Eva cried.

"He is our bait," I snapped. "William will take him and run. I will not lose him again."

"Let someone else do it."

I ignored her. "Vlad!" I rode quickly to where he was shouting a stream of orders. "Radu has been taken from the rear. Taken to William. I will bring him back."

"Why?" he said.

"William wants him. He is my bait. You command the *sluji* and attack one flank of the enemy, there. Break through the men there and join the rest of your army. If we are separated, I will see you at Bucharest."

I turned and rode toward the rear, past my immortal soldiers. It seemed wrong to abandon them but I knew Vlad would lead them well enough and I would return to them soon. Worse would be abandoning Rob and losing my one chance at snaring my brother.

Walt, Eva and Stephen fell in behind me and a handful of squires came with us. The group of monks were standing together at the rear with the lay brothers in the centre, the abbot at the forefront. He waved his hand to beckon me to him.

"You should flee, you fools," I shouted, "you will be killed."

"We shall stay," the abbot said, firmly. "None shall kill us."

"The bloody Turks will," I cried. "Where is Radu?"

"Gone. There." He pointed through the woods. "You should flee also, Richard. Do not pursue him. Let Serban go, he is nothing but trouble."

I left them to their impending deaths and rode in the direction he had indicated. We had not gone far into the cold dark of the woodland before I found three bodies upon the ground.

Throwing myself from the saddle I found Rob on his back with a sword thrust up through his neck and out of the top of his skull. His eyes were open and unseeing and he lay soaked in blood.

"God, no," I cried. "Rob!"

A few steps away, Radu lay on his back in his monk's robe, alive for the moment but

744

clutching at his throat where it had been cut. Blood gushed through his fingers, soaking his robe, and when his eyes met mine they were wild. He knew he was about to die.

Serban crawled away on his belly through the pine needles, though he glanced over his shoulder and sighed, rolling onto his back. I strode over to him and saw his loins were drenched with blood. His guts were spilling from the wound and he stank of his innards. He should not have been alive but he was and I knew then that he was an immortal.

"He should not have tried to stop me," Serban said, snarling. "I warned him but he would not—"

I reached down and wrapped two hands around his throat and pulled him up, lifting him off his feet and throttled him. His eyes bulged.

After a moment, I threw him against a tree trunk and released my grip enough for him to breathe.

"Why?" I growled through clenched teeth. "Why betray me? Why kill Rob?"

He coughed. "Never betrayed you. Was never yours."

A chill seized my heart. "You are William's?"

He smiled. "Not his either. Our people have been here since before the Christ was born."

"Your people? What people? Immortals?"

"Tried to make you see. Understand. But you want only to kill us all."

I leaned down. "Did you tell William we were coming? Where to ambush us?" I saw in his eyes that it was true. "You must have, you have been gone since we reached the monastery."

He coughed blood and clutched at his slippery guts. "I wish it did not have to be so."

"Why take Radu? Why kill Rob?"

"You have lost. William will control Wallachia. Radu was... a gift."

I grabbed his hair and pulled his head back. "Where are the other immortals? Who are the other *vampirs* in Wallachia?"

He smiled again and winced. In the distance, the guns fired and men shouted. Hooves drummed on the earth. Steel rang out on steel. I had already tarried too long.

I drew my dagger and sawed through Serban's neck until his head was cut from it. I threw it down, disgusted with him and with myself.

Walt cradled Rob in his lap after having drawn the sword from his skull. Eva knelt beside him and had one arm around Walt's shoulder and her other stroked Rob's blood-soaked hair. Walt wept freely but I was numb. From beside Radu, Stephen shook his head. Radu Dracula was dead also.

"We will return for Rob's body," I said to Walt. "And bury him properly. But now we still have work to do."

Walt cuffed his cheeks and when he looked at me I saw white rage and black despair.

We rode back through the wood directly toward the sounds of battle to find hundreds of bodies lying in the meadow. The *sluji* had dismounted and were fighting in a ragged line against the Blood Janissaries. So many had fallen on both sides and more were being killed every moment. With horror I realised that the Janissaries had the upper hand. There were more of them alive and the *sluji* were dying quicker.

I looked for Vlad as I advanced and saw him hammering his sword against the breastplate of a fallen figure in elaborate Turkish armour.

William.

My brother fought against Vlad, one against the other. Dracula in his magnificent plate and William on his back, his face twisted in hatred as Vlad whipped his sword down on him. William held his blade up to defend himself, holding it with two hands, one on the blade itself.

The men around them fought their own desperate battles to the death, bodyguards fighting bodyguards, and immortals against immortals. My *sluji* were almost wiped out. My captains had all fallen.

And yet Vlad had almost achieved victory. He had William down, almost at his mercy.

I aimed my horse for their fight, drew my sword, and charged at them.

Vlad's sword blade broke and he fell upon William with a dagger in hand and they grappled. Vlad worked his arm down and his blade under William's helm, cutting and stabbing into him.

By God, I thought with a thrill as I came closer. *He has done it.*

Just then, four Janissaries rushed forward, raised their hand-guns and fired them as one into Vlad from a yard away.

The shots ripped through Vlad's armour and through his flesh, deep into his body. He jerked and fell back from William and the Janissaries pulled their fallen master away.

"No!" I roared, almost upon them.

Vlad lay as if he was dead and I was running out of time before William's men got him away from me. My horse was nervous of the noise and the stink of smoke and the mass of men I was forcing him towards but I had to force my way through the line to reach William. Vlad had wounded William severely and there would never be a better chance to finish him once and for all.

My horse fell under me, shot by a dozen Janissaries behind the line. The beast went down hard, as if his legs had been cut off, throwing me and I fell on my neck. It hurt like the devil and I was dazed but I rolled to my feet to find a company of Janissaries rushing me with their swords and axes.

I killed one as I fell back and then Eva and Stephen arrived on horseback, flattening some and driving the rest back. We rushed into them together and killed them.

But the rest were fleeing. Some mounted, others on foot.

"I need a horse!" I shouted and a squire rode over, leaping off and offering me his hands to boost me into the saddle. Once seated, I looked for the fleeing enemy. They were retreating through the woods, with companies of Janissaries covering the escape.

"*Sluji!* Form on me!"

We had been all but obliterated. Many of my men lay wounded and were calling for blood but there were dead squires all over the field and my immortals were bleeding to death in their dozens. Others were dead and limbs and heads littered the field.

Vlad Dracula lay on the field with two of his men at his side. His helm had been removed and his eyes stared up at the sky, blood soaking his hair.

"Is he dead?" Walt shouted. "Is he dead?"

His men seemed stunned. I could not spare time to deal with Dracula or his men.

"*Sluji!*" I cried to any that yet lived. "Our enemies flee. There. We stop for nothing. Every one of them will fall."

Despite all they had been through, they found their horses and formed up on me. We were so few and they were exhausted and wounded but still they formed up and we chased the enemy into the woods.

The Turks had engaged the Wallachian army further along the track and the fighting there continued. Whatever the outcome, it did not matter to me. All that mattered was catching William. I prayed that he was already dead, killed by Dracula's blade and his men carried nothing but William's corpse back toward the Danube, but I doubted God would grant me such luck.

A half dozen immortal Janissaries rushed suddenly from hiding behind a stand of trees with their lances up and we had to pull up and cut them down before continuing. Two of my men were killed in the exchange. But then we were on again.

Every half a mile or so we crashed into another ambush in the woodland. Each time we killed them but I lost men in turn and so our numbers dwindled and our progress slowed.

"His men spend their lives to grant him a few yards more," Walt shouted, wiping his blade off on a Janissary's red robes.

"And mine spend theirs to gain it back," I said, looking at the few men I had left. Our horses were hanging their heads and if they survived the day, not one of them would be fit for anything other than food for the hounds by the morrow.

"Be full dark soon," Walt said, looking up. "How will we find him then?"

"When we reach the Danube, we will follow the bank in both directions. You will take half the men one way and I the other. If you find him, send a man back to me and I will do the same."

Walt puffed his cheeks and shook his head but we rode on for the river and came out of the trees with the moon already up. It was cold and my men shook and there was not one of us who was not disheartened.

"By God," Eva said, riding up to my side with her hand outstretched. "Is that them?"

"It is. A score of the bastards."

"They see us," Eva said.

I squinted, trying and failing to see what their eyes could. "Is he with them?"

"Can't tell," Walt said, drawing his sword and sighing. "Is that a boat drifting across the river?"

A dark shape moved slowly out there, not far from the bank.

"William may be within?" Stephen suggested.

"Another boat is drawn up on the bank," Eva cried. "I see it in the grass."

"And twenty Janissaries guarding it," Walt growled. "Letting their master get away."

"Dismount," I ordered. "Form a line!"

We pushed our useless horses away and formed up with the Danube shining in the moonlight nearby. From the long grasses by the river, the remnants of the Blood Janissaries advanced. They outnumbered us two to one but I would not let them stop me. William was so close, I could almost taste him.

I led the charge, pulling ahead of my tired men.

The Janissaries were superb and fought with ferocity and skill. My men fell, fighting with every last breath.

I cut them down and killed the last of them, running my sword through his face.

All that remained of the *sluji*, who were once five hundred, were three badly wounded men who sat on ground soaked with the blood of their brothers and their enemies.

William's dark boat was crossing the river, a single rower within, moving slowly.

Wading through the grass and into the freezing mud, I reached the boat which was pulled half up onto the muddy bank. It was big enough for thirty men, with four oars aside. Clutching my sword I pulled myself up and over the side, splashing into deep water within.

They had hacked holes through the bottom of it, rendering it unusable.

"William!" I shouted across the river, standing in the ruined boat. "You coward!"

Out in the gloom, he stopped rowing and stood. No more than a shadow upon shadows. "Damn you to hell, Richard!" His voice was loud, travelling across the water and the still night air.

"Find a hand-gun," I muttered to my men. "Crossbow, anything." They splashed away toward the corpses on the bank and I raised my voice again. "I will find you, William. No matter where you run, I will find you."

"Ha!" he shouted. I saw him raise his hands to his mouth as he did so. "You leave me be, brother!"

"I defeated you, William," I shouted. "Again and again, I defeated you. And now you flee. All your men, dead! Your Sultan despises you. You are finished!"

"I have barely begun!" he cried out.

Walt splashed over to me, hissed, and held out a hand-gun. "The only one still dry. Loaded. You aim, I will fire it." He had the end of a burning match cupped in his hand.

I took it and squeezed the wooden end under my arm and looked down the iron barrel. It was practically full night and William was drifting further on the current with every moment. The river and the boat and the man had blended into one shadow.

"Radu is dead!" I called.

He said nothing in return. I scanned left and right while Walt blew on the match, ready.

"Did you hear me? I killed your only friend in all the world, William. He died in agony!"

Silence, and then. "And my men killed Vlad!" he shouted. "And he was your—"

"Now!" I hissed at Walt.

He touched the match on the firing pan and the gun banged in my hand. Across the river, William cried out and I was sure I heard him fall into the water.

We stood and listened. There was nothing but the wind in the trees behind me and the gentle sound of the great river in front.

1 9

The Vampir

1 4 7 6

IT WAS MORNING when we cautiously returned to the battlefield. Exhausted beyond measure, our horses dragging their feet with each step.

We were dejected and heartbroken.

I was not certain whether William had in fact been killed but I strongly doubted it. At least I had given him a parting gift. Whether Dracula was dead, I was not certain either but it seemed likely, considering the lifeless state I had last seen him in. Either way, I had to return to the field. Above all, Rob had to be buried. I would not leave him to be tossed into a mass grave or allow his body to be scavenged and lay unburied.

We crept through the dark trees to the edge of the meadow and found the usual sight after a battle. Figures crouched over the dead and dying, collecting bodies and weapons and armour. Hand carts trundling along, horses standing here and there. Locals mixed with soldiers and servants. Crows hopped and squawked and were chased away, only to land on some other poor body.

"Where is the prince?" I asked a Wallachian captain who stood at the edge by his horse.

"My lord?"

"Where is Vlad Dracula?"

The captain was somewhat out of his wits and he stared for a moment, despair in his eyes. "We fell back. The Turks came up here to this field. We gathered the men and pushed the Turks off. They fled south, back to the river."

"Where is he?"

The Wallachian frowned, looking at me. "They took his head."

"The Turks took Dracula's head?" I asked. "You are certain?"

He shook as he recalled it. "They had it raised on a spear. They celebrated as they fled."

"You recognised him?"

"It was his helm, yes. The only one like it."

I sighed, rubbing my eyes. "What about the rest of him?"

"My lord?"

"Where is your prince's body, sir?"

"The monks took it."

"What monks? They took it where?"

He stared. "Monks."

I sighed. "Where are your friends, Captain? Where are your servants?"

"Dead." He looked around. "Or fled. Or..."

Walt approached and patted him on the shoulder. "Come on, son. Let's find your mates, shall we." He led the man away across the meadow and passed him off to a group of soldiers.

We retraced our steps back along the track to find the place where Rob fell. He was right where we had left him. However, the others were not.

"Where is Radu's body?" Eva said.

"Serban's is gone also," Stephen said. "Head and body both. Could Radu have been alive after all?"

"Not a chance," I said. "His people must have taken him."

"And Serban also?" Stephen asked. "Why would they do that?"

"Where shall we take dear Rob?" Eva asked, kneeling by him.

"What about the monastery at Snagov?" Stephen said. "He appeared to like it there."

We all instinctively turned to Walt who nodded his assent. "The monks will bury him proper."

The sun rose as high as it would on that winter day by the time we reached the monastery at Snagov. We rowed across the lake and moored up, leaving Rob's body on the shore while we approached the buildings, calling out for any of the monks or servants who had stayed or, we hoped, had returned from the battlefield with the bodies of Vlad, Radu, and Serban.

It was deserted.

Walking through the empty buildings, I called for anyone. I called for Theodore, who had stayed, and headed for the library.

"They were not at the battlefield," Stephen said beside me, his dagger in his fist. "And they are not here. So, where have they gone?"

"They must have come here," Eva said. "Where else could they go?"

"There is nowhere else," Walt said, his face a mask of anguish.

We stopped as one at a noise up ahead. The screeching of iron hinges and the shuffling of feet.

"You have returned, my dear brothers," a raspy voice called out up ahead. It was Theodore. The ancient, blind monk stood filling the doorway to the library, like a bag of bones beneath his robes.

Walt scoffed behind me. "Silly old sod."

I raised my voice as I continued toward him. "It is not your brothers who have returned, Father Theodore. We also are looking for them. It is I, Richard Ashbury, who fought with—"

"I know who it is returning," Theodore said, his voice seeming suddenly stronger. "Come and speak with me a while, Richard Ashbury, the *vampir*."

I followed him into the library in time to see him ease himself into his chair by the window, the place I had first seen him. It was open and the cold afternoon air smelled of pine and woodsmoke.

"You call me a *vampir*?" I asked him, crossing the library to stand over him. "Why do you say that?"

"Have a seat, brother," he said, indicating the seat opposite.

I ignored him. "You called me a *vampir*. And you are right. But how did you know it?"

Theodore smiled. "I know it, Richard, because I am a *vampir*, also."

A chill spread up my spine. I was shocked and at the same time, it seemed as if I already knew. With a sigh, I sat across from Theodore while he smiled through me. Cold air poured in through the window but the old man did not seem to feel it.

"You call yourself a *vampir*, Theodore?" I looked at his lined face and the broad yet bony shoulders under his robes. I wondered how he could be an immortal and also aged and infirm. "What did you do to the other monks? Did they return here after the battle?"

"They came with men to bury," Theodore said, pointing toward the graveyard outside his window. "And then my brothers had to leave. You see, they were afraid of you and *your* brother and what you might do."

"Afraid of me? But it is William who means to conquer your people."

Theodore smiled. "And you, Richard, are the one who is hunting *strigoi*. You are both young and dangerous. Both of you are quite mad."

"I am not young," I said. "But I am dangerous. And yet William is the mad one."

He raised a large, bony finger. "Both of you are tearing through the world like mad bulls, not knowing our ways. It is not your fault. But you are a danger to us and my brothers had to go into the wild once more."

"The wild?"

Sighing, he turned his unseeing gaze to the world. "We were here for a good while. We dwelled here in peace, our lives safe from notice, from interference. They will go on, at least for a time, but I am tired of this life. It is time for mine to end."

I shook my head, more confused than ever. "You call yourself *vampir*. How can that be so when you are so..?" I gestured at him, searching for the right word.

"Aged?" he said, smiling. "Decrepit? Frail?"

"How old are you?"

"I do not remember. Is it eight centuries? Or nine, now?" He shrugged. "Enough. Yes, enough, now."

"Do you drink blood? You feed on your monks?"

"You misunderstand. Our lay brothers, the servants, provide our blood. When it is required, some few of those are chosen to join us and so we go on."

I laughed at my own idiocy. "So you were all immortals? All the monks? The entire time I was searching for *strigoi* but I already found them all?"

"All of my brothers are *strigoi* but not all the *strigoi* were here. They are everywhere in these lands. The places they now call Albania, Serbia, Hungary. In all these places they have their own names for us. The Hungarians call us *izcacus*, the blood drinkers, and believe we are demons. Others that we are risen from the dead."

"How did you come to be made?"

He opened his arms, presenting himself. "I am like you. We are born *vampir*, from our *vampir* fathers, though we must die in our lives to become all that we might be. We have greater power and the ability to make *strigoi* with our own blood. But we, you and I, are lesser than our fathers. We cannot mate with woman. As you will know."

I rubbed my face and sat back. I did not know where to begin. "Who is your father?"

"A son of a creature that we call the Ancient One. The First *Vampir*. He has many names. My father was born of him and later my father made me. My father taught me many things. But he is long dead."

"So we are... cousins, you and I. We share a grandfather. The Ancient One." I hesitated. "Did you meet him, Theodore?"

"Alas, no. He has not been heard of in a thousand years. Lost and likely dead, though some say he will one day return and rule over all *vampir*, *strigoi*, and human alike. If he does, I shall not be here to see it."

I almost told him that Priskos yet lived but I held my tongue. It seemed to be an even greater secret than I had imagined.

"So you made your brothers? The monks? I thought the abbot led them?"

"Ioánnis is young. Not yet four hundred years. He has heart enough to go on. I have remained to guide my brothers, my sons, for many years beyond my desire to do so. But they have to go into the wilderness once more and to wander until they find a new home. I am old and broken and do not wish to travel. Only to die."

"I do not understand. How it that you are an immortal and yet you have aged?"

He sighed. "Aged, yes. But slowly. Some *vampir* live for a thousand years and seem to hardly age a decade, as did my father. But for centuries now I have drunk only the blood of lowly servants, many of them old men. In my youth, I was a warrior and I drank the blood of the warriors that I defeated. If I had continued to drink the blood of the strong, I would have my sight and a straight back and the strength of my legs. Alas, I chose the path of peace."

"You ceased to be a soldier in order to become a monk? Why? To hide from those who would harm you?"

"If I had continued to live as a warrior, I would have died many centuries ago. Even a warrior as strong as we cannot cheat fate forever. All those I made died. I came to a monastery in Constantinople and discovered the rules of Saint Basil. I was entranced. For a time, I was consumed by it. I raised my head and argued with matters of Church and the empire. I argued with emperors and wrote and wrote and wished to reform this rule or that. So many words. You will find my writings here and elsewhere." He smiled, his wrinkled face creasing deeply as he turned his blind eyes to the scrolls lining the walls. "It seems so foolish now. Self-indulgent and naïve. And I angered one emperor too many and then I had to leave Constantinople and I took some of my brothers with me. We have lived in many monasteries in the centuries since. And we were here so briefly but this was a good place. A good place for our troubled souls to search for peace. And it is a good place to die."

"You are the one who created all the *strigoi* in these lands? And they were all were monks?"

"No, they do not all come from me. Once, I had brothers. My father had brothers and so we had cousins. We *vampir* of Rome made many *strigoi* and with them we fought to keep the barbarians from Rome's door. My father and his brothers were soldiers and *strategoi* for many emperors but we could do only so much as the empire slowly declined. It took us centuries to realise that it is not military power but moral supremacy that keeps a people strong. We did not do enough to stem the moral decline of our people and when we realised, it was too late. My father, his brothers, my brothers and cousins, they all died fighting the enemies of Rome. I believed the *vampir* were all dead, other than me, for it seemed I found only *strigoi* in my travels. Some I gave sanctuary. Others, wild and mad, had to be killed. But then you came to me and I knew."

"You knew what I was? How?"

"Even without my sight, I could see it in you. In your bearing, in your manner, I could feel your age. You reminded me of my brothers. Even so, I was not certain but young Serban confirmed he had seen your power. You were young and yet somehow you were *vampir*. I must ask, who is your father, Richard? Can it be that one of my father's brothers survived after all and you are his son?"

"No, I have a different lineage. My father did not know what he was and he died in ignorance. And so I did not know either. Neither did my brother William. We had to be killed before we discovered the truth about our nature."

Theodore smiled. "The truth? To be raised in ignorance must have been terrible. And even now, you have discovered so little, I pity you. And you have sworn to kill your brother, and his strigoi? That is not our way."

"It is my way. Besides, you said not moments ago that you killed your own."

He made a growling sound as he cleared his throat. "Only when the rogue strigoi's actions threatened to bring down us all."

I leaned toward him. "And William's actions threaten to bring down Christendom. Even if they did not, he has committed murders that must be revenged."

Theodore's thin lips drew even thinner. "Revenge, is it? Ah, I see."

"It is justice."

"Because he broke the laws of man?"

"Because he sinned. He killed innocent women and children. Many times."

"Ah, children." Theodore tilted his head back and breathed deeply. "It has been so very long since I drank a child. I remember the sweet taste upon my lips. Such power in a child's blood."

I swallowed my revulsion. "So I have heard. But why is it so?"

"God is mysterious. But the child is like a sprouting seed, is it not? Within the acorn is the strength of the oak."

"Whatever the benefit, it is wrong, surely you see that? You profess to be a man of God, do you not believe the murder of children to be a sin?"

"It is a sin, for men. But are we men, you and I?"

"I do not know. Once, I knew I was a man but as the centuries have gone by, I have begun to wonder. Am I to understand that you do not believe the laws of man, the morality of God, applies to us? To *vampir*? You are convinced, then, that we are not men?"

"For centuries, I have asked this question."

I waited for him to continue but he did not. "And you have an answer?"

"I have many answers. But which is the truth? I do not know. Perhaps I was incapable or perhaps I needed more time. But my time is up, and so I must die without knowing. I am ready to die and you will kill me."

"You want me to kill you?" I said. "Why?"

"I cannot kill myself. That is certainly a sin, for men and for *vampir*. And yet I cannot go on in this broken body. Can you do this thing?"

"Killing men, or immortals, has never troubled me. And yet I have so many more questions before you die."

"I am so tired, Richard. After my eyes failed, I wished to die and yet my brothers begged for me to stay with them. I have given them decades against my will. If you wish for another hour of my life then when our time has run through you must give me what I want in turn."

"And what is that?" I asked, though I could guess.

"I will answer your questions and then you will end my life swiftly, striking my head from my body and burying my remains in the manner I wish. Do you agree to grant me this mercy in exchange?"

"Certainly."

"Then go on with your questions, Richard."

"How many of us are there in the world?"

"*Vampir*? Only me, you, and your brother. There were many but they all died. Their offspring are yet walking the earth."

I knew of at least two sons of the Ancient One still serving Priskos but I said nothing about that. "And their offspring? The *strigoi* that they made? How many of them are there?"

"I know of a mere few wild ones still out there but they have learned to be wary of me and my brothers. They cannot be very many."

"What about Serban? Did you place him in my service? I was deceived by him and because of my foolishness, he murdered my friend."

"Serban came here, dying and Ioánnis asked me to save him. I believed he would stay and become one of us but he fled and stayed away, fearing I would have him killed for his betrayal. When you brought him here, he told us what you were, hoping to find favour with us. He wished to know whether he should side with you or with your brother in this war that you are waging. I told Serban to embrace peace, to join his brothers in contemplation of God, and to devote his life to prayer. He cursed me for a fool and said that he would have power and wealth instead."

"You could have warned me," I said. "Because you did not, my friend is dead."

"It is no fault of mine. I can tell you are naïve and trusting and entirely without cunning. In truth, I am surprised you have survived this long. I doubt you will live much longer. Why not come to an understanding with your brother? Make peace and live."

"As you have chosen peace, Theodore? It is peace that has withered your body. Peace has withered your mind and your soul. Man was not meant to live in peace. Only through struggle and conflict and war can we find our fulfilment and live as we are meant to."

Theodore smiled as I spoke. "My father and my brothers spoke as you do. They all died."

"I see now it is your fear of death that has made you this way. Death is not failure. To give up is failure. All of you here, this brotherhood, it is failure. It is contemptible. While you sit here in contemplation, Constantinople fell to the barbarians. If you had fought, if your monks were soldiers, perhaps it would yet stand. You are nothing but a coward."

"The difference between you and I is that I once thought as you do." Theodore sneered. "My time is almost up, oh great soldier. Ask your questions."

I sighed and looked out of the window, thinking on what might help me to know. "I have met immortals in my life, *strigoi*, who themselves turned mortals by their blood. These men so turned became like savages, filled always with a madness for blood. Their skin would blister and burn in the sun. We named them revenants, for they resembled creatures from stories told in England that went by such a name. Do you know about these creatures?"

Theodore scowled. "These are *moroi*. They are abominations. They bring nothing but destruction and chaos and so we do not allow such creatures to live."

"Oh? When have you seen them made?"

"Ah, many *strigoi* grow lonely in their isolation. They make a companion out of lust or love. Sometimes the *moroi* turns on their creator and kills them. A *moroi* is always mad. My brothers and my strigoi have always done their duty and killed all *moroi* that are made. We hear of their madness and murders and track down and kill the abomination. This you must do always."

"So just as I kill *strigoi*, you kill *moroi* but you believe only I am at fault."

Theodore's brow knitted over his sightless eyes. "Your ignorance is vile, cousin. A *strigoi* keeps his soul. He may lose it through his actions, just as any man, but a *moroi* is nothing but a man made into a beast. A beast in the likeness of a man. Like a wild beast, it acts without thought. And like a wild beast, it must be slain to protect the people. It is our duty, *vampir* and *strigoi* alike, to do so. My brothers have cleansed them from the world for centuries and they will continue to do so after I am gone, until they themselves dwindle into nothing."

"There was an old woman up near Poenari who told me her village was almost destroyed by two strigoi. She sent me to Snagov. She said her husband went away for a long time and returned to her as a strigoi, for a while. Do you know about this?"

Theodore frowned. "Petru, yes. It was not long ago. Forty years, perhaps. Two of my brothers fled and it took Ioánnis and the others days to find them. Weeks, perhaps, weeks of murder and violence against the peasants. When they found them, they were bleeding Petru. Once, in his youth, Ioánnis was a desperately violent man and he unleashed that violence on our rogue brothers. Petru was almost dead when they brought him to me. He took his oaths. But he did not stay more than a few years."

"You let him go? Why?"

"He was quiet. He lived with his wife, for a time, supping on her blood. Then he went away and found some way to feed without causing trouble. Or he was killed, or he murdered himself. I should never have made him, and I should never have made Serban. Saving a man's life is not reason enough to make him strigoi. But my sentimentality and my weakness in the face of my brothers' compassion is the least of my sins. They take pity on others far more than I ever could but I find myself indulging their compassion, as a father indulges a son who brings home a wounded animal."

I nodded at the graveyard outside. "Your monks took Serban, Radu and Vlad from the battlefield and buried them here?"

"They buried Serban here, yes."

I was confused. "Where did the abbot take Dracula's body?"

Thedore smirked. "His body?"

I sighed. "The Turks took Dracula's head but the monks were seen removing his body from the battlefield. So where is his grave? His tomb?"

"Ah," Theodore smiled. "Our poor former ward Radu was killed in your little skirmish, yes. His body was swiftly exchanged for Vlad Dracula and the men guarding their fallen lord were killed."

I could barely believe it. "By the monks?"

"They sought to rescue one of their own. They left the body of Radu in Vlad Dracula's armour so that the people would believe their prince was dead. My brothers returned here with him and he was submerged in the font."

"The font?"

"The blood font. It required a number of sacrifices to fill it but then Lord Dracula was close to death. He rose stronger than ever and left with my brothers."

He rose.

"Vlad is alive? Where did they go?"

Theodore smiled. "You will not find them."

"They can have no more than half a day on me. I will track them."

I stood and he thrust his hand out to grasp my wrist. His grip was iron. "Why do you wish to slay your family?"

"I wish only to slay my brother and the evil that he spawns with his blood."

"Vlad Dracula is *strigoi*. Made by your brother. You will kill him?"

"He has been my ally. My friend, even. I wish for him to help me in slaying William but if he will not then perhaps he must die also."

"But why?"

"He has done evil. Great evil."

Theodore tilted his head. "What evil has he done?"

"Killed innocent women and children."

"Those of his enemies. It is the work of kings. A kingdom cannot be maintained without sacrifice. Indeed, my young cousin, nothing of value can be maintained without it."

"You speak of peace and yet you have no sympathy for the innocent. Are you a man of God or not?"

"What is a kingdom, Richard? What is a nation? A people?" He paused, expecting an answer.

"It is... a family."

Theodore made an approving growl in his throat. "Yes, good. And what is a family?"

I sighed. "I do not know."

"A man, a woman, their sons and daughters, this family is a stone. One stone amongst others just like it forming the foundation of a clan, a tribe, a people, a nation. The family and the nation both are the foundation of order. Outside it is chaos and destruction that will shatter any family or nation that is not united, and which does not protect itself against the chaos. It must be strong and maintain itself at all costs. At all costs. Maintenance of family and nation takes sacrifice. It costs blood. But it must be done or all comes crumbling to dust and ash."

"Dracula sacrificed a little too much, do you not think? Spent so much blood and yet his people are not safe now, no safer than they were. What did he achieve with his bloodletting?"

"It is not something one ever achieves. It is something one does. It never ends. Blood sacrifice every day until the end of days. How old are you to not know this? Did you never have a family of your own, Richard?"

"You want me to let Dracula live because he did his best?"

"You must let them all live because they are your family. They are your people."

"The English are my people."

"The English would kill you if they knew what you were."

"Perhaps. But they are my family all the same and I will maintain them through *my* sacrifice. The *strigoi* who do not protect Christendom are my enemies."

"You would kill my sons, though they do that very thing for their own people? They serve the Vlach, the Serbs, Albanians, Bulgars. We bring them wisdom and guidance."

I could barely believe how wrong he was. "Your people are being overwhelmed by the Turks as we speak. They will be no more if Dracula and your sons do not *fight*. Perhaps I will not kill them but they must be brought into the fight so that the Turks can be defeated and your people can have peace."

"This is the crux of it, Richard," Theodore said. "The fight will *never* be won. I pray it will never be lost also but it will never end. In my youth, fighting for the Emperor, I thought as you do. But I learned there is no end to these things."

"You were a Greek. You fought for Rome and lived in Constantinople but because you stopped fighting your great city has fallen to the Turks. So your homeland is conquered by an enemy who wants nothing but the eradication of you and your people and everything you ever achieved and you decide only that it is time now for you to die? You may have once been a warrior but you hid yourself away for so long that you have grown weak not only in body but in your soul. And now you abandon your monks to their fate. You even admit that without you to make more of them as they die off over time, they will dwindle into nothing. You are nothing but a broken old man who has given up."

"My body is dying. I did not understand until it was too late that I needed to drink the blood of warriors or infants to maintain my strength. Whether I wish to abandon them or not, that is what has happened. They will endure for centuries yet, I hope. And perhaps you might one day help them. If they need more *strigoi*, you might grant them your blood."

"No."

Theodore smiled, sadly. "We shall see. If not you, perhaps your brother would grant his."

"He has no interest in maintaining this world, Theodore. William *is* the chaos swirling outside."

"Perhaps. What will be, will be. It is in God's hands. But my time is long past. Now, I have answered your questions at length and it is time that you do as you agreed."

I was sick of him and his weakness. But still, he was family, of sorts. "You are certain you wish to die?"

"It pleases me that you do not wish to kill me, cousin. I pray that you one day feel the same way about all of your family. Now, help me to stand."

"Would you not rather kneel?" I asked.

"Help me to the lectern." I held his bony elbow and supported him as he shuffled across the room. Once beside the lectern he felt for the book that lay upon it. A liturgical gospel book, closed, with a cover of wood and leather inlaid with rubies and shining with gold leaf. Theodore sighed as his fingers brushed the cover. "Make the blow clean, brother. Take my body and bury it well with my head between my feet and with a rod of iron driven through my heart so that I will not rise before God raises me by His hand." He closed his eyes. "I am ready."

I felt as though I should say something, offer him something in his last moments. But he wanted only one thing from me and I could see no good reason to deny him it.

His fingers brushed the cover of the book and he smiled, with a prayer on his lips, as my sword cut through his neck. Theodore's blood sprayed across the gold cover and his body fell while his head rolled and came to a stop by his chair. The smile still on his lips.

***

As the sun went down on a cold, clear day, we buried him as he wished in the graveyard, overlooking the lake.

There, also, we buried poor Rob. As good a friend and as good a man as any who ever lived. My heart ached to know he was dead and to have died in such ignominy instead of in glory. But then he had lived a long life filled with glory on the battlefield and nothing, not even an inglorious death, could take that away from him. Sir Robert Hawthorn had saved my life more times than I could count and he had given his hand when he killed the lunatic immortal Joan of Arc, saving an innocent young woman and captive children by his actions. Off the battlefield, he had been my constant friend and I could barely believe he would be at my side no longer. In his mortal life, he had fathered and raised children and been a faithful husband to his wife, leaving them prosperous, secure, and respected, which is the most honourable duty a man can fulfil. The world was a worse place now that he was dead but he left it a better one because he had lived.

"It is a good place," I said over his grave.

"He should be buried in English soil," Walt said. "Ain't right that he is here. Ain't right that he died here, amongst these people. They are mad. They are hopeless. He should have been fighting for England."

"You are right, Walt," I said. "You are right."

"Still some food in the kitchens," Eva said. "Sleep here and go after William at first light?"

I nodded, looking at the wooden crosses we had pushed into the earth.

"Why not go after Dracula first?" Stephen suggested.

"We will not find him," Eva said. "This is his land."

"I am inclined to leave him and the monks alone," I said. "For now, at least. Not only are they a distraction from William, they are doing no harm and may be doing good."

"William, then," Stephen said. "Who has either returned to Sultan Mehmed or fled elsewhere."

"Probably burrowed into the mud," Walt said, "like the worm he is. Don't really expect to find him, do we?"

None of us answered for a time. We watched the sun sink beyond the hills and almost at once the air grew colder.

"Wherever he has gone, we will pursue him."

Walt was right, of course. William slithered away and abandoned all he had worked for.

Sultan Mehmed had grown tired of Zaganos Pasha and instead turned his attention elsewhere. In the years that followed, he conquered the Mamluks of Egypt and the Turks, known as the Ottoman Empire, dominated the entire region for another four hundred years until its eventual collapse.

Mehmed's sons and grandsons would conquer in all directions. They pushed Christendom back all the way to the gates of Vienna, first in 1529 and then for the last time in 1683, which was the point that the tide finally began to turn.

Every Christian kingdom in the Balkans fell to them, from Serbia to Albania and even much of Hungary, these places were subject to direct Ottoman rule. It was only Wallachia, Transylvania, and Moldavia that remained as vassal states with their own rulers.

I am certain that Vlad Dracula and his strigoi monks were to thank for that, and they continued to watch over their people for generations. It would be centuries before I saw Dracula again.

William fled to Greece and from there to Italy. We followed his trail for a long time but we could never corner him and after many years had to admit defeat. Having lost William's trail, I returned to England once more. So much had changed in our absence and yet it was a delight to return home, to be surrounded everywhere by my own people.

In my long absence, the Plantagenets had been overthrown and England had a new king, a miserable sod named Henry VII. Stephen and Eva wormed themselves into the machinations of the new lords during the reign of his son, Henry VIII while I fought in a handful of minor wars. We recruited men, I made some into immortals and built the Order of the White Dagger for the day when William emerged once more.

That day would come during the reign of Queen Elizabeth. Unbeknownst to us, William ingratiated himself at the courts of Spain and worked to create an army of immortals large enough and powerful enough to conquer England for ever.

It would be my greatest challenge yet.

A vampire armada.

AUTHOR'S NOTE

Richard's story continues in *Vampire Armada: the Immortal Knight Chronicles Book 8*

You can find out more and get in touch with me at dandavisauthor.com

BOOKS BY DAN DAVIS

The IMMORTAL KNIGHT Chronicles
Historical Fantasy

Vampire Crusader
Vampire Outlaw
Vampire Khan
Vampire Knight
Vampire Heretic
Vampire Impaler
Vampire Armada

GODS OF BRONZE
Bronze Age Fantasy

The Wolf God
Godborn

The GALACTIC ARENA Series
Science fiction

Inhuman Contact
Onca's Duty
Orb Station Zero
Earth Colony Sentinel
Outpost Omega

For a complete and up-to-date list of Dan's available books, visit:
http://dandavisauthor.com/books/

Printed in Great Britain
by Amazon

20103214R00441